SPECIAL TOPICS
IN CALAMITY PHYSICS

Marisha Pessl was born in 1977 and lives in New York City. This is her first novel.

SPECIAL TOPICS
IN CALAMITY
PHYSICS

Marisha Pessl

VIKING
an imprint of
PENGUIN BOOKS

VIKING

Published by the Penguin Group
Penguin Books Ltd, 80 Strand, London WC2R ORL, England
Penguin Group (USA) Inc., 375 Hudson Street, New York, New York 10014, USA
Penguin Group (Canada), 90 Eglinton Avenue East, Suite 700, Toronto, Ontario, Canada M4P 2Y3
(a division of Pearson Penguin Canada Inc.)
Penguin Ireland, 25 St Stephen's Green, Dublin 2, Ireland (a division of Penguin Books Ltd)
Penguin Group (Australia), 250 Camberwell Road,
Camberwell, Victoria 3124, Australia (a division of Pearson Australia Group Pty Ltd)
Penguin Books India Pvt Ltd, 11 Community Centre,
Panchsheel Park, New Delhi – 110 017, India
Penguin Group (NZ), cnr Airborne and Rosedale Roads, Albany,
Auckland 1310, New Zealand (a division of Pearson New Zealand Ltd)
Penguin Books (South Africa) (Pty) Ltd, 24 Sturdee Avenue,
Rosebank, Johannesburg 2196, South Africa

Penguin Books Ltd, Registered Offices: 80 Strand, London WC2R ORL, England

www.penguin.com

First published in the United States of America by Viking Penguin,
a member of Penguin Group (USA) Inc. 2006
First published in Great Britain by Viking 2006
1

Printed in Great Britain by Clays Ltd, St Ives plc

A CIP catalogue record for this book is available from the British Library

ISBN-13: 978–0–670–91611–5
ISBN-10: 0–670–91611–0

For Anne and Nic

SPECIAL TOPICS
IN CALAMITY PHYSICS

Core Curriculum
(Required Reading)

Introduction

Dad always said a person must have a magnificent reason for writing out his or her Life Story and expecting anyone to read it.

"Unless your name is something along the lines of Mozart, Matisse, Churchill, Che Guevara or Bond—*James* Bond—you best spend your free time finger painting or playing shuffleboard, for no one, with the exception of your flabby-armed mother with stiff hair and a mashed-potato way of looking at you, will want to hear the particulars of your pitiable existence, which doubtlessly will end as it began—with a wheeze."

Given such rigid parameters, I always assumed I wouldn't have my Magnificent Reason until I was at least seventy, with liver spots, rheumatism, wit as quick as a carving knife, a squat stucco house in Avignon (where I could be found eating 365 different cheeses), a lover twenty years my junior who worked in the fields (I don't know what kind of fields—any kind that were gold and frothy) and, with any luck, a small triumph of science or philosophy to my name. And yet the decision—no, the grave necessity—to take pen to paper and write about my childhood—most critically, the year it unstitched like a snagged sweater—came much sooner than I ever imagined.

It began with simple sleeplessness. It had been almost a year since I'd found Hannah dead, and I thought I'd managed to erase all traces of that night within myself, much in the way Henry Higgins with his relentless elocution exercises had scrubbed away Eliza's Cockney accent.

I was wrong.

By the end of January, I again found myself awake in the dead of night, the hall hushed, dark, spiky shadows crouching in the edges of the ceiling. I had nothing and no one to my name but a few fat, smug textbooks like *Introduction to Astrophysics* and sad, silent James Dean gazing down at me where he was trapped in black and white and taped to the back of our door. I'd stare back at him through the smudged darkness, and see, in microscopic detail, Hannah Schneider.

She hung three feet above the ground by an orange electrical extension cord. Her tongue—bloated, the cherry pink of a kitchen sponge—slumped from her mouth. Her eyes looked like acorns, or dull pennies, or two black buttons off an overcoat kids might stick into the face of a snowman, and they saw nothing. Or else that was the problem, they'd seen *everything*; J. B. Tower wrote that the moment before death is "seeing everything that has ever existed all at once" (though I wondered how he knew this, as he was in the prime of life when he wrote *Mortality*). And her shoelaces—an entire treatise could be written on those shoelaces—they were crimson, symmetrical, tied in perfect double knots.

Still, being an inveterate optimist ("Van Meers are natural idealists and affirmative freethinkers," noted Dad) I hoped lurid wakefulness might be a phase I'd quickly grow out of, a fad of some kind, like poodle skirts or having a pet rock, but then, one night early in February as I read *The Aeneid*, my roommate, Soo-Jin, mentioned without looking up from her *Organic Chemistry* textbook that some of the freshmen on our hall were planning to crash an off-campus party at some doctor of philosophy's but I wasn't invited because I was considered more than a little "bleak" in demeanor: "Especially in the morning when you're on your way to Intro to '60s Counterculture and the New Left. You look so like, *afflicted.*"

This, of course, was only Soo-Jin talking (Soo-Jin whose face employed the same countenance for both Anger and Elation). I did my best to wave away this remark, as if it were nothing more than an unpleasant odor coming off a beaker or test tube, but then I *did* start to notice all kinds of unquestionably bleak things. For example, when Bethany brought people into her room for a Friday night Audrey Hepburn marathon, I was distinctly aware, at the end of *Breakfast at Tiffany's*, unlike the other girls sitting on pillows chainsmoking with tears in their eyes, I actually found myself hoping Holly *didn't* find Cat. No, if I was completely honest with myself, I realized I wanted Cat to stay lost and abandoned, mewing and shivering all by its Cat self in those splintery crates in that awful Tin Pan Alleyway, which from the rate of that Hollywood downpour would be submerged under the Pacific Ocean in less than an hour. (This I disguised, of course, smiling gaily when George Peppard feverishly grasped Audrey feverishly grasping Cat who no longer looked like a cat but a drowned squirrel. I believe I even uttered one of those girly, high-pitched, "Ewws," in perfect harmony with Bethany's sighs.)

And that wasn't the end of it. A couple of days later, I was in American Biography, led by our Teaching Assistant, Glenn Oakley, with his cornbread complexion and habit of swallowing right in the middle of a word. He was discussing Gertrude Stein's deathbed.

" 'So what is the answer, Gertrude?' " Glenn quoted in his pretentious whisper, his left hand up as if holding an invisible parasol, pinky outstretched. (He resembled Alice B. Toklas with that specter-mustache.) " 'Well, Alice, what is the quest-*gurgh*-tion?' "

I stifled a yawn, happened to glance down at my notebook and saw, in horror, I'd absentmindedly been scribbling in strange loopy cursive a very disturbing word: good-bye. On its own it was breathy and harmless, sure, but I'd happened to scrawl it like some heartbroken lunatic at least forty times down the entire margin of the page—a little bit on the *preceding* page too.

"Can anyone tell me what Ger-*gulp*-trude meant by such a statement? Blue? No? Could you stay with us please? What about you, Shilla?"

"It's *ob*vious. She was talking about the insufferable vacuity of subsistence."

"Very good."

It appeared, in spite of my concerted efforts to the contrary (I wore fuzzy sweaters in yellow and pink, fixed my hair into what I considered a very upbeat ponytail), I had started to twist into that very something I'd been afraid of, ever since all of it had happened. I was becoming Wooden and Warped (mere rest stops on the highway to Hopping Mad), the kind of person who, in middle age, winced at children, or deliberately raced into a dense flock of pigeons minding their own business as they pecked at crumbs. Certainly, I'd always felt chills tiptoeing down my spine when I came across an eerily resonant newspaper headline or advertisement: "Steel Magnate Sudden Death at 50, Cardiac Arrest," "CAMPING EQUIPMENT LIQUIDATION SALE." But I always told myself that everyone—at least everyone fascinating—had a few scars. And scars didn't necessarily mean one couldn't be, say, more Katharine Hepburn than Captain Queeg when it came to overall outlook and demeanor, a little more Sandra Dee than Scrooge.

My gradual decent into grimdom might have continued unabated, had it not been for a certain startling phone call one cold March afternoon. It was almost a year to the day after Hannah died.

"You," said Soo-Jin, barely turning from Diagram 2114.74 "Amino Acids and Peptides" to hand me the phone.

"Hello?"

"Hi. It's me. Your past."

I couldn't breathe. It was unmistakable—her low voice of sex and highways, equal parts Marilyn and Charles Kuralt, but it had changed. If once it had been sugared and crackly, now it was porridged, grueled.

"Don't worry," Jade said. "I'm not catching up with you." She laughed, a short, *Ha* laugh, like a foot kicking a rock. "I no longer smoke," she announced, obviously quite proud of herself, and then she went on to explain that after St. Gallway she hadn't made it to college. Instead, due to her "troubles" she'd voluntarily admitted herself to a "Narnia kind of place" where people talked about their feelings and learned to watercolor fruit. Jade hinted excitedly that a "really huge rock star" had been in residence on *her* floor, the comparatively well-adjusted *third* floor ("not as suicidal as the fourth or as manic as the second") and they'd become "close," but to reveal his name would be to forsake everything she'd learned during her ten-month "growth period" at Heathridge Park. (Jade now, I realized, saw herself as some sort of herbaceous vine or creeper.) One of the parameters of her "graduation," she explained (she used this word, probably because it was preferable to "release") was that she tie up Loose Ends.

I was a Loose End.

"So how are you?" she asked. "How's life? Your dad?"

"He's fantastic."

"And Harvard?"

"Fine."

"Well, that brings me to the purpose of the call, an apology, which I will not dodge or do unconvincingly," she said officially, which made me sort of sad, because it sounded nothing at all like the Real Jade. The Jade I knew, as a rule, *always* dodged apology and, if forced, did it unconvincingly, but this was the Jade Vine (*Strongylodon macrobotrys*), a member of the *Leguminosae* family, distantly related to the humble garden pea.

"I'm sorry for the way I behaved. I know what happened had nothing to do with you. She just lost it, you know. People do that all the time and they always have their own reasons. Please accept my request for forgiveness."

I thought about interrupting her with my little cliff-hanger, my about-face, my kick in the teeth, my fine print: "Actually, to be technical about the whole thing, uh . . ." But I couldn't do it. Not only did I not have the courage,

I didn't see the point of telling her the truth—not now. Jade was blooming, after all, receiving ideal amounts of sun exposure and water, displaying promising signs of reaching her maximum height of seventy feet, and would eventually expand via seeds, stem-cutting in the summer, layering in the spring, to overtake the entire side of a stone wall. My words would have the effect of a one-hundred-day drought.

The rest of the call was a fervid exchange of "so give me your e-mail," and "let's plan big reunions"—paper-doll pleasantness that did little to cover the fact we'd never see each other again and would rarely speak. I was aware as ever that she, and maybe the others too, would occasionally float over to me like pollen off a withered dandelion with news of sugarplum marriages, gooey divorces, moves to Florida, a new job in real estate, but there was nothing keeping them and they'd drift away as simply and randomly as they'd come.

Later that day, as Fate would have it, I had my "Greek and Roman Epic" lecture with Professor of the Humanities, Emeritus, Zolo Kydd. Students called Zolo "Rolo," because, if only in stature and complexion, he happened to resemble that particular chewable chocolate caramel candy. He was short, tan and round, wore bright plaid Christmas pants regardless of the time of year, and his thick, yellow-white hair encrusted his shiny freckled forehead as if, ages ago, Hidden Valley Ranch salad dressing had been dribbled all over him. Customarily, by the end of Zolo's lectures on "Gods and Godlessness" or "The Beginning and the End," most students had nodded off; unlike Dad, Zolo had an anesthetizing delivery style, which had to do with his run-on sentences and tendency to repeat a certain word, usually a preposition or adjective, in a way that brought to mind a small green frog bouncing across lily pads.

And yet, on this particular afternoon, my heart was in my throat. I hung on his every word.

"Came across a–a–a funny little editorial the other day about Homer," Zolo was saying, frowning down at the podium and sniffing. (Zolo sniffed when he was nervous, when he'd made the brave decision to leave the safe bank of his lecture notes and drift away on a shaky digression.) "It was in a small journal, I encourage all of you to take a look at it in the library, the–the– the little-known, *Classic Epic and Modern America*. Winter volume, I believe. It turns out, a year ago, a couple of wacko Greek and Latinists like myself wanted to conduct an experiment on the power of the epic. They arranged to give copies of *The Odyssey* to–to–to a hundred of the most hardened criminals at a maximum-security prison—Riverbend, I think it was—and would you know it, twenty of the convicts read the thing cover to cover, and three of them sat down and wrote their own epic tales. One is going to be published next year by Oxford University Press. The article discussed epic poetry as a very viable means to reform the–the–the deadliest offenders in the world. It–it appears, funnily enough, there's something within it that lessens the rage, the–the stress, pain, brings about, even to those who are far, far, gone, a sense of *hope*—because there's an absence in this day and age of real heroism. Where *are* the noble heroes? The great deeds? Where are the gods, the muses, the warriors? Where is ancient Rome? Well, they have to–to–to be somewhere, don't they, because according to Plutarch, history repeats itself. If only we'd have the nerve to look for it in–in ourselves, it just–it just might—"

I don't know what came over me.

Maybe it was Zolo's perspiring face, festively reflecting the overhead fluorescents like a river reflecting carnival light, or the way he gripped the podium as if without it he'd collapse into a pile of brightly colored laundry—direct contrast to Dad's posture on any stage or raised platform. Dad, as he expounded upon Third World Reform (or whatever he *felt* like expounding upon; Dad was neither intimidated by, nor nervy around, the Verbal Foray on-the-Fly or the Apropos Excursion), always stood without the slightest slouch or sway. ("While lecturing, I always imagine myself a Doric column on the Parthenon," he said.)

Without thinking, I stood up, my heart heaving against my ribs. Zolo stopped midsentence and he, along with the other three hundred drowsy students in the lecture hall, stared at me as I, head down, hacked through backpacks, outstretched legs, overcoats, sneakers and textbooks to get to the nearest aisle. I lurched toward the double EXIT doors.

"There goes Achilles," Zolo quipped into the microphone. There were a few tired laughs.

I ran back to the dorm. I sat down at my desk, laid out a three-inch stack of white paper and hastily began to scrawl this Introduction, which originally started with what happened to Charles, after he'd broken his leg in three places and had been rescued by the National Guard. Supposedly he'd been in such pain he couldn't stop shouting, "God help me!" over and over again. Charles had a terrifying voice when he was upset, and I couldn't help but think those words had minds of their own, floating up like helium balloons through the sterile halls of the Burns County Hospital, all the way to the

Maternity Ward, so every child entering the world that morning heard his screams.

Of course, "Once upon a time there was a beautiful, sad little boy named Charles" wasn't exactly fair. Charles was St. Gallway's dreamboat, its Doctor Zhivago, its *Destry Rides Again*. He was the gold-limbed kid Fitzgerald would've picked out of the senior class photo and described with sun-soaked words like "patrician" and "of eternal reassurance." Charles would fiercely object to my beginning any story with his moment of indignity.

Again I was at a standstill (I wondered how those hard-edged convicts had managed, against the odds and with such flair, to conquer the Blank Page), yet just as I threw those crumpled pages into the trash can under Einstein (miserably held hostage on the wall next to Soo-Jin's ill-conceived "To Do or Not to Do" bulletin board), I suddenly remembered something Dad once said back in Enid, Oklahoma. He was paging through a remarkably attractive course catalogue for the University of Utah at Rockwell, which, if memory serves, had just offered him a visiting professorship.

"There is nothing more arresting than a disciplined course of instruction," he said abruptly.

I must have rolled my eyes or grimaced, because he shook his head, stood up and shoved the thing—an impressive two inches thick—into my hands.

"I'm serious. Is there anything more glorious than a professor? Forget about his molding the minds, the future of a nation—a dubious assertion; there's little you can do when they tend to emerge from the womb predestined for Grand Theft Auto Vice City. No. What I mean is, a professor is the only person on earth with the power to put a veritable frame around life—not the whole thing, *God* no—simply a fragment of it, a small *wedge*. He organizes the unorganizable. Nimbly partitions it into modern and postmodern, renaissance, baroque, primitivism, imperialism and so on. Splice that up with Research Papers, Vacation, Midterms. All that order—simply divine. The symmetry of a semester course. Consider the words themselves: the seminar, the tutorial, the advanced whatever workshop accessible *only* to seniors, to graduate fellows, to doctoral candidates, the practicum—what a marvelous word: *practicum*! You think me crazy. Consider a Kandinsky. Utterly muddled, put a frame around it, voilà—looks rather quaint above the fireplace. And so it is with the curriculum. That celestial, sweet set of instructions, culminating in the scary wonder of the Final Exam. And what *is* the Final Exam? A test of one's deepest understanding of giant concepts. No wonder so many adults long to return to university, to all those deadlines—ahhh, that structure! Scaffolding to which we may cling! Even if it *is* arbitrary, without it, we're lost, wholly incapable of separating the Romantic from the Victorian in our sad, bewildering lives . . ."

I told Dad he'd lost his mind. He laughed.

"One day you'll see," he said with a wink. "And remember. Always have everything you say exquisitely annotated, and, where possible, provide staggering Visual Aids, because, trust me, there will always be some clown sitting in the back—somewhere by the radiator—who will raise his fat, flipperlike hand and complain, 'No, no, you've got it all wrong.' "

I swallowed, staring down at the blank page. I triple-lutzed the ink pen in my fingers, my gaze falling out the window where, down in Harvard Yard, solemn students, winter scarves wrapped tightly around their necks, hurried down the paths and across the grass. " 'I sing of arms and of the man, fated to be an exile,' " Zolo had sung only a few weeks ago, bizarrely tapping his foot on every other word so the cuffs of his plaid pants raised and you caught an unwelcome glimpse of his toothpick ankles and dainty white socks. I took a deep breath. At the top of the page, I wrote in my neatest handwriting, "Curriculum," and then, "Required Reading."

That was always how Dad began.

PART 1

Othello

Before I tell you about Hannah Schneider's death, I'll tell you about my mother's.

At 3:10 P.M. on September 17, 1992, two days before she was to pick up the new blue Volvo station wagon at Dean King's Volvo and Infiniti dealership in Oxford, my mother, Natasha Alicia Bridges van Meer, driving her white Plymouth Horizon (the car Dad had nicknamed Certain Death) crashed through a guardrail along Mississippi State Highway 7 and hit a wall of trees.

She was killed instantly. I would've been killed instantly too if Dad had not, by that strange, oily hand of Fate, telephoned my mother around lunch to tell her that she didn't need to pick me up from Calhoun Elementary as she always did. Dad had decided to blow off the kids who always hung around after his Political Science 400a: Conflict Resolution class to pose ill-considered questions. He'd pick me up from Ms. Jetty's kindergarten and we'd spend the rest of the day at the Mississippi Wildlife Conservatory Project in Water Valley.

While Dad and I learned that Mississippi had one of the best deer management programs in the country with a population of 1.75 million white-tailed deer (surpassed only by Texas), rescue crews were trying to extricate my mother's body from the totaled car with the Jaws of Life.

Dad, on Mom: "Your mother was an *arabesque*."

Dad was fond of using ballet terms to describe her (other favorites include *attitude*, *ciseaux* and *balancé*), in part because she trained as a girl for seven years at the famed Larson Ballet Conservatory in New York (quitting, per her parents wishes, to attend The Ivy School on East 81st Street) but also because she lived her life with beauty and discipline. "Though classically trained, early in life Natasha developed her own technique and was seen by her family and friends as quite radical for the era," he said, alluding to her parents, George and Geneva Bridges, and her childhood peers who didn't understand why Natasha chose to live not in her parents' five-story townhouse near Madison Avenue but in a studio in Astoria, why she worked not for American Express or Coca-Cola, but for NORM (Non-profit Organization for Recovering Mothers), why she fell for Dad, a man thirteen years her senior.

After he'd had three shots of bourbon, Dad was known to talk about the night they met in the Pharaoh Room of the Edward Stillman Collection of Egyptian Art on East 86th Street. He saw her across a crowded room of mummified limbs of Egyptian kings and people eating duck at $1,000 a head with proceeds going toward a charity for orphaned children in the Third World. (Dad, quite fortuitously, had been given the two tickets by a tenured university colleague unable to attend. I can therefore thank Columbia Political Science Professor Arnold B. Levy and his wife's diabetes for my existence.)

Natasha's dress had a tendency to change colors in his memory. Sometimes she was "wrapped in a dove-white dress accenting her perfect figure, which made her as arresting as Lana Turner in *The Postman Always Rings Twice.*" Other times she was wearing "all red." Dad had brought a date, a Miss Lucy Marie Miller of Ithaca who was a new Associate Professor in Columbia's English Department. Dad could never remember what color *she* was wearing. He didn't even remember seeing Lucy, or saying good-bye to her after their brief discussion about King Taa II's hip's remarkable state of preservation, because, moments later, he spotted the pale blond, aristocratically nosed Natasha Bridges standing in front of the knee and lower thigh of Ahmosis IV, chatting absentmindedly with her date, Nelson L. Aimes of the San Francisco Aimeses.

"The kid had the charisma of a throw rug," Dad liked to recall, though sometimes in his accounts the unfortunate Mr. Aimes was only guilty of "weak posture" and "a hedge of a hairline."

Theirs was a brutal romance of fairy tales, replete with wicked queen, bungling king, stunning princess, impoverished prince, a love that was enchanted (caused birds and other furry creatures to congregate on a windowsill)—and one Final Curse.

"You vill die unhappy vith him," Geneva Bridges allegedly said to my mother during their last telephone conversation.

Dad was at a loss when asked to articulate exactly *why* George and Geneva Bridges were so unimpressed with him when the rest of the world was. Gareth van Meer, born July 25, 1947, in Biel, Switzerland, never knew his parents (though he suspected his father was a German soldier in hiding) and grew up in a Zurich orphanage for boys where Love (*Liebe*) and Understanding (*Verständnis*) were as likely to make personal appearances as the Rat Pack (*Der Ratte-Satz*). With nothing but his "iron will" pushing himself toward "greatness," Dad earned a scholarship to the University of Lausanne to study economics, taught social science for two years at the Jefferson International School in Kampala, Uganda, worked as Assistant to the Director for Guidance and Academics at the Dias-Gonzales School in Managua, Nicaragua, and came to America for the first time in 1972. In 1978, he earned his Ph.D. from Harvard's Kennedy School of Government, completing a highly regarded dissertation, "The Curse of the Freedom Fighter: Fallacies of Guerrilla Warfare and Third-World Revolution." He spent the next four years teaching in Cali, Colombia, and then Cairo, while in his spare time conducting fieldwork in Haiti, Cuba and various African countries, including Zambia, Sudan and South Africa, for a book on territorial conflict and foreign aid. Returning to the United States he became a Harold H. Clarkson Professor of Political Science at Brown, and in 1986, an Ira F. Rosenblum Professor of World Order Studies at Columbia University, also publishing his first book, *The Powers That Be* (Harvard University Press, 1987). That year he was awarded six different honors, including the Mandela Award of the American Political Science Institute and the esteemed McNeely Prize of International Affairs.

When George and Geneva Bridges of 16 East 64th Street met Gareth van Meer, however, they didn't award him any prizes, not even an Honorable Mention.

"Geneva was Jewish and she loathed my German accent. Never mind that her family was from St. Petersburg and *she* had an accent too. Geneva complained that every time she heard me she thought of Dachau. I tried to curb it, an effort that brought me to the squeaky clean accent I have today. Ah, *well*," Dad sighed and waved in the air, his gesture of When All's Said and Done. "I suppose they didn't think I was good enough. They had plans to marry her off to one of those pretty boys with hair mannerisms and a preponderance of real estate, someone who hadn't seen the world, or if he had, only through the windows of a Presidential Suite at the Ritz. They didn't understand her."

And so my mother, "tying her duty, beauty, wit and fortunes / In an extravagant and wheeling stranger / Of here and everywhere," fell for Dad's tales of flood and field. They were married at a registrar in Pitts, New Jersey, with two witnesses recruited from a highway Huddle House: one, a truck driver; the other, a waitress named Peaches who hadn't slept in four days and yawned thirty-two times (Dad counted) during the exchange of vows. Around this time Dad had been having disagreements with the conservative head of the Political Science Department at Columbia, culminating in a major blowout over an article Dad published in *The Federal Journal of Foreign Affairs* entitled "Steel-Toe Stilettos: The Designer Fashions of American Foreign Aid" (Vol. 45, No. 2, 1987). He quit midsemester. They moved to Oxford, Mississippi. Dad took a position teaching Conflict Resolution in the Third World at Ole Miss, while my mother worked for the Red Cross and began to catch butterflies.

I was born five months later. My mother decided to call me Blue, because for her first year of Lepidoptera study with the Southern Belles' Association of Butterflies, with its Tuesday night meetings at the First Baptist Church (lectures included "Habitat, Conservation and Hindwing Coupling," as well as "Attractive Showcase Display"), the Cassius Blue was the only butterfly Natasha could catch (see *"Leptotes cassius," Butterfly Dictionary*, Meld, 2001 ed.). She tried different nets (canvas, muslin, mesh), perfumes (honeysuckle, patchouli), the various stalking techniques (upwind, downwind, crosswind) and the many netting swings (the Swoop, the Shorthanded Jackknife, the Lowsell-Pit Maneuver). Beatrice "Bee" Lowsell, President of SBAB, even met privately with Natasha on Sunday afternoons to coach her on Modes of the Butterfly Chase (the Zigzag, the Indirect Pursuit, the Speedy Snag, the Recovery) as well as the Art of Hiding One's Shadow. Nothing worked. The Shy Yellow, the White Admiral, the Viceroy were repelled from my mother's net like two same-sided magnets.

"Your mother decided it was a sign, so she decided to adore *only* catching Cassius Blues. She'd come home with about fifty of them every time she went into the fields and managed to become quite an expert on them. Sir Charles Erwin, Principal Lepidoptera Survival Specialist at the Surrey Museum of Insects in England, a man who evidently had appeared not once but *four* times on *Bug Watch* on the BBC, he actually phoned your mother to discuss *Leptotes cassius* feeding patterns on matured flowers of the lima bean."

Whenever I voiced a particular hatred of my name, Dad always said the same thing: "You should be happy she wasn't always catching the Swamp Metalmark or the Scarce Silver-spotted Flambeau."

The Lafayette County Police told Dad Natasha had apparently fallen asleep at the wheel in broad daylight, and Dad admitted that, four or five months prior to the accident, Natasha had been known to work through the night on her butterflies. She'd fallen asleep in the oddest of places: cooking Dad Irish oatmeal at the stove, on the examination table as Dr. Moffet listened to her heart, even while riding the escalator between the first and second floors of Ridgeland Mall.

"I told her not to work so hard on the bugs," Dad said. "After all, they were only a hobby. But she insisted on working through the night on those display cases, and she could be very bullheaded. When she had an idea, when she *believed* something, she wouldn't let go of it. And still—she was as fragile as her own butterflies, an artist who feels things deeply. To be sensitive is fine, but it makes day-to-day living—life—rather painful, I'd imagine. I used to joke that when someone cut down a tree in the Brazilian Amazon, or stepped on a fire ant, or when a sparrow flew smack into a sliding glass door, it hurt her."

If it weren't for Dad's anecdotes and observations (his *pas de deux* and *attitudes*), I don't know how much of her I'd remember. I was five when she died, and unfortunately, unlike those geniuses who boast vivid memories of their own births ("An earthquake underwater," said renowned physicist Johann Schweitzer of the event. "Petrifying."), my memory of life in Mississippi stutters and stalls like an engine that refuses to turn over.

Dad's favorite photograph of Natasha is the one in black and white, taken before she ever met him, when she was twenty-one and dressed for a Victorian costume party (Visual Aid 1.0). (I no longer have the original photograph and so, where appropriate, I've supplied illustrations, drawn from what I can remember.) Although she is in the foreground, she seems about to drown in the rest of the room, a room overflowing with "bourgeois belongings," as Dad would note with a sigh. (Those are real Picassos.)

And although Natasha stares almost directly at the camera and has an elegant yet approachable look on her face, I never feel a spark of recognition while surveying this blonde of pronounced cheekbone and superb hair. Nor can I associate this refined person with the cool and assured sense I *do* remember, however vaguely: the feel of her wrist in my hand, smooth as polished wood, as she led me into a classroom with orange carpet and a stench

VISUAL AID 1.0

of glue, the way, when we were driving, her milky hair covered almost all of her right ear, though the edge still peeked out, barely, like a fish fin.

The day she died is thin and insubstantial too, and though I think I remember Dad sitting in a white bedroom making strange, strangled noises into his hands, and everywhere the smell of pollen and wet leaves, I wonder if this is not a Forced Memory, born of necessity and "iron will." I do remember looking out to the spot where her white Plymouth had been parked by the lawn-mower shed, and seeing nothing but oil drips. And I remember, for a few days, until Dad was able to rearrange his lecture schedule, our next-door neighbor picked me up from kindergarten, a pretty woman in jeans who had short red porcupine hair and smelled of soap, and when we pulled into our driveway, she wouldn't immediately unlock the car, but gripped the steering wheel, whispering how sorry she was—not to me, but to the garage door. She'd then light a cigarette and sit very still as the smoke squirmed around the rearview mirror.

I recall, too, how our house, once cumbersome and wheezing as a rheumatoid aunt, seemed tense and restrained without my mother, as if awaiting her return so it could feel comfortable to croak and groan again, allow the wooden floors to grimace under our hurried feet, let the screen door spank the door frame 2.25 times with every opening, consent to the curtain rods belching when an uncouth breeze barged through a window. The house simply refused to complain without her, and so until Dad and I packed up and left Oxford in 1993, it remained trapped in the ashamed, tight-lipped deportment required for Reverend Monty Howard's dull sermons at the New Presbyterian Church, where Dad dropped me every Sunday morning while he waited in the parking lot of the McDonald's across the street, eating hashbrowns and reading *The New Republic*.

However not really remembered, you might imagine how a day like September 17, 1992, could float around in one's mind when a particular teacher couldn't remember one's name and finally called one "Green." I thought of September 17 at Poe-Richards Elementary, when I'd snuck into the murky stacks of the library to eat my lunch and read *War and Peace* (Tolstoy, 1865–69) or when Dad and I were driving a highway at night, and he'd lapsed into such strict silence, his profile looked carved on a totem pole. I'd stare out the window, at that black doily silhouette of passing trees, and experience an attack of the What Ifs. What If Dad hadn't picked me up from school and *she'd* come to get me and, knowing I was in the backseat, made particular effort *not* to fall asleep—unrolling the window so her glossy hair flew all over the place (exposing her *entire* right ear), singing along with one of her favorite songs on the radio, "Revolution" by the Beatles? Or What If she hadn't been asleep? What If she'd *deliberately* veered to the right at 80 mph crashing through the guardrail, colliding, head-on, with the wall of tulip poplar trees nine meters from the shoulder of the highway?

Dad didn't like to talk about that.

"That very morning your mother had talked to me of plans to enroll in a night class, Intro to Moths of North America, so rid yourself of such dour thoughts. Natasha was the victim of one too many butterfly nights." Dad gazed at the floor. "A sort of moth moon madness," he added quietly.

He smiled then and looked back at me, where I was standing in the door, but his eyes were heavy, as if it required strength to hold them to my face.

"We'll leave it at that," he said.

A Portrait of the Artist as a Young Man

We traveled.

Due to the surprisingly high sales of *The Powers That Be* (compared to the other page-turners published by Harvard University Press that year, including *Currency Abroad* [Toney, 1987] and *FDR and His Big Deal: A New Look at the First 100 Days* [Robbe, 1987]), his impeccable twelve-page curriculum vitae, the frequent appearance of his essays in such respected, highly specialized (yet little-read) journals as *International Affairs and American Policies* and Daniel Hewitt's *Federal Forum* (not to mention a nomination in 1990 for the heralded Johann D. Stuart Prize for American Political Science Scholarship), Dad had managed to make enough of a name for himself to be a perennial visiting lecturer at political science departments across the country.

Mind you, Dad no longer wooed top-tiered universities for their esteemed multinamed teaching positions: the Eliza Grey Peastone-Parkinson Professor of Government at Princeton, the Louisa May Holmo-Gilsendanner Professor of International Politics at MIT. (I assumed, given the extreme competition, these institutions weren't mourning Dad's absence from their "tight-knit circle of incest"—what he called highbrow academia.)

No, Dad was now interested in bringing his erudition, international fieldwork experience and research to the bottom tiers ("bottom-*feeders*," he called them in a Bourbon Mood), the schools no one had ever heard of, sometimes not even the students enrolled in them: the Cheswick Colleges, the Dodson-Miner Colleges, the Hattiesburg Colleges of Arts and Sciences and the Hicksburg State Colleges, the universities of Idaho and Oklahoma and Alabama at Runic, at Stanley, at Monterey, at Flitch, at Parkland, at Picayune, at Petal.

"Why should I waste my time teaching puffed-up teenagers whose minds are curdled by arrogance and materialism? No, I shall spend my energies enlightening America's unassuming and ordinary. 'There's majesty in no one but the Common Man.'" (When questioned by colleagues as to why he no longer wished to educate the Ivy League, Dad adored waxing poetic on the Common Man. And yet, sometimes in private, particularly while grading a frighteningly flawed final exam or widely-off-the-mark research paper, even the illustrious, unspoiled Common Man could become, in Dad's eyes, a "half-wit," a "nimrod," a "monstrous misuse of matter.")

An excerpt from Dad's personal University of Arkansas at Wilsonville Web page (www.uaw.edu/polisci/vanmeer):

> Dr. Gareth van Meer (Ph.D. Harvard University, 1978) is the Visiting Professor of Political Science for the 1997–1998 school year. He hails from Ole Miss, where he is Chair of the Department of Political Science and Director of the Center for the Study of the United States. He is interested, broadly, in political and economic revitalization, military and humanitarian involvement, and post-conflict renewal of Third World nations. He is currently working on a book entitled *The Iron Grip*, about African and South American ethnic politics and civil war.

Dad was always hailing from somewhere, usually Ole Miss, though we never went back to Oxford in the ten years we traveled. He was also always "currently working on *The Iron Grip*," though I knew as well as he did that the *Grip*—fifty-five legal pads filled with unintelligible handwriting (much of it water damaged), stored in a large cardboard box labeled in black permanent marker, GRIP—had not been worked on, currently or otherwise, in the last fifteen years.

"America," Dad sighed as he drove the blue Volvo station wagon across another state line. *Welcome to Florida, the Sunshine State*. I flipped down the visor so I wasn't blinded. "Nothing like this country. No indeedy-o. Really is the Promised Land. Land of the Free and the Brave. Now how about that Sonnet number 30? You didn't finish. 'When to the sessions of sweet silent thought / I summon up remembrance of things past.' Come on, I know you know this one. Speak up. 'And with old woes . . .'"

From second grade at Wadsworth Elementary in Wadsworth, Kentucky, until my senior year of high school at the St. Gallway School in Stockton,

North Carolina, I spent as much time in the blue Volvo as I did in a class-room. Although Dad always maintained an elaborate explanation for our itinerant existence (see below), I secretly imagined we wandered the country because he was fleeing my mother's ghost, or else he was looking for it in every rented two-bedroom house with a grouchy porch swing, every diner serving waffles tasting of sponge, every motel with pancake pillows, bald car-peting and TVs with a broken CONTRAST button so newscasters resembled Oompa Loompas.

Dad, on Childrearing: "There's no education superior to travel. Think of *The Motorcycle Diaries*, or what Montrose St. Millet wrote in *Ages of Explo-ration*: 'To be still is to be stupid. To be stupid is to die.' And so we shall *live*. Every Betsy sitting next to you in a classroom will only know Maple Street on which sits her boxy white house, inside of which whimper her boxy white parents. After your travels, you'll know Maple Street, sure, but also wilderness and ruins, carnivals and the moon. You'll know the man sitting on an apple crate outside a gas station in Cheerless, Texas, who lost his legs in Vietnam, the woman in the tollbooth outside of Dismal, Delaware, in possession of six children, a husband with black lung but no teeth. When a teacher asks the class to interpret *Paradise Lost*, no one will be able to grab your coattails, sweet, for you will be flying far, far out in front of them all. For them, you will be a speck somewhere above the horizon. And thus, when you're ultimately set loose upon the world . . ." He shrugged, his smile lazy as an old dog. "I suspect you'll have no choice but to go down in history."

Typically, our year was divided between three towns, September though December in one, January through June in another, July through August in a third, though occasionally this increased to a maximum of five towns in the span of one year, at the end of which I threatened to start sporting a burden-some amount of black eyeliner and baggy clothing. (Dad decided we'd return to the median number of three towns per year.)

Driving with Dad wasn't cathartic, mind-freeing driving (see *On the Road*, Kerouac, 1957). It was mind-taxing driving. It was Sonnet-a-thons. It was One Hundred Miles of Solitude: Attempting to Memorize *The Waste Land*. Dad could meticulously divide a state end to end, not into equal driv-ing shifts but into rigid half-hour segments of Vocabulary Flash Cards (words every genius should know), Author Analogies ("the analogy is The Citadel of thought: the toughest way to condition unruly relationships"), Essay Recita-tion (followed by a twenty-minute question-and-answer period), War of the

Words (Coleridge/Wordsworth face-offs), Sixty Minutes of an Impressive Novel (selections included *The Great Gatsby* [Fitzgerald, 1925] and *The Sound and the Fury* [Faulkner, 1929], and The Van Meer Radio Theater Hour, featuring such plays as *Mrs. Warren's Profession* (Shaw, 1894), *The Importance of Being Earnest* (Wilde, 1895) and various selections from Shakespeare's oeuvre, including the late romances.

"Blue, I can't fully distinguish Gwendolyn's sophisticated upper-class accent from Cicely's girlish country one. Try to make them more distinct and, if I may give you a little Orson Wellian direction here, understand, in this scene they're quite angry. Do not lie back and pretend you're sitting down to a leisurely tea. No! The stakes are *high*! They both believe they're engaged to the same man! Ernest!"

States later, eyes watery and focus sore, our voices hoarse, in the highway's evergreen twilight Dad would turn on, not the radio, but his favorite A. E. Housman *Poetry on Wenlock Edge* CD. We'd listen in silence to the steel-drum baritone of Sir Brady Heliwick of the Royal Shakespeare Company (recent roles included Richard in *Richard III*, Titus in *Titus Andronicus*, Lear in *King Lear*) as he read "When I Was One-and-Twenty" and "To an Athlete Dying Young" against a sinuous violin. Sometimes Dad spoke the words along with Brady, trying to outdo him.

Man and boy stood cheering by,
And home we brought you shoulder-high.

"Could have been an actor," said Dad, clearing his throat.

*　　*　　*

By examining the U.S. Rand-McNally map on which Dad and I marked with a red pushpin every town in which we'd lived, however brief the period ("Napoleon had a similar way of marking out his regime," Dad said), I calculate that, from my years six to sixteen we inhabited thirty-nine towns in thirty-three states, not including Oxford, and I thus attended approximately twenty-four elementary, middle and high schools.

Dad used to joke that in my sleep I could pound out the book *Hunting for Godot: Journey to Find a Decent School in America*, but he was being unusually harsh. He taught at universities where "Student Center" referred to a deserted room with nothing but a foosball table and a vending machine with a few candy bars bravely tipped toward the glass. I, however, attended sprawling, freshly painted schools with slender corridors and beefy gyms: Schools of Many Teams (football, baseball, spirit, dance) and Schools of Many Lists (attendance, honor, headmaster's, detention); Schools Full of Newness (new arts center, parking lot, menu) and Schools Full of Oldness (which used the words *classic* and *traditional* in their admissions brochure); schools with snarling, sneering mascots, schools with pecking, preening mascots; the School of the Dazzling Library (with books smelling of glue and Mr. Clean); the School of the Bog Library (with books smelling of sweat and rat droppings), the School of Teary-Eyed Teachers; of Runny-Nosed Teachers; of Teachers Never Without Their Lukewarm Coffee Mug; of Teachers Who Cakewalked; of Teachers Who Cared; of Teachers Who Secretly Loathed Every One of the Little Bastards.

When I introduced myself into the culture of these relatively well-developed nations, with firmly established rules and pecking orders, I didn't immediately don the status of the Drama Queen with Shifty Eyes or the Obnoxious Brain Who Wore Meticulously Ironed Madras. I wasn't even the New Girl, as that glittery title was always stolen from me within minutes of my arrival by someone fuller lipped and louder laughed than I.

I'd *like* to say I was the Jane Goodall, a fearless stranger in a stranger land doing (groundbreaking) work without disturbing the natural hierarchy of the universe. But Dad said, based on his tribal experiences in Zambia, a title only has meaning when others fully support it, and I'm sure if someone asked the Tanned Sporto with Shiny Legs, she'd say if I *had* to be a Jane, I *wasn't* the Jane Goodall, nor was I the Plain Jane, the Calamity Jane, the What Ever Happened to Baby Jane, and certainly not the Jayne Mansfield. I was more along the lines of the Pre-Rochester Jane Eyre, which she'd call by either of its pseudonyms, the I Don't Know Who You're Talking About or the Oh Yeah, *Her*.

A brief description might be due here (Visual Aid 2.0). Obviously, I am the half-obscured, dark brown-haired girl wearing glasses who looks apologetically owl-like (see "Scops Owl," *Encyclopedia of Living Things*, 4th ed.). I am paninied between (starting in the lower right-hand corner and continuing clockwise): Lewis "Albino" Polk, who would soon be suspended for bringing a handgun to Pre-Algebra; Josh Stetmeyer, whose older brother, Beet, was arrested for dealing LSD to eighth graders; Howie Easton, who went through girls the way a deer hunter in a single day of shooting could go through hun-

VISUAL AID 2.0

VISUAL AID 2.1

dreds of rounds of ammunition (some claimed his list of conquests included our art teacher, Mrs. Appleton); John Sato, whose breath always smelled like an oil rig; and the much ridiculed, six-foot-three Sara Marshall who, only a few days after this class photo was taken, left Clearwood Day, supposedly to go revolutionize German women's basketball in Berlin. ("You're the spitting image of your mother," Dad commented when first observing this photo. "You have her prima ballerina grit and grace—a quality all the plains and uglies of the world would kill for.")

I have blue eyes, freckles and stand approximately five-foot-three in socks.

I should also mention that Dad, despite having received embarrassing marks from the Bridges on both his Technical and Freestyle programs, had that brand of good looks which only reach full force at the onset of middle age. As you can see, while at the University of Lausanne, Dad's look was uncertain and squinty—his hair too angrily blond, his skin too severely fair, his large frame uneven and indecisive (Visual Aid 2.1). (Dad's eyes are considered hazel, but during this period, simple "haze" was a more fitting description.) Over the years, however (and due in a large part to the African kilnlike conditions), Dad had hardened nicely into one with a coarse, slightly ruined appearance (Visual Aid 2.2). This made him the target, the lighthouse, the light*bulb*, of many women across the country, particularly in the over thirty-five age group.

Dad picked up women the way certain wool pants can't help but pick up lint. For years I had a nickname for them, though I feel a little guilty using it now: June Bugs (see "Figeater Beetle," *Ordinary Insects*, Vol. 24).

There was Mona Letrovski, the actress from Chicago with wide-set eyes and dark hair on her arms who liked to shout, "Gareth, you're a *fool*," with her back to him, Dad's cue to run over to her, turn her around and see the Look of Bitter Longing on her face. Only Dad never turned her around to see the Bitter Longing. Instead, he stared at her back as if it was an abstract painting. Then he went into the kitchen for a glass of bourbon. There was Connie Madison Parker, whose perfume hung in the air like a battered piñata. There was Zula Pierce of Okush, New Mexico, a black woman who was taller

VISUAL AID 2.2

than he was, so whenever Dad kissed her she had to bend down as if peeking through a peephole to see who was ringing her bell. She started out calling me, "Blue, honey," which, like her relationship with Dad, slowly began to erode, becoming "Bluehoney" and then "Blueoney," ultimately ending with "Baloney." ("Baloney had it in for me from the very beginning!" she screamed.)

Dad's romances could last anywhere between a platypus egg incubation (19–21 days) and a squirrel pregnancy (24–45 days). I admit sometimes I hated them, especially the ones teeming with Ladies' Tips, How-tos and Ways to Improve, the ones like Connie Madison Parker, who muscled her way into my bathroom and chastised me for hiding my merchandise (see "Molluscs," *Encyclopedia of Living Things*, 4th ed.).

Connie Madison Parker, age 36, on Merchandise: "You got to put your goods on display, babe. Otherwise, not only will the boys ignore you but—an' trust me on this, my sister's flat as you—we're talkin' the Great Plains of East Texas—*no* landmarks—one day you'll look down and have no wares at all. What'll you do then?"

Sometimes June Bugs weren't too terrible. Some of the sweeter, more docile ones like poor, droopy-eyed Tally Meyerson, I actually felt sorry for, because even though Dad made no attempt to hide the fact they were as temporary as Scotch tape, most were blind to his indifference (see "Basset Hound," *Dictionary of Dogs*, Vol. 1).

Perhaps the June Bug understood Dad had felt that way about all the *others*, but armed with three decades' worth of *Ladies Home Journal* editorials, an expertise in such publications as *Getting Him to the Altar* (Trask, 1990) and *The Chill Factor: How Not to Give a Damn (and Leave Him Wanting More)* (Mars, 2000) as well as her own personal history of soured relationships, most of them believed (with the sort of unyielding insistence associated with religious fanatics) that, when under the spell of her burnt-sugar aura, Dad wouldn't feel that way about *her*. Within a few fun-filled dates, Dad would learn how intoxicating she was in the kitchen, what an Old Sport she was in the bedroom, how enjoyable during carpools. And so it always came as a complete surprise when Dad turned out the lights, swatted her ruthlessly off his screen, and subsequently drenched his entire porch in Raid Pest Control.

Dad and I were like the trade winds, blowing through town, bringing dry weather wherever we went.

Sometimes the June Bugs tried to stop us, foolishly believing they could reroute a Global Wind and permanently impact the world's weather system. Two days before we were scheduled to move to Harpsberg, Connecticut, Jessie Rose Rubiman of Newton, Texas, heiress to the Rubiman Carpeting franchise, announced to Dad she was pregnant with his child. She tearfully demanded she move with us to Harpsberg or Dad would have to pay a One-time Initiation Fee of $100,000 with an ongoing direct debit of $10,000 per month for the next eighteen years. Dad didn't panic. When it came to such matters, he prided himself with having the air of a maître d' in a restaurant with an exorbitant wine list, preordered soufflé, and roving cheese cart. He calmly asked for confirmation with blood.

As it turned out, Jessie wasn't pregnant. She had an exotic strain of stomach flu, which she'd eagerly confused with morning sickness. While we prepared for Harpsberg, now a week behind schedule, Jessie performed sad, sobbing monologues into our answering machine. The day we left, Dad found an envelope on the porch in front of the front door. He tried to hide it from me. "Our last utilities bill," he said, because he'd rather die than show me the "hormonal ravings of a madwoman," which he himself had inspired. Six hours later, however, somewhere in Missouri, I stole the letter from the glove compartment when he stopped at a gas station to buy Tums.

Dad found love letters from a June Bug as monumental as an extraction of aluminum, but for me it was like coming across a vein of gold in quartz. Nowhere in the world was there a nugget of emotion more absolute.

I still have my collection, which tallies seventeen. I include below an excerpt from Jessie's four-page Ode to Gareth:

You mean the very world to me and I'd go to the ends of the earth for you if you asked me. You didn't ask me though and I will accept that as a friend. I will miss you. I'm sorry about that baby thing. I hope we keep in touch and that you will consider me a good friend in the future who you can relie on in thickness and thin. In lou of yesterday's phone call I am sorry I called you a pig. Gareth all I ask is to remember me not as I have been over the past couple days but as that happy woman you met in the parking lot of K-Mart.

Peace be to you forever more.

Most of the time, though, despite the occasional buzzing sounds reverberating through a quiet evening, it was always Dad and me, the way it was always George and Martha, Butch and Sundance, Fred and Ginger, Mary and Percy Bysshe.

On your average Friday night in Roman, New Jersey, you wouldn't find me in the darkened corner of the parking lot of Sunset Cinemas with the Tanned Sporto with Shiny Legs, puffing on American Spirits waiting for the Spoiled Pretender (in his father's car) so we could speed down Atlantic Avenue, scale the chain-link fence surrounding long-out-of-business African Safari Minigolf, and drink lukewarm Budweiser on the tatty Astroturf of Hole 10.

Nor would you find me in the back of Burger King holding sweaty hands with the Kid Whose Mouthful of Braces Made Him Look Simian, or at a sleepover with the Goody Two-Shoes Whose Uptight Parents, Ted and Sue, Wished to Prevent Her Ascent into Adulthood as if It Were the Mumps and certainly not with the Cools or the Trendies.

You'd find me with Dad. We'd be in a rented two-bedroom house on an unremarkable street lined with bird mailboxes and oak trees. We'd be eating overcooked spaghetti covered in the sawdust of parmesan cheese, either reading books, grading papers or watching such classics as *North by Northwest* or *Mr. Smith Goes to Washington*, after which, when I was finished with the dishes (and only if he'd sunk into a Bourbon Mood), Dad could be entreated to perform his impression of Marlon Brando as Vito Corleone. Sometimes, if he was feeling especially inspired, he'd even stick a piece of paper towel into his gums to re-create Vito's mature bulldog look. (Dad always pretended I was Michael.):

> Barzini will move against you first. He'll set up a meeting with someone you absolutely trust, guaranteeing your safety. And at that meeting you'll be assassinated . . . it's an old habit. I've spent my entire life trying not to be careless.

Dad said "careless" regretfully, and stared at his shoes.

> Women and children can be careless, but not men . . . Now listen.

Dad raised his eyebrows and stared at me.

Whoever comes to you with this Barzini meeting, he's the traitor. Don't ever forget that.

This was the moment for my only line in the scene.

Grazie, Pop.

Here Dad nodded and closed his eyes.

Prego.

On one particular occasion however, when I was eleven in Futtoch, Nebraska, I remember quite distinctly I *didn't* laugh at Dad doing Brando doing Vito. We were in the living room, and as he spoke, he happened to move directly over a desk lamp with a red lampshade; and suddenly, the crimson light Halloweened his face—ghosting his eyes, witching his mouth, beasting his jaw so his cheeks resembled a withered tree trunk into which some kid could crudely carve his initials. He was no longer my Dad, but someone else, some*thing* else—a terrifying, red-faced stranger bearing his dark, moldy soul in front of the worn velvet reading chair, the slanted bookshelf, the framed photograph of my mother with her bourgeois belongings.

"Sweet?"

Her eyes were alive. She stared at his back, her gaze mournful, as if she were an old woman in a nursing home who pondered and probably answered every one of Life's Great Questions, but nobody took her seriously in those sticky rooms of *Jeopardy!*, pet therapy and Makeup Hour for Ladies. Dad, directly in front of her, stared at me, his shoulders seesawed. He looked uncertain, as if I'd just entered the room and he wasn't sure if I'd seen him stealing.

"What is it?" He stepped toward me, his face again soaked in the harmless yellow light of the rest of the room.

"I have a stomachache," I said abruptly, and then turned, ran upstairs to my room and pulled from the shelf an old paperback, *Souls for Sale: Unveiling John Doe Sociopath* (Burne, 1991). Dad himself had picked it up for me at some psychology professor's pre-retirement garage sale. I actually flipped through all of Chapter 2, "Character Sketch: A Lack of Connection in Romantic Relationships," and parts of Chapter 3, "Two Missing Pieces: Scruples and a Conscience," before I realized how hysterical and foolish I was. While it was true that Dad displayed a "marked disregard for others' feelings" (p. 24), could "charm the pants off people" (p. 29), and wasn't "concerned with the moral codes of society" (p. 5), he *did* "love things other than himself" (p. 81) or the "splendid sage he saw whenever he regarded himself in the bathroom mirror" (p. 109): my mother and, of course, me.

Wuthering Heights

Princeton professor and leading sociologist Dr. Fellini Loggia made the somewhat gloomy statement in *The Imminent Future* (1978) that nothing in life is authentically astonishing, "not even being struck by lightning" (p. 12). "A person's life," he writes, "is nothing more than a series of tip-offs of what's to come. If we had the brains to notice these clues, we might be able to change our futures."

Well, if *my* life had a hint, a whisper, a cute, well-placed clue, it was when I was thirteen and Dad and I moved to Howard, Louisiana.

While my nomadic life with Dad might sound daring and revolutionary to the outside observer, the reality was different. There is a disturbing (and wholly undocumented) Law of Motion involving an object traveling across an American interstate, the sense that, even though one is careening madly forward, nothing is actually happening. To one's infinite disappointment, one always arrives at Point B with energy and all physical characteristics wholly unchanged. Every now and then, at night, before I fell asleep, I found myself staring at the ceiling, praying for something *real* to happen, something that would transform me—and God always took on the personality of the ceiling at which I was staring. If the ceiling was imprinted with moonlight and leaves from the window, He was glamorous and poetic. If there was a slight tilt, He was inclined to listen. If there was a faint water stain in the corner, He'd weathered many a storm and would weather mine too. If there was a smear cutting through the center by the overhead lamp where something with six or eight legs had been exterminated via newspaper or shoe, He was vengeful.

When we moved to Howard, God answered my prayers. (He turned out to be smooth and white, otherwise, surprisingly unremarkable.) On the long, dry drive through Nevada's Andamo Desert, listening to a book-on-tape, Dame Elizabeth Gliblett reading in her grand ballroom of a voice *The Secret Garden* (Burnett, 1909), I offhandedly mentioned to Dad that none of the houses we rented ever had a decent yard, and so, the following September when we arrived in Howard, Dad chose 120 Gildacre Street, a worried house of pale blue stranded in the middle of a tropical biosphere. While the rest of Gildacre Street cultivated prim peonies, dutiful roses, placid yards plagued only by the rare clump of crabgrass, Dad and I fought escalating plant life indigenous to the Amazon Basin.

Every Saturday and Sunday for three weeks, armed with nothing but pruning shears, leather gloves and Off, Dad and I rose early and trekked deep into our rain forest in a heroic attempt to scale back the growth. We'd rarely last two hours, sometimes less than twenty minutes if Dad happened to spot what was allegedly a Stag Beetle the size of his foot scuttling under the leaves of a talipot palm (men's size 12).

Never one to admit defeat, Dad attempted to rally the troops with "Nothing defeats the Van Meers!" and "You think if Patton lived here, he'd throw in the towel?" until that fateful morning he was mysteriously bitten by something ("*Ahhhhhhh!*" I heard him cry from the front porch where I was trying to curtail knotted liana.) His left arm inflated to the size of a football. That evening, Dad answered an advertisement of an experienced gardener in *The Howard Sentinel*.

"Yardwork," it read. "Anyhow. Anywhere. I do."

His name was Andreo Verduga, and he was the most beautiful creature I'd ever seen (see "Panther," *Glorious Predators of the Natural World*, Goodwin, 1987). He was tan, with black hair, gypsy eyes and, from what I could deduce from my upstairs bedroom window, a torso smooth as a river rock. He was from Peru. He wore heavy cologne and spoke in the language of an old-fashioned telegram.

HOW YOU DO STOP NICE DAY STOP WHERE IS HOSE STOP

Every Monday and Thursday at four o'clock, I'd procrastinate working on my French compositions or Algebra III and spy on him working, though most of the time he didn't work so much as hang out, chill, loiter, loaf, enjoy a laid-back cigarette in a scarce patch of sun. (He always threw the stub in a clandestine place, tossing it bchind a bromeliad or into a dense section of bamboo without even making sure it was extinguished.) Andreo really only started working two to three hours after his arrival, when Dad came home from the university. With an array of showy gestures (heavy panting, wiping his brow), he'd then push the lawnmower ineffectively along the forest floor, or prop up the wooden stepladder on the side of the house in a futile attempt to hack back the canopy. My favorite observation was when Andreo muttered to himself in Spanish after Dad confronted him, demanding to know exactly *why* the knotted liana was still creating a Greenhouse Effect on the back porch, or why a brand new crop of strangler figs now lined the back of our property.

One afternoon I made sure I was in the kitchen when Andreo slipped inside to steal one of my orange push pops from the freezer. He looked at me shyly and then smiled, revealing crooked teeth.

YOU DON'T MIND STOP I EAT STOP BAD BACK STOP

In the Howard Country Day library during lunch, I consulted Spanish textbooks and dictionaries and taught myself what I could.

Me llamo Azul.
My name is Blue.

El jardinero, Mellors, es una persona muy curiosa.
The gamekeeper, Mellors, is a curious kind of person.

¿Quiere usted seducirme? ¿Es eso que usted quiere decirme?
Would you like me to seduce you? Is that what you're trying to tell me?

¡Nelly, soy Heathcliff!
Nelly, I am Heathcliff!

I waited in vain for Pablo Neruda's *Twenty Love Songs and a Song of Despair* (1924) to be returned to the library. (The Girlfriend Who Wore Nothing But Tight Tank Tops had checked it out and lost it at the Boyfriend Who Should Shave Those Gross Hairs on His Chin's.) I was forced to steal a copy from the Spanish room and fitfully memorized XVII, wondering how I'd ever find the courage to do The Romeo, publicly proclaim those words of love, shout them so loudly that the sound had wings and carried itself up to balconies. I doubted I could even handle The Cyrano, writing the words on a card, signing someone else's name and covertly dropping it through the cracked window of his truck while he lounged in the backyard reading *¡Hola!* under the rubber trees.

As it turned out, I did neither The Romeo nor The Cyrano.
I did The Hercules.

*   *   *

At approximately 8:15 P.M. on a brisk Wednesday night in November, I
was upstairs in my room studying for a French test. Dad was at a faculty dinner in honor of a new dean. The doorbell rang. I was terrified and immediately imagined all kinds of wicked Bible salesmen and bloodthirsty misfits
(see O'Connor, *The Complete Stories*, 1971). I darted into Dad's room and
peered through the window in the corner. To my astonishment, in the night-
plum darkness, I saw Andreo's red truck, though he'd driven clear off the
driveway into a dense cluster of violin ferns.

I didn't know what was more gruesome, imagining The Misfit on my
front porch or knowing it was *he*. My first inclination was to lock my bedroom door and hide under the comforter, but he was ringing the doorbell
over and over again—he must have noticed the bedroom lights. I tiptoed
down the stairs, stood for at least three minutes in front of the door, biting my
fingernails, rehearsing my icebreaker (*¡Buenas Noches! ¡Qué sorpresa!*). Finally, hands clammy, mouth like half-dry Elmer's glue, I opened the door.

It was Heathcliff.

And yet it wasn't. He was standing away from me by the steps, like a wild
animal afraid to come close. The evening light, what little managed to hack
its way through the branches crisscrossing the sky, cut into the side of his
face. It was contorted as if he was screaming, but there was no sound, only
a low hum, nearly imperceptible, like electricity in walls. I looked at his
clothes and thought to myself he'd been housepainting, but then I realized
stupidly it was *blood*, everywhere, on his hands, inky and metallic-smelling,
like pipes under the kitchen sink. He was standing in it too—around his half-
laced combat boots were mudlike splatters. He blinked at me, his mouth still
open, and stepped forward. I had no idea if he was going to hug me or kill
me. He fell, slumped at my feet.

I ran to the kitchen, dialed 911. The woman was a hybrid between person
and machine and I had to repeat our address twice. Finally, she said an ambulance was on the way and I returned to the porch, kneeling next to him. I
tried to remove his jacket, but he moaned and grabbed at what I realized was
a gunshot wound in his lower left side, under his ribs.

"*Yo telefoneé una ambulancia,*" I said. (I called an ambulance.)

I rode in the back with him.

NO STOP NO GOOD STOP PAPA STOP

"Usted va a estar bien," I said. (You're going to be fine.)

At the hospital, the paramedics raced his gurney through the smudged, white double doors and the nurse in charge of the emergency room roster, petite, perky Nurse Marvin, handed me a bar of soap and paper-towel pajamas and told me to use the bathroom at the end of the hall; the cuffs of my jeans were splattered with blood.

After I changed, I left a message on the machine for Dad and then sat quietly on a pastel plastic seat in the waiting room. I sort of dreaded Dad's inevitable appearance. Obviously I loved the man, but unlike some of the other fathers I observed at Pappy-Comes-to-School Day at Walhalla Elementary, dads who were shy and talked in cottony voices, my dad was a loud, uninhibited man, a man of resolute action with little patience or innate tranquility, more Papa Dop in temperament than Paddington Bear, Pavlova or Petting Zoo. Dad was a man who, due to his underprivileged background perhaps, never hesitated when it came to the verbs *to get* or *to take*. He was always getting something off the ground, his act together, his hands dirty, the show on the road, someone's goat, the message, out more, on with things, lost, laid, away with murder. He was also always taking charge, the bull by the horns, back the night, something in stride, someone to the cleaners, a rain check, an ax to something, Manhattan. And when it came to looking at things, Dad was something of a Compound Microscope, one who viewed life through an adjustable eyepiece lens and thus expected all things to be in focus. He had no tolerance for The Murky, The Blurry, The Hazy or The Soiled.

He charged into the emergency room shouting, "What the hell is going on here? *Where is my daughter?*" causing Nurse Marvin to scuttle off her chair.

After ensuring that I too had not suffered a gunshot wound, nor had any open cuts or scrapes through which I might have been fatally contaminated by "that Latino son-of-a-bitch," Dad barged through the smudged, white double doors with the giant red letters screaming AUTHORIZED PERSONNEL ONLY (Dad was always electing himself an AUTHORIZED PERSON) and demanded to know what had happened.

Any other dad would have been cursed, expelled, expunged, maybe even arrested, but this was Dad, part Pershing missile, part People's Prince. Within minutes, various excitable nurses and the odd redheaded intern were scurrying around the major shock–trauma unit, working not for the third-degree burn victim or the boy who'd overdosed on ibuprofen now weeping silently into the crook of his arm, but for Dad.

"Well, he's upstairs in surgery and he's stable," said the odd redheaded intern, standing very close to Dad and smiling up at him (see "Bulldog Ant," *Meet the Bugs*, Buddle, 1985).

"We will have some more up-to-date information for you as soon as the doctor comes down from surgery. Let's pray it'll be good news!" exclaimed a nurse (see "Wood Ant," *Meet the Bugs*).

Shortly Dr. Michael Feeds appeared from Floor 3, Surgery, and told Dad Andreo had suffered a gunshot wound to his abdomen, but was going to live.

"Do you know what he was up to tonight?" he asked. "From the look of the bullet wound, he was shot at close range, which could mean it was an accident, his own gun maybe. He could have been cleaning the barrel and it accidentally discharged. Some semiautomatics can do that . . ."

Dad stared down at poor Dr. Mike Feeds until Dr. Mike Feeds was cross-sectioned, positioned on a spotless examination slide and firmly clamped to the specimen stage.

"My daughter and I know nothing about that human being."

"But I thought—"

"He happened to mow our lawn twice a week and did an inadequate job at that, so exactly why in Christ's name he chose to *drip* up onto our porch is beyond my comprehension. Of course," Dad said, glancing at me, "we understand the situation is tragic. My daughter was more than happy to save his life, getting him proper treatment or what have you, but I will tell you quite bluntly, Dr. . . ."

"Dr. Feeds," said Dr. Feeds. "Mike."

"I will tell you, Dr. Meeds, that we are of no relation to this individual and I will not involve my daughter in whatever it was that got him into such a predicament—gang warfare, gambling, any number of those insalubrious activities of the underworld. Our involvement ends here."

"Oh, I see," said Dr. Feeds softly.

Dad gave a curt nod, planted a hand on my shoulder, and steered me through the smudged, white double doors.

That night in my room, I stayed awake imagining a humid reunion with Andreo surrounded by Philippine figs and peacock plants. His skin would smell of cacao and vanilla, mine of passion fruit. I wouldn't be paralyzed with shyness, not anymore. After a person had come to you with his/her gunshot wound, after his/her blood had been all over your hands, socks and jeans, you were tied together by a powerful bond of human existence that no one, not even a Dad, could comprehend.

¡No puedo vivir sin mi vida! ¡No puedo vivir sin mi alma! (I cannot live without my life! I cannot live without my soul!)

He ran his hand through his black hair, oily and thick.

YOU SAVE MY LIFE STOP ONE NIGHT I MAKE YOU COMIDA CRIOLLA STOP

But such an exchange was not meant to be.

✳   ✳   ✳

The following morning, after the police called and Dad and I made a statement, I made him drive me to St. Matthew's hospital. I carried in my arms a dozen pink roses ("You will not take that boy *red* roses, I draw the line," Dad bellowed in the Seasonal Flowers aisle at Deal Foods, causing two mothers to stare) and a melted chocolate milkshake.

He was gone.

"Disappeared from his room 'round five this morning," reported Nurse Joanna Cone (see "Giant Skink," *Encyclopedia of Living Things*, 4th ed.). "Ran a check on his insurance. The card he gave was a fake. Doctors think that's why he hightailed it outta here, but the *thing is*," Nurse Cone leaned forward, jutting out her round, pink chin and speaking in the same emphatic whisper she probably used to tell Mr. Cone to stay awake during church, "he didn't speak aworda English so Dr. Feeds never got outa him how he got the bullet. Police don't know either. What I'm thinkin', and this is just a hunch, but I wonder if he was one of them illegal aliens who come to this country to find steady work and a good benefit program with disability and unlimited sick days. They've been spotted in this area before. My sister Cheyenne? She saw a whole slew of them in a checkout aisle at Electronic Cosmos. Know how they do it? Rubber rafts. The dead of night. Sometimes all the way from Cuba, fleeing Fidel. You know what I'm talking about?"

"I believe I have heard a few rumors," said Dad.

Dad made Nurse Cone call AAA from the Recovery Unit desk, and when we returned home, Andreo's truck was being towed. A large white van, discreetly marked Industrial Cleaning Co., was parked under our banyan tree. At Dad's request, ICC, specializing in the sanitization of former crime scenes, had driven the half hour north from Baton Rouge to attend to the trail of Andreo's blood staining the walkway, the front porch and a few maidenhair ferns.

"We're putting this sad incident behind us, my little cloud," Dad said, squeezing my shoulder as he waved to grim-faced ICC employee Susan, age 40–45, wearing a blinding white slicker and green rubber gloves that extended beyond her elbows to her upper arms. She stepped onto our porch like an astronaut stepping on the moon.

*　*　*

The appearance of Andreo's blurb in *The Howard Sentinel* (FOREIGNER SHOT, VANISHES) marked the end of The Verduga Incident, as Dad called it (a minor scandal that had only briefly tarnished an otherwise spotless Administration).

Three months later, when the allspice and cassava plants had successfully quarantined the lawn, when twisting liana had choked every porch pillar and gutter and begun its murderous designs on the roof, when rays of sunlight, even at noon, rarely had the nerve to trespass beyond the understory to the ground, we still knew nothing about Andreo, and in February, Dad and I left Howard for Roscoe, Michigan, official homeland of the Red Squirrel. Though I never said his name and remained silent in supposed indifference whenever Dad mentioned him ("Wonder what ever happened to that Latino thug"), I thought about him all the time, my stop-spoken gamekeeper, my Heathcliff, my Something.

There was one more incident.

When Dad and I were living in Nestles, Missouri, immediately following my fifteenth birthday celebration at The Hashbrown Hut, we were loafing around Wal-Mart so I could pick out a few birthday presents. ("Sundays at Wal-Mart," said Dad. "Parkies feasting for an afternoon on a football stadium of spectacular savings so the Waltons may buy an extra château in the south of France.") Dad had gone to Jewelry and I was perusing Electronics when I looked up and noticed a man with shaggy hair black as an eight ball. He was moving past the display of digital cameras with his back to me. He wore faded jeans, a gray T-shirt and an army camouflage baseball cap pressed way down over his forehead.

His face was hidden—apart for a bit of tan, unshaved cheek—and yet, as he rounded into the aisle of TVs, my heart began to pound, because instantly I recognized the showy sigh, the slouch, that slow, underwater movement— his overall sense of Tahiti. No matter what time of day or amount of work to be done, someone with Tahiti could close his eyes and the reality of moody lawnmowers, scruffy lawns, threats of termination of employment would recede and in seconds he'd simply be in Tahiti, stark naked and drinking from a coconut, aware only of the percussion of the wind and girlish sighs of the ocean. (Few people were born with Tahiti, although there was a natural proclivity in Greeks, Turks and male South Americans. In North America, there was prevalence amongst Canadians, particularly in the Yukon territories, but in the United States it could be found only in first- and second-generation hippies and nudists.)

I slipped after him, so I could find out it wasn't him but only someone who looked like him with a flat nose or Gorbachev birthmark. Yet, when I reached the aisle of TVs, as if he was in one of his restless, drowsy moods (exactly why he'd never tended the Neptune orchids), he'd drifted out the other end of the aisle, seemingly headed toward Music. I darted back the other way, slipping past the CDs, the cardboard CLEARANCE display of Bo Keith Badley's "Honky-tonk Hookup," but, again, when I peered around the FEATURED ARTIST OF THE MONTH sign, he'd already disappeared into the Photo Center.

"Find some respectably rolled-back prices?" Dad suddenly asked behind me.

"Oh—no."

"Well, if you'd accompany me to Garden and Patio, I believe I've found a winner. The Beech Total Ovation Symphony Hot Tub Spa with Stereo. Typhoon back and neck jets. Maintenance free. Eight people may pile in for the fun at once. And price? *Firmly* rolled back. Hurry. We don't have much time."

I managed to extricate myself from Dad under the somewhat shaky guise of wanting to peruse Apparel, and after I saw him head merrily toward Pets, I quickly circled back to the Photo Center. He wasn't there. I checked Pharmacy; Gifts & Flowers; Toys, where a red-faced woman was spanking her kids; Jewelry, where a Latino couple was trying on watches; the Vision Center, where an old woman bravely considered life behind brown-tinted billboard frames. I ran through a slew of cranky mothers in Baby; dazed newlyweds in Bath; Pets, where I covertly observed Dad discussing freedom with a goldfish ("Life ain't so good in the slammer, is it, old boy?"); and Sewing, where a bald man weighed the pros and cons of pink-and-white cotton chintz. I patrolled the café and the checkout aisles, including Customer Service and the Express Lane where a fat toddler screamed and kicked the candy bars.

But again—he was gone. There'd be no awkward reunion, no WHEN LOVE SPEAKS STOP THE VOICE OF THE GODS MAKE HEAVEN DROWSY WITH THE HARMONY STOP.

It wasn't until I dejectedly returned to the Photo Center that I noticed the shopping cart. Abandoned by the Drop-Off counter, jutting out into the middle of the aisle, it was empty—as I could have sworn his had been—apart from one item, a small plastic package of something called, ShifTbush™ Invisible Gear, Fall Mix.

Puzzled, I picked up the bag. It was stuffed with crunchy nylon leaves. I read the back: "ShifTbush™ Fall Mix, a blend of 3-D, photo-enhanced, synthetic forest leaves. Apply it using EZStik™ to your existing camo and you'll be instantly invisible in your woodland surroundings, even to the keenest of animals. ShifTbush™ is the accomplished hunter's dream."

"Don't tell me you're about to go through a deer-hunting phase," Dad said behind me. He sniffed. "What is that horrific smell—men's cologne, acidic sap. I couldn't find you. Figured you'd disappeared into that black hole known as the public restroom."

I tossed the package back into the cart. "I thought I saw someone."

"Oh? Now tell me your gut reaction to the following words. Colonial. Dellahay. Wood. Patio. Five Pieces. Sun resistant, wind resistant, Judgment Day resistant. Amazing value at just $299. And consider the Dellahay motto neatly inscribed on their cute little tags: 'Patio furniture isn't furniture. It's a state of mind.'" Dad smiled, putting his arm around me as he pushed me gently toward Garden. "I'll give you ten thousand dollars if you can tell me what that means."

Dad and I left Wal-Mart with patio furniture, a coffee machine and one paroled goldfish (freedom was too much for him; he went belly up after a day of living on the outside), and yet, weeks later, even when the Improbables and Highly Unlikelies had taken over my head, I couldn't let go of the thought that it had, in fact, been he, restless and moody Heathcliff. Day after day, he floated through all the Wal-Marts in America, searching for me in a million lonely aisles.

The House of the Seven Gables

Naturally, for me, the idea of a Permanent Home (the definition of which I took to be any shelter Dad and I inhabited in excess of ninety days—the time an American cockroach could go without food) was nothing more than a Pipe Dream, Cloud-Cuckoo-Land, the hope to purchase a brand new Cadillac Coupe DeVille with baby blue leather interior for any Soviet during the drab winter of 1985.

On countless occasions, I pointed out New York City or Miami on our Rand-McNally map. "Or Charleston. Why can't you teach Conflict Resolution at University of South Carolina at This Is Actually a Civilized Location?" My head mashed against the window, seatbelt strangling me, my gaze dazed by the ceaseless rewinding of cornfields, I'd fantasize that one day, Dad and I would quietly settle somewhere—anywhere—like dust.

Due to his stock refusals over the years, however, during which he ridiculed my sentimentality ("How can you eschew travel? I don't understand. How can *my* daughter wish to be dimwitted and dull as some handmade ashtray, as floralized wallpaper, as that sign—yes, *that* one—Big Slushy. Ninety-nine cents. That's your name from now on. Big Slushy."), during our highway discussions of *The Odyssey* (Homer, Hellenistic Period) or *The Grapes of Wrath* (Steinbeck, 1939), I'd stopped even *alluding* to such literary themes as the Homestead, Motherland or Native Soil. And thus it was with great fanfare Dad unveiled over rhubarb pie at the Qwik Stop Diner outside of Lomaine, Kansas ("Ding! Dong! The Witch Is Dead," he sang facetiously, causing the waitress to frown at us suspiciously), that for the *entirety* of my high school senior year, all seven months and nineteen days, we would reside in a single location: Stockton, North Carolina.

I'd heard of it oddly enough, not only because I'd read, a few years back, the cover story in *Ventures* magazine, "Fifty Top Retirement Towns," and Stockton (pop. 53,339), marooned in the Appalachian Mountains, evidently quite pleased with its nickname (The Florence of the South) had been written up as #39, but also because the mountain city had featured prominently in a fascinating FBI account of the Jacksonville fugitives, *Escaped* (Pillars, 2004), the true story of the Vicious Three who escaped from Florida State Prison and survived for twenty-two years in the Great Smoky Mountain National Park. They roamed the thousands of trails veining the foothills between North Carolina and Tennessee, living on deer, rabbit, skunk and the refuse of weekend campers, and would have remained at large ("The Park is so expansive it could effectively hide a herd of pink elephants," wrote the author, retired Special Agent Janet Pillars) had one of them not acted on the apparently uncontrollable urge to hang at the local mall. On a Friday afternoon in fall 2002, Billy "The Pit" Pikes wandered into a West Stockton shopping center, Dinglebrook Arcade, bought a few dress shirts, ate a calzone and was identified by a cashier at Cinnabon. Two of the Vicious Three were captured, but the last, known simply as "Sloppy Ed," remained at large, somewhere in the mountains.

Dad, on Stockton: "As dreary a mountain town as any in which I'll collect a frighteningly diminutive paycheck from UNCS and you'll secure your place next year at Harvard."

"Hot diggity dog," I said.

The August before our arrival, while living at the Atlantic Waters Condotel in Portsmouth, Maine, Dad had been in close contact with one Ms. Dianne L. Seasons, a Senior Associate with a very impressive sales and long-term lease record at the Stockton-based Sherwig Realty. Once a week, Dianne mailed Dad glossy photos of Featured Sherwig Properties, each one accompanied with her handwritten note on Sherwig memo stationary, paper-clipped to the corner: "A lovely mountain oasis!" "Full of Southern charm!" "Exquisite and special, one of my all-time *faves*!"

Dad, famous for toying with Salespersons Desperate to Close like grassland cats with a limping wildebeest, deferred making a final decision on a house and responded to Dianne's evening phone calls ("Just wanted to know how ya'll liked 52 Primrose!") with melancholic indecision and plenty of sighing and thus, Dianne's handwritten memos became increasingly frenzied ("Won't last the summer!!" "Will go like a hot cake!!!").

Finally, Dad put Dianne out of her misery when he chose one of the most exclusive of all Featured Sherwig Properties, the fully furnished 24 Armor Street, #1 on the Hot List.

I was shocked. Dad, hailing from his visiting professorship at Hicksburg State College or the University of Kansas at Petal, certainly had not been amassing great reserves of wealth (*Federal Forum* paid a derisory $150 per essay) and almost every other address at which we'd lived, the 19 Wilson Streets, the 4 Clover Circles, had been tiny, forgettable houses. And yet Dad had selected the SPRAWLING 5BR TUDOR FURNISHED IN KINGLY LUXURY, which looked, at least in Dianne's glossy photo, like an enormous two-humped Bactrian Camel at rest. (Dad and I would discover that the Sherwig photographer took particular care to conceal the fact that it was a *molting* Bactrian Camel at rest. Almost all of the gutters were detaching and many of the wooden beams decorating the exterior fell down during Fall Term.)

Within minutes of our arrival at 24 Armor Street, Dad began his customary effort to transform himself into Leonard Bernstein, orchestrating the men of Feathery Touch Moving Co. as if they weren't simply Larry, Roge, Stu and Greg hoping to get off early and go for a beer, but sections of Brass, Woodwinds, Strings and Percussion.

I snuck away and did my own tour of the house and grounds. Not only did the mansion come with 5BR, a COOK'S HEAVEN ON EARTH W/GRANITE, HARDWOODS, IN-DRAWER FRIDGE and CUSTOM HEART PINE CABINETS, but also a MASTER SUITE W/ MARBLE BATH, an ENCHANTING FISH POND and a BOOKWORM'S FANTASY LIBRARY.

"Dad, how are we *paying* for this place?"

"Hmm, oh, don't worry about that—excuse me, must you carry that box on its side? See the arrow there and those words that read, 'This End Up'? Yes. That means, this end up."

"We can't afford it."

"Of course we—I ask you once and I will ask you again, that goes in the living room, not here, please don't drop—there are valuables—I've saved a little in the last year, sweet. Not *there*! You see, my daughter and I employ a *system*. Yes, if you read the boxes you will discover that there are *words* written there in permanent marker and those words correspond to a particular *room* in this house. That's right! You get a gold star!"

Carrying a gigantic box, Strings lumbered past us into COOK'S HEAVEN ON EARTH.

"We should leave, Dad. We should go to 52 Primrose."

"Don't be ridiculous. I worked out a fine price with Miss Seasons

Greetings—yes, now *that* goes downstairs into my study, and please, there are actual butterflies in that box, do not drag—don't you read? Yes, lighten your grip."

Brass clumsily made his way down the stairs with the giant box marked BUTTERFLIES FRAGILE.

"Hmm? Now, yes, simply relax and enjoy—"

"Dad, this is too much money."

"I'm, well, yes, I understand your point, sweet, and certainly, this is . . ." Dad's eyes drifted up to the giant, brass light hanging from the ten-foot plaster ceiling, an upside-down representation of the 1815 Mt. Tambora eruption (see *Indonesia and the Ring of Fire*, Priest, 1978). "It's somewhat more ornate than we're used to, but why *not*? We're going to be here the entire year, aren't we? It's the last chapter, so to speak, before you go off, conquer the world. I want to make it memorable."

He adjusted his glasses and looked back down into the opened box labeled LINENS like Jean Peters gazing into the Trevi Fountain, about to throw in a coin and make a wish.

I sighed. It was evident, and had been for some time, that Dad was determined to make *une grande affaire* out of this year, my senior year (hence, the Bactrian Camel and other perplexing Auntie Mame–like lavishes I shall soon detail). Yet he was dreading it too (hence, the gloomy gaze into LINENS). Part of it was that he didn't want to think about me leaving him at the end of the year. I didn't particularly want to think about leaving him either. The thought was difficult to fathom. Abandoning Dad felt like de-boning all the old American musicals, separating Rodgers from Hammerstein, Lerner from Loewe, Comden from Green.

The other reason why I thought Dad was feeling a little blue, and perhaps the more significant one, was that our scheduled year-long stay in a single location would mark an undeniably monotonous passage within chapter 12, "American Teachings and Travel" of Dad's otherwise thrilling mental biography.

"Always live your life with your biography in mind," Dad was fond of saying. "Naturally, it won't be published unless you have a Magnificent Reason, but at the very least you will be living grandly." It was painfully obvious Dad was hoping his posthumous biography would be reminiscent not of *Kissinger: The Man* (Jones, 1982) or even *Dr. Rhythm: Living with Bing* (Grant, 1981) but something along the lines of the New Testament or the Qur'an.

Though he certainly never said so, it was evident Dad adored being in motion, in transit, in the midst. He found standstills, halts, finishing points, termini, to be unappetizing, dull. Dad wasn't concerned with the fact that he was seldom at a university long enough to learn his students' names and was forced, for the sake of assigning their grades correctly at the end of term, to give them certain pertinent monikers, such as Too Many Questions, Tadpole Glasses, Smile Is All Gums and Sits on My Left.

Sometimes I was afraid Dad felt having a daughter was a last stop, a finishing point. Sometimes when he was in a Bourbon Mood, I worried he wanted to ditch me and America and return to former Zaire, presently the Democratic Republic of the Congo (*democratic* in Africa, a word like the slang usage of *totally* and *bobbing for fries,* used purely for cool effect) in or-der to play a Che-cum-Trotsky-cum-Spartacus to the native people's fight for freedom. Whenever Dad spoke of the four treasured months spent in the Congo River Basin in 1985, hobnobbing with the "kindest, hardest-working, most genuine" people he'd ever met, he adopted an unusually flimsy appear-ance. He resembled an aged silent movie star photographed with buttery lights and lens.

I'd accuse him of secretly wanting to return to Africa in order to spear-head a well-organized revolution, single-handedly stabilizing the DRC (ex-punging Hutu-aligned forces), then moving on to other countries waiting to be freed like exotic maidens tied to railroad tracks (Angola, Cameroon, Chad). When I voiced these suspicions, he'd laugh of course, but I always felt the laugh wasn't *quite* hard enough; it was conspicuously hollow, which made me wonder if I'd haphazardly thrown in my line and caught the biggest, most unlikely of fishes. This was Dad's deep-sea secret, never be-fore photographed or scientifically classified: he wished to be a hero, a poster boy for freedom, silk-screened, reduced to bright colors and printed on a hundred thousand T-shirts, Dad with Marxist beret, martyr-ready eyes, and a threadbare mustache (see *The Iconography of Heroes,* Gorky, 1978).

There was too a certain uncharacteristic, boyish gusto he reserved solely for sticking another pushpin through the Rand-McNally map and briefing me on our next location in a show-offy factoid riff, his version of Gangsta Rap: "Next stop Speers, South Dakota, homeland of the Ring-necked Pheas-ant, the Black-footed Ferret, the Badlands, Black Hills Forest, Crazy Horse Memorial, capital, Pierre, largest city, Sioux Falls, rivers, Moreau, Cheyenne, White, James . . ."

"You take the large bedroom at the top of the stairs," he said now, watch-ing Percussion and Woodwinds as they carried a heavy box across the yard toward the separate gabled entrance of the EXPANSIVE MASTER SUITE, "Hell, have the upstairs wing to yourself. Isn't it nice, sweet, to have a *wing?* Why shouldn't we live it up like Kubla Khan for a change? If you go up there, you'll find a surprise. I think you'll be pleased. I had to bribe a housewife, a real estate agent, two furniture salesmen, a UPS Head of Operations—now *listen,* yes, I'm talking to you—if you could go downstairs and aid your compatriot in unpacking the materials for my study, it would be most effective. He seems to have fallen down a rabbit hole."

* * *

Over the years, Dad's surprises, large and small, had been scholarly in nature, a set of 1999 Lamure-France *Encyclopedias of the Physical World* translated from the French and unavailable for purchase in the United States. ("All Nobel Prize–winners have a set of these," Dad said.)

But as I pushed open the bedroom door at the top of the stairs and walked into the large blue-walled room covered in pastoral oil paintings, giant arc windows along the far wall blistered with bubble curtains, I discovered not a rare, underground edition of *Wie schafft man ein Meisterwerk*, or *The Step-by-Step Manual for Crafting Your Magnum Opus* (Lint, Steggertt, Cue, 1993), but astonishingly, my old Citizen Kane desk pushed into the corner by the window. It was the real thing: the elephantine, walnut, Renaissance Revival library table I'd had eight years ago at 142 Tellwood Street in Wayne, Oklahoma.

Dad had found the desk at the Lord and Lady Hillier Estate Sale just outside of Tulsa, to which antiques wheeler-and-dealer June Bug, Pattie "Let's Make a Deal" Lupine, had dragged Dad one stuffy Sunday afternoon. For some reason, when Dad saw the desk (and the five struggling Arnies it took to get it on the auction platform), he saw me and only me presiding over it (though I was only eight with a wingspan less than half its length). He paid a huge, undisclosed amount for it and announced with great flourish that this was "Blue's Desk," a desk "worthy of my little Eve of St. Agnes, upon which she will unmask all the Great Ideas." A week later, two of Dad's checks bounced, one at a grocery store, another at the university bookstore. I secretly believed it was because he'd paid "way above treasure price" for the desk, according to Let's Make a Deal, though Dad claimed he'd simply been slapdash with his bookkeeping. "Snubbed a decimal point," he'd said.

And then, rather anticlimactically, I was only able to unmask Great Ideas in Wayne, because we weren't able to take the desk with us to Sluder,

Florida—something to do with the movers (the falsely advertised You *Can* Take It With You Moving Co.) being unable to fit it in the van. I shed ferocious tears and called Dad a reptile when we had to leave it, as if it wasn't just an oversized table with elaborate talon legs and seven drawers requiring seven individual keys, but a black pony I was abandoning in a barn.

Now I hurried back down the TWELVE OAKS STAIRCASE, finding Dad in the basement carefully opening the BUTTERFLIES FRAGILE box containing my mother's specimen—the six glass display cases she'd been working on when she'd died. When we arrived at a new house, he took hours to mount them, always in his office, always on the wall opposite his desk: thirty-two lined up girls in a petrified beauty pageant. It was why he didn't like June Bugs—or anyone, for that matter—nosing around his study, because the most devastating aspect of the Lepidoptera was not their color, or the unexpected furriness of the Polyphemus Moth antennae, not even the gloomy feeling you felt whenever you stood in front of something that had once zigzagged madly through the air, now still, wings uncouthly spread, body pinned to a piece of paper in a glass case. It was the presence of my mother within them. As Dad

VISUAL AID 4.0

said once, they allowed you to see her face in greater close-up than any photographic likeness (Visual Aid 4.0). I'd always felt too that they held a strange adhesive power, so when a person looked at them, it was difficult to yank his/her gaze away.

"So how do you like it?" he asked cheerfully, lifting out one of the cases, frowning as he inspected the corners.

"It's perfect," I said.

"Isn't it? The perfect surface on which to draft an admissions essay to make any Harvard graybeard shiver in his dress slacks."

"But how much did it cost for you to buy it again—and then the shipping!"

He glanced at me. "Hasn't anyone told you it's blasphemous to ask the price of a gift?"

"*How much*? In total."

He stared at me. "Six hundred dollars," he said with a resigned sigh, and then, returning the case to the box, squeezed my shoulder and moved past me, back up the stairs, shouting at Brass and Woodwinds to speed up the tempo of their last movement.

He was lying. I knew this, not only because his eyes had flicked to the side when he'd said "six hundred" and Fritz Rudolph Scheizer, MD, had written in *The Conduct of Rational Creatures* (1998) that the cliché of a person's eyes flicking to the side when he or she lies is "utterly true," but also because, while surveying the underside of the desk, I'd spotted the tiny red price tag still knotted around the leg in the far corner ($17,000).

I hurried back upstairs, into the foyer where Dad was looking through another box, BOOKS LIBRARY. I felt bewildered—a little upset, too. Dad and I had long put into effect the Sojourner Agreement, the understanding we'd always give each other The Truth "even if she was a beast, frightening and foul smelling." Over the years, there'd been countless occasions when the average dad would've cooked up an elaborate story, just to preserve the Parental Ruse, that they were sexless and morally flawless as Cookie Monsters—like the time Dad disappeared for twenty-four hours and when home, sported the tired yet satisfied look of a ranch hand who'd successfully horsewhispered a touchy Palomino. If I asked for The Truth (and sometimes I chose not to ask), he never let me down—not even when it let me hold his character up to the light and I could see him for what he sometimes was: harsh, scratchy, a few unexpected holes.

I had to confront him. Otherwise, the lie could wear me away (see "Acid

Rain on Gargoyles," *Conditions*, Eliot, 1999, p. 513). I ran upstairs, removed the price tag and kept it in my pocket for the rest of the day, waiting for the perfect checkmate moment to fling it at him.

But then, just before we left for dinner at Outback Steakhouse, he was in my room examining the desk, and he looked so absurdly cheerful and proud of himself ("I'm *good*," he said, animatedly rubbing his hands together like Dick Van Dyke. "Fit for St. Peter, hmm, sweet?"). I couldn't help but feel to call him out on this well-intentioned extravagance, to embarrass him, was sort of unnecessary and cruel—not unlike informing Blanche Dubois that her arms looked flabby, her hair dry and that she was dancing the polka dangerously close to the lamplight.

It was better not to say anything.

The Woman in White

We were in the Frozen section of Fat Kat Foods when I first saw Hannah Schneider, two days after our arrival in Stockton.

I was standing by our shopping cart, waiting for Dad to choose which flavor of ice cream he preferred.

"America's greatest revelation was not the atom bomb, not Fundamentalism, not fat farms, not Elvis, not even the quite astute observation that gentlemen prefer blondes, but the great heights to which she has propelled ice cream," Dad was fond of commenting while standing with the freezer door open and inspecting every flavor of Ben and Jerry's, oblivious to the customers swarming around him, waiting for him to move.

As he scrutinized the cartons on the shelves like a scientist engaged in creating an accurate DNA profile from a hair root, I became aware of a woman standing at the far end of the aisle.

She was dark haired, thin as a riding crop. Dressed in funeral attire, a black suit with black 1980s stilettos (more dagger than shoe), she looked incongruous, bleached in the neon lights and achey tunes of Fat Kat Foods. It was obvious, however, in the way she examined the back of the box of frozen peas that she liked being incongruous, the lone Bombshell slinking into a Norman Rockwell, the ostrich amongst buffalo. She exuded that mix of satisfaction and self-consciousness of beautiful women used to being looked at, which made me sort of hate her.

I'd long decided to hold in contempt all people who believed themselves to be the subject of everyone else's ESTABLISHING SHOT, BOOM SHOT, REACTION SHOT, CLOSE-UP or CHOKER, probably because I couldn't imagine myself turning up on anyone's storyboard, not even my own. At the same time, I (and the man staring at her with his mouth in an O holding a Lean Cuisine) couldn't help but shout, "Quiet on the set!" and "Roll 'em!" because, even at this distance, she was unbelievably stunning and strange, and as Dad was famous for quoting in one of his Bourbon Moods, 'Beauty is truth, truth beauty,—that is all / Ye know on earth, and all ye need to know.' "

She returned the peas to the freezer and began to walk toward us.

"New York Super Fudge or Phish Food?" asked Dad.

Her heels stabbed the floor. I didn't want to stare, so I made an unconvincing attempt to examine the nutritional content of various popsicles.

Dad didn't see her. "There's always Half Baked, I suppose," he was saying. "Oh, look. Makin' Whoopie Pie. I believe that's a new one, though I'm not sure how I feel about marshmallow with what, devil's food. Seems a bit overwrought."

As she passed, she glanced at Dad gazing into the freezer. When she looked at me, she smiled.

She had an elegant sort of romantic, bone-sculpted face, one that took well to both shadows and light, even at their extremes. And she was older than I'd realized, somewhere in her late thirties. Most extraordinary though was the air of a Chateau Marmont bungalow about her, a sense of RKO, which I'd never before witnessed in person, only while Dad and I watched *Jezebel* into the early hours of the morning. Yes, within her carriage and deliberate steps like a metronome (now retreating behind the display of potato chips) was a little bit of the Paramount lot, a little neat scotch and air kisses at Ciro's. I felt, when she opened her mouth, she wouldn't utter the crumbly speech of modernity, but would use moist words like *beau, top drawer* and *sound* (only occasionally *ring-a-ding-ding*), and when she considered a person, took *in* him/her, she would place those nearly extinct personality traits— Character, Reputation, Integrity and Class—above all others.

Not that she wasn't *real*. She was. There were hairs out of place, a quiver of white lint on her skirt. I simply felt somewhere, at some time, she'd been the toast of something. And a confident, even aggressive look in her eyes, made me certain she was planning a comeback.

"I'm thinking Heath Bar Crunch. What do you think? Blue?"

*   *   *

If her appearance in my life had amounted only to that single, Hitchcock cameo, I still think I would have remembered her, perhaps not in the same detail I remembered the ninety-five-degree summer night I watched *Gone with the Wind* for the first time at the Lancelot Dreamsweep Drive-in and Dad found it necessary to provide ongoing commentary on which constellations were visible ("There's Andromeda"), not only while Scarlett took on Sherman and when she got sick on the carrot but even when Rhett said he didn't give a damn.

As the oily hand of Fate would have it, I'd only wait twenty-four hours to see her again, this time in a speaking role.

School began in three days and Dad, in keeping with his recent Open-a-New-Window persona, insisted on spending the afternoon at Blue Crest Mall in the Adolescent Department of Stickley's, urging me to try on various articles of Back-2-School clothing and soliciting the fashion expertise of one Ms. Camille Luthers (see "Curly Coated Retriever," *Dictionary of Dogs*, Vol. 1). Camille was Adolescent Department Manager, who not only had worked in Adolescent for the last eight years but knew which Stickley styles were de rigueur this season due to her own esteemed daughter around my age named Cinnamon.

Ms. Luthers, on a pair of green pants, which resembled those worn by Mao's Liberation Army, size 2: "These look like they'd suit you perfectly." She eagerly pressed the hanger against my waist and stared at me in the mirror with her head tilted, as if hearing a high-pitched noise. "They suit Cinnamon perfectly too. I just got her a pair and she lives in them. Can't get her to take them off."

Ms. Luthers, on a boxy white button-down shirt, which resembled those worn by the Bolsheviks when they stormed the Winter Palace, size o: "Now this is you, too. Cinnamon has one of these in every color. She's around your size. Bird boned. Everyone thinks she's anorexic, but she's not and a lot of her peers get jealous living on fruit and bagels just to squeeze into a size 12."

After Dad and I left the Adolescent Department of Stickley's with most of Cinnamon's rebel wardrobe, we made our way to Surely Shoos on Mercy Avenue in North Stockton, per Ms. Luthers' helpful tip-off.

"I believe these are right up Cinnamon's alley," said Dad, holding up a large black platform shoe.

"No," I said.

"Thank God. I can safely say Chanel's rolling in her grave."

"Humphrey Bogart wore platform shoes throughout the filming of *Casablanca*," someone said.

I turned, expecting to see a mother circling Dad like a Hooded Vulture eyeing carrion, but it wasn't.

It was *she*, the woman from Fat Kat Foods.

She was tall, wearing skintight jeans, a tailored tweed jacket, and large black sunglasses on her head. Her dark brown hair hung idly around her face.

"Though he wasn't Einstein or Truman," she said, "I don't think history would be the same without him. Especially if he had to look *up* at Ingrid Bergman and say, 'Here's looking at you, kid.' "

Her voice was wonderful, a flu voice.

"You aren't from around here, are you?" she asked Dad.

He stared at her blankly.

The phenomenon of Dad interacting with a beautiful woman was always an odd, sort of uninspired chemical experiment. Most of the time there was no reaction. Other times, Dad and the woman might *appear* to react vigorously, producing heat, light, and gas. But at the end, there was never a functional product like plastics or glassware, only a foul stench.

"No," said Dad. "We're not."

"You've just moved down here?"

"Yes." He smiled, though it didn't do a fig leaf's job of hiding his desire to end the conversation.

"How do you like it?"

"Magnificent."

I didn't know why he wasn't friendlier. Usually, Dad didn't mind the odd June Bug spiraling over to him. And he certainly wasn't above encouraging them, opening all the curtains, turning on all the lights by launching into certain extemporaneous lectures on Gorbachev, Arms Control, the 1-2-3s of Civil War (the gist of which the June Bug missed like a rare raindrop), often dropping hints about the impressive tome he was authoring, *The Iron Grip*.

I wondered if she was too attractive or tall for him (she was almost his height) or perhaps her unsolicited Bogie comment had rubbed him the wrong way. One of Dad's pet peeves was to be "informed" of something he already knew and Dad and I were well aware of her crumb of trivia. Driving between Little Rock and Portland, I'd read aloud all of the eye-opening *Thugs, Midgets, Big Ears and Dentures: A Real Profile of Hollywood's Leading Men* (Rivette, 1981), and *Other Voices, 32 Rooms: My Life as L. B. Mayer's Maid* (Hart, 1961). Between San Diego and Salt Lake City I'd read aloud countless celebrity biographies, authorized and unauthorized, including those of Howard Hughes, Bette Davis, Frank Sinatra, Cary Grant and the highly memorable *Christ, It's Been Done Before: Celluloid Jesuses from 1912–1988,*

Why Hollywood Should Cease Committing the Son of God to Screen (Hatcher, 1989).

"And your daughter," she said, smiling at me, "what school will she be attending?"

I opened my mouth, but Dad spoke.

"The St. Gallway School."

He was looking at me intently with his I'm-Thumbing-a-Lift-Here look, which soon slipped into his Please-Pull-a-Ripcord face, and then, If-You-Would-Be-So-Kind-as-to-Administer-a-Rabbit-Punch. Normally, he reserved those faces for instances when a June Bug with some sort of physical deformity was actively pursuing him, like a faulty sense of direction (extreme near-sightedness) or an erratic wing (facial tic).

"I'm a teacher there," she said, extending her hand to me. "Hannah Schneider."

"Blue van Meer."

"What a wonderful name." She looked at Dad.

"Gareth," he said, after a moment.

"Nice to meet you."

With the brazen self-confidence present only in one who had shucked off the label of Sweater Girl and proved herself to be a dramatic actress of considerable range and talent (and enormous box-office draw), Hannah Schneider informed Dad and me that for the last three years she had taught Introduction to Film, an elective class for all grades. She also told us with great authority that the St. Gallway School was a "very special place."

"I think we should be getting along," Dad said, turning to me. "Don't you have piano?" (I hadn't, nor have I ever, had piano.)

But, quite unabashedly, Hannah Schneider did not stop talking, as if Dad and I were *Confidential* reporters who'd waited six months to interview her. Still, there was nothing outright haughty or overbearing in her manner; she simply assumed you were deeply interested in whatever she was saying. And you *were*. She asked where we were from ("Ohio," seethed Dad), what year I was ("Senior," fumed Dad), how we liked our new house ("It's fun," frothed Dad) and explained that she had moved here three years ago from San Francisco ("Astonishing," fizzed Dad). He really had no choice but to throw her a scrap.

"Perhaps we'll see you at a home football game," he said, waving good-bye (a one-hand-in-the-air "So long" that could also pass for "Not now") and steering me toward the exit at the front of the store. (Dad had never attended a home football game and had no intention of attending one. He considered most contact sports, as well as the hooting and woofing spectators, to be "embarrassing," "very, very wrong," "pitiful exhibitions of the *Australopithecus* within." "I suppose we *all* have an inner *Australopithecus*, but I'd prefer mine to remain deep in his cave, whittling away at Mammoth carcasses with his simple stone tools.")

"Thank God we made it out alive," said Dad, starting the car.

"What *was* that?"

"Your guess is as good as mine. As I've told you, these aged American feminists who pride themselves on opening their own doors, paying for themselves, well, they're not the fascinating, modern women they imagine themselves to be. Oh no, they're Magellan space probes looking for a man they can orbit without end."

One of Dad's favorite personal comments regarding the sexes was his likening assertive women to Spacecraft (fly-by probes, orbiters, satellites, landers) and men to the unwitting subjects of these missions (planets, moons, comets, asteroids). Dad, of course, saw himself as a planet so remote it had suffered only a single visit—the successful but brief *Natasha* Mission.

"I'm talking about *you*," I said. "You were rude."

"Rude?"

"Yes. She was nice. I liked her."

"Someone is not 'nice' when they intrude upon your privacy, when they force a landing and take the liberty of discharging radar signals that bounce off your surface, formulating panoramic images of your landscape and transmitting them ceaselessly through space."

"What about Vera Strauss?"

"Who?"

"Vera P. Strauss."

"Oh. The veterinarian?"

"Check-out girl in the express lane at Hearty Health Foods."

"Of course. She wanted to *be* a veterinarian. I remember."

"She accosted us in the middle of your—"

"Birthday dinner. At Wilber Steak, yes, I know."

"Wil*son* Steakhouse in Meade."

"Well, I—"

"You invited her to sit down for dessert and for three hours we listened to those awful stories."

"About her poor brother getting all that psychosurgery, yes, I remember, and I *told* you I was sorry. How was I supposed to know she herself was a candidate for shock treatment, that we should've called those same people who arrive at the end of *Streetcar* to cart the woman off?"

"At the time I didn't hear you bemoaning *her* panoramic images."

"Point taken. But I remember with Vera, very distinctly, she had an unusual quality. The fact that this unusual quality turned out to be of the Sylvia Plath variety, well, it wasn't *my* fault. And at least she was extraordinary on some level. At least she provided us with a raw, uncensored view of complete lunacy. This last woman, this—I don't even remember her name."

"Hannah Schneider."

"Well, yes, she was . . ."

"What?"

"Commonplace."

"You're nuts."

"I didn't spend six hours quizzing you on those 'Far, Far Beyond the SAT' flashcards for you to use the word 'nuts' in everyday speech—"

"You're *outré*," I said, crossing my arms, staring out the window at the afternoon traffic. "And Hannah Schneider was"—I wanted to think of a few decent words to blow Dad's hair back—"prepossessing. Yet abstruse."

"Hmm?"

"You know, she walked by us in the grocery store last night."

"Who?"

"Hannah."

He glanced over at me, surprised. "That woman was in Fat Kat Foods?"

I nodded. "Walked right by us."

He was silent for a moment, then sighed. "Well, I only hope she's not one of those defunct Galileo probes. I don't think I could withstand another crash landing. What was her name? The one from Cocorro—"

"Betina Mendejo."

"Yes, Betina, with the sweet little asthmatic four-year-old."

"She had a nineteen-year-old daughter studying to be a dietician."

"Of course," Dad said, nodding. "I remember now."

Brave New World

D ad said he'd first heard about the St. Gallway School from a fellow professor at Hicksburg State College, and for at least a year or so, a copy of
the school's shiny 2001–2004 admissions catalogue, breathlessly entitled *Higher Learning, Higher Grounds*, had been riding around in a box
in the back of our Volvo (along with five copies of *Federal Forum*, Vol. 10, Issue 5, 1998, featuring Dad's essay, "*Nächtlich*: Popular Myths of Freedom
Fighting").

The catalogue featured the proverbial wound-up rhetoric drenched in
adjectives, sunny photos filled with bushy autumn trees, teachers with the
kind faces of mice and kids grinning as they strolled down the sidewalk holding big textbooks in their arms like roses. In the distance, looking on (and apparently bored stiff) sat a crowd of glum plum mountains, a sky in wistful
blue. "Our facilities leave nothing to be desired," moaned p. 14, and sure,
there were football fields so smooth they looked like linoleum, a cafeteria
with bay windows and wrought-iron chandeliers, a monster athletic complex
that resembled the Pentagon. A diminutive stone chapel did its best to hide
from the massive Tudor buildings slouched all over the lawns, structures
christened with names like Hanover Hall, Elton House, Barrow and Vauxhall, each sporting a façade that brought to mind early U.S. presidents: gray-
topped, heavy brow, wooden teeth, mulish bearing.

The booklet also featured a delightfully eccentric blurb about Horatio
Mills Gallway, a rags-to-riches paper industrialist who'd founded the school
back in 1910, not in the name of altruistic principles like civic duty or the per-
sistence of scholarship, but for a megalomaniacal desire to see *Saint* in front

of his surname; establishing a private school proved to be the easiest way to achieve this.

My favorite section was "Where Have All the Gallwanians Gone?" which featured a proud blurb written by the Headmaster, Bill Havermeyer (a big old Robert Mitchum type), then went on to summarize the unparalleled achievements of Gallwanian alumni. Rather than the typical boasts of most puffed-up private schools—stratospheric SAT scores, the vast number of seniors who vaulted into the Ivy League—St. Gallway touted other, more extraordinary achievements: "We have the highest number of graduates in the country who go on to be revolutionary performance artists; . . . 7.27 percent of all Gallway graduates in the last fifty years have registered with the U.S. Patent and Trademark Office; one out of every ten Gallway students becomes an inventor; . . . 24.3 percent of all Gallwanians become published poets; 10 percent will study stage-makeup design; 1.2 percent puppetry; . . . 17.2 percent will reside in Florence at some point; 1.8 percent in Moscow; 0.2 percent in Taipei." "One out of every 2,031 Gallwanians gets into *The Guinness Book of World Records*. Wan Young, Class of 1982, holds the record for Longest Operatic Note Held . . ."

As Dad and I sped down the school's main road for the first time (the aptly named Horatio Way, a narrow drive that teased you through a forest of pin-thin pines before abandoning you at the center of campus), I found myself holding my breath, inexplicably awed. To our immediate left tumbled a lawn of Renoir green, which pitched and swelled so excitedly, it appeared as if it might float away had it not been for the oak trees nailing it to the ground ("The Commons," sang the catalogue, "a lawn expertly cultivated by our ingenious caretaker, Quasimodo, who some say is the original Gallwanian . . ."). To our right, chunky and impassive, was Hanover Hall, poised to cross the Delaware under icy conditions. Beyond a square stone courtyard ringed with birch trees, sat an elegant auditorium of glass and steel, colossal yet chic: Love Auditorium.

Our intentions were strictly business. Dad and I had come, not only to take a campus tour with Admissions guru Mirtha Grazeley (an elderly woman in fuchsia silk who led us like an old moth in dazed zigzags across the grounds: "Eh, we haven't seen the art gallery have we? Oh dear, the cafeteria slipped my mind. And that horse weathervane on top of Elton, not sure if you remember, it appeared in *Southern Architecture Monthly* last year.") but also to ingratiate ourselves with the administrator in charge of translating the credits from my last school into the St. Gallway Grading

System and hence, determining my class rank. Dad approached this task with the seriousness of Reagan approaching Gorbachev with the Nuclear Forces Treaty.

"Let me do the talking. You sit and look erudite."

Our target, Ms. Lacey Ronin-Smith, was tucked away in the Rapunzel-like clock tower of Hanover. She was sinewy, salt voiced, and unequivocally dreary haired. Now in her late sixties, she'd served as St. Gallway Academic Chancellor for the past thirty-one years, and, according to the photographs on display around her desk, was keen on quilting, nature hikes with her lady friends and a lapdog sporting more greasy black hair than an aged rock star.

"What you have in your hands is an official copy of Blue's high school transcript," Dad was saying.

"Yes," said Ms. Ronin-Smith. Her thin lips, which even in repose tended to look as if she were sucking on a lime, trembled slightly at the corners, hinting at vague dismay.

"The school Blue is coming from—Lamego High in Lamego, Ohio—is one of the most dynamic schools in the country. I want to make sure her work is adequately recognized here."

"Of course you do," said Ronin-Smith.

"Naturally, students will be threatened by her, especially those who anticipate they'll be first or second in the class. We don't wish to upset anyone. However, it's only fair that she is placed in close proximity to where she was when my work forced us to relocate. She was number *one*—"

Lacey gave Dad the Bureaucratic Stare—regret, with a hint of triumph. "I hate to discourage you, Mr. Van Meer, but I must inform you, Gallway policy is very clear in these matters. An incoming student, no matter how outstanding his or her marks, can not be placed higher than—"

"Good God," Dad said abruptly. Eyebrows raised, mouth an enraptured smile, he was leaning forward in his seat the precise angle of the Tower of Pisa. I realized, in horror, he was pulling his Yes-Virginia-There-Is-a-Santa-Claus face. I wanted to hide under my chair. "That is a very impressive diploma you have there. May I ask what it is?"

"Eh—what?" squeaked Ronin-Smith (as if Dad had just pointed out a centipede inching along the wall behind her), and she swiveled around to survey the giant, gold-sealed, cream, calligraffitied diploma mounted next to a photo of the Mötley Crüe dog in a bowtie and top hat. "Oh. That's my N.C. certificate for Distinguished Academic Counseling and Arbitration."

Dad gasped a little. "Sounds like they could use you at the U.N."

"Oh, please," said Ms. Ronin-Smith, shaking her head, reluctantly break-ing into a small yellowed smile of rickrack teeth. A flush was starting to seep into her neck. "*Hard*ly."

Thirty minutes later, after Dad had sufficiently wooed her (he worked like a ferocious evangelist; one had no choice but to be saved), we descended the corkscrew stairs leading from her office.

"Only one twerp ahead of you now," he whispered with unmitigated glee. "Some little tarantula named Radley Clifton. We've seen the type be-fore. I surmise three weeks into Fall Term, you'll turn in one of your research papers on relativism and he'll go 'splat.' "

*   *   *

The following morning at 7:45, when Dad dropped me off in front of Hanover, I felt absurdly nervous. I had no idea why. I was as familiar with First Days of School as Jane Goodall her Tanzanian chimps after five years in the jungle. And yet, my linen blouse felt two sizes too big (the short sleeves creased off my shoulders like stiffly ironed dinner napkins), my red-and-white checkered skirt felt sticky and my hair (usually the one feature I could count on not to disgrace me) had opted to try a dried-dandelion frizz: I was a table in a bistro serving Bar-B-Q.

" 'She walks in beauty, like the night,' " Dad shouted through the un-rolled window as I climbed from the car. " 'Of cloudless climes and starry skies; / And all that's best of dark and bright / Meet in her aspect and her eyes'! Knock them dead, kiddo! Teach them what *educated* means."

I nodded weakly and slammed the door (ignoring the Fanta-haired woman who'd stopped on the steps and turned around for Dad–Dr. King's drop-off sermon). A campus-wide Morning Announcements was scheduled for 8:45, so after I found my locker on the third floor of Hanover, collected my books (throwing a friendly smile to the teacher frantically running in and out of her classroom with photocopies—the soldier who'd woken up to real-ize she had not sufficiently planned the day's offensive), I made my way out-side along the sidewalk to Love Auditorium. I was still nerdily early, and the theater was empty apart from one diminutive kid in front trying to look ab-sorbed in what was clearly a blank spiral notebook.

The section for seniors was in the back. I sat down in my assigned seat, given to me by Ronin-Smith, and counted the minutes until the deafening student stampede, all the "What ups" and "How wuz your summers," the smell of shampoo, toothpaste and new leather shoes, and that scary kinetic energy kids emitted whenever they were in large numbers so floors throbbed, walls buzzed and you thought if only you could figure out how to harness it, get it through a few parallel circuits and straight through a power station, you could safely and economically light up the East Coast.

I'm obliged to reveal an old trick: implacable self-possession can be attained by all, not by pretending to look absorbed in what's clearly a blank spiral notebook; not by trying to convince yourself you're an undiscovered rock star, movie star, top model, tycoon, Bond, Bond Girl, Queen Elizabeth, Elizabeth Bennett or Eliza Doolittle at the Ambassador's Ball; not by imagining you're a long-lost member of the Vanderbilt family, nor by tilting up your chin fifteen to forty-five degrees and pretending to be Grace Kelly in her prime. These methods work in theory, but in practice they slip away, so one is left hideously naked with nothing but the stained sheet of self-confidence around one's feet.

Instead, stately dignity can be possessed by all, in two ways:

1. Diverting the mind with a book or play
2. Reciting Keats

I discovered this technique early in life, in second grade at Sparta Elementary. When I couldn't help but overhear details of Eleanor Slagg and Her Recent Exclusive Sleepover, I pulled a book out of my bag, *Mein Kampf* (Hitler, 1925), which I'd randomly stolen from Dad's library. I tucked my head between the hardback covers and, with the severity of the German Chancellor himself, made myself read and read until the words on the page invaded Eleanor's words and Eleanor's words surrendered.

* * *

"Welcome," said Headmaster Havermeyer into the microphone. Bill was built like a Saguaro cactus that had ultimately had gone too long without water, and his clothes—the navy jacket, blue shirt, the leather belt with a giant silver buckle portraying either the Siege of the Alamo or the Battle of Little Bighorn—looked as dried out, faded and dusty as his face did. He paced the stage, slowly, as if reveling in the imaginary clinks of his spurs; he held the cordless microphone lovingly: it was his high-crowned Stetson.

"Here we go," whispered the hyperactive Mozart next to me who wouldn't stop tapping out *The Marriage of Figaro* (1786) in the space of seat between his legs. I was next to Amadeus and some sad kid who was the spitting image of Sal Mineo (see *Rebel Without a Cause*).

"For those of you who've never heard Dixon's Words of Wisdom," Bill went on, "those of you who're new, well, you're lucky 'cause you get to hear it for the first time. Dixon was my grandfather, Pa Havermeyer, and he liked young people who listened, who learned from their elders. When I was growing up he'd pull me aside and he'd say, 'Son, don't be afraid to change.' Well, I can't say it any better. Don't be afraid to change. That's right."

He certainly wasn't the first headmaster to suffer from the Ol'-Blue-Eyes-at-The-Sands Effect. Countless headmasters, particularly male, confused the slick floors of a dimly lit cafeteria or the muddled acoustics of a high school auditorium for the ruby-walled Copa Room, mistook students for a doting public who'd made their reservations months in advance and shelled out $100 a pop. Tragically, he believed he could sing "Strangers in the Night" off-key, croon "The Best Is Yet to Come," lose a strand of the lyrics and never mar his reputation as Chairman of the Board, The Voice, Swoonatra.

In truth, of course, he was being ridiculed, mocked and mimicked.

"Hey, what're you reading?" a boy asked behind me.

I did not think the words were directed at me until they were repeated very close to my right shoulder. I stared down at the worn-out play in my hand, p. 18. *Do ya make Brick happy?*

"Hello, miss? Ma'am?" He leaned even closer, leaving breath-hotness on my neck. "You speak English?"

A girl next to him giggled.

"Parlay vu fronsai? Sprekenzee doyche?"

According to Dad, in every circumstance when it was difficult to flee, there was what he called The Oscar Shapeley, a man of great repugnance who'd mysteriously come to the conclusion that what he had to offer in the way of conversation was intensely fascinating and what he had to offer in the way of sex was wholly irresistible.

"Parlate Italiano? Hello?"

The dialogue in *Cat on a Hot Tin Roof* (Williams, 1955) trembled before my eyes. "One of those no-neck monsters hit me with some ice cream. Their fat little heads sit on their fat little necks without a bit of connection . . ." Maggie the Cat wouldn't withstand such harassment. She'd cross her legs in her flimsy slip and say something passionate and shrill and everyone in the room, including Big Daddy, would choke on the ice they were chewing from their mint juleps.

"What's a guy gotta do to get a little attention around here?"

I had no choice but to turn around.

"What?"

He was smiling at me. I expected him to be a no-neck monster, but to my shock, he was a *Goodnight Moon* (Brown, 1947). Goodnight Moons had duvet eyes, shadowy eyelids, a smile like a hammock and a silvered, sleepy countenance that most people wore only during the few minutes prior to sleep, but which the Goodnight Moon sported all day and well into the evening. Goodnight Moons could be male or female and were universally adored. Even teachers worshiped them. They looked to Goodnight Moons whenever they asked a question and even though they answered with a drowsy, wholly incorrect answer, the teacher would say, "Oh, wonderful," and twist the words around like a thin piece of wire until they resembled something glorious.

"Sorry," he said. "Didn't mean to disturb you."

He had blond hair, but he wasn't the sort of washed-out Scandinavian blond person who desperately looked as if he needed to be dyed, tinted, hand dipped in something. He wore a crisp white shirt, a navy blazer. His red-and-blue striped tie was loose and slightly askew.

"So what are you, a famous actress? Headed to Broadway?"

"Oh, no—"

"I'm Charles Loren," he said, as if revealing a secret.

Dad was a devotee of Sturdy Eye Contact, but what Dad never addressed was that staring directly into a person's eyes was nearly impossible at close range. You had to *choose* an eye, right or left, or veer back and forth between the two, or simply settle for the spot *between* the eyes. But I'd always thought that was a sad, vulnerable spot, unkempt of eyebrow and strange of tilt, where David had aimed his stone at Goliath and killed him.

"I know who *you* are," he said. "Blue something. Don't tell me—"

"What on earth is that *hubbub* in the back there?"

Charles jerked back in his seat. I turned.

A stocky woman with sour orange hair—the same person who'd glowered at Dad shouting Byron when he dropped me off—had replaced Havermeyer on the auditorium stage. Wearing a turnip-pink suit that strained like a weight lifter to remain buttoned, she stared up at me with her arms crossed and legs planted firmly apart resembling Diagram 11.23, "Classic Turkish Warrior during the Second Crusade" in one of Dad's favorite texts, *For the Love of God: History of Religious War and Persecution* (Murgg, 1981). And she wasn't the only one staring. All sound had been sucked out of Love Auditorium. Heads were turned toward me like a troop of Seljuk Turks noticing a lone, unwitting Christian taking a shortcut through their camp on his way to Jerusalem.

"You must be a new student," she said into the microphone. Her voice sounded like amplified heel scuffs along pavement. "Allow me to let you in on a little secret. What's your name?"

I hoped it was a figurative question, one I might not be expected to answer, but she was waiting.

"Blue," I said.

She made a face. "What? What did she say?"

"She said *blue*," someone said.

"*Blue?* Well, *Blue*, at this school, when people take the stage, we give them the respect they deserve. We pay *attention*."

Perhaps I need not point out that I was not accustomed to being stared at, not by an entire school. The Jane Goodall was accustomed to doing all the staring, always in solitude and always from a location of dense foliage, which made her in her khaki shorts and linen blouse virtually indistinguishable from the bamboo canopy. My heart stuttered as I stared back at all the eyes. Slowly, they began to peel off me like eggs on a wall.

"As I was saying. There are critical changes in the Add-Drop Deadlines and I will not make exceptions for anyone. I don't care how many Godiva chocolates you bring me—I'm talking to *you*, Maxwell. I ask you be on time when you make decisions about coursework, and I mean it."

"Sorry about that," Charles whispered behind me. "I should've warned you. Eva Brewster, you want to lie low around her. Everyone calls her Evita. It's a bit of a dictator situation. Technically, though, she's only a *secretary*."

The woman—Eva Brewster—dismissed the school to class.

"Now listen, I wanted to ask you something—hey, wait a sec—!"

I darted past Mozart, pushing my way to the end of the row and into the aisle. Charles managed to keep up with me.

"Hold on." He smiled. "Dang, you're really gung ho about classes—typical A personality, sheesh—but, uh, seeing how you're brand *new,* a few of my friends and I were hoping . . ." He was apparently talking to me, but his eyes were already floating up the stairs to the EXIT. Goodnight Moons all had heliumed eyes. They could never be tied to anyone for long. "We were hoping you'd have lunch with us. We snagged a pass to go off campus. So don't go to the cafeteria. Meet us at the Scratch. 12:15." He leaned in, his face inches from mine: "And don't be late, or there'll be serious consequences. Understand?" He winked and dashed away.

I stood for a moment in the aisle, unable to move until kids started pushing against my backpack and I was forced up the stairs. I had no idea how Charles knew my name. I *did*, however, know exactly why he'd rolled out the red carpet: he and his friends were hoping I'd join their Study Group. I'd toiled through a long history of Study Group invites extended by everyone from the Almond-Eyed Football Hero Who'd Have a Son by Senior Year to the Rita Hayworth Sunday Newspaper Coupon Model. I used to be *thrilled* when I was asked to join a Study Group, and when I arrived at the designated living room equipped with note cards, highlighters, red pens, and supplemental textbooks, I was euphoric as any Chorus Girl who'd been asked to understudy the Lead. Even Dad was excited. As he drove me to Brad's, or Jeb's or Sheena's, he'd start muttering about this being a wonderful opportunity, one that would allow me to spread my Dorothy Parker wings and singlehandedly spearhead a contemporary Algonquin Round Table.

Once he dropped me off, though, it didn't take long to realize I hadn't been invited for my scathing wit. If Carla's living room was the Vicious Circle, I was the waiter everyone ignored unless they wanted another scotch or there was something wrong with the food. Somehow, one of them had discovered I was a "geek" (a "cardigan" at Coventry Academy), and I'd be assigned to research one out of every two questions on the Study Sheet, sometimes the entire Study Sheet.

"Let her do that one, too. You don't mind do you, Blues?"

The turning point came at Leroy's. Right in the middle of his living room crowded with porcelain Dalmatian miniatures, I started to cry—though I didn't know why I decided to cry on *that* particular occasion; Leroy, Jessica and Schyler had only assigned me one out of every *four* questions on the Study Sheet. They began to chant in high-pitched, saccharine voices, "Oh, my God, what's *wrong?*" causing the three live Dalmatians to run into the living room, circling and barking, and Leroy's mother emerged from the kitchen wearing pink dishwashing gloves shouting, "Leroy, I told you not to egg them on!" I ran out of the house, all the way home, about six miles. Leroy never returned my supplemental textbooks.

"So how do you know Charles?" asked Sal Mineo next to me as we reached the glass doors.

"I don't know Charles," I said.

"Well, you're lucky because everyone wants to know him."

"Why?"

Sal looked troubled, then shrugged and said in a soft, regretful voice: "He's royalty." Before I could ask what that meant, he skipped down the cement steps and disappeared into the crowd. Sal Mineos were always talking in spongy voices and making comments that were as vague as the outline of an angora sweater. Their eyes weren't like everyone else's but had enlarged tear glands and extra optic nerves. I thought about hurrying after him, letting him know by the end of the movie he'd be acknowledged as a character of great sensitivity and pathos, an archetype of all that was lost and injured about his generation, but would be gunned down by trigger-happy police if he wasn't careful, if he didn't come to an understanding about himself and who he was.

Instead, I'd spotted the royal: Prince Charles, backpack slung over his shoulder, a playful grin, was striding quickly across the courtyard toward a tall, dark-haired girl wearing a long brown wool coat. He snuck up behind her, threw his arm around her neck with an "Ah-haahhhh!" She shrieked, and then, when he jumped in front of her, laughed. It was one of those chime-laughs that knifed cleanly through the morning, through the tired muttering of all the other kids, hinting this person had never known embarrassment or awkwardness, that even her grief would be gorgeous in the off chance she ever experienced it. Obviously, this was his dazzling girlfriend, and they were one of those tan, hair-tossing *Blue Lagoon* couples (one per every high school) who threatened to destroy the bedrock of the chaste educational community simply by the muggy way they looked at each other in the halls.

Students observed them with wonder, like they were fast-sprouting pinto beans in a clammy covered aquarium. Teachers—not all, but some—stayed awake all night hating them, because of their weird grown-up youth, which was like gardenias blooming in January, and their beauty, which was both stunning and sad as racehorses, and their love everyone except them knew wouldn't last. I deliberately stopped staring (you'd seen one version of *Blue Lagoon*, you'd seen them all), but when I'd walked to Hanover and pulled open the side door, I nonchalantly glanced back in their direction and realized with shock, I'd made a major blunder in observation.

Charles now stood at a respectful distance (though the look on his face was still like a kitten staring at string) and she was talking to him with a teacherly frown (a frown all decent teachers mastered; Dad had one that instantly turned his forehead into rippled potato chips). She wasn't a student. In fact, I had no idea how I, given that stance, could possibly have mistaken her for one. A hand on her hip, chin tilted as if trying to make out a falcon circling above the Commons, she wore brown leather boots that resembled Italy and dug the heel of one into the pavement, grinding out an invisible cigarette.

It was Hannah Schneider.

*　*　*

When Dad was in a Bourbon Mood, he'd make a five-minute toast to old Benno Ohnesorg, shot by Berlin police at a student rally in 1967. Dad, nineteen years old, was next to him: "He was standing on my shoelace when he went down. And my life—asinine things I'd wasted time worrying about—my marks, my standing, my *girl*—it all congealed when I looked into his dead eyes." Here, Dad fell silent and sighed (though it wasn't so much a sigh as a Herculean exhale one could use to play a bagpipe). I could smell the alcohol, a strange hot smell, and when I was little I guessed it was what the Romantic poets smelled of, or those nineteenth-century Latin generals Dad enjoyed talking about who "surfed in and out of power on waves of revolution and resistance juntas."

"And that was my Bolshevik moment, so to speak," he said. "When I decided to storm the Winter Palace. If you're lucky, you'll have one."

And every now and then, after Benno, Dad might go on to expound upon one of his most beloved principles, that of the Life Story, but only if he didn't have a lecture to compose, or wasn't midway through a chapter in a new book on war written by someone he'd known at Harvard. (He'd dissect it like a gung-ho coroner hoping to find evidence of foul play: "Here it is, sweet! Evidence Lou Swann's a hack! Counterfeit! Listen to this dung! 'In order to be successful, revolutions require a highly visible armed force to unleash widespread panic; this violence must then gain momentum, escalating into out-and-out civil war.' Fool wouldn't know civil war if it bit him on the ass!")

"Everyone is responsible for the page-turning tempo of his or her Life Story," Dad said, scratching his jaw thoughtfully, arranging the limp collar of his chambray shirt. "Even if you have your Magnificent Reason, it could still be dull as Nebraska and that's no one's fault but your own. Well, if you feel it's miles of cornfields, find something to believe in other than yourself, preferably a cause without the stench of hypocrisy, and then charge into battle. There's a reason they still put Che Guevara on T-shirts, why people *still* whisper about The Nightwatchmen when there's been no evidence of their existence for twenty years.

"But most critically, sweet, never try to change the narrative structure of someone *else's* story, though you will certainly be tempted to, as you watch those poor souls in school, in life, heading unwittingly down dangerous tangents, fatal digressions from which they will unlikely be able to emerge. Resist the temptation. Spend your energies on *your* story. Reworking it. Making it better. Increasing the scale, the depth of content, the universal themes. And I don't care what those themes are—they're yours to uncover and stand behind—so long as, at the very least, there is courage. Guts. *Mut*, in German. Those around you can have their novellas, sweet, their short stories of cliché and coincidence, occasionally spiced up with tricks of the quirky, the achingly mundane, the grotesque. A few will even cook up Greek tragedy, those born into misery, destined to die in misery. But you, my bride of quietness, you will craft nothing less than epic with your life. Out of all of them, your story will be the one to last."

"How do you know?" I always asked, and when I spoke it sounded tiny and uncertain, compared to Dad.

"I just know," he said simply, and then closed his eyes, which indicated that he didn't want to talk anymore.

The only sound in the room was the ice melting his glass.

Les Liaisons Dangereuses

Knowing that Charles was on familiar terms with Hannah Schneider tempted me a little, but in the end I decided not to meet him at the Scratch.

I didn't have a clue what the Scratch was and didn't have time to care. I was, after all, weighed down with six AP courses ("Enough to sink a fleet of USS Anythings," Dad said) and only a single free period. My professors had shown themselves to be sharp, methodical, altogether on the ball (not "entirely in the outhouse," as Dad described Mrs. Roper of Meadowbrook Middle who boldly brought a grand finale to her every sentence with a preposition: "Where's your copy of *The Aeneid* at?"). Most of them had perfectly respectable vocabularies (Ms. Simpson of AP Physics used *ersatz* within fifteen minutes of the bell) and one, namely Ms. Martine Filobeque of AP French, had Permanently Pursed Lips, which could present a serious threat as the year unfolded. "The enduring pursed lip, a trait associated exclusively with the female educator, is a sign of erratic academic anger," Dad said. "I'd think seriously about flowers, candy—anything to get yourself associated in her mind with all that's right in the world, rather than all that's wrong."

My peers too—they were not exactly airheads or fools (*pasta*, as Dad called every kid at Sage Day). When I'd raised my hand in AP English to answer Ms. Simpson's question regarding Primary Themes in *Invisible Man* (Ellison, 1952) (which turned up on Summer Reading Lists with the regularity of corruption in Cameroon), incredibly, I wasn't *quite* fast enough; another kid, Radley Clifton, pudgy, with an eroded chin, already had his fat hand in the air. While his answer wasn't brilliant or inspired, it also wasn't crude or Calibanesque, and it dawned on me, as Ms. Simpson handed out a nineteen-page syllabus solely covering Fall Term, perhaps St. Gallway wouldn't be such Child's Play, such Easy Victory. Perhaps if I actually wanted to be Valedictorian (and I think I did, though sometimes What Dad Wanted blatantly made its way into What I Wanted without having to go through Customs), I'd have to launch an aggressive campaign with all the ferocity of Attila the Hun. "One is only eligible for Valedictorian once in one's life," Dad noted, "just as one only gets one body, one existence, and thus one shot at immortality."

* * *

I also didn't respond to the letter I received the next day, though I read it twenty times, even in the middle of Ms. Gershon's introductory AP Physics lecture, "From Cannonballs to Light Waves: The History of Physics." Paleo-anthropologist Donald Johanson, when stumbling upon early hominid "Lucy" in 1974, probably felt the way I did when I opened my locker door and that cream envelope fell at my feet.

I had no idea what I'd found: a wonder (that would forever change history) or a hoax.

Blue,

What the heck happened?? You missed out on a nice broccoli cheddar baked potato at Wendy's. Guess you're playing hard to get. I'll play. Shall we try this again? You're filling me with longing. (Kidding.)

Same place. Same time.

Charles

I also ignored the two letters discovered in my locker the next day, Wednesday: the first in the cream envelope, the second written in pointy cursive on celery green paper emblazoned at the top with an elaborate tangle of initials: JCW.

Blue,

I'm hurt. Well, I'll be there again today. Every day. Until the end of time. So give a guy a break already.

Charles

Dear Blue,

Charles has obviously made a mess of this situation, so I'm staging a family intervention. I'm assuming you think he's stalkerish. I don't blame you. The truth is, our friend Hannah told us about you and suggested we introduce ourselves. None of us have you in a class so we'll have to meet after school. This Friday at 3:45 go to the second floor of Barrow House, room 208, and wait for us there! Don't be late. We're DYING to meet you and hear all about Ohio!!!

Kisses,
Jade Churchill Whitestone

These letters would have charmed the average New Student. After a day or two of wordy resistance, like some silly eighteenth-century virgin, she'd tiptoe into the dark shadows of the Scratch, excitedly biting her cherry-plump bottom lip, and await Charles, the wigged aristocrat who'd carry her away (*culottes* flying) to ruin.

I, on the other hand, was the implacable nun. I remained unmoved.

Well, I'm exaggerating. I'd never received a letter from someone I didn't know (rather, never received a letter from someone who wasn't Dad) and there is an undeniable thrill when faced with a mysterious envelope. Dad once observed that personal letters (now alongside the Great Crested Newt on the Endangered Species list) were one of the few physical objects in this world that held magic within them: "Even the Dull and the Dim, those whose presences can barely be stomached in person, can be tolerated in a letter, even come off as mildly amusing."

To me, there was something strange and insincere about their letters, something a little too "Madame de Merteuil to the Vicomte de Valmont at the Chateau de—", a little too "Paris. 4 August 17—".

Not that I thought I was the latest pawn in their game of seduction. I wouldn't go *that* far. But I knew all about knowing people and not knowing people. There was drudgery and danger in introducing a newcomer into that exclusive circle of belonging, *le petit salon*. Seating was limited, and thus it was inevitable someone old would have to move (a horrifying sign of losing one's foothold in the court, of turning into *une grande dame manqué*).

To be safe, the newcomer was best ignored, if her background was obscure enough, shunned (coupled with insinuations of illegitimate birth), unless there was someone, a mother with a title, an influential aunt (affectionately called *Madame Titi* by all) who had the time and power to present the newcomer, to squeeze her in (never mind that everyone's birdcage wig knocked together) rearranging the others to positions which were comfortable, or at least bearable until the next revolution.

Even more bizarre were the references to Hannah Schneider. She had no grounds to be *my* Madame Titi.

I wondered if I'd come off at Surely Shoos as a particularly sad and despondent person. I *thought* I'd exuded "watchful intelligence," which was how Dad's colleague, hearing-impaired Dr. Ordinote described me when he came over for lamb chops one evening in Archer, Missouri. He complimented Dad on raising a young woman of "startling power and acumen."

"If only everyone could have one of her, Gareth," he said, raising his eyebrows as he twisted the knob in his hearing aid. "The world would spin a little faster."

There was the possibility that during her ten-minute exchange with Dad, Hannah Schneider had set her romantic sights on him and resolved that I, the quiet daughter, was the small, portable stepladder she'd use to reach him.

Such had been the machinations of Sheila Crane of Pritchardsville, Georgia, who'd only encountered Dad for twenty seconds at the Court Elementary Art Show (she tore his ticket in half) before she decided he was Her Guy. After the Art Show, Miss Crane, who worked part-time at the Court Elementary Infirmary, had a habit of materializing during Break near the seesaws, calling out my name, holding up a box of Thin Mints. When I was in close proximity, she held out a cookie as if trying to tempt a stray dog.

"Can you tell me a little more about your daddy? I mean," she said nonchalantly, though her eyes bored into me like an electrician's drill, "what kinda things duzzie like?"

Usually I stared blankly at her, grabbed the Thin Mint and spirited away, but once I said, "Karl Marx." Her eyes widened in fear.

"He's homosexshull?"

*   *   *

Revolution is slow burning, occurring only after decades of oppression and poverty, but the exact hour of its unleashing is often a moment of fateful mishap.

According to one of Dad's little-known history texts, *Les Faits Perdus* (Manneurs, 1952), the Storming of the Bastille would never have happened, if one of the demonstrators outside the prison, a barley farmer by the name of Pierre Fromande, had not noticed a prison guard pointing at him and calling him *un bricon* ("fool").

On the morning of July 14, 1789, Pierre was on a short fuse. He'd had a fight with his voluptuous wife, Marie-Chantal, for her flirting *sans scrupule* with one of their field hands, Louis-Belge. Pierre, overhearing the insult, dimly aware the prison guard had the same chunky Roqucfort torso of Louis-Belge, lost all self-control and charged forward screaming, "*C'est tout fini!*" ("It's all over.") The frenzied crowd followed, believing he was speaking of the reign of Louis XVI, though Pierre was, in fact, referring to the image of Marie-Chantal screaming in pleasure in barley fields, Louis-Belge melting all over her. Yet, Pierre had misunderstood the well-meaning guard, who'd simply pointed at Pierre and shouted, "Votre *bouton;*" when dressing that morning, Pierre had missed the third button on his chemise.

According to Manneurs, most of history has played out under similar circumstances, including the American Revolution (the Boston Tea Party was the work of 1777-era frat boys) and World War I (Gavrilo Princip, after a day with his drinking buddies, the Black Hands, fired a few rounds into the air, simply to show off, just as Archduke Ferdinand cruised by in his royal arcade) (p. 199, p. 243). Hiroshima was unintentional too. When Truman told his Cabinet, "I'm going in," he wasn't, as was believed, referring to a Japanese invasion, but giving voice to the simple desire to take a dip in the White House pool.

My revolution was no less accidental.

That Friday, a Know-Your-School Sorbet Social was held after lunch. Students mingled with teachers on the stone patio outside the Harper Racey '05 Cafeteria, feasting upon a selection of exclusive French sorbet, doled out by the Head Chef, Christian Gordon. Eager students (including Radley Clifton with his belly peeking out of his partially untucked shirt) swarmed around the key Gallway administrators (doubtlessly those in charge of end-of-year honors; "Brown-nosing in this day and age backfires," Dad attested. "Networking, hobnobbing—it's all painfully out of season."). After saying modest helloes to a few of my teachers (smiling at Ms. Filobeque who stood rather forlornly under a hemlock, though in reply she only pursed her lips) I headed to my next class, AP Art History in Elton House, and waited in the empty classroom.

After ten minutes, Mr. Archer appeared, carrying his tub of Mango sherbet and I'M EARTH FRIENDLY biodegradable satchel (see "Red-eyed Tree

Frog," *The World of Ranidae: From Frog Princes to Tadpoles*, Showa, 1998).
He had so much sweat on his forehead he looked like a glass of iced tea.

"Would you mind helping me set up the slide projector for the lecture?"
he asked. (Mr. Archer being EARTH FRIENDLY was APPARATUS HOSTILE.)

I agreed, and was just finishing loading the 112 slides, as the other students began to arrive, most of them with big, slurpy grins on their faces, tubs of sorbet in hand.

"Thank you for your assistance, Babs," Mr. Archer said, smiling at me and affixing his long, sticky fingers to the top of his desk. "Today we finish up with Lascaux and turn to the rich artistic tradition that emerged in the area that is now southern Iraq. James, will you get the lights?"

Unlike Pierre Fromande, I'd heard the man correctly. Unlike Truman's cabinet members, I'd understood his true meaning. Certainly, I'd been given aliases by teachers before, from Betsy and Barbara to "You in the Corner" and "Red, No, I'm Kidding." From years twelve to fourteen, I actually believed the name was cursed, that it was whispered among instructors "Blue" had the erratic properties of a ballpoint pen at high altitudes; if they uttered the name, a permanent blueness, dark and inexorable, could very well leak all over them.

Lottie Bergoney, Instructor of the Second Grade in Pocus, Indiana, actually telephoned Dad and suggested he rechristen me.

"You won't believe this!" Dad mouthed, cupping his hand over the receiver, gesturing for me to listen on the other line.

"I'll be honest with you, Mr. Van Meer. The name's not healthy. The kids in class make fun of it. They call her navy. A few of the smart ones call her cobalt. And cordon *bleu*. Maybe you should think about alternatives."

"Might you suggest some possibilities, Miss Bergie?"

"Sure! I don't know about you, but I've always loved Daphne."

Perhaps it was Mr. Archer's particular choice of name, Babs, the nickname of a restless wife wearing no bra during her tennis lesson. Or perhaps it was the confidence with which he said it, without a trace of uncertainty or second thought.

Suddenly, at my desk, I couldn't breathe. At the same time, I wanted to leap from my chair and shout, *"It's Blue, you sons of bitches!"*

Instead, I reached into my backpack and removed the three letters, still tucked into the cover of my assignment notebook. I reread each one, and then, with the same clarity that overtook Robespierre as he lounged in a bath and *liberté, egalité* and *fraternité* sailed into his head—three great merchant ships coming into port—I knew what I had to do.

*   *   *

After class, I used the student payphone in Hanover to call Dad at the university. I left a message explaining I wouldn't need a ride home until 4:45; I was meeting with Ms. Simpson, my AP English teacher, to discuss her Great Expectations for research papers. At 3:40, after confirming in the Hanover ground-floor ladies room that I had sat on neither gum nor chocolate, that I had nothing in my teeth and had not accidentally pressed my ink-stained hand against the side of my face leaving it a mosaic of black fingerprints (as I had once before), I walked, as composedly as I could, over to Barrow. I knocked on the door of 208 and was instantly greeted with a few flat, unsurprised voices: "It's open."

Slowly, I opened the door. Four flour-pale kids sat at desks in a circle at the center of the classroom, none of them smiling. The other desks had been pushed to the walls.

"Hi," I said.

They stared at me sullenly.

"I'm Blue."

"You're here for the Dungeons & Dragons Demonology Guild," a kid pronounced in a squeaky voice like air being let out of a bicycle tire. "There's an extra player's handbook *there*. Right now we're choosing our roles for the year."

"*I'm* Dungeon Master," clarified a kid quickly.

"Jade?" I asked hopefully, turning to one of the girls. It wasn't a terrible guess: this one, wearing a long black dress with tight sleeves that ended in medieval Vs on top of her hands, had green hair that resembled dried spinach.

"Lizzie," she said, narrowing her eyes suspiciously.

"You know Hannah Schneider?" I asked.

"The *Film* Studies teacher?"

"What's she talking about?" the other girl asked the Dungeon Master.

"Excuse me," I said. Holding onto my tight smile like some crazed Catholic her rosary, I backed out of Room 208, hurried back down the hall and stairs.

In the aftermath of being brazenly hoodwinked or swindled, it's difficult to accept, particularly if one has always prided oneself on being an intuitive and scorchingly observant person. Standing on the Hanover steps, waiting for Dad, I reread Jade Whitestone's letter fifteen times, convinced I'd missed something—the correct day, time or location to meet, or perhaps *she'd* made a mistake; perhaps she'd written the letter while watching *On the Waterfront* and had been distracted by the pathos of Brando picking up Eva Marie Saint's tiny white glove and slipping it onto his own meaty hand, but soon, of course, I realized her letter was teeming with sarcasm (particularly in the final sentence), which I hadn't originally picked up on.

It had all been a hoax.

Never had there been a rebellion more anticlimactic and second rate, except perhaps the "Gran Horizontes Tropicoco Uprising" in Havana in 1980, which, according to Dad, was composed of out-of-work big band musicians and El Loro Bonito chorus girls and lasted all of three minutes. ("Fourteen-year-old lovers last longer," he'd noted.) And the longer I sat on the steps, the cruddier I felt. I pretended not to stare enviously at the happy kids slinging themselves and their giant backpacks into their parents' cars, or the tall boys with untucked shirts rushing across the Commons, shouting at each other, cleats slung over their bony shoulders like tennis shoes over traffic wires.

By 5:10 P.M. I was doing my AP Physics homework on my knees and there was no sign of Dad. The lawns, the roofs of Barrow and Elton, even the sidewalks, had tarnished in the fading light of Depression-era photographs, and apart from a few teachers making their way to the Faculty Parking Lot (coal miners plodding home) it was all quite sad and silent, except for the oak trees fanning themselves like bored Southerners, a coach whistle far off on the fields.

"Blue?"

To my horror, it was Hannah Schneider, descending the steps behind me.

"What are you doing here at this hour?"

"Oh," I said, smiling as joyously as I could. "My dad's running late at work." It was critical to appear happy and well loved; after school, teachers stared at kids unattended by parents like they were suspicious packages abandoned in an airport lounge.

"You don't drive?" she asked, stopping next to me.

"Not yet. I *can* drive. I just haven't gotten my license." (Dad didn't see the point: "What, so you can cruise around town for a year before you go off to college like a nurse shark lazing around a reef desperate for guppies? I don't think so. Next thing I know you'll be wearing biker leather. Wouldn't you prefer, anyway, to be chauffeured?")

Hannah nodded. She wore a long black skirt and a yellow button-down sweater. While most teachers' hair at the end of the day resembled crusty windowsill plants, Hannah's—dark, but rusting a little in the late-day light—posed provocatively around her shoulders like Lauren Bacall in a doorway. It was strange for a teacher to be so guiltily watchable, so addictive. She was *Dynasty*, *As the World Turns*; one felt something fantastically bitchy was about to happen.

"Jade will have to swing by and pick you up then," she announced matter-of-factly. "It's just as well. The house is difficult to find. This Sunday. Twoish, two-thirty. You like Thai food?" (She didn't wait for my answer.) "Every Sunday I cook for them and you're the guest of honor from now until the end of the year. You'll get to know them. Gradually. They're *wonderful* kids. Charles is adorable and sweet, but the others can be difficult. Like most people they hate change, but everything good in life is an acquired taste. If they give you a hard time, remember it's not *you*—it's them. They'll just have to get over themselves." She gave one of those housewife commercial sighs (kid, carpet stain) and waved away an invisible fly. "How do you like your classes? Are you adjusting?" She spoke quickly and for some reason my heart was hitch-kicking excitedly in the air as if I was Orphan Annie and she was that wonderful character played by Anne Reinking who Dad said had spectacular legs.

"Yes," I said, standing up.

"Wonderful." She clasped her hands together—sort of like a fashion designer admiring his own fall line. "I'll get your address from the office and give it to Jade."

At this point, I noticed Dad in the Volvo, parked by the curb. He was probably watching us, but I couldn't see his face, only his splotchy outline in the driver's seat. The windshield and windows mirrored the oak trees and the yellowed sky.

"That must be your ride," Hannah said following my stare. "See you Sunday?"

I nodded. Her arm lightly around my shoulder—she smelled like pencil lead and soap, and, oddly enough, a vintage clothing store—she walked me toward the car, waving at Dad before continuing down the sidewalk toward the Faculty Parking Lot.

"You're absurdly late," I said, pulling the door closed.

"I apologize," Dad said. "I was walking out of the office when the most appalling student marched in, held me hostage with the most mundane questions—"

"Well, it doesn't look good. Makes me look like one of those unloved latchkey children they make after-school specials about."

"Don't sell yourself short. You're more *Masterpiece Theatre*." He started the car, squinting in the rearview mirror. "And that, I deduce, was the meddling woman from the shoe store?"

I nodded.

"What'd she want this time?"

"Nothing. Just wanted to say hello."

I intended to tell him the truth; I'd have to, if on Sunday I wanted to run off with some "slack-jawed Suzy," some "invertebrate," a "post-pubescent wasteoid who imagines the Khmer Rouge to be makeup and Guerrilla Warfare to be that rivalry which occurs between apes"—but then we were accelerating past Bartleby Athletic Center and the football field where a crowd of shirtless boys leapt into the air like trout as they hit soccer balls with their heads. And as we rounded the chapel, Hannah Schneider was directly in front of us unlocking the door to an old red Subaru, one of the back doors dented like a Coke can. She brushed her hair off her forehead as she watched our passing car, and smiled. It was the distinct, secret smile of adulterous housewives, bluffing poker players, consummate con artists in mug shots and I decided, in that split second, to hold onto what she said, cup it tightly in my hands, setting it free only at the last possible second.

Dad, on Having a Secret, Well-Laid Plan: "There is nothing more delirious to the human mind."

Madame Bovary

There was a poem Dad was quite fond of and knew by heart, entitled "My Darling" or "Mein Liebling" by the late German poet, Schubert Koenig Bonheoffer (1862–1937). Bonheoffer was crippled, deaf, had only one eye, but Dad said he was able to discern more about the nature of the world than most people in possession of all their senses.

For some reason, and perhaps unfairly, the poem always reminded me of Hannah.

"Where is the soul of my Darling?" I ask,
Oh, somewhere her soul must be,
It lives not in words, nor in promises,
Mutable as gold hers can be.

"It's in the eyes," the great poets say,
" 'Tis where the soul must dwell."
But watch her eyes; they glisten bright
At news of heaven and of hell.

I once believed her crimson lips,
Marked her soul soft as winter's snow,
But then they curled at tales dismal, sad;
What it meant, I could not know.

I thought her fingers, then, her slender hands,
'Cross her lap, they're delicate doves,

Though sometimes cold as ice to touch,
They surely hint of all she loves.

Aye, but there are moments she waves farewell,
I confess my Darling I do not follow,
She vanishes from view 'fore I reach the road,
Windows bare, house quiet and hollow.

And at times I wish I might read her walk,
Like a sailor his map o' the sea,
Or find instructions for her looks,
Explaining all she hopes will be.

How curious such an enlightened life!
God Himself wouldn't deign to doubt her,
Instead, I'm left a-wondering,
Darling's shadows lurking about her.

Dinner at Hannah's was a honey-bunch tradition, held more or less every Sunday for the past three years. Charles and his friends looked forward to the hours at her house (the address itself, a little enchanting: 100 Willows Road) much in the way New York City's celery-thin heiresses and beetroot B-picture lotharios looked forward to noserubbing at the Stork Club certain sweaty Saturday nights in 1943 (see *Forget About El Morocco: The Xanadu of the New York Elite, the Stork Club, 1929–1965,* Riser, 1981).

"I can't remember how it all started, but the five of us just got on with her famously," Jade told me. "I mean, she's an *amazing* woman—anyone can see that. We were freshman, taking her film class, and we'd spend hours after school sitting in her classroom talking about any old thing—life, sex, *Forrest Gump*. And then we started going to dinner and things. And then she invited us over for Cuban food and we stayed up all night howling. About what I don't remember, but it was *amazing*. Of course, we had to be hush-hush about it. Still do. Havermeyer doesn't like relationships between teachers and students that go beyond faculty advising or athletic coaching. He's afraid of shades of gray, if you know what I mean. And that's what Hannah is. A shade of gray."

Of course, I didn't know any of this that first afternoon. In fact, I wasn't even positive I knew my own name as I rode next to Jade, the very disturbing person who only two days prior had maliciously directed me toward the De-monology Guild.

I'd actually assumed I'd been stood up again; by 3:30 P.M. there'd been no sign of her, or anyone. That morning, I'd hinted to Dad that I might have a Study Group later that afternoon (he'd frowned, surprised I was willing to subject myself again to such torture), but in the end, there was no need to give him a lengthier explanation; he'd disappeared to the university, having left a critical book on Ho Chi Minh in his office. He'd phoned to say he'd simply finish his latest *Forum* essay there—"The Trappings of Iron-Clad Ide-ologies," or something to that effect—but would be home for dinner. I'd sat down in the kitchen with a chicken salad sandwich, resigned to an afternoon of *Absalom, Absalom!: The Corrected Text* (Faulkner, 1990), when I heard the extended howl of a car horn in the driveway.

"I'm appallingly late. I am *so sorry*," a girl shouted through the inch-opened, tinted window of the blubbery black Mercedes beached at the front door. I couldn't see her, only her squinting eyes of indeterminate color and some beach-blond hair. "Are you ready? Otherwise I might have to take off without you. Traffic's a bitch."

Hastily, I grabbed keys to the house and the first book I could find, one of Dad's favorites, *Civil War Endgames* (Agner, 1955), and ripped a page from the back. I scrawled a terse note (Study Group, *Ulysses*) and left it for him on the round table in the foyer without even bothering to sign it "Love, Christa-bel." And then I was in her killer whale of a Mercedes, all Disbelief, Awk-wardness and Outright Panic as I compulsively glanced at the speedometer trembling toward 80 mph, her lazy manicured hand slung atop the steering wheel, her blond hair in the cruel bun, the sandal straps XXXing up her legs. Candelabra earrings broadsided her neck every time she took her eyes off the highway to survey me with a look of "corroding tolerance." (It was how Dad described his mood waiting for June Bug Shelby Hollow tending to her acrylic nails, creative half-a-head highlights and pedicured feet—"With bunionettes," Dad noted—at Hot-2-Trot Hair & Nails.)

"Yeah, so this"—Jade touched the front of the elaborate, parrot-green ki-mono dress she was wearing; she must have thought I was silently admiring her outfit—"this was a gift to my mom Jefferson when she entertained Hiro-fumi Kodaka, some loaded Japanese businessman for three grisly nights at the Ritz in 1982. He had jetlag and didn't speak English so she was his twenty-four-hour translator if you know what I mean—*Get off the fucking road!*" She leaned on the horn; we veered in front of a lowly gray Oldsmobile driven by an old lady no bigger than a Dixie cup. Jade craned her neck around to give her a dirty look, then flipped her off. "Why doncha go to a graveyard and kick the bucket, old bag."

We darted down Exit 19.

"That reminds me," she said, tossing me a look. "Why didn't you show?"

"What?" I managed to ask.

"You weren't there. We *waited*."

"Oh. Well, I went to room 208—"

"208?" She made a face. "It was 308."

She wasn't fooling anyone. "You wrote 208," I said quietly.

"I did *not*. I remember perfectly—308. And you *totally* missed out. We had a cake for you and a lot of icing and candles and everything," she added sort of absentmindedly (I was bracing myself for tales of hired belly dancers, elephant rides, whirling dervishes), but then, to my relief, she leaned forward and with a haughty, "God, I love Dara and the Bouncing Checks," turned the CD *way* up, a heavy metal band with a lead singer that sounded as if he were being gouged by bulls at Pamplona.

We drove on, not a word spoken between us. (She'd resolved to shake me off like a hit funnybone.) She checked her watch, winced, huffed, damned stop lights, road signs, anyone abiding the speed limit in front of us, proudly surveyed her blue eyes in the rearview mirror, brushed specks of mascara off her cheeks, dabbed her lips with glittery pink lip gloss and then *more* glittery lip gloss so some of it started to ooze off the side of her mouth—a detail I didn't have the guts to point out. In fact, driving to Hannah's made the girl so apparently restless and anxiety ridden, I couldn't help but wonder if at the end of this nauseating parade of woods and pastures and nameless dirt roads, and shoe-box barns and gaunt horses waiting by fences, I'd find not a house, but a black door barred by a velvet rope, a man with a clipboard who'd look me over and, when ascertaining I didn't know Frank or Errol or Sammy personally (nor any other titan of entertainment), would declare me unfit to enter, by inference, to continue living.

But at last, at the very end of the twisting gravel road was the house, an awkward, wooden-faced coy mistress clinging to half a hill with bulky additions stuck to her sides like giant faux pas. As soon as we parked by the other cars and rang the bell, Hannah swung open the front door in a wave of Nina Simone, Eastern spices, perfume, Eau de Somethingfrench, her face warm as the living room light. A pack of seven or eight dogs, all different breeds and sizes, crept nervously behind her.

"This is Blue," Jade said indifferently, walking inside.

"Of course," said Hannah, smiling. She was barefoot, wearing chunky gold bracelets and an African batik caftan in orange and yellow. Her dark hair was a perfect swish of ponytail. "The lady of the hour."

To my surprise, she hugged me. It was an Epic Hug, heroic, big budget, sprawling, with ten thousand extras (not short, grainy and made on a shoe-string). When she finally let go, she grabbed my hand and squeezed it the way people at airports grab the hands of people they haven't seen in years, asking how the flight was. She pulled me next to her, her arm around my waist. She was unexpectedly thin.

"Blue meet Fagan, Brody, he's got three legs—though it doesn't stop him from going through the garbage—Fang, Peabody, Arthur, Stallone, the Chi-huahua with half-a-tail—accident with a car door—and the Old Bastard. Don't look him in the eye." She was referring to a skin-and-bones greyhound with the red eyes of a middle-aged, midnight tollbooth collector. The other dogs glanced at Hannah doubtfully, as if she were introducing them to a pol-tergeist. "Somewhere around here are the cats," she continued. "Lana and Turner, the Persians, and in the study we have our lovebird. Lennon. I'm in desperate need of an Ono, but there aren't many birds that show up at the shelter. Want some oolong tea?"

"Sure," I said.

"Oh, and you haven't met the others yet, have you?"

I looked up from the black-and-tan Chihuahua, who'd snuck over to me to consider my shoes, and saw them. Including Jade, who'd flopped down onto a half-melted chocolate couch and lit a cigarette (aiming it at me like a dart), they each stared with eyes so immobile and bodies so stiff, they might have been the series of paintings Dad and I scrutinized in the nineteenth-century Masters Gallery at the Chalk House outside Atlanta. There was the scrawny girl with brown seaweed hair, hugging her knees on the piano bench (*Portrait of a Peasant Girl*, pastel on paper); a tiny kid wearing Ben Franklin spectacles, Indian-style by a mangy dog, Fang (*Master with Foxhound*, Brit-ish, oil on canvas); and another, a huge, boxy-shouldered boy leaning against a bookshelf, his arms and ankles crossed, brittle black hair sagging across his forehead (*The Old Mill*, artist unknown). The only one I recognized was Charles in the leather chair (*The Gay Shepherd*, gilt frame). He smiled en-couragingly, but I doubted it meant much; he seemed to hand out smiles like a guy in a chicken costume distributing coupons for a free lunch.

"Why don't you introduce yourselves?" Hannah said cheerfully.

They said their names with paint-by-numbers politeness.

"Jade."

"We've met," said Charles.

"Leulah," said the Peasant Girl.

"Milton," said the Old Mill.

"Nigel Creech, very pleased to meet you," said the Master with Fox-hound, and then he flashed a smile, which disappeared instantly like a spark off a defunct lighter.

* * *

If all histories have a period known as The Golden Age, somewhere between The Beginning and The End, I suppose those Sundays during Fall Semester at Hannah's were just that, or, to quote one of Dad's treasured characters of cinema, the illustrious Norma Desmond as she recalled the lost era of silent film: "We didn't need dialogue. We had faces."

I sort of like to think the same was true back in those days at Hannah's (Visual Aid 8.0). (Forgive my regrettable rendering of Charles—and Jade for that matter; they were much more beautiful in real life.)

Charles was the handsome one (handsome in the opposite way of Andreo). Gold-haired, mercury-tempered, he was not only St. Gallway's Track and Field star, excelling at both hurdles and the high jump, but also its Travolta. It wasn't unusual to see him sliding between classes engaged in a shameless, campus-wide soft shoe, involving not only known Gallway beauties but also the less physically heralded. Somehow he was able to twirl one girl away by the Teacher's Lounge just as another rumbaed over to him, and they pachangaed down the hall. (Amazingly, no one's feet were ever stepped on.)

Jade was the terrifying beauty (see "Tawny Eagle," *Magnificent Birds of Prey*, George, 1993). She swooped into a classroom and girls scattered like chipmunks and squirrels. (The boys, equally afraid, played dead.) She was brutally blond ("bleached to the hilt," I heard Beth Price remark in AP English), five-feet-eight ("wiry"), stalked the halls in short skirts, her books in a black leather bag ("Guess she's Donna fucking Karan") and what I took to be a severe and sad look on her face, though most took it for conceit. Due to Jade's fortresslike manner, which, like any well-built castle, made access challenging, girls found her existence not only threatening, but flat out wrong. Although Bartleby Athletic Center featured the latest advertising campaign of Ms. Sturds's three-member Benevolent Body-Image Club (laminated *Vogue*

VISUAL AID 8.0

and *Maxim* covers above captions, "You Can't Have Thighs Like This and Still Walk" and "All Airbrushing"), Jade would only have to swan by, munching on a Snickers to reveal a disturbing truth: you *could* have thighs like that and still walk. She emphasized what few wanted to accept, that some people did win Trivial Pursuit: The Deity Looks Edition and there wasn't a thing you could do about it, except come to terms with the fact *you'd* only played Trivial Pursuit: John Doe Genes and come away with three pie pieces.

Nigel was the cipher (see "Negative Space," *Art Lessons*, Trey, 1973, p. 29). At first glance (even at second and third), he was ordinary. His face—rather his entire being—was a buttonhole: small, narrow, uneventful. He stood no more than five-feet-five with a round face, brown hair, features weak and baby-feet pink (neither complemented nor marred by the wire glasses he wore). At school, he sported thin, tonguelike neckties in neon orange, a fashion statement I guessed was his effort to force people to take notice of him, much like a car's hazard lights. And yet, upon closer examination, the ordinariness was extraordinary: he bit his nails into thumbtacks; spoke in hushed spurts (uncolored guppies darting through a tank); in large groups, his smile could be a dying light bulb (shining reluctantly, flickering, disappearing); and a single strand of his hair (once found on my skirt after sitting next to him), held directly under a light, shimmered with every color in a rainbow, including purple.

And then there was Milton, sturdy and grim, with a big, cushiony body like someone's favorite reading chair in need of reupholstering (see "American Black Bear," *Meat-Eating Land Animals*, Richards, 1982). He was eighteen, but looked thirty. His face, cluttered with brown eyes, curly black hair, a swollen mouth, had a curdled handsomeness to it, as if, incredibly, it wasn't what it'd once been. He had an Orson Wellian quality, Gerardepardieuian too: one suspected his large, slightly overweight frame smothered some kind of dark genius and after a twenty-minute shower he'd still reek of cigarettes. He'd lived most of his life in a town called Riot in Alabama and thus spoke in a Southern accent so gooey and thick you could probably cut into it and spread it on dinner rolls. Like all Mysteriosos, he had an Achilles' heel: a giant tattoo on his upper right arm. He refused to talk about it, went to great pains to conceal it—never removing his shirt, always wearing long sleeves—and if some clown during P.E. asked him what it was, he either stared at the kid as if he were a *Price Is Right* rerun, barely blinking, or replied in his molasses accent: "Nunna ya goddamn business."

And then there was the delicate creature (see *Juliet*, J. W. Waterhouse, 1898). Leulah Maloney was pearl skinned, with skinny bird arms and long brown hair always worn in a braid, like one of those cords aristocracy pulled in the nineteenth century to summon servants. Hers was an eerie, old-fashioned beauty, a face at home in amulets or carved into cameos—a romantic look I actually used to wish *I* had whenever Dad and I were reading about Gloriana in *The Faerie Queene* (Spenser, 1596) or discussing Dante's love for Beatrice Portinari. ("Know how difficult it is to find a woman that looks like Beatrice in today's world?" asked Dad. "You've a better chance running at the speed of light.")

Early in the Fall, when I least expected it, I'd spot Leulah in a long dress (usually white or diaphanous blue) strolling the Commons in the middle of a downpour, holding her little antique face up to the rain while everyone else streaked past her screaming, textbooks or disintegrating *Gallway Gazettes* held over their heads. Twice I noticed her like this—another time, crouched in Elton House shrubbery, apparently fascinated by a piece of bark or tulip bulb—and I couldn't help but think such faerielike behavior was all very calculated and irritating. Dad had carried on a tedious five-day affair with a woman named Birch Peterson in Okush, New Mexico, and Birch, having been born outside Ontario on a "terrific" free-loving commune called Verve, was always entreating Dad and me to walk untroubled in rain, bless mosquitoes, eat tofu. When she came for dinner she said a prayer before we "consumed," a fifteen-minute plea asking "Shod" to bless every slime mold and mollusk.

"The word *God* is inherently male," said Birch, "so I came up with *she, he,* and *God* rolled into one. *Shod* exemplifies the truly genderless Higher Power."

I concluded Leulah—Lu, as they all called her—with her gossamer dresses, reedy hair, decisions to skip daintily along everything but sidewalks, had to have Birch's persona of bean curd, that esprit de spirulina, until I discovered someone had actually hexed the girl, cast a powerful spell, so her oddities were eternally unthinking, careless and unscripted, so she never questioned what people thought or how she looked, so the cruelties of the entire kingdom ("There's something sour about her. She's *totally* past her Eat-by date," I heard Lucille Hunter remark in AP English) dissolved miraculously—never reaching her ears.

Since much has already been made of Hannah's paramount face, I won't mention it again, except to say, unlike other Helens of Troy, who can never quite get over their own magnificence, like a pair of perilously high heels they're always wandering around in (self-consciously stooped over or haughtily towering over everyone), Hannah managed to wear hers day and night and still be only vaguely aware she was wearing shoes. With her, you noticed how exhausting beauty actually was, how used up one might feel after a day of strangers rubbernecking to watch you pour Sweet'N Low into your coffee or pick out the tin of blueberries with the least mold.

"Whatever," Hannah said, without a trace of false modesty when, one Sunday, Charles commented how great she looked in a black T-shirt and army fatigues. "I'm just a tired old lady."

There was, too, the problem of her name.

While it cartwheeled off the tongue nimbly enough, more elegantly than, say, Juan San Sebastién Orillos-Marípon (the lip-calisthenics name of Dad's teaching assistant at Dodson-Miner), I couldn't help but think there was something criminal about it. Whoever had named her—mother, father, I didn't know—was a person harrowingly out of touch with reality, because even as an infant, Hannah could never have been one of those troll-babies, and a troll-baby was what you dubbed "Hannah." (Granted, I was biased: "Thank God that thing's incarcerated in his carriage. Otherwise, people might start to panic, thinking we have a veritable *War of the Worlds* on our hands," Dad said, peering down at a happy, yet decidedly elderly baby parked in an aisle at Office Depot. Then the mother arrived. "I see you've met Hannah!" she cried.) If she *had* to have a common name, she was Edith or Nadia or Ingrid, at the very least, Elizabeth or Catherine; but her glass-slipper name, the one that *really* fit, was something along the lines of Countess Saskia Lepinska, or Anna-Maria d'Aubergette, even Agnes of Scudge or Ursula of Poland ("Hideous names on beautiful women tend to rumplestiltskin quite nicely," Dad said).

"Hannah Schneider" fit her like stonewashed Jordache jeans six sizes too big. And once, oddly enough, when Nigel said her name during dinner, I could have sworn I noticed a funny delay in her response, as if, for a split second, she had no idea he was talking to her.

It made me wonder, even if it was solely on the subconscious level, maybe Hannah Schneider didn't love "Hannah Schneider" either. Maybe she wished she was Angelique von Heisenstagg too.

✳   ✳   ✳

Many people speak enviously of the Fly on a Wall. They yearn for its characteristics: virtually invisible, yet privy to the secrets and shifty dialogues of an exclusive group of people. And yet, as I was nothing more than a fly on a wall for those first six, maybe seven Sunday afternoons at Hannah's, I can say with some authority such disregard gets old fairly quickly. (Actually, one could argue flies elicited more attention than I did, because someone always rolled up a magazine and doggedly chased them around a room, and no one did that to me—unless one counted Hannah's erratic attempts to insert me into the conversation, which I found more embarrassing than the others' disdain.)

Of course, that very first Sunday ended up nothing more than a disastrous humiliation, in many ways worse than the Study Group at Leroy's, because at least Leroy and the others had *wanted* me there (granted, wanted me as their beast of burden, so I could haul them up the steep hill toward eighth grade), but these kids—Charles, Jade and the others—they made it clear my presence at the house was entirely Hannah's idea, not theirs.

"Know what I hate?" Nigel asked pleasantly as I helped him clear the plates off the dinner table.

"What?" I asked, grateful he was attempting small talk.

"Shy people," he replied, and of course there was no ambiguity about *what* shy person had prompted this announcement; I'd remained entirely mute during both dinner and dessert and the one instance Hannah had asked me a question ("You just moved here from Ohio?"), I was so taken aback my voice stumbled on the curb of my teeth. And then, minutes later, when I was pretending to be fascinated by the paperback cookbook Hannah had wedged next to her CD player, *Cooking Without Processed Foods* (Chiobi, 1984), I overhead Milton and Jade in the kitchen. He was asking her—in all seriousness it seemed—if I spoke English.

She laughed. "She must be one of those Russian mail-order brides," she said. "With those looks though, Hannah got seriously ripped off. I wonder what the return policy is. Hopefully we can send her back COD."

Minutes later, Jade was driving me home like a bat out of hell (Hannah must have only paid minimum wage) and I stared out the window, thinking it had been the most horrible night of my life. Obviously I'd never speak to these halfwits, these simpletons ("banal, spiritless teenagers," Dad would add) *ever again*. And I wouldn't give that sadistic Hannah Schneider the time of day either; it was she, after all, who'd lured me to that snake pit, let me flail around with nothing but a chic smile on her face as she chitchatted about homework or what fifth-tier college those slack-jawed mopes hoped to squeeeeze their way into, and then after dinner, that unforgivable way she calmly lit a cigarette, her manicured hand tipped into the air like a delicate teakettle, as if all was fantastic with the world.

But then I don't know what happened. The following Tuesday, I passed Hannah briefly in Hanover Hall—"See you this weekend?" she called out brightly through the crowd of students; naturally my reaction was that of a deer in headlights—and then, on Sunday, Jade appeared in the driveway again, this time at 2:15 P.M. and the *entire* window unrolled.

"Coming?" she shouted.

I was powerless as a maiden who'd been fed upon by vampires. Zombielike, I told Dad I'd forgotten about my Study Group and before he could protest, I'd kissed him on the cheek, assured him it was a St. Gallway-sponsored event and fled the house.

Embarrassedly—and then, after a month, kind of resignedly—I settled into my appointed role as fly on the wall, as barely tolerated mute, because the truth was, when it came down to it (and I could never admit this to Dad), being snubbed at Hannah's was infinitely more electrifying than being mulled over back at the Van Meer's.

*   *   *

Wrapped up like an expensive gift in her emerald batik caftan, her purple and gold sari or some wheat-colored housedress straight out of *Peyton Place* (for this comparison you had to pretend you didn't see the cigarette burn at the hip), on Sunday afternoons, Hannah *entertained*, in the old-fashioned, European sense of the word. Even now, I don't understand how she managed to prepare those extravagant dinners in her tiny mustard-yellow kitchen— Turkish lamb chops ("with mint sauce"), Thai steak ("with ginger-infused potatoes"), beef noodle soup ("Authentic Pho Bo"), on one less successful occasion, a goose ("with cranberry rub and sage carrot fries").

She cooked. The very air began to sauté in a reduction of candle, wine, wood, her perfume, and damp animal. We picked through the remains of our homework. The kitchen door swung open, and she stepped forth, a *Birth of Venus* in a red apron smeared with mint sauce, walking with the fast, swingy grace of Tracy Lord in *The Philadelphia Story*, all soft bare feet (if those were toes, what you had was something else altogether, tuds), twinkles at her earlobes, the pronunciation of certain words with little shivers on the endings. (The same word, when you said it, went limp.)

"How's everything? Getting everything done, I hope?" she said in her alwaysalittlehoarse voice.

She carried the silver tray to the hunchback coffee table, kicking a paperback on the floor missing half its cover (*The Lib Wo* by Ari So): more Gruyère and British farmhouse cheddar fanned around the plate like Busby Berkeley girls, another pot of oolong tea. Her appearance caused the dogs and cats to come out of their salooned shadows and band around her, and when she returned in a swoosh to the kitchen (they weren't allowed, when she was cooking), they roamed the living room like dazed cowboys, unsure what to do with themselves with no showdown.

Her house ("Noah's Arc," Charles called it) I found fascinating, schizophrenic, in fact. Its original personality was old-fashioned and charming, albeit slightly outmoded and wooden (the two-floor log cabin structure built in the late 1940s with a stone fireplace and low, beamed ceilings). Yet there was another persona lurking inside as well, which could spring forth unexpectedly as soon as one turned a corner, a profane, common, at times embarrassingly crude disposition (the boxy aluminum-siding additions she'd made to the ground floor the previous year).

Every room was crammed with so much worn, mismatched furniture (stripe married to plaid, orange engaged to pink, paisley coming out of the closet), at any position in any of the rooms, you could take a haphazard Polaroid and end up with a snapshot that bore a startling resemblance to Picasso's *Les Demoiselles d'Avignon*. Instead of misshapen cube-ladies filling the frame, the angular shapes would be Hannah's skewed bookshelf (used, not for a library, but for displaying plants, Oriental ashtrays and her chopstick collection, with a few notable exceptions: *On the Road* [Kerouac, 1957], *Change Your Brain* [Leary, 1988], *Modern Warriors* [Chute, 1989], a Bob Dylan book of lyrics and *Queenie* [1985] by Michael Korda), Hannah's blistered leather chair, Hannah's samovar by the hat rack devoid of hats, the end table without an end.

Hannah's furnishings weren't the only things tired and poor. I was surprised to observe that, despite her immaculate appearance, which rarely, upon even the closest inspections, had an eyelash out of place, some of her clothes were somewhat fatigued in appearance, though this was only obvious if you were sitting next to her and she happened to shift a certain way. *There*, suddenly, the lamplight stone-skipped across hundreds of tiny lint balls rippling through the front of her wool skirt, or, very faintly, as she picked up her wineglass and laughed like a man, the unmistakable smell of mothballs embedded in all that Palais de Anything.

A lot of her clothes looked as if they'd gone a night without sleeping or had taken the red-eye, like her canary-and-cream Chanel-like suit with the weary hem, or her white cashmere sweater with the haggard elbows and debilitated waist, and a *few* articles, like the silver blouse with the drooping rose safety-pinned to the neck, actually looked like runner-ups in a three-day Depression dance marathon (see *They Shoot Horses, Don't They?*).

I overheard the others referring to Hannah's "secret trust fund" on countless occasions, but I assumed these suppositions were incorrect and a precarious financial situation lay at the heart of Hannah's evident thrift store purchases. I once watched Hannah over a rump of lamb "with tea leaves and cherry-rose compote" and envisioned her teetering, like a cartooned man, drunk and blindfolded, on the craggy cliffs of Bankruptcy and Ruin. (Even Dad lamented teachers' salaries in a Bourbon Mood: "And they wonder why Americans can't locate Sri Lanka on a map! I hate to break the news to them, but there ain't no grease for the wheel of American education! *Non dinero! Kein Geld!*")

As it turned out, money had nothing to do with it. On one occasion, when Hannah was outside with the dogs, Jade and Nigel were laughing about the gigantic peeling wagon wheel that had just appeared that day, leaning against the side of the garage like a fat man on a cigarette break. It was missing half its spokes and Hannah had announced she was planning to turn it into a coffee table.

"St. Gallway must not pay her enough," I noted quietly.

Jade turned to me. "*What?*" she asked, as if I'd just insulted her.

I swallowed. "Maybe she should ask for a raise."

Nigel suppressed his laughter. The others seemed content to ignore me, but then, something unexpected happened: Milton lifted his head from his Chemistry textbook.

"Oh, no," he said smiling. I felt my heart shudder and stall. Blood began to flood my cheeks. "Junkyards, dumps—Hannah goes nuts for 'em. All this stuff? She found it in *sad* places, trailer parks, parkin' lots. She's been known to stop in the middle of a highway—cars honkin' crazy, *mad* pile-up—just so she can rescue a chair from the side of the road. The animals too—she saved them from shelters. I was with her once, last year when she stopped for a freaky-ass hitchhiker—muscles, head shaved, total skinhead. The back of his neck read, 'Kill or Be Killed.' I asked her what she was doin' and she said she had to show him kindness. That maybe he never had any. And she was right. Guy was like a kid, smilin' the whole way. We dropped him off at Red Lobster. He shouted, 'God bless you!' Hannah had made his year." He shrugged and returned to his Chemistry. "S'just who she is."

Who she was, too, was a woman surprisingly daring and competent, whine and whimper free. The woman could fix, in a matter of minutes, any clog, drip, leak, seep—slacker toilet flushes, pipe clangs before sunrise, a dazed and confused garage door. Frankly, her handyman expertise made Dad look like a twitchy-mouthed grandmother. One Sunday, I watched in awe while Hannah fixed her own recessed doorbell with electrician gloves, screwdriver and voltmeter—not the easiest of processes, if one reads *Mr. Fix-It's Guide to Rewiring the Home* (Thurber, 2002). Another occasion, after dinner, she disappeared into the basement to fix the temperamental light on her water heater: "There's too much air in the flue," she said with a sigh.

And she was an expert mountaineer. Not that she boasted: "I *camp*," was all she'd say. One could infer it, however, from the overload of Paul Bunyan paraphernalia: carabiners and water bottles lying around the house, Swiss army knives in the same drawer as junk mail and old batteries; and in the garage, brawny hiking boots (seriously gnarled soles), moth-eaten sleeping bags, rock-climbing rope, snowshoes, tent poles, crusty sunscreen, a first-aid kit (empty, apart for blunt scissors and discolored gauze). "What're those?" Nigel asked, frowning at what looked like two vicious animal traps atop a pile of firewood. "Crampons," Hannah said, and when he continued to stare confusedly: "So you don't fall off the mountain."

She once admitted as a footnote to dinner conversation, she'd saved a man's life while camping as a teenager.

"Where?" asked Jade.

She hesitated, then: "The Adirondacks."

I'll admit I almost leapt from my seat and boasted, "*I've* saved a life too! My shot gardener!" but thankfully I had some tact; Dad and I held in contempt people forever interrupting fascinating conversations with their own rinky-dink story. (Dad called them What-About-Mes, accompanying said phrase with a slow blink, his gesture of Marked Aversion.)

"He'd fallen, injured his hip."

She said it slowly, deliberately, as if playing Scrabble, concentrating on sorting the letters, compiling clever words.

"We were alone, in the middle of nowhere. I panicked—I didn't know what to do. I ran and ran. Forever. Thankfully, I found campers who had a radio and they sent help. After that, I made a pact with myself. I'd never be helpless again."

"So the man was okay?" Leulah asked.

Hannah nodded. "He had to have surgery. But he was fine."

Of course, further inquiry into this intriguing incident—"Who was the guy?" Charles asked—was trying to scratch a diamond with a toothpick.

"Okay, okay," Hannah said, laughing as she cleared Leulah's plate, "that's enough for tonight, I think." She kneed the swish door (a little aggressively I thought) and vanished into the kitchen.

*　　*　　*

We usually sat down for dinner around 5:30 P.M. Hannah turned off the lights, the music (Nat King Cole demanding to be flown to the moon, Peggy Lee sermonizing you're nobody 'til somebody loves you), lighting the thin red candles at the center of the table.

Dinner conversation wasn't anything Dad would be particularly impressed with (no debates about Castro, Pol Pot and the Khmer Rouge, though sometimes she brought up materialism; "It's hard, in America, not to equate happiness with things."), but Hannah, chin in her hand, eyes dark as caves, was a master of the Art of Listening, and thus dinners could last two, three hours, maybe even longer, if *I* hadn't been the one who had to get home by eight. ("Too much Joyce isn't good for you," Dad said. "Bad for digestion.")

To describe this singular quality of hers (which I believe holds one of the brightest lanterns to her sometimes shadowy profile) is impossible, because what she did had nothing to do with words.

It was just this　　　　　　way about her.

And the　　　　　　wasn't premeditated, condescending, or forced (see Chapter 9, "Get Your Teen to Consider You The 'In' Crowd," *Befriending Your Kids*, Howards, 2000).

Obviously, being able to simply　　　　　　, was a skill supremely underestimated in the Western world. As Dad was fond of pointing out, in America, apart from those who won the lottery, generally all Winners were in possession of a strident voice, which was successfully used to overpower the thrum of all the competing voices, thereby producing a country that was insanely loud, so loud, most of the time no actual meaning could be discerned—only "nationwide white noise." And thus when you met someone who *listened*, someone content to do nothing but　　　　　　, so overwhelming was the difference, you had the startling and quite lonely epiphany that everyone else, every person you'd encountered since the day you were born who'd *supposedly* listened, had really not been listening to you at all. They'd been subtly checking out their own reflection in the glass bureau a little to the west of your head, thinking what they had to do later that evening, or deciding that next, as soon as you shut up, they were going to tell that classic story about their bout of Bangladeshi beachside dysentery, thereby showcasing how worldly, how wild (not to mention how utterly enviable) a human being they were.

Hannah did ultimately speak, of course, but it wasn't to tell you what she thought or what you had to do, but only to ask you certain relevant questions, which were often laughable in their simplicity (one, I remember, was, "Well, what do you think?"). Afterward, when Charles cleared the plates, Lana and Turner jumped into her lap, fashioning her arm bracelets out of their tails, and Jade turned on the music (Mel Tormé detailing how you were getting to be a habit with him), you didn't feel the edgy feeling of being alone in the world. As stupid as this sounds—you felt you had an answer.

It was this quality, I think, that made her have such an influence on the others. She was the reason Jade, for example, who sometimes talked of becoming a journalist, joined *The Gallway Gazette* as a freelance staff writer even though she downright loathed Hillary Leech, the editor-in-chief who pulled out a copy of *The New Yorker* and read it before every class (sometimes chuckling irritatingly at something in "The Talk of the Town"). And Charles sometimes carried around a three-inch textbook, *How to Be a Hitchcock* (Lerner, 1999), which I secretly paged through one Sunday and beheld the first-page inscription: "To my master of suspense. Love, Hannah." Leulah tutored fourth-graders in Science every Tuesday after school at Elmview Elementary, Nigel read *The Definitive Foreign Service Exam Study Guide* (2001 ed.), and Milton had taken an acting class at the UNCS the previous summer, Introduction to Shakespeare: The Art of the Body—acts of humanitarianism and self-improvement I couldn't help but think had originally been Hannah's suggestions, though proposed in her   way, they probably believed they'd thought of it themselves.

I, too, was not immune to her brand of inspiration. At the beginning of October, Hannah arranged with Evita for me to drop out of AP French with drapery-drab Ms. Filobeque and enroll with a bunch of freshmen in Beginning Drawing with the Dalí-decadent Mr. Victor Moats. (I did so without breathing a word to Dad.) Moats was Hannah's favorite teacher at Gallway.

"I absolutely *adore* Victor," she said, biting her bottom lip. "He's wonderful. Nigel's in one of his classes. Isn't he wonderful? I think he's *wonderful.* Really."

And Victor *was* wonderful. Victor sported faux suede shirts in Permanent Magenta and Burnt Sienna and had hair that, under the art room lights, channeled the gleam of film noir streets, Humphrey Bogart's wingtips, opera footlights and tar, all at the same time.

Hannah also bought me a sketchbook and five ink pens, which she wrapped in old-fashioned parcel paper and sent to my school mailbox. (She never talked about things. She simply did them.) On the inside cover, she'd written (in a handwriting that was a perfect extension of her—elegant, with tiny mysteries in the curves of her *n*'s and *h*'s): "For your Blue Period. Hannah."

In the middle of class, occasionally I'd take the thing out and covertly try to draw something, like Mr. Archer's ranidae hands. Though I showed no signs of being an untapped El Greco, I enjoyed pretending I was a rheumatoid artiste, some Toulouse concentrating on the outline of bony arm of a can-can girl, instead of plain old Blue van Meer, who might go down in history for the talent of feverishly copying down every syllable a teacher uttered (including *um*s and *eh*s) in case it showed up on the Unit Test.

*   *   *

In her absorbing memoir, *There's a Great Day Coming Mañana* (1973), Florence "Feisty Freddie" Frankenberg, a 1940s their-girl-Friday actress whose great claim to fame was appearing on Broadway with Al Jolson in *Hang on to Your Handkerchiefs* (she also palled around with Gemini Cervenka and Oona O'Neill), wrote in Chapter 1 that at first glance, Saturday night at the Stork Club was an "oasis of rarified fun" and that, despite WWII grimly unfolding across the Atlantic like a telegram delivering bad news, when one was in a "new gown, perched on those comfy banquettes," one had the feeling "nothing bad could happen" because one was protected by "all the money and the mink" (p. 22–3). At second glance, however, as Feisty Freddie goes on to reveal in Chapter 2, the swanky Stork Club was in fact "as vicious as Rudolph Valentino with a dame who wouldn't knock knees with him" (p. 41). She writes that everyone, from Gable and Grable to Hemingway and Hayworth, was so anxious about where the proprietor, Sherman Billingsley, placed them in the room, whether they'd be allowed into that rarefied-room-of-the-already-absurdly-rarefied, the Cub Room, one could "use the space between folks' necks and shoulders as a nutcracker" (p. 49). Freddie further reveals in Chapter 7 that on more than one occasion, she overheard certain studio honchos admitting they wouldn't think twice about "letting off a bullet or two into some balmy broad," in order to permanently secure that coveted banquette in the corner, Table 25, the Royal Circle, with its ideal view of the bar and the door (p. 91).

And thus I have to mention tensions ran quite high at Hannah's, too, though I often wondered if I, like Feisty Freddie, was the only one who noticed. Sometimes it felt as if Hannah was J. J. Hunsecker and the others were sinuous Sidney Falcos vying to be her chosen charlie, her preferred pajama playboy, her dreamy de luxe.

I remember those occasions Charles was working on his Third Reich timeline or his research paper on the USSR collapse for AP European History. He'd throw his pencil across the room. "I can't do this fucking assignment! Fuck Hitler! Fuck Churchill, Stalin and the Red Fuckin' Army!" Hannah would run upstairs to get a history book or an *Encyclopaedia Britannica* and when she returned, for an hour, their brown and gold heads huddled together like cold pigeons under the desk lamp, trying to figure out the month of Germany's invasion of Poland or exactly when the Berlin wall fell (September 1939, November 9, 1989). Once I spoke up, tried giving them a hand by pointing them in the direction of the 1200-page history text Dad always put at the top of his Required Reading, Hermin-Lewishon's famed *History Is Power* (1990) but Charles looked through me, and Hannah, flipping through the *Britannica*, was apparently one of those people who, while reading, could sit through an entire civil war between Sandinistas and U.S.-backed Contras and hear nothing. During these interludes, though, I always noticed Jade, Lu, Nigel and Milton stopped working, and if their perpetual glances across the room were any indication, they sort of became hyperaware of Hannah and Charles, maybe even a little jealous, like a pride of starving lions in a zoo when only one of them is singled out and hand-fed.

To be honest, I didn't particularly care for the way they acted around her. With me, they were edgy and aloof, but with Hannah—they seemed to confuse her rapt attention for Cecil B. DeMille's camera and a couple of klieg lights turned in their direction for principal shooting of *The Greatest Show on Earth*. Hannah would only have to ask Milton a question, commend him on some B+ he received in Spanish, and without delay he'd shuck off his usual

deliberating Alabama drawl and weirdly take to the stage as plucky lil'
Mickey Rooney, posturin', posin', moonin' and muggin' all over the place
like a six-year-old vaudeville veteran.

"Spent all night studyin', never worked so hard in my life," he'd gush, his
eyes running around her face, desperate for praise like spaniels after retrieving a shot duck. Leulah and Jade, too, were not above turning into lil' Bright
Eyes and Curly Tops themselves. (I especially detested the occasions Hannah
referred to Jade's beauty, as she turned into the sweetiest of all sweetie pies,
Little Miss Broadway.)

These manic tap dances were nothing compared to the awful occasions
Hannah gave *me* the spotlight, like the night she mentioned I had the highest
rank in school and was thus poised to be valedictorian. (Lacey Ronin-Smith
had announced the coup d'etat during Morning Announcements. I'd ousted
Radley Clifton who'd reigned, uncontested, for three years, and apparently
believed, because his brothers, Byron and Robert, had been valedictorian,
he, Radley the Razor-dull, held Divine Right to the title. Passing me in Barrow, his eyes narrowed and his mouth shrank, doubtlessly praying I'd be
found guilty of Cheating and exiled.)

"Your father must be so proud of you," Hannah said. "*I'm* proud of you.
And let me tell you something. You're a person who can do anything with
your life. I *mean* that. Anything. You can be a rocket scientist. Because you
have the rare thing everyone wants. The smarts, but also the sensitivity. Don't
be afraid of it. Remember—God, I can't remember who said it—'Happiness
is a hound dog in the sun. We aren't on Earth to be happy, but to experience
incredible things.' "

This happened to be one of Dad's favorite quotations (it was Coleridge
and Dad would tell her she'd butchered it; "If you're using your own words it
isn't *quite* a quotation, is it?"). And she wasn't smiling as she said it to me, but
looked solemn, as if talking about death (see *I'll Think About That Tomorrow*,
Pepper, 2000). (She also sounded like FDR declaring war against Japan in his
historical 1941 radio address, Track 21 on Dad's *Great Speeches, Modern Times*
three-CD boxed set.)

On the very best of days I was their burden, their bête noire, and so, if
you considered Newton's Third Law of Motion, "All actions have an equal
and opposite reaction," and the five of them spontaneously turned into lil'
Baby Face Nelsons and Dimples, they *also* had to turn into old Lost Weekends and Draculas, which best describes the looks on their faces in *that* instance. For the most part though, I did my best to deflect such personal

attention. I didn't especially long for Table 25, The Royal Circle. I was still elated to be one of the jelly beans allowed in off the street, and was thus perfectly content to spend the evening, rather the entire swank decade, sitting at wholly undesirable Table 2, too close to the orchestra and with an obscured view of the door.

Hannah, during their song'n'dance antics, remained impassive. She was all diplomatic smiles and kind "Fantastic, darlings," and it was during these moments I found myself wondering if I'd made a few errors in my breathless reading of her, if, as Dad said bluntly in the rare event he admitted he was wrong (accompanying said sentence with a contrite gaze at the floor): "I'd been a blind ass."

She was, after all, highly peculiar when it came to talking about herself. Attempts to exhume details about her life, indirectly or otherwise, went nowhere. You think it'd be impossible for someone not to give *some* semblance of an answer when asked a question point-blank, making some very revealing dodge (sharp intake of breath, shifty eyes), which you could subsequently translate into a Dark Truth About Her Childhood using Freud's *The Psychopathology of Everyday Life* (1901) or *The Ego and the Id* (1923). But Hannah had a very plain way of saying, "I lived outside Chicago, then San Francisco for two years. I'm not that interesting, guys."

Or she'd shrug.

"I—I'm a teacher. I wish I could say something more interesting."

"But you're part-time," Nigel said once. "What do you do with the other part?"

"I don't know. I wish I knew where the time went."

She laughed and said nothing more.

There was also the question of a certain word: Valerio. It was their mythical, tongue-and-cheek nickname for Hannah's secret Cyrano, her cloak-and-dagger Darcy and her QT Oh Captain! My Captain! I'd heard them mention the word on countless occasions, and when I finally found the courage to inquire who, or what it was, so exciting was the subject, they forgot to ignore me. Eagerly, they recounted a puzzling incident. Two years ago, when they were sophomores, Leulah had left behind an Algebra textbook at Hannah's house. When her parents drove her back for the book the following day, while Hannah retrieved it upstairs, Lu went into the kitchen for a glass of water. She noticed, by the telephone, a small yellow notepad. On the topmost page, Hannah had doodled a strange word.

"She'd written *Valerio* all over it," Lu said heatedly. She had a funny way of wrinkling her nose, which made it look like a tiny bunched-up sock. "Like a *million* times. Kind of crazily too, the way psycho killers write things when the investigator breaks into his house on *CSI*. The one word over and over, like she was talking on the phone, unaware of what she was drawing. Still, *I* do stuff like that, so I didn't think anything of it. Until she walked in. She picked up the notepad immediately, facing the pages toward her so I couldn't see it. I don't think she put it down until I was in my car, driving away. I'd never seen her act so strange."

Strange indeed. I took the liberty of looking up the word in Cambridge etymologist Louis Bertman's *Words, Their Origin and Relevance* (1921). *Valerio* was a common Italian patronymic meaning "brave and strong," derived from the Roman name Valerius, derived in turn from the Latin verb *valere*, "to be in healthy sprits, to be robust and sturdy." It was also the name of several minor saints in the fourth and fifth centuries.

I asked them why they didn't simply ask Hannah outright who he was.

"Can't do that," said Milton.

"Why?"

"We already did," said Jade with irritation, exhaling smoke from her cigarette. "Last year. And she turned a weird red color. Almost purple."

"Like we'd smacked her in the head with a baseball bat," said Nigel.

"Yeah, I couldn't tell if she was sad or pissed," Jade went on. "She just stood there with her mouth open, then disappeared into the kitchen. And when she came out, like, five minutes later, Nigel apologized. And she said in a fake administrator voice, oh, no, it's *fine*, it's just that she doesn't like us snooping or talking about her behind her back. It's hurtful."

"Total bullshit," said Nigel.

"It wasn't bullshit," Charles said angrily.

"Well, we can't bring it up again," Jade said. "We don't want to give her another heart attack."

"Maybe it's her Rosebud," I said, after a moment. Naturally, none of them were ever thrilled when I opened my mouth, but this time, every one of their heads swiveled toward me, almost in unison.

"Her *what*?" asked Jade.

"Have you seen *Citizen Kane*?" I asked.

"Sure," said Nigel with interest.

"Well, Rosebud is what the main character, Kane, searches for his entire life. It's what he's desperate to get back to. An unrequited, aching yearning for a simpler, happier time. It's the last thing he says before he dies."

"Why didn't he just go to a florist?" asked Jade distastefully.

And thus Jade (who, although sometimes very literal, had a flair for the dramatic) enjoyed fashioning all kinds of exciting conclusions out of Hannah's mysteriousness whenever Hannah happened to be out of the room. Sometimes *Hannah Schneider* was an alias. At other times, Hannah was a member of the Federal Witness Protection Program after testifying against crime-tsar Dimitri "Caviar" Molotov of the Howard Beach Molotovs, and was thus chiefly responsible for his being found guilty of sixteen counts of fraud. Or else, she figured Hannah was one the Bin Ladins: "That family's big as the Coppolas." Once, after she happened to watch *Sleeping with the Enemy* at midnight on TNT, she told Leulah Hannah was hiding in Stockton in order to avoid detection by her ex-husband, who happened to be both physically abusive and clinically insane. (Naturally, Hannah's hair was dyed, her eyes, colored contacts.)

"And that's why she hardly ever goes out and pays cash for everything. She doesn't want him to trace her credit cards."

"She doesn't pay cash for everything," said Charles.

"*Some*times she does."

"Everyone on the planet *some*times pays cash."

I humored these wild speculations, even designed a few interesting ones of my own, but of course, I didn't genuinely believe them.

Dad, on Double Lives: "It's fun to imagine they're as epidemic as illiteracy or chronic fatigue syndrome or any other cultural malaise that graces the covers of *Time* and *Newsweek*, but sadly, most Bob Joneses off the street are just that, Bob Jones, with no dark secrets, dark horses, dark victories, or dark sides of the moon. It's enough to make you give up on Baudelaire. Mind you, I'm not counting adultery, which isn't dark in the slightest, but rather clichéd."

I thus secretly concluded Hannah Schneider was a typo. Destiny had been sloppy. (Most likely because she was overworked. Kismet and Karma were too flighty to get anything done and Doom couldn't be trusted.) Quite by accident, she'd assigned an outstanding person of breathtaking beauty to a buried mountain town, where grandeur was like that slighted tree always falling in the woods and no one noticing. Somewhere else, in Paris, or Hong Kong probably, someone named Chase H. Niderhann with a face compelling as a baked potato and a voice like a throat clearing, happened to be living *her* life, a life of opera, of sun and lakes and weekend excursions to Kenya (pronounced "keen-YA"), of gowns that went "Shhhhh" across a floor.

I decided to take control of the situation (see *Emma*, Austen, 1816).

*   *   *

It was October. Dad was dating a woman named Kitty (whom I hadn't yet had the pleasure of swatting away from our screen), but she was of no consequence. Why should Dad settle for a Standard American Wirehair when he could have a Persian? (I can blame Hannah's croony music taste for my wayward vision, old Peggy Lee and her incessant whining about the crazy moon and Sarah Vaughan sniveling about her lover man.)

I acted with uncharacteristic vehemence that rainy Wednesday afternoon as I set my Disney-inspired plan into action. I told Dad I had a ride and then asked Hannah to drive me home. I made her wait in the car, giving her a lame excuse ("Hold on, I have a great book for you.") before I ran inside to pry Dad away from Patrick Kleinman's latest tome published by Yale University Press, *The Chronicle of Collectivism* (2004), so he'd come outside and talk to her.

He did.

In short, there was no world on a string, no tender trap, no wee small hour of the morning and certainly no witchcraft. Dad and Hannah exchanged moonless pleasantries. I believe Dad even said, "Yes, I've been meaning to attend one of those home football games. Blue and I will see you there," in an effort to clothespin the silence.

"That's right," said Hannah. "You like football games."

"Yes," said Dad.

"Don't you have a book to lend me?" Hannah asked me.

Within minutes, she was driving away with my only copy of *Love in the Time of Cholera* (García Márquez, 1985).

"Touched as I am by your efforts to play Cupid, my dear, in the future, please allow me to do my own riding into the sunset," Dad said as he walked inside.

*   *   *

That night I couldn't sleep. Even though I'd never said anything to Hannah, and she'd never said anything to me, a certain foolproof Thesis had been floating around in my head, that the only plausible explanation for her including me in the Sunday soirees, for her brutally shoehorning me in with the others (determined to pry open their airtight clique like a frenzied housewife with a jar opener) was that she wanted Dad. Because I couldn't have mistaken, at least back at Surely Shoos, her eyes hovering a little fretfully over his face like green dragontails over a flower (Family *Papilionidae*), that sure, she'd smiled at *me* back at Fat Kat Foods, but it was Dad whom she wanted to notice her, Dad whom she wanted to stun.

But I was wrong.

I tossed and turned, analyzing every look Hannah had thrown me, every word, smile, hiccup, throat clear and distinctly audible swallow until I was so confused, I could only lie on my left side staring at the windows with its swollen blue and white curtains where night melted so slowly it hurt. (Mendelshon Peet wrote in *Loggerheads* [1932], "Man's wobbly little mind isn't equipped for hauling around the great unknowns.")

Finally I fell asleep.

"Very few people realize, there's no point chasing after answers to life's important questions," Dad said once in a Bourbon Mood. "They all have fickle, highly whimsical minds of their own. Nevertheless. If you're patient, if you don't rush them, when they're ready, they'll smash into you. And don't be surprised if afterwards you're speechless and there are cartoon tweety birds chirping around your head."

How right he was.

Pygmalion

The legendary Spanish conquistador Hernando Núñez de Valvida (*La Serpiente Negra*) wrote, in his diary entry of April 20, 1521 (a day he allegedly slaughtered two hundred Aztecs), "*La gloria es un millón ojos asustados,*" roughly translated as, "Glory is a million frightened eyes."

This never meant much to me, until I became friends with them.

If the Aztecs regarded Hernando and his henchmen with fright, then the entire St. Gallway student body (more than a few teachers too) regarded Charles, Jade, Lu, Milton and Nigel with awe and outright panic.

They had a name, as all choice societies do. Bluebloods.

And daily, hourly (possibly even minutely) that posh little word was whispered and whined over in envy and agitation in every classroom and corridor, every lab and locker room.

"The Bluebloods catwalked into the Scratch this morning," said Donnamara Chase, a girl who sat two seats away from me in AP English. "They stood in the corner and went, 'Ew,' to everyone who walked by to the point that Sam Christenson—you know that mannish sophomore girl? Well, she actually broke down at the beginning of Chemistry. They had to cart her off to the Infirmary and all she'd say was that they made fun of her shoes. She was wearing Aerosole pink suede penny loafers in a size nine and a half. Which isn't even that *bad*."

Obviously at Coventry Academy, at Greenside Junior High, there'd been the popular ones, the VIPs who cruised the halls like an arcade of limousines and invented their own tongue in order to intimidate like fierce Zaxoto tribesmen in the Côte d'Ivoire (at Braden Country I was a "mondo nuglo," whatever that meant), but the asthma-inducing mystique of the Bluebloods was unparalleled. I think it was due in part to their diva foxiness (Charles and Jade were the Gary Cooper and Grace Kelly of our time), their for-real fabulousity (Nigel was so tiny he was trendy, Milton so vast he was vogue), their trippy confidence (there goes Lu proudly across the Commons, her dress on inside-out), but also, most singularly, because of certain tabloidal rumors about them, a lil' somethin' somethin' and Hannah Schneider. Hannah kept a surprisingly low profile; she taught only the one class, Intro to Film, in a squat building at the edge of campus called Loomis, famous for laundering credit fillers like Intro to the Fashion Business and Woodshop. And as Mae West is quoted in the out-of-print *Are You Just Happy to See Me* (Paulson, 1962): "Y'ain't nobody 'til you've had a sex scandal."

Two weeks after my first dinner at Hannah's, I overheard two senior girls slinging such sleaze in my second period Study Hall, held in the Central Reading Room of the Donald E. Crush Library, monitored by crossword-puzzle enthusiast, Mr. Frank Fletcher, a bald man who taught Driver's Ed. The girls were fraternal twins, Eliaya and Georgia Hatchett. With curly auburn hair, stout frames, shepherd's-pie potbellies and alehouse complexions, they resembled two oily portraits of King Henry VIII, each painted by a different artist (see *The Faces of Tyranny*, Clare, 1922, p. 322).

"I don't get how she got a job at this school," said Eliaya. "She's three sandwiches short of a picnic."

"Who're you talking about?" asked Georgia absentmindedly as she poured over colored photos in a magazine, *VIP Weekly*, her tongue sticking out the side of her mouth.

"*Duh.* Hannah Schneider." Eliaya tipped her chair backward and drummed her fat fingers on the cover of the textbook on her lap, *An Illustrated History of Cinema* (Jenoah, 2002 ed.). (I could only assume she was enrolled in Hannah's class.) "She totally wasn't prepared today. She disappeared for fifteen minutes 'cause she couldn't find the DVD we were supposed to watch. We were supposed to watch *The Tramp*, but she comes back with friggin' *Apocalypse Now*, which Mom and Dad would go mental over—the movie's three hours of harlotry. But Hannah was like *plan*etary—didn't have a *clue*. She puts it in, doesn't even *think* about the rating. So we see the first twenty minutes and the bell rings, and then that kid Jamie Century, he asks her when we're gonna see the rest and she says tomorrow. That she's changing the syllabus around a little. I'll bet by the end of the year we're watching *Debbie Does Dallas*. It was ghetto."

"Your point?"

"She's tweaked. Wouldn't be shocked if she went Klebold."

Georgia sighed. "Well, everyone and their grandmother knows she's still banging Charles after all these years—"

"Like a screen in a tornado. Sure."

Georgia leaned closer to her sister. (I had to be very still to hear what she said.) "You really think the Bluebloods go all Caligula on the weekends? I'm not sure if I believe Cindy Willard."

"Of course," said Eliaya. "Mom said royals *only* bed royals."

"Oh, *right*," said Georgia, nodding, then breaking into toothy laughter, a sound like a wooden stool being dragged across a floor. "That's how they keep their gene pool from getting contaminated."

Unfortunately, as Dad pointed out, there's often a seed of Truth within the Flash and Trash (he himself wasn't above perusing a few supermarket tabloids while standing in line: " 'Plastic Surgery Smash-ups of the Stars'— there's something rather compelling about that headline.") and I'll admit, ever since I saw Hannah and Charles together in the courtyard on the first day of school, I suspected there *was* something clammy going on between them (though I'd decided, after a Sunday or two, while Charles was almost certainly infatuated with Hannah, her attitude toward him was pleasantly platonic). And though I was in the dark regarding the Bluebloods' weekend activities (and would be until the middle of October) I *did* know they were quite preoccupied with maintaining the superiority of their line.

I, of course, was the one contaminating it.

* * *

My inclusion into their Magic Circle was as painless as the invasion of Normandy. Sure, we had *faces* eventually, but for the first month or so— September, the very beginning of October—though I saw them all the time peacocking through campus, and acted as hushed, horrified journalist to the anxieties they inspired ("If I ever see Jade injured, facedown in the street, homeless, riddled with leprosy—I'll do humanity a favor and run her over," pledged Beth Price in my AP English class), I only ever hung out with them at Hannah's.

And obviously, during those first few evenings, the scenario was more than a little humiliating. Obviously it made me feel like a dumpy bachelorette on a reality show called *In-sta-love* no one wanted to take for drinks and I sure as hell could forget about dinner. I'd sit on Hannah's shabby chaise longue with one of her dogs, pretending to be transfixed by my AP Art History homework while the five of them talked in hushed voices about how "hard-core," how "juiced," they'd been on Friday at mysterious places they'd nick-named "The Purple" and "The Blind," and when Hannah emerged from the kitchen, immediately they'd hurl me greasy little sardine-smiles. Milton would blink, aw-shucks his knee and say, "So how's it goin', Blue? You're aw-ful quiet over there." "She's shy," Nigel would observe, deadpan. Or Jade, who without fail dressed like a famous person working the red carpet at Cannes: "I *love* your shirt. *I* want one. You'll have to tell me where you got it." Charles smiled like a talk show host with poor Neilsen Ratings and Lu never said a word. Whenever my name was mentioned, she examined her feet.

Hannah must have sensed we were heading toward a stalemate, because shortly thereafter, she launched her next assault.

"Jade, why don't you take Blue with you when you go to Conscience? It might be fun for her," she said. "When are you going again?"

"Don't know," Jade said drearily, sprawled on her stomach on the living room carpet, reading *The Norton Anthology of Poetry* (Ferguson, Salter, Stall-worthy, 1996 ed.).

"I thought you said you were going this week," Hannah persisted. "Maybe they can squeeze her in?"

"Maybe," she said without looking up.

I forgot this conversation, until that Friday, a worn, gray afternoon. After my last class, AP World History with Mr. Carlos Sandborn (who used so much gel, one always thought he'd just come from swimming laps at the Y), I returned to the third floor of Hanover to find Jade and Leulah standing by my locker: Jade, in a black Golightly dress, Leulah, a white blouse and skirt. Standing with her hands and feet together as if waiting for choir practice, Leulah looked pleasant enough, but Jade looked like a kid in a nursing home impatiently waiting for her designated fogey to be wheeled in so she could read him *Watership Down* in a monotone, thereby earning her Community Outreach credit, thereby graduating on time.

"So we're going to get our hair and nails and eyebrows done and you're coming," Jade informed me with a hand on her hip.

"Oh," I said, nodding, spinning through the combination of my padlock, though I don't think I was actually entering the combination, only vigorously turning it in one direction, then the other.

"Ready?"

"Now?" I asked.

"Of course *now*."

"I can't," I said. "I'm busy."

"*Busy?* With *what?*"

"My dad's picking me up." Four sophomore girls who'd drifted by had snagged, like garbage in a river, by the German Language Bulletin Board. They blatantly eavesdropped.

"Oh, God," said Jade, "not your *wonder*dad again. You'll have to let us know his civilian name and what he looks like without the mask and the cape." (I'd made the serious mistake of bringing Dad up the previous Sunday. I think I actually said the phrase "brilliant man" in relation to him, also "one of the preeminent commentators on American culture at work in this country today," a line lifted verbatim from the two-page spread on Dad in *TAP-SIM*, the American Political Science Institute's quarterly [see "Dr. Yes," Spring 1987, Vol. XXIV, Issue 9]. I'd said it because Hannah had asked what he did for a living, how he "kept busy," and something about Dad simply invited the boast, the brag, the self-congratulating monologue.)

"She's just kidding," Lu said. "Come on. It'll be fun."

I collected my books and walked outside with them to inform Dad my *Ulysses* Study Group had decided to meet for a few hours, but I'd be home for dinner. He frowned at the sight of Jade and Lu standing on the Hanover steps: "Those two tartlets think they can read Joyce? *Heh.* Good luck to them—let me revise that—pray for a miracle."

I could tell he wanted to say no, but was reluctant to make a scene.

"Very well," he said with a sigh and a pitying look. He started the Volvo. "Tallyho, my dear."

As we walked to the Student Parking Lot, I heard his rave reviews.

"Shit," Jade said, looking at me with surprised esteem. "Your dad's *magnifico*. You said he was brilliant but I didn't realize you meant in a Clooney way. If he wasn't your dad, I'd ask you to set me up with him."

"He looks like what's his name . . . the father in *The Sound of Music*," said Lu.

Frankly, it could get a little stale how Dad, within minutes, could elicit such worldwide acclaim. Sure—I was the first person to stand up and throw him roses, shout, "Bravo, man, bravo!" But sometimes I couldn't help but feel Dad was an opera diva who garnered reverential ratings even when he was too lazy to hit the high notes, forgot a costume, blinked after his own death scene; something about him seized approval from everyone, regardless of the performance. For instance, when I passed Ronin-Smith, the guidance counselor, in Hanover Hall, it seemed she'd never gotten over the minutes Dad had spent in her office. She asked not "How are your classes?" but "How's your father, dear?" The only woman who'd met him and not inquired after him ad nauseam was Hannah Schneider.

"*Right* . . . Mr. Von Trapp," said Jade thoughtfully, nodding, "Yeah, I always had a thing for him. So where's your mom in all this?"

"She's dead," I said in a dramatic, bleak voice, and for the first time, enjoyed their astonished silence.

*   *   *

They took me to purple-walled, zebra-couched Conscience, located in downtown Stockton across from the public library, where Jaire of the alligator boots (pronounced "jay-REE") gave me copper highlights and cut my hair so it no longer looked "like she did it herself with a pair of toenail scissors." To my surprise, Jade insisted my new grooming initiative was complimentary, care of her mother, Jefferson, who'd left Jade her black American Express card "in case of Emergency" before disappearing for six weeks in Aspen with her new "hottie," a ski instructor "named Tanner with permanently chapped lips."

"I'll give you a thousand dollars if you can do something with those broom-bangs," Jade instructed my hairdresser.

Also funded by Jefferson, over the next two weeks, was my six-month supply of disposable contact lenses procured from ophthalmologist Stephen J. Henshaw, MD, with eyes like an Arctic Fox's and a bad head cold, as well as clothes, shoes and undergarments hand-selected for me by Jade and Lu *not* from the Adolescent Department of Stickley's, but at Vanity Fair Bodiwear on Main Street, at Rouge Boutique on Elm, at Natalia's on Cherry, even at Frederick's of Hollywood ("If you ever decide to get kinky, I suggest *this* for the occasion," Jade instructed, thrusting something at me that resembled the harness one dons before skydiving, only in pink). The final coups de grâce to my previous dull appearance were moisturizing makeups, the thyme and myrtle lip shimmers, the day (shiny) and evening (murky) eye shadows exhumed especially for my skin tone from Stickley's cosmetics main floor, as well as the fifteen-minute application tutorial by gum-chewing Millicent with her powdery forehead and spotless lab coat. (She artfully crammed the entire white light color spectrum onto both of my eyelids.)

"You are a goddess," Lu said, smiling at me in Millicent's hand mirror.

"Who would've thought," cracked Jade.

I was no longer apologetically owl-like, but impenitently pastrylike (Visual Aid 9.0).

* * *

Dad, of course, witnessing this transformation, felt the way Van Gogh would probably feel, if, one hot afternoon, he happened to wander into a Sarasota Gift Shoppe and found next to the cardboard baseball caps and Fun-in-the-Sun seashell figurines, his beloved sunflowers printed on one side of two-hundred beach towels on SALE for just $9.99.

"Your hair appears to *blaze*, sweet. Hair is not supposed to blaze. Fires are supposed to blaze, illuminated clock towers, lighthouses, Hell perhaps. Not human hair."

Soon, however, rather miraculously, apart from the odd gripe or humph, most of his indignation subsided. I assumed it had to do with his absorption with Kitty, or, as she called herself on our answering machine, "Kitty Cat." (I hadn't met her, but had heard the latest headlines: "Kitty Swoons in Italian Restaurant Due to Dad's Musings on Human Nature," "Kitty Begs Dad's Forgiveness for Spilling Her White Russian on Cuff of His Irish Tweed," "Kitty Plans Her Fortieth Birthday and Hints at Wedding Bells.") It was bizarre, but Dad appeared to have accepted the fact that his work of art had been shamelessly commercialized. He even seemed to harbor no ill will.

"You're satisfied? You're responsible? You respect the youths in this *Ulysses* Study Group, which unsurprisingly, spend more time roaming the mall and bleaching their hair than tracking the whereabouts of Stephen Dedalus?"

(No, I never quite disabused Dad of the idea that I spent Sunday afternoons trying to scale that Himalayan tome. Thankfully, Dad had no real taste for Joyce—excessive wordplay bored him, so did Latin—but in order to avoid even the most basic questioning, I told him periodically that due to the weak constitutions of others, we were still unable to make it past Base Camp, Chapter 1, "Telemachus.")

"They're actually pretty sharp," I said. "Just the other day, one of them used 'obsequious' in conversation."

"Don't be cheeky. They're thinkers?"

"Yes."

"Not lemmings? Not leg warmers? Not nitwits, net-heads, neo-Nazis? Not anarchists or antichrists? Not pedestrian youths who believe they're the first people on earth to be *mizundahstood?* Sadly, American teenagers are to a weightless vacuum as seat cushions are to polyurethane foam—"

"Dad. It's fine."

"You're positive? Never rely on intoxicating surfaces."

"Yes."

"I'll accept it then." He frowned as I stood on my tiptoes to kiss his rough cheek. I made my way to the front door. It was Sunday and Jade was resting her elbow on the car horn. "Have a swell time with your chicks and charlies," he said and sighed a little theatrically, though I ignored him. " 'If others have their will, Ann hath a way.' "

*   *   *

There were a handful of occasions when Jade, Lu and I screeched with laughter over something, like the one time they invited me "mall slumming" and a crew of chickenheads with their boxers on display trailed us with stupid smiles around Blue Crest Mall ("Serious mafuglies—just as I suspected," Jade said, surveying them through a rack of scrunchies at Earringz N' Thingz) or when Jade debated the mysterious dimensions of Nigel's candlestick ("Given his shortness, it could be powerful, it could be pygmy"; "Oh, God," said Lu slapping a hand to her mouth) or driving to Hannah's, the time Jade and I flipped off a scab (her word for any "forty-plus hideous male") who had the gall to drive a meandering Volkswagen in front of her. (Following her lead, I unrolled the window to stick my hand out and my hair—now a fascinating Bornite color, Atomic number 29—thrashed in the wind.)

During such moments, I thought to myself, maybe these were my friends, maybe I'd confide in them about sex over rhubarb pie in a diner at 3:00 A.M. and someday we'd phone each other to chat about Tuskawalla Trails Retirement Community and back pain and our turtle-bald husbands, but then their smiles fell off their faces like Visual Aids on bulletin boards missing a tack. They'd look at me irritably, as if I'd tricked them.

They drove me home. I'd sit in the backseat doing my best to lip-read due to the ear-splitting levels of the heavy-metal CD (I decoded agonizingly shadowy phrases: "meet us later," "hot-ass date"), knowing full well because I hadn't said anything breathtaking (because I was about as cool as Bermuda shorts), they'd drop me like laundry and accelerate into the whispery night with its plum sky and black mountains snooping over the spiked tops of the pine trees. At an undisclosed location, they'd join Charles, Nigel and Black (what they called Milton), and probably park and neck, and race cars off cliffs (don leather jackets emblazoned with T-BIRD or PINK LADY).

"Astalowaygo," Jade said to my general vicinity as she smeared on red lipstick in the rearview mirror. I slammed the car door, heaved my backpack onto my shoulder.

Leulah waved. "See you Sunday," she said sweetly.

I trudged inside, the veteran who wished war had lasted longer.

"What on earth did you find compulsory to purchase at a store called Bahama-Me-Tan?" shouted Dad from the kitchen when he returned from his date with Kitty. He appeared in the doorway of the living room with the orange plastic shopping bag I'd thrown on the foyer floor, holding it as if it were the carcass of a hedgehog.

"Bali-Me Bronzer," I said drearily without looking up from some book I'd yanked off the shelf, *The South American Joven Mutiny* (Gonzalez, 1989).

Dad nodded and wisely decided not to probe further.

There was a turning point. (And I'm sure it had everything to do with Hannah, although her role, what she must have said to them—an ultimatum perhaps, a bribe or one of her   suggestions—was never clear.)

It was the first week of October, on a Friday, during sixth period. It was a harsh, bright day for fall, glaring as a washed car, and Mr. Moats, my instructor for Beginning Drawing, had entreated the class to go outside with our No. 2 pencils and sketch—"Find your melting clocks!" he'd ordered, swooshing open the door as if freeing mustangs, his other hand *Oléing* in the air so for four seconds he was a Flamenco dancer in tight pants of Cadmium Green. Slowly, lazily, the class floated out across the campus with their giant sketch pads. I found it tricky to choose what to draw, and wandered for fifteen minutes before deciding upon a faded package of M&Ms hiding in a bed of pine needles behind Elton. I was sitting on the cement wall, drawing my first few wimpy lines, when I heard someone traipsing down the sidewalk. Instead of passing me, the person stopped.

"Hey, there," he said.

It was Milton. His hands were stuffed in his pockets and his stringy hair mumbo-jumboed over his forehead.

"Hi," I said, but he didn't answer or even smile. He simply stepped over to my sketchpad and tilted his head to inspect my rickety pencil lines like a teacher looming over your shoulder, blithely helping himself to what you scribbled during an Essay Test.

"What're you doing out of class?" I asked.

"Oh, I'm sick," he said, smiling. "Flu. Goin' to the infirmary, then home to rest."

I should mention: while Charles was the obvious Cassanova at St. Gallway, popular among chicks, charlie-boys and cheerleaders, Milton, I'd learned, was sort of the Studhorse for the smart and strange. A girl in AP

English, Macon Campins, who drew henna-style swirling designs in permanent ink on her palms, claimed to be obsessively in love with him, and before the bell, before flustered Ms. Simpson shuffled into the room muttering in escalating whispers—"no toner, nothing but legal paper, no staples, everything in this school, no, this country, no, the *world*, all going to seed"—you could hear Macon discussing Milton's mystery tattoo with her best friend, Engella Grand: "I think he did it himself. See, I was staring at his rolled-up sleeve in Biology? And I'm pretty sure it's a huge freakin' oil slick on his arm. That's sooo sexy."

I, too, felt there was something undercover and sexual about Milton, which made me act sort of inebriated whenever I was alone with him. I was once rinsing plates, loading them into Hannah's dishwasher when he came in with seven water glasses in his giant hands and, as he leaned past me to put them in the sink, my chin accidentally touched his shoulder. It was damp and muggy as a greenhouse and I thought I was going to fall down. "Sorry, Blue," he said when he stepped away. Whenever he said my name, which he did often (so often, I felt it came tantalizingly close to satire), his accent yo-yoed it, or else, turned it into a piece of elastic. *Bluuue.*

"Got plans tonight, Blue?" he asked me now.

"Yes," I said, though my response didn't seem to register. (I think they'd figured by now, unless Hannah had actively arranged a suitor, no one came calling—not an outrageous assumption.)

"Well, we're hangin' at Jade's tonight if you want to come. I'll get her to pick you up. Should be mad crazy. If you can handle it."

He continued past me, down the sidewalk.

"I thought you had the flu," I said under my breath, but he heard me, because he turned and, walking backward, winked at me, saying: "Feelin' better by the minute."

He then began to whistle and, tightening his green-and-blue plaid tie as if about to interview for a job, he swung open the back doors of Elton and disappeared inside.

                        *   *   *

Jade lived in a thirty-five-room Tara-inspired McMansion (what she called the Wedding Cake) built atop a hill in a hick town "sprinkled with trailer parks and people without molars" known as Junk Spread (pop. 109).

"The house is vulgar when you see it for the first time," she said cheerfully, swinging open the massive front door. (From the moment Jade had picked me up, her spirits had approached *Gidget*-like gladness, which made me wonder what kind of stellar deal she'd cut with Hannah; it had to have had something to do with immortality.)

"Yeah," she said, fixing the front of her black-and-white silk wrap dress so her electric yellow bra didn't show. "I made the suggestion to Jefferson that she have on hand some of those airplane sick bags, you know, right when you first walk in. She hasn't gotten them yet. Oh, and no you're not hallucinating. That really is Cassiopeia. Ursa Minor's in the dining room, Hercules in the kitchen. Jefferson dreamed it up, constellations of the Northern Hemisphere on all the ceilings. She was dating this guy Timber, an Astrologist and Dream Translator, when they were designing the house, and by the time Timber unloaded her and she was going out with Gibbs from England who hated the idea of all the fucking twinkling lights — 'How the devil will you change those *bulbs?*' — it was too late. The electricians had already done Corona Borealis and half of Pegasus."

The foyer was white-on-white-on-white with a slick marble floor on which one could probably triple-lutz and double-toe-loop with little difficulty. I stared up at what really *was* Cassiopeia twinkling above us in the pale blue ceiling, which also seemed to hum that acid note of Frozen Food sections. It was freezing too.

"No, you're not coming down with something. Living in cool temperatures stalls, sometimes even reverses the aging process so Jefferson doesn't allow the thermostat in the house to get above forty." Jade flung the car keys onto the massive Corinthian column by the door, messy with change, toenail clippers, brochures for meditation classes at something called The Suwanee Centre for Inner Life. "Don't know about you, but I'm in dire need of a cocktail. Nobody's here yet, they're late, the motherfuckers, so I'll show you around."

Jade made us mudslingers, the first alcoholic drink I'd ever had; it was sweet yet fascinatingly throat scalding. We embarked on the Grand Tour. The house was ornate and filthy as a flophouse. Under the pulsing constellations (many of them with extinguished stars, supernovas, white dwarfs) almost every room looked confused, in spite of the very explicit title Jade gave it (Rec Room, Museum Room, Drawing Room). For example, the Imperial Room displayed an ornate Persian *vahze* and some large oily portrait of an "eighteenth-century Sir Somebodyorother"; but also a stained silk blouse over a sofa arm, a sneaker capsized under a stool, and on a gilded end table, gruesome cotton balls huddled together in miserable commiseration after having removed blood-red polish from somebody's nails.

She took me to the TV Room ("three thousand channels and nothing on"), the Toy Room with a life-sized rearing carousel horse ("That's Snowpea") and the Shanghai Room, empty, apart from a big bronze Buddha statue and ten or twelve cardboard boxes. "Hannah really likes it if we get rid of as much material possession as possible. I take stuff to Goodwill all the time. You should think about doing the same," she said. In the basement, under Gemini, was the Jefferson Room ("where my mother pays *ohmage* to her heyday"). It was a 1600-square-foot family room with a Drive-In-sized TV, carpeting the color of spareribs and wooden walls lined with thirty advertisements for brands like "Ohh!" Perfume, Slinky Silk™ Pantyhose, Keep Walkin' Bootwear, Orange Bliss Lite® and other obscure products. Each featured the same carrot-topped woman flashing a banana-grin that walked the fine line between ecstatic and fanatic (see Chapter 4, "Jim Jones," *Don Juan de Mania*, Lerner, 1963).

"That's my mom, Jefferson. You can call her Jeff."

Jade frowned as she surveyed one of the ads for Vita Vitamins in which Jeff, sporting blue terry-cloth wristbands, did a jackknife over VITA VITAMIN YOUR WAY TO A BETTER LIFE.

"She was big in New York in 1978 for two minutes. See here, how her hair curves way up over, then ends right there above her eye? Well, she invented that hairstyle. When she came out with it everyone went bonkers. It was called The Crimson Marshmallow. She was also friends with Andy Warhol. I guess he let her see him without his wig all the time. Oh, wait."

She walked to the table beneath the Sir Albert's Spicy Sausages ads ("If it's good enough for royals, it's good enough for you.") returning with a framed photograph of Jefferson, apparently in the present day.

"This is her last year posing for her Christmas cards."

The woman had wandered deep into her forties and, to her evident panic, had been unable to make her way back. She still flashed the banana-smile, though it'd gone mushy on the ends, and her hair no longer had enough kinetic energy to swing itself up into The Crimson Marshmallow, but frizzled stiffly off her head in a Red Zinger Silo. (If Dad saw her he would not hesitate to call her "a badly aged Barbarella." Or he'd use one of his Stale Candy remarks reserved for women who spent the greater portion of their week attempting to halt Middle Age as if Middle Age was nothing but a team of runaway stallions: "a melted red M&M," a "stale strawberry Sweet Tart.")

Jade was looking at me intently, arms crossed, eyes narrowed.

"She looks very nice," I said.

"About as nice as Hitler."

After the tour, we retreated to the Purple Room, "where Jefferson gets to really know her boyfriends if you know what I mean. Avoid the paisley couch by the fireplace." The others still hadn't arrived, and after Jade busied herself with making more mudslingers and turning over the Louis Armstrong record on the antique gramophone, she finally sat down, though her eyes flew around the room like canaries. She checked her watch a fourth time, then a fifth.

"How long have you lived here?" I asked, because I sort of wished we'd get along so when the others arrived we were performing our favorite number, "Just Two Little Girls from Little Rock," Jade, a skinnier, angrier Marilyn to my unquestionably-more-flat-chested Jane Russell. But, much to my own disappointment, the odds didn't look good for being bosom buddies.

"Three years," she said distractedly. "Oh, where the fuck *are* they? I loathe when people are late and Black swore he'd be here by seven, the *fraud*," she complained not to me, but the ceiling. "I'll *cas*trate him." (Orion, the constellation under which we sat, had not had his light bulbs changed and thus he'd lost his legs and head. He was nothing but a belt.)

Soon the others arrived wearing quirky accessories (plastic bead necklaces, fast-food crowns; Charles wore an old fencing shirt, Milton a blazer in navy velveteen) and they stormed the room, Nigel crawling over the leather couch, hitching his legs on the coffee table, Leulah air-kissing Jade hellos. She only smiled at me, then glided to the bar, her eyes glassy and red. Milton wandered toward a wooden box on the writing desk in the corner and unlatched it, removing a cigar.

"Jadey, where's the cutter?" he asked, sniffing it.

She dragged on her cigarette and glared at him. "You said you'd be on time and you're late. I'll hate you until I die. Top drawer."

He chuckled, a muffled sound, as if he was being smothered with a pillow, and I realized I wanted him to say something to me—"Glad you could join us," "Hey, *Bluuue*,"—but he didn't. He didn't see me.

"Blue, how about a dirty martini?" Leulah asked.

"Or something else," said Jade.

"A Shirley Temple," suggested Nigel with a smirk.

"A cosmo?" asked Leulah.

"There's milk in the fridge," Nigel said, deadpan.

"A—a dirty martini would be quite nice. Thank you," I said. "Three olives, please." *Three Olives, Please:* it was what Eleanor Curd specified, the emerald-eyed heroine that caused men to shudder with hungry desire in A *Return to Waterfalls* (DeMurgh, 1990), pilfered from June Bug Rita Cleary's gold leather purse when I was twelve. ("Where's my book?" she repeated to Dad for days like a woman with mental illness who'd wandered away from her sanitarium. She searched our every couch, rug and closet, at times on her hands and knees, frantic to find out if Eleanor ended up with Sir Damien or they stayed apart because he believed she believed he believed he'd impregnated a vicious tattletale with an illegitimate child.)

As soon as Leulah handed me my martini, I was forgotten like Line 2 on a Corporate Headquarters Switchboard.

"So Hannah had a date tonight," Nigel said.

"No, she didn't," said Charles, smiling, though he sat up imperceptibly as if he'd felt the prick of a needle in his seat cushion.

"She did," said Nigel. "I saw her after school. She was wearing red."

"Oh, boy," said Jade exhaling cigarette smoke.

They talked on and on about Hannah; Jade again said something about Goodwill and "bourgeois pigs," words that startled me (I hadn't heard the phrase since Dad and I, driving across Illinois, read Angus Hubbard's *Acid Trips: The Delusions of '60s Counterculture* [1989]) though I didn't know who or what she was referring to, because I found it impossible to focus on the conversation; it was like that cruel little blurry line at the bottom of an eye chart. And I didn't feel like myself. I was a swirl of Interstellar Material, a mist of Dark Matter, a case in point of General Relativity.

I stood up and tried to make my way to the door, but my legs felt as if they were being asked to measure the universe.

"*Jesus,*" said Jade from somewhere. "What's wrong with her?"

The floor was transmitting in a wide array of wavelengths.

"What'd you give her to drink?" Milton asked.

"Nothing. A mudslinger."

"*Told* you to give her milk," Nigel said.

"I gave her a martini," added Leulah.

Suddenly I was on the floor, gazing at the stars.

"Is she going to die?" asked Jade.

"We should take her to the hospital," Charles said.

"Or call Hannah," said Lu.

"She's *fine.*" Milton was leaning over me. His tendriled black hair resembled squid. "Let her sleep it off."

A tidal wave of nausea was starting to flood my stomach and there was nothing I could do to stop it. It was like the black seawater overtaking a crimson *Titanic* stateroom, as recounted in one of Dad's favorite autobiographies of all time, the gripping eyewitness account *Black in My Mind, Yellow in My Legs* (1943) by Herbert J. D. Lascowitz, who finally, in his ninety-seventh year, came clean about his Machiavellian behavior aboard the legendary ocean liner, admitting he strangled an unidentified woman, stripped her body, donned her clothes in order to pretend he was a woman with child, thereby securing a choice spot for himself on one of two remaining lifeboats. I tried to roll over and stand, but the carpet and the couch swerved upward and then, as shocking as lightning striking inches from my shoes, I was sick: cartoonishly sick all over the table and the carpet and the paisley couch by the fireplace and Jade's black leather Dior sandals, even on the coffee-table book, *Thank God for the Telephoto Lens: Backyard Photos of the Stars* (Miller, 2002). There were also small but identifiable splatters on the cuffs of Nigel's pants.

They stared at me.

And this, I am ashamed to say, is where memory abruptly drops off (see Figure 12, "Continental Shelf Cliff," *Oceanic Terrain*, Boss, 1977). I can recall only a few flimsy sentences ("What if her family presses charges?"), faces peering down at me as if I'd tumbled down a well.

Yet I don't really need a memory here, because that Sunday at Hannah's, when they were calling me Gag, Retch, Hurl and Olives, they each went to great lengths to give me their eyewitness account of what happened. According to Leulah, I passed out on the South Lawn. Jade claimed I'd muttered a phrase in Spanish, something along the lines of "*El perro que no camina, no encuentra hueso,*" or "The dog that doesn't walk, doesn't find a bone," and then my eyes rolled into the back of my head and she thought I'd died. Milton said I got "nekkid." Nigel claimed I "partied like Tommy Lee during the Theater of Pain tour." Charles rolled his eyes when hearing these versions, these "gross distortions of the truth." He said I walked up to Jade and she and I began to make out in flawless reenactment of his favorite film, the cult masterpiece of French fetishist director, Luc-Shallot de la Nuit, *Les Salopes Vampires et Lesbiennes de Cherbourg* (Petit Oiseau Prod., 1971).

"Guys spend *whole lives* wishing to see that kind of thing, so thank you, Retch. Thank you."

"Sounds like you really enjoyed yourselves," Hannah said with a smile, her eyes glistening as she sipped her wine. "Don't tell me any more. It's not fit for a teacher's ears."

I could never decide which version I believed.

* * *

It was after I had a nickname that everything changed.

Dad said my mother, the woman who "left people holding their breaths in awe when she entered a room," always acted the same no matter who she talked to or where she was, and sometimes Dad couldn't tell when she answered the phone, if she was talking to "her childhood best friend from New York or a telemarketer, because she was so thrilled to hear from both." " 'Believe me, I'd be overjoyed to schedule a carpet cleaning—your product is obviously terrific—but I have to be honest, we don't actually have any carpets.' She could go on and on with apologies for hours," Dad said.

And I let her down, because I'll admit, I *did* act differently now that I was friends with them, now that Milton, immediately following Morning Announcements shouted "Retch!" and the entire courtyard of students looked ready to Stop, Drop and Roll. Not that overnight I morphed into a tyrannical foulmouthed girl who'd started out in Chorus, and managed to claw her way to the Lead. But, strolling through first-floor Hanover with Jade Whitestone between third and fourth periods ("I'm bushed," Jade would sigh, hitching her elbow around my neck the way Gene Kelly does to a lamppost in *Singin' in the Rain*) was an unforgivably paparazzi moment; I thought I understood, completely, what Hammond Brown, the actor in the 1928 Broadway hit *Happy Streets* (known throughout the Roaring Twenties simply as The Chin) meant when he said "a crowd's eyes have a touch like silk" (*Ovation*, 1952, p. 269).

And at the end of the school day, when Dad picked me up and we fought about something, like my "tinseled" hair or a new slightly edgier essay I'd written—"Tupac: Portrait of a Modern Romantic Poet," on which I received a derisory B ("Your senior year of high school is not the time to suddenly become alternative, hip and cool.")—afterward, it was strange; before my friendship with the Bluebloods, after an argument with Dad, when I retreated to my room I'd always felt like a smudge; I couldn't perceive where I began and where I ended. But now, I felt as if I could still see myself, my outline—a thin, but perfectly respectable black line.

Ms. Gershon of AP Physics perceived the change too, if solely on the subconscious level. For example, when I first arrived at St. Gallway, whenever I raised my hand to ask a question in her class, she couldn't immediately make me out; I blended effortlessly with the lab tables, the windows, the poster of James Joule. Now, I only had to hold my hand up for three, maybe four seconds before her eyes snapped to me: "Yes, Blue?" It was the same with Mr. Archer—all delusions he'd entertained about my name were gone. "*Blue*," he said, not with shakiness or unease, but supreme faith (similar to the tone he used for *Da Vinci*). And Mr. Moats, when he wandered over to my easel to inspect my Figure Drawing, his eyes almost always veered away from the drawing to my head, as if I were more worthy of scrutiny than a few wobbly lines on a page.

Sal Mineo noticed the difference too, and if *he* noticed, it had to be Agonizingly True.

"You should be careful," he said to me during Morning Announcements.

I glanced over at his intricate wrought-iron profile, his soggy brown eyes.

"I'm happy for you," he said, looking not at me but at the stage where Havermeyer, Eva Brewster and Hilary Leech were unveiling the new look of *The Gallway Gazette*: "A colored front page, advertisements," Eva was saying. Sal swallowed and his Adam's apple, which pushed against his neck like a metal coil in an old couch, trembled, rose and fell. "But they only hurt people."

"What are you talking about?" I asked, irritated by his ambiguity, but he didn't answer, and when Evita dismissed the school to class, he flew out of the aisle, quick as a wren off a lamppost.

* * *

The twins in my second period Study Hall, the Great Social Commentators of the Age, Eliaya and Georgia Hatchett (Nigel and Jade, who had them in a Spanish class, called them *Dee* for Tweedledee and *Dum* for Tweedledum, respectively) naturally had all kinds of dirt on my association with the Bluebloods. Before, they'd always gossiped messily about Jade and the others, their slurpy voices splattering all over each other and everyone else, but now they sat in the back, next to the water fountain and Hambone Reading Recommendations, carrying on in crackly, roast-potato whispers.

I ignored them for the most part, even when the words *blue* and *Shhh, she'll hear you*, hissed over to me like a couple of Gaboon Vipers. But when I didn't have any homework to do, I asked Mr. Fletcher if I could be excused to the restroom and slipped into row 500 and then the densest section of row 900, Biography, where I repositioned some of the larger books from row 600 to the holes between the shelves, in order to avoid detection. (Librarian

Hambone, if you're reading this, I apologize for the biweekly repositioning of H. Gibbons' bulky *African Wildlife* [1989] from its proper place in the 650s to just above *Mommie Dearest* [Crawford, 1978] and *Notorious: My Years with Cary Grant* [Drake, 1989]. You weren't going mad.)

"So do you or don't you want to hear the icing, the cake, the double whammy, the Crown Jewel, the Jewel après orthodontia, the Madonna abs après hatha yoga"—she took a swift breath, swallowed—"the Ted Danson après hair plugs, the J-Lo avant *Gigli*, the Ben avant J-Lo but après psychiatric treatment for gambling, the Matt après—"

"You think you're like a blind bard and all?" asked Dum, glancing up from *Celebrastory Weekly*. "I don't *think* so."

"Okay, so Elena Topolos."

"Elena Topolos?"

"Mediterranean freshman who needs to wax that lip. She told me the blue person's some weird autistic savant. Not only that, but we lost a man to her."

"*What?*"

"Hard Body. He's neurotic for her. It's already myth. Everyone on the soccer team calls him Aphrodite and he doesn't even care. He and the blue person have a class together and someone saw him digging through the garbage can to find a paper she threw away because she'd *touched* it."

"Whatever."

"He's asking her to Christmas formal."

"WHAT?" shrieked Dee.

Mr. Fletcher looked up from *The Crossword Fanatic's True Challenge* (Albo, 2002) and fired a disapproving glace at Dee and Dum. They were unfazed.

"Formal's like three months away," Dee said, wincing. "That's all a holy war in high school. People get pregnant, caught with pot, get a bad haircut so you find out it was their only decent feature and they have awful ears. It's *way* too soon to ask. Is he out of his *mind?*"

Dee nodded. "He's *that* haunted. His ex, Lonny, is pissed. She vows she's gonna jihad her ass by the end of the year."

"Ouch."

* * *

Dad was fond of pointing out the rule of thumb that "at times, even fools are right," but I was still surprised when, a day later, as I collected books from my locker, I noticed a kid from my AP Physics class passing me not once, but three times, faux-frowning at some giant hardback open in his hands, which I realized the second time he passed was our class textbook, *Fundamentals of Physics* (Rarreh & Cherish, 2004). I assumed he was waiting for Allison Vaughn, the sedate yet mildly popular senior with a locker near mine who wandered around with a wan smile and polite hair, but when I slammed my locker door, he was behind me.

"Hi," he said. "I'm Zach."

"Blue." I spasm-swallowed.

He was a tall, tan, supremely American-looking kid: square chin, big straight teeth, eyes an absurd Jacuzzi blue. I knew, vaguely, based on chatter during labs, he was shy, a little bit funny (my partner, Krista, was forever neglecting our experiment to giggle at something he said), also captain of the soccer team. His lab partner was his supposed ex-girlfriend, Lonny, cocaptain of Gallway Spirit, a girl with soggy platinum hair, a fake tan and a marked tendency to break the equipment. No cloud chamber, potentiometer, friction rod or alligator clip was safe with her. On Mondays, when the class wrote up our results on the dry-erase board, our teacher, Ms. Gershon, consistently threw out Lonny and Zach's findings, as they always flew daringly in the face of Modern Science, discrediting Planck's constant, undermining Boyle's law, amending the theory of relativity from $E=mc^2$ to $E=mc^5$. According to Dee and Dum, Lonny and Zach had gone out since sixth grade, and for the past few years had partaken in something called "lion sex" every Saturday night in the "hineymooner's suite," Room 222 at the Dynasty Motel on Pike Avenue.

He was handsome, sure, but as Dad once said, there were people who'd completely missed their decade, were born at the wrong time—not in the intellectually gifted sense, but due to a certain look on their face more suitable to the Victorian Age than, say, the Me Decade. Well, this kid was some twenty years too late. He was the one with thick brown hair that flying-saucered over an eye, the one who inspired girls to make their own prom dress, the one from the country club. And maybe he had a secret diamond earring, maybe a sequin glove, maybe he even had a good song at the end with three helpings of keyboard synthesizer, but no one would know, because if you weren't born in your decade you never made it to the ending, you floated around in your middle, unresolved, in oblivion, confused and unrealized. (Pour some sugar on him and blame it on the rain.)

"I was kinda hoping you could help me out with something," he said, contemplating his shoes. "I have a serious problem."

I felt irrationally frightened. "What?"

"There's a girl . . ." He sighed, hooked his thumbs through his belt loops. "I like her. Yeah. I really do." He was doing an embarrassed thing with his head, chin down, eyes sticking to me. "I've never talked to her. Never said a *word*. And normally this wouldn't throw me—normally, I'd go right up to her, ask her for pizza . . . movie . . . yeah. But *this* one. She throws me."

He ran his right hand through his hair and it was absurdly knot free like a shampoo commercial. His left hand was still cradling our Physics textbook, bookmarking, for some bizarre reason p. 123, which featured a sizeable diagram of a magenta Plasma Ball. I was able to make out, upsidedown, around the crook of his arm: *"Plasma is the fourth state of matter."*

"So I say to myself, *fine*," he said with a shrug. "It's not meant to be. 'Cause if you don't feel comfortable talking to someone, how're you gonna handle . . . well, you have to trust the person, right, or what's the point. But then" —frowning, he gazed all the way down the hall toward the EXIT—"it's like every time I see her I feel . . . I feel . . ."

I didn't think he was going to continue, but then he broke into a smile. "Fucking. *Great.*"

The smile was pinned to his face, delicate as a prom corsage.

It was my turn to speak. Words were in my throat—advice, council, some pithy line from a screwball comedy—but they were grinding together, disappearing fast like celery in a sink disposal.

"I . . ." I began.

I could feel his minty breath on my forehead, and he was staring at me with his eyes the color of a kiddy pool (blue, green, suspicious hints of yellow). He was searching my face as if he took me to be a cruddy masterpiece in somebody's attic and if he scrutinized my deft use of color and shading as well as the direction of my brushstrokes, he'd figure out who my artist was.

"Hurl?"

I turned. Nigel was inching his way toward us, visibly amused.

"I really can't help you, so if you'd be so kind as to excuse me," I blurted quickly, then darted past his shoulder and the Physics textbook. I didn't turn around, not even when I reached Nigel and the German Language Bulletin Board and then the EXIT. I assumed he stood in the hall staring after me with his mouth open like a newscaster reading Breaking News when the teleprompter goes dead.

"What'd the Chippendale want?" Nigel asked as we headed downstairs.

I shrugged. "Who knows. I–I couldn't really follow his logic."

"Oh, you're terrible." Nigel laughed, a quick, skidding sound, then linked his arm through mine. We were Dorothy and the Cowardly Lion.

Obviously, a few short months ago, I would have been astounded, maybe even knock-kneed that the El Dorado rode over to me and made a long speech about A Girl. ("All of history comes down to a girl," Dad said with a hint of regret as we watched *The Dark Prince*, the award-winning documentary on Hitler's youth.) In the past, I had all sorts of Hidden Desire moments when I gazed at El Dorados riding through the hushed corridors, the empty football fields of a lonesome school—like old Howie Easton at Clearwood Day with the cleft chin and gap in his teeth making him such a sophisticated whistler he could've whistled Wagner's entire *Der Ring des Nibelungen* (1848–74) if he'd wanted to (he didn't want to)—and I'd wished, just once, I might ride into the wilderness with them, that I, *not* Kaytee Jones with the Hawaiian eyes nor Priscilla Pastor Owensby with legs as long as highways, could be their favorite Appaloosa.

But now things were different. Now I had copper hair and sticky, myrtle lips, and as Jade said that Sunday dinner at Hannah's: "The Zach Soderbergs of the world are cute, sure, but they're boring as Saltines. Okay—you hope if you scratch one you'll find Luke Wilson. Even Johnny Depp with his clothing missteps at major award ceremonies you'd be happy with. But trust me, all you get is bland cracker."

"Who's this?" asked Hannah.

"Some kid in my physics class," I said.

"He's a pretty popular senior," said Lu.

"You should see his rug," Nigel said. "I think he has hair plugs."

"Well, he's barking up the wrong tree," Jade said. "Retch is already in a puddle over someone."

She gazed triumphantly at Milton, but to my relief, he was cutting into his Danish roasted chicken with sunflower seasoning and hash of sweet potato and didn't see her.

"So Blue's breaking hearts," Hannah said and winked at me. "It's about time."

*   *   *

I did wonder about Hannah.

And I felt guilty wondering about her, because the others trusted her in the uncomplicated way an old horse accepts a rider, a child grabs an outstretched hand to cross the street.

Yet immediately following my attempt to Parent Trap her with Dad, sometimes at her house, I'd find myself falling out of the dinner conversation. I'd look around the room as if I was a snooping stranger outside, pressing my nose to the window. I wondered why she took so much interest in my life, my happiness, my haircut ("A*dorable*," she said. "You look like a dispossessed flapper," Dad said); why, for that matter, *any* of them were of interest to her. I wondered about her adult friends, why she hadn't married or done any of the things Dad referred to as "domesticated hooey" (SUVs, kids), the "sitcom script people stick to as they hope for meaning in their canned-laughter lives."

In her house, there were no photographs. At school, I never once saw her conversing with other teachers apart from Eva Brewster, and only then on a single occasion. As much as I adored her—particularly those moments she let herself be silly, when a favorite song came on and she did a funny little jig with her wineglass in her bare feet in the middle of the living room and the dogs stared at her the way fans stared at Janis Joplin singing "Bobby McGee" ("I was in a band once," Hannah said shyly, biting her lip. "Lead singer. I dyed my hair red.")—I couldn't overlook a certain book by leading neuro-physicist and criminologist Donald McMather MD, *Social Behaviors and Nimbus Clouds* (1998).

"An adult with a fastidious interest in those considerably younger than him or herself can not be completely sincere or even rational," he writes on p. 424, Chapter 22, "The Allure of Children." "Such a preoccupation often hides something very dark."

The Mysterious
Affair at Styles

I'd been in thick with the Bluebloods three, maybe four weeks, when Jade invaded, Sherman-style, my nonexistent sex life.

Not that I took her assault too seriously. When it came down to the nitty-gritty, I knew I'd probably flee without warning, like Hannibal's elephants during the Battle of Zama in 202 B.C. (I was twelve when Dad wordlessly presented me with various tomes to read and reflect upon, including C. Allen's *Shame Culture and the Shadow World* [1993], *Somewhere Between Puritans and Brazil: How to Have a Healthy Sexuality* [Mier, 1990], also Paul D. Russell's terrifying *What You Don't Know About White Slavery* [1996].)

"You've never gotten laid, have you, Retch?" Jade accused one night, deliberately ashing her cigarette in the cracked blue vahze next to her like some movie psychiatrist with switchblade fingernails, her eyes narrowed, as if hoping I'd confess to violent crime.

The question hung in the air like a national flag with no wind. It was obvious the Bluebloods, including Nigel and Lu, approached sex as if it were cute little towns they had to whizz through in order to make good time on their way to Somewhere (and I wasn't so sure they knew their final destination). Immediately, Andreo Verduga flashed into my head (shirtless, trimming shrubs) and I wondered if I could speedily make up a steamy experience involving the bed of his pickup truck (propped up against mulch, rolling onto tulip bulbs, hair snagging the lawnmower) but prudently decided against it. "Virgins advertise their stunning lack of insight and expertise with the subtlety and panache of Bible salesmen," wrote British comic Brinkly Starnes in *A Harlequin Romance* (1989).

Jade nodded knowingly at my silence. "We'll have to do something about it then," she said, sighing.

After this painful revelation, on Friday nights, after I got clearance from Dad to spend the night at her house ("And this Jade individual—she's one of your Joycean aficionados?"), Jade, Leulah and I, decked out in Jefferson's Studio 54 prom getup, drove an hour to a roadside bar in Redville, just over the South Carolina border.

It was called the Blind Horse Saloon (or lin ors loon, as the sign whispered in dying pink neon), a grouchy place Jade claimed the five of them had been frequenting for "years," which, from the outside looked like a burnt loaf of pound cake (rectangular, black, no windows) stranded in an expanse of stale-cookie pavement. Armed with farcically fake IDs (I was brown-eyed Roxanne Kaye Loomis, twenty-two, five-feet-seven, a Virgo organ donor; I attended Clemson with a major in Chemical Engineering; "Always say you're seriously into engineering," Jade instructed. "People don't know what it is and they won't ask because it sounds mind-numbing."), we edged past the bouncer, a large black man who stared at us as if we were cast members of Disney on Ice who'd forgotten to remove our costumes. Inside, the place was stuffed with country music and middle-aged men in plaid shirts clutching their beers like handrails. Most of them stared openmouthed at four televisions suspended from the ceiling broadcasting some baseball game or local news. Women, standing in tight circles, fiddled with their hair as they talked, as if putting finishing touches on a sagging flower arrangement. They always glared at us, particularly Jade (see "Snarling Coon Dogs," *Appalachian Living*, Hester, 1974, p. 32).

"Now we find Blue's lucky man," Jade announced, her eyes creeping all over the room, past the linebacker jukebox, the bartender pouring shots with a strange brawny energy, as if he were a GI who'd just arrived in Saigon, and the wooden benches along the far wall where girls waited with foreheads so hot and oily you could fry eggs on them.

"I don't see any melted Milk Duds," I said.

"Maybe you should hold out for true love," Leulah said. "Or Milton."

It was a running joke between Jade and Lu that I "had it bad for Black," that I desperately wanted to be "Black and Blue," make "the beast with two Blacks," and so on—allegations I refused to admit to (even though they were true).

"Haven't you heard the expression, 'Don't shit where you eat?' " Jade said. "God, you people have no faith. *There*. The cute one at the end of the bar talking to that malaria mosquito. He's wearing tortoiseshell glasses. Know what tortoiseshell glasses mean?"

"No," I said.

"Stop pulling down your dress, it makes you look five. It means he's intellectual. You can never be too far in the backwoods if someone at the bar's wearing tortoiseshell glasses. He's perfect for you. I'm parched."

"Me too," I said.

"I'll go," said Leulah. "What do you want?"

"We didn't drive all the way to this shantytown to purchase our own beverages," said Jade. "Blue? My cigarettes please."

I took them out of my purse and handed them to her.

Jade's pack of Marlboro Lights was the instrument (*boleadoras*) she used to ambush unsuspecting men (*cimarron*). (Jade's best subject—the only one at which she excelled—was Spanish.) She began by roaming the bar (*estancias*), singling out an attractive, beefy guy standing a little apart from everyone else (*vaca perdida*, or lost cow). She approached him slowly and with no sudden jerks of the head or hands, tapped him lightly on the shoulder.

"Got a light, *hombre*?"

There were two inevitable scenarios this opening evoked:

1. He eagerly obliged.
2. If he didn't have a light, he started a frantic quest to find one.

"Steve, got a light? Arnie, you? Henshaw? A light. Matches okay too. McMundy, you? Cig—know if Marcie has one? Go ask—right. Does Jeff? No? I'll go ask the bartender."

Unfortunately, if the outcome was #2, by the time the *cimarron* returned with fire, Jade was already on the lookout for more lost cattle. He'd stand motionlessly at her back for a minute, sometimes up to five or *ten* minutes, not doing anything but chewing his lower lip and staring straight ahead, occasionally mooing a dreary "Excuse me?" at her back or shoulder.

Eventually, she acknowledged him.

"Hmm? Oh, gracias, *chiquito*."

If she was feeling at home on the range, she tossed him two questions:

1. Where do you see yourself in, say, twenty years, *cavron*?
2. What's your favorite position?

Most of the time he was unable to answer either off the top of his head, but even if he answered #2 without hesitation, if he said, "Assistant Manager of Sales and Marketing at Axel Corp, where I work and I'm months away from a promotion," Jade had no choice but to butcher him and cook him immediately over an open fire (the *asado*).

"Unfortunately we have nothing else to talk about. Beat it, *muchacho*."

Most of the time he didn't react, only stared at her with drippy, red eyes.

"*Vamos!*" she shouted. Biting our lips in suppressed laughter, Leulah and I raced after her, hacking our way across the room (*pampas*), fertile with elbows, shoulders, big hair and beer cups, all the way to GIRLS. Jade elbowed past the dozen *muchachas* standing in line, telling them I was pregnant and about to be sick.

"Bullshit!"

"If she's pregnant how come she's so scrawny?"

"And why's she drinkin'? Don't alcohol cause preemies?"

"Oh, stop hurting your cerebrums, *putas*," said Jade.

We took turns laughing and peeing in the handicapped stall.

Sometimes, if the lighting of Jade's cigarette was done with swift precision, she began to have a real conversation, though it was usually so loud, most of it consisted of Jade firing off more questions and the guy mooing, "Huh?" over and over as if trapped in a Beckett play.

Occasionally, the guy had a friend who rested his heavy load of a gaze on Leulah, and once, a man with apparent color blindness and more hair than an Old English Sheepdog fixed his gaze on *me*. Jade nodded excitedly and pulled her own earlobe (her sign for "This is the one"), but when the guy bent his bushy head down to inquire how I was "likin' Leisure City," for some reason I couldn't think of anything to say. (" 'Fine' is mind-numbing. Never ever say, 'fine,' Retch. And, another thing. Granted, he's hot as hell, but if you bring up your *dad* in conversation *one* more time, I'll cut out your tongue.") After too long a pause I said, "Not much."

Frankly, I was a little terrified of how he leaned over me, so confident of his beer breath and his chin, which, underneath the masses of hair, appeared to be modeled after a sugar cone, how his eyes looked down my front as if he'd like nothing better than to lift my hood and inspect my carburetor. "Not much" wasn't the answer he was looking for, because he forced a smile and set about trying to raise Leulah's hood.

There were times too, when I'd glance back to the spot by the door where Jade, minutes before, had been inspecting her Angus bull, trying to decide if he was worth buying to improve her herd—and she wasn't there. She wasn't *any*where, not by the jukebox, or by the girl showing another girl her gold necklace—"He got me this, innit sweet?" (it looked like a gilded thumbnail)—not in the breath-dampened hallway that lead to the back by the couches and pinball machines, not by the man fossilized at the bar mesmerized by closed captions ("A tragedy coming out of Burns County this evening with a robbery that left three dead. Cherry Jeffries is live at the scene."). The first time it happened, I was terrified (I'd read *The Girl Done Gone* [1982] by Eileen Crown when I was too young and thus it'd made a gruesome impression) and immediately, I alerted Leulah (who, though she looked prim and old-fashioned, could turn pretty vixeny with her nosegay smile, the way she coiled her thick braid around her hand and spoke in a little-girl voice so men tilted over her like big beach umbrellas trying to block the sun).

"Where's Jade?" I asked. "I don't see her."

"Around," she said airily, not looking away from a guy named Luke with a white T-shirt like cling film and arms like basement lead pipes. Using words with no more than two syllables, he was telling her the fascinating story of how he'd been kicked out of West Point for hazing.

"But I don't see her," I said nervously, my eyes wandering the room.

"She's in the bathroom."

"Is she all right?"

"Sure." Leulah's eyes were hooked to Luke's face; it was like the guy was Dickens, fucking Samuel Clemens.

I pushed my way into the GIRLS bathroom.

"Jade?"

It was sticky, murky as unclean aquariums. Girls in tube tops and tight pants swarmed the mirror, applying lipstick, running fingernails through hair stiff as soft-drink straws. Unrolled toilet paper wormed along the floor and the hand dryer shrieked, though no one dried their hands.

"Jade? Jade? Hello?"

I crouched down and spotted her green metallic sandals in the handicapped stall.

"Jade? Are you okay?"

"Oh, for fuck's sake, what is it? WHAT?!"

She unlatched the door. It bashed against the wall. She marched out.

Behind her, stuffed between the toilet and the toilet-paper dispenser, was a man, approximately forty-five years old with a thick brown beard that cut his face into crude shapes first graders tape to windows during Art Time. He wore a jean jacket too short in the sleeves and looked as if he'd respond to various shouted commands, including, "C'mere boy!" and "Sick 'em!" His belt was undone, hanging like a rattlesnake.

"Oh, I–I–" I stuttered. "I–"

"Are you dying?" Her face was pale green in the light, seal slick. Fine gold hairs stuck to her temples in question marks and exclamation points.

"No," I said.

"Are you planning to die anytime soon?"

"No—"

"Then what are you bothering me for? What am I, your fucking mother?"

She turned on her heel, slammed the door, and locked it.

"What a bitchy slut," said a Hispanic woman reapplying liquid eyeliner at the sink, her top lip stretched tight over her teeth like Saran Wrap over left-overs. "That your friend?"

I nodded, somewhat dazed.

"You kick her skanky ass."

There were times, to my infinite horror, Leulah disappeared, too, for fifteen, sometimes twenty, minutes into GIRLS (Beatrice had come a long way in seven hundred years; so had Annabel Lee) and afterward, she and Jade both sported pleased, even conceited looks on their faces, as if, in that handicapped stall they believed they'd single-handedly come to the last digit of pi, discovered who killed Kennedy, found the Missing Link. (From the looks of some the guys they brought in with them, maybe they had.)

"Blue should try it," Leulah said once on the drive home.

"No *way*," Jade said. "You have to be a pro."

Obviously, I wanted to ask them what they thought they were doing, but I sensed they didn't care to know what Robard Neverovich, the Russian who'd volunteered in more than 234 American runaway shelters, wrote in *Kill Me* (1999) or his follow-up account of his trip to Thailand to investigate the child porn industry, *Wanting It All, All At Once* (2003). It was evident Jade and Leulah were doing just fine, thank you, and certainly didn't need the feedback of a girl who stands "deaf and dumb when some dude wants to buy her a hurricane," who "wouldn't know what to do with a guy if she had a manual with illustrations and an interactive CD-rom." But at the same time, as scared as I was every time one of them vanished, afterward, when we were back in the Mercedes; when they were howling over some scab they'd taken into GIRLS together, who'd emerged from that handicapped stall with a sort of madness and, as we walked outside, chased after them shouting, "Cammie! Ashley!" (the names on their fake IDs) before the bouncer threw him down like a sack of potatoes; when Jade was speeding back to her house, crisscrossing between semis and Leulah screamed for no reason, head back, hair tangling around the headrest, her arms reaching out of the sunroof as if grabbing at the tiny stars sticking to the sky and picking them off like lint, I noticed there was something incredible about them, something brave, that no one in my immediate recollection had written about—not really.

I doubted *I* could write about it either, being "the total flat tire in any bar or club," except that they seemed to inhabit a completely different world than the one I did—a world that was hilarious, without repercussion or revolting neon light or stickiness or rug burn, a world in which they ruled.

*   *   *

There was one night that wasn't like the others.

"This is it, Hurl," Jade said. "The night that will change your everything."

It was the first Friday of November and Jade had gone to considerable lengths to pick out my outfit: four-inch malevolent gold sandals two sizes too big and a gold lamé dress that rippled all over me like a Shar-pei (see "Traditional Wife's Bound Feet," *History of China*, Ming, 1961, p. 214; "Darcel," *Remembering "Solid Gold,"* LaVitte, 1989, p. 29).

It was one of the rare occasions someone at the Blind actually approached *me*—a guy in his thirties named Larry, heavy as a keg of beer. He was attractive only in the way of a seriously unfinished Michelangelo sculpture. There were tiny patches of remarkable detail in his delicate nose, full lips, even in his large, well-molded hands, but the rest of him—shoulders, torso, legs—had not been liberated from the raw slab of marble, nor would they be any time soon. He'd bought me an Amstel Light and stood close to me while he talked about quitting smoking. It had been the most difficult thing he'd ever done in his life. "Patch is the greatest thing medical science's come up with. They should use that technology for everything. Don't know 'bout you, but I got no problem eatin' and drinkin' with the patch. Days you're really busy. 'Stead of fast food, ya stick on the patch. Half hour later? You're full. We could all have *sex* with the patch too. Sure save everyone a lot of time and energy. What's yer name?"

"Roxanne Kaye Loomis."

"What do you do, Roxy?"

"I attend Clemson University with a major in engineering. I'm from Dukers, N.C. Also an organ donor." Larry nodded and took a long drink of his beer, shifting his heavy body toward me so my leg pressed against his chunky one. I took a tiny step in the only other possible direction, bumping into the back of a girl with thorny blond hair.

" 'Scuse you," she said.

I tried stepping back in the other direction but effigy-Larry was there. I was a piece of hard candy stuck in a throat.

"Where do you see yourself in, say, twenty years?" I asked.

He didn't answer. In fact, he looked as if he didn't speak English anymore. He was losing altitude, and fast. It was like the afternoon Dad and I parked the Volvo station wagon a few meters from the end of the airport runway in Luton, Texas, and spent an hour sitting on the hood, eating pimento cheese sandwiches and watching the planes land. Watching the planes was like floating in the depths of the ocean and observing a 105-foot Blue Whale drift over you, but unlike the private jets, the airbuses, and the 747s, Larry actually crashed. His lips hit my teeth and his tongue darted into my mouth like a tadpole escaping from a jar. He slapped a hand onto my chest, squeezing my right breast like a lemon over dover sole.

"Blue?"

I tore myself away. Leulah and Jade stood next to me.

"We're blowing this joint," Jade said.

Larry shouted (a markedly unenthusiastic "Wait a minute, Roxy!"), but I didn't turn around. I followed them outside to the car.

"Where are we going?"

"To see Hannah," Jade said flatly. "By the way, Retch, what's up with your taste in men? That guy was fugly."

Lu was staring at her apprehensively, her green Bellmondo prom dress sagging open at the neck in a permanent yawn. "I don't think it's a good idea."

Jade made a face. "Why not?"

"I don't want her to see us," Lu said.

Jade yanked on her seatbelt. "We'll take another car. Jefferson's boy-friend's. His heinous Toyota's in our driveway."

"What's going on?" I asked.

"We'll probably bump into Charles," Jade said, ignoring me, glancing at Lu as she jammed the key in the ignition and started the car. "He'll be wear-ing camouflage and those night-vision goggle things."

Lu shook her head. "He's with Black on a double date. Sophomores."

Jade turned around to see if I'd overheard this (a triumphantly sympa-thetic look on her face), then accelerated out of the parking lot, merging onto the highway and heading toward Stockton. It was a cold night, with thin, greasy clouds streaking the sky. I pulled the gold lamé tight over my knees, staring at the passing cars and Lu's fancy parenthesis profile, the taillights sig-naling her cheekbones. Neither of them spoke. Their silence was one of those tired adult silences, that of a married couple driving home from a din-ner party, not wanting to talk about someone's husband getting too drunk or how they secretly didn't want to go home with each other but someone new, someone whose freckles they didn't know.

Forty minutes later, Jade had disappeared inside her house for the car keys—"Only be a sec"—and when she emerged, still in her rickety red san-dals and firebird dress (it looked like she'd gone through the garbage at a rich kid's birthday, removed the most exotic scraps of wrapping paper and taped them to herself), she carried a six-pack of Heineken, two giant bags of potato chips and a pack of spaghetti licorice, one piece dangling from her mouth. Looped around her shoulder was a giant pair of binoculars.

"We're going to Hannah's house?" I asked, still confused, but Jade only ignored me again, dumping the food into the backseat of the beat-up white Toyota parked by the garage. Leulah looked furious (her lips were pulled tightly together like a fabric change purse), but without a word, she walked across the driveway, climbed into the front seat and slammed the door.

"Fuck." Jade squinted at her watch. "We don't have much time."

Minutes later, we were in the Toyota, merging onto the highway again, this time heading north, the opposite direction of Hannah's house. I knew it was pointless to ask where we were going; both of them had fallen into that trench-silence again, a silence so deep it was difficult and tiring to heave one-self out. Leulah stared at the road, the sputtering white lines, the drifting red sequins of the cars. Jade was more or less her usual self, though as she chewed a strand of licorice (the girl was chain-licoricing; "Hand me another one," she demanded three times before I wedged the packet by the emergency brake), she wouldn't stop fiddling with the radio.

We drove a half hour before swerving down Exit 42—"Cottonwood," read the sign—barreling across the deserted two-lane road into a truck stop. A gas station was off to our left, and, in front of the eighteen-wheelers slung across the pavement like dead whales, a wooden A-framed restaurant sat glumly on bald hill. STUCKEY'S, announced the yellow letters over the entrance. Jade was slinking the Toyota between the trucks.

"See her car?" she asked.

Leulah shook her head. "It's already 2:30. Maybe she's not coming."

"She's coming."

We circled the lot until Leulah tapped a fingernail on the window.

"There." She was indicating Hannah's red Subaru; it was sandwiched between a white pickup truck and a van.

Jade swung into the next row and reversed into a spot by a bank of pine needles and the road. Leulah flung off her seatbelt, crossed her arms, and Jade blithely helped herself to another black shoelace, gnawing one end, and wrapping the other fast around her knuckles like a boxer before he puts on his gloves. Hannah's Subaru was in front of us, two lines of cars away. Across the parking lot on the hill slumped the restaurant, legally blind (three windows in the back boarded up) and seriously balding (roofing coming off in clumps). You couldn't see much in the dimmed windows—a few shifts of tired color, a row of green lamps hanging down like moldy showerheads—but one didn't have to go inside to know the menus were sticky, the tables seasoned with pie crumb, the waitresses crabby, the clientele beefy. One definitely had to beat the saltshaker senseless—maggotlike grains of rice visible inside—to coax out a mere *speck* of salt. ("If they can't do salt, I wonder what makes them think they can do chicken cacciatore," Dad would say in such a place, holding the menu at a safe distance from his face in case it sprang to life.)

I hunched forward and cleared my throat, a signal for Jade or Lu to explain what we were doing at this awful roadie watering hole (a place Dad and I would go to great distances to avoid; it wasn't unheard for us to take a twenty-mile detour simply to avoid breaking bread with "men and women who, if one squinted, resembled piles of tires") but when they *still* said nothing (Lu, too, was stuffing her mouth with licorice now, chewing goatishly) I realized it was one of those things they couldn't put into words. Putting it into words made it real and they'd be guilty of something.

For ten minutes, the only sound was an occasional door slam—some loot-stomached trucker coming, going, starving, stuffed—and the angry hisses of the freeway. Visible through the dark trees edging the parking lot was a bridge with an endless bullet-fire of cars, red-and-white sparks shooting into the night.

"Who'll it be?" Jade asked blandly, looking through the binoculars.

Lu shrugged, chewing her licorice cud. "Don't know."

"Fat or skinny."

"Skinny."

"See, I think pork this time."

"She doesn't like pork."

"Yes, she does. They're her Beluga. Reserved for special occasions. *Oh.*" Jade jolted forward, banging the binoculars on the windshield. "Oh, *fuck me* . . . shit."

"What—is he a baby?"

Jade's mouth was open. Her lips moved, but there were no words. Then she exhaled heavily: "Ever seen *Breakfast at Tiffany's?*"

"*No,*" Lu said sarcastically, putting her hands on the dashboard and leaning forward to survey the two people who'd just emerged from the restaurant.

"Well"—without looking away from the binoculars, Jade's right hand plunged into the bag of chips and stuffed a clump into her mouth—"it's that awful Doc person. Only ancient. Normally, I'd say at least it's not Rusty Trawler, but in this case I'm not so sure." She sat back, swallowed, and, with a grim look, handed Lu the binoculars. "Rusty has teeth."

After a quick glimpse (a revolted expression spilled all over her face), Lu handed me the binoculars. I swallowed and pressed them to my eyes: Hannah Schneider had just left the restaurant. She was walking with a man.

"I always hated Doc," Lu said softly.

Hannah was dolled up as I'd never seen her before ("painted," they'd say at Coventry Academy) wearing a furry black coat—I guessed rabbit, due to its teenybopperish look (the zipper graced with a pompom)—gold hoops, dark lipstick charring her mouth. Her hair recoiled from her shoulders and sharp, white high heels peered out of the cuffs of her Saran-tight jeans. When I shifted the binoculars to inspect her companion, I immediately felt sick, because in comparison to Hannah, he was shriveled. Wrinkles Etch A Sketched his face. He was in his late sixties, maybe even early seventies, shorter than she and skinny as a roadside curb. His torso and shoulders were meatless, like thick plaid flannel had been chucked over a picture frame. His hair was pretty thick, his hairline not eroding (his lone, remotely attractive feature). It mopped up whatever light was around, going green as they passed under the floodlight, then an oxidized, bicycle-spoke gray. As he moved down the steps after her—Hannah was walking swiftly, unzipping a weird pink fur purse, searching for her car keys—his bony legs jerked out to the sides like a retractable drying rack.

"Retch, you going to let anyone else look or what?"

I handed Jade the binoculars. She peered through them, gnawing her lip.

"Hope he brought Viagra," she muttered.

Lu slouched down in her seat and froze as they climbed into Hannah's car.

"Oh, for God's sake, you idiot, she can't *see* us," Jade said irritably, though she, too, sat very still, waiting for the Subaru to move out of its space, sneaking behind one of the semis, before starting the car.

"Where are they going?" I asked, though I wasn't sure I wanted to know.

"Fleabag motel," Jade said. "She'll bang the guy for a half-hour to forty-five minutes, then throw him out. I'm always surprised she doesn't bite off his head like a praying mantis."

We followed the Subaru (maintaining a polite distance) for three, maybe four miles, soon entering what I assumed was Cottonwood. It was one of those skin-and-bone towns Dad and I had driven through a million times, a town wan and malnourished; somehow it managed to survive on nothing but gas stations, motels, and McDonald's. Big scablike parking lots scarred the sides of the road.

After fifteen minutes, Hannah switched on her blinker and turned left into a motel, the Country Style Motor Lodge, a white flat arc-shaped building sitting in the middle of a barren lot like a lost pair of dentures. A few maple trees sulked close to the road, others slouched suggestively in front of the Registration Office, as if mimicking the clientele. We pulled in thirty seconds after her, but quickly swung to the right, stopping by a gray sedan, while Hannah parked by the office and disappeared inside. Two or three minutes later, when she reappeared, slimy light from the carport splattered her face and her expression scared me. I saw it only for a few seconds (and she wasn't exactly close) but to me, she looked like an off TV—no breathy soap opera or courtroom drama, not even a wan western rerun—just blank. She climbed back into the Subaru, started the car, and slowly pulled past us.

"Shit," squeaked Lu, slipping down in the seat.

"Oh *please*," Jade said. "You'd be the crummiest assassin."

The car stopped in front of one of the rooms on the far left. Doc emerged with his hands in his pockets, Hannah with a minute grin spearing her face. She unlocked the door and they disappeared inside.

"Room 22," Jade reported from behind the binoculars. Hannah must have immediately pulled the curtains, because when a light flicked on, the drapes, the color of orange cheddar, were completely closed, without a splinter through them.

"Does she know him?" I asked. It was more a far-flung hope than an actual question.

Jade shook her head. "Nope." She turned around in the seat, staring at me. "Charles and Milton found out about it last year. They were out one night, decided to swing by her house but then passed her car. They followed her all the way out here. She starts at Stuckey's at 1:45. Eats. Picks one out. The first Friday of every month. It's the one date she keeps."

"What do you mean?"

"*You* know. She's pretty disorganized. Well, not about this."

"And she doesn't . . . know you know?"

"No *way*." Her eyes pelted my face. "And don't even think about telling her."

"I won't," I said, glancing at Lu, but she didn't seem to be listening. She sat in her seat as if strapped to an electric chair.

"So what happens now?" I asked.

"A taxi pulls up. He'll emerge from the room with half his clothes, sometimes his shirt balled in his hands or without his socks. And then he'll limp away in the taxi. Probably back to Stuckey's where he'll get into his truck, drive off to who knows where. Hannah leaves in the morning."

"How do you know?"

"Charles usually stays the whole time."

I didn't especially want to ask any more questions, so the three of us lapsed into silence again, a quiet that went on even after Jade moved the car closer so we could make out the 22, the safari leaf pattern on the pulled curtains and the dent in Hannah's car. It was strange, the wartime effect of the parking lot. We were stationed somewhere, oceans from home, afraid of things unseen. Leulah was shell-shocked, back straight as a flagpole, her eyes magnetized to the door. Jade was the senior officer, crabby, worn-out and perfectly aware nothing she said could comfort us so she only reclined her seat, turned on the radio and shoved potato chips into her mouth. I sort of Vietnamed too. I was the cowardly homesick one who ends up dying unheroically from a wound he accidently inflicts upon himself that squirts blood like a grape Capri Sun. I would've given my left hand to be away from this place. My Pie in the Sky was to be next to Dad again, wearing cloud flannel pajamas and grading a few of his student research papers, even the awful ones by the slacker who employed a huge bold font in order to reach Dad's minimum requirement of twenty to twenty-five pages.

I remembered what Dad said when I was seven at the Screamfest Fantasy Circus in Choke, Indiana, after we'd taken the House of Horrors ride and I'd been so terrified I'd ridden the thing with my fingers nailed to my eyes— never peeking, never once glimpsing a single horror. After I pried my hands off my face, rather than chastising my cowardice, Dad had looked down at me and nodded thoughtfully, as if I'd just revealed startling new insights on revolutionizing welfare. "Yes," he'd said. "Sometimes it takes more courage not to let yourself see. Sometimes knowledge is damaging—not enlightenment but enleadenment. If one recognizes the difference and prepares oneself—it is extraordinarily brave. Because when it comes to certain human miseries, the only eyewitnesses should be the pavement and maybe the trees."

"Promise I won't ever do this," Lu said suddenly in a mousey voice.

"What," said Jade in a monotone, her eyes papercuts.

"When I'm old." Her voice was something frail you could tear right through. "Promise me I'll be married with kids. Or famous. That . . ."

There wasn't an end to her sentence. It just stopped, a grenade that'd been thrown but hadn't exploded.

None of us said anything more, and at 4:03 A.M. someone turned off the lights in Room 22. We watched the man emerge, fully clothed (though his heels, I noticed, were not fully inside his shoes) and he drove away in the rusty Blue Bird Taxicab (1-800-BLU-BIRD), purring as it waited for him by the Registration Office.

It was just as Dad said (if he'd been in the car with us he would have tipped up his chin, just a little, raised an eyebrow, his gesture for both Never Doubt Me and I Told You So) because the only eyewitnesses should have been the neon sign shuddering VACANCY, and the thin asthmatic trees seductively trailing their branches down the spine of the roof, and the sky, a big purple bruise fading too slowly over our heads.

We drove home.

PART 2

Moby-Dick

Two weeks after the night we spied on Hannah ("*Observed*," Chief Inspector Ranulph Curry clarified in *The Conceit of a Unicorn* [Lavelle, 1901]), Nigel found an invitation in the wastepaper basket in her den, the tiny room off the living room filled with world atlases and half-dead hanging plants barely surviving on her version of flora life support (twenty-four-hour plant lights, periodic Miracle-Gro).

It was elegant, printed on a thick, cream, embossed card.

The Burns County Animal Shelter
cordially invites you to
our annual charity event
in support of all animals in need,
at 100 Willows Road,
on Saturday, November the 22nd,
at eight o'clock in the evening.

Price: $40 per person.
RSVP.

Costume Required. Masks Preferred.

"I think we should go," Nigel announced that Friday at Jade's.

"Me too," said Leulah.

"You can't," Charles said. "She didn't invite you."

"A minor detail," Nigel said.

In spite of Charles' words of warning, the following Sunday, halfway through dinner, Nigel removed the invitation from his back pocket and brazenly placed it next to the platter of veal chops, without saying a word.

In that instant, the dining room became nail-bitingly unbearable (see *Midday Face-Off at Sioux Falls: A Mohave Dan Western*, Lone Star Publishers, Bendley, 1992). Dinners had already become a teensy bit unbearable since I'd gone to Cottonwood. I found it impossible to look at Hannah's face, to smile gaily, to shoot the breeze about schoolwork or term papers or Mr. Moats' penchant for textured shirts without envisioning Doc and his accordion legs, his wrinkled face like wood once infested with termites, not to mention the horror of their Hollywood Kiss, which granted, had taken place offscreen, but was still scary. (It was two different movies crudely edited together—*Gilda* with *Cocoon*.)

Of course, when I considered Jade, Lu, and the handicapped stall, I also felt queasy; but with Hannah it was worse. As Dad said, the difference between a dynamic and a wasted uprising depends upon the point at which it occurs within a country's historic timeline (see Van Meer, "The Fantasy of Industrialization," *Federal Forum*, Vol. 23, Issue 9). Jade and Lu were still developing nations. And thus, while it wasn't fantastic, it also wasn't *too* terrible for them to have a backward infrastructure and a poor human development index. But Hannah—she was much farther along. She should have already established a robust economy, peacefulness, free trade—and as these things weren't yet assured, frankly, it wasn't looking good for her democracy. She could very well struggle forever, with "corruption and scandal perpetually undermining [her] credibility as a self-ruled state."

Milton had opened a window. A puppyish draft tore around the dining room, causing my paper napkin to fly off my lap, the flames to dance violently atop the candles like lunatic ballerinas. I couldn't believe what Nigel had done, acted like a jealous husband presenting his wife with an incriminating cufflink.

And yet, Hannah gave no reaction.

She didn't even seem to *notice* the invitation, concentrating instead on her veal chop, cutting it into identically sized pieces with an elegant handbag of a smile on her face. Her blouse, satin and sea-green (one of her few articles of clothing that didn't carry itself like a refugee), clung to her as a languid, iridescent skin, moving when she moved, breathing when she breathed.

This uneasiness continued for what felt like an hour. I toyed with the idea of stretching my arms over my veal chop in the direction of the sautéed spinach, grabbing the thing, stealthily slipping it under my leg, but, to be honest, I didn't have the moral aplomb to perform such things as The Sir Thomas More or The Jeanne d'Arc. Nigel was sitting in his chair staring at Hannah, and the way his eyes were buried behind his glasses, reflecting the candles, until he turned his head and they emerged for a moment like beetles in sand, the way he sat so straight, so small yet so substantial, he looked like Napoleon, especially the unappealing oil rendering of the diminutive French Emperor on the cover of Dad's foundational seminar textbook, *Mastering Mankind* (Howards & Path, 1994). (He looked as if he could perform a coup d'état in his sleep and had no qualms being at war with every major European power.)

"I didn't tell you," Hannah said suddenly, "because if I did, you'd want to come. And you can't. I'm inviting Eva Brewster, which makes your attendance out of the question if I'm to keep my job."

Not only was her reaction surprising (also a bit of a letdown; I suppose I was in the stands, drinking Anis del Toro, awaiting the matador), but also remarkable and slick was the way she'd *seen* the invitation but appeared *not* to have seen it.

"Why'd you invite Eva Brewster?" asked Leulah.

"She heard I was planning the fund-raiser and asked if she could come. I couldn't say no. Nigel, I don't appreciate your going through my things. Please give me the courtesy of privacy."

No one said anything. It was Nigel's cue to explain himself, to give some semblance of an apology, attempt some flea-bitten joke about his sticky fingers or refer to *Cool Parenting*'s Chapter 21, "Teenagers and the Joy of Kleptomania," quoting one of the surprising statistics, that it was common for teenagers to go through a period of "appropriation" and "embezzlement" (Mill, 2000). Sixty percent of the time it was something "the youngster eventually grew out of, like Gothic eye makeup and skateboarding" (p. 183).

But Nigel wasn't paying attention. He was cheerfully helping himself to the last veal chop.

Soon the food was cold. We cleared the plates, collected our books, said weak good-byes into the monstrous night. Hannah leaned against the doorway, saying what she always did—"Drive home safely!"—but something in the timbre of her voice, that certain campfire quality, was gone. As Jade and I drove down the driveway, I looked back and saw her still standing on the porch, watching us, her green blouse in the gold light shivering like a swimming pool.

"I feel sick," I said.

Jade nodded. "Utterly wretched."

"Wonder if she'll forgive him."

"Of course she will. She knows him like the back of her hand. Nigel was born without the feeling gene. Other people have no appendix, not enough white blood cells. He doesn't have enough feeling. I guess they did a scan of his brain when he was kid and where other people have emotion, he has a vacuum of total space, poor kid. And he's gay, too. And sure, everyone's open-minded and accepting—all that jazz—but it *still* can't be easy in high school."

"He's gay?" I asked in amazement.

"Earth to Retch? He*llo*?" She looked at me as if I were a snag in tights. "You know, sometimes I wonder if you're all there, if you know what I mean. Have you ever gone to a doctor to make sure you have all your furniture upstairs? Because I have serious doubts about it, Gag. I really do."

*　*　*

Such things as anguish, woe, affliction, guilt, feelings of awfulness and utter wretchedness, the bread and butter of Days of Yore and Russians, sadly have very little staying power in these lickety-split Modern Times.

One has only to consult the 2002 edition of R. Stanbury's *Illuminating Statistics and Cross-Century Comparisons*, under "Grieving," to learn that the very idea of being Brokenhearted, Wretched, Desolate and Despairing is a thing of the past, soon to take on the amusing novelty of such archaic things as the Jalopy, the Jitterbug and Jams. The average American widower in 1802 waited an average of 18.9 years before remarrying, while in 2001 he holds out for an average 8.24 months. (In the "By State" snapshot, you will see in California he holds out for a horrifying 3.6 months.)

Of course, Dad made it his business to rage against this "cultural anes-thetizing," this "ironing out of deep human sentiment, leaving only a flat, unwrinkled vacuity," and thus he'd deliberately raised me to be an insightful, sensitive sort of person, someone aware, beneath even the most tedious sur-faces, of good, evil and the smoky shades in between. He made sure I took the time between Muders, Ohio, and Paducah, Washington, to commit to

memory not one or two, but *all* of Blake's "Songs of Innocence and Experience," and thus I couldn't look at a fly buzzing around a hamburger without
fretting, "Am not I / A fly like thee? / Or art not thou / A man like me?"

When I was with the Bluebloods though, it was easy to pretend I hadn't
committed anything to memory except the lyrics of a thousand corn syrup
R&B songs, that I'd never heard of anyone named Blake except that junior who always had his hands in his pockets and looked like he wanted to
hit someone, that I could simply notice a fly and not think anything but
shrill girlish expressions (Ew). Naturally, if Dad knew about my attitude, he
would've called it "stomach-turning conformity," maybe even "a disgrace to
the Van Meers." (It often slipped his mind he was an orphan.) Yet I saw it as
thrilling, Romantic, if I allowed the current to take me along the "willowy
hills and fields," or wherever it wanted, regardless of the consequences (see
"The Lady of Shalott," Tennyson, 1842).

This was why I had no objections the following slattern Saturday night,
November 22, when Jade made an entrance in the Purple Room wearing a
black wig and a billowing white pantsuit. Colossal shoulder pads jutted off of
her like the White Cliffs of Dover and she'd drawn *duomo* eyebrows over her
eyes with what appeared to be a burnt sienna Crayola crayon.

"Guess who I am."

Charles turned to survey her. "Dame Edna."

" 'I never go out unless I look like Joan Crawford the movie star. You
want The Girl Next Door? Go next door.' " She threw her head back and
villain-laughed, falling onto the leather couch, and putting her feet with their
big, dinghy-like, black pumps in the air. "Guess where I'm headed."

"Hell," said Charles.

She rolled over, sitting up. A clump of wig stuck to her lipstick.

"The Burns County Animal Shelter cordially invites you to our annual—"

"Not a chance."

"—charity soir*ay*—"

"We can't."

"—RSVP—"

"Absolutely not."

"Rowdy sex *very* possible."

"No."

"I'll go," said Leulah.

*   *   *

In the end, we couldn't agree on a group costume, so Charles was Jack the Ripper (for blood, Leulah and I doused him with A.1. Steak Sauce), Leulah was a French maid (helping herself to the array of Hermès silk scarves in various equestrian motifs, folded into neat squares in Jefferson's bureau), Milton, refusing to dress up, was Plan B (the ambiguous sense of humor that bubbled up whenever he smoked pot), Nigel was Antonio Banderas as Zorro (he used Jeff's toenail scissors to cut small holes around the rhinestone zzzzzs of her black sleeping mask), Jade was Anita Ekberg of *La Dolce Vita* replete with stuffed kitten (she duct-taped it to a headband). I was one very unlikely Pussy Galore in shrublike red wig and baggy, teal nylon bodysuit (see "Martian 14," *Profiling Little Green Men: Sketches of Aliens from Eyewitness Accounts*, Diller, 1989, p. 115).

We were drunk. Outside, the air was supple and warm as a dance hall girl after her opening number; and in our costumes, we sprinted sloppily across the nighted lawn, laughing at nothing.

Jade, in her giant conch-shell gown, crunchy with crinolines, ruffles and ribbons, screamed and threw herself against the grass, rolling down the hill.

"Where are you going?" shouted Charles. "It started at eight! It's nine-thirty!"

"Come on, Retch!" shouted Jade.

I crossed my arms over my chest and hurled myself forward.

"Where *are* you?"

I rolled. Grass needled me and my wig ripped off. Stars catapulted between dull pauses of ground, and at the bottom, the quiet hit me. Jade was lying a few feet away, her face serious and blue. Staring at the stars naturally encouraged one's face to appear serious and blue, and Dad had a variety of theories explaining this phenomenon, the majority of which centered on human insecurity and sobering realizations of absolute smallness when measured against such unfathomable things as the Spiral, the Barred Spiral, the Elliptical and the Irregular Galaxy.

But I remember, I couldn't recall a single one of Dad's theories at that moment. The black sky, pinpricked with light, couldn't help but show off like Mozart at five. Voices scratched the air, words wobbly and unsure of themselves, and soon Milton was hurtling through the darkness, and Nigel's loafers rocketed past my head, and Leulah fell right next to me with a teacup sound ("Ahh!"). The silk scarf escaped her hair and settled over my neck and chin. When I breathed, it bubbled like a pond when something drowns in it.

"You bastards!" screamed Charles. "By the time we get there, it'll be over! We need to leave *now!*"

"Shut up, Nazi," Jade said.

"Think Hannah will be mad?" asked Leulah.

"Probably."

"She'll kill us," said Milton. He was only a few feet away. When he breathed it was dragon breaths.

"Hannah shmanna," Jade said.

Somehow, we peeled ourselves off the ground and trekked up the hill to the Mercedes, where Charles was waiting in a bad mood wearing Jade's eighth-grade clear plastic raincoat so he didn't get A.1. Steak Sauce all over the driver's seat. I was the smallest, and Jade said it was necessary to take one car, so I acted as the human seat belt across Nigel, Jade and Leulah, who was making babies' feet with her fist in the fogged window. I concentrated on the car light, my big white high heels touching the door handle, the cloud of smoke loitering around Milton's head in the front seat where he smoked one of his joints thick as lipstick.

"Gonna be messy," he said, "showin' up there unannounced. Not too late to change the plan, friends."

"Stop being mind-numbing," Jade said, plucking the joint from his fingers. "We see Evita, we hide. Make like rugs. It'll be fun."

"Perón won't be there," said Nigel.

"Why not?"

"Hannah didn't really invite her. She was lying. She said it just to have a valid reason why we couldn't come."

"You're paranoid."

Nigel shrugged. "She showed the classic signs of lying. I'd bet my life Eva Brewster will not be at the party. And if anyone asks her about it on Monday, she wouldn't have a clue what you're talking about."

"*You* are the spawn of Satan," Jade pronounced, then accidentally bumped her head against the window. "Ow."

"Want some?" asked Leulah, handing me the joint.

"Thanks," I said.

At the risk of protesting too much, I'd become well acquainted with the crafty behavior of both ceilings and floors under the influence of nip, tipple, hooch, booze, jet fuel, grog, zip, ex, pippin, poison and snifter (the Tremble, the Swoop Out of Nowhere, the Apparently Sinking Ship, the Fraudulent

Earthquake). Much of the time when I was with them, I was only *pretending* to take all those superhuman swigs from Milton's silver M.E.B. flask full of his preferred liquid arsenic, Wild Turkey, passed around the Purple Room like a Native American Peace Pipe.

Unbeknownst to the others, midway through any given evening, I was not, as it appeared, throwing them back with the best of them. "Look. Hurl's deep in thought," Nigel once commented as I stared into space on the couch. I *wasn't* deep in thought, I was trying to pin down a covert means via which I might dispose of Leulah's latest potion, something she simply called "Claw," a deceitfully clear concoction that charred one's esophagus and entire digestive system. One of my preferred scenarios was walking outside unaccompanied for some "fresh air" and, with the porch light off, stealthily pouring whatever it was down one of Jeff's bronze, open-mouthed lions, final gifts from Andy Warhol in January 1987, a month before he died from complications after a gallbladder operation. Obviously, I could have simply dumped it in the grass, but I found a certain woozy satisfaction in feeding it to the lions, who obediently held their giant mouths open and stared up at me as if hoping with this final batch I'd finish them off. I only prayed Jeff never decided the hulking beasts would look better by the front door; when she uprooted them, she'd drown in a tidal wave of nip, tipple, hooch, booze, jet fuel, poison and snifter.

Nearly an hour later, we turned down Hannah's driveway. Charles expertly navigated the Mercedes through the corridor of empty cars parked along the road. Frankly, I was surprised he was able to drive so well given his state of impairment (see "Unidentified Fluid," Chapter 4, "Engine Troubleshooting," *Automobile Mechanics*, Pont, 1997).

"Don't get a ding," said Jade. "If you get a ding I'm in trouble."

"She knows more people than we thought," Leulah said.

"Shit," said Milton.

"This is perfect," said Jade, clapping her hands. "Absolutely ideal. We'll blend. I just hope we don't see Hannah."

"You're worried about seeing Hannah?" shouted Charles. "Then we need to go back, because let me give you the heads up, honey bunch! We're going to see her!"

"Keep your eyes on the road. It's fine." Jade huffed. "It's just . . ."

"*What?*" Charles slammed his foot on the brake. We all went forward and backward together like children on a bus.

"It's just a party. And Hannah won't really *mind*. We're not doing anything terrible or anything. Right?"

Anxiety, Doubt and Uncertainty had unexpectedly stood up in Jade's voice and now they were meandering through it making Helluva Good Time quite nervous.

"Kind of," said Leulah.

"No," said Nigel.

"Could go either way," said Milton.

"Somebody make a fucking decision!" shouted Charles.

"Let Gag decide," said Jade. "She's the responsible one."

To this day, I'm not sure how or why I said what I did. Perhaps it was one of those uncanny occasions when it really isn't *you* speaking, but Fate, who intervenes every so often to make sure that, rather than your choosing the easy road, recently paved, with clearly labeled street signs and maple trees, she, with the cruelty of drill sergeants, dictators, and office personnel, makes certain you stick to the dark, thorny path she's already laid out for you.

"We're going in," I said.

*   *   *

Hannah was a Snowy Egret, and when one heard she was planning a social affair, one couldn't help but expect a Snowy Egret kind of party—flutes of champagne, cigarette holders and a string quartet, people asking each other to dance with delicate rests of cheeks against shoulders and very few clammy palms, adulterous intrigues behind laurel hedges and grandiflora roses—the sort of elegant, whispery affair the Larrabees could host with their eyes closed, the kind Sabrina observed from her tree.

As we approached the house, however, and saw the weird crowd of animal, vegetable and mineral dribbling through the front yard and across the driveway, Milton suggested we cut into the woods and head to the other side of the house, maybe sneak in the door off the patio where Hannah had a kidney-shaped swimming pool, which she never used.

"We can still leave if we want to," said Jade.

We parked the car behind a van and sat in the dark, at the edge of pine trees, watching in the loose light of fourteen tiki torches, some fifty or sixty people crowding Hannah's patio. They all wore surprisingly complicated costumes (ghouls, alligators, devils, the entire crew of the USS *Enterprise*), those in masks sipping straws in blue and red plastic cups, others eating pretzels and crackers, trying to make themselves heard over the meat-cleaving music.

"Who're all these people?" asked Charles, frowning.

"I don't recognize them," said Jade.

"I guess they're friends of Hannah's," said Leulah.

"You see her?"

"No."

"Even if she was here," said Milton, "it'd be impossible to tell which one she was. Everyone's wearin' masks."

"I'm freezing," said Jade.

"*We* should have masks," Milton said. "That's what the invite said."

"Where the fuck are we going to find masks *now*?" asked Charles.

"There's Perón," said Lu.

"Where?"

"The woman with the sparkly halo thing."

"That's not her."

"Seriously," said Jade uneasily, "what are we even *doing* here?"

"You guys can sit here all night," said Nigel, "but I, for one, am going to enjoy myself." He was wearing his Zorro mask *and* his glasses. He looked like an erudite raccoon. "Who else wants to have some fun?"

For some reason, he was looking at me.

"What do you say, old broad? Shall we dance?"

I adjusted my wig.

We left the others, hurrying across the yard—one nerdy raccoon and an inverted carrot—to Hannah's patio.

It was jam packed. Four men dressed as rats and a mermaid beauty queen with a half-mask of blue sequins were actually in the swimming pool, laughing, throwing a volleyball. We decided to make our way inside (see "Walking upstream in the Zambezi River during a flood period," *Quests*, 1992, p. 212). We crammed ourselves into a space between the plaid couch and a pirate talking to a devil oblivious to the repercussions of his massive sweaty back when he suddenly and without warning backed it into two much smaller people.

For twenty minutes, we didn't do anything but sip vodka out of the red plastic cups and watch the people—none of whom we recognized—crawling, slithering, waddling their way around the room in costumes ranging from the teensy-weensy to the wholly insurmountable.

"Butterfly hazy!" Nigel shouted, shaking his head.

I shook my head and he repeated himself.

"This is totally crazy!"

I nodded. Hannah, Eva Brewster and the animals were nowhere to be found, only graceless birds, doughy sumo wrestlers, unvelcroed reptiles, a Queen who'd removed her crown and distractedly gnawed on it as her eyes strolled the room, probably searching for a King or Ace to come royally flush her.

If Dad had been present, he'd undoubtedly have commented that most of the adults present were "dangerously close to relinquishing their dignity" and that it was sad and disturbing, because "they were all searching for something they'd never recognize, even if they found it." Dad was notoriously severe when it came to commenting upon the behaviors of all people other than himself. Yet, watching a midforties Wonder Woman stumble backward into Hannah's neat stack of *Traveler* magazines made me wonder if the very idea of Growing Up was a sham, the bus out of town you're so busy waiting for, you don't notice it never actually comes.

"What are they speaking?" Nigel shouted in my ear.

I followed his eyes to the astronaut standing a few feet away. He was holding his pressure helmet, a stocky man with a sideways sigma hairline (Σ) talking vigorously to a gorilla.

"I think it's Greek," I said, surprised. ("The language of the Titans, the Oracles, η γλῶσσα των ηρώων," said Dad. (This last bit apparently meant "the language of heroes.") Dad loved showing off his bizarre aptitude when it came to foreign languages. (He claimed to be fluent in twelve; yet *fluent* often meant *yes* and *no*, plus a few impressive phrases, and enjoyed repeating a certain witticism about Americans and their dearth of language skills: "Americans need to master *lingual* before they attempt *bi*lingual.")

"I wonder who that is," I said to Nigel. The gorilla took off its head, revealing a small Chinese woman. She nodded, but answered in some other guttural language that made a person's mouth break-dance. I wasn't even sure I'd heard Greek in the first place. I leaned closer.

"Aye, Savannah," said Nigel, squeezing my arm.

"Again," I shouted.

"I see Hannah."

He grabbed my hand and yanked me through two Elvises.

"So where'd you come from?" asked *Elvis: Aloha from Hawaii*. "Reno," said a very sweaty *Elvis on Tour* drinking from a blue plastic cup.

"She went upstairs," Nigel said into my ear, trying to get us past Sodom and Gomorrah, Leopold and Loeb, Tarzan and Jane, who'd just managed to find each other in this jungle and were talking with a great deal of clothing fiddling. I didn't know why Nigel *wanted* to find Hannah, but midway up, I saw only a six-ton Tyrannosaurus Ex who'd unzipped his costume and sat down on his rubber head.

"Fuck."

"Why do you want to find her?" I shouted, "I thought the—" and just as I turned to look out over the bobbing wigs and masks, I saw her.

Her face was eclipsed by the brim of a top hat (only a white sliver of chin and red mouth was visible) but I knew it was she, due to the oil and vinegar reaction her presence had with all backdrops, atmospheres and given conditions. The young, the old, the pretty and plain merged to compose some standard room of talking people, but Hannah was permanently separate and distinctive, as if there was always an unmistakable, thin black line drawn around her, or a YOU ARE HERE arrow discreetly floated in her wake reading, SHE IS HERE. Or perhaps, due to a certain relationship she had with incandescence, her face exerted a gravitational pull on 50 percent of all the light in the room.

She was dressed in a tuxedo and heading our way, leading a man up the stairs. She held his left hand as if it was expensive, something she couldn't afford to lose.

Nigel saw her too. "Who's she dressed as?"

"Marlene Dietrich, *Morocco*, 1930. We need to hide."

But Nigel shook his head and held on to my wrist. As we were trapped by a sheikh waiting for someone to come out of the upstairs bathroom and a group of men dressed as tourists (Polaroids, Hawaiian shirts) I could do nothing but brace myself for what was coming.

I was marginally reassured, however, when I saw the man. If she'd been with Doc three weeks ago, at least she'd traded up and was now arm in arm with Big Daddy (see *The Great Patriarchs of American Theatre: 1821–1990*, Park, 1992). Though he was gray haired, overweight in that Montgomery, Alabama way (when the stomach looked like a great big bag of loot and the rest of the body ignored that rude, uncouth section, going about its business of being perfectly fit and trim), something about him was satisfying, impressive. Dressed in a Red Army uniform (presumably as Mao Zedong), he had a chancellor's posture, and his face, if not flat-out handsome, was at the very least, splendid: rich, glistening and rosy, like a block of salted ham at a state dinner. It was also evident he was a little bit in love with her. Dad said being in love had nothing to do with words, action or the heart ("the most overrated of organs"), but with the eyes ("Everything essential concerns the eyes.") and this man's eyes couldn't stop slipping and sliding off every curve of her face.

I wondered what she could possibly be *saying* to him, her profile puzzling into the space between his jaw and shoulder. Maybe she was wowing him with an ability to recite pi out to sixty-five decimal places, which I secretly thought would be sort of electrifying if some kid heatedly whispered it into my ear ("3.14159265 . . ."). Or maybe she was repeating a Shakespearean sonnet, #116, Dad's favorite ("If there are authentic words of love that exist in this English language, *these* are the ones people with any real affection should say, rather than the shopworn, 'I love you,' which can be uttered by any hebetudinous Tom, Dick or Moe"): "Let me not to the marriage of true minds admit impediments . . ."

Whatever it was, the man was mesmerized. He looked as if he couldn't wait for her to garnish him with fresh bay leaves, slice him, pour him all over with gravy.

They were three stairs away now, passing the cheerleader, the woman dressed as Liza Minnelli leaning against the wall with makeup clogging her eyes like rotten leaves in old gutters.

And then she saw us.

There was a skid of her eyes, a brief suspension of smile, a catch, a soft sweater snagging a tree branch. All Nigel and I could do was stand with lousy smiles safety-pinned to our faces like HELLO MY NAME IS name tags. She didn't say anything until she was next to us.

"Shame on you," she said.

"Hi," said Nigel brightly, as if he thought she'd said, "Overjoyed to see you," and to my horror, he was now extending his hand to the man, who'd turned his large, soggy face curiously in our direction. "I'm Nigel Creech."

The man raised one white eyebrow and tilted his head, smiling good-naturedly. "Smoke," he said. His eyes were a crisp seersucker blue, and shrewd—surprisingly so. Dad said you could tell how sharp someone was by the tempo of his/her eyes on your face when you were introduced. If they barely did the box step or took to being wallflowers somewhere between your eyebrows, the person had "the IQ of caribou," but if they waltzed from your eyes to your shoes, not nervously, but with easy, untroubled curiosity, then the person had "a respectable acumen." Well, Smoke's eyes macumbaed from Nigel to me back to Nigel and I felt in that simple movement he grasped every embarrassment of our lives. I couldn't help but like him. Laugh lines parenthesized his mouth.

"You're visiting for the weekend?" Nigel asked.

Smoke glanced at Hannah before he answered. "Yes. Hannah's been kind enough to show me around."

"Where are you from?"

Nigel's aggressive curiosity wasn't lost on Smoke. Again, he looked at Hannah. "West Virginia," he said.

And then it was horrifying because Hannah didn't say a *word*. I could see she was angry: redness soaked her cheeks, her forehead. She smiled, some-what shyly, and then (and I noticed this because I was one step up from Nigel and could see her entirely, her too-long cuff and sleeve, the cane in her hand) she squeezed, tightly, Smoke's bicep. This seemed to be a signal of sorts, because he smiled again, and said in his bear-hug voice: "Well, nice meeting you. So long."

They continued on, passing the sheikh and the tourists ("Not many peo-ple realize the electric chair's not a bad way to go," shouted one) and some private dancer, a dancer for money in a tiny silver dress and white go-go boots.

At the top of the stairs, they turned down the hall, out of sight.

"Shit," said Nigel, grinning.

"What's the matter with you?" I asked. I wanted to slap the smile off his face.

"What?"

"How could you do that?"

He shrugged. "I wanted to know who her boyfriend was. Could have been Valerio."

Doc do-si-doed into my head. "I'm not sure Valerio exists."

"Well, you, doll face, may be an atheist but *I'm* a believer. Let's get some air," he said, and then he grabbed my hand and yanked me down the stairs after him, stepping around Tarzan and Jane (Jane pressed against the wall, Tarzan leaning *way* in) and outside onto the patio.

Jade and the others had joined the crowd by now, which hadn't thinned, but buzzed like a porch wasp nest after a housewife stabs it with a broom. Leulah and Jade shared a deck chair talking to two men who wore their swollen, fleshy masks as hats. (They depicted Ronald Reagan, Donald Trump, Clark Gable, or any renowned man over fifty with formidable ears.) I didn't see Milton (Black could come and go like stormy weather) but Charles was by the barbecue flirting with a woman in a lioness costume who'd pulled her mane down around her neck and casually stroked it every time Charles said something. Abraham Lincoln threw himself against a jackrabbit, banging into the picnic table so a platter of wilted lettuce fireworked into the air. Rock music screamed from speakers rigged by the hanging plants, and the electric guitar, the roars of the singer, so many shrieks and laughs, the moon, a sickle stabbing the pine trees off to the right—it all fused into a strange suffocating violence. Maybe it was because I was a little drunk and my thoughts moved slowly like blobs in a lava lamp, but I felt it was a crowd that could attack, loot, rape, cause a "violent uprising that detonated like a bomb, and ended a day later with the whimper of a silk scarf pulled from the flabby neck of an old lady—as *all* rebellions do, if they arise purely from emotion and no forethought" (see "The Last of the Summer Whine: A Study of the Novgorod Rebellion, USSR, August 1965," Van Meer, *The SINE Review*, Spring, 1985).

Sharp light from the tiki torches cut into the masks, turning even the sweet costumes, the cute black cats and tutu angels into ghouls with buried eyes and dagger chins.

And then, my heart stopped.

On the brick wall, staring out over the crowd, stood a man. He wore a black hooded cloak and a gold mask with a hooked nose. Not a centimeter of human was visible. It was that horrible Brighella mask, worn during carnivals in Venice and Mardi Gras—Brighella, the lascivious villain from the Commedia dell'arte—but the sick thing, the thing that made the rest of the beasts at the party shiver out of focus, was *not* that the mask was demonic, that it turned eyes to bullet holes, but the fact that it was Dad's costume. In Erie, Louisiana, June Bug Karen Sawyer had coerced him into participating in her Junior League Halloween Fashion Show and she'd brought the outfit back for him from her trip to New Orleans. ("Is it me or do I look robustly absurd?" Dad had asked when he'd first tried on the velvet robe.) And the figure opposite me, far across the patio, as tall as Dad so he rose out of the crowd like a crucifix, what he wore was identical, down to the bronze color of the mask, the blistered nose, the satin trim around the hood, the tiny fish-eye buttons down the front. The man didn't move. He seemed to watch me. I could see cigarette cinders in his eyes.

"Retch?"

"I see—my dad—" I managed to say. My heart rolling in my chest, I pushed through the Flintstones, red-faced Rapunzel, squeezing past shoulders and tinseled backs and elbows and stuffed tails stabbing me in the stomach. The wire edge of an angel wing knifed my cheek. "I—excuse me." I pushed a caterpillar. "Screw you!" it shouted, its bloodshot eyes infected with glitter. I was shoved hard and fell onto the brick, snaring in sneakers and fishnet stockings and plastic cups.

Seconds later, Nigel was crouching next to me. "What a beaatch. I'd shout 'catfight,' but I don't think you want to go there."

"The man," I said.

"Hmm?"

"Standing on the wall. A tall man. I–is he there?"

"Who?"

"He's wearing a mask with a long nose."

Nigel looked at me, puzzled, but stood up, and I watched his red Adidas sneakers turn in a circle. He bent down again. "I don't see anyone."

My head felt if it were unstitching from my neck. I blinked and he helped me up. "Come on, old girl. Easy does it." Holding onto his shoulder, I craned my neck around the orange wig, the halo, to catch another glimpse of that face, to be *sure*, to realize I was only intoxicated, imagining impossible, highly dramatic things—but there were only Cleopatras on the brick wall now, their wide faces sweaty and rainbowed like oil puddles in parking lots: "*Haaaaarveeeeey!*" one screamed, shrilly, pointing at someone in the crowd.

"We have to get the fuck out of here or we might be trampled," Nigel said. He tightened his grip on my wrist. I assumed he was going to lead me out into the yard, but instead he was pulling me back inside.

"I have an idea," he said with a smile.

*   *   *

As a rule, Hannah's bedroom door remained closed.

Charles once told me she was peculiar about it—she hated people in her "private space"—and, rather incredibly, none of them, in the three years they'd known her, had ever been inside or seen it, except at a passing glance.

I wouldn't have intruded in a million Ming Dynasties if I hadn't been tipsy and marginally catatonic after conjuring Dad as Brighella, or if Nigel hadn't been there, hauling me up the stairs past the hippies and the cavemen, knocking three times on the closed door at the end of the hall. And though I certainly knew it was wrong to take refuge in her bedroom, I also felt, as I removed my shoes—"We don't want heavy footprints on the carpet,"

Nigel said, as he closed and locked the door behind us—that perhaps Hannah herself wouldn't mind so much, if it was only this once, and besides, it was *her* fault everyone was so curious about her, so spellbound. If she hadn't cultivated her own *aire de mystère*, always being reluctant to answer even the most humdrum of questions, maybe we wouldn't have gone into her bedroom in the first place—maybe we'd have gone back to the car or even home. (Dad said all criminals have complicated means of rationalizing their aberrant behavior. This twisty logic was mine.)

"I'll fix you right up," Nigel said, planting me on the bed and switching on the bedside lamp. He disappeared into the bathroom and returned with a glass of water. Away from the music and ferocious crowd, I realized, with a little wonder, I was much more lucid than I'd thought, and after only a few sips of water, some deep breaths, staring at the starkness of Hannah's bedroom, I began to come around, feel twinges of what was commonly known in palcontologist circles as "Dig Fever," a blind, untiring enthusiasm for unearthing the history of life. (It was allegedly experienced by both Mary and Louis Leakey when they first wandered around Oldupai Gorge in the eastern Serengeti Plains of Tanzania, a location that would go on to become one of the most revealing archeological sites in the world.)

Her bedroom walls were beige, without a single picture or painting. The carpet under the bed was preppy green. Considering the rest of her house, muddled with animals, cat hair, oriental wall hangings, handicapped furniture, every *National Geographic* since 1982, the austere furnishings here were bizarre and, I felt, a definitive sign of something ("A man's bedroom is direct insight into his character," wrote Sir Montgomery Finkle in 1953's *Gory Details*). The few pieces of humble furniture—chest of drawers, wooden Quaker chair, a vanity table—had been relegated to the corners of the room as if they'd been punished. The bed was queen sized, neatly made (although where I was sitting it wrinkled) and the comforter (or bedspread, as there was nothing comforting about it) was a thorny blanket the color of brown rice. The bedside table featured a lamp, and on the bottom shelf only a single well-worn book, *I Ching, or The Book of Changes*. ("There's nothing more irritating than Americans hoping to locate their inner Tao," Dad said.) Standing up, I noticed a faint but unmistakable smell hanging in the air, like a flashy guest that refused to go home: men's musky cologne, the sort of persistent syrup a Miami hunk doused on his trunk-thick neck.

Nigel was having a look around too. He'd stuffed his Zorro mask into his pocket and had a subdued, almost reverential look on his face, as if we'd snuck into a monastery and he didn't want to disturb nuns at prayer. He crept over to Hannah's closet and, very slowly, slid open the door.

I was about to follow him—the closet was crowded with clothes, and when he tugged the string to turn on the light, a black pump fell from a shelf piled with shoe boxes and shopping bags—but then, I noticed something I'd never seen in the house before, three framed photographs positioned along the edge of the chest of drawers. They each strictly faced forward like suspects in a police lineup. I tiptoed over to them, but realized immediately they were not the obvious evidence of an extinct species (ex-boyfriend) or Jurassic period (fierce Goth phase) I'd been hoping to discover.

No, they each featured (one in black and white, the others in outdated 1970s colors, *Brady Bunch* brown, *M*A*S*H** maroon) a girl who was presumably Hannah between the ages of, say, nine months and six, and yet the baby with hair like a squirt of icing on its bald cupcake head, the toddler wearing nothing but a diaper, looked nothing like her—not at *all*. This thing looked portly and red as an alcoholic uncle; if you squinted, it looked like it'd passed out in its crib from too much scotch. Even the eyes were dissimilar. Hannah's were almond-shaped, and these were the same color, black-brown, but round. I was prepared to accept that maybe these pictures weren't of Hannah, but a beloved sister—and yet, peering closer, particularly at the one of her at four, sitting atop a fierce Whitman-shaggy pony, the resemblance *did* surface: the perfect mouth, upper lip fitting with bottom lip like delicate pieces of a jigsaw puzzle, and as she stared down at the reigns held tightly in her fists, that intense yet secret expression.

Nigel was still in Hannah's closet—he seemed to be trying on shoes—so I slipped into the adjacent master bathroom and switched on the light. In terms of décor, it was an extension of the bedroom, austere, stark as a penitentiary cell: a white-tiled floor, neat white towels, the sink and mirror meticulous, without a single splatter or smear. Words from a certain book flashed into my head, the paperback June Bug Amy Steinman had left at our house, *Stranded in the Dark*, by P.C. Mailey, Ph.D. (1979). The book detailed in frantic, husky prose, "the surefire signs of depression in single women," one of which was "a stark living space as a form of self-torture" (p. 87). "A severely depressed woman either lives in squalor or in a strict, minimalist living space—without anything that could remind her of her own taste or personality. In other rooms, however, she certainly might have 'stuff' in order to appear normal and happy to her friends" (p. 88).

I found it somewhat disheartening. However, it was when I knelt down and opened the cabinet under the bathroom sink that I was *really* taken aback, and I don't think it was the same joyful disbelief Mary Leakey felt in 1959 when she stumbled upon *Zinjanthropus* or "Zinj."

Inside, assembled in a pink plastic basket, was a collection of prescription bottles that made anything Judy Garland had popped in her glory days look like a few rolls of Smarties. I counted nineteen orange containers (barbiturates, amphetamines, I was chanting to myself, *Seconal, Phenobarbital, Dexedrine*; Marilyn and Elvis would've had a heyday) but, rather frustratingly, it was impossible to know what they were; there wasn't a single label, not even evidence they'd been ripped off. On each PUSH DOWN AND TURN cap was a piece of colored tape in blue, red, green or yellow.

I picked up one of the larger ones, shaking the tiny blue tablets, each marked with a tiny 50. I was tempted to steal it, then at home, try to decipher what it was by consulting the Internet or Dad's twenty-pound *Encyclopedia of Medicine* (Baker & Ash, 2000), but then—What If Hannah had a secret terminal illness and this was the treatment that kept her alive? What If I swiped one of these vital drugs and tomorrow she couldn't take her necessary dosage and lapsed into a coma like Sunny von Bulow and I thus became the shifty Claus character? What If I had to hire Alan Dershowitz who talked about me incessantly with his mob of irksome college students who stuffed themselves with spaghetti and ginger prawns while waxing poetic on Degrees of Innocence and Guilt while my life danced in their hands like a marionette poorly rigged with sewing thread?

I returned the container.

"Blue! Come *here!*"

Nigel was buried in the closet behind a few garment bags. He was one of those passionate yet chaotic excavators who shamelessly contaminated the site; he'd removed at least ten shoe boxes from the top shelf and left them heedlessly on the floor. Faded cotton sweaters had been strewn between balled up tissue paper, plastic bags, a rhinestone belt, jewelry case, one sweat-petrified burgundy shoe. He was wearing a strand of fake pink pearls around his neck.

"I'm Hannah Schneider and I'm mys*terious*," he said in a vampish voice, tossing the end of the necklace over his shoulder as if he were Isadora Duncan, the Mother of Modern Dance (see *This Red, So Am I*, Hillson, 1965).

"What're you doing?" I asked, giggling.

"Window shopping."

"You have to put this stuff back. She's going to know we were here. She could come back—"

"Oh, check this out," he said excitedly and plopped a heavy, intricately carved wooden case into my hands. Biting his bottom lip, he opened the lid. Inside glinted a silver machete approximately eighteen inches long, the sort of horrifying weapon rebels used to cut the arms off of children in Sierra Leone ("Romancing the Stones," Van Meer, *The Foreign Quarterly*, June 2001). I was speechless. "There's a whole knife collection up here," he was saying. "She must be into S & M. Oh, I also found a picture."

He cheerfully took back the knife (as if he were the enthusiastic manager of a pawnshop), throwing it on the carpet, and after digging through another shoe box, handed me a faded square photo.

"She kind of looked like Liz when she was young," he said dreamily. "Very *National Velvet*."

The picture was of Hannah when she eleven or twelve. It was a photo taken from the waist up so you couldn't tell if she was outside or inside, but she was smiling hugely (frankly, I'd never seen her so happy). Her arm was mink-shrugged around the neck of another girl who was also probably quite beautiful, but she'd shyly twisted away from the camera, smiling, but blinking just as the photo was taken so you could only see into the foyer of her face (cheek, a bit of regal forehead, rumors of eyelash) and maybe a bit of parlor room (perfect ski slope nose). They wore the same school uniform (white blouse, a navy jacket—on Hannah's, a gold lion insignia on the breast pocket) and it was one of those snapshots that seemed to have trapped not only an image but a grainy reel of life—their ponytails were full of static, stands of hair cobwebbed in the wind. You could almost hear their laughs twisting together.

And yet—there was something eerie about them. I couldn't help but think of Holloway Barnes and Eleanor Tilden, the girls who'd conspired to murder their parents in Honolulu in 1964, subject of Arthur Lewis' chilling nonfiction account, *Little Girls* (1988). Holloway killed Eleanor's parents with a pick-ax as they slept and Eleanor killed Holloway's with a rifle, shooting them in the face as if playing a game, hoping to win a stuffed panda, and in the photographs section in the middle of the book, there'd been a picture of the girls almost exactly like this one, the two of them in Catholic schoolgirl uniforms, their arms pretzeled, their brutal smiles piercing their faces like fish hooks.

"Wonder who the other one is," Nigel said. He sighed wistfully. "Two people that beautiful should die. Im*me*diately."

"Does Hannah have a sister?" I asked.

He shrugged. "Don't know."

I moved back over to the three framed photographs on the chest of drawers.

"What?" he asked, walking up behind me.

I held up the picture for comparison. "It's not the same person."

"Huh?"

"These photos. They're not of Hannah."

"Aren't those baby pictures?"

"But it's not the same face."

He leaned closer, nodding. "Maybe it's a fat cousin."

I turned over the picture of Hannah with the blonde. There was a date written in the corner in blue pen: 1973.

"*Wait*," Nigel whispered suddenly, a hand pressed to the pearls around his neck, his eyes wide. "Oh, fuck. Listen."

The music downstairs, which had been beating with the steadiness of a healthy heart, had stopped, leaving total silence.

I moved toward the door, unlocked it and peered down the hall.

It was deserted.

"Let's get out of here," I said.

Nigel, with a small squeak, was already at the closet, madly trying to re-fold the sweaters and matching lids to shoe boxes. I considered swiping the photograph of Hannah and the other girl—but then, did Howard Carter blithely help himself to treasures in the tomb of Tutankhamen? Did Donald Johanson covertly pocket a piece of Lucy, the 3.18-million-year-old hominid? Reluctantly, I handed the photograph back to Nigel who slipped it into the Evan Picone shoe box, standing on his tiptoes to return it to the shelf. We switched off every light, grabbed our shoes, did a final check of the room to make sure we hadn't dropped something ("All thieves leave behind a calling card because the human ego craves recognition the way junkies crave smack," noted Detective Clark Green in *Fingerprints* [Stipple, 1979]). We closed Hannah's bedroom door and hurried down the hall.

The stairs were empty, and below, in the whirlpools of people, some sweaty bird in a crooked feather headdress was screeching something, a hysterical "Ooooooouu" that went on and on, cutting through the noise like a sword during any climatic fight scene. Charlie Chaplin was trying to restrain her. "Breathe! Fuckin' breathe, Amy!" Nigel and I glanced at each other, baffled, then continued down the stairs, only to find ourselves drowning in a flood of feet, plastic masks, tails, wands, wigs, all of them trying to shove their way toward the back door, out onto the patio.

"*Stop pushing!*" someone shouted. "*Stop pushing, motherfucker!*"

"I saw it," said a penguin.

"But what about the police?" wailed a fairy. "I mean, why aren't they *here?* Did someone call nine-one-one?"

"Hey," said Nigel, grabbing the shoulder of the merman pushing in front of us. "What's going on?"

"Someone's dead," he said.

A Moveable Feast

When he was seven years old, Dad almost drowned in Lake Brienz. He claimed it was the second most illuminating experience of his life, trailing in significance only to one other occasion, the day he saw Benno Ohnesorg die.

In customary fashion, Dad was trying to outperform one Hendrik Salzmann, a twelve-year-old, another boy at the Zurich *Waisenhaus*. Although Dad "showed dogged endurance and athleticism" as he splashed past the weary Hendrik, when he was some thirty or forty meters beyond the swimmer's boundary, Dad found himself too exhausted to go on.

The bright green shore floated far behind him. "It appeared to be waving good-bye," Dad said. As he slumped into the gurgling darkness, arms and legs heavy as bags of stones, after an initial panic, which was "really nothing more than surprise, that this was *it*, what it all comes down to," Dad claimed he felt what is frequently referred to as the "Socrates Syndrome," a feeling of utter tranquility moments before death. Dad closed his eyes and saw not a tunnel, not blinding light, not a slide show of his short, Dickensian life, not even a Smiling Bearded White Man in a Robe, but sweets.

"Caramel truffles, marmalade," Dad said, "Babel cookies, marzipan. I could smell them. I really believed I was falling not to my watery grave, but into a *Café Conditorei*."

Dad also swore he heard, somewhere in the depths, Beethoven's Fifth, which some beloved nun named Fraulein Uta (the first June Bug in recorded history, *der erste Maikäfer in der Geschichte*) played in her room on Saturday evenings. When he was wrenched from this sugary euphoria and hauled ashore by none other than Hendrik Salzmann (experiencing a heroic second wind), Dad said his first conscious thought was that he wanted to go back, down into the dark water, for dessert and the Allegro-Presto.

Dad, on Death: "When it's your time—and naturally, none of us know when we'll be drafted—there's no use sniveling. *Please.* You should walk out a warrior, even if the revolution you waged in your life was for biology or neurology, the origins of the sun, bugs, the Red Cross, like your mother. Might I remind you of the way Che Guevara went out? He was a deeply flawed man—his pro-Chinese, pro-Communist viewpoints were blinkered, naïve at best. *Yet*"—Dad sat up in his chair and leaned forward, his hazel eyes huge behind his glasses, his voice rising up then plunging deep into himself—"on October 9, 1967, after a traitor alerted CIA operatives to the secret location of Guevara's guerrilla encampment, after he was so badly injured he couldn't stand and he surrendered to the Bolivian army and René Barrientos ordered his execution, after a lily-livered officer drew the short straw and, trembling so severely witnesses thought he was having a seizure, entered the windowless schoolhouse in order to put a bullet in Guevara's head. He was going to murder, once and for all, the man who charged into battle for those he believed in, the man who said, 'Freedom,' and 'Justice,' without a hint of sarcasm, Guevara, who *knew* what was coming, he turned to the officer . . ." Here, Dad turned to an imaginary officer standing to his left. "They say he wasn't afraid, sweet, not a bead of sweat, not the *slightest* tremor in his voice—he said, 'Shoot, coward. You are only going to kill a man.' "

Dad stared at me.

"May you and I aspire to such certainty."

After Hannah told us about Smoke Harvey, with a raw voice and a certain grayness seeping around her eyes (as if something inside her had spilled), and her every detail about him laid a pink brick in the re-creation of his big, noisy plantation of a life, I found myself wondering about Smoke's certainty. As he drowned, I tried to imagine what it was that wooed him, if not Dad's childhood loves of sugar and Beethoven, then Cuban cigars, or his first wife's doll hands ("She was so tiny she couldn't wrap her arms all the way around him," said Hannah), or a glass of Johnnie Walker on the rocks (Blue Label probably, as Hannah said he enjoyed "the fine things"), anything to gently push him away from the fact that the culmination of his life, sixty-eight years lived with great vigor and force ("gusto" and "zest" Hannah said) was to be in her swimming pool, inebriated and dressed as Mao Zedong, drifting over a concrete floor eight feet under and no one noticing.

His full name was Smoke Wyannoch Harvey, age 68. Not many people knew who he was, unless they lived in Findley, West Virginia, or used him as a Portfolio Manager when he worked at DBA LLC, or found the book he'd written in the 80-percent off bin, *The Doloroso Treason* (1999), or browsed the two articles about his death in *The Stockton Observer* on November 24 and November 28 (see "West Virginia Man Drowns in Pool," "Weekend Drowning Ruled Accidental," Local News, 2B, 5B, respectively).

He was, of course, the distinguished gray-haired man Nigel and I had met with Hannah on the stairs, the one I'd liked (Visual Aid 12.0).

*   *   *

After we heard someone was dead, Nigel and I pushed our way to one of the windows overlooking the patio. We could only see the backs of people, all of them staring at something in front of them, as if watching a stirring street performance of *King Lear*. Most of them were half-birthed from their costumes, so they looked between species, and the ground was littered with pipe-cleaner antennae and beached-jellyfish wigs.

VISUAL AID 12.0

Screams from an ambulance ripped through the night. Red light hurtled around the lawn. Everyone on the patio was herded into the living room.

"Things'll go quick soon as everyone gets quiet," the blond police officer said from the door. He chewed gum. From the way he leaned against the doorjamb, rested one foot on Hannah's jug of umbrellas and took seconds too long to blink, you could tell his body was present, but his mind was back at some red felt pool table where he'd missed an easy draw shot, or else, back with his wife in their swayback bed.

I was in an O-mouthed state of shock—wondering who it was, wanting to make sure it wasn't Milton or Jade or any of them (*if it has to be someone, it could be that sick caterpillar*)—but Nigel was acting like a Boy Scout Leader. Grabbing my hand again, he forced us across the room, stepping on the hippies who'd sat down on the floor to give each other contrition massages. He ejected a sick Jane from the bathroom (she'd lost Tarzan) and, locking the door, instructed me to start drinking water.

"We don't want to be asked by a flatfoot to take a Breathalyzer," he said agitatedly. I was shocked by his intensity. Dad said emergencies created an elemental shift in everyone, and while most people liquefied immediately, Nigel was turning into a denser, somewhat more formidable version of himself. "I'm going to find the others," he said with Rockette-kick fervor. "We have to come up with a good story as to why we're here because they're going to be securing the scene, taking names and addresses," he said as he opened the door, "and I'll be *damned* if I'm getting kicked out of school for some slob who can't hold his liquor and never took a swimming lesson."

※　※　※

Some people have a knack for finding themselves, if not the star of every Detective Film, Skin Flick, Love Story or Spaghetti Western, at the very least, one of the supporting players, or appearing in an unforgettable cameo for which they garner critical acclaim and considerable buzz.

Unsurprisingly, it was Jade who was cast as Unwitting Eyewitness. She was outside talking to Ronald Reagan, who, in a drunken desire to show off, flopped into the heated pool, and, backstroking in his blue suit, avoiding the four rats playing Marco Polo, he shouted out names as Jade looked on, trying to guess who she was dressed as ("Pam Anderson! Ginger Lynn!"). He accidentally kicked the dark, submerged body with his foot.

"What the—?" The Gipper said.

"Someone's unconscious! Call nine-one-one! Who knows CPR? *Get me a fucking doctor!*" Jade claimed she screamed, though Milton, who'd just returned to the patio after smoking the remainder of his joint in the woods, said she didn't do or say anything until the Great Communicator and one of the rats hauled the great whale of a body out of the water, at which point she sat down in the deck chair and only watched, biting her nails while people began to murmur their "Oh, my fucking Gods." A man in zebra print tried to resuscitate him.

Jade was still on the patio with Dutch and the other main characters waiting to be interviewed by the police, but Nigel returned to the bathroom with Charles, Milton and Lu. Charles and Lu looked as if they'd barely survived the War of 1812, but Milton looked as he always did, laid-back and lumpy, a smear of smile on his face.

"Who died?" I asked.

"A very large man," Leulah said, sitting down on the edge of the bathtub, an unfocused look in her eyes. "And he really is *dead*. There's a dead body on Hannah's patio. He's sopping wet. And this terrible blubbery color." She pressed a hand to her stomach. "I might throw up."

"Life, death," sighed Nigel. "It's all so Hollywood."

"Did anyone see Hannah?" asked Charles quietly.

It was a grisly thought. Even if it was an accident, it was never a good thing for someone to die unexpectedly at one's house while one is entertaining, for a person to "walk out of this outrageous world" (as Dad was fond of saying) on one's property, in one's kidney-shaped pool. None of us spoke. Behind the closed door, a few tadpole-words wriggled free of the noise ("Ow," "Sheila!" "Did you know him?" "Hey, what's going on?") and through the open window by the tub, the police car radios fizzed, ceaseless and indecipherable.

"Well, I'd say run for it," Nigel said, slipping behind the shower curtain, and hunching down as he peered out the window as if someone might open fire. "I doubt they even have a squad car at the end of the driveway. But we can't leave Jade, so we'll have to take our chances following police procedure."

"Of *course* we can't flee the crime scene," said Charles irritably. "What are you—nuts?" His face was red. He was obviously worried about Hannah. I noticed, whenever Jade or Nigel did a little guesswork in the Purple Room about what she did on the weekends (if they so much as whispered, "Cottonwood"), he became fiery and short tempered as a Latin American dictator. In a matter of seconds, his entire body—face, hands too—could go the pink of Tropical Punch.

Milton, as usual, said nothing, only chuckled as he leaned against the burgundy hand towels.

"It wouldn't be a big deal," Nigel said. "Drownings are *obvious*. They can see by the skin if it's an accident or foul play and in this case, there's a high rate of drownings that are linked to alcohol. Some bombed guy falls in the water? Knocks himself out? Dies? What can you do? He did it to himself. And it happens all the time. The Coast Guard's always finding sloshed mother-fuckers floating in the ocean who had too many rum and Cokes."

"How do you know this?" I asked, though I'd read something similar in *Murder in La Havre* (Monalie, 1992).

"My mom's a huge crime fiction fanatic," he said proudly. "Diana could perform her own autopsy."

*   *   *

When we decided we weren't visibly drunk (Death had the effect of six cups of coffee and a dip in the Bering Sea), we returned to the living room. A new officer had taken charge, Officer Donnie Lee with globular, off-centered features reminiscent of a wrecked urn on a potter's wheel. He was trying to line people up "in orderly fashion, folks," with the sort of manic patience of an Activities Director on a cruise ship organizing a Shore Excursion. Gradually, the crowd ringed around the room.

"Let me go first," said Nigel. "And don't say anything. I'll give you the advice my mom gave me. No matter what happens, look like you're having a Christ experience."

Officer Donnie Lee happened to have saturated himself in Paul Revere-like cologne (it rode far ahead of him, alerting all of his impending arrival) so by the time he came to Nigel, wrote down his name, phone number, and asked, "How old are you, son?" Nigel was prepared for the impending massacre.

"Seventeen, sir."

"Uh-huh."

"I assure you Ms. Schneider knew nothing about our showing up this evening. My friends and I mistakenly thought it'd be fun to crash an adult party. To see what it was like. *Not*, let me add, to partake in illegal substances. I've been a Baptist all my life, head of my own worship circle for two years, and it's against my religion to partake in alcohol of any kind. Abstinence works well enough for me, sir."

I thought his performance campy and over-the-top, but to my surprise, he went over like Vanessa Redgrave in *Mary, Queen of Scots.* Officer Donnie Lee, those big wrinkles pressing through his great clay forehead (as if invisible hands were starting to rework him into a vase or ashtray), only tapped his end-chewed blue Bic pen on the side of his notepad.

"You kids watch yourselves. I don't wanta hear or see you in this kinda venue again. Do I make myself clear?"

Without even waiting for our "Yes, sir, absolutely, sirs," he moved on to take the contact details of the whiney Marilyn shivering next to us in her skimpy *Seven Year Itch* dress with a gruesome brown stain down the front.

"How long's this gonna take anyway? I got a babysitter."

"Ma'am, if you'd just bear with us now . . ."

Nigel grinned. "Nothing like a well-placed honey pot to attract flies," he whispered.

Officer Lee didn't let anyone leave until after 5:00 A.M. When we were finally allowed outside, we discovered a blued, tubercular morning: sky wan, grass sweaty, a cold breeze wheezing through the trees. Purple feathers roamed the lawn, chasing each other under the POLICE LINE DO NOT CROSS tape, pestering a Hulk mask playing dead.

We followed the wearied procession to the parked cars, bypassing the crowd who wanted to stay to see something (a fairy, a gorilla, a blond golfer struck by lightning), the two police cars, the empty ambulance, the paramedic with dark, sunken eyes smoking a cigarette. Gold-chromed Nefertiti in front of us prattled on and on as she wobbled down the driveway in silver heels like ice picks: "There's respons'bility comes with ownin' a puwl," she said, "second I got outta bed, I had a *bad* feelin', I'm serius."

In numb silence, we climbed into the car and waited another fifteen minutes for Jade.

"I made a statement," she said proudly as she climbed into the backseat, mashing me against Nigel as she pulled the door closed. "It was exactly like TV only the cop wasn't hot or tan."

"What was he?" asked Nigel.

Jade waited until our eyes were crawling all over her.

"Lieutenant Arnold Trask was a pig."

"You see the guy who died?" asked Milton from the front seat.

"I saw everything," she said. "What do you want to know? First thing I'll tell you, which I found *really* weird, was that he was *blue*. I'm not even kidding. And the arms and legs just flopped there. Arms and legs don't usually *flop*, you know what I mean? He was inflated like a raft. Something had blown him up a little—"

"If you don't stop I'm going to be sick," said Leulah.

"What?"

"Did you see Hannah?" asked Charles, starting the car.

"Sure," said Jade, nodding. "That was the worst of it. They brought her outside and she started screaming like some clinically insane person. One of the officers had to take her away. I felt like I was watching an after-school special about a mother who's not granted custody of her kids. After that I didn't see her. Someone said the guy from the ambulance gave her a sedative and she went to lie down."

In the pale blued morning, hundreds of bare trees crowded the guardrail, nodding at us, extending condolences. I could see Charles clenching his jaw as he turned onto the highway, heading back to Jade's. His cheek looked unusually hollow, as if someone had hacked at it with a knife. I thought about Dad, those awful instances he fell into a Bourbon Mood with *The Great White Lie* (Moon, 1969) or E. B. Carlson's *Silence* (1987) slung over his corduroy knee. He was known to mention what he rarely mentioned, how my mother died. "It was my fault," he'd tell not me but my shoulder or leg. "Honestly, sweetheart. It's disgraceful. I should have been there." (Even Dad, who prided himself on never dodging anything, like many people, preferred to address a body part when drunk and afflicted.)

And I hated those moments, when Dad's face, the one thing I secretly believed strong and permanent, fixed as volcanic rock Head Sculptures on Easter Island (if anyone was still going to be standing after nine hundred years, it'd be Dad). For a brief moment, in the kitchen, or in some corner of smudged darkness in his study, I saw him fragile and smaller somehow, human certainly, but forlorn, frail as tissue pages in a motel Bible.

Of course, he always recovered splendidly. He mocked his self-pity, quoted something about Man's worst enemy being Himself. And even though, when he stood up, he was Dad again, Dad, my Man of the Moment, my *Man Who Would Be King*, he'd been highly contagious because *I* was moody for hours afterward. It was what accidental deaths did to people, made everybody's sea floor irregular and uneven, causing tidal currents to collide, surge upwards, thereby resulting in small yet volatile eddies churning at everybody's surface. (In the more dangerous cases, it created a lasting whirlpool in which the strongest swimmers could drown.)

*   *   *

There was no dinner at Hannah's that Sunday.

I spent the weekend in a swampy mood: stifling afternoons of homework, thoughts about Death and Hannah leaching my head. I hated when people participated in what Dad called "Sing-along Sorrow" ("Everyone's eager to mourn so long as it's not *their* child who was decapitated in the car accident, not *their* husband stabbed by a gutter binger desperate for crack."); yet when I read the brief article about Smoke Harvey in *The Stockton Observer*, staring at the accompanying photo (some horrific Christmas shot: tuxedo, grin, a forehead shiny as chrome), I couldn't help but feel, if not Loss or Sadness, then a sense of Missed Conversation, what one felt on the interstate when seeing an arresting person sleeping in the passenger seat of a passing van, a secret cirrus-smudge on the window.

"So tell me," Dad said dryly, folding down a corner of *The Wall Street Journal* to look at me, "how were your Joycean hooligans? You didn't fill me in when you got home. Have you made it to Calypso yet?"

I was curled up on the couch by the window, trying to get my mind off the costume party by reading British chick-lit classic *One Night Stand* (Zev, 2002), hidden within the larger hardback *Thus Spake Zarathustra* (Nietzsche, 1883–85), for Dad's sake.

"They're fine," I said, trying to sound blasé. "How was Kitty?"

Dad had had a date with her, and the fact that their dirty wine glasses were still in the sink when I returned home (on the counter, an empty bottle of cabernet), I could presume whatever drunk delusion I'd entertained about Dad's looming presence at Hannah's party, decked in the costume he himself had said made him "look like the love child of Marie Antoinette and Liberace," was exactly that—a delusion. (Kitty wore copper lipstick, and judging from the bristly strand of hair I'd found clinging to the back of the couch in the library, she brutally assaulted her locks with Clorox. It was the color of a Yellow Page.)

Dad looked confounded by my question. "How shall I answer that? Let's see. Well, she's lively as ever."

If *I* felt the Everglades, I couldn't imagine what Great Dismal Swamp Hannah was trudging through, when she woke up in her strange blank bedroom in the night and thought about Smoke Harvey, the man whose arm she'd squeezed like a giddy teenager when she was on the stairs, a man now dead.

That Monday, however, I was marginally reassured when Milton found me at my locker after school. He said Charles had gone to see her on Sunday.

"How is she?" I asked.

"She's okay. Charles said she's still kinda in a state of shock, but otherwise peachy."

He cleared his throat, stuck his hands in his pockets with ox-in-sun slowness. I suspected Jade had recently tipped him off to my feelings—"Gag's gaga over you," I could just hear her saying, "like *so gone*, like *fixated*,"—because lately, when he looked at me, a shabby smile drifted across his face. His eyes circled over me like old flies. I suffered no hope, no daydreams, that he felt anything similar to the way I did, which wasn't lust or love ("Juliet and Romeo be damned, you can't be in *love* until you've flossed your teeth next to the person at least three hundred times," Dad said) but acute electricity. I'd spot him lumbering across the Commons; I'd feel struck by lightning. I'd see him in the Scratch and he'd say, "Howdy, Retch"; instantly I was a light bulb in a series circuit. I wouldn't have been surprised if, in Elton, when he trudged by my AP Art History class on his way to the infirmary (he was always on the verge of measles or mumps), my hair rose off my neck and stood on end.

"She wants to take us to dinner tonight," he said. "Wants to talk about what happened. Can you make it at five?"

I nodded. "I'll have to make up something good for my dad."

He squinted. "What chapter are we on?"

"Proteus."

He laughed as he turned away. His laugh was always a big bubble rising through a quagmire: one gurgle and it was gone.

*   *   *

Charles was right. Hannah *was* peachy.

At least she looked peachy initially, when Jade, Leulah and I were ushered by the maître d' into the dining room and saw her waiting for us, alone at the round table.

She'd taken the others to Hyacinth Terrace restaurant before. It was where she took them for special occasions—birthdays, holidays, someone's grand achievement on a Unit Test. The restaurant attempted, with the intensity of any dedicated Emergency Medicine physician, to resuscitate Victorian England with a "heady culinary voyage that artfully blends The Old with

The New" (see www.hyacinthterracewnc.net). Housed in a pristine green and pink Victorian house, the restaurant was perched on one side of Marengo Mountain and resembled a depressed Yellow-shouldered Amazon Parrot desperate to return to its natural habitat. Walking in, one could see no sprawling view of Stockton from the giant fan-shaped windows, nothing but that notorious local fog frothing off the greasy chimneys of Horatio Mills Gallway's old paper mill twenty-seven miles east (now Parcel Supply Corp.), a haze with a fondness for hitching a ride on a recurring Westerly and smothering Stockton's valley like a maudlin lover in a humid hug.

It was early, approximately 5:15 P.M., and Hannah was the only one in the dining room apart from an elderly couple eating by the window. A gold, five-tiered chandelier at the center of the room hung like an upside-down duchess shamelessly exposing to the paying public her ankle boots and froufrou petticoat.

"Hello," Hannah said, as we made our way to the table.

"The boys should be here in ten minutes," said Jade, sitting down. "They had to wait for Charles to finish practice."

She nodded. She wore a black turtleneck sweater, a gray wool skirt and the starched-and-pressed expression of someone running for office in the heat of an election, moments before he/she is to appear on a televised stage for a debate. There was a series of nervous gestures (a sniff, swipe of the tongue over teeth, a smoothing of skirt) and one weak attempt at conversation ("How was school?") with ensuing lack of follow-up ("I'm glad."). I could tell she was planning to say something very specific to us on this Special Occasion, and I grew worried as I watched her press her lips together and smile at her wineglass, as if mentally reviewing her cordial-yet-threatening greeting of the candidate of the opposing party.

I didn't know what to do. I pretended to be enchanted by the giant menu with the dishes floating down the page in lacy handwriting: *Puree of Parsnip-Pear Soup with Infusion of Black Truffle and Micro Greens.*

My suspicions were confirmed when Charles and the others arrived, though she waited to deliver her speech until the skinny waiter took our orders then bounded away like a deer hearing rifle shots.

"If our friendship is to continue," she said in a stiff voice, sitting too straight, sweeping her hair officially behind her shoulders, "and there were moments yesterday when I really thought it wouldn't be possible—in the future, when I tell you not to do something, *don't* do it."

Staring at each of us, she let those words march all over the table, through the hummingbird plates and the wooden napkin rings and the bottle of pinot noir, around the glass centerpiece of roses craning their thin necks and yellow heads over the rim like newly hatched chicks desperate to be fed.

"Is that clear?"

I nodded.

"Yes," said Charles.

"Yes," said Leulah.

"Mmm," said Nigel.

"What you did on Saturday was inexcusable. It hurt me. Deeply. On top of everything, everything so, so *awful* that happened, I still can't quite fathom what you did to me. That you'd put me at risk, disrespect me so—because, let me tell you, in the *only* stroke of luck that night, Eva Brewster ended up not coming because her terrier was sick. So if it weren't for a fucking *terrier* I'd be fired right now. Do you under*stand*? We'd all be fired, because if she *had* come, if she'd seen any of you, you would've been expelled. I guarantee it. I'm sure you weren't drinking fruit punch and I couldn't have pulled strings to get you out of it. No. Everything you've worked for, college, it'd be lost. And for what? A prank you thought would be *fun*? Well, it wasn't fun. It was sickening."

Her voice was too loud. Also jarring was her use of the word *fucking*, because she never swore. Yet Hyacinth Terrace gave no surprised stares, no waiterly raised eyebrows. The restaurant was meandering along like some humming grandmother refusing to accept the fact that the price of milk had gone up 600 percent since Her Day. The waiters bowed, deeply immersed in table settings, and across the room, a turnip-haired kid in a loose tuxedo walked to the piano, sat down, began to play Cole Porter.

She took a deep breath. "Since I've known each of you, I've treated you as adults. As my equals and friends. That you would treat our friendship with such flagrant contempt, it knocks the wind out of me."

"We're sorry," said Charles in a thimble-voice I'd never heard before.

She turned to him, lacing her long, manicured fingers together in perfect This-is-the-church-this-is-the-steeple architecture.

"I know you're sorry, Charles. It isn't the point. When you grow up—and from the looks of things, you have a while—you learn things never go back to normal simply because everyone's sorry. Sorry is ridiculous. A good friend of mine is *dead*. And, and I'm *upset* . . ."

Hannah's demoralizing soliloquy lasted all through the Appetizer and well into the Main Course. By the time our attending antelope sprung through the dining room to place dessert menus in front of us, we resembled a band of political dissidents in 1930s USSR after a year of laboring in Siberia and other brutal Arctic Lands. Leulah's shoulders slumped. She looked harrowingly close to collapsing. Jade did nothing but stare into her hummingbird plate. Charles looked puffy and miserable. A doomed expression had torpedoed Milton and was in the process of sinking his entire bulky body under the table. Though Nigel showed no discernible signs of either sorrow or regret, I noticed he'd been able to eat only half of his Pride Hills lamb shank and had not touched his leek whipped potatoes.

I, of course, listened to every word she said and felt renewed sadness every time she looked at me without bothering to disguise her Utter Disappointment and Disillusion. Her Utter Disappointment and Disillusion didn't seem as severe when she looked at the others, and I was certain my observation wasn't an example of Dad's "Theory of Arrogance"—that everyone always assumes they're the Principal Character of Desire and/or Loathing in everybody else's Broadway play.

Sometimes, apparently so distraught, Hannah let go of the rope of her words and came to a dead stop in a silence that stretched on and on, arid and relentless as far as the eye could see. The restaurant with its shines and clinks, its fanned napkins and resplendent forks (in which you could identify microscopic things lodged in your teeth), its dowager duchess hanging there, desperate to be let down to go dance a quadrille with an eligible man of society—it all felt indifferent and damned, hopeless as a Hemingway short story teeming with mean conversations, hopes lost between their bullet point words, voices voluptuous as rulers. Perhaps it was because on my personal timeline there was a small red rectangle positioned solely between the years 1987 and 1992, discreetly labeled NATASHA ALICIA BRIDGES VAN MEER, MOTHER, but I was aware now, as ever, that between all people there were First Times You See Them and Last Times You See Them. I felt certain this was a Last Time I See Them. We were going to have to say good-bye and this shiny place served as well a setting as any to be our terminus.

The only thing that kept me from melting onto my dessert menu was Hannah's bedroom. The objects in that room annotated her relentlessly, gave me what I felt were secret insights into her every word and dart of her eyes, every crumple in her voice. I knew it was an appallingly professorial thing to do—Hannah finishing off an entire bottle of wine by herself illustrated how distressed she was; even her hair was exhausted as it slung itself across her shoulders and stopped moving—but I couldn't help myself: I was Dad's daughter and thus prone to bibliography. Hannah's eye sockets looked gray, as if they'd been lightly shaded with one of Mr. Moats' drawing pencils.[1] She sat schoolhouse-strict.[2] When she wasn't berating us, she sighed, rubbed the stem of her wineglass between her thumb and forefinger the way commercial housewives notice dust.[3] I sensed, somewhere within the context of these singular details, within her knife collection, empty walls, shoe boxes and thatch bedspread was Hannah's Plot, her Principal Characters—most significantly, her Primary Themes. Maybe she was simply a matter of Faulkner: she had to be read very closely, word by painful word (never skimmed, pausing to make critical notes in the margin), including her bizarre digressions (costume party) and improbabilities (Cottonwood). Eventually, I'd come to her last page and discover what she was all about. Maybe I could even *Cliffs Note* her.

"Can you tell us about the man who died?" Leulah asked suddenly, without looking Hannah in the eye. "I don't mean to be nosy and I understand if you don't want to talk about it. But I think I'd sleep better if I knew a little about him. What he was like."

Rather than replying in a bleak voice that, in light of our cavalier betrayal, it certainly *was* nosy and none of her business, after a thoughtful stare at the dessert menu (her eyes fell somewhere between the Passion Fruit Sorbet and the Petit Fours), Hannah drained the rest of her wine and began a surprising and quite captivating exposition of *Smoke Wyannoch Harvey: The Life*.

---

1. A pallor hinting at acute insomnia, melancholy or the unknown illness that necessitated her having a small pharmacy in her bathroom cabinet.

2. A bearing that mimicked the stiff Quaker chair in the corner of her bedroom.

3. The tired and contemplative look on Hannah's face gave her an odd sort of fill-in-the-blankness, which made me wonder if my initial suspicions had been incorrect, that she *was*, in fact, that little round-eyed girl in the three framed photographs positioned on that bureau. And yet, why would she put *those* photos on display? The absence of her mother or father in the pictures seemed to indicate she wasn't on the cheeriest of terms with them. Yet Dad said happy photos on exhibition as a representation of deep feeling was a facile assumption; he said if a person was so insecure he/she had to have constant reassurance of all "gay ol' times," well, then "the sentiments obviously weren't all that profound to begin with." For the record, there were no framed pictures of *me* around our house, and the only class portrait Dad had ever ordered was the one from Sparta Elementary in which I'd sat, knees glued together, in front of a background that looked like Yosemite, sporting pink overalls and a lazy eye. "This is classic," Dad said. "That they shamelessly send me an order form so I can pay $69.95 for prints large and small of a photo in which my daughter looks as if she just suffered a great blow to her head—it just shows you, we are simply strapped to a motorized assembly line moving through this country. We're supposed to pay out, shut up or get tossed in the rejects bin."

"I met him in Chicago," she said, clearing her throat as the waiter vaulted forth to fill her glass with what little was left in the wine bottle. "The Valhalla chocolate cake with the . . ."

"White chocolate ice cream and caramel crème sauce?" he chirped.

"For everyone. And can I see your list of brandies?"

"Certainly, madam." He bowed and retreated into his peachy grassland of round tables and gold chairs.

"God. It was ages ago," Hannah said. She picked up her dessert spoon and began to somersault it in her fingers. "But, yes. He was a remarkable man. Excruciatingly funny. Generous to a fault. A great storyteller. Everyone wanted to be around him. When Smoke—*Dubs*, I mean, everyone important to him called him Dubs—when Dubs told a story you laughed so hard your stomach hurt. You thought you'd die."

"People who tell a good story are amazing," said Leulah sitting up eagerly in her chair.

"The house alone was straight out of *Gone with the Wind*. Enormous. White columns, you know, and a long white fence and big magnolias. Built in eighteen-something. It's in southern West Virginia, outside of Findley. He called it Moorgate. I–I can't remember why."

"Have you been to Moorgate?" asked Leulah breathlessly.

Hannah nodded. "Hundreds of times. It used to be a tobacco plantation, four thousand acres, but Smoke only has a hundred and twenty. And it's haunted. There's an awful story about the house—what was it, I can't remember. Something to do with slavery . . ."

She tilted her head, trying to remember, and we leaned forward like first graders during Story Hour.

"It was just before the Civil War. Dubs told me all of this. I guess the master's daughter, beautiful, the belle of the county, she fell in love with a slave and became pregnant with his child. When it was born, the master had the servants take it down to the basement and put it in the furnace. So every now and then, during thunderstorms, or on summer nights when there were crickets in the kitchen—Smoke was very specific about the crickets—you can hear a baby crying, way, way down in the basement. In the walls. There's also a willow tree in the front yard, which had supposedly been used for beatings, and if you go up to the trunk, carved faintly into the bark are the initials of that girl and the slave who loved each other. Dorothy Ellen, his first wife, hated the tree, thought it was evil. She was very religious. But Smoke refused to cut it down. He said you couldn't pretend the terrible things in life didn't happen. You can't clean it up. You keep all the refuse and the scars. It's how you learn. And try to make improvements."

"That's one old willow tree," Nigel said.

"Smoke was a person with a sense of history. Do you know what I mean?" She happened to be looking at me with a very intense look, so I automatically nodded. But in truth, I *did* know what she meant. Da Vinci, Martin Luther King, Jr., Genghis Kahn, Abraham Lincoln, Bette Davis—if you read their definitive biographies, you learned that even when they were a month old, cooing in some wobbly crib in the middle of nowhere, they already had something historic about them. The way other kids had baseball, long division, Hot Wheels and hula hoops, these kids had History and thus tended to be prone to colds, unpopular, sometimes plagued with a physical deformity (Lord Byron's clubfoot, Maugham's severe stutter, for example), which pushed them deep into exile in their heads. It was there they began to dream of human anatomy, civil rights, conquering Asia, a lost speech and being (within a span of only four years) a jezebel, a marked woman, a little fox and an old maid.

"He sounds dreamy," said Jade.

"Sounded," said Nigel very quietly.

"So were you two, uh . . . ?" asked Charles. He let the sentence make its own way into that renowned motel bed with sandpaper sheets and proverbial shrieking mattress.

"He was a *friend*," Hannah said. "I was too tall for him. He liked women who were little dolls, porcelain baby dolls. All of his wives, Dorothy Ellen, Clarisse, poor Janice. They were all under five feet." She giggled girlishly—a much-welcomed sound—sighed and rested her head in her hand, the pose of an unknown woman one came across in some second-hand biography, in a black-and-white photo accompanied by the caption, "At a Cuernavaca party, late 1970s." (It wasn't *her* biography, but the portly Nobel Prize–winner she sat next to; but so arresting were the dark eyes, the sleek hair, the strict expression, one wondered who she was, and didn't want to keep reading when there was no other mention of her.)

She talked on and on about Smoke Harvey, through the warm Valhalla chocolate cake, through the selection of English Farmhouse Cheeses, through two piano renditions of "I Could Have Danced All Night." She was like Keats' Grecian Urn left under a running faucet, overflowing, unable to stop herself.

The waiter returned her credit card and she still didn't stop talking. Frankly, at this point, it made me a little edgy. As Dad said famously after his first date with June Bug Betina Mendejo in Cocorro, California (Betina managed to air her every piece of Dirty Linen at Tortilla Mexicana, telling Dad how her ex-husband, Jake, stole everything from her, including her Pride and Ego): "Funnily enough, it is the subject one dreads talking about at length one ends up talking about at length, often without the slightest provocation."

"Anyone want the last selection of English Farmhouse Cheese?" asked Nigel, pausing only for a second before helping himself to the last selection of English Farmhouse Cheese.

"It was my fault," Hannah said.

"No, it's wasn't," said Charles.

She didn't hear him. Sticky redness had oozed into her face. "I invited him," she said. "We hadn't seen each other in years, exchanged a few calls, sure, but, you know, he was busy. I wanted him to come to the party. Richard, whom I work with at the shelter, had invited some of his friends from all over the world—he'd worked in the Peace Corps for thirteen years, still keeps in touch with a lot of the people he worked with. An international crowd. It was supposed to be fun. And I sensed Smoke needed a break from things. One of his daughters, Ada, had just gotten a divorce. Shirley, another daughter, had just had a baby and named it Chrysanthemum. Can you imagine, a person with the name Chrysanthemum? He called me up, howling about it. It was the last thing we talked about."

"What'd he do for a living?" asked Jade quietly.

"He was a banker," Nigel said, "but he also wrote a book, didn't he? *Devil's Treason* or something."

Again, Hannah didn't seem to hear. "The last thing we talked about was chrysanthemums," she said to the tablecloth.

The darkness in the fan-shaped window had soothed the room and the gold chairs, the fleur-de-lys wallpaper; even the dowager chandelier relaxed a little, like a family finally rid of an affluent guest and they could now squash the seat cushions, eat with their fingers, remove their stiff, uncomfortable shoes. The kid at the piano was playing, "Why Can't a Woman Be More Like a Man," which happened to be one of Dad's favorites.

"Some people are fragile as—as butterflies and sensitive and it's your responsibility not to destroy them," she went on. "Just because you *can*."

She was staring at *me* again, minute reflections of light dancing in her eyes, and I tried to smile reassuringly, but it was difficult because I could see how drunk she was. Her eyelids sagged like lazy window shades and she was trying too hard to herd her words together so they jostled, bumped, stepped all over each other.

"Grow up in a country," she said, "a house of–of privilege, endless commodity, you think you're better than other people. You think you belong to a fucking country club so you can kick people in the face on your way to acquiring more *things*." She was staring at Jade now and said *things* as if biting it off the end of a candy bar. "It takes years to overturn th–this conditioning. I tried my whole life and I *still* exploit people. I'm a pig. Show me what a man hates and I'll show you what he is. Can't remember who said that . . ."

Her voice went dead. Her teary eyes drifted toward the center of the table, bobbing around the rose centerpiece. All of us were sort of madly *eyeing* each other, holding our breaths in mutual queasiness—what people do in restaurants when a soiled drunk person walks in and starts shouting through a mouthful of kernel teeth about working for The Man. It was as if Hannah had sprung a leak and her character, usually so meticulous and contained, was spilling all over the place. I'd never seen her speak or behave in this way, and I doubted the others had either; they stared at her with sickened yet fascinated expressions, as if watching crocodiles mate on the Nature Channel.

Her teeth snagged her bottom lip, there was a little manifestoed frown between her eyebrows. I was deathly afraid she'd go on about needing to go live on a kibbutz or relocating to Vietnam where she'd become a hash-smoking beatnik ("Hanoi Hannah," we'd have to call her) or else she'd turn on us, chastise us for being like our parents, odious and square. Even more frightening was the possibility she might cry. Her eyes were wet, murky tide-pools where things unseen lived and glowed. I felt there were few things in the world more horrific than the adult weep—not the rogue tear during a long-distance commercial, not the stately sob at a funeral, but the cry on the bathroom floor, in the office cubicle, in the two-car garage with one's fingers frantically pressing down on one's eyelids as if there was an ESC key somewhere, a RETURN.

But Hannah didn't cry. She lifted her head, looking around the dining room with the confused expression of someone who'd just woken up in a bus station with seams and the button of a shirtsleeve imprinted on her forehead. She sniffed.

"Let's get out of this fucking place," she said.

*   *   *

For the rest of the week, even a little bit after that, I noticed Smoke Wyannoch Harvey, age 68, was still sort of alive.

Hannah had brought him back to life like Frankenstein his Monster by her deluge of detail, and thus, in all of our heads (even that of the painfully pragmatic Nigel) Smoke didn't really seem dead, but simply offstage somewhere, kidnapped.

Jade, Leulah, Charles and Milton had been outside on the patio as Smoke lurched to his death (Nigel and I simply told the others we were "amusing ourselves inside," which technically was the truth). They were plagued by the If Onlys.

"If only I'd been paying attention," said Lu.

"If only *I* hadn't smoked the rest of that joint," said Milton.

"If only I hadn't been hitting on Lacey Laurels from Spartanburg who just graduated from Spartan Community College with a major in Fashion Merchandizing," said Charles.

"Oh, *pu-leese*," said Jade rolling her eyes, turning to stare at the freshmen and sophomores standing in line to buy their two-dollar hot chocolates. They appeared to be afraid of her gaze, as certain diminutive mammals must tremble at the thought of a Golden Eagle.

"*I'm* the one who was *there*. How hard is it to notice some green polyester person floating facedown in a pool? I could have dived in and *saved* the man, done one of those good deeds that more or less guarantees entry through the Pearly Gates. But *no*, now I'm going to suffer from Post Traumatic Stress. I mean, it's a possibility I never get over this. Not for years and years. And when I'm thirty I'll have to be submitted into some asylum, with the walls all green and I wander around in an unflattering nightgown with hairy legs because they don't allow razors in case you feel the urge to tiptoe into the communal bathroom and slit your wrists."

That Sunday, I was relieved to find Hannah back to her old self, spiriting around the house in a red-and-white floral housedress.

"Blue!" she called cheerfully as Jade and I walked through the front door. "Good to see you! How is everything?"

Hannah neither commented on, nor apologized for, her tipsy behavior at Hyacinth Terrace, which was fine, because I wasn't so sure she *needed* to apologize. Dad said certain people's sanity, in order to maintain a healthy equilibrium, required getting messy once in a while, what he called "going

Chekhovian." Some people, every now and then, simply *had* to have One Too Many, go drifty voiced and slouch mouthed, swimming willfully around in their own sadness as if it were hot springs. "Once a year, they say Einstein had to blow off steam by getting so inebriated on *hefeweizen,* he was known to go skinny-dipping at 3:00 A.M. in Carnegie Lake," Dad said. "And it's perfectly understandable. You carry the weight of the world on your shoulders, in his case, the unification of all space and time—you can imagine it'd get quite exhausting."

Smoke Harvey's death—*any* death, for that matter—was as perfectly noble a reason as any for words to stagger out of one's mouth, for eyes to take almost as much time to blink as it takes for an old man with a cane to descend stairs—especially if, afterward, you looked as epically spic and span as Hannah did. She busied herself with Milton setting the table, slipping into the kitchen to remove a shrieking kettle from the stove, swooping back into the dining room and, as she speedily folded the dinner napkins into cute geisha fans, holding a glorious smile up to her face like a glass during a wedding toast.

And yet, I must have been overly zealous in my attempt to convince myself Hannah was all Fiddle Dee Dee and La Dee Da, that our dinners would return to the weightlessness of Pre-Cottonwood, Pre-costume party days. Or maybe it was the other way around. Maybe Hannah was trying too hard to make things chic and upbeat, and it was akin to beautifying one's cell; no matter what kind of curtains you hung, or rug you placed by your cot, it was still prison.

The Stockton Observer had published the second and final article on Smoke Harvey that day, detailing what we'd already assumed, that his death had been an accident. There'd been "no indication of trauma to the body" and his "blood-alcohol level had been .23, nearly three times the North Carolina legal limit of .08." It seemed he'd inadvertently fallen into the pool, been too drunk to swim or cry for help and, in less than ten minutes, he'd drowned. Hannah had been so eager to tell us about Smoke at Hyacinth Terrace, and was in such well-adjusted spirits *now,* I don't think Nigel thought twice about bringing him up again.

"You know the number of drinks Smoke would've had to knock back to get his BAC to that level?" he asked us, tapping the end of his pencil against his chin. "I mean, we're talking, for a man about what? Two hundred and fifty pounds? Like, ten drinks in an hour."

"Maybe he was doing shots," said Jade.

"I wish the article said more about the autopsy."

Hannah spun around from the coffee table, where she'd just placed the tray of oolong tea.

"For God's sake! Stop it!"

There was a long silence.

I find it difficult to sufficiently describe how strange, how disconcerting her voice was in that moment. It was neither outright angry (though anger was certainly in there somewhere) nor exasperated, neither weary nor bored, but *strange* (with the "a" of that word drawn out in "ayyy").

Without saying anything more, head down, her hair quickly falling over the sides of her face like a curtain when a magic trick goes wrong, she vanished into the kitchen.

We stared at each other.

Nigel shook his head, stunned. "First she gets sloshed at Hyacinth Terrace. Now she just *snaps*—?"

"You are a fucking asshole," said Charles through his teeth.

"Keep your voices down," Milton said.

"Hold on, though," Nigel went on excitedly. "That was exactly what she did when I asked her about Valerio. Remember?"

"It's Rosebud again," Jade said. "Smoke Harvey's another Rosebud. Hannah has *two* Rosebuds—"

"Let's not get graphic," said Nigel.

"Shut the fuck up," said Charles angrily. *"All* of you, I—"

The door thumped and Hannah emerged from the kitchen carrying a platter of sirloin steaks.

"I'm sorry, Hannah," Nigel said. "I shouldn't have said that. Sometimes I get caught up in the drama of a situation and I don't think about how it sounds. How it might hurt someone. Forgive me." His voice I thought a little hollow and bland, but he went over with rave reviews.

"It's okay," Hannah said. And then her smile appeared, a promising little towrope for all of us to grab onto. (You wouldn't be surprised at all if she said, "When I lose my temper, honey, you can't find it anyplace," or "It's the kissiest business in the world," one hand poised in the air, holding an invisible martini.) She brushed Nigel's hair off his forehead. "You need a haircut."

We never mentioned Smoke Wyannoch Harvey, age 68, around her again. And thus concluded his Lazarus-like resurrection, fuelled by her boozey Hyacinth Terrace monologue, our If Onlys and Might Have Dones. Out of empathy for Hannah (who, as Jade said, "must feel like a person who killed someone in a car accident") we tactfully returned the Great Man—a latter-day Greek hero, I liked to imagine, an Achilles, or an Ajax prior to going mad ("Dubs lived the lives of a hundred people, all at once," Hannah had said, baton-twirling that dessert spoon expertly in her fingers like a late-night Swingin' Door Suzie)—to that unknown place people go when they die, to silence and ever afters, to cursivy The Ends materializing out of black-and-white streets and his-and-her deliriously happy faces pressed together against a soundtrack of scratchy strings.

Rather, we returned him there for the time being.

Women in Love

I'd like to make a minor adjustment to Leo Tolstoy's oft-quoted first sentence: "All happy families resemble one another, but each unhappy family is unhappy in its own way, *and when it comes to the Holiday Season, happy families can abruptly become unhappy and unhappy families can, to their great alarm, be happy.*"

The Holiday Season was, without fail, a special time for the Van Meers.

Since I was very small, over any December dinner, during which Dad and I cooked our acclaimed spaghetti with meat sauce (J. Chase Lamberton's *Political Desire* [1980] and L. L. MacCaulay's 750-page *Intelligensia* [1991] were also known to join us), Dad was fond of asking me to explain, in great detail, how my latest school was getting into the Holiday Mood. There was Mr. Pike and his Infamous Yule Log in Brimmsdale, Texas, and Santa's Secret Shoppe in the Cafeteria Featuring Twisty Rainbow Candles and Crude Jewelry Boxes in Sluder, Florida, the Forty-Eight-Hour Toymaker Village Hideously Vandalized by Spiteful Seniors in Lamego, Ohio, and one appalling recital in Boatley, Illinois, "The Christ Child Story: A Mrs. Harding Musical." For some reason, this subject made me as sidesplitting as Stan Laurel in a two-reel comedy for Metro in 1918. Within minutes, Dad was in stitches.

"For the life of me," he said between howls, "I cannot comprehend why no producer has realized its untapped potential as a horror movie, *Nightmare of the American Christmas* and such. There's even enormous commercial promise for a number of sequels and television spin-offs. *St. Nick's Resurrection, Part 6: The Final Nativity.* Or perhaps, *Rudolph Goes to Hell* with a certain ominous tagline, '*Don't* Be Home for Christmas.'"

"Dad, it's a time of good *cheer*."

"So I am thus inspired to good cheerfully inject fuel into the U.S. economy by purchasing things I don't need and can't afford—most of which will have funny little plastic parts that suddenly snap off, rendering it inoperative within weeks—thereby digging myself a debt of elephantine proportions, causing me extreme anxiety and sleepless nights yet, more importantly, arousing a sexy economic growth period, hoisting up droopy interest rates, breeding jobs, the bulk of which are inessential and able to be executed faster, cheaper and with greater precision by a Taiwanese-manufactured central processing unit. Yes, Christabel. I *know* what time it is."

Ebenezer had very little criticism and no remarks at all on "the plague of American consumerism," "corporate gluttons and their Botswana-sized bonuses" (not even a passing allusion to one of his choice social theories, that of the "Tinseled American Dream") when I detailed how lavishly St. Gallway was celebrating the season. Every banister (even the one in Loomis, Hannah's banished building) was wrapped in boughs of pine, thick and bristly as a lumberjack's mustache. Massive wreaths had been posted Reformation-style with what had to be iron spikes to the great wooden doors of Elton, Barrow and Vauxhall. There was a Goliath Christmas tree, and, looping around the iron gates of Horatio Way, white lights blinking like demented fireflies. A brass menorah, staunch and skeletal, flickering at the end of second-floor Barrow stalwartly staved off, as best it could, Gallway's Christian proclivities (AP World History professor Mr. Carlos Sandborn was responsible for this brave line of defense). Sleigh bells the size of golf balls fell around the handles of Hanover's main doors and they jingle-sighed every time a kid hurried through them, late for class.

I believe it was the sheer force of the school's festivities that allowed me to set the uneasiness of the preceding weeks a little bit off to the side, pretend it wasn't there like a largish stack of unopened mail (which, when finally confronted at a belated date, indicated I'd have to declare bankruptcy). Besides, if Dad was to be believed, the American holidays were a time for "coma-inspired denial" anyway, an occasion of "pretending the working poor, widespread famine, unemployment and the AIDS crisis were simply exotic, tart little fruits that, mercifully, were out of season," and thus I wasn't completely responsible for letting Cottonwood, the costume party, Smoke, the unusual behavior of Hannah herself be upstaged by the encroaching cloud of Finals Week, Perón's used clothing drive (the kid who brought in the most trash bags of clothes won a Brewster's Gold Ticket, ten points added onto any Final Exam; "Hefty Cinch Sak Lawn and Leaf Bags," she roared during Morning Announcements, "Thirty-nine gallons!") and, most dizzying of all, Student Council President Maxwell Stuart's pet project, the Christmas formal, which he'd rechristened "Maxwell's Christmas Cabaret."

Love, too, had something to do with it.

Unfortunately, little of it was my own.

* * *

The first week of December, during second period Study Hall, a freshman entered the library and approached the desk in the back where Mr. Fletcher sat working on a crossword.

"Headmaster Havermeyer needs to see you immediately," the boy said. "It's an emergency."

Mr. Fletcher, visibly annoyed he'd been pried away from *The X-word X-pert's Final Face-off* (Pullen, 2003), was led out of the library and up the hill toward Hanover.

"This is it!" shrieked Dee. "Fletcher's wife, Linda, has finally attempted suicide because Frank would rather do a crossword than have *sex*. It's her cry for help!"

"It *is*," cooed Dum.

A minute later, Floss Cameron-Crisp, Mario Gariazzo, Derek Pleats and a junior I didn't know the name of (though from his alert expression and soggy mouth he looked like some sort of Pavlovian response) entered the library with a CD player, a microphone with amplifier and stand, a bouquet of red roses and a trumpet case. They proceeded to set up for a rehearsal of some kind, plugging in the CD player and microphone, relocating the tables in the very front to the side wall by the Hambone Bestseller Wish List. This included relocating Sibley "Little Nose" Hemmings.

"Maybe I don't *want* to move," Sibley said, wrinkling her perky, symmetrical nose, which, according to Dee and Dum, had been handcrafted for her face by an Atlanta plastic surgeon who'd fashioned a host of other high-quality facial features for some CNN anchors and an actress on *Guiding Light*. "Maybe *you* should move. Who are you to tell me? Hey, don't touch that!"

Floss and Mario unceremoniously picked up Sibley's desk scattered with her personal belongings—her suede purse, a copy of *Pride and Prejudice* (unread), two fashion magazines (read)—and carried it to the wall. Derek Pleats, a member of the Jelly Roll Jazz Band (with whom I also had AP Physics), was standing off to the side with his trumpet, playing ascending and descending scales. Floss started to roll back the cruddy mustard carpet and Mario crouched over the CD player, adjusting the sound levels.

"Excuse me," said Dee, standing up, walking over to Floss, crossing her arms, "but what exactly do you think you're doing? Is this an attempt at anarchy, to like, gain control of the school?"

"Because we'll tell you right now," said Dum, striding over to Floss, crossing her arms next to Dee, "it's not going to work. If you want to start a movement you'll have to plan better because Hambone's in her office and she'll summon the authoritates in no time."

"If you want to make a strong personal statement, I suggest you save it for Morning Announcements when the whole school is all in one place and can be held captive."

"Yep. So you can make your demandations."

"And the administration knows you're all a force to be reckoned with."

"So you can't be *ignored*."

Floss and Mario acknowledged neither Dee nor Dum's demandations as they secured the rolled-back rug with a few extra chairs. Derek Pleats was gently shining his trumpet with a soft purple rag and the Pavlovian response, tongue out, was absorbed with checking the microphone and amplifier: "Testing, testing, one, two, three." Satisfied, he signaled to the others and all four of them huddled together, whispering, nodding excitedly (Derek Pleats doing fast flexing exercises with his fingers). Finally, Floss turned, picked up the bouquet and without saying a word, he handed it to me.

"Oh, my God," said Dee.

I held the flowers dumbly in front of me as Floss spun on his heels and jogged away, disappearing around the corner in front of the library doors.

"Aren't you going to open the card?" Dee demanded.

I ripped open the small, cream-colored envelope and pulled out a note. The words were written in a woman's handwriting.

LET'S GROOVE.

"What's it say?" asked Dum, leaning over me.

"It's some kind of threat," said Sibley.

By now everyone in second period Study Hall—Dee, Dum, Little

Nose, the horse-faced Jason Pledge, Mickey "Head Rush" Gibson, Point Richardson—swarmed around my table. Huffing, Little Nose grabbed the card and reviewed it with a pitying look on her face, as if it was my Guilty verdict. She passed it to Head Rush, who smiled at me and passed it to Jason Pledge, who passed it to Dee and Dum who huddled over the thing as if it were a piece of WWII intelligence encrypted by the German Enigma Cipher Machine.

"Too weird," said Dee.

"Totally—"

Suddenly, they were quiet. I looked up to see Zach Soderberg bent over me like a windswept rhododendron, his hair plummeting dangerously across his forehead. I felt as if I hadn't seen him in *years*, probably because ever since he'd talked to me about A Girl, I'd gone out of my way to look zealously preoccupied in AP Physics. I'd also strong-armed Laura Elms into being my laboratory partner until the end of the year by offering to write up *her* lab reports as well as mine, never copying or even using an identical turn of phrase (in which case I'd be suspended for cheating), but faithfully adopting Laura's restricted vocabulary, illogical mind-set and blubbery calligraphy when I wrote the report. Zach, no longer wanting to partner with his ex, Lonny, had to partner with my old partner Krista Jibsen who never did her homework because she was saving for a breast reduction. Krista worked three jobs, one at Lucy's Silk and Other Fine Fabrics, one at Bagel World and one in the Outdoors department at Sears, the minimum-waged drudgery of which she felt pertinent to the study of Energy and Matter. Thus we all knew when one of her coworkers was new, late, sick, stealing, let go, jerking off in the storeroom, also that one of her managers (if I remember correctly, some poor overseer at Sears) was in love with her and wanted to leave his wife.

Floss reached down and pressed the Play button on the CD player. Robotic sounds from a 1970s disco exploded out of the speakers. To my infinite horror, while watching me (as if on my face he could see his reflection, monitor his tempo, the height of his kicks), Zach began to take two steps forward, two steps back, pulsing his knees, the boys shadowing him.

" 'Let this groove. Get you to move. It's alright. Alright," Zach and the others sang in falsetto along with Earth, Wind & Fire. " 'Let this groove. Set in your shoes. So stand up, alright! Alright!' "

They sang "Let's Groove." Floss and the boys shrugged, snapped and foxtrotted with such concentration, one could almost see the moves running through their brains like Stock Exchange ticker tape (*kick left front, touch back left, kick left, step left, kick right front, knee right).* "I'll be there, after a while, if you want my looove. We can boogie on down! On *down!* Boogie on *down!*" Derek on his trumpet was playing a rudimentary melody. Zach sang solo with the occasional side step and shoulder lunge. His voice was earnest yet awful. He spun in place. Dee squeaked like a crib toy.

A sizable crowd of sophomores and juniors gathered in front of the library doors, watching the Boy Band with their mouths open. Mr. Fletcher reappeared with Havermeyer, and Ms. Jessica Hambone, the librarian, who'd been married four times and resembled Joan Collins in her more recent years, had emerged from her office and was now standing by the Hambone Reserves Desk. Obviously, she'd intended to shut down the disturbance because shutting down disturbances, with the exception of fire drills and lunch, was the only reason Ms. Hambone ever emerged from her office, where she allegedly spent her day shopping www.QVC.com for Easter Limited-quantity Collectibles and Goddess Glamour Jewelry. But she wasn't coming over to the scene with her arms in the air, her favorite words, "This is a library, people, not a gym," darting out of her mouth like Neon Tetra, her metallic green eye shadow (complimenting her Enchanted Twilight Leverback earrings, her Galaxy Dreamworld bracelet) reacting against the overhead fluorescent lights to give her that explicit Iguana Look for which she was famous. No, Ms. Hambone was speechless, hand pressed against her chest, her wide mouth, deeply lip-lined like the chalk outline of a body at a crime scene, curled into a soft, wisteria-fairy-pin of a smile.

The boys were diligently Lindy Hopping behind Zach, who spun in place again. Ms. Hambone's left hand twitched.

At last, the music faded and they froze.

It was silent for a moment, and then everyone—the kids at the door, Ms. Hambone, those in second period Study Hall (all except Little Nose)—erupted into mind-numbing applause.

"Oh, my *God*," said Dee.

"That did *so* not happen," said Dum.

I clapped and beamed as everyone stared at me with big astonished faces as if I were a Crop Circle. I beamed at Ms. Hambone dabbing her eyes with the frilly cuff of her Rococo poet's blouse. I beamed at Mr. Fletcher who looked so happy you'd think he just finished an exceptionally grueling crossword, like last week's Battle of Bunker Hill, "Not Waving but Drowning?" I even beamed at Dee and Dum, who were staring at me with incredulous yet fearful looks on their faces (see Rosemary at the end of *Rosemary's Baby* when the old people shout, *"Hail Satan!"*).

"Blue van Meer," said Zach. He cleared his throat and approached my desk. The fluorescent lights made a soured halo around his hair so he looked like a hand-painted Jesus one finds hanging on clammy walls of churches that smell of Gruyère. "How about going to the Christmas formal with me?"

I nodded and Zach didn't pick up on my acute reluctance and horror. A Cadillac-sized smile drove away with his face as if I'd just agreed to pay him "in cayash," as Dad would say, for a Sedona Beige Metallic Pontiac Grand Prix, fully loaded, two grand over sticker price, driving it off the lot right then and there. He also didn't pick up on—no one did—the fact that I was experiencing a very severe lost *Our Town* feeling, which only intensified when Zach left the library with his Temptations, a supremely satisfied look on his face (Dad had described a similar look on Zwambee tribesmen in Cameroon after they'd impregnated their tenth bride).

"Think they've had *sex?*" asked Dum with slitty eyes. She was sitting with her sister a few feet behind me.

"If they had sex, you think he'd be skadiddiling over her? It's publicized knowledge the nanosecond you have sex with a guy you go from being a headline to being all blurbatized in the obituary section. He just Timber-laked in front of our *very eyes.*"

"She must be insane in bed. She must be man's best friend."

"It takes six Vegas strippers and a leash to be man's best friend."

"Maybe her mom works at The Crazy Horse." They began to laugh shrilly, not even bothering to quiet down when I turned around to glare at them.

Dad and I had seen *Our Town* (Wilder, 1938) during a torrential down-pour at the University of Oklahoma at Flitch (one of his students was making his Flitch stage debut as the Stage Manager). Although the play had its share of faults (there seemed to be great confusion with the address, as "In the Eye of God" came before "New Hampshire") and Dad found the carpe diem premise much too syrupy ("Wake me up if someone gets shot," he said as he nodded off), I still found myself more than a little moved when Emily Webb, played by a tiny girl with hair the color of sparks off railroad tracks, realized no one could see her, when she knew she had to say good-bye to Grover's Corners. In my case, though, it was skewed. I felt invisible though *every*one had seen me, and if Zach Soderberg and his mantelpiece hair were Grover's Corners, I could think of nothing I'd rather do than get the hell out of town.

This grim feeling reached a record high when, that same day, as I walked to AP Calculus in Hanover I passed Milton walking hand in hand with Joalie Stuart, a sophomore, one of those highly petite girls who could fit into a carry-on suitcase and look at home on a Shetland pony. She had a baby-rattle laugh: a jelly-bean sound that irked even if you were minding your own business about a light year away. Jade had informed me Joalie and Black were a magnificently happy couple in the Newman and Woodward tradition. "Nothing will come between those two," she said with a sigh.

"Hey there, Hurl," Milton said as he passed me.

He smiled and Joalie smiled. Joalie was wearing a blue icing sweater and a thick brown velvet headband that looked like a giant woolly worm was rummaging behind her ears.

I'd never contemplated relationships very much (Dad said they were preposterous if I was under twenty-one and when I was over twenty-one Dad considered it Fine Points, Minutiae, a question of transportation or ATM location in a new town; "We'll figure it out when we get there," he said with a wave of his hand) and yet, in that moment, when I moved past Milton and Joalie, both of them smiling confidently in spite of the fact at distances greater than fifteen feet they looked like a gorilla walking a teacup Yorkie, I actually felt awed by the remote possibilities of the person *you* liked ever liking you back a corresponding amount. And this mathematical conundrum started its long division in my head at breakneck speed, so by the time I sat down in the front row of AP Calculus and Ms. Thermopolis at the dry-erase board was trying to wrestle to the ground a robust function from our homework, I was left with a disturbing number.

I suppose it was why, after years of playing the odds, some people cashed in their measly chips for their Zach Soderberg, the kid who was like a cafeteria, so rectangular and brightly lit there wasn't a millimeter of exciting murk or thrilling secret (not even under the plastic chairs or behind the vending machines). The only saturnine miasma to be found in him was maybe a bit of mold on the orange Jell-O. The boy was all creamed spinach and stale hot dog.

You couldn't make a grisly shadow on his wall if you tried.

* * *

I suppose it was just one of those December *Dog Day Afternoons*, when Love and its wired cousins—Lust, Crush, Eat Up, Have It Bad (all of whom suffered from ADHD or Hyperkinetic Syndrome) were on the loose and in heat, terrorizing the neighborhood. Later that day, when Dad dropped me at home before heading back to the university for a faculty meeting, I was only five minutes into my homework when the telephone rang. I picked it up and no one said anything. A half hour later, when it rang again, I switched on the answering machine.

"Gareth. It's me. Kitty. Look, I need to talk to you." *Click.*

Less than forty-five minutes later, she called again. Her voice was cratered and barren as the moon, exactly as Shelby Hollow's voice had been, and Jessie Rose Rubiman's before her, and Berkley Sternberg's, old Berkley who used *The Art of Guiltless Living* (Drew, 1999) and *Take Control of Your Life* (Nozzer, 2004) as coasters for her potted African violets.

"I–I know you don't like it when I call, but I *do* need to speak to you, Gareth. I have a feeling you're home and choosing not to pick up. Pick up the phone."

She waited.

Whenever they waited, I always pictured them on the other end, standing in their yellowed kitchens, twisting the telephone cord around an index finger so it turned red. I wondered why it never occurred to them *I* was the one listening, not Dad. I think if one of them had said my name, I would've picked up and done my best to console them, explained that Dad was one of those theories you could never know for certain, never prove beyond a reasonable doubt. And though there was a chance you could be struck by the lightning of genius it took to solve the man, the odds were so infinitesimal, so unbearable, the act of trying only had the effect of making one feel very small (see Chapter 53, "Superstrings and M-Theory, or Mystery Theory, the Theory of Everything," *Incongruities*, V. Close, 1998).

"Okay. Call me when you get a chance. I'm at home. But you can reach me on my mobile if I go out. I might go out. I need eggs. On the other hand, I might stay home and make tacos. Okay. Forget this message. Speak to you soon."

In a seemingly astute statement Socrates wrote, "The hottest love has the coldest end." By these words, by their very definition—because I'm sure Dad never lied to them, never pretended his affections were anything not perfectly encapsulated by the words *lackadaisical* and *lukewarm*—every one of Dad's ends should have been a sun-drenched, rosy affair. They should have been polo matches. They should have been picnics.

I don't think Dad ever quite understood it himself, treating these sobs as he did, with a muddle of embarrassment and regret. When he came home that night, he did what he always did. He played the messages (turning down the volume when he realized who it was) and deleted them.

"Have you eaten, Christabel?" he asked.

He knew I'd heard her messages, but like Emperor Claudius in 54 A.D. upon hearing the thrum of Roman rumor that his dear wife, Agrippina, was plotting to poison him with a dish of mushrooms presented to him by his favorite eunuch, for some unknown reason, Dad chose to ignore these signs of impending doom (see *Lives of the Caesars*, Suetonius, 121 A.D.).

He never learned.

*　　*　　*

Two weeks later, the Saturday night of Maxwell's Christmas Cabaret, I was being unlawfully detained at Zach Soderberg's house. I was wearing one of Jefferson Whitestone's old black cocktail dresses, which Jade claimed Valentino himself had designed specifically for her, though when they feuded for the affections of "a shirtless bartender at Studio 54 named Gibb," she'd furiously ripped out the label, leaving the dress an amnesiac. ("This is how empires fall," Jade had said, sighing dramatically as she and Leulah pinned the armholes and waist so the thing no longer fit like a life jacket. "Trust me. You start breeding with the nimrods and that's the end of your civilization. But I suppose you couldn't help it. I mean, he asked you in front of all the whole *school*. What could you say, except that you'd be ecstatic to be his saltine? I feel sorry for *you*. That you have to spend an entire evening with the coupon." It's what they called Zach now, "the coupon," and it fit him. He really *was* all bar code, all Great Savings, all $5-Off with Proof of Purchase.)

"Have some bonbons," said Zach's dad, Roger, holding out a bowl of powdery chocolates.

"Don't force her to eat," said Zach's mom, Patsy, shooing his hand.

"You like chocolate? You must. Everyone likes chocolate."

"Roger," protested Patsy. "No girl wants to eat before a party, when she's got the jitters! *Later's* when she gets the munchies. Zach, make sure she eats something."

"Okay," said Zach, blushing like a nun. He raised his eyebrows and tossed me a repentant smile as Patsy got down on one knee in the snowdrift carpet of the living room and squinted at us through the Nikon's viewfinder.

Unbeknownst to Patsy, Roge had moved to my left and was holding out the ceramic bowl again.

"*Go on*," he mouthed, winking. It seemed Roge, in his yellow cotton sweater and khaki pants—creases down each leg, clear cut as the International Date Line—would make a very convincing wholesaler of junk, white girl, afghan black, billy whiz and joy powder.

I obliged, took one. It began to melt in my hand.

"*Roger!*" said Patsy, *tisking* (two dimples snagging her cheeks) as she took what was now our sixteenth picture, this one with Zach and me on the floral couch, our knees positioned at a perfect ninety degrees.

Patsy was a self-proclaimed "picture nut," and all around us, covering every hard, flat surface like thousands of wet, unraked leaves in a gazebo, were framed photos of skew-smiled Zach, urn-eared Bethany Louise, a few with Roge when he had sideburns and Patsy when her hair was a redder brown, which she wore as an amaretto bundt cake atop her head, drizzled with ribbons. The only hard, flat surface in the living room devoid of pictures—the coffee table in front of us—supported a paused game of Parcheesi.

"I hope Zach didn't embarrass you with his dance," said Patsy.

"Not at all," I said.

"He was practicing all the time. So *nervous*! He had Bethany Louise up all hours of the night going over the steps."

"Mom," said Zach.

"He knew it was risky," said Roge. "But I told him to take that leap of faith."

"It runs in the family," said Patsy, nodding toward Roge. "You should have seen this one when he proposed."

"Sometimes you just can't help yourself."

"Thank goodness for that!"

"Mom, we should get going," said Zach.

"All right! All right! One more by the window."

"Mom."

"Just one. There's gorgeous light over there. One. I promise."

I'd never been inside a household full of ! and even more !!! I wasn't even aware these nests of goodwill, these bubble baths of clasps and cuddles actually existed, except in one's head when one compared one's own fitful family to the seemingly blissful one across the street.

An hour ago, as Zach and I drove up the driveway and I saw his wooden house—up-front as an open-faced sandwich, served to the sky on skinny wooden stilts—Patsy in her beetle-green blouse scurried down the porch steps to greet us before Zach had even parked the car ("You said she was pretty, you didn't say *drop dead!* Zach never tells us anything!" she exclaimed. And that was her voice, even when she wasn't greeting people on the driveway, an exclaimation).

Patsy was pretty (though some twenty-five pounds heavier than her bundt cake days) with a cheerful, round face suggestive of a fresh vanilla cake blessed with a cherry and placed lovingly in a sweet shoppe's window. Roge was handsome, but in the opposite way of Dad. Roge (Have enough gas in the car Zachary, Just had her filled, Good boy) displayed the sparkling air of a brand new bathroom fixture in sought-after White Heat tile. He had sparkling blue eyes and skin so clear, you almost expected to see your own reflection winking back at you when you peered into his face.

Finally, after logging photo number twenty-two (Patsy made that word all her own, *foe-toe*) Zach and I were finally granted permission to leave. We were heading out of the living room into the neat beige foyer when Roge stealthily passed me a cloth napkin full of bonbons he ostensibly hoped I'd traffic out of the house.

"Oh, wait," said Zach. "I wanted to show Blue the Turner. I think she'd like it."

"Of course!" said Patsy, clapping her hands.

"Just for a second," Zach said to me.

Grudgingly, I followed him up the stairs.

For the record, Zach had held up remarkably well during his encounter with Dad when he picked me up in his Toyota. He'd shaken Dad's hand (from the looks of things it wasn't a "wet washcloth," Dad's pet peeve), called him "Sir," jumpstarted a conversation about what a beautiful night it was going to be and what Dad did for a living. Dad gave him the thrice-over and answered in stark replies that would've frightened Mussolini: *"Is it?"* and *"I teach civil war."* Other dads would have felt sorry for Zach, recalling their own wobbly days of adolescence, and they'd take pity, try to Make the Kid Feel Comfortable. Unfortunately, Dad decided to Make the Kid Feel Small and Less Than a Man, simply because Zach hadn't known, innately, what Dad did for a living. Even though Dad knew the readership of *Federal Forum* was less than 0.3 percent of the United States and hence only a handful of individuals had scoured his essays or noted his romantic (a June Bug would say "rugged" or "dashing") black-and-white *foe-toe* on display in "Contributors of

Note," Dad *still* didn't like to be reminded that he and his educational efforts weren't as recognizable as say, Sylvester Stallone and *Rocky*.

Yet Zach displayed the optimism of a cartoon.

"*Midnight*," decreed Dad as we walked outside. "I *mean* it."

"You have my word, Mr. Van Meer!"

At this point, Dad wasn't bothering to hide his You've-Got-to-Be-Kidding face, which I ignored, though it quickly dissolved into his This-Is-the-Winter-of-My-Discontent look, and then, Shoot-If-You-Must-This-Old-Gray-Head.

"Your dad's nice," Zach said as he started the car. (Dad was an infinite number of things, yet clammy handed, sigh-by-night Nice was the one thing the man absolutely wasn't.)

Now I trailed after him, down the airless, carpeted hallway, which he presumably shared with his sister if one went by the his-n-her hallkill along the floor and the onslaught of sibling odor (smell of athletic socks bullying peach perfume, cologne competing with fumes off a limp gray sweatshirt and threatening to go tell mom). We walked by what had to be Bethany Louise's room, painted gum pink, a pile of clothes on the floor (see "Mount McKinley," *Almanac of Major Landmarks*, 2000 ed.). We then passed a second bedroom, and through the crack of the not-quite-closed door I made out blue walls, trophies, a poster of an overcooked blonde in a bikini. (Without much imagination, I could fill in the other obvious detail: held captive under the mattress, a ravished *Victoria's Secret* catalogue with the majority of its pages stuck together.)

At the end of the hall, Zach stopped. In front of him was a small painting, no bigger than a porthole, illuminated by a crooked gold light on the wall.

"So my father's a minister at the First Baptist Church. And when he did one of his sermons last year, 'The Fourteen Hopes,' there was a man in the congregation visiting from Washington, D.C. A guy by the name of Cecil Roloff. Well, this guy was so inspired he told my dad afterward he was a changed man." Zach pointed at the painting. "So a week later this came by UPS. And it's real. You know Turner, the artist?"

Obviously I was familiar with the "King of Light," otherwise known as J.M.W. Turner (1775–1851), having read Alejandro Penzance's eight hundred-page X-rated biography of the man, published only in Europe, *Poor and Decayed Male Artist Born in England* (1974).

"It's called *Fishermen at Sea*," Zach said.

Nimbly I stepped around the pair of green plastic gym shorts dead on the floor and leaned in to examine it. I guessed it probably *was* real, though it wasn't one of the "light fests" where the artist "screwed convention and took painting by the testicles," as Penzance described Turner's hazy, almost completely abstract work (p. viii, Introduction). This painting was an oil, yet dark, depicting a tiny boat seemingly lost in a storm at sea, painted in hazy grays, browns and greens. There were slurpy waves, a wooden boat forceful as a matchbox, a moon, wan and small and a little bit of an acrophobe as it peered fretfully through the clouds.

"Why is it hanging up here?" I asked.

He laughed shyly. "Oh, my mom wants it close to my sister and me. She says it's healthy to sleep close to art."

"A very interesting use of light," I said. "Faintly reminiscent of *The Burning of the Houses of Lords and Commons*. Especially in the sky. But a different palette obviously."

"My favorite part's the clouds." Zach swallowed. A soup spoon had to be stuck in his throat. "Know what?"

"What."

"You kind of remind me of that boat."

I looked at him. His face was about as cruel as a peanut butter sandwich with the crusts cut off (and he'd had a haircut so his Panama-hat hair didn't slant *quite* so low over his forehead) but his remark still made me—well, suddenly unable to *stand* him. He had likened me to a diminutive vessel manned by faceless dots of brown and yellow—*poorly* manned at that, because in a matter of seconds (if one took into account the oiled swell curled to strike down with vengeance), the thing was about to go under and that brown smudge on the horizon, that unwitting passing ship, wasn't coming to rescue the dots anytime soon.

It was the cause of many of Dad's outrages too, when people elected themselves his personal oracle of Delphi. It was the grounds for many of his university colleagues going from nameless, harmless peers to individuals he referred to as "anathemas" and "bête noires." They'd made the mistake of abridging Dad, abbreviating Dad, putting Dad in a nutshell, watering Dad down, telling Dad How It Was (and getting it all wrong).

Four years prior, at Dodson-Miner College's opening day World Symposium, Dad had delivered a forty-nine-minute lecture entitled, "Models of Hate and the Organ Trade," a lecture he was particularly fond of, having traveled in 1995 to Houston to interview one mustachioed Sletnik Patrutzka who'd sold her kidney for freedom. (Through tears, Sletnik had showed us her scars; "Steel hurts," she'd said.) Immediately following Dad's speech, College Provost Rodney Byrd scuttled across the outdoor stage like a shooed cockroach, dabbed his sloppy mouth with a handkerchief and said, "Thank you, Dr. Van Meer, for your keen insight into post-Communist Russia. It is very rare that we have a bona fide Russian *émigré* on campus"—he said it as if it were some mysterious individual who was a no-show, a very elusive Ms. Emmie Gray—"and we look forward to spending the semester with you. If anyone has a question about *War and Peace* I suspect he's your man." (Of course, Dad's lecture had covered the organ trade rife in Western *Europe* and he'd never set foot in Russia. Though proficient in other languages, Dad actually knew no Russian at all except, " На бога надейся, а сам не плошай," which meant, "Trust in God, but lock your car," a well-known Russian proverb.)

"The act of being personally misconstrued," Dad said, "informed to one's face one is no more complex than a few words haphazardly strung together like blotchy undershirts on a clothesline—well, it can gall the most self-possessed of individuals."

There was no sound in the claustrophobic hallway except Zach's breathing, which heaved like the interior of a conch shell. I could feel his eyes dripping down me, coursing through the folds of Jefferson's crispy black dress that resembled an upside-down shitake mushroom if you squinted at it. The silvery-black fabric felt flimsy, as if it could stiffly peel away like tinfoil around cold fried chicken.

"Blue?"

I made the grave error of glancing up at him again. His face—head light-bright from the light on the Turner, eyelashes absurdly long like those of a Jersey Cow—was heading straight toward me, drifting on down like Gondwanaland, the giant Southern landmass that inched toward the South Pole 200 million years ago.

He wanted our tectonic plates to collide, forcing one on top of the other so molten material from the earth's interior gives rise to a wild and unstable volcano. Well, it was one of those sweaty moments I'd never had before except in dreams, when my head was in the cul-de-sac of Andreo Verduga's arm, my lips by his alcoholic cologne in the dead end of his neck. And as I stared up at Zach's face hovering at the intersection of Desire and Shyness, patiently waiting for a green light (even though there wasn't a soul around), you'd think I'd flee, run for my life, lie back and think of Milton (throughout the evening, I'd been engaged in covert Neverlanding, fantasizing it'd been *he* who'd met Dad, *his* mother and father who'd squirreled around the living room), but no, at this bizarre moment, Hannah Schneider slipped into my head.

I'd seen her at school just that afternoon, right after sixth period. She was dressed in a long-sleeved black wool dress, a tight black coat, moving unevenly down the sidewalk toward Hanover carrying a cream canvas bag, her head bent toward the ground. While Hannah had *always* been thin, her figure, particularly her shoulders, looked unusually hunched and narrow, dented even—like she'd been smashed in a door.

Now, caught in some gluey moment with this kid, feeling like I was still in Kansas, the reality of her getting so close to Doc she could count the number of gray hairs on his chin felt gruesome. How could she stomach his hands, his rocking-chair shoulders or the next morning, the sky sterile as a hospital floor? What was *wrong* with her? Something was wrong, of course, yet I'd been too preoccupied with myself, with Black and the number of times he sneezed, with Jade, Lu, Nigel, my hair, to take it to heart. ("The average American girl's principal obsession is her hair—simple bangs, a perm, straightening, split ends—to the breathtaking rebuff of all else, including divorce, murder and nuclear war," writes Dr. Michael Espiland in *Always Knock Before Entering* [1993].) What had happened to Hannah to make her descend into Cottonwood the way Dante had willfully descended into Hell? What had caused her to perpetuate a marked pattern of self-annihilation, which was obviously replicating at an alarming rate with the death of her friend Smoke Harvey, the drinking and swearing, her thinness, which made her look like a starved crow? Misery multiplied unless it was treated immediately. So did misfortune, according to Irma Stenpluck, author of *The Credibility Gap* (1988), which detailed on p. 329 one had only to suffer a tiny misfortune before one found one's "entire ship sinking into the Atlantic." Maybe it was none of our business, but maybe it was what she'd been hoping for all along, that one of us would unstick from our self and ask about *her* for once, not out of snoopy intrigue but because she was our friend and obviously crumbling a little bit.

I hated myself, standing there in the hallway, next to the Turner and Zach still hovering on the edge of his dry canyon of a kiss.

"You have something on your mind," he quietly observed. The kid was Carl Jung, fucking Freud.

"Let's get out of here," I said harshly, taking a small step backward.

He smiled. It was incredible; his face had no expression for anger or annoyance, just as some Native Americans, the Mohawks, the Hupa, had no word for purple.

"You don't want to know why you're like that boat?" he asked.

I shrugged and my dress sighed.

"Well, it's because the moon shines right on it and nowhere else in the picture. Right here. On the side. She's the only thing that's incandescent," he said, or some other word-of-the-day response to that effect, full of oozing lava, lumps of rock, ash and hot gas I opted not to stick around for because I'd already turned and headed down the stairs. At the bottom, I again encountered Patsy and Roge, positioned right where we'd left them like two shopping carts abandoned in the cookie aisle.

"Isn't it *some*thing?" Patsy exclaimed.

They waved good-bye as Zach and I climbed into the Toyota. Big smiles fireworked through their faces when I waved and shouted out the unrolled window, "Thank you! Look forward to seeing you again!" How strange it was that people like Zach, Roge and Patsy floated through the world. They were the cute daisies twirling past the mirror orchids, the milk thistle of the Hannah Schneiders, the Gareth van Meers snared in the branches and the mud. They were the sort of giddy people Dad loathed, called *fuzz*, *frizz* (or his most contemptuous put-down of all, *sweet people*) if he happened to be standing behind one of them in a checkout aisle and eavesdropped on what was always a painfully bland conversation.

And yet—and I didn't know what was wrong with me—though I couldn't wait to unload Zach as soon as we arrived at the Cabaret (Jade and the others would be there, Black and Joalie too, Joalie, I hoped, suffering from a unforeseen skin irritation that refused to budge, even with persistent entreaties of various over-the-counter medications) I sort of marveled at the kid's buoyancy. I'd approached his would-be kiss with no less dread than if a plague of locusts had started to descend upon my lands, and yet, now, he smiled at me and cheerfully asked if I had enough leg room.

Incredibly too, at the bottom of the driveway, when we were about to make a right, I glanced back, up the sharp wooded hill toward his house, and saw that Patsy and Roge were still standing there, most likely with their arms *still* snug around each other's waist. Patsy's green blouse was visible, shredded by the matchstick trees. And though I'd never confess it to Dad, I *did* wonder, for a second, as Zach turned up the pop song on the radio, if it was really so atrocious to have a family like that, to have a dad that twinkled and a boy with eyes so blue you wouldn't be shocked to see sparrows winging through them, and a mother who stared, unwaveringly, at the last place she'd seen her son like a dog in a supermarket parking lot, never taking its eyes off the automatic doors.

"Are you excited about the dance?" asked Zach.

I nodded.

"The Housebreaker
of Shady Hill"

The Christmas Cabaret was held in the Harper Racey '05 Cafeteria, which, under Student Council President Maxwell's iron fist, had transformed into a sweltering, Versailles-styled nightclub with imitation-Sèvres vases on the side tables, French cheeses and pastries, gold tinsel, big, crudely painted posters of deformed girls on makeshift swings affixed over the "World Enough and Time" Wall (Gallway class photos from 1910 to present) which were meant to invoke the flouncing fiddle-dee-dee of Fragonard's *The Swing* (c. 1767), but inadvertently conjured *The Scream* (Munch, c. 1893).

At least half of all St. Gallway faculty had shown up, those who'd been asked to chaperone, and there they were, the Mondo-Strangos, turned out in their monkey suits. Havermeyer stood next to his pale, rawboned wife, Gloria, in black velvet. (Gloria only rarely made public appearances. They said she rarely left the house, preferring to laze around, nibbling marshmallows and reading romance novels by Circe Kensington, a beloved author of many June Bugs, and thus I knew the most popular title, *The Crown Jewels of Rochester de Wheeling* [1990].) And there was bulge-eyed Mr. Archer gripping the window ledge, neatly fitted into his navy suit like an invitation into an envelope, and Ms. Thermopolis talking to Mr. Butters in flighty Hawaiian oranges and reds. (She'd done something to her hair, a styling mousse that turned locks to lichen.) There was Hannah's favorite, Mr. Moats, nearly as tall as the door frame by which he stood, wearing a jacket in Prussian Blue and plaid pants. (His was a disastrous face; his nose, puffy mouth, chin, even most of his cheeks seemed to crowd into the lower half of his face, like passengers on a sinking ship trying to avoid sea water.)

Jade and the others had promised (sworn on a range of grandparents' graves) they'd show up at nine, but now it was ten-thirty and there was no sign of them, not even Milton. Hannah was supposed to be here, too—"Eva Brewster asked me to drop by," she'd told me—but she was nowhere. And thus I was stuck deep in the heart of Zachville, homeland of the Sticky Palm, the Hazardous Wingtip, the Rickety Arm, the Calcutta Breath, the Barely Discernable Off-Key Hum Annoying as Any Wall's Drone of Electricity, largest city, cluster of freckles on his neck beneath left ear, rivers of sweat at his temples, in that small gorge at his neck.

The dance floor was meatpacked. To our right, less than a foot away, Zach's ex-girlfriend, Lonny Felix, danced with her date, Clifford Wells, who had an upturned, elfin face and wasn't as tall as she was. He didn't weigh as much either. Every time she instructed him to dip her (*"Dip me,"* she coached) he gnashed his teeth together as he struggled to keep her from falling to the floor. Otherwise, she seemed to be enjoying her self-styled tornado-twirls, flinging her elbows and thorny bleached hair harrowingly near my face every time Zach and I completed one revolution, when I was facing the buffet table (where Perón was making Nutella crêpes, uncharacteristically subdued in a puff-sleeved Rhapsody in Blue) and Zach faced the windows.

Maxwell, a sort of mad Phineas T. Barnum in crimson velvet jacket and cane, completely ignored his date, Kimmie Kaczynski (a sad, dejected mermaid in green satin unable to lure her sailor) and presided with delight over his sideshow of freaks, the bleary-eyed, burnt-out Jelly Roll Jazz Band.

"Pardon me," said a voice behind me.

It was Jade, my knight in shining armor. Immediately, however, I noticed something was wrong. Donnamara Chase in her unwieldy pink Liberty Bell dress and her date, lip-licking Trucker, and a few others, like Sandy Quince-Wood, Joshua Cuthbert and Dinky, a living, breathing booby trap, arms tightly clamped around the neck of poor, destined-for-captivity Brett Carlson, they'd all stopped dancing and were staring at her.

I saw why.

She was wearing a thin silk dress the color of tangerines, the neckline plunging down her front with the force of a skydiver's free fall. She was drunk, in possession of neither a bra nor shoes, and though she surveyed Zach and me with a hand on her hip, her customary gesture of intimidation, now it simply looked as if she was doing her best to hold onto herself, in case her self fell over. She was holding a pair of black stilettos.

"If you don't mind, coup—coupon"—she lurched forward; I was terrified she might fall—"I need to borrow Gag for a minute."

"Are you okay?" Zach asked.

Quickly, I stepped forward and grabbed her arm. Force-feeding a smile to my face, I pulled her after me, *hard*, but not so hard she dissolved into a puddle of orange juice on the dance floor.

"Geez. I'm *sorry* I'm late. What can I say? I hit traffic."

I managed to move her away from most of the faculty chaperones, and pushed her straight into a crowd of freshmen tasting the *gâteaux au chocolat et aux noisettes* and the French cheeses. ("This tastes like ass," someone said.)

My heart was pounding. Within minutes, no, seconds, she'd be spotted by Evita and would be arrested, in Gallwanian terms, "roundtabled," inevitable suspension, Saturday morning community service with men who licked their lips at her when she served them lukewarm vegetable soup—perhaps even expulsion. In my head, I began to stitch together an excuse, something to do with an accidental pill slipped into her 7-Up by some pimply psycho; there were plenty of articles I could reference on the subject. There was also, of course, simply pretending to be stupid ("*When in doubt, feign oblivion,*" Dad chanted in my head. "*No one can fault you for being born with a lean IQ.*"). But before I knew it, we were slipping past the buffet table and the bathrooms and out the wooden doors, undetected. (Mr. Moats, if you are reading this, I'm certain you saw us. I thank you for simply replacing your look of marked boredom with one of cynical delight, sighing, and doing nothing more. And if you have no idea what I'm talking about, ignore the above.)

Outside, I yanked her across the brick patio ringed with wrought-iron love seats ("Ow. That *hurts*, you know.") where Gallway's most earnest couples were marooned.

Glancing over my shoulder to be certain no one followed, I yanked Jade across the lawn, down the mineral-gritty sidewalks, through the orange floodlights where our thin shadows dragged farther and farther behind us. I didn't let go of her until we were in front of Hanover, where it was dark and desolate, where everything—the black windows, the wooden steps, a folded sheet of Algebra homework mumbling in its sleep—was nightwashed, uniformed in grays and blues.

"*Are you out of your mind?*" I shouted.

"What?"

"How can you show *up* like this?"

"Oh, stop yelling, Gag. Gaggle."

"I—are you trying to get kicked out?"

"Fuck you," she said, giggling. "And your little dog too."

"Where is everyone? Where's Hannah?"

She made a face. "At her house. They're making apple pie and watching *Heaven & Earth*. You guessed it. They ditched you. Thought this scene would be a bore. *I'm* the one with loyalty. You should thank me. I take cash, check, MasterCard, Visa. No American Express."

"Jade."

"The others are traitors. In our midst. Aye too brew tays. And in case you're wondering, Black and that little petunia are off somewhere doing the nasty in a cheap motel. He's so in love I want to kill him. That girl's a Yoko Ono and we're going to break *up*—"

"Get a hold of yourself."

"For Pete's sake, I'm *fine*." She smiled. "Let's go somewhere. Some bar where the men are men and the women are hairy. And have smiles of beer."

"You have to go home. *Now*."

"I was thinking Brazil. Gag?"

"What."

"I think I'm going to throw up."

She did look ill. Her lips had faded into her face and she stared at me with huge nocturnal eyes, touching a hand to her throat.

I took her arm with the intention of directing her toward the crowd of now ill-fated young pines to our right, but suddenly, she made the short, high-pitched squeak of a kid when it didn't want to eat some final piece of cauliflower or get strapped into a car seat, and she tore free, sprinting up the stairs and across the porch. I thought the doors would be locked, but they weren't. She disappeared inside.

I found her in Mirtha Grazeley's admissions bathroom on her knees in one of the stalls getting sick.

"I hate throwing up. I'd rather die. Kill me, would you? *Kill* me. I beg you."

For fifteen sickened minutes, I held her hair.

"Better," she said, wiping her eyes and mouth.

After she rinsed her face in the sink, she collapsed facedown on one of the couches in Mirtha's Greeting Room.

"We should go home," I said.

"Give me a second."

Sitting there in the quiet, the lights off, the green floodlights from the M. Bella Chancery lawn spilling through the windows, it felt as if we were at the bottom of the ocean. The thin shadows from the bare trees outside stretched across the wooden floor like sea grass and sargassum weed, the grit dappling the windows, a little bit of zooplankton, the floor lamp in the corner, a glass-rope sponge. Jade sighed and turned over onto her back, her hair stuck to her cheeks.

"We should get out of here," I said.

"You like him," she said.

"Who?"

"Coupon."

"Like I like noise pollution."

"You're going to run off with him."

"Right."

"You're going to have tons of sex with him and have his gift certificates. Seriously. I know these things. I'm psychic."

"Shut up."

"Hurl?"

"What."

"I hate the others."

"Who?"

"Leulah. Charles. I hate them. I like *you. You're* the only one who's decent. The others are all sick. And I hate Hannah most of all. Ugh."

"Oh, come on."

"*No.* I pretend I don't because it's easy and fun to go over and have her cook and watch her act like St. Francis of friggin' Assisi. Sure. Blah blah. But deep down I know she's sick and repulsive."

I waited for a moment, enough time for, say, a spinner shark to swim by seeking a school of sardines, for that peculiar word she used, *repulsive,* to disband, dissolve slightly, like ink from a cuttlefish.

"Actually," I said, "it's a common feeling for people to feel intermittent antipathy toward individuals they're familiar with. It's the Derwid-Loeverhastel Principle. It's discussed in *Beneath the Associated—*"

"*Fuck* David Hasselhoff." She raised herself up on an elbow, narrowing her eyes. "I don't like the woman." She frowned. "*You* like her?"

"Sure," I said.

"Why?"

"She's a good person."

Jade huffed. "Not *that* good. I don't know if you're aware of it, but she killed that guy."

"Who?"

Obviously, I knew she was talking about Smoke Harvey, but I chose to feign ignorance, volunteer only the barest words as a question, much in the reserved manner of Ranulph (pronounced "RALF") Curry, the intemperate chief inspector of Roger Pope Lavelle's three standoffish detective master-pieces composed in a decade-long fit of inspiration, from 1901 to 1911, works ultimately overshadowed by the sunnier tomes of Sir Arthur Conan Doyle. It was a pretext artfully assumed by Curry while interviewing all eyewitnesses, bystanders, informants and suspects, and, more often than not, leading to the discovery of a certain sharp detail that ripped open the case. "Tut, tut, Ho-race," says Curry in the 1017-page *Conceit of a Unicorn* (1901). "It is a capital error in the art of detection to insert one's own voice into the ungoverned words of another. The more one speaks, the less one hears."

"That Smoke person," Jade went on. "*Dubs.* Knocked him off. I'm positive."

"How do you know?"

"I was watching when they told her about him, remember?" She paused, staring at me, her eyes snatching, then holding on to what little light there was in the room. "You weren't around, but I saw the performance. Com-pletely overdone. She's really the worst actress on the planet. If she was an ac-tress she wouldn't even make the B movies. She'd be in the D or the E movies. I don't even think she's good enough for porn. Of course, she *thinks* that she's going on *Inside the Actor's Studio* like next friggin' *week.* She went over the top, shouting like a crazy person when she saw the guy dead. For a second I thought she was screaming, 'The dingo ate my baby.' "

She rolled off the sofa and walked toward the kitchenette behind Mirtha's desk. She opened the small refrigerator door and, crouching down, was illuminated by a rectangle of gold light so her dress became transparent and you could see, in this X-ray, how thin she was, how her shoulders were no wider than a coat hanger.

"There's that eggnog in here," she said. "Want some?"

"No."

"There's tons. Three full containers."

"Mirtha probably measures how much is left at the end of every day. We don't want to get in trouble."

Jade stood up with the pitcher, banging the door closed with her foot.

"It's Mirtha Grazeley, who everyone knows is the Mad freakin' Hatter. Who'll listen to her if she croaks there's something missing? Besides. Most people just aren't that organized. Isn't that what *you* said the other *soir*, 'no method to the madness' and such?" She opened one of the cabinets and took out two glasses. "All I'm saying is that I happen to think Hannah got *rid* of the man like I happen to know my mother's the Loch Ness Monster. Or Bigfoot. I haven't decided what monster she is but I'm positive she's one of the big ones."

"What was her motive then?" I asked. ("In my opinion," said Curry, "it is also a very useful achievement to make certain the speaker remains on course, does not skirt around what he knows, prattling on about latchkeys and boilers.")

"Monsters don't need a motive. They're monsters so they just—"

"I mean Hannah."

She looked at me, exasperated. "You don't get it, do you? No one *needs* a motive in this day and age. People look for motives and such because they're afraid of like, total chaos. But motives are out like clogs. The truth is, some people just like to execute, like some people have a thing for ski bums with moles all over like God spilled peppercorns or paralegals with full-sleeve tattoos."

"Then why him?"

"Who?"

"Smoke Harvey," I said. "Why him and not me, for example?"

She made a sarcastic *Ha* sound as she handed me the glass and sat down. "I don't know if you're aware of it but Hannah's completely obsessed with you. It's like you're her freaking lost *child*. I mean, we knew about you before you even freaking showed up at this place. It was so freaking weird."

My heart stopped. "What are you talking about?"

Jade sniffed. "Well, you met her at that shoe store, correct?"

I nodded.

"Well, like, immediately after that, or maybe even the day *of*, she was talking on and on about this Blue person who was so amazing and wonderful and we'd have to become friends with you or like, *die*. Like you were the fucking Second Coming. She still acts that way. When you're not around she's always, 'Where's Blue, anyone seen Blue?' Blue, Blue, Blue, for Christ sake. But it's not just you. She has all kinds of abnormal fixations. Like the animals and the furniture. All those men in Cottonwood. Sex for her's like shaking hands. And Charles. She's completely fucked him up and doesn't even realize it. She thinks she's doing all of us a big favor by being friends with us, educating us or whatever—"

I swallowed. "Something really did happen between Charles and Hannah?"

"Hel*lo?* Of course. I'm like, *ninety* percent positive. Charles won't tell anyone a thing, not even Black, because she's brainwashed him. But last year? Lu and I went to pick him up and we found him crying like I'd never seen a person cry in my whole life. His face was screwed up like this." She demonstrated. "He'd had a tantrum. The whole house was destroyed. He'd thrown paintings, attacked the wallpaper—huge chunks ripped right off the walls. We found him crying in a little ball by the TV. There was a knife on the floor, too, and we were afraid he was going to try to commit suicide or something—"

"He didn't, did he?" I asked quickly.

She shook her head. "No. But I think the reason he was freaking out was that Hannah told him they'd have to stop. Or who knows, maybe it just happened the one time. I mean, it was *probably* an accident. I don't think she set out to fuck him up, but she definitely did *some*thing, because he's not himself anymore. I mean, you should have seen him last year, the year before. He was amazing. This really happy person everyone loved. Now he's always pissed off."

She took a long drink of the eggnog. The darkness hardened her profile so her face looked like one of the colossal decorative jade masks Dad and I observed in the Olmec Room at the Garber Natural History Museum in Artesia, New Mexico. " 'The Olmec people were a singularly artistic civilization, deeply intrigued by the human face,' " Dad read grandly from the printed explanation on the wall. " 'They believed that though the voice often lies, the face itself is never deceitful.' "

"If you really think these things about Hannah," I managed to say, "how can you spend time with her?"

"I know. It's weird." She scrunched her mouth to one side, thinking. "I guess she's like crack." She sighed, hugging her shins. "It's a mint chocolate chip ice cream thing."

"What does that mean?" I asked, when she didn't immediately elaborate.

"Well." She tilted her head. "Have you ever felt that you loved, *loved* mint chocolate chip? That it was always your favorite flavor over every other in the entire world? But then one day you hear Hannah going on and on about butter pecan. Butter pecan this and butter pecan that and then you find yourself ordering butter pecan all the time. And you realize you like butter pecan best. That you probably liked it all along and just hadn't known." She was quiet for a moment. "You never eat mint chocolate chip again."

At this point, I felt as if I was drowning in the shadowed floats and the holdfasts and the Blood Henry Starfish clinging to the overhead lamp, but I told myself to take a deep breath, remember I couldn't believe all or any of what she said—not necessarily. Much of what Jade swore by, when she was drunk or sober, could be trapdoors, quicksand, trompe l'oeil, the hoax of light as it speeds through the air at a variety of temperatures.

I'd made the mistake of taking her words at face value for the first and last time when she confided to me how much she "hated" her mother, was "dying" to go live with her father, a judge in Atlanta, who was "decent" (despite having run off some four years prior with a woman she simply referred to as Meathead Marcy, about whom little was known, except that she was a paralegal with full-sleeve tattoos) and then, not fifteen minutes later, I watched her pick up the phone to call her mother, who was still in Colorado, happily trapped in some avalanche of a love affair with the ski instructor.

"But when are you coming home? I hate being looked after by Morella. I need you for my proper emotional development," she said tearfully, before noticing me, shouting, "What the fuck are *you* looking at?" and slamming the door in my face.

Though lovable (her signature tic, that absentminded way of blowing her hair out of her face couldn't be surpassed in charm by Audrey Hepburn), also blessed with the enviable properties of a mink coat—graceful, unreasonable and impractical no matter what she was draped over, whether it be couches or people (a quality that didn't diminish even when she was marginally torn and tatty, as she was now)—Jade was nevertheless one of those people whose personality proved to be the bane of modern mathematicians. She was neither a flat nor a solid shape. She showed no symmetry at all. Trigonometry, Calculus and Statistics all proved useless. Her Pie Chart was a muddle of arbitrary wedges, her Line Graph, the silhouette of the Alps. And just when one listed her under Chaos Theory—Butterfly Effects, Weather Predictions, Fractals, Bifurcation diagrams and whatnot—she showed up as an equilateral triangle, sometimes even a square.

Now she was on the floor with her filthy feet over her head, demonstrating a Pilates exercise that she explained, "made more blood flow along the spinal cord." (Somehow this translated into living longer.) I downed my glass of eggnog.

"I say we go to her classroom," she said in a keyed-up whisper. She swung her skinny legs back onto the carpet in the fast, violent movement of a guillotine. "We could take a look around. I mean, it's not completely insane to imagine that she'd keep evidence in her classroom."

"Evidence of *what?*"

"I told you. Murder. She killed that Smoke person."

I took a deep breath.

"Criminals put things where people are the least likely to look, right?" she asked. "Well, who'd think to look in her classroom?"

"We would."

"We find something? Then we *know.* Not that it means anything. I mean, giving her the benefit of the doubt, maybe Smoke had it coming to him. Maybe he clubbed seals."

"Jade—"

"We don't find anything? Who cares? No harm, no foul."

"We can*not* go to her classroom."

"Why not?"

"Any number of reasons. One, we might get caught and kicked out of school. Two, it makes no logical sense—"

"*Oh, fuck off!*" she shouted. "*Can you forget your fucking stellar college career for once and have a good time? You're a fucking drag!*" She looked furious, but then almost immediately, the anger slipped off her face. She sat up, an inchworm smile. "Just *think,* Olives," she whispered. "We have a higher cause. Undercover investigations. Recon work. We could end up on the *news.* We could be America's fucking sweethearts."

I stared at her. " 'Once more unto the breach, dear friends,' " I said.

"Good. Now help me find my shoes."

*　　*　　*

Ten minutes later, we were scurrying down the hall. Hanover had an old accordion floor, wheezing flat notes with every step. We pushed open the door, rushed down the hollow stairwell, outside into the cold, down the sidewalk trickling in front of the courtyard and Love. Stalactites of shadow grew around us, making Jade and me instinctively pretend we were nineteenth-century schoolgirls pursued by Count Dracula. We shivered and leaned into each other tightly, pretzeling our arms. We began to run, her hair splashing against my bare shoulder and face.

Dad once noted (somewhat morbidly, I thought at the time) that American institutions would be infinitely more successful in facilitating the pursuit of knowledge if they held classes at night, rather than in the daytime, from 8:00 P.M. to 4:00 or 5:00 in the morning. As I ran through the darkness, I understood what he meant. Frank red brick, sunny classrooms, symmetrical quads and courts—it was a setting that mislead kids to believe that Knowledge, that Life itself, was bright, clear and freshly mowed. Dad said a student would be infinitely better off going out into the world if he/she studied the periodic table of elements, *Madame Bovary*, the sexual reproduction of a sunflower, for example, with deformed shadows congregating on the classroom walls, silhouettes of fingers and pencils leaking onto the floor, gastric howls from unseen radiators and a teacher's face not flat and faded, not delicately pasteled by a golden late afternoon, but serpentine, gargoyled, Cyclopsed by the inky dark and feeble light from a candle. He/she would understand "everything and nothing," Dad said, if there was nothing discernible in the windows but a lamppost mobbed by blaze-crazy moths and darkness, reticent and unfeeling, as darkness always was.

Two tall pines somewhere to our left inadvertently touched branches, the sound of a madman's prosthetic limbs.

"Someone's coming!" Jade whispered.

We raced down the hill, past silent Graydon, and the basement of Love Auditorium, and Hypocrite's Alley, where the music classrooms with their long windows were vacant and blind like Oedipus after he hollowed out his eyes.

"I'm scared," she whispered, tightening her grip on my wrist.

"I'm terrified. And freezing."

"Have you seen *School of Hell?*"

"No."

"Serial killer's a Home Ec teacher."

"Ow."

"Baking 203. Bakes the students into soufflés. Isn't that sick?"

"I stepped on something. I think it went through my shoe."

"We have to hurry, Retch. We can't get caught. We'll *die.*"

She broke away from me and skipped up the steps of Loomis, yanking on the doors covered with dark, leafy announcements for Mr. Crisp's production of *The Bald Soprano* (Ionesco, 1950). They were locked.

"We'll have to go in another way," she whispered excitedly. "Through the window. Or the roof. I wonder if there's a chimney. We'll pull a Santa, Retch. A *Santa.*"

She grabbed my hand. Taking cues from movies featuring cat burglars and silent assassins, we circled the building, crunching through the shrubs and pine needles, trying the windows. Finally, we found one that wasn't latched, which Jade forced open into a narrow space of inward-leaning glass leading into Mr. Fletcher's Driver's Ed classroom. She slipped through the opening easily, landing on one foot. As I went through, I skinned my left shin on the window catch, my stockings ripped, and then I crashed onto the carpet, hitting my head on the radiator. (A poster on the wall featuring a kid wearing braces and a seat belt: "Always Check Your Blind Spot, on the Road and in Life!")

"Move it, slowpoke," Jade whispered and disappeared through the door.

Hannah's classroom, Room 102, was located at the very end of the root-canal hallway, a *Casablanca* poster taped to the door. I'd never been in her classroom before, and inside, when I opened the door, it was surprisingly bright; yellow-white floodlight from the sidewalk outside radiated through the wall of windows, X-raying the twenty-five or thirty desks and chairs and flinging long, skeletal shadows across the floor. Jade was already perched cross-legged on the stool at the front desk, one or two of the drawers hanging open. She paged intensely through a textbook.

"Find any smoking guns?" I asked.

She didn't answer, so I turned and walked down the first row of desks, staring up at the row of framed movie posters on the walls (Visual Aid 14.0).

In total, there were thirteen, including the two in the back by the bookshelf. Maybe it was because of the eggnog, but it only took a minute to realize how odd the posters were—not the fact that every one was foreign, or an American movie in Spanish, Italian or French, or even that they were each spaced some three inches apart and straight as soldiers, a level of exactitude you learned never to expect from the Visual Aids caking the walls of a classroom, not even one of Science or Mathematics. (I went up to *Il Caso Thomas Crown,* moved back the frame and saw, around the nail, distinct pencil lines, where she'd made the measurements, the blueprint of meticulousness.)

With the exception of two (*per un Pugno di Dollari, Fronte del Porto*), all the posters featured an embrace or kiss of some kind. Rhett was there grasping Scarlett, sure; and Fred holding onto Holly and Cat in the rain (*Colazione da Tiffany*); but there was also Ryan O'Neal Historia del Amoring with Ali MacGraw; Charlton Heston clutching Janet Leigh, making her head

VISUAL AID 14.0

fall at an uncomfortable angle in *La Soif du Mal*; and Burt Lancaster and Deborah Kerr getting a great deal of sand in their bathing suits. In a funny way too, I noticed—and I didn't think I was getting too carried away—the way the woman was positioned in each of the posters, it could very well have been *Hannah* embraced from there to eternity. She had their same fine china bones, their hairpin, coastal-road profiles, the hair that tripped and fell down their shoulders.

It was surprising, because she'd never struck me as the dizzy type to surround herself with firework displays of untold passion (as Dad called it, a "big to-don't"). That she'd so meticulously assembled these Coming Attractions that had come and gone—it made me a little sad.

"Somewhere in a woman's room there is always something, an object, a detail, that is her, wholly and unapologetically," Dad said. "With your mother, of course, it was the butterflies. Not only could you ascertain the extreme care she took in preserving and mounting them, how much they meant to her, but each one shed a tiny yet persistent light on the complex woman she was. Take the glorious Forest Queen. It reflects your mother's regal bearing, her fierce reverence for the natural world. The Clouded Mother of Pearl? Her maternal instinct, her understanding of moral relativism. Natasha saw the world not in blacks or whites, but as it really is—a decidedly dim landscape. The Mechanitis Mimic? She could impersonate all the greats, from Norma Shearer to Howard Keel. The insects themselves were her in many ways—glorious, heartbreakingly fragile. And so you see, considering each of these specimens, we end up with—if not your mother *precisely*—at the very least, a close approximation of her soul."

I wasn't sure why, at this moment, I thought of the butterflies, except that these posters seemed to be the details that were Hannah, "wholly and unapologetically." Maybe Burt Lancaster and Deborah Kerr getting sand in their bathing suits were her ardor for living coupled with a passion for the sea, the origin of all life, and *Bella di giorno* featuring Catherine Deneuve with her mouth hidden, was her need for shiftiness, secrets, Cottonwood.

"Oh, God," Jade said behind me. She threw a thick paperback into the air and it fluttered, crashing against the window.

"What?"

She didn't say anything, only pointed at the book on the floor, her breathing exaggerated. I walked over to the windows and picked it up.

It was a gray book with the photograph of a man on the front, its title in orange letters: *Blackbird Singing in the Dead of Night: The Life of Charles Milles Manson* (Ivys, 1985). The cover and pages were extremely tattered.

"So?" I asked.

"Don't you know who Charles Manson *is?*"

"Of course."

"Why would she have that book?"

"A lot of people have it. It's the definitive biography."

I didn't feel like going into the fact that *I* had the book too, that Dad included it on the syllabus for a course he'd last taught at the University of Utah at Rockwell, Seminar on Characteristics of a Political Rebel. The author, Jay Burne Ivys, an Englishman, had spent hundreds of hours interviewing assorted members of the Manson Family, which, in its heyday, included at least one hundred and twelve people, and thus the book was remarkably comprehensive in Parts II and III explaining the origins and codes of Manson's ideology, the daily activities of the sect, the hierarchy (Part I entailed a fastidious psychoanalysis of Manson's difficult childhood, which Dad, not being a Freud aficionado, found less effective). Dad addressed the book, juxtaposed with Miguel Nelson's *Zapata* (1989), for two, sometimes three classes under the lecture title "Freedom Fighter or Fanatic?" "Fifty-nine people who encountered Charles Manson during his years living in Haight-Ashbury went on the record saying he had the most magnetic eyes and most stirring voice of any human being they'd ever encountered," Dad boomed into the microphone at the lectern. "Fifty-nine *different* sources. So what was it? The It-factor. Charisma. He had it. So did Zapata. Guevara. Who else? Lucifer. You're born with, what? That certain je ne sais quoi, and according to history, you can move, with relatively little effort, a group of ordinary people to take up guns and fight for your cause, whatever cause it is; the nature of the cause actually matters very little. If you say so—if you toss them something to believe in—they'll murder, give their lives, call you Jesus. Sure, you laugh, but to this day, Charles Manson receives more fan mail than any other inmate in the entire U.S. penitentiary system, some sixty thousand letters per year. His CD, *Lie*, continues to be a mover on Amazon .com. What does that tell us? Or, let me rephrase that. What does that tell us about *us?*"

"There's no other book in here, Gag," Jade said in a nervous voice. "Look."

I walked over to the desk. Inside the open drawer were a pile DVDs, *All the King's Men, The Deer Hunter, La Historia Oficial,* a few others, but no books.

"I found it in the back," she said. "Hidden."

I opened the shabby cover, flipped through a few pages. Maybe it was the stark light in the room, slashing and deboning everything, including Jade (her emaciated shadow fell to the floor, crawled toward the door), but I felt genuine chills skidding down my neck when I saw the name written in faded pencil in the upper corner of the title page. *Hannah Schneider.*

"It doesn't mean anything," I said, but noticed, with surprise, I was trying to convince myself.

Jade's eyes widened. "You think she wants to kill us?" she whispered.

"Oh, please."

"Seriously. We're targets because we're bourgeois."

I frowned. "What is it with you and that word?"

"It's Hannah's word. Ever noticed when she's drunk everyone's a pig?"

"She's just kidding," I said. "Even my Dad jokes about that sometimes." But Jade, her teeth bricked into a tiny wall, grabbed the book from my hands and started furiously spinning through the pages, stopping at the black-and-white photographs in the middle, tilting them so they caught the light. " 'Charles called Susan Atkins Sexy Sadie,' " she read slowly. "Ew. Look how freaky this woman looks. Those eyes. Honestly, they kind of look like *Hannah's—*"

"Stop it," I said, snatching the book from her. "What's the matter with you?"

"What's the matter with *you?*" Her eyes were narrowed, tiny incisions. Sometimes, Jade had a very severe way of looking at you that made you feel as if she was a 1780 sugarcane plantation owner and you, the branded slave on the Antiguan auction block who hadn't seen your mother and father in a year and probably never would again. "You miss your coupon, is that it? You want to give birth to food stamps?"

At this point, I think we would have broken into an argument, which would have ended with me fleeing the building, probably in tears, her laughing and shouting a variety of names. The terrified look on her face, however, caused me to turn and follow her stare out the windows.

Someone was walking down the sidewalk toward Loomis, a heavy-set figure wearing a bulging, bruise-colored dress.

"It's Charles Manson," Jade whimpered. "In *drag.*"

"No," I said. "It's the dictator."

In horror, we watched Eva Brewster move to the front doors of Loomis, yanking on the handles before turning and walking out onto the lawn by the giant pine tree, shading her eyes as she peered into the classroom windows.

"Oh, fuck *me*," said Jade.

We leapt across the room, to the corner by the bookshelf where it was pitch black (under Cary and Grace, as it so happened, *Caccia al ladro*).

"Blue!" Eva shouted.

The sound of Evita Perón shouting one's name could make anyone's heart lurch. Mine thrashed like an octopus thrown to the deck of a ship.

"Blue!"

We watched her come to the window. She wasn't the most attractive woman in the world: she had a fire-hydrant's bearing, hair the fluffy texture of home insulation and dyed a hideous yellow-orange, but her eyes, as I'd observed once in the Main Office in Hanover, were shockingly beautiful, sudden sneezes in the dull silence of her face—big, wide-set, in a pale blue that tiptoed toward violet. She frowned now and deliberately pressed her forehead to the glass so it became one of those Ramshell Snails feeding on the side of aquariums. Although I was petrified and held my breath and Jade dug her nails into my right knee, the woman's puffy, slightly blued face, flanked by large, garish pine-cone earrings, didn't *look* particularly angry or devious. Frankly, she appeared more frustrated, as if she'd come to the window with the express hope of glimpsing the rare Barkudia Skink, the limbless lizard notorious among the reptilian elite as something of a Salinger, gallingly incommunicado for eighty-seven years, and now it was choosing to stay hidden under a moist rock in the exhibit, ignoring her no matter how many times she shouted, tapped on the glass, waved shiny objects or took flash pictures.

"Blue!" she called again, a little more emphatically, craning her neck to glance over her shoulder. *"Blue!"*

She muttered something to herself, and hurried around the corner of the building, ostensibly to search the opposite side. Jade and I couldn't move, our chins conjoined to our knees, listening for the footsteps that reverberate down the linoleum asylum corridors of one's most terrifying dreams.

But the minutes dripped by and there was only silence and the occasional coughs, sniffs, and throat clearings of a room. After five minutes, I crawled past Jade (she was frozen solid in fetal position) and moved toward the window where I looked out and saw her again, this time standing on the front steps of Loomis.

It would have been a stirring view, one of the Thomas Hardy variety, if she'd been someone else—someone with decent posture, like Hannah—because her cottony hair was blowing up off her forehead and insistent wind had seized her dress and pushed it far behind her, giving her the wild, secret air of a widow staring at the sea, or a magnificent ghost, pausing for a moment before continuing a sad search along the mottled moors for relics of dead love, a Ruined Maid, a Trampwoman's Tragedy. But she was Eva Brewster: stout and sobering, bottlenecked, jug-armed and cork-legged. She tugged at the dress, scowled at the dark, took a last look at the windows (for a harrowing second, I thought she saw me) and then turned, heading briskly back down the sidewalk and disappearing.

"She's gone," I said.

"You sure?"

"Yeah."

Jade lifted her head and pressed a hand to her chest.

"I'm having a heart attack," she said.

"No, you're not."

"It's possible. My family has a history of heart failure. It happens just like this. Out of the blue."

"You're fine."

"I feel a tightness. *Here.* That's what happens when you're having pulmonary embrosis."

I stared out the window. Where the sidewalk twisted out of sight around Love Auditorium, a lone tree stood guard with a thick black trunk, its shivering, thin limbs with the tops bent backward into tiny wrists and hands, as if feebly holding up the sky.

"That was really strange, huh?" Jade made a face. "How she called your name like that—wonder why she wasn't calling my name."

I shrugged, trying to act nonchalant, though in truth I felt ill. Maybe I had the gauzy constitution of a Victorian woman who fainted because she heard the word *leg*, or perhaps I'd read *L'Idiot* (Petrand, 1920) too attentively with its lunatic hero, the sickly and certifiable Byron Berintaux, who saw in every upholstered armchair his upcoming Death waving at him enthusiastically. Maybe I'd simply had too much darkness for one night. "Night is not good for the brain or the nervous system," contends Carl Brocanda in *Logical Effects* (1999). "Studies show neurons are constricted by 38 percent in individuals who live in locations with little daylight, and nerve impulses are 47 percent slower in prison inmates who go forty-eight hours without seeing the light of day."

Whatever it was, it wasn't until Jade and I crept our way outside, sneaking past the cafeteria, still lit but silent (a few teachers lingered on the patio, including Ms. Thermopolis, a dying ember by the wooden doors), hightailing it out of St. Gallway in the Mercedes without encountering Eva Brewster, roaring down Pike Avenue past Jiffy's Eatery, Dollar Depot, Dippity's, Le Salon Esthetique—when I realized I'd forgotten to return the *Blackbird* book to Hannah's desk. I was actually still holding it and in my haste, confusion, the darkness, only dimly aware I'd been doing so.

"How come you still have that book?" Jade demanded as we swung into a Burger King drive-thru. "She's going to know it's gone. Hope she doesn't dust for fingerprints—hey, what do you want to eat? Hurry and decide. I'm starved."

We ate Whoppers drenched in the acid light of the parking lot, barely speaking. I suppose Jade was one of those people who flung handfuls of wild accusations into the air, smiling as they rained on everyone's head, and then the festivities were over and she went home. She looked contented, refreshed even, as she jostled fries into her mouth, waved at some scab making his way to his pick-up balancing a tray of Cokes in his arms, and yet, deep in my chest, unavoidable as the sound of your heart when you stopped to hear it beating, I felt, as deadbeat gumshoe Peter Ackman (who had a weakness for the chalk-tube and flutes of skee) said at the end of *Wrong Twist* (Chide, 1954), "like the bean-schnozzle been jammed far up my lousy, threatening to sneeze metal." I stared at the wrinkled cover of that book, where, despite the faded ink, the creases, the man's black eyes rose off the page.

"So these are the eyes of the Devil," Dad remarked thoughtfully once, picking up and scrutinizing his own copy. "He looks out and sees you— doesn't he?"

Sweet Bird of Youth

There was an anecdote Dad recounted like clockwork whenever he had a colleague over for dinner. Having a guest was rare, occurring only once every two or three towns in which we lived. Customarily, Dad found it difficult to withstand the echoing howls of his associates at Hattiesburg College of Arts and Science, the displays of chest-beating rampant among his Cheswick College cronies or professors at the University of Oklahoma at Flitch, eternally absorbed with feeding, grooming and being territorial to the exclusion of all else. (Dad regarded silverbacks—professors over sixty-five who had tenure, dandruff, rubbery shoes and quadrangle glasses that bugified their eyes—with particular disdain.)

Once in a while, however, under the wild oak trees, Dad bumped into his own kind (if not his exact subspecies or species, at least the same genus), a compatriot who'd made his way down from the foliage and learned to walk on two feet.

Naturally, this person never was as sophisticated an academic as Dad, nor as handsome. (The man was almost always saddled with a flattish face, an extensive, slanted forehead and an awning brow.) But Dad would cheerfully extend a Van Meer dinner invitation to this uncommonly advanced lecturer; and on a quiet Saturday or Sunday night, big, fig-eyed Professor of Linguistics Mark Hill would turn up, with his hands enduringly tucked into the patch pockets of his shapeless dinner jacket, or Associate Professor of English Lee Sanjay Song, with his quince-and-cream complexion and teeth in a traffic jam, and somewhere between the spaghetti and the tiramisu Dad treated him to the story of Tobias Jones the Damned.

It was a straightforward tale about a nervous, pale-skinned chap Dad encountered in Havana working at OPAI *(Organización Panamaricana de la Ayuda Internacional)* during the hot rum-soaked summer of 1983, a British kid from Yorkshire who, in the span of a single luckless week in August, lost his passport, wallet, wife, right leg and dignity—in that order. (Every now and then, to illicit even more extreme cries of amazement from his audience, Dad reduced the tragedy to a neat span of twenty-four hours.)

Never one for paying attention to physical details, Dad was disappointingly hazy on what the face of the Exceedingly Ill-fated looked like, but I was able to discern, out of Dad's poorly lit verbal portrait, a tall, pale man with stalklike legs (after he was hit by the Packard, leg), maize-colored hair, a clammy gold pocket watch repeatedly removed from his breast pocket and blinked at disbelievingly, a propensity for sighing, for cufflinks, for lingering too long in front of the chrome metal fan (the only one in the room) and for spilling café con leche on his trousers.

Dad's dinner guest listened in rapt attention as Dad narrated the beginning of the ill-starred week, which found Tobias showing off his new fiesta linen shirt to his coworkers at OPAI while a pack of *gente de guarandabia* ransacked his bungalow back at Comodoro Neptuno, all the way to the tale's miserable end, a mere seven days later, with Tobias prostrate in his lumpy bed at *el hospital Julio Trigo* missing a right leg and recuperating from an attempted suicide (fortunately, the attending nurse had been able to pry him off the window ledge).

"And we never knew what happened to him," Dad said in closing with a thoughtful sip of wine. Professor of Psychology Alfonso Rigollo stared dolefully at the edge of the dinner table. And after he muttered, "Shit," or "Tough luck," Dad and he would discuss predestination, or the waywardness of a woman's love, or how Tobias might've had a chance for canonization if he hadn't tried to kill himself and had stood for something. (According to Dad, Tobias had definitely performed one of the three miracles required for sainthood: back in 1979 he'd somehow convinced the ocean-eyed Adalia to marry him.)

Within twenty minutes, though, Dad would twist the conversation around to the *real* reason he'd brought up Tobias Jones in the first place, to detail one of his favorite theories, "The Theory of Determination," because his final position (related with the intensity of Christopher Plummer murmuring, "The rest is silence.") was that Tobias was not, as it might appear, a defenseless victim of fate, but a victim of himself, of his own "sallow head."

"And thus we are faced with the simple question," said Dad. "Is man's destiny determined by the vicissitudes of environment or free will? I argue that it is free will, because what we think, what we dwell upon in our heads, whether it be fears or dreams, has a direct effect upon the physical world. The more you think about your downfall, your ruin, the greater the likelihood that it will occur. And conversely, the more one thinks of victory, the more likely one will achieve it."

Dad always paused here for dramatic effect, staring across the room at the trite little daisy landscape hanging on the wall, or the pattern of horse heads and riding crops running up and down the faded dining room wallpaper. Dad adored all Suspensions and Silences, so he could feel everyone's eyes madly running all over his face like Mongol armies in 1215 sacking Beijing.

"Obviously," he continued with a slow smile, "it's a concept that has been bastardized of late in Western Culture, associated with the runny-nosed Why-Nots and How-Comes of self-help and PBS marathons that drone on into the wee hours, begging you to pledge money and in return, receive forty-two hours of meditation tapes one can chant to when one is mired in traffic. Yet visualization is a concept that was once considered not so frothy, dating back to the founding of the Buddhist Mauryan Empire, around 320 B.C. History's great leaders understood it. Niccolò Machiavelli tipped Lorenzo de' Medici off to it, though he called it 'prowess' and 'foresight.' Julius Caesar understood it—he saw himself conquering Gaul decades before he actually did so. Who else? Hadrian, Da Vinci certainly, another great man, Ernest Shackleton—oh, and Miyamoto Musashi. Take a look at his *The Book of Five Rings*. Members of *Nächtlich*, The Nightwatchmen, also followed it, of course. Even America's most dashing leading man, the circus-educated Archibald Leach, understood it. He is quoted, in that funny little book we have, what is it, the—"

"*Talk of the Town: Hollywood Heroes Have Their Moment*," I chirped.

"Yes. He said, 'I pretended to be somebody I wanted to be until I became that person. Or he became me.' In the end, a man turns into what he thinks he is, however large or small. It is the reason why certain people are prone to colds and catastrophe. And why others can dance on water."

Dad obviously thought he was one of the ones who could dance on water, because for the next hour or so, he went on to discuss his premise in meticulous detail—the necessity of discipline and reputation, the curbing of emotion and feeling, modes for quietly implementing change. (I'd sat in the wings during so many performances, I was a natural choice for the understudy, though Dad never missed a show.) Although Dad's concert was filled with sweetness and light, none of his melodies were all that ground-breaking. He was pretty much summarizing the French ghostwritten *La Grimace*, a funny little book on power published in 1824. His other ideas were cherry-picked from H. H. Hill's *Napoleon's Progress* (1908), *Beyond Good and Evil* (Nietzsche, 1886), *The Prince* (Machiavelli, 1515), *History Is Power* (Hermin-Lewishon, 1990), obscure works like Aashir Alhayed's *The Instigations of a Dystopia* (1973) and *The Con Game* (1989) by Hank Powers. He even referenced a few folktales by Aesop and La Fontaine.

Our dinner guest was nothing more than a cavity of reverential silence by the time I served coffee. His mouth was always open. His eyes resembled harvest moons. (If it'd been 1400 B.C. there was a chance he'd have crowned Dad leader of the Israelites and asked him to lead the way to the Promised Land.)

"Thank you, Dr. Van Meer," he said as he was leaving, vigorously shaking Dad's hand. "It's been a–a pleasure. Everything you talked about—it–it was informative. I'm honored." He turned to me, blinking in surprise, as if he was seeing me for the first time all evening. "It was a privilege to meet you as well. I look forward to seeing you again."

I never did see him again, nor any of the others. For these colleagues, the Van Meer dinner invitation was like Birth, Death, the Senior Prom, a once in a lifetime event, and though there were enthusiastic promises of some future rendezvous shouted into the cricketed night as Teaching Assistant to Poetic and Narrative Forms dizzily lumbered to his car, in the ensuing weeks, Dad's kind always withdrew into the concrete corridors of the University of Oklahoma at Flitch or Petal or Jesulah or Roane, never to emerge again.

Once, I asked Dad why.

"I don't think the man's presence was titillating to the degree that I wish to put myself through a repeat performance. He was neither dope, money nor jiggy with it," he said, barely glancing up from Christopher Hare's *Social Instability and the Narcotics Trade* (2001).

I found myself thinking about the story of Tobias the Damned quite often, in particular, when Jade drove me home after the Christmas Cabaret. Whenever anything strange happened, even the most trivial of occurrences, I found myself sort of going back to him, secretly afraid with just a little heave-ho I might turn *into* him—by my own fear and nervousness, setting off some awful spiral of misfortune and misery, thereby severely disappointing Dad. It'd mean I'd missed every one of the principles of his beloved Determination

Theory, with its extensive section on handling emergencies. ("There are very few men who have the shrewdness to think and feel beyond the commotion of the present moment. *Try*," he commanded, recapitulating Carl von Clausewitz.)

* * *

As I walked up the lighted path to our porch, I could think of nothing I wanted to do more than forget Eva Brewster, Charles Manson, everything Jade had told me about Hannah, and simply disintegrate into bed, in the morning, maybe curl up next to Dad with *The Chronicle of Collectivism*. Maybe I'd even help him trek through a few student essays on future methods of war or have him read aloud *The Waste Land* (Eliot, 1922). Normally I couldn't stand it—he did it in a very grandiose way, channeling John Barrymore (see "Baron Felix von Geigern," *Grand Hotel*). But now, it seemed like the perfect antidote to my gloom.

When I opened the front door and walked into the foyer, I noticed the lights were still on in the library. I quickly tucked the *Blackbird* book into my backpack, still slumped next to the stairs where I'd heaved it Friday afternoon, and hurried down the hall to find Dad. He was in his red leather armchair, a cup of Earl Gray tea on the table next to him, head bent over a legal pad, doubtlessly scribbling another lecture or an essay for *Federal Forum*. His illegible handwriting tangled down the page.

"Hi," I said.

He glanced up. "Know what time it is?" he asked pleasantly.

I shook my head as he checked his watch.

"One twenty-two," he said.

"Oh. I'm sorry. I—"

"Who was it that dropped you off?"

"Jade."

"And where is Joe Public?"

"He's—well, I'm not sure."

"And where is your coat?"

"Oh, I left it. I forgot it at the—"

"And what in God's name did you do to your *leg*?"

I looked down. Blood had crusted around a cut on my shin, and my stockings had seized the opportunity to Go West, Young Man, ripping all the way up and around my leg, staking a claim somewhere in my shoe.

"I skinned it."

Dad slowly removed his reading glasses. He placed them delicately on the table next to him.

"We're through here," he said.

"What?"

"Finito. Kaput. I've had enough of the deceit. I'll tolerate it no longer."

"What are you talking about?"

He stared at me, his face calm as the Dead Sea.

"Your fabricated Study Group," he said. "The flagrant bravado you've cultivated when it comes to lying, which, to be frank, is more than a little pedestrian in its execution. My dear, *Ulysses* is an implausible choice for a study group in a secondary institution, however academically progressive. I think you might have done better with Dickens." He shrugged. "Austen perhaps. But as you're standing there in stunned silence, I'll go on. The returning at all hours. The running around town like a hairless stray dog. The alcoholic binges, which, granted, I have no proof of, but can infer with little difficulty from the innumerable tales of America's wayward youths saturating the airwaves and those unattractive caves around your eyes. I have said little, every time you so eagerly ran out of that door resembling a Cocoa Puff, wearing what the freethinking world would unanimously identify as a piece of Kleenex, because I *assumed*—unwisely it seems—that given the advanced degree of your education, you'd eventually come to the realization at the end of this hootchy-cootchy-with-the-ho-dawgs game, that these *friends* of yours, these *puppy fats* with whom you choose to *pal around*, are a waste of time, their thoughts about themselves and the world, stale. Instead, you seem to be suffering from a severe case of blindness. And poor judgment. I have to step in for your sake."

"Dad—"

He shook his head. "I've accepted a position at the University of Wyoming for next term. A town called Fort Peck. One of the best salaries I've seen in years. After your final exams next week, we'll orchestrate the move. You can call Harvard Admissions on Monday and notify them of the change of address."

"What?"

"You heard me quite well."

"Y–you can't do this." It came out a shrill, quivering whine. And it's embarrassing to admit, but I was trying not to cry.

"And that is precisely my point. If we'd had this conversation a mere three or four months ago you would have recognized this as an opportunity to quote *Hamlet*. 'O! that this too too solid flesh would melt / Thaw and resolve itself into a dew.' No, this town seems to have affected you like television on Americans. It's turned you into a side order of sauerkraut."

"I won't go."

Thoughtfully, he twisted the cap on his ink pen. "My dear, I understand in full the melodrama that is about to transpire. After you inform me you're running away to go live at the Dairy Queen, you'll go to your room, sob into your pillow that *lahf ain't fair,* throw things—I suggest socks; we're renting— tomorrow you'll refuse to speak to me, a week from today you'll have fallen into a pattern of one-word replies and amongst your Peter Pan *playas* you'll refer to me as the Red Mafia, one whose life's sole intent is to reduce to rubble your every chance at happiness. This pattern of behavior will doubtlessly continue until we *blow this here town,* and after three days in Fort Peck, you'll be speaking again, albeit between eye rolls and grimaces. And in a year, you'll thank me. Tell me it was the best thing I ever did. I thought by having you read *The Annals of Time* we'd circumvented such sludge. *Scio me nihil scire.* But if you still insist on putting both of us through this tedium, I suggest you get the ball rolling. I have a lecture to write on the Cold War and four- teen research papers to grade, each penned by a student with no concept of irony."

He sat there, his face burnt-tan and brutal in the gold lamplight, supremely arrogant and unapologetic (see "Picasso enjoying the fine weather in the South of France," *Respecting the Devil,* Hearst, 1984, p. 210). He was waiting for me to retire, retreat, as if I was one of his limp-jawed students who'd shown up during Office Hours, interrupting his research to pose some crackpot question about right and wrong.

I wanted to *kill* him. I wanted to take a fire poker to his too, too solid flesh (anything hard and pointy would do) so his hard-bitten face would de- form in fear and out of his mouth, not that perfect piano sonata of words, but a strangled, soul-ripped *Ahhhhhhhhh!,* the kind of sob one hears reverberat- ing through damp chronicles of medieval torture and the Old Testament. Hot tears had begun their exodus, making their slow, stupid way down my face.

"I–I'm not leaving," I said again. "*You* go. Go back to the Congo."

He gave no indication he'd even heard me, because his cherished lec- ture on the ABCs of Reaganism had already snagged his attention. His head was down, glasses returned to the end of his nose, an implacable smile. I tried to think of something to say, something huge and thrilling—a hypothesis of some kind, an obscure quotation that would knock him off his seat, turn his eyes to quarters. But as so often happens when one is thinking and feeling in the commotion of the present moment, I couldn't think of a thing. All I could do was stand with my arms at my sides, arms that felt like chicken wings.

The next few moments transpired in a detached haze. I felt the same sensation convicted murderers saturated in inmate orange describe in detail when asked by a keen news reporter wearing crummy bronze makeup how he/she, so seemingly *average* a human being, came to brutally wring the life out of a certain harmless person. Such offenders speak, a little dizzily, of the lonely clarity that settled over them on that fateful day, light as a swooping cotton sheet, an awake anesthesia that permitted them for the first time in their quiet lives, to ignore Prudence and Discretion, to give Good Sense the cold shoulder, to snub Self-Preservation and look right through Second Thoughts.

I walked out of the library, down the hall. I stepped outside, closing the front door behind me as softly as I could, so the Prince of Darkness didn't hear. I stood for two or three minutes on the steps, staring at the barebones trees, the strict light from the windows quilting the lawn.

I began to run. It was awkward at first in Jefferson's high heels, so I took them off, flung them over my shoulder. I hurried down the driveway and then down the street, past the empty cars and the flower beds cruddy with pinecones and dead flower stalks, past the potholes and mailboxes and the fallen branches grasping the street and the greenish puddles of light leaking from the streetlights.

* * *

Our house, 24 Armor Street, was buried in a densely forested section of Stockton known as Maple Grove. Though it wasn't one of those Orwellian gated communities like Pearl Estates (where we lived in Flitch) with identical white houses lined up like post-orthodontics teeth and the entry gate an aging actress (shrill, rusty, temperamental), Maple Grove still boasted its own exclusive Town Hall, Police Force, Zip Code and its own Unfriendly Welcome Sign ("You are now entering the Township of Maple Grove, an elegant and private residential community").

The fastest way out of the Grove was to cut directly south off our street, head into the woods and skulk through some twenty-two elegant and private backyards. I carefully made my way, hiccupping and crying at the same time,

the houses noiseless and sedate, slumped against the smooth lawns like dozing elephants on ice rinks. I crawled through a barricade of blue spruce,
scrambled through a reef of pines, shimmied down a hill, until I was unceremoniously emptied out, like water from a gutter, onto Orlando Avenue,
Stockton's answer to the Sunset Strip.

I was without plan, plum out of ideas, at a loss. Even within fifteen minutes of running away from home, unmooring oneself from one's parent, one
was struck by the vastness of things, the typhoon ferocity of the world, the
frailty of one's boat. Without thinking, I hurried across the street to the BP
gas station and pushed open the door to the Food Mart. It dinged a pleasant
hello. The kid always working, Larson, was incarcerated in the front in his
bulletproof holding pen, talking to one of his girlfriends dangling in front of
his window like an air freshener. I ducked into the nearest aisle.

Well, it just so happened Hello, My Name Is LARSON was a kid Dad took
to like a Surinam Cockroach to bat droppings. He was one of those unsink-
able eighteen-year-olds, with a Hardy Boy face no one had anymore, all freckles and gee-whiz grin, thick brown hair that grew around his face like an urn
plant and a lanky body in constant motion as if he was being operated by a
ventriloquist on speed (see Chapter 2, "Charlie McCarthy," *The Puppets That
Changed Our Lives*, Mesh, 1958). Dad found Larson *wondrous*. And that was
the thing with Dad: he'd teach Modes of Mediation to a thousand John
Dorys he was barely able to stomach, and then he'd pay a kid for berry-
flavored Tums and fall head over heels, declaring him a veritable dolphin
who'd spiral through the air when you whistled. "Now *that's* a promising
young man," said Dad. "I'd exchange every Happy, Sleepy and Doc to teach
him. He has spark. You don't find that often."

"If it ain't the girl with the dad," announced the store intercom. "Innit
past yer bedtime?"

Doused in the dead light of the Food Mart, I felt absurd. My feet hurt, I
was wearing an overcooked marshmallow and my face (I could see it plainly
in the reflective shelving) was decaying by the minute into an unstable mess
of crusty tears and bad makeup (see "Radon-221," *Questions of Radioactivity*,
Johnson, 1981, p. 120). I was also festooned with one billion pine needles.

"Come on over here and say hello! Whatcha doin' out so late?"

Reluctantly, I made my way to the cashier window. Larson was wearing
jeans and a red T-shirt that read MEAN REDS, and he was grinning. And that
was the thing with Larson; he was one of those people who grinned all the

time. He had ticklish eyes too, which had to explain the multitude of nutty-eyed peanut-butter parfaits thawing all over his Food Mart on any given night. Even when you were standing in front of his window innocuously paying for gas, his eyes, the clear-cut color of milk chocolate or mud, had a way of oozing all over you, so you couldn't help but have a feeling he was seeing something private about you—you stark naked, for example, or you saying humiliating things in your sleep, or worst of all, you in your favorite dumb fantasy, in which you walked a red carpet and wore a long beaded gown everyone took great pains not to step on.

"Lemme guess," he said. "Boyfriend trouble."

"Oh. I, uh, had a fight with my dad." I sounded like scrunched aluminum foil.

"Yeah? Saw him the other day. Came by with his girlfriend."

"They broke up."

He nodded. "Hey, Diamanta, go get her a Slurpee."

"Whut," said Diamanta, making a sour face.

"Seventy-ounce. Any flavor. On me."

Diamanta, in glittery pink shirt and sparkly jean miniskirt, was Pixy-stick skinny and had that wan, white parchment skin through which, in harsher lights, you could glimpse thin blue veins swimming through her arms and legs. Scowling at me, she removed her black platform boot from the bottom of the greeting card stand, turned and twinkled down the aisle.

"Sure," Larson said, shaking his head. "Old mans. They can be tough. When I was fourteen my pops cleared out. Left me nothin' but work boots and his subscription to *People* magazine, I kid you not. Two years? Did nothin' but glance over my shoulder, look for him every place. Think I'd see him 'cross the street. Passin' by on a bus. An I'd tail the bus one enda town to the other, thinkin' it was *him*, waitin', waitin' like a crazy man, just for him to get out at the stop. Only when he got out, it was someone else's old man. Wudn't mine. Things turned out, though, what he did? Best thing ever happened to me. Wanta know why?"

I nodded.

He leaned down, hitching his elbows on the counter.

"Cuza him I kin play King Layer."

"What flavor?" yelled Diamanta by the Slurpee machine.

"What flavor?" asked Larson. Without blinking, he recounted the names like an auctioneer overseeing a livestock sale. "Rootbeer, Blue Bubbagum,

7-Up, 7-Up Trop*icale,* Grapermelon, Crystallat, 'Nana Split, Code Red, Live-War—"

"Rootbeer is fine. Thanks."

"Lady without shoes would like Rootbeer," he said into the intercom.

"King what did you say?" I asked.

He grinned, revealing two severely crooked front teeth, one peeking out from behind the other as if it had stage fright.

"Layer. Shakespeare personage. Contrary to popular belief, person needs heartbreak an' betrayal. Else you got no stayin' power. Can't play a lead for five whole acts. Can't play two performances inna day. Can't fashion a character arch from Point A ta Point G. Can't get through the denewment, create a convincin' through line—all that stuff. See whut I'm sayin'? Person's *gotta* get banged up. Gotta get jerked around, lived in. So he's got somethin' to use, see. Hurts like hell. Sure. Feels bad. Not sure you wanna go on. But that gives way to what they commonly call emotive re-*zone*-ance. An emotive re-zonance makes it impossible fer people to take their eyes offa you, when yer onstage. Ever turned round in a good movie and seen the faces? Pretty intense. Diamanta?"

"Ain't coming out right," she cried.

"Turn off the machine, put it back on and try again."

"Where's the switch at?"

"On the side. Red."

"Looks all nasty," she said.

I stared up at him. Dad was right. There *was* something riveting about the kid. It was his outdated earnestness, the way his eyebrows did the polka when he talked and his mountain accent, which made the words jut out like pointy, slippery rocks on which he might get hurt. It was also the thousands of copper freckles dusting him head to toe as if he'd been dipped in glue, then in fine, penny-iridescent confetti.

"See," he said, leaning in and widening his eyes, "ya ain't felt pain, you kin only play yerself. And that ain't gonna move people. Maybe yer good for toothpaste, hemorrhoid commercials and such. But that's it. You'll never be a legend in yer own time. Ain't that what ya wanna be?"

Diamanta shoved the gigantic Slurpee into my hands and resumed her droop by the greeting cards.

"Now," Larson said, slapping his hands together, "ya got to tell us what yer name is."

"Blue."

"Got to tell us. *Blue.* Came to my doorstep tonight in yer hour a' need. Whud we do now?"

I looked from Larson to Diamanta, back to Larson again.

"What do you mean?" I asked.

He shrugged. "Ya turned up here ona dark stormy night. At"—he glanced at his watch—"2:06." He peered at my feet and nodded. "No shoes. Swut they call dramatic action. Swut happens in the beginnin' of a scene."

He stared at me, his face grave as any photo of Sun Yat-sen.

"Gotta tell us if we're in a comedy or a mellow drama or a whodidit or what they call a theater of the absurd. Ya just can't leave us standin' on stage with no dialogue."

I was aware of a certain convenience-store calm coursing through me, steady and ho-hum as the thrum of the beer fridge. Where I wanted to go, whom I had to talk to, was plain as the mirrored windows, the display of gum and batteries, Diamanta's hoop earrings.

"It's a whodunit," I said. "I was wondering if I could borrow your car."

Laughter in the Dark

Hannah was wearing a housedress the color of sandpaper, crudely scissored off at the hem so tiny threads hula-danced around her shins when she opened the door. Her face was bare as an unpainted wall, but it was obvious she hadn't been sleeping. Her hair hung serenely by her cheekbones and her bright black eyes bumblebeed from my face to my dress to Larson's truck to my face—all in a matter of seconds.

"Goodness," she said in a hoarse voice. "Blue."

"I'm sorry I woke you," I said. It was the sort of thing you said when you arrived on someone's doorstep at 2:45 A.M.

"No, no—I was awake." She smiled, but it wasn't a real smile, more of a cardboard cutout, and instantly I wondered if I'd made a mistake in coming, but then she put her arm around me. "God, come on in. It's freezing."

I'd only ever been in her house with Jade and the others, with Louis Armstrong warbling like toads, the air full of carrots, and it felt claustrophobic now, forsaken and dim like the cockpit of an old crashed plane. The dogs peered at me from behind her bare legs, their gaunt army of shadows slowly advancing toward my feet. There was a light on, the goosenecked lamp in the living room, and it spotlighted papers on the desk, bills, a few magazines.

"Why don't I fix you some tea?" she asked.

I nodded and after squeezing me again on the shoulder, she disappeared into the kitchen. I sat down on the lumpy plaid armchair next to the stereo. One of the dogs, Brody with three legs and the face of a senile sea captain *woofe*d in disgust, then hobbled over to me, pressing his cold wet nose into my hand, smuggling a secret. Pots coughed behind the kitchen door, a tap whimpered, a few moans from a drawer—I tried to concentrate on these mundane sounds, because frankly, I wasn't feeling all that marvelous about being there. When she'd opened the door, I'd expected a terrycloth bathrobe, her hair a hornet's nest, a heavy-eyed, "Sweet Jesus, what's happened?" Or, hearing the doorbell, she should have taken me for a mulleted highwayman thirsty for gruel and a warm lady, or a livid ex-boyfriend with tattoos on his knuckles ("V-A-L-ER-IO," it spelled).

I had not foreseen the stiff, clapboard manner with which she'd greeted me, the bare bones welcome, the whisper of a frown—as if I'd been wired for sound all night and she'd been privy to every defamatory chat, banter and tête-à-tête, including the one in which Jade accused her of Mansonian ties, *and* the one from my head, when the reality of Cottonwood smashed into the reality of Zach Soderberg and I was temporarily manslaughtered. I'd driven to her house (40 mph, barely able to merge, out of my mind when passing a semi or what resembled a wall of tulip poplars) because I loathed Dad, and could think of no other decent place to go, but I also sort of hoped seeing Hannah would lay to rest those other conversations, render them funny and invalid, the way a single scientific sighting of a Mysterious Starling (*Aplonis marvornata*) could tear it right off the Extinct Species list, throw it up on the dire, but decidedly more encouraging Critically Endangered.

Seeing her, however, had made it worse.

Dad always warned that it was misleading when one *imagined* people, when one saw them in the Mind's Eye, because one never remembered them as they *really* were, with as many inconsistencies as there were hairs on a human head (100,000 to 200,000). Instead, the mind used a lazy short-hand, smoothed the person over into their most dominating characteristic— their pessimism or insecurity (sometimes really being lazy, turning them into either Nice or Mean)—and one made the mistake of judging them from this basis alone and risked, on a subsequent encounter, being dangerously surprised.

A gasp of the kitchen door, and she reappeared, carrying a tray piled with a sagging piece of apple pie, a wine bottle, a glass, a pot of tea.

"Let's turn on some lights," she said, pushing with her bare foot a *National Geographic*, a *TV Guide* and some mail off the coffee table before sliding the tray across it. She switched on the yellow lamp by an ashtray, cruddy with dead-worm cigarette butts and thick light splashed all over me and the furniture.

"I'm sorry to be bothering you like this," I said.

"Blue. *Please.* I'm always here for you. You know that." She said the words and the meaning—well, it was there, but it was also sort of grabbing its suitcase and heading for the door. "I'm sorry if I seem a bit . . . out of sorts. It's been a long night." She sighed, and staring at me, reached forward and squeezed my hand. "Really, I'm glad you showed up. I could use the company. You can stay in the guest room, so forget about driving home tonight. Now tell me everything."

I swallowed, jittery about where to begin. "I had a fight with my dad," I said, but then to my surprise—just as she picked up the paper napkin and, biting her lip a little, set about folding it into an isosceles triangle—the phone began to ring. It sounded like human screams—Hannah had one of those bleating 1960s telephones, probably picked up for a dollar at a yard sale—and the sound made my heart throw itself melodramatically against my ribs (see Gloria Swanson, *Shifting Sands*).

"Oh, God," she whispered, visibly annoyed. "Hold on."

She disappeared into the kitchen. The ringing stopped.

I strained to hear her voice, but there was nothing to eavesdrop on, only silence and the pings of the dogs' collars; they nervously raised their heads off the floor.

Almost immediately, she reappeared, again with that small smile shoved onto her face like a tiny child forced onstage.

"That was Jade," she said, returning to the couch. With secretarial concentration she became absorbed with the teakettle, lifting the lid, scrutinizing the floating tea bags, tapping them with one finger as if they were dead fish.

"I take it you two had quite a night?" she asked. Glancing at me, she poured the tea, handed me the I HEART SLUGS coffee mug (not reacting when some hot water dripped off the side onto her knee) and then, as if I'd been begging her all night to pose for an oil portrait, she stretched out across the entire couch, glass of red wine in hand, her bare feet pushed beneath the cushions (Visual Aid 16.0).

"You know, we had a terrible fight," she said. "Jade and I. She left here absolutely enraged with me." She was speaking in an odd, teacherish voice, as if explaining Photosynthesis. "I don't even remember what it was about. Something mundane." She tilted her head toward the ceiling. "I think it was college applications. I told her she needed to get organized or she might not make it. She flew off the handle."

She took a sip of wine and I sipped my oolong tea feeling pangs of guilt. It was harrowingly clear Hannah knew the things Jade had said about her—

VISUAL AID 16.0

either for certain, if Jade had called her and confessed (Jade could never be a confidence woman, mortgage shark or shyster due to her overwhelming need to explain things to her victim), or simply assumed it given their argument. Most spectacular of all though, Hannah was visibly irked by it. Dad said people do all kinds of odd things when they're on the defensive, and now Hannah was frowning as she rubbed her thumb around the rim of her wineglass, and her eyes, they kept moving between my face and the wineglass and the piece of apple pie (that looked like it'd been stepped on) back to her wineglass.

I couldn't help but stare at her (her left arm boa-constricting her hip) like an investigator inspecting fingerprints on a bedpost, desperate to find the truth—if only a smudge of it. I knew it was an absurd thing—lunacy, guilt and love couldn't be eked out by connecting freckles, or shining a tiny light in the dugout of a collarbone—but I couldn't help myself. Some of the things Jade had said had stuck to me. *Could* she have purposefully drowned that man? Had she really slept with Charles? Was there a lost love hiding somewhere in her outskirts, her periphery—Valerio? Even when she was in a sullen, distracted mood, as she was now, Hannah *still* grabbed one's headlines, shoved other less captivating stories (Dad, Fort Peck) to page 10. FADE OUT: Dad, Fort Peck (my dream he'd go play Che in the Democratic Republic of the Congo). FADE IN: Hannah Schneider twisted along the couch like a piece of shimmering trash that had washed up on a beach, her face speckled with sweat, her fingertips nervously playing with the seam meandering through her dress.

"So you didn't make it to the dance?" I probed, my voice flimsy.

The question shook her awake; it was obvious she'd forgotten the question of why I was here, that I'd just shown up in a four-door Chevy Colorado truck in Sunburst Orange, unannounced, with no shoes. Not that I minded; Dad was a man who always assumed he was the Primary Subject, Group Focus, Chief Plan Under Discussion, so the fact that Hannah, after I'd mentioned my fight with him, blatantly snubbed him, shook him off as a nonevent—it was kind of fantastic.

"Things ran late," she said blandly. "We made pie." She looked at me. "Jade went, didn't she? She stormed out of here saying she was going to find you."

I nodded.

"She can be a strange girl. *Jade.* Sometimes she can say things that are— how should I . . . well, they're horrifying."

"I don't think she means anything by it," I suggested quietly.

Hannah tilted her head. "No?"

"Sometimes people say things simply to fill silence. Or as a way to shock and provoke. Or as exercise. Verbal aerobics. Loquacious cardio. There are any number of reasons. Only very rarely are words used strictly for their denotative meanings," I said, and yet Dad's comments from "Modes of Oration and the Brawn of Language" weren't making the slightest dent in Hannah. She wasn't paying attention. Her gaze was snagged somewhere near the piano in the dark corner of the room. And then, scowling (lines I'd never noticed before darting through her forehead), she reached over the arm of the couch, yanked open the end-table drawer and seized a half-empty pack of Camel cigarettes. She tapped one out, windmilled it agitatedly between her fingers and looked at me with anxious interest, like I was a dress on sale, the last in her size.

"Surely, you must realize," she said. "You're such a perceptive person; you don't miss anything"—she interrupted herself—"or maybe *not.* No. She hasn't told you. I think she's jealous—you speak so lovingly of your father. I'm sure it's hard for her."

"Tell me what?" I asked.

"Do you know anything at all about Jade? Her history?"

I shook my head.

Hannah nodded, and sighed again. She fished a pack of matches from the drawer and lit the cigarette quickly. "Well, if I tell you, you have to promise me you won't say anything to any of them. But I think it's important that you know. Otherwise, on nights like this, when she comes to you so angry . . . she was drunk, wasn't she?"

Slowly, I nodded.

"Well, on occasions like—well, like *tonight*, I can understand if you'd feel"—Hannah thought hard about what'd I'd feel, biting her lip like she was deciding what to order off a menu—"*confused*. Disturbed, even. I know *I* would. Knowing the truth will put everything into context for you. Maybe not immediately. No—you can't understand what something *is* when you're close to it. That's like looking at a billboard an inch away. We're all . . . what do they say . . . farsighted . . . or is it near—but later, no, that's when"—she was talking all of this over with herself—"yes, that's when it always becomes clear. Afterward."

She didn't immediately continue. She contemplated, with narrowed eyes, the fuming end of her cigarette, the tatty ears of Old Bastard who'd crept over to her, licked her kneecap and then slumped to the rug, tired as a summer fling.

"What do you mean?" I asked softly.

A shy, sort of mischievous smile was sneaking into her face—though I couldn't be certain of this; every time she moved her head the yellow lamplight raced across her cheekbones and mouth, but when she faced me fully it dashed away.

"You can't tell anyone what I tell you," she said sternly. "Not even your father. Promise me."

I felt a nervous knife-stab in my chest. "Why?"

"Well, he's protective, isn't he?"

I supposed Dad *was* protective. I nodded.

"Yes, well, it'd traumatize him, I'm sure," she said distastefully. "And what's the point of that?"

Fear began to course through me. It made me woozy, like I'd injected it into my arm. I found myself rewinding the last six minutes, trying to figure out how we'd taken this bizarre detour. I'd shown up, intent to perform a quiet, un-choreographed routine on Dad, but I'd been shoved into the wings, and here she was, the seasoned artiste commanding the stage, about to begin her monologue—a terrifying monologue by the sound of things. Dad said it was imperative to avoid people's fervent confidences and confessions. "Tell the person that you must leave the room," he instructed, "that you ate something, that you're ill, that your father has scarlet fever, that you feel the end of the world is imminent and you must rush to the grocery store to stock up on bottled water and gas masks. Or simply fake a seizure. Anything, sweet, anything at all to rid yourself of that intimacy they plan to lay on you like a slab of cement."

"You won't say anything?" she asked.

For the record, I *did* consider telling her Dad was riddled with smallpox, that I had to race to his bedside to hear his humble and heartfelt Final Words. But in the end, I found myself nodding, the unavoidable human response when someone asks if you'd like to hear a secret.

"When Jade was thirteen, she ran away from home," she said, waiting for a moment, letting those words land somewhere in the darkness on the other side of the room before continuing.

"From what she told me, she was raised to be a very rich, spoiled girl. Her father gave her everything. But he was the worst kind of hypocrite—he was from oil money, so he had the blood and suffering of thousands on his hands, and her mother"—Hannah raised her shoulders, shivered theatrically—"well, I don't know if you've ever had the pleasure of meeting her, but she's someone who doesn't bother to get dressed. She wears a bathrobe in the middle of the day. Anyway, Jade had a best friend growing up—she told me this—a beautiful girl, fragile. They were like sisters. She could confide in her, tell her everything under the sun—you know, the kind of friend everyone wants but never has—for the life of me, I can't remember her name. What *was* it? Something elegant. Anyway"—she flicked ashes off her cigarette—"she was considered problematic. Was caught stealing for the third or fourth time. She was going to be sent to a juvenile detention center. So she ran away. Made it all the way to San Francisco. Can you imagine? *Jade?* Atlanta to San Francisco—she was in Atlanta at the time, before her parents divorced. That's twenty-nine-hundred miles. She hitchhiked with truckers, families she encountered at rest stops and was finally picked up by the police at a drug store—Lord's Drugstore, I think it was. Of all names, *Lord's* Drugstore." Hannah smiled and exhaled, the smoke tripping over itself. "She said it changed the course of her life. Those six days."

She paused for a moment. The living room seemed to have sunk a few inches deeper into the ground, weighed down with the story.

As she'd started to speak, her voice weirdly relentless, trudging its way through the words, instantly my head switched off the lights and film-reeled: I saw Jade in grainy twilight (tight jeans, umbrella-thin) marching determinedly through the weedy junk along a highway—one in Texas or New Mexico—her gold hair ignited by the headlights, her face red from the unblinking eyes of the cars. But then, when I barreled past her in my mental eighteen-wheeler, I looked back and saw with surprise, it wasn't Jade: only a girl that looked like her. Because "hitchhiked with truckers" didn't sound like her and neither did the "beautiful, fragile" friend. Dad said it took a certain, rare revolutionary spirit to abandon "one's home and family, however bleak the conditions, and hurtle oneself into the unknown." Sure, every now and then, Jade slipped into handicapped stalls with *hombres* taking their fashion Must Haves off of Wanted posters, got so drunk her head hung from her shoulders like a squirt of glue, but for the girl to take such a chance, a running leap into the air and not be sure where she'd land, if she'd even make it to the other side—it seemed unbelievable. Of course, no detailed history of a human being could be laughed at or dismissed out of hand: "Never presume to know what a person is, was, or will be capable of," Dad said.

"Leulah was in a similar situation," Hannah continued. "Ran away with her math teacher when she was thirteen, too. She said he was handsome and passionate. In his late twenties. Mediterranean. I want to say Turkish. She thought she was in *love*. They made it all the way to—where was it . . . Florida, I think, before he was arrested." She took a long drag on her cigarette, letting the smoke drool out of her mouth as she talked on. "This was at her school before St. Gallway, somewhere in South Carolina. Anyway, Charles was a ward of a state for most of his life. His mom was a prostitute, junkie—the usual fare. No dad. Finally, he was adopted. Nigel, too. Both of his parents are in a Texas prison for killing a police officer. I can't remember the exact circumstances. But they shot him dead."

She raised her chin, staring at the cigarette smoke cowering above the lamp. It seemed deathly afraid of Hannah—as I was, in that moment. I was afraid of her tone of voice, which threw out these secrets impatiently as if she'd been forced to play a dull game of horseshoes.

"It's kind of funny," she continued (and she must have sensed my alarm because her voice was now pasteled, the harsher edges shaded with fingertips), "the moments on which life hinges. I think growing up you always imagine your life—your success—depends on your family and how much money they have, where you go to college, what sort of job you can pin down, starting salary." Her lips curled into a laugh before there was sound. (She'd been poorly dubbed.) "But it doesn't, you know. You wouldn't believe this, but life hinges on a couple of seconds you never see coming. And what you decide in those few seconds determines everything from then on. Some people pull the trigger and it all explodes in front of them. Other people run away. And you have no idea what you'll do until you're there. When your moment comes, Blue, don't be afraid. Do what you need to do."

She pulled herself upright, swung her bare feet onto the carpet, stared at her hands. They sat on each leg crumpled and useless like Dad's discarded lecture beginnings. A piece of her hair had fallen over her left eye turning her into a pirate and she didn't bother tucking it behind her ear.

Meanwhile, my heart was trying to crawl into my mouth. I didn't know if it was right to passively sit there, listening to these awful skin-and-bones confessions, or to try to run for it, scramble to the door, fling it open with the force of Scipio Africanus when he ruthlessly sacked Carthage, sprinting to the truck, taking off into the pillaged night, gravel flying, tires wailing like captives. But where would I go? Back to Dad, like some president's middle initial no one remembered, like some day in History on which nothing groundbreaking occurred apart from a few Catholic missionaries arriving in the Amazon and a minor native uprising in the East.

"And then Milton," Hannah said, her voice sort of caressing his name. "He was involved in that street gang—I can't remember what it was, something 'night'—"

"*Mil*ton?" I repeated. I saw him immediately: junkyard, leaning against a chain-link fence (he was always swaybacked against something), combat boots, one of those scary nylon scarves in red or black knotted over his head, his eyes tough, his skin faintly rifle colored.

"Yes. *Mil*ton." She repeated, mimicking me. "He's older than everyone thinks. Twenty-one. God—don't let on you know. He had a few lost years, blackouts, when he doesn't even remember what he did. He lived on the streets . . . raised hell. But of course, I understand. When you don't know what to believe, you feel like you're sinking, so you grab on to as many different ideas as possible. Even the crazy ones. Eventually one will keep you afloat."

"So this was when he was in Alabama?" I asked.

She nodded.

"So that must be why he got his tattoo," I said.

I'd seen it by now—the tattoo—and the breathtaking occasion in which he'd shown it to me had become a timeless film clip I replayed incessantly in my head. We'd been alone in the Purple Room—Jade and the others had gone to the kitchen to make pot brownies—and Milton was fixing himself a drink at the bar, plopping ice cubes into his glass, leisurely, as if counting out ducats. He'd pushed up the long shirtsleeves of his Nine Inch Nails T-shirt, so on his right bicep I could *just* make out the black toes of something. "You wanta see it?" he'd asked suddenly, and then strolled over to me, whiskey in hand, sitting down, hard, so his back collided with my left knee, the couch wincing. His brown eyes stapled to mine, he pulled up the sleeve, sloooowly—obviously enjoying my rapt attention—to reveal, not the crude black splotch everyone at St. Gallway whispered about, but a cheeky cartoon angel the size of a beer can. She was winking like a lascivious grandpa, one chubby knee in the air, the other leg straight down as if she'd frozen solid doing a jackknife off a diving board. "There she is," Milton said in his drooping voice, "Miss America." Before I could speak, hunt and gather a few words, he'd stood, pushed the sleeve down and wandered from the room.

"Yes," Hannah said abruptly. "So anyway," she was tapping out another cigarette, "they all had things happen to them, earthquakes, you know, when they were twelve, thirteen, things most people don't have the guts to recover from." She lit it swiftly, tossed the matches onto the coffee table. "Know anything about The Gone?"

Hannah, I noticed, had been about to run out of gas when she talked about Milton. If she'd started out in a slick and self-assured Monte Carlo roadster with Jade's story, by the time Milton's yarn rolled around, she was in one of those rusty jalopies panting along the side of the highway, hazards on. I sensed she was experiencing pangs of remorse about what she was doing, weighing me down with this confession; her face looked like a pause between sentences as her mind ran back over to the words she'd just said, poking them, listening to their little heartbeats, hoping they weren't fatal.

But now, with this new question, she seemed to have regained speed. She stared at me, a fierce look on her face (her eyes gripping my eyes, not letting go), a look that reminded me of Dad; as he combed supplemental textbooks on Rebellion and Foreign Affairs in order to find that bright bloom of evidence that, when transplanted into his lecture, would have the capacity to stun, to intimidate, make the "little shits melt in their seats, leaving them mere stains on the carpet," he often sported this militant look, making his features look so hard, I felt if I was blind and had to run my hand over his face to recognize him, he'd feel like a bit of stone wall.

"They're missing persons," Hannah said. "They fall through those ubiquitous cracks, in the ceiling, on the floor. Runaways, orphans, they're kidnapped, killed—they vanish from public record. After a year, the police stop looking. They leave behind nothing but a name, and even that's forgotten in the end. 'Last seen in the evening hours of November 8, 1982, as she was completing her shift at an Arby's in Richmond, Virginia. She drove away in a blue 1988 Mazda 626, which was later found abandoned on the side of the road, in what was possibly a staged accident.' "

She fell silent, lost in memory. Certain memories were like that—swamps, bogs, pits—and while most people avoided these muggy, unmapped, wholly uninhabited recollections (wisely understanding they were liable to disappear in them forever), Hannah seemed to have taken the risk and tiptoed into one of hers. Her gaze had fallen, lifeless, to the floor. Her bent head eclipsed the lamp and a thin ribbon of light clung to her profile.

"Who are you talking about?" I asked as gently as I could. Noah Fishpost, MD, in his captivating book on the adventures of modern psychiatry, *Meditations on Andromeda* (2001), mentioned one had to proceed as unobtrusively as possible when questioning a patient, because truth and secrets were cranes, dazzling in size yet notoriously shy and wary; if one made too much noise, they'd disappear into the sky, never to be seen again.

She shook her head. "No—I used to collect them as a girl. I'd memorize the listings. I could recite hundreds of them. 'The fourteen-year-old girl disappeared on October 19, 1994, when she was walking home from school. She was last seen at a pay telephone booth between 2:30 and 2:45 on the corner of Lennox and Hill.' 'Last seen by her family in their residence in Cedar Springs, Colorado. At approximately 3:00 A.M. a family member noticed the television still on in her bedroom, but she was no longer inside.' "

Goose bumps pinched my arms.

"I think it was why I sought them out," she said. "Or they sought me—I can't even remember anymore. I was worried they'd fall through the cracks, too."

Her gaze finally picked itself up and I saw, with horror, her face was red. There were giant tears looming in her eyes.

"And then there's you," she said.

I couldn't breathe. *Run for Larson's truck,* I told myself. *Run for the high-*

way, for Mexico, because Mexico was where everyone went when they had to escape (though no one ever got there; they were all killed tragically, mere yards from the border) or if not Mexico, then Hollywood, because Hollywood was where everyone went when they wanted to reinvent themselves and end up a movie star (see *The Revenge of Stella Verslanken*, Botando, 2001).

"When I saw you in that grocery store back in September, I saw a lonely person." She didn't say anything for a moment, just let those words rest there like tired workmen on a curb. "I thought I could help."

I felt like a wheeze. No—I was a cough, a bed creak, something humiliating, the frayed ruffle on discolored pantaloons. But just as I was going to glue together some childish excuse to run out of her house, never to return ("The most catastrophic thing to befall any man, woman or child is abject pity," wrote Carol Mahler in the Plum Award–winning *Color Doves* [1987])—I glanced over at Hannah and was struck dumb.

Her anger, irk, aggravation—whatever that mood was she'd been mired in since I'd first arrived, when the phone screamed, when she'd sworn me to secrecy, even the apparent melancholy of moments ago—had fizzled. She was now disturbingly peaceful (see "Lake Lucerne," *A Question of Switzerland*, Porter, 2000, p. 159).

True, she'd lit yet another cigarette, and smoke tangled out of her fingers. She'd also fluffed her hair and so it swayed one way, then the other across her forehead as if seasick. But her face, rather bluntly, boasted the relieved and somewhat satisfied expression of a person who'd just accomplished something, a harrowing feat; it was a face of slammed-shut textbooks, doors dead bolted, switched-off lights, or else, after a bow, amidst a drizzle of applause, heavy red curtains swinging closed.

Jade's words slammed into my head: *"She's really the worst actress on the planet. If she was an actress, she wouldn't even make the B movies. She'd be in the D or the E movies."*

"Anyway," Hannah went on, "who cares about any of that now—the reasons for things. Don't think about it. Ten years from now—*that's* when you decide. After you've taken the world by storm. Are you sleepy?" She asked this quickly and evidently had no interest in my answer because she yawned into her fist, stood up, and stretched in the lazy royal way of her own white Persian cat—Lana or Turner, I wasn't sure which—who, with a heralding thrash of tail, strolled out of the darkness beneath the piano bench and meowed.

The Sleeping Beauty
and Other Fairy Tales

I couldn't sleep.

Oh, no—now that I was alone in a strange, stiff bed, a pale morning soaking through the curtains, the overhead lamp a giant eye staring down at me, The Histories of the Bluebloods began to creep out of the underbrush like exotic nocturnal animals at nightfall (see "Zorilla," "Shrew," "Jerboa," "Kinkajou" and "Small-Eared Zorro," *Encyclopedia of Living Things*, 4th ed.). I had very little experience dealing with Dark Pasts, apart from close readings of *Jane Eyre* (Brontë, 1847) and *Rebecca* (Du Maurier, 1938) and though I'd always secretly seen splendor in melancholic chills, ashy circles stamped under the eyes, wasted silence, now, knowing each of them had suffered (if Hannah could be believed), it worried me.

After all, there was Wilson Gnut, the calmly handsome kid I knew at Luton Middle in Luton, Texas, whose father hanged himself on Christmas Eve. Wilson's own ensuing tragedy had nothing to do with his father, but in the way he was treated at school. People weren't mean to him—quite the contrary, they were sweet as pie. They held open doors, offered homework to plagiarize, allowed him to cut in line at all water fountains, vending machines and gym uniform distributions. But lurking within their benevolence was the universal understanding that because of his father, a Secret Door had been opened for Wilson, and anything and everything dark and deviant could fly out of it—suicide, sure, but other frightening things too, like Necrophilia, Polyorphantia, Menazoranghia, maybe even Zootosis.

With the quiet precision of Jane Goodall alone at her observation post in a tropical forest of Tanzania, I observed and documented the array of looks elicited in Wilson's presence by students, parents and faculty alike. There was the Relieved Glance of "Darn Glad I Ain't You" (after smiling amiably at Wilson, performed covertly to a commiserating third party), the Sorry Look of "He'll Never Git Over It" (performed to the floor and/or immediate space around Wilson), the Meaningful Gaze of "Kid'll End Up Crooked as a Dog's Hind Leg" (performed deep into Wilson's brown eyes) and the Simple Gawk of the Unbelieving (mouth open, eyes unfocused, overall demeanor near vegetative, performed at Wilson Gnut's back as he sat quietly at his desk).

There were gestures too, like the Just-Whistlin'-Dixie Wave (performed after school in car windows as students drove away with their parents and noticed Wilson still waiting for his mother, who had stringy hair, a goat laugh and wore beads, a gesture always accompanied by one of three remarks: "So sad, what happened," "Cain't imagine what he's goin' through" or the bluntly paranoid, "Dad's not goin' kill himself anytime soon. Is he?"). There was also the That's-Him-Thar Point, the That's-Him-Thar Point in the Opposite Direction of Wilson Gnut (a Texan's attempt at subtlety) and worst of all, the Quick Conniption (performed by students when Wilson Gnut's hands accidentally touched theirs, on door handles, for example, or passing Unit Tests around class, as if Wilson Gnut's misfortune was an illness transmitted via hands, elbows or fingertips).

In the end—and this was the tragedy—Wilson Gnut ended up agreeing with everyone. He, too, began to believe a Secret Door had been opened just for him and awaited something dark and deviant, which, any moment now, would come flying out. It wasn't his fault, of course; if the world insinuates you're a Dog That Don't Hunt, a Cowboy With No Shit Kickers, In Low Cotton, you tend to believe it's true. Wilson stopped spearheading basketball games at break, disappeared from Olympics of the Mind. And even though, on multiple occasions, I overheard a few well-meaning kids asking him if he wanted to accompany them after school to KFC, Wilson avoided eye contact, mumbled, "No, thanks," and disappeared down the hall.

I thus concluded, with the same awe of Jane Goodall discovering the chimpanzees' nimble use of tools to extract termites, it really wasn't so much the tragic event itself, but others having knowledge of it that prevented recovery. Individuals could live through almost anything (see *Das unglaubliche Leben der Wolfgang Becker*, Becker, 1953). Even Dad was in awe of the human body and Dad was never in awe of anything. "It really is staggering, what the corpus can withstand."

After this observation, if he was in a Bourbon Mood and feeling theatrical, Dad did Brando as Colonel Kurtz.

" 'You have to have men who are moral,' " droned Dad, slowly turning his head toward me, widening his eyes in an attempt to portray Genius and Insanity simultaneously, " 'and at the same time, able to use their primordial instincts to kill without feeling, without passion, without judgment . . .' " (Dad always raised his eyebrows and stared at me pointedly on "judgment.") " 'Because it's judgment that defeats us.' "

Of course, I had to question the soundness of what Hannah had told me, of Hannah herself. There had been an undeniable sound-staginess to her words, evidence of fake palms (vagueness over exact locations), a prop warehouse (wineglass, endless cigarettes), wind machines (tendency to romanticize), publicity stills (heavy gazes at the ceiling, the floor)—theatrical flairs that brought to mind the lovelorn posters caking her classroom. It was *also* true, plenty of confidence men were capable of spinning grim fairy tales under pressure, replete with backstory, artful cross-reference, dashes of irony and twists of fate without a single flick of the eyes. And yet, while such villainous scheming was *remotely* plausible, it didn't exactly seem feasible for Hannah Schneider. Sharpies and shortchangers concocted such elaborate fictions to escape the slammer; what was Hannah's motivation for making up forlorn pasts for each of the Bluebloods, brutally pushing them outside, locking the door, making them stand in the rain? No, I felt certain there was a basic truth to what she'd told me, even if it had Hannified studio lighting and white people in pancake makeup playing savages.

With these thoughts, morning sneaking toward the windows, flimsy curtains whispering to a draft, I fell asleep.

*   *   *

There's nothing like a bright and chipper morning to briskly send running all demons of the night before. (Contrary to popular belief, Unease, Inner Demons and Guilt Complexes were remarkably unsure of themselves and usually fled in the strong presence of Ease and Squeaky-Clean Conscience.)

I woke up in Hannah's tiny guest room—walls the color of bluebells— and slumped out of bed. I pulled back the thin white curtain. The front lawn shivered excitedly. Blue sky ballooned overhead. Crisp brown leaves, *en pointe*, were busy practicing *glissades* and *grand jêtés* down the driveway. On Hannah's moldy bird feeder (usually as forsaken as a house with asbestos insulation and lead paint) two fat cardinals lunched with a chickadee.

I made my way downstairs and found Hannah dressed, reading the newspaper.

"There you are," she said cheerfully. "Sleep well?"

She gave me clothes, old gray corduroy pants she said had shrunk in the wash, black shoes and a pale pink cardigan with tiny beads around the neck.

"Keep this stuff," she said, smiling. "It looks adorable on you."

Twenty minutes later, she drove behind me in her Subaru all the way to the BP gas station, where I left Larson's truck and keys with Big Red who had raw-carrot fingers and worked mornings.

Hannah suggested we grab a bite to eat before she drove me home, so we stopped at Pancake Haven on Orlando. A waitress took our order. The restaurant had an uncomplicated frankness: square windows, worn brown carpet that stuttered Pancake Haven Pancake Haven all the way to the bathrooms, people sitting quietly with their food. If there was Darkness or Doom in the world, it was remarkably courteous, waiting for everyone to finish breakfast.

"Is Charles . . . in love with you?" I asked suddenly. It shocked me, how easy it was to ask the question.

Her reaction wasn't outrage, but amusement. "Who told you that—Jade? I thought I explained it last night—her need to exaggerate everything, pit people against each other, make everything more exotic than it is. They all do it. I have no idea why." She sighed. "They also have me pining after some person—what's the name . . . *Victor.* Or Venezia, something out of *Braveheart*. It begins with V—"

"Valerio?" I suggested quietly.

"Is *that* it?" She laughed, a loud flirty sound, and a man in orange flannel sitting at the table next to us looked over at her, hopeful. "Believe me, if my knight in shining armor was wandering around out there—Valerio, right?— I'd be hightailing it after him. And when I found him, I'd hit him over the head with my club, toss him over my shoulder, bring him back to my *lair* and have my way with him." Still sort of giggling to herself, she unzipped her leather purse and handed me three quarters. "Now call your father."

*   *   *

I used the payphone by the cigarette machine. Dad answered after the first ring.

"Hi—"

"*Where in God's name are you?*"

"At a diner with Hannah Schneider."

"Are you all right?"

(I have to admit, it was thrilling to hear the tremendous anxiety in Dad's voice.)

"Of course. I'm having french toast."

"Oh? We'll I'm having a Missing Person's Report for breakfast. Last Seen. Approximately two-thirty. Wearing. I'm not sure. Glad you called. Was that a dress you were wearing last night or a Hefty-Hefty Cinch Sak?"

"I'll be home in an hour."

"Delighted you've decided to again grace me with your presence."

"Well, I'm not going to Fort Peck."

"Eh—we can discuss it."

And then it came to me, like Alfred Nobel his idea of a weapon to end all war (see Chapter 1, "Dynamite," *History's Missteps*, June, 1992).

" 'In fear, one flees,' " I said.

He hesitated, but only for a second. "A valid point. But we'll have to see. On the other hand, I am in dire need of your assistance with these piteous student essays. If it meant putting myself at your disposal, say, trading Fort Peck for three or four hours of your time, I suppose I'd be willing to do so."

"Dad?"

"Yes?"

I don't know why, but I couldn't say anything.

"Don't tell me you've gotten a tattoo across your chest that reads, 'Raised in Hell,' " he said.

"No."

"You've obtained a piercing."

"No."

"You wish to join a cult. A division of extremists who practice polygamy and call themselves Man's Agony."

"No."

"You're a lesbian and you'd like my blessing before asking out a field hockey coach."

"No, Dad."

"Thank God. Sapphic love, while natural and as old as the seas, is, regrettably, still considered by Middle Amcrica something of a fad, akin to the Melon Diet or Pantsuits. It wouldn't be an easy way of life. And as we both know, having me for a father is no cakewalk. It'd be strenuous, I think, to shoulder both loads."

"I love you, Dad."

There was silence.

I felt ludicrous, of course, not only because when one throws out those particular words, one needs them to boomerang back without delay, not even because I realized the previous evening had turned me into a sap, a cuckoo, a walking *For the Love of Benji* and a living *Lassie Come Home,* but because I knew full well Dad couldn't stomach those words, just as he couldn't stomach American politicians, corporate executives who were quoted in *The Wall Street Journal* saying either "synergy" or "out of the box," third-world poverty, genocide, game shows, movie stars, *E.T., or* for that matter, Reese's Pieces.

"I love you too, my dear," he said at last. "Really though, I thought you'd have figured that out by now. Yet I suppose it's to be expected. The clearest, most palpable things in life, the elephants and white rhinos if you will, standing around quite plainly in their watering holes, chewing on leaves and twigs, they often go unnoticed. And why is that?"

It was a Van Meer Rhetorical Question followed by the Van Meer Pregnant Pause, so I simply waited, pressing the receiver against the bottom of my chin. I'd heard him use such oratorical devices before, the few times I'd come to watch him lecture in one of the big amphitheaters with carpeted walls and buzzing light. The last time I'd heard him speak, on Civil Warfare at Cheswick College, I remember, quite distinctly, I was horrified. Without a doubt, I thought to myself, as Dad went on frowning center stage (occasionally breaking into a variety of showy gestures, as if he was a deranged Mark Antony or manic King Henry VIII), everyone could see, plain as day, Dad's embarrassing truth: he wanted to be Richard Burton. But then I really looked around, and noticed every student (even the one on the third row who'd shaved an anarchy symbol into the back of his head) was behaving like a feeble white moth spiraling through Dad's light.

"America is asleep," Dad boomed. "You've heard it before—perhaps by a homeless man you passed on the street and he smelled like a Porta-John so you held your breath and pretended he was a mailbox. Well, is it *true? Is* America hibernating? Getting forty winks, a bit of shut-eye? We're a country of boundless opportunity. Aren't we? Well, I know the answer's 'yes' if you happen to be a CEO. Last year, the average compensation for a Chief Executive

Officer soared 26 percent, compared to blue-collar salaries inching up a pitiable 3 percent. And the fattest paycheck of all? Mr. Stuart Burnes, CEO of Remco Integrated Technologies. Tell him what he's won, Bob! One-hundred-sixteen-point-four million dollars for a year's labor."

Here Dad crossed his arms and looked fascinated.

"What's Stu *doing* to warrant such a windfall, a salary that would feed all of Sudan? Sadly, not much. Integrated missed fourth-quarter earnings. Stock prices fell 19 percent. Yet board members picked up the tab for the crew on Stu's hundred-foot yacht, also paid the Christie's curator fees for his fourteen-hundred-piece Impressionist art collection."

Here Dad inclined his head as if hearing faint, far-off music.

"So this is greed. And is it *good?* Should we listen to a man wearing suspenders? With many of you, when you come and chat with me during office hours, I sense an air of inevitability, not of *defeat,* but resignation, that such iniquities are simply the way it is and they can't be changed. This is America and what we do is grab as much *cash* as we can before we all die of heart disease. But do we want our lives to be a bonus round, a Money Grab? Call me an optimist, but I don't think so. I think we hope for something more meaningful. But what do we *do?* Start a revolution?"

Dad asked this of a small brown-haired girl wearing a pink T-shirt in the front row. She nodded apprehensively.

"Are you out of your *mind?*"

Instantly, she turned six shades pinker than the T-shirt.

"You might have heard of various imbeciles who waged war on the U.S. government in the sixties and seventies. The New Communist Left. The Weather Underground. The Students for the Blah-Blah-No-One-Takes-You-Seriously. In fact, I think they were worse than Stu, because they smashed, not monogamy, but hope for productive protest and objection in this country. With their delusional self-importance, ad hoc violence, it became easy to dismiss anyone voicing dissatisfaction with the way things are as freaky flower chiles.

"*No.* I contend we should take a cue from one of the greatest American movements of our time—a revolution in itself really, nobly warring as it does against time and gravity, also accountable for the most widespread perpetuation of alien-looking life forms on Earth. Cosmetic surgery. That's right, ladies and gentlemen. America is in dire need of a nip-tuck. No mass uprising, no widespread revolution. Rather, an eye lift here. A boob job there. Some well-placed liposuction. A minuscule cut behind the ears, tug it up, staple it into place—confidentiality is key—and *voilà*, everyone will be saying we look mahvelous. Greater elasticity. No sags. For those of you who are laughing, you'll see precisely what I mean when you do the reading for Tuesday, the treatise in Littleton's *Anatomy of Materialism*, 'The Nightwatchmen and Mythical Principles of Practical Change.' And Eidelstein's 'Repressions of Imperialist Powers.' And my own meager piece, 'Blind Dates: Advantages of Silent Civil War.' Do not forget. You will be pop quizzed."

Only when Dad, with a small, self-satisfied smile, closed his worn leather folder full of chicken-scratch notes (placed on the podium for effect, because he never looked at them), removed the linen handkerchief from his jacket pocket, and delicately touched it to his forehead (we'd driven through Nevada's Andamo Desert in the middle of July and he hadn't needed to blot his forehead like that a single time), only then did anyone move. Some of the kids grinned in disbelief, others walked out of the lecture hall with surprised faces. A few were starting to page through the Littleton book.

Now, Dad answered his own question, his voice low and scratchy in the receiver.

"We are under an invincible blindness as to the true and real nature of things," he said.

A Room with a View

The late great Horace Lloyd Swithin (1844–1917), British essayist, lecturer, satirist and social observer, wrote in his autobiographical *Appointments, 1890–1901* (1902), "When one travels abroad, one doesn't so much discover the hidden Wonders of the World, but the hidden wonders of the individuals with whom one is traveling. They may turn out to afford a stirring view, a rather dull landscape or a terrain so treacherous one finds it's best to forget the entire affaire and return home."

I didn't see Hannah during Finals Week and only encountered Jade and the others once or twice before an exam. "See ya next year, Olives," Milton said when we passed each other outside the Scratch. (I thought I detected wrinkles in his forehead hinting at his advanced age when he winked at me, but I didn't want to stare.) Charles, I knew, was off to Florida for ten days, Jade was going to Atlanta, Lu to Colorado, Nigel to his grandparents—Missouri, I think—and I was thus resigned to an uneventful Christmas vacation with Dad and Rikeland Gestault's latest critique of the American justice system, *Ride the Lightning* (2004). After my last exam, however, AP Art History, Dad announced that he had a surprise.

"An early graduation present. A final *Abenteuer*—I should say, *aventure*—before you're rid of me. It's only a matter of time before you refer to me as—what do they say in that mawkish film with the cranky elderly? An old poop."

As it turned out, an old friend of Dad's from Harvard, Dr. Michael Servo Kouropoulos (Dad affectionately called him "Baba au Rhum," and thus I assumed he bore a resemblance to rum-soaked sponge cake), had, for some time, been entreating Dad to visit him in Paris, where he'd been teaching archaic Greek literature at La Sorbonne for the past eight years.

"He invited us to stay with him. Which we will, certainly; I understand he has a palatial apartment somewhere along the Seine. Comes from a family drowning in money. Imports and exports. First, however, I thought it'd be *swell* to stay a few nights in a hotel, get a taste of *la vie parisienne*. I booked something at the Ritz."

"The *Ritz?*"

"A suite *au sixième étage*. Sounds quite electrifying."

"Dad—"

"I wanted the Coco Suite, but it was taken. I'm sure everyone wants the Coco Suite."

"But—"

"Not a word about the cost. I told you I've been saving for a few extravagances."

I was surprised by the trip, the proposed lavishness, sure, but even more by the childlike zeal that'd overtaken Dad, a Gene Kelly Effect I had not witnessed in him since June Bug Tamara Sotto of Pritchard, Georgia, invited Dad to Monster Mash, the statewide tractor pull in which it was impossible for someone without trucker connections to get tickets. ("Do you think if I slip one of those toothless marvels a fifty, he'd allow me to get behind the wheel?" Dad asked.) I'd also recently discovered (crumpled paper sadly staring out of the kitchen trash) *Federal Forum* had declined to print Dad's latest essay, "The Fourth Reich," an offense which, under normal circumstances, would have caused him to grumble under his breath for days, perhaps launch into spontaneous lectures on the dearth of critical voices in American media forums, both popular and obscure.

But, no, Dad was all "Singin' in the Rain," all "Gotta Dance," all "Good Mornin'." Two days before our scheduled departure, he came home laden with guidebooks (of note, *Paris, Pour Le Voyageur Distingué* [Bertraux, 2000]), city shopping maps, Swiss Army suitcases, toiletry kits, miniature reading lights, inflatable neck pillows, Bug Snuggle plane socks, two strange brands of hearing plug (EarPlane and Air-Silence), silk scarves ("All Parisian women wear scarves because they wish to create the illusion of being in a Doisneau photo," said Dad), pocket phrase books and the formidable, hundred-hour La Salle Conversation Classroom ("Become bilingual in five days," ordered the side of the box. "Be the toast of dinner parties.").

With the nervous expectation "one can only feel when one parts with one's personal baggage and holds fast to the shabby hope of reuniting with it after journeying two thousand miles," Dad and I, on the eve of December 20, boarded an Air France flight out of Atlanta's Hartsfield airport and safely landed in Paris at Charles de Gaulle, the cold, drizzling afternoon of December 21 (see *Bearings, 1890–1897*, Swithin, 1898, p. 11).

We weren't scheduled to meet up with Baba au Rhum until the 26 (Baba was supposedly visiting family in the south of France), so we spent those first five days in Paris alone as we'd been in the old Volvo days, speaking to no one but each other and not even noticing.

We ate crêpes and coq au vin. At night, we dined in expensive restaurants crawling with city views and men with bright eyes that fluttered after women like caged birds hoping to find a tiny hole through which they might escape. After dinner, Dad and I entombed ourselves at jazz clubs like au Caveau de la Huchette, a smoky crypt in which one was required to remain mute, motionless and alert as a coonhound while the jazz trio (faces so sweaty, they had to have been lined with Crisco) ripped, riffed and warped with their eyes closed, their fingers tarantuling up and down keys and strings for over three and a half hours. According to our waitress, the place had been a favorite of Jim Morrison, and he'd shot up heroin in the same dark corner in which Dad and I were sitting.

"We'd like to move to that table there, *s'il vous plaît*," said Dad.

Despite these rousing environs, I thought about home all the time, about that night with Hannah, the strange stories she told me. As Swithin wrote in *State of Affairs: 1901–1903* (1902), "Whilst man is in one location, he thinks of another. Dancing with one woman, he can't help but long to see the quiet curve of another's nude shoulder; to never be satisfied, to never have the mind and body cheerfully stranded in a single location—this is the curse of the human race!" (p. 513).

It was true. Contented as I was (especially those moments Dad was unaware of the bit of éclair at the corner of his mouth, or when he rattled off a sentence in "perfect" French and was met with confused stares), I found myself staying awake at night, worried about them. And, this is awful to admit, because the correct thing was to be wholly unfazed by what Hannah had told me—I really couldn't help but see them all in a slightly different light now, a very severe overhead light in which they bore a startling resemblance to smudged street urchins who sang and marched in the chorus of "Consider

Yourself" in *Oliver!*, which Dad and I watched over salty popcorn one dull evening in Wyoming.

After nights such as these, the next morning I found myself squeezing Dad's arm a little tighter as we dashed in front of traffic crossing the Champs Élysées, giggling a little louder over his comments regarding fat Americans in khaki when a fat American in khaki asked the madame at the pâtisserie counter where the bathrooms were. I began to behave like someone with a grave prognosis, searching Dad's face all the time, feeling on the verge of tears when I noticed the delicate wrinkles blooming around his eyes, or the prick of black in his left iris, or the frayed cuffs of his corduroy jacket—a direct result of my childhood, of my tugging on his sleeve. I found myself thanking God for these dusty details, these things no one else noticed, because they, fragile as spiderwebs and thread, were the only things separating me from *them*.

I must have thought about the others more than I realized, because they began to make Hitchcock cameos. I saw Jade on countless occasions. There she was, just in front of us, walking a haughty pug down Rue Danton—wheat-bleached hair, blunt red lipstick, gum and jeans—perfectly jaded. And there was Charles, the thin, sullen blond kid melting into the bar at Café Ciseaux, drinking his café, and poor Milton, beached outside the Odéon Métro with nothing but a sleeping bag and a recorder. With gnarled fingers he played a woeful Christmas song—some sad, four-note tune—his feet raw, his skin heavy as a wet pair of jeans.

Even Hannah made a brief appearance, in what turned out to be the only incident of our stay Dad had not planned (at least, not to my knowledge). There was a bomb scare in the early morning of December 26. Alarms screamed, hallways flashed, all guests in the hotel, as well as employees—bathrobes, bald heads, bare chests a-flying—were emptied out into Place Vendôme like cream of potato soup from a can. Smooth Efficiency, the implacable quality exuded by all Ritz staff, turned out to be nothing more than a flimsy magic spell, valid only when workers were physically *inside* the hotel. Dumped into the night, they pumpkined back into shivery humans, red-eyed, runny-nosed people with windswept hair.

Naturally, Dad found this dramatic interlude all very exciting, and as we awaited the arrival of the fire brigade ("I imagine we'll be on France 2," Dad speculated with glee) in front of a waxen bellboy, draped in rippling silk pajamas the color of peas, I spotted Hannah. She was much older, still slim, but most of her beauty had corroded. The sleeves of her pajamas were rolled up like a truck driver's.

"What's going on?" she asked.

"Eh," said the frightened bellboy. "*Je ne sais pas, madame.*"

"What d'ya mean *tu ne sais pas?*"

"*Je ne sais pas.*"

"Does anyone know *any*thing around here? Or are you all just a bunch of frogs on lily pads?"

(The "bomb scare," to Dad's evident displeasure, turned out to be nothing more than an electrical malfunction, and the following morning, our last in the hotel, Dad and I awoke to free breakfast in our suite and a note calmly printed in gold, apologizing for *le dérangement.*)

✻   ✻   ✻

On the windy afternoon of the 26, we said good-bye to the Ritz and took our suitcases across the city to Baba au Rhum's five-bedroom apartment, occupying the top two floors of a seventeenth-century stone building on Île St. Louis.

"Not bad, hmmm?" said Servo. "Yes, the girls enjoyed this old *shed* growing up. All their French friends wanted to come over every weekend, couldn't get *rid* of them. How do you like Paris, mmm?"

"It's extr—"

"Elektra does not like Paris. Prefers Monte Carlo. I agree. Tourists make life difficult for us true Parisians, and Monte's a theme park you can't enter unless you have, what, Soc—one, two million? Been on the phone with Elektra all morning. Calls me up. 'Daddy,' she says, 'Daddy, they want me for the embassy.' Salary they offered her, I fall off my chair. Barely nineteen, skipped three grades. They adore her at Yale. Psyche too. She just started as a freshman. And they still want her for all the modeling, did top modeling in the summers. Made enough to buy all of Manhattan, and what is his name with the underwear, Calvin Klein. He fell madly in love with her. Nine years old, she was writing like Balzac. Her teachers would cry when they read her work, they were always telling me she's a *poet*. And poets are born, you see, they're not made. Only one comes along in a single, what do they say? Mmm? A single century."

Dr. Michael Servo Kouropoulos was a severely tanned Greek man of many opinions, tales and chins. He was overweight, in his mid- to late sixties with white sheep's hair and dull brown dice eyes that never stopped rolling around a room. He sweated, suffered from the strange tic of slapping then rubbing in circular motions his own chest, threaded each of his sentences together with a belly-deep "mmm" and treated idle conversations that had nothing to do with his family as if they were termite-infested houses in dire need of being exterminated with another story about Elektra or Psyche. He moved speedily, in spite of the limp that warped his walk and the wooden cane that, after propping it against some counter while ordering *un pain au chocolat*, came clattering noisily to the floor, sometimes hitting people on the shin or foot ("Mmmm? Oh, dear, excusez-moi.").

"He always hobbled," Dad said. "Even when we were at Harvard."

As it turned out, too, he was severely averse to having his picture taken. The first time I removed my disposable camera from my backpack, Dr. Kouropoulos put his hand over his face and refused to remove it. "Mmmm, no, I don't photograph well." The second time, he disappeared for ten minutes in the Men's Room. "Excuse me, hate, hate to break up the photo op, but, nature. She's calling." The third time, he threw out that shopworn detail people loved to repeat about the Masai people, thereby drawing attention to their sensitivity and savoir faire when it came to primitive cultures: "They say it steals the soul. I don't want to take any chances." (This factoid was painfully outdated. Dad had spent time in the Great Rift Valley, and said for five dollars, most Masai under seventy-five would let you steal their soul as many times as you wished.)

I asked Dad what his problem was.

"I'm not sure. But I wouldn't be surprised if he was wanted for tax evasion."

To imagine that Dad had deliberately chosen to spend five minutes with this man, let alone *six, days,* was inconceivable. They were not friends. In fact, they appeared to loathe each other.

Meals with Baba au Rhum were not joyous affairs, but prolonged torture. He ended up so filthy after pulling apart his braised beef or leg of lamb, I found myself wishing he'd taken the gauche yet critical precaution of tucking his napkin around his neck. His hands behaved like fat, startled tabby cats; without warning, they'd pounce two to three feet across the table in order to seize the saltshaker or the bottle of wine. (He'd pour himself a glass first, then in a dull afterthought, one for Dad.)

My primary discomfort during these meals derived not from his table manners, but from the general repartee. Midway through the appetizers, sometimes even before, Dad and Servo became engaged in a strange, spoken locking-of-horns, a masculine battle of one-upmanship widespread among such species as the Rutting Bull Elk and the Sabre-toothed Ground Beetle.

From what I gathered, the competition sprung from Servo's subtle insinuations that while it was all fine and dandy Dad had raised *one* genius ("When we go home, a little bird told me we're going to find good news from Harvard," Dad pompously unveiled during dessert at Lapérouse), he, Dr. Michael Servo Kouropoulos, hailed professor of *littérature archaïque*, had raised *two* ("Psyche was tapped by NASA for the Lunar Mission V in 2014. I'd tell you more, but these things are classified. I must remain, for *her* sake and the sake of the world's declining superpower, *mum* . . .").

After considerable word-to-word combat, Dad showed signs of strain—that is, until he located Servo's Achilles' heel, some disappointing younger son apparently mislabeled Atlas, who'd been unable not only to shoulder the world, but a single freshman course load at Río Grande Universidad in Cuervo, Mexico. Dad made him admit the poor kid was now adrift somewhere in South America.

I did my best to ignore these ridiculous skirmishes, spending my time eating as daintily as I could, raising White Mercy Flags in the form of long, apologetic stares at the various aggravated waiters and cranky close-at-hand clientele. Only when there appeared to be a stalemate did I placate Dad.

" 'Our love of what is beautiful does not lead to extravagance. Our love of things of the mind does not make us soft,' " I said as gravely as I could after Servo's forty-five minute oration on the famous son of a billionaire (Servo couldn't name names) who in 1996 fell madly in love with tan twelve-year-old Elektra in Cannes, as she sat on the beach making sandcastles with all the modern design sense and keen eye for craftsmanship of Mies van der Rohe. So haunted was the World's Most Eligible Bachelor, Servo was afraid he'd have to get a restraining order, so the man and his four-hundred-foot yacht (which he was threatening to rename Elektra, replete with Pilates gym and helicopter landing pad) couldn't come within a thousand feet of the mesmeric girl.

Hands folded in my lap, I tilted my head and set loose a Powerful Gaze of Omniscience across the room, a gaze reminiscent of the doves Noah set loose from the deck of his Ark, doves that returned to him with twigs.

"So said Thucydides, Book Two," I whispered.

Baba au Rhum's eyes bulged.

After three days of such agonizing meals, I deduced from the defeated look in Dad's eyes he'd come to the same conclusion I had, that it was best we find alternative accommodation, because, although it was all well and good they'd had bell-bottoms and sideburn length in common back at Harvard, this was the era of the ohs, epoch of serious hair and cigarette pants. Being Bon Amis at Harvard in the late 1970s with shirts fashioned out of cheesecloth and a widespread popularity of clogs and clip-on suspenders was certainly not greater than or equal to being Bon Amis *now* with minimalist fitted shirts in cotton blends and a widespread popularity of collagen and clip-on headsets so one could give orders hands free.

I was wrong, however. Dad had been severely brainwashed (see "Hearst, Patty," *Almanac of Rebels and Insurgents*, Skye, 1987). He cheerfully announced he was going to spend the *entire day* with Servo at La Sorbonne. There was an opening for a government professor at the school, which would be an interesting fit for him while I was marooned at Harvard, and as I'd undoubtedly find an entire day of faculty hobnobbing tedious, I was instructed to go amuse myself. Dad handed me three hundred euros, his MasterCard, a key to the apartment, scribbled down Servo's home and mobile phone numbers on a piece of graph paper. We'd reconvene at 7:30 P.M. at Le Georges, the restaurant on the top of the Centre Pompidou.

"It'll be an adventure," said Dad with faux enthusiasm. "Didn't Balzac write in *Lost Illusions* that the only way to see Paris is on your own?" (Balzac wrote nothing of the kind.)

Initially, I was relieved to be rid of the two of them. Dad and Baba au Rhum could have each other. But after six hours of wandering the streets, the Musée d'Orsay, stuffing myself with *croissants* and *tartes*, at times, pretending I was a young duchess in disguise ("The gifted traveler can't help but affect a traveling persona," notes Swithin in *Possessions*, 1910 [1911]. "Whilst at home he may merely be a hoi polloi husband, one of a million dull suited financiers, in a foreign land, he can be as majestic as he desires."), my feet were blistered, I had a sugar nadir; I felt drained and entirely irritated. I decided to make my way back to Servo's apartment, resolving (with more than a little satisfaction) to take the opportunity of Me Time to peruse a few of Baba au Rhum's personal belongings, namely, to locate some mislaid *foe-toe* drowning at the bottom of a sock drawer that revealed his girls not to be the chiseled Olympians their father led everyone to believe, but flabby, pimpled mortals, with dim eyes shoved deep into their heads, mouths long and bendy like pieces of licorice.

Somehow I'd managed to walk all the way to Pigalle, so I entered the first métro I could find, switched trains at Concorde and was walking out of the

St. Paul station, when I passed a man and a woman moving quickly down the stairs. I stopped in my tracks, turning to watch them. She was one of those short, dark, severe-looking women who didn't walk, but *mowed*, with jaw-length brown hair and a boxy green coat. He was considerably taller than she, in jeans, a suede bomber jacket, and as she talked to him—in French, it seemed—he laughed, a loud but supremely lethargic sound, the unmistakable laugh of a person reclining in a hammock soaked with sun. He was reaching into his back pocket for the ticket.

Andreo Verduga.

I must have whispered it, because an elderly French woman with a floral scarf wrapping her withered face tossed me a look of contempt as she pushed past me. Holding my breath, I hurried back down the stairs after them, jostled by a man trying to exit with an empty stroller. Andreo and the girl were already through the turnstiles, strolling down the platform and I would have followed, but I'd only purchased a single ride and four people were waiting in line at the ticket counter. I could hear the shudders of an approaching train. They stopped walking, far to my right, Andreo with his back to me, Green Coat facing him, listening to what he said, probably something along the lines of, YES STOP I SEE WHAT YOU MEAN STOP (OUI ARRETTE JE COMPRENDS ARRETTE), and then the train rushed in, the doors groaned open and he turned, chivalrously letting Green Coat enter in front of him. As he stepped into the car, I could just make out a splinter of his profile.

A smack of the doors, the train belched and pulled out of the station.

I wandered back to Servo's apartment in a daze. It couldn't have been he; no, not *really*. I was like Jade, making things more exotic than they actually were. I *thought* I'd noticed, as he moved past me, unzipping his jacket as he hurried down the stairs, a heavy silver watch hanging on his wrist, and Andreo the Gardener, Andreo of the Bullet Wound and Badly Fractured English wouldn't have that kind of watch, unless, in the three years since I'd seen him (not counting the Wal-Mart sighting), he'd become a successful entrepreneur or inherited a small fortune from a distant relative in Lima. And yet—the shard of face I'd seen, the passing blur on the stairs, the muscular cologne that strolled through the air behind him like pompous tan men on yachts—it added up to something real. Or perhaps I'd just witnessed his doppelgänger. After all, I'd been spotting Jade and the others all over the city, and Allison Smithson-Caldona in her relentless study of all things double and dittoed, *Twin Paradox and Atomic Clocks* (1999), actually tried to scientifically prove the somewhat mystical theory that everyone had a twin wandering the planet. She was able to confirm this as fact in three out of every twenty-five examined individuals, no matter their nationality or race (p. 250).

When I finally eased open the front door to Servo's apartment, I was surprised to hear Dad and Servo in the living room just off the dark foyer and hall. *The bloom was finally off the rose,* I noted with satisfaction. They were fighting like Punch and Judy.

"Highly hysterical over—" That was Dad (Judy).

"*You* can't comprehend what it actually means—!" That was Servo (Punch).

"Oh, don't *give me*—you're hot-headed as—go, go—"

"—*always* content, aren't you, to hide behind the lecture podium?"

"—*you* act like a hormonal preteen! Go take a cold shower, why—!"

They must have heard the door (though I tried to close it silently), because their voices cut off like a big ax had just swung down on their words. A second later, Dad's head materialized in the doorway.

"Sweet," he said, smiling. "How was the sightseeing?"

"Fine."

Servo's white round head bobbed into view by Dad's left elbow. His shiny roulette eyes tripped ceaselessly around my face. He didn't say a word, but his lips twitched in evident irritation, as if there were invisible threads knotted to his mouth's corners and a toddler was yanking the ends.

"I'm going to take a nap," I said brightly. "I'm exhausted."

I shrugged off my coat, tossed my backpack to the floor and, smiling nonchalantly, headed upstairs. The plan was to remove my shoes, stealthily tiptoe back to the first floor, eavesdrop on their heated dispute resumed in irate hisses and fizz (hopefully not in Greek or some other unfathomable language)—but when I did this, standing stone still on the bottom step in my socks, I heard them banging around the kitchen, bickering about nothing more calamitous than the difference between absinthe and anisette.

*   *   *

That night we decided not to go to Le Georges. It rained, so we stayed in, watching Canal Plus, eating leftover chicken and playing Scrabble. Dad combusted with pride when I won two games in a row, *hologram* and *monocular* being the *coups de grâcey* that caused Servo (who insisted the Cambridge

Dictionary was wrong, license was spelled "lisence" in the UK, he was sure of it) to turn crimson, say something about Elektra being president of the Yale Debate Team and mutter he himself had not fully recovered from the flu.

I hadn't been able to get Dad alone, and even at midnight, neither of them showed signs of tiring or, regrettably enough, any residual bitterness toward each other. Baba was fond of sitting in his giant red chair sans shoes and socks, his chunky red feet propped in front of him on a large velvet pillow (veal cutlets to be served to a king). I had to resort to my A-Little-Bread-a-Crust-a-Crumb look, which Dad, frowning over his row of letters, didn't pick up on, so I resorted to my A-Dying-Tiger-Moaned-for-Drink look, and when that went unobserved, A-Day!-Help!-Help!-Another-Day!

At long last, Dad announced he'd see me to bed.

"What were you fighting about when I came home?" I asked when we were upstairs, alone in my room.

"I would have preferred if you hadn't heard that." Dad shoved his hands into his pockets and gazed out the window where the rain seemed to be drumming its fingernails on the roof. "Servo and I have a great deal of lost baggage between us—mislaid items, so to speak. We both think the other is to blame for the deficiency."

"Why did you tell him he was acting like a hormonal preteen?"

Dad looked uncomfortable. "Did I say that?"

I nodded.

"What else did I say?"

"That's pretty much all I heard."

Dad sighed. "The thing with Servo is—everyone has a *thing*, I suppose; but nevertheless, Servo's *thing*—everything is an Olympic competition. He derives great pleasure from setting people up, putting them in the most discomforting of situations, watching them flounder. He's an idiot, really. And now he has the absurd notion that I must remarry. Naturally, I told him he was preposterous, that it's none of his business, the world does not revolve around such social—"

"Is *he* married?"

Dad shook his head. "Not for years. You know, I don't even remember what happened to Sophie."

"She's in an insane asylum."

"Oh, no," Dad said, smiling, "when controlled, given parameters, he's harmless. At times, ingenious."

"Well, I don't like him," I pronounced.

I rarely, if ever, used such petulant one-liners. You had to have a strong, experienced, ain't-no-other-way-'round-it face to say them with any authority (see Charlton Heston, *The Ten Commandments*). Sometimes, though, when you had no sound reason for your sentiments—when you simply had a *feeling*—you had to use one no matter what kind of face you had.

Dad sat down next to me on the bed. "I suppose I can't disagree. One can only take so much inflated self-importance before one feels ill. And I'm a bit angry myself. This morning, when we went to the Sorbonne, me with my briefcase full of notes, essays, my résumé—like a fool—it turned out there was no job opening as he'd led me to believe. A Latin professor had requested three months' leave this fall, and that was *it*. Then came the actual reason we'd ventured to the school—Servo spent an hour trying to get me to ask Florence of the guttural r's to dinner, some *femme* who was a leading expert in Simone de Beauvoir—of all hellish things to be an expert in—a woman who wore more eyeliner than Rudolph Valentino. I was trapped in her crypt-office for hours. I didn't leave in *love* but with lung cancer. The woman chainsmoked like nobody's business."

"I don't think he has children," I said in a hushed voice. "Maybe just the one in the Colombian rain forest. But I think he's making the others up."

Dad frowned. "Servo has children."

"Have you *met* them?

He considered this. "No."

"Seen pictures?"

He tilted his head. "No."

"Because they're figments of his unhinged imagination."

Dad laughed.

And then I was about to tell him about the other incredible incident of the day, Andreo Verduga with the suede jacket and the silver watch shuffling through the métro, but I stopped myself. I noticed how outlandish it was, such a coincidence, and reporting it in all seriousness made me feel stupid—tragic even. "It is adorable and healthily childlike secretly to believe in fairy tales, but the instant one articulates such viewpoints to other people, one goes from darling to dumbo, from childlike to chillingly out of touch with reality," wrote Albert Pooley in *The Imperial Consort of the Dairy Queen* (1981, p. 233).

"Can we go home?" I asked quietly.

To my surprise, Dad nodded. "I was actually going to ask you the very same thing this afternoon, after my dispute with Servo. I think we've had enough of *la vie en rose*, don't you? Personally, I prefer to see life as it actually is." He smiled. "*En noir.*"

*   *   *

Dad and I said farewell to Servo, to Paris, two days before we were scheduled to depart. Perhaps it wasn't so incredible a thing, Dad calling the airline and changing the tickets. He looked deflated, eyes bloodshot, his voice prone to sighs. For the first time since I could remember, Dad had very little to say. Saying good-bye to Baba au Rhum, he managed only "thank you" and "see you soon" before climbing into the waiting taxi.

I, however, took my time.

"Next time I look forward to meeting Psyche and Elektra in person," I said, staring straight into the man's hole-punched eyes. I almost felt sorry for him: the bristly white hair drooped over his head like a plant that hadn't had nearly enough water or light. Tiny red veins were taking root around his

VISUAL AID 18.0

nose. If Servo were in a Pulitzer Prize–winning play, he'd be the Painfully Tragic character, the one who wore bronze suits and alligator shoes, the man who worshipped all the wrong things so Life had to bring him to his knees.

" 'One's real life is, so often, the life that one does not lead,' " I added as I turned toward the taxi, but he only blinked, that nervous, sly smile again twitching through his face.

"So long, my dear, mmmm, safe flight."

On the drive to the airport, Dad barely said a word. He rested his head against the taxi window, mournfully staring out at the passing streets—such an unusual pose for him, I covertly took the disposable camera out of my bag, and while the taxi driver muttered at people dashing across the intersection in front of us, I took his picture, the last photo on the roll.

They say when people didn't know you were taking their picture, they appeared as they really were in life. And yet Dad didn't know I was taking his picture and he appeared as he *never* was—quiet, forlorn, somehow lost (Visual Aid 18.0).

"As far as one journeys, as much as a man sees, from the turrets of the Taj Mahal to the Siberian wilds, he may eventually come to an unfortunate conclusion—usually while he's lying in bed, staring at the thatched ceiling of some substandard accommodation in Indochina," writes Swithin in his last book, the posthumously published *Whereabouts, 1917* (1918). "It is impossible to rid himself of the relentless, cloying fever commonly known as Home. After seventy-three years of anguish I have found a cure, however. You must go home again, grit your teeth and however arduous the exercise, determine, without embellishment, your exact coordinates at Home, your longitudes and latitudes. Only then, will you stop looking back and see the spectacular view in front of you."

PART 3

Howl and Other Poems

Upon my return to St. Gallway and the commencement of Winter Term, the first odd thing I noticed about Hannah—rather, what the whole school noticed ("I think that woman was committed to an institution over vacation," surmised Dee during second period Study Hall)—was that over Christmas Break, she'd cut off all her hair.

No, it was not one of those cute 1950s haircuts labeled by fashion magazines as *chic* and *gamine* (see Jean Seberg, *Bonjour Tristesse*). It was harsh and choppy. And, as Jade noticed when we were at Hannah's for dinner, there was even a tiny bald patch behind her right ear.

"What the *hell?*" said Jade.

"What?" asked Hannah, spinning around.

"There's a—hole in your haircut! You can see your scalp!"

"Really?"

"You cut your own hair?" asked Lu.

Hannah stared at us and then nodded, visibly embarrassed. "Yes. I know it's crazy and looks, well—different." She touched the back of her neck. "But it was late at night. I wanted to try something."

The acute masochism and self-hatred behind a woman willfully defacing her appearance was a concept that featured prominently in the angry tome by proto-feminist Dr. Susan Shorts, *Beelzebub Conspiracy* (1992), which I'd noticed peeking out of the L. L. Bean canvas tote belonging to my sixth-grade science teacher, Mrs. Joanna Perry of Wheaton Hill Middle. In order to better understand Mrs. Perry and her mood swings, I procured my own copy. In Chapter 5, Shorts contends that since 1010 B.C., many women who'd tried and failed to be self-governing were forced to take action upon their very selves, because their physical appearance was the lone thing on which they could immediately "exert power," due to the "colossal masculine plot at work since the beginning of time, ever since man began to walk on his two stubby, hairy legs and noticed that he was taller than poor woman," growls Shorts (p. 41). Many women, including St. Joan and Countess Alexandra di Whippa, "crudely chopped off their hair," and cut themselves with "clippers and knives" (p. 42–43). The more radical ones branded their stomachs with hot irons to the "distress and revulsion of their husbands" (p. 44). On p. 69, Shorts goes on to write, "A woman will mar her exterior because she feels she is a part of a greater scheme, a plot, which she cannot control."

Of course, one never thinks about damning feminist texts at the time, and even if one does, it's to be theatrical and over-the-top. So I simply imagined there came a point in a mature woman's life when she needed to radically change her appearance, discover what she *really* looked like, without all the bells and whistles.

Dad, on Understanding Why Women Do the Things They Do: "One has a better chance of squeezing the universe onto a thumbnail."

And yet, when I sat next to Hannah at the dinner table and looked over at her as she daintily cut her chicken (haircut poised boldly atop her head like an atrocious hat worn to church), I suddenly had the nerve-racking feeling I'd *seen* her somewhere before. The haircut strip-searched her, uncovered her in a shoulder-cringing fashion, and now, crazily enough, the carved cheekbones, the neck—it was all vaguely familiar. I recognized her, not from an encounter (no, she was not one of Dad's long-lost June Bugs; it'd take more than glamorous hair to camouflage *their* brand of monkey face); the feeling was smokier, more remote. I sensed instead I'd seen her in a photograph somewhere, or in a newspaper article, or maybe in a snapshot in some discount biography Dad and I had read aloud.

Instantly, she noticed I was staring at her (Hannah was one of those people who kept tabs on all eyes in a room) and slowly, as she took an elegant bite of food, she turned her head toward me and smiled. Charles was talking on and on about Fort Lauderdale—God, it was hot, stuck at the airport for six hours (telling this rambling story as he always did, as if Hannah was the only person at the table)—and the haircut drew attention to her smile, did to her smile what Coke-bottle lenses did to eyes, made it huge (pronounced, "HYOOOGE"). I smiled back at her and sat for the remainder of the meal with my eyes taped to my plate, shouting silently to myself in a dictator voice

(Augusto Pinochet commanding the torture of an opponent) — to *stop staring* at Hannah.

It was rude.

* * *

"Hannah's going to have a nervous breakdown," Jade announced flatly that Friday night. She was wearing a jittery black-beaded flapper dress and sitting behind a huge gold harp, plucking the strings with one hand, a martini in the other. The instrument was covered with a thick film of dust like the layer of fat in a pan after frying bacon. "You can quote me on that."

"You've been sayin' that all fuckin' year," said Milton.

"Yawn," said Nigel.

"Actually I kind of agree," said Leulah solemnly. "That haircut's scary."

"Finally!" Jade shouted. "I have a convert! I have one, do I hear two, two, going, going, *sold* at the pathetic number of *one*."

"Seriously," Lu went on, "I think she might be clinically depressed."

"Shut up," Charles said.

It was 11:00 P.M. Sprawled across the leather couches in the Purple Room, we were drinking Leulah's latest, something she called Cockroach, a mishmash of sugar, oranges and Jack Daniel's. I don't think I'd said twenty words the entire evening. Of course, I was excited to see them again (also grateful Dad, when Jade picked me up in the Mercedes, said nothing but "See you soon, my dear," accompanied with one of his bookmark smiles, which would hold my place until I returned), but something about the Purple Room now felt stale.

I'd had fun on these types of nights before, hadn't I? Hadn't I always laughed and sloshed a little bit of Claw or Cockroach on my knees, and said quick things that sailed across the room? Or, if I'd never said quick things (Van Meers were not known for stand-up comedy), hadn't I allowed myself to drift in a pool with a deadpan expression on an inflatable raft wearing sunglasses as Simon and Garfunkel went "Woo woo woo"? Or if I hadn't allowed myself to drift with a deadpan expression (Van Meers did not excel at poker), hadn't I let myself become, at least while I was in the Purple Room, a shaggy-haired counterculture biker on my way to New Orleans in search of the real America, hobnobbing with ranchers, hookers, rednecks and mimes? Or if I hadn't let myself be a counterculture roadie (no, the Van Meers were not naturally hedonistic) hadn't I let myself wear a striped shirt and shout in a frankfurter American accent, *"New York Herald Tribune!"* with eyeliner jutting out from my eyes, subsequently absconding with a small-time hood?

If you were young and mystified in America you were supposed to find something to be a part of. That something had to be either shocking or rowdy, for within this brouhaha you'd find yourself, be able to locate your Self the way Dad and I had finally located such minuscule, hard-to-find towns as Howard, Louisiana, and Roane, New Jersey, on our U.S. Rand-McNally Map. (If you didn't find such a thing, your fate would sadly be found in plastics.)

Hannah has ruined me, I thought now, pressing the back of my head into the leather couch. I'd resolved to dig an unmarked grave in the middle of nowhere and bury what she'd told me (shoe box it, save it for a rainy day much like her own alarming knife collection) but of course, when you deep-sixed something precipitously, inevitably it rose from the dead. And so, as I watched Jade pluck the harp strings in the absorbed manner of plucking hairs from an eyebrow, I couldn't help but envision her tossing her skinny arms around the barrel torsos of various truck drivers (three per state, thus the grand total for her journey from Georgia to California was twenty-seven grease-prone gear-jammers; roughly one per every 107.41 miles). And when Leulah took a sip of her Cockroach and some of it dribbled down her chin, I actually saw the twenty-something Turkish math teacher looming behind her, sinuously grooving to Anatolian rock. I saw Charles as one of those golden babies gurgling next to a woman with her eyes punched in, body naked, curled up on a carpet like overcooked shrimp, grinning madly at nothing. And then *Milton* (who'd just arrived from his movie date with Joalie, Joalie who'd spent Christmas vacation skiing with her family at St. Anton, Joalie who sadly had not fallen into a mile-deep crevice on an unmarked trail), when he dug into his jean pocket to remove a piece of Trident, I thought for a split second he was actually removing a switchblade, similar to the ones the Sharks danced with in *West Side Story* as they sang—

"Retch, what in hell's the matter with you?" demanded Jade, squinting at me suspiciously. "You've been staring at everyone with freaky-ass eyes *all night*. You didn't see that Zach person over the break, did you? There's a good chance he turned you into a Stepford wife."

"Sorry. I was just thinking about Hannah," I lied.

"Yeah, well, maybe we should do something instead of just thinking all the time. At the very least, we should stage an intervention so she doesn't keep going to Cottonwood, 'cause if something happens? If she does something *extreme?* We'll all look back on this moment and detest ourselves. It'll be a thing we won't get over for years and years and then we'll die alone with tons of cats or be hit by cars. We'll end up road pizzas—"

"Will you shut the fuck up?" shouted Charles. "I–I'm tired of hearing this shit *every fucking weekend!* You're a fucking moron! All of you!"

He banged his glass on the bar and raced from the room, his cheeks red, his hair the color of the palest, barest wood, the soft kind you could dent with your thumbnail, and then seconds later—none of us spoke—we heard the front door thump, the whining motor of his car as he sped down the driveway.

"Is it me or is it obvious none of this ends happily," Jade said.

*   *   *

Around 3:00 or 4:00 A.M., I passed out on the leather couch. An hour later, someone was shaking me.

"Want to take a walk, old broad?"

Nigel was smiling down at me, his glasses pinching the end of his nose.

I blinked and sat up. "Sure."

Blue light velveted the room. Jade was upstairs, Milton had gone home ("home," I suspected, meant a motel rendezvous with Joalie) and Lu was sound asleep on the paisley couch, her long hair ivying over the armrest. I rubbed my eyes, stood and blearily plodded after Nigel, who'd already slipped into the foyer. I found him in the Parlor Room: walls painted mortified pink, a yawning grand piano, spindly palms and low sofas that resembled big, floating graham crackers you didn't dare sit on for fear they'd break and you'd get crumbs everywhere.

"Put this on if you're cold," Nigel said, picking up a long black fur coat that'd been left for dead on the piano bench. It sagged romantically in his arms, like a grateful secretary who'd just fainted.

"I'm okay," I said.

He shrugged and slipped it on himself (see "Siberian Weasel," *Encyclopedia of Living Things*, 4th ed.). Frowning, he picked up a large, blue-eyed crystal swan that had been swimming across the top of an end table toward a large silver picture frame. The frame featured not a photo of Jade, Jefferson or some other beaming relative, but the black-and-white insert it had ostensibly been purchased with (FIRENZE, it read, 7" x 91/2").

"Poor fat drowned bastard," Nigel said. "No one remembers him anymore, you know?"

"Who?"

"Smoke Harvey."

"Oh."

"That's what happens when you die. Everyone makes a big deal about it. Then everyone forgets."

"Unless you kill a state employee. A senator, or–or a police officer. Then everyone remembers."

"Really?" He looked at me with interest, nodding. "Yeah," he said cheerfully. "You're probably right."

Customarily, when one stopped to consider Nigel—his face, ho-hum as a penny, his fiercely gnawed fingernails, his thin, wired glasses that forever evoked the image of an insect brazenly resting its tired, transparent wings on his nose—one was hard pressed to imagine *what*, exactly, he was thinking, what was the reason for the eyes that sparked, the tiny smile, reminiscent of those cute red pencils used to mark voting ballots. Now I couldn't help but assume he was thinking of his *real* parents, Mimi and George, Alice and John, Joan and Herman, whoever they were, tucked away in maximum-security prison. Not that Nigel ever looked particularly glum or brooding; if Dad were ever permanently incarcerated (if a handful of June Bugs had their way, he would be) I'd probably be one of those kids always jaw clenching and teeth grinding, fantasizing about killing my fellow students with cafeteria lunch trays and ball point pens. Nigel did a remarkable job of remaining positive.

"So what do you think about Charles?" I whispered.

"Cute but not my type."

"No, I mean." I wasn't exactly sure how to phrase it. "What's happened between him and Hannah?"

"What—you've been talking to Jade?"

I nodded.

"I don't think *anything's* happened except he thinks he's madly in love with her. He's *always* been madly in love with her. Since we were freshmen. I don't know why he wastes his time—hey, you think I could pass for Liz Taylor?" He set down the glass swan, twirled. The mink dutifully Christmas-treed around him.

"Sure," I said. If he was Liz, I was Bo Derek in *Ten*.

Smiling, he pushed his glasses higher onto his nose. "So we need to find the loot. The bounty. The big payoff." He spun on his heel, then darted out the door, across the foyer, up the white marble stairs.

At the top of the landing, he stopped, waiting for me to catch up. "Actually I wanted to tell you something."

"What?" I asked.

He pressed a finger to his lips. We were outside Jade's bedroom, and though it was completely dark and silent, her door was half open. He motioned for me to follow him. We crept down the carpeted hall and into one of the guest rooms at the very end.

He switched on a lamp by the door. Despite the rose-colored carpet and floral curtains, the room was claustrophobic, like being inside a lung. The musty, forsaken smell doubtlessly was what *National Geographic* correspondent Carlson Quay Meade was talking about in the account of his excavation of the Valley of the Kings with Howard Carter in 1923, in *Revealing Tutankhamen*: "I daresay I was troubled of what we might find in that eerie sepulcher, and though there was most certainly an air of excitement, due to the sickening stench, I was forced to remove my linen handkerchief and place it over my nose and mouth, proceeding thus into the cheerless tomb" (Meade, 1924).

Nigel closed the door behind me.

"So Milton and I went over to Hannah's early last Sunday, before you showed up," he said in a low, serious voice, leaning against the bed. "And Hannah had to slip away to the grocery store. While Milton was doing homework, I went outside and took a look inside her garage." His eyes widened. "You wouldn't *believe* the stuff I found. For one thing, there's all that old camping equipment—but then, I checked out some of the cardboard boxes. Most of them were full of junk, mugs, lamps, stuff she'd collected, a photo too—guess she went through a serious punk phase—but one huge box only contained trail maps, a *thousand* of them. She'd marked some with a red pen."

"Hannah used to go camping all the time. She told us about that incident when she saved someone's life. Remember?"

He held up his hand, nodding. "Right, well, then I came across a folder sitting right on top of everything. It was full of newspaper articles. Photocopies. A couple from *The Stockton Observer*. Every single one was about a kid disappearing."

"Missing Persons?"

He nodded.

I was surprised how the reappearance of two simple words, *Missing*

Persons, could instantly make me feel so, well, *disturbed*. Obviously, if Hannah hadn't launched into that hair-raising sermon about The Gone, if I hadn't witnessed her stonily reciting all those Last Seens, one by one, like some sort of severely unbalanced person, I wouldn't have been unsettled by what Nigel reported in the least. We knew Hannah, at some point in her life, had been a seasoned mountaineer, and the folder of photocopies as an isolated item didn't mean much. Dad for one, was a person with a highly impulsive intellectual mind and he was forever taking sudden explosive interest in a variety of haphazard subjects, from Einstein's early versions of the atomic bomb and the anatomy of a sand dollar, to gruesome museum installations and rappers who'd been shot nine times. But no subject matter for Dad was ever a fixation, an obsession—a *passion*, sure; mention Che or Benno Ohnesorg and a gauzy look would appear in his eyes—but Dad did not memorize random facts and recite them in a brutal Bette Davis voice while puffing on cigarettes, his eyes whizzing madly around the room like balloons losing air. Dad did not pose, posture, cut off his own hair leaving a bald spot the size of a Ping-Pong ball. ("Life has few absolute pleasures and one is sitting back in that barber chair, getting one's hair trimmed by a woman with capable hands," Dad said.) And Dad did not, at unanticipated moments, fill me with *fear*, a fear I couldn't put my hands on because as soon as I noticed it, it slipped through my fingers like steam, evaporated.

"I have one of the articles if you want to read it," Nigel said.

"You *took* it?"

"Just a page."

"Oh, *great*."

"What?"

"She's going to know you were snooping."

"No way, there were fifty pages there at *least*. She couldn't notice. Let me go get it. It's in my bag downstairs."

Nigel headed from the room (before disappearing out the door he gave a sort of delighted bulge of the eyes—a silent-movie Dracula expression). He returned a minute later with the article. It was a single page. Actually, it *wasn't* an article, but an excerpt from a paperback published by Foothill Press of Tupock, Tennessee, in 1992, *Lost But Not Found: People Who Vanished Without a Trace, and Other Baffling Events* by J. Finley and E. Diggs. Nigel sat down on the bed and wrapped the mink tightly around himself, waiting for me to finish reading.

96.

Chapter 4

Violet May Martinez

So do not fear, for I am with you;
so do not be dismayed, for I am your God.

—*Isaiah, 41:10*

On August 29, 1985, Violet May Martinez, 15, vanished without a trace. She was last seen in the Great Smoky Mountains National Park between Blindmans Bald and the parking lot near Burnt Creek.

Today her disappearance remains a mystery.

* * *

It was a sunny morning on August 29, 1985, when Violet Martinez took off with her Bible study group of Besters Baptist Church in Besters, N.C. They were heading to the Great Smoky Mountains National Park for a nature appreciation trip. A sophomore at Besters High, Violet was known by her peers as fun and outgoing and had been voted Best Dressed by the yearbook.

Violet's father, Roy Jr., dropped her off at church that morning. Violet had blond hair and was 5'4". She was wearing a pink sweater, blue jeans, a gold "V" necklace and white Reeboks.

The church trip was chaperoned by Mr. Mike Higgis, a favorite church leader and Vietnam Vet who'd been active at the church for seventeen years.

Violet rode in the back of the bus next to her best friend, Polly Elms. The bus arrived at the Burnt Creek parking lot at 12:30 P.M. Mike Higgis announced they'd hike the trail to Blindmans Bald, returning to the bus by 3:30 P.M.

" 'Stand still,' " he said, quoting the Book of Job, " 'and consider the wondrous works of God.' "

Violet hiked to the summit with Polly Elms and Joel Hinley. Violet had snuck a pack of Virginia Slims in her jeans pocket and smoked a cigarette at the summit before Mike Higgis told her to

put it out. Violet posed for pictures and ate trail mix. She became anxious to start back, so she left the summit with Joel and
two friends. A mile from the parking lot, Violet started walking
faster than everyone else. The group had to slow down because
Barbee Stuart had a cramp. Violet didn't stop.

"She called us slow pokes and skipped ahead," said Joel.
"When she reached the last visible part in the trail, she stopped
to light another cigarette and waved at us. She walked around the
bend and out of sight."

Joel and the others moved on, assuming Violet would be
waiting at the bus. But at 3:35 P.M., when Mike Higgis took roll,

"Where's the rest?" I asked.

"That's all I took."

"All the articles were about disappearances like this?"

"Pretty odd, huh?"

I only shrugged. I couldn't remember if my oath of secrecy extended exclusively over the Blueblood Histories or the *entire* night's conversation with
Hannah, and so all I said was: "I think Hannah's always been interested in
the subject. Disappearances."

"Oh, yeah?"

I feigned a yawn and handed him the page. "I wouldn't worry about it."

He shrugged, obviously disappointed by my reaction, and folded the paper.

I prayed—for my continued sanity—that would be the end of it. Unfortunately, for the next forty-five minutes, as we wandered the Whitestone rooms,
the dust-iced tables, the never-sat-in chairs, no matter *what* I said to pacify
him, he wouldn't stop blathering about the articles (poor Violet, wonder
what happened, why would Hannah have those papers, why should she
care). I assumed he was simply vamping, doing Liz in *The Last Time I Saw
Paris*, until his little face caught the light of a constellation—Hercules the
Giant—flickering in the kitchen ceiling and I saw his expression: it wasn't affected, but genuinely concerned (surprisingly weighty, too, a seriousness usually associated only with unabridged dictionaries and old gorillas).

Soon we drifted back into the Purple Room, and Nigel, removing his
glasses, instantly fell asleep in front of the fireplace, clutching the mink pos-
sessively like he was afraid it'd tiptoe out before he woke. I returned to the
leather couch. A marmalade smear of morning was spreading through the
sky, visible beyond the trees through the glass-pane doors. I wasn't tired. No,

thanks to Nigel (now snoring), my mind was circling like a dog after its tail. What was the reason for Hannah's addiction to disappearances—Life Stories brutally cut off so they remained beginnings and middles, never an end? ("A Life Story without a decent ending is sadly no story at all," Dad said.) Hannah couldn't be a Missing Person herself, but perhaps her brother or sister had been one, or one of the girls in the photographs Nigel and I had glimpsed in her room, or else the lost love she refused to confirm the existence of—Valerio. A connection between these Missing Persons and her life, however distant or gauzy, had to exist: "People only very, very rarely develop fixations wholly unrelated to their private histories," wrote Josephson Wilheljen, MD, in *Wider Than the Sky* (1989).

There was, too, the supremely itchy feeling I'd *seen* her somewhere before, when she had a similar eggshell haircut—a feeling *so* persistent, the next day, sunny and freezing, when Leulah dropped me off at home, I found myself weeding through some of the contemporary biographies in Dad's library, *Fuzzy Man: The Life and Times of Andy Warhol* (Benson 1990), *Margaret Thatcher: The Woman, The Myth* (Scott 1999), *Mikhail Gorbachev: The Lost Prince of Moscow* (Vadivarich, 1999), flipping to the centers and inspecting the photographs. It was a pointless exercise, I knew, but frankly, the feeling, though relentless, was also sort of vague; I couldn't vouch that it was authentic, that I wasn't simply mixing Hannah up with one the Lost Boys in a production of *Peter Pan* Dad and I caught at the University of Kentucky at Walnut Ridge. At one point, I actually thought I'd found her—my heart swooped when I saw a black-and-white picture of what *had* to be Hannah Schneider reclining on a beach in a chic vintage bathing suit and headlight sunglasses—until I read the caption: "St. Tropez, Summer of 1955, Gene Tierney." (I'd stupidly picked up *Fugitives from a Chain Gang* [De Winter, 1979], an old biography of Darryl Zanuck.)

My next foray into Private Investigation led me down into Dad's study where I searched for "Schneider" and "Missing Person" on the Internet, a survey that belched up nearly five thousand pages. "Valerio" and "Missing Person" yielded 103.

"Are you down there?" Dad called into the stairwell.

"Doing research," I shouted.

"Have you eaten lunch?"

"No."

"Well, get your skates on—we just received twelve coupons in the mail for Lone Steer Steakhouse—ten percent off All-You-Can-Eat Sparc Ribs,

Buffalo Wings, Molten Onions and something they call, rather disturbingly, a Volcanic Bacon-Bit Potato."

Quickly, I scanned a few pages, seeing nothing remotely interesting or relevant—court documents detailing motions of Judge Howie Valerio of Shelburn County, records of Loggias Valerio born in 1789, Massachusetts—and switched off Dad's laptop.

"Sweet?"

"I'm coming," I called.

*   *   *

I hadn't had time to conduct any more recon work on Hannah or Missing Persons by the time Jade picked me up that Sunday, and when we arrived at Hannah's house, I thought to myself—more than a little relieved—perhaps I'd never have to again; Hannah, with renewed exhilaration, was dashing around the house in bare feet and a black housedress, smiling, engaged in six things at once and speaking in chic sentences that snubbed punctuation: "Blue did you meet Ono—is that the timer going off—oh Christ the asparagus." (Ono was a tiny green shaving of bird missing an eye who apparently hadn't taken to Lennon at all; she was putting as much birdcage between herself and him as she could.) Hannah also had taken the trouble to make the haircut look marginally more stylish, urging some of the edgier, meaner parts to lie down, chill out off to the side of her forehead. Everything was fine—perfect really—as the seven of us sat in the dining room eating our steaks, asparagus and corn on the cob (even Charles was smiling and when he told one of his stories he actually told it to *all* of us, not Hannah exclusively)—but then she opened her mouth.

"March twenty-sixth," she said. "The beginning of Spring Break. It's our big weekend. So mark your calendars."

"Big weekend for what?" asked Charles.

"Our camping trip."

"Who said anything about a camping trip?" asked Jade.

"I did."

"Where?" asked Leulah.

"The Great Smokies. It's less than an hour's drive."

I almost choked on my steak. Nigel and I locked eyes across the table.

"You know," continued Hannah brightly, "campfires and ghost stories and gorgeous vistas, fresh air—"

"Ramen noodles," muttered Jade.

"We don't have to eat ramen noodles. We can eat anything we like."

"*Still* sounds wretched."

"Don't be like that."

"My generation doesn't do wilderness. We'd rather go to a mall."

"Well, maybe you should aspire to something beyond your generation."

"Is it safe?" Nigel interjected, as offhandedly as he could.

"Of course." Hannah smiled. "So long as you're not stupid. But I've been up there a million times. I know the trails. I just went actually."

"With who?" asked Charles.

She smiled at him. "Myself."

We stared at her. It was, after all, January.

"When?" Milton asked.

"Over vacation."

"You weren't freezin'?"

"Forget about freezing," said Jade. "Weren't you *bored*? There's nothing to do up there."

"No, I wasn't *bored*."

"And what about the bears?" Jade went on. "Even worse, the bugs. I'm *so* not an insect person. They *love me* though. Every bug is obsessed with me. They stalk me. They're crazed fans."

"When we go in March, there won't be bugs. And if there are, I'll drown you in Off," Hannah said in a severe voice (see "1940 publicity still for *Torrid Zone*," *Bulldog in a Henhouse: The Life of James Cagney*, Taylor, 1982, p. 339).

Jade said nothing, bulldozing her spinach with a fork.

"For goodness' sake," Hannah continued, frowning at us, "what—what's the matter with you? I try to plan something fun, a little different—didn't you read, weren't you *inspired* by Thoreau, *Walden*? Didn't you read it in English class? Or don't they teach that anymore?"

She looked at me. I found it difficult to look back. In spite of her styling efforts, the haircut was still distracting. It looked like one of those alarming styles directors used in 1950s movies to illustrate that the main character had recently spent time in an institution or been branded a harlot by bigoted townsfolk. And the longer you looked at her, the more her shorn head seemed to isolate and float on its own like Jimmy Stewart's in *Vertigo*, when he suffers from a nervous breakdown and psychedelic colors, the pinks and greens of madness, swirl behind him. The haircut made her eyes unhealthily huge, her neck pale, her ears vulnerable as snails missing shells. Perhaps Jade was right; she *was* going to have a nervous breakdown. Perhaps she was "sick and tired of going along with Man's Great Lie" (see *Beelzebub*, Shorts, 1992, p. 212). Or a more frightening possibility: perhaps she'd read too much of the Charles Manson *Blackbird* book. Even Dad said—Dad who wasn't in the least superstitious or fainthearted—such an explicit dissection of the workings of evil was truly not safe for the "impressionable, the confused, or the lost." For this very reason, he no longer included it on his syllabus.

"*You* know what I'm talking about, don't you?"

Her eyes were bumper-stickered to my head.

" 'I went to the woods because I wished to live deliberately,' " she started to recite. " 'I wanted to suck all that marrow out of life, and—and afterwards, learn that if I had not lived, that—that I,' what is it, something or other deliberately . . .' "

Her words slumped to the ground and stopped moving. No one spoke. She chuckled, but it was a sad, dying sound.

"I need to read it again myself."

The Taming of the Shrew

Leontyne Bennett skillfully dissected in *The Commonwealth of Lost Vanities* (1969) Virgil's renowned quotation: "Love conquers all."

"For centuries upon centuries," he writes on p. 559, "we have been misinterpreting this famed trio of words. The uninformed masses breathlessly hold up this dwarfish phrase as a justification for snogging in public squares, abandoning wives, cuckolding husbands, for the escalating divorce rate, for swarms of bastard children begging for handouts in the Whitechapel and Aldgate tube stations—when in fact, there is nothing remotely encouraging or cheerful about this oft-quoted phrase. The Latin poet wrote '*Amor vincit omnia*,' or 'Love conquers all.' He did not write, 'Love *frees* all' or '*liberates*' all, and therein lies the first degree of our flagrant misunderstanding. Conquer: to defeat, subjugate, massacre, cream, make mincemeat out of. Surely, this cannot be a positive thing. And then, he wrote 'conquers *all*'—*not* exclusively the unpleasant things, destitution, assassination, burglary, but *all*, including pleasure, peace, common sense, liberty and self-determination. And thus we may appreciate that Virgil's words are not encouragement, but rather a caveat, a cue to evade, shirk, elude the feeling at all costs, else we risk the massacre of the things we hold most dear, including our sense of self."

Dad and I always snickered about Bennett's long-winded protestations (he never married and died, in 1984, of cirrhosis of the liver; no one attended his funeral but a housekeeper and an editor from Tyrolian Press) but by February, I actually noticed the value in what he prattled on about for over eight hundred pages. Because it was love that caused Charles to act increasingly sullen and inconsistent, wandering St. Gallway with his hair disheveled, a consumed look on his face (something told me he wasn't contemplating The

Eternal Why). During Morning Announcements, he fidgeted restlessly in his seat (often banging the back of my chair) and when I turned around to smile at him, he didn't see me; he gazed at the stage the way sailor widows probably stared at the sea. ("I've had it with him," Jade announced.)

Love, too, could pick me up and chuck me into a bad mood with the relative easiness of a tornado uprooting a farmhouse. Milton would only have to say, "Old Jo" (what he called Joalie now—a pet name the most devastating of all high school relationship developments; like superglue, it could hold any couple together for months), and instantly I'd feel like I was dying inside, as if my heart, lungs and stomach were all punching their time card, closing up shop and heading home, because there was no point of beating, breathing, day in, day out, if life was this sore.

And then there was Zach Soderberg.

I'd completely forgotten about him, with the exception of thirty seconds during the plane ride home from Paris, when a frazzled stewardess accidentally spilled Bloody Mary mix on an elderly gentleman across the aisle. Instead of growling, the man's face crinkled into a smile as he dabbed his now gruesome-looking jacket with napkins, and he said without a smidgin of sarcasm: "Don't worry about it, my dear. Happens to the best of us." I'd thrown Zach contrite little smiles every now and then during AP Physics (but didn't wait to find out if he caught them or let them fall to the floor). I was taking Dad's counsel: "The most poetic of endings to love affairs isn't apology, excuse, extensive investigation into What Went Wrong—the St. Bernard of options, droopy-eyed and slobbery—but stately silence." One day, however, immediately following lunch, when I slammed my locker door, I found Zach standing directly behind me, smiling one of those tent smiles, one side hoisted way up, the other limp.

"Hello, Blue," he said. His voice was stiff as new shoes.

My heart, rather unexpectedly, began to jump-rope. "Hi."

"How are you?"

"Fine." I had to come up with something decent to say, of course, an excuse, an apology, my reason for forgetting him at the Christmas Cabaret like a winter glove. "Zach, I'm sorry abo—"

"I have something for you," he interrupted, his voice not angry, but cheerfully official, as if he was Deputy Manager of Such-and-Such, happily emerging from his office to inform me I was a valued customer. He reached into his back pocket and handed me a thick blue envelope. It was emphatically sealed, even at the very, very corners, and my name had been written in schmaltzy cursive across the front.

"Feel free to do whatever you want with them, you know," he said. "I just got a part-time job at Kinko's, so I could inform you of some printing options. You could do a blow-up, poster-size, then total lamination. Or you could go the greeting card route. Or a calendar, wall or desk. Then there's the T-shirt option. That's pretty popular. We just got in some baby tees. And then, what do they call it—there's art print on canvas. That's very nice. Higher quality than you'd expect. We also offer sign and banner options in a range of sizes, including vinyl."

He nodded to himself and seemed on the verge of saying something more—his lips were cracked, barely, like a window—but then, frowning, he appeared to change his mind.

"I'll see you in Physics," he said, turning on his heel and heading down the hall. Instantly, he was greeted by a girl who'd walked by only a minute ago—watching us out of the corner of her coin-slot eyes, then stopping by the water fountain and taking a drink of water. (She must have just trekked the Gobi Desert.) She was Rebecca of the camel teeth, a junior.

"Is your dad preaching this Sunday?" she asked him.

With a pang of irritation (as they continued their sacred conversation down the hall) I ripped open the giant envelope and inside, found glossy *foe-toes* of Zach and me stationed around his living room, our shoulders rigid, irregular smiles pressed deep into our faces.

In six of them, to my horror, my right bra strap was visible (so white it was almost neon purple and if one looked at the bra strap, then at something else, it drifted in one's vision), but in the last *foe-toe*, the one Patsy had taken in front of the sun-lit window (Zach's left arm rigid around my waist; he was a metal stand, I a collector's doll) the light between us had gone buttery, splattering the lens, dissolving the outline of Zach's left side and my right so we blended together and our smiles went the same color of the white sky poured between the naked trees behind us.

Frankly, I barely recognized myself. Usually in pictures I was either Stork Stiff or Ferret Frightened, but in this, I looked strangely bewitching (*literally*: my skin was gold, there were paranormal pinpricks of green in my eyes). I looked relaxed too, like the kind of person one might find squealing in delight while kicking up sand on a piña-colada beach. I looked like I could be a woman who could forget herself entirely, let go of all the strings, let her self float away like a hundred helium balloons and everyone, everyone bound to the earth, stared at her enviously. ("A woman for whom reflection is as rare as a Giant Panda," Dad said.)

Without thinking, I turned to look after Zach—maybe I wanted thank him, maybe I wanted to say something more—but realized stupidly he was gone and I was left staring at the EXIT sign, the stampede of kids in stockings and shabby shoes rushing toward the stairs on their way to class.

*   *   *

A week or two later, on a Tuesday evening I was sprawled across my bed, trudging through the battlefields of *Henry V* for AP English when I heard a car. Immediately, I went to the window and, peering through the curtains, watched a white sedan slink down the driveway like a punished animal, coming to a timid halt by the front door.

Dad wasn't home. He'd left an hour before to go have dinner at Tijuana, a Mexican restaurant, with Professor Arnie Sanderson who taught Intro to Drama and History of the World Theater. "A sad young man," said Dad, "with funny little moles all over his face like enduring chicken pox." Dad said he wouldn't be home until eleven o'clock.

The headlights switched off. The engine died with a bloated belch. After a moment of stillness, the driver's door opened and a pillarlike white leg fell out of the car, then another. (This entrance of hers, at first glance, seemed to be an attempt to act out some red-carpet fantasy, yet when the woman came into full view, I realized it was nothing but the sheer challenge of maneuvering in what she wore: a tight white jacket doing its best to bind her waist, a white skirt like plastic wrap around a bouquet of stocky flowers, white stockings, exceedingly high white heels. She was a giant cookie dipped in icing.)

The woman closed the door, and, somewhat hilariously, set about trying to lock the doors, having a hard time finding the keyhole in the dark, then the correct key. Adjusting her skirt (a movement akin to twisting a pillowcase around a pillow), she turned and tried *not* to make a sound as she boosted herself up onto our porch, her swollen hair—a citrus yellow color—shuddering over her head like a loose lamp shade. She didn't ring the bell, but stood for a moment at the door, an index finger in her front teeth (the actor about to enter, suddenly uncertain of his first line). She shaded her eyes, bent to the left and looked in the window of our dining room.

I knew who she was, of course. There'd been a series of anonymous phone calls just prior to our departure for Paris (my "Hello?" was met with silence, then the hiccup of hanging up), and another less than a week ago. Swarms of June Bugs before her had shown up like this, out of the blue, in as many moods, conditions, and colors as a box of Crayola crayons (Brokenheart Burnt Umber, Seriously Pissed Cerulean, etc.).

They all had to see Dad again, wanted to pin him down, corner, cajole (in Zula Pierce's case, maim) him, make a Final Appeal. They approached this doomed confrontation with the weightiness of appearing in federal court, tucking their hair behind their ears, sporting no-nonsense suits, pumps, perfume and conservative brass earrings. June Bug Jenna Parks even toted an unwieldy leather briefcase for *her* final showdown, which she primly rested on her knees, opened with the clichéd bite of all briefcase openings and, not wasting any time, returned to Dad a bar napkin on which he'd written, in happier days, " 'A woman's face with Nature's own hand painted / Hast thou, the master-mistress of my passion.' " They always made sure to add sexy punctuation to this expert appearance (crimson mouth, complex lingerie under a faintly transparent blouse) to tempt Dad, hint at what he was missing.

If he was home, he ushered them into the den in the manner of a cardiologist about to deliver bad news to a heart patient. Before closing the door, however, he'd ask me (Dad the all-knowing doctor, me the flighty nurse) to prepare a tray of Earl Gray tea.

"Cream and sugar," he'd say with a wink—a suggestion that made an unlikely smile sprout on the June Bug's bleak face.

After I put on the kettle, I'd return to the closed door in order to eavesdrop on her deposition. No, she couldn't eat, couldn't sleep, couldn't touch or even look at another man ("Not even Pierce Brosnan and I used to think he was wonderful," Connie Madison Parker confessed). Dad would speak— something muffled, inaudible—and then the door would open and the June Bug emerged from the courtroom. Her blouse was untucked, her hair full of static and, in the most disastrous part of this metamorphosis, her face, before, so meticulously made up, now, a Rorschach test.

She fled to her car, a little frown between her eyebrows like pleated fabric, and then she drove away in her Acura or Dodge Neon, as Dad, all resigned and weary sighs, settled comfortably into his reading chair with the Earl Gray tea I'd fixed for him (as he'd planned all along) to tackle another lecture on Third-World Mediation, another tome on Principles of Revolt.

It was always a tiny detail that made me feel guilty: the dirty grosgrain bow barely hanging on to the front of Lorraine Connelly's left high heel, or Willa Johnson's ruby triangle of polyester blazer; caught in the car door, it flapped in terror as she sped down the driveway not bothering to check for oncoming traffic before making the left onto Sandpiper Circle. Not that I hoped Dad would permanently keep one. It was an irksome thought, watching *On the Waterfront* with a woman who smelled like apricot potpourri from a restaurant bathroom (Dad and I rewinding our favorite scene, the glove scene, ten sometimes twelve times as the June Bug crossed and uncrossed her legs in huffy annoyance), or listening to Dad explain his latest lecture concepts (Transformationism, Starbuckization) to a woman who did forceful, newscaster "Uh-huh uh-huhs," even when she didn't understand a word. Still, I couldn't help but feel ashamed when they cried (an empathy I wasn't entirely sure they deserved; apart from a few flat questions about boys or my mother, none of them ever talked to me, eyeing me as if I were a few grams of plutonium, unsure if I was radioactive or benign).

Obviously it wasn't fantastic what Dad was doing, making perfectly realistic women act like—well, as if they were determined to resurrect old story lines of *Guiding Light*—but I did wonder if it was entirely his fault. Dad never lied about the fact he'd already logged his one Great Love. And everyone knew *one* was the maximum of Great Loves a person could stumble upon in a lifetime, though some gluttonous people refused to accept it, mistakenly muttering on about seconds and thirds. Everyone was quick to hate the heartbreaker, the Casanova, the libertine, completely overlooking the fact that *some* libertines were completely candid about what they wanted (excitement between lectures) and if it was all so appalling why did everyone keep flying onto their porches? Why didn't they spiral off into the summer night, expiring with peace and poise in the soft shadows of the tulip trees?

If Dad wasn't home when a June Bug unexpectedly materialized, I was to follow his specific instructions: under no circumstances should I allow her into the house. "Smile and tell her to hold on to that fabulous human quality which, unfortunately, people no longer have the slightest sense of—*pride*. No, there was never anything wrong with Mr. Darcy. You may also elucidate that the saying is true: it *will* all feel better in the morning. And if she still insists, which is likely—some of them have dispositions of pit bulls with bones—you'll have to let drop the word *police*. That's all you need to say, *poelease*, and with any luck she'll fly from the house—if my prayers are answered, from our lives—like a chaste soul out of hell."

Now I was tiptoeing downstairs, more than a little nervous (it wasn't easy being Dad's Human Resource) and just as I reached the front door, she rang the bell. I looked through the peephole, but she'd turned to look over her shoulder at the yard. With a deep breath, I switched on the porch light and opened the door.

"Howdy," she said.

I froze. Standing in front of me was Eva Brewster, Evita Perón.

"Nice to see you," she said. "Where is he?"

I couldn't speak. She grimaced, burped "ha," and pushed both the door and me to the side as she walked inside.

"*Gareth, honey, I'm home!*" she shouted, her face upturned as if expecting Dad to materialize from the ceiling.

I was so shocked, I could only stand and stare. "Kitty," I realized, had been a pet name, which she'd doubtlessly had at some point in her life and resurrected so they'd have a secret. I should have known—at the very least *thought* about it. They'd had them before. Sherry Piths had been Fuzz. Cassie Bermondsey had been both Lil' and Squirts. Zula Pierce had been Midnight Magic. Dad found it humorous when they had catchy names that tripped off the tongue, and his smile, when saying this name, she probably mistook for Love, or, if not Love, some seed of Caring, which would eventually grow into the massive vine of Affection. It might be a nickname her father gave her when she was six or her Secret Hollywood Name (the name she *should* have been called, the one that would have been her passport to the Paramount lot).

"You going to speak? Where is he?"

"At dinner," I said, swallowing, "with a–a colleague."

"Uh-huh. Which one?"

"Professor Arnie Sanderson."

"Right. *Sure.*"

She made another sulky noise, crossed her arms so her jacket winced, and continued down the hall to the library. Dimly, I followed. She sauntered over to Dad's legal pads neatly stacked on the wooden table by the bookshelves. She grabbed one, ruffling the pages.

"Ms. Brewster—?"

"Eva."

"Eva." I took few steps closer. She was approximately six inches taller than me and sturdy as a silo. "I–I'm sorry, but I don't know if you should be here. I have homework."

She threw her head back and laughed (see "Shark Death Cry," *Birds and Beasts*, Barde, 1973, p. 244).

"Oh, come *on*," she said looking at me, flinging the legal pad to the floor. "One of these days you're going to have to lighten up. Though with *him,* yeah, I got you—it's a tall order. I'm sure I'm not the only one he keeps in a constant state of terror." She moved past me, out of the library, down the hall toward the kitchen, affecting the air of a real estate agent inspecting the wallpaper, rugs, doorjambs and ventilation in order to determine a price the market could bear. I understood now: she was drunk. But she was a concealed drunk. She'd vigorously zipped up most of the drunkenness so it was scarcely visible, only in her eyes, which weren't red, but swollen (and a little bit sluggish when they blinked), also in her walk, which was slow and forced, as if she had to organize every step or she'd topple like a FOR SALE sign. Every now and then, too, a word jammed in her mouth and began to slide back into her throat until she said something else and it coughed out.

"Just taking a teensy-weensy look around," she muttered, trailing her chubby, manicured hand along the kitchen counter. She pressed PLAY on the answering machine ("You have no new messages.") and squinted at June Bug Dorthea Driser's ugly cross-stitch quotations hanging in rows along the wall by the telephone ("Love Thy Neighbor," "To Thine Own Self Be True").

"You knew about me, didn't you?" she asked.

I nodded.

"Because he was weird that way. All the secrets and lies. Remove one from the ceiling and the whole thing collapses on top of you. Nearly kills you. He lies about everything—even 'Nice to see you,' and 'Take *care.*' " She tilted her head, thinking. "Any idea how you get to be a man like that? What happened to him? Did his mother drop him on his head? Was he the nerd who wore an ugly brace on his leg and everyone beat him to a pulp at lunchtime—?"

She was opening the door leading down to Dad's study.

"—If you could shed some light on that it'd be great, because I, for one, am pretty con*found*ed—"

"Ms. Brewster—?"

"—keeps me awake at night—"

She was clunking down the stairs.

"I–I think my dad would prefer that you wait up here."

She ignored me, walking the rest of the way down. I heard her fumble with the switch to the overhead lights, then yank the chain of Dad's green desk lamp. I hurried after her.

When I entered the study she was, as I both expected and feared, inspecting the six butterfly and moth cases. Her nose was almost touching the glass of the third case from the window and a small cloud had formed over the female *Euchloron megaera*, the Verdant Sphinx Moth. It wasn't her fault she was drawn to them; they were the most riveting things in the room. Not that Lepidoptera displayed in Ricker cases was a unusual thing ("Let's Make a Deal" Lupine told Dad and me they were a dime a dozen at estate sales, and could be purchased on the street in New York City for "forty big ones") but many of these specimens were exotics, rarely seen outside of a textbook. Apart from the three Cassius Blues (which looked quite dreary in comparison to the Paris Peacock just next to them—three wan orphans standing beside Rita Hayworth), my mother had purchased the others from butterfly farms in South America, Africa and Asia (all of them supposedly humane, allowing the insects a full life and natural death before collection; "You should have heard her on the phone drilling them about the living conditions," Dad said. "You'd have thought we were adopting a child."). The Cairns Birdwing (4.8 in.), the Madagascan Sunset Moth (3.4 in.) were so luminescent, they looked as if they weren't real, but crafted by Nicholas and Alexandra's legendary toymaker, Sacha Lurin Kuznetsov. With the most dazzling materials at his fingertips—velvet, silks, furs—he could craft chinchilla teddy bears, 24-carat dollhouses in his sleep (see *Imperial Indulgence*, Lipnokov, 1965).

"What is this stuff?" asked Eva, moving to examine the fourth box, jutting out her chin.

"Just some bugs." I was standing *right* behind her. Gray lint balls pimpled the sides of her white wool jacket. A strand of her sulphur orange hair swerved into a ? on her left shoulder. If we'd been in a film noir it would've been the moment I jammed a pistol into her back through the pocket of my trench coat and said, through teeth: "Make a funny move and I'll blow you from here to next Tuesday."

"I don't like this kinda thing," she said. "Gives me the creeps."

"How'd you meet my dad?" I asked as cheerfully as I could.

She turned around, narrowing her eyes. They really *were* an incredible color: the softest blue-violet in all the world, so pure, it actually seemed cruel to make it witness this scene.

"He didn't tell you?" she asked suspiciously.

I nodded. "I think he did. I just can't remember."

She stepped away from the cases and bent over Dad's desk to scrutinize his desk calendar (stuck in May 1998) covered with his illegible scrawl.

"I'm the type of person who stays professional," she said. "A lot of the other teachers don't. Some father comes by, tells them he likes their teaching style and suddenly they're in the throes of some cheap romance. And I tell them over and over, you're meeting at lunch hours, you're driving by his house in the middle of the night—you really think it's going to turn into something cute? Then your dad comes along. He wasn't fooling anyone. The average woman, sure. But me? I *knew* he was a fraud. That's the funny thing, I *knew*, but I didn't know, you know what I mean? Because he also had such a *heart*. I've never been one of those romantic types. But suddenly I thought I could save him. Only you can't save a fraud."

With her long fingernails (painted the pink of kitten noses) she was riffling through Dad's mug of pens. She picked one out—his favorite actually, an 18-carat gold Mont Blanc, a good-bye gift from Amy Pinto, one present from a June Bug he'd actually liked. Eva turned it in her fingers, sniffing it like a cigar. She put it in her purse.

"You can't take that," I said, horrified.

"If you don't win *Hollywood Squares*, you still get a consolation prize."

I couldn't breathe. "Maybe you'd be more comfortable in the living room," I suggested. "He'll be home"—I looked at my watch and to my panic it was only nine-thirty—"in a few minutes. I can make you some tea. I think we have some Whitman's chocolates—"

"Tea, huh? How civilized. *Tea*. That's something *he* would say." She threw me a look. "You should watch that, you know. Because sooner or later we all turn into our parents. *Poof.*"

She slumped down into Dad's office chair, pulled open a drawer and started to page through the legal pads.

"Won't know what hit . . . 'Interrelationships Between Domestic and International Politics from Greek Site-Cit–City States to the Present-Day.'" She frowned. "You get any of this crap? I had a good time with the guy, but mostly I thought what he said was a load of dung. 'Quantitative methods.' 'The role of external powers in peacekeeping processes—'"

"Ms. Brewster?"

"Yeah."

"What are your . . . plans?"

"Making it up as I go along. Where'd you move from, anyway? He was always fuzzy about it. Fuzzy about a lot of things—"

"I don't mean to be rude, but I think I might have to call the police."

She threw the legal pads back in the drawer, hard, and looked at me. If her eyes had been buses I'd have been run over. If they'd been guns I'd have been shot dead. I found myself wondering—ridiculously—if she perhaps had a gun on her and perhaps she wasn't afraid to use it. "You really think that's a good idea?" she asked.

"No," I admitted.

She cleared her throat. "Poor Mirtha Grazeley, you know, crazy as a dog struck by lightning, but pretty organized when it comes to that Admissions Office. Poor Mirtha came back to school on Monday. Last term. Found her place, not as she'd left it but with a couple of moved chairs and messy seat cushions, a liter of eggnog gone. It also looked like someone had lost her cookies in the bathroom. Not pretty. I know it wasn't a professional job because the vandal left her shoes behind. Black. Size 9. Dolce & Gabbana. Not a lot of kids can afford the hoity-toity stuff. So I narrow it down to the big donors' kids, Atlanta types who let their kids run around in the Mercedes. I cross-reference that with the kids who went to the dance and come up with a list of suspects that, surprisingly, ain't all that long. But I have a conscience, you know. I'm not one of those people who get a kick out of wrecking some kid's future. It'd be sad. From what I hear the Whitestone girl has enough problems. Might not graduate."

I couldn't speak for a moment. The hum of the house was audible. As a child, some of our house hums were so loud, I used to think an invisible glee club had gathered in the walls, wearing burgundy choir robes, mouths open in earnest Os, chanting all night and all day.

"Why were you calling out my name?" I managed to ask. "At the dance—"

She looked surprised. "You heard me?"

I nodded.

"I *thought* I saw you two running toward Loomis." She made an odd "rumph" sound and shrugged. "Just wanted to chew the fat. Talk about your dad. Kinda like we're doing now. Not that there's much to say anymore. Jig is up. I *know* who he is. Thinks he's God, but really, he's just a small . . ."

I thought she was going to stop there, at the searing declaration, "He's just a small," but then she ended it, her voice soft.

"A small little man."

She was silent, crossing her arms, tipping back in Dad's office chair. Even though Dad himself had warned me, one should never take notice of the words that barged out of an irate person's mouth, I still *hated* what she said. I noticed too, it was the cruelest thing to say about a person—that they were small. I was only consoled by the fact that, in truth, *all* humans were small when one considered them in the Grand Scheme of Things, put them side by side with Time, the Universe. Even Shakespeare was small and Van Gogh—Leonard Bernstein too.

"Who is she?" Eva demanded suddenly. She should have been triumphant, having made all those groundbreaking assertions about Dad, but there was a discernible sprain in her voice.

I waited for her to continue, but she didn't. "I'm not sure what you mean."

"You don't have to tell me who she is, but I'd appreciate it."

She was obviously referring to Dad's new girlfriend, but he didn't have one—at least, not to my knowledge.

"I don't think he's seeing anyone, but I could ask him for you."

"*Fine*," she said, nodding. "I believe you. He's good. I'd never know, never even *suspect* if I hadn't been friends since second grade with Alice Steady who owns the Green Orchid on Orlando. 'What's the name of the guy you're dating again?' 'Gareth.' 'Uh-huh,' she says. Guess he came in, blue Volvo, used a credit card to buy a hundred bucks' worth of flowers. Said no to Alice's offer of free delivery. And that was sneaky, see—no delivery address, no evidence, right? And I know the flowers weren't for himself because Alice said he asked for one of the little message cards. And from the look on *your* face, they weren't for *you* either. Alice's one of those romantic types, says no man buys a hundred bucks' worth of barbaresco orientals for someone he isn't madly in love with. Roses, sure. Every cheap piece of ass gets roses. But not barbaresco orientals. I'll be the first to admit I was upset—I'm not one of those people who pretends they never cared in the first place, but then he started not returning my calls, sweeping me under the rug like I'm crumbs or something. Not that I *care*. I'm seeing someone else now. An optometrist. Divorced. His first wife I guess was a real clinker. Gareth can do whatever he wants with himself."

She fell silent, not out of exhaustion or reflection, but because her eyes had again snagged on the butterflies in front of her.

"He really loves those things," she said.

I followed her gaze to the wall. "Not really."

"No?"

"He barely looks at them."

I actually saw the thought, the light bulb illuminating her head as if she were a comic book character.

She moved quickly, but so did I. I stood in front of them and hastily said something about receiving the flowers myself ("Dad talks about you all the time!" I cried rather pathetically) but she didn't hear me.

A garish flush bleeding into the back of her neck, she yanked open Dad's desk drawers and hurled every one of his legal pads (he organized them by university and date) into the air. They flew around the room like giant scared canaries.

I guess she found what she was looking for—a steel ruler, which Dad used for orderly cross-comparison diagrams in his lecture notes—and to my shock, she brutally shoved me aside and tried to stab it through the glass of one of the Ricker's cases. The ruler, silver aluminum, would have no part of it however, so with an infuriated "Fuckin' A," she threw it to the floor and tried punching one of the boxes with her bare fist, and then with her elbow, and when that didn't work, she scratched the glass with her nails as if she were some lunatic scraping the silver skin off a lottery ticket.

Still thwarted, she turned, her eyes swerving around Dad's desk until they stopped on the green lamp (a parting gift from the agreeable Dean at the University of Arkansas at Wilsonville). She seized it, jerking the cord out of the wall, and raised it over her head. She used the base, solid brass, to shatter the glass of the first case.

At this point, I ran at her again, lurching at her shoulders, also shouting, "Please!" but I was too weak and, I suppose, too stunned by it all to be effective. She pushed me again, elbowing me right in the jaw so my neck twisted to the side and I fell down.

Glass rained everywhere, all over Dad's desk, the rug, my feet and hands, all over her, too. Tiny shards glittered in her hair and stuck to her thick white tights, trembling like beads of water. She couldn't remove the cases from the wall (Dad used special screws to hang them) but she ripped through the pieces of mounting paper and tore the brown cardboard backing from the frames, ripping every butterfly and moth from their pins, squashing their wings so they became colored confetti, which, with eyes wide, her face creased like a wad of paper smoothed out, she tossed around the room, making something of a sacrament out of it like a priest gone mad with holy water.

At one point, with a muffled growl, she actually bit into one, and resembled for a horrifying and faintly surreal moment, a massive orange tabby eating a blackbird. (In the most peculiar of instances, one is struck by the most peculiar of thoughts, and in this case, as Eva bit into the wing of the Night Butterfly, *Taygetis echo*, I remembered the occasion when Dad and I were driving from Louisiana to Arkansas, when it was ninety degrees and the air-conditioning was broken, and we were memorizing a Wallace Stevens poem, one of Dad's favorites, "Thirteen Ways of Looking at a Blackbird." " 'Among twenty snowy mountains / The only thing moving / was the eye of the black-bird,' " Dad explained to the highway.)

When she stopped, when she finally stood still, astonished herself by what she'd just done, there was the utterest of all utter silences, reserved, I imagined, for the aftermath of massacres and storms. You could probably hear the rustle of the moon if you concentrated, the earth too, its *whoosh* as it whirled around the sun at 18.5 miles per second. Eva then began to shiver an apology in a trembling voice that sounded as if it were being tickled. She cried a little too, a disquieting, low-pitched seeping sound.

I can't be sure of her crying, actually; I, too, had been hauled into a state of disorientation under which I could only repeat to myself, *this did not actually happen* as I gazed at the surrounding debris, in particular, at the top of my right foot, my yellow sock, on which rested a brown and furry torso of some moth, the Bent-Wing Ghost Moth perhaps, slightly crooked, as if it were a bit of pipe cleaner.

Eva then put the lamp down on Dad's desk, tenderly, the way one handles a baby, and, avoiding my eyes, walked past me, up the stairs. After a moment, I heard the front door slam and the sputter of her car as she drove away.

*   *   *

With a samurai-like precision and clarity of mind that promptly settles over one following the weirder episodes of one's life, I resolved to clean everything up before Dad returned home.

I obtained a screwdriver from the garage and, one by one, removed the destroyed boxes from the wall. I swept up the glass and the wings, vacuumed under Dad's desk, along the edges of the floor, the bookshelves and stairs. I returned the legal pads to their respective drawers, organizing them by university and date, and then carried to my room their cardboard moving box (BUTTERFLIES FRAGILE) in which I'd put all that was salvageable. It wasn't much—only torn white paper, a handful of brown wings still in one piece and the single Small Postman, *Heliconius erato*, which had emerged from the slaughter miraculously unscathed after hiding behind Dad's filing cabinet. I tried to read more of *Henry V* as I waited for Dad to return home, but the words snagged my eyes. I found myself staring at a single point on the page.

Despite the throb in my right cheek, I had no illusions Dad was anything other than the pitiless villain in this evening's freaky drama. Sure, I hated her, but I hated him, too. Dad had finally gotten what was coming to him, except he'd been otherwise engaged, so *I*, his guiltless direct descendant, had gotten what was coming to him. I knew it was melodramatic, but I found myself wishing Kitty had *killed* me (at the very least, knocked me provisionally unconscious) so when Dad returned home, he'd see me lying on his study floor, my body saggy and gray as a hundred-year-old sofa, my neck twisted at the disturbing angle indicating Life caught a bus out of town. After Dad fell to his knees, uttered King Learean cries ("No! Noooo! Don't take her God! I'll do anything!") my eyes would open, I'd gasp, then deliver my mesmerizing speech, touching upon Humanity, Compassion, the fine line between Kindness and Pity, the necessity of Love (a theme rescued from the trite and the maudlin by sturdy support from the Russians: ["Everything that I understand, I understand only because I love."] and a little Irving Berlin to keep things snappy ["They say that falling in love is wonderful, it's wonderful, so they say."]). I'd end with the pronouncement that the Jack Nicholson, Dad's customary modus operandi, would henceforth be replaced by the Paul Newman, and Dad would nod with his eyes lowered, his face pained. His hair would turn gray, too, a uniform steel-gray, like Hecuba's, the emblem of Purest Sorrow.

What about the others? Had he hurt the others as much as he'd hurt Eva Brewster? What about Shelby Hollows with her bleached moustache? Or Janice Elmeros with cactus-prickly legs under her sundresses? And the others, like Rachel Groom and Isabelle Franks who never came to see Dad without bearing gifts like contemporary Wise Men (Dad, mistaken for a Christ Child), cornbread, muffins and straw dolls with wincing faces (as if they'd all just eaten a Sour Patch Kid), their gold, frankincense and myrrh? How many hours had Natalie Simms slaved constructing the birdhouse out of popsicle sticks?

The blue Volvo cruised down the driveway at a quarter to twelve. I heard him unlock the front door.

"Sweet, come down at once! You'll laugh your eyes out!"

(Laughing one's eyes out was a particularly irritating Dadism, as was crying until the bulls come home and being the pear of one's eye.)

"Turns out little Arnie Sanderson couldn't hold his liquor! He fell down, I swear to you, fell *down* in the restaurant on his way to the men's room. I had to drive the thug home, to his Calcutta-inspired university housing. A terrifying place—tatty carpeting, a stench of curdled milk, graduate fellows wandering the halls with feet that appeared to support more exotic life forms than the Galápagos Islands. I had to carry him up the stairs. Three *flights!* Do you remember *Teacher's Pet*, that rather delightful film starring Gable and Doris we watched—where was it? Missouri? Well, I lived it this evening, only without the perky blonde. I believe I deserve a drink."

He was silent.

"Have you gone to bed?"

Dad dashed up the stairs, knocked lightly, pushed open the door. He was still wearing his coat. I was sitting on the edge of my bed, staring at the wall with my arms crossed.

"What's happened?" he asked.

When I told him (doing my best to keep my manner like that of the Loosened Steel Girder, dangerous and unforgiving) Dad turned into one of those things twirling outside of vintage barber shops: he went red when he saw the red splotch on my face, white when I escorted him downstairs and expertly reenacted the scene (including snippets of actual dialogue, the exact position in which I was ruthlessly chucked to the ground and Eva's revelation that Dad was "*a small*"), and upstairs again, when I showed him the box full of butterfly and moth remains, red again.

"If I'd known such a thing was possible," Dad said, "that she could became a Scylla—*worse* than a Charybdis in my book—I'd have *murdered* that nut." He pressed the washcloth full of ice to my cheek. "I must think what measures to take."

"How'd you meet her?" I asked gloomily, without looking at him.

"Of course, I've heard stories of this nature from colleagues, seen the movies, *Fatal Attraction* being the gold stand—"

"*How, Dad?*" I screamed.

He was taken aback by my voice, but rather than getting angry, he only lifted the ice, and frowning in grave concern (his impression of the nurse in *For Whom the Bell Tolls*), touched my cheek with the back of his fingers.

"How did I—let's see if, what was it—late September," he said, clearing his throat. "I made that second trip to your school to discuss your class ranking. Remember? I found myself lost. That officer in charge, that off-the-wall Ronin-Smith—she told me to meet her in a different room because her office was being repainted. But she gave me the wrong location, and thus I made an imbecile of myself knocking on Hanover 316 and encountered an unpleasantly bearded History professor attempting to clarify—rather unsuccessfully, I gathered from the benumbed expressions of his class—the Hows and Whys of the Industrial Age. I stopped by the main office to inquire after the correct location and encountered the manic Miss Brewster."

"And it was love at first sight."

Dad gazed at the box of remains on the floor. "To think all this might have been avoided if that goat had simply told me *Barrow* 316."

"It isn't funny."

He shook his head. "It was wrong not to tell you. I apologize. But I was uncomfortable with it, my"—he held his breath in discomfort—"*connection* with someone from your school. I certainly didn't mean for it to escalate as it did. In the beginning, it all seemed rather harmless."

"That's what the Germans said when they lost World War II."

"I take full responsibility. I was an ass."

"A liar. A *cheat. She* called you a liar. And she was right—"

"Yes."

"—you lie about anything and everything. Even, 'Nice to see you.' "

He didn't respond to this, only sighed.

I crossed my arms, still glowering at the wall, but I didn't move my head away when he pressed the cold washcloth to my cheek again.

"As I see it," he said, "I'll have to call the police. That, or the more appealing option. Going to her house with an illegally obtained firearm."

"You can't call the police. You can't do anything."

He looked at me. "But I thought you'd want that beast behind bars."

"She's just a normal woman, Dad. And you didn't treat her with respect. Why didn't you return her phone calls?"

"I suppose I didn't feel much like talking."

"Not returning phone calls is the severest form of torture in the civilized world. Haven't you read *Hit and Run: Crisis in Singlehood America*?"

"I don't believe I have—"

"The least you can do now is leave her alone."

He was about to add something, but stopped himself.

"Who'd you send the flowers to anyway?" I asked.

"Hmm?"

"Those flowers she was talking about—"

"Janet Finnsbroke. One of the administrators in the department who dates back to the Paleozoic Period. Her fiftieth wedding anniversary. I thought it'd be nice—" Dad caught my eye "—no, I most certainly am *not* in love with her. For Pete's sake."

I pretended not to notice, but Dad looked sort of deflated there on the edge of my bed. A lost, even humbled look was wandering around his face (quite surprised to be there). Seeing him like this, so un-Dad, made me feel sorry for him—though I didn't let on. His befuddled expression reminded me of those unflattering photographs of presidents *The New York Times* and other newspapers adored sticking on their front page in order to show the world how the Great Leader looked between the staged waves, the scripted sound-bites, the rehearsed handshakes—not staunch and stately, not even steady, but frail and foolish. And though these candid photographs were amusing, when you actually *thought* about it, the underlying implication of such a photograph was scary, for they hinted how delicate the balance of our lives, how tenuous our calm little existences, if this was the man in charge.

Deliverance

And so, I come to the perilous part of my story.

If this narrative were a quotidian account of the history of Russia, this chapter would be a proletarian's account of the Great October Soviet Socialist Revolution of 1917, if a history of France, the beheading of Marie Antoinette, if a chronicle of America, the assassination of Abraham Lincoln by John Wilkes Booth.

"All worthwhile tales possess some element of violence," Dad said. "If you don't believe me, simply reflect for a moment on the utter horror of having something threatening lurking outside your front door, hearing it huff and puff and then, cruelly, callously, *blowing your house down*. It's as horrifying as any story on CNN. And yet where would the 'Three Little Pigs' be without such brutality? No one would have heard of them, for happiness and placidity are not worth recounting by the fire, nor, for that matter, reporting by a news anchor wearing pancake makeup and more shimmer on her eyelids than a peacock feather."

Not that I am trying to imply my story can hold a candle to complex world histories (each one worth over one thousand pages of fine print) or three-hundred-year-old fables. Yet one can't help but notice that violence, although officially abhorred in modern Western and Eastern cultures (only officially, for no culture, modern or otherwise, hesitates using it for the pursuit of their own interests) is unavoidable if there is to be change.

Without the disturbing incident of this chapter, I'd never have taken on the task of writing this story. I'd have nothing to write. Life in Stockton would have continued exactly as it was, as placid and primly self-contained as Switzerland, and any strange incidents—Cottonwood, Smoke Harvey's death, that strange conversation with Hannah prior to Christmas Break—might be regarded as unusual, certainly, but in the end, nothing that couldn't be dully reviewed and accounted for by Hindsight, forever unsurprised and shortsighted.

I cannot help but anticipate a little, run on ahead (much in the manner of Violet Martinez in the Great Smoky Mountains), and so, given this lapse in patience, I will only hopscotch through the two months between Eva's destruction of my mother's butterflies and moths and the camping trip, which Hannah, in spite of our patent lack of enthusiasm ("Won't do it, couldn't pay me," pledged Jade), maintained was scheduled for the weekend of March 26, the beginning of Spring Break.

"Make sure you bring hiking shoes," she said.

St. Gallway doggedly marched on (see Chapter 9, "The Battle of Stalingrad," *The Great Patriotic War*, Stepnovich, 1989). With the exception of Hannah, most teachers had returned from Christmas vacation cheerfully unchanged, apart from small, pleasant enhancements to their appearance: a new red Navajo sweater (Mr. Archer), shiny new shoes (Mr. Moats), a new boysenberry rinse that turned hair into something that had to be consciously matched, like paisley (Ms. Gershon). These distracting details caused one to daydream in class about *who* had given Mr. Archer that sweater, or how Mr. Moats must be insecure about his height because all of his shoes possessed soles thick as sticks of butter, or the exact look on Ms. Gershon's face when her hairdresser removed the towel from her head and said, "Don't worry. The plum tones just look extreme now because it's wet."

St. Gallway students were also the same, rodentlike in their ability to carry on foraging, storing, burrowing and eating a huge amount of plant food in spite of humiliating national scandals and harrowing world events. ("This is a critical time in our nation's history," Ms. Sturds was always informing us during Morning Announcements. "Let's make sure we look back in twenty years and feel proud. Read the newspaper. Take sides. Have an opinion.") Student Council President Maxwell Stuart unveiled elaborate plans for a Spring Term Barbecue Hoedown, replete with square dancing, bluegrass band and Faculty Scarecrow Contest; Mr. Carlos Sandborn of AP World History stopped using gel in his hair (it no longer looked wet, as if it'd been swimming laps, but windblown, as if it'd been doing figure-eights in a propeller plane) and Mr. Frank Fletcher, crossword maharishi and monitor of second period Study Hall, was in the throes of a divorce; his wife, Evelyn, had apparently made him move out (though whether the deep circles under his eyes were due to the divorce or crosswords, no one knew), citing Irrecon-cilable Differences.

"I guess when they were doing the nasty on Christmas Eve, Mr. Fletcher shouted out, 'Oh, Eleven Down!' not 'Evelyn, Down!' That was the last straw," said Dee.

I saw Zach all the time in Physics, but apart from a handful of hellos, we didn't speak. He never materialized at my locker anymore. Once, during the Dynamics Lab we found ourselves at the back of the room together and just as I looked up from my notebook to smile at him, he bumped into the corner of one of the lab tables and spontaneously dropped what he was carrying, a ring stand and a set of known masses. But even as he picked up the equip-ment, he didn't say anything, only returned swiftly to the front of the room (and his lab partner, Krista Jibsen) with an official spokesperson look on his face. I couldn't tell what he was thinking.

Clumsy, too, were the occasions I passed Eva Brewster in the hallway. We both pretended to be suffering from the effects of Walking and Thinking an Elaborate Thought at the Same Time (Einstein suffered from it, Darwin, de Sade too), and hence the person suffered from an obliviousness toward his/her immediate surroundings that approached that of a temporary black-out or complete loss of consciousness (this, though as we slipped past each other, our eyes fell like curtains when a hooker strolls through a prairie town searching for accommodation). I felt as if I was now privy to a dark, grisly se-cret about Eva (in certain rare instances, she transformed into a werewolf) and she begrudged me for knowing it. At the same time, as she marched down the hall with an absorbed expression, a hint of lemony perfume, as if she'd spritzed herself with a cleaner for kitchen countertops, I swore I de-tected in the hunch of her beige sweater, in the angle of her meaty neck, that she was sorry and she'd take it all back if she could. Even if she didn't have the guts to say it to me outright (so few people had the guts to really say things), it made me feel less anxious, as if I understood her a little.

Ms. Brewster's rampage *did* have some constructive effects, as all disas-ters and tragedies do (see *The Dresden Upshot*, Trask, 2002). Dad, still guilty about Kitty, had adopted a permanently contrite manner, which I found re-freshing. The day we returned from Paris, I'd learned I'd been admitted to Harvard, and we finally celebrated this milestone on a blustery Friday eve-ning in early March. Dad donned his Brooks Brothers, French-cuffed dress shirt, his gold GUM cufflinks; I, a gum-green dress from Au Printemps. Dad chose the four-star restaurant purely on the basis of its name: Quixote.

The dinner was unforgettable for many reasons, one of them being that Dad, in an uncharacteristic display of self-command, paid no attention at all to our gorgeous waitress with the voluptuous body of a swan-necked flask and an astoundingly cleft chin. Her coffee-colored eyes trespassed all over Dad when she took our order and again when she asked Dad if he wanted fresh pepper ("*Had enough* [pepper]?" she inquired breathily). Yet Dad willfully remained indifferent to this intrusion, and so, somewhat dejectedly, her eyes went back the way they came ("Dessert menu," she announced grimly by the end of the meal).

"To my daughter," Dad said grandly, clinking his wineglass on the rim of my Coke. A middle-aged woman at the table next to us with heavy hardware jewelry and a thickset husband (whom she seemed anxious to unload like armfuls of shopping bags) beamed at us for the thirtieth time (Dad, a stirring example of Paternity: handsome, devoted, wearing tweed). "May your studies continue to the end of your days," he said. "May you walk a lighted path. May you fight for truth—your truth, not someone else's—and may you understand, above all things, that you are the most important concept, theory and philosophy I have ever known."

The woman was practically blown off her seat by Dad's eloquence. I thought he was paraphrasing an Irish drinking toast, but later I did check Killing's *Beyond Words* (1999) and couldn't find it. It was Dad.

* * *

On Friday, March 26, with the same innocence of the Trojans as they gathered around the strange wooden horse standing at the gate to their city in order to marvel at its craftsmanship, Hannah drove our yellow Rent-Me truck into the dirt lot of Sunset Views Encampment and parked in Space 52. The lot was empty, with the exception of a swayback blue Pontiac parked in front of the cabin (a wooden sign slapped crookedly over the door like a Band-Aid: MAIN) and a rusty towable trailer ("Lonesome Dreams") chucked under an evangelist oak tree. (It was in the midst of some violent enlightenment, branches stretched heavenward as if to grab hold of His feet.) A white sky ironed, starched, folded itself primly behind the rolling mountains. Garbage floated across the lot, cryptic messages in bottles: Santa Fe Ranch Lay's potato chips, Thomas' English Muffins, a frayed purple ribbon. Sometime in the last week or so, it had sleeted cigarette butts.

None of us knew how we'd gotten there. We'd been unenthused with the idea of a camping trip from the beginning (including Leulah, who was always the first to go along with something) and now, here we were, in old jeans and uncomfortable hiking shoes, our distended camping backpacks rented from Into the Blue Mountaineering slumped against the van's back-seat windows like fat men who'd dozed off. An empty, nervous canteen, a tired bandana, Special K and ramen noodles rattling, the sudden evaporation of an entire can of contact solution, fitful whines of "Wait, who took my wind-resistant parka?"—it was a testament to Hannah's influence, her startling yet subtle way of getting you to do something when you'd sworn to everyone, including yourself, you never would.

For reasons we never discussed, Nigel and I hadn't said anything to the others about the articles he'd found or Violet May Martinez, though when we were alone, he hashed them over incessantly. True tales of unsolved vanishings tended to hang around the darkest confines of one's mind long after one read about them—doubtlessly the reason why Conrad Hiller's poorly written and scrappily researched 2002 account of two teenage kidnappings in Massachusetts, *The Beautiful Ones*, hung around the *New York Times* Bestseller List for sixty-two weeks. Such stories were as pervasive as bats, flying around at the slightest provocation, circling over your head, and though you knew they had nothing to do with you, that your fate would probably not be like theirs, you still felt a mixture of fear and fascination.

"Everyone have what they need?" sang Hannah as she retied the bright red laces on her leather boots. "We can't come back to the truck, so make sure you have your backpacks and maps—*do not* forget the maps I gave you. It's very important you know where we are as we hike. We're following Bald Creek Trail, past Abram's Peak to Sugartop Summit. It moves northeast and the campground's four miles away from Newfound Gap Road, U.S. 441, that thick red line. See it on the map?"

"Yep," said Lu.

"The first aid kit. Who has it?"

"Me," said Jade.

"Fantastic." Hannah smiled, her hands on her hips. She was dressed for the occasion: khaki pants, a long-sleeved black T-shirt, a puffy green vest, mirrored sunglasses. There was an enthusiasm in her voice I hadn't heard since Fall Term. During Sunday dinners of late, we were all aware she wasn't herself. Something very slight had shifted within her, a change difficult to pinpoint; it was as if a painting in one's house had secretly been moved an inch to the right of where it'd hung for years. She listened to us as she always did, took the same interest in our lives, talked about her volunteer work at the animal shelter, a parrot she was hoping to adopt—but she didn't seem to laugh anymore, that girlish giggle like a kick through pebbles. (As Nigel said, that haircut was an "eternal rain on her parade.") She was prone to silent nods and abstracted stares, and I couldn't tell if she simply couldn't help this new reticence, if it was born of some unaccountable grief, which had rooted and spread inside of her like leafy liverwort, or if it was deliberate, so we'd all worry about what was troubling her. Certain June Bugs, I knew, willed themselves into abnormal moods that ranged from dour to delicate, simply so Dad would ask them, in tormented tones, if there was anything in the world he could do. (Dad's actual response to such calculated behavior was to comment she looked tired and suggest making it an early night.)

After dinner, Hannah no longer put on Billie Holiday's "No Regrets," singing along in her low, bashful, tone-deaf voice, but sat meditatively on the couch, stroking Lana and Turner, not saying a word while the rest of us hashed over college, or Headmaster Havermeyer's wife, Gloria, who was expecting twins and hauled her great stomach around campus with the same pleasure of Sisyphus with his boulder, or the outrageous story that broke in early March, that Ms. Sturds had been secretly engaged to Mr. Butters since Christmas (a pairing as dubious as an American Bison with a Grass Snake).

Efforts, both stealthy and obvious, to have Hannah join our conversations was like playing volleyball with a shot put. And she hardly ate the dinner she'd so painstakingly prepared, just pushed the food around her plate like an uninspired painter with a palette of dreary oils.

Now, for the first time in months, she was in a grand mood. She moved with the bright quickness of a sparrow.

"Are we ready?" she asked.

"For what?" asked Charles.

"Forty-eight hours of hell," said Jade.

"For being at one with nature. Everyone have their maps?"

"For the twentieth time, we have the goddamn *maps*," said Charles, slamming the doors at the back of the van.

"Perfect," Hannah said cheerfully and, making sure the doors were locked, she hoisted her enormous blue backpack onto her shoulders and began to walk away, briskly heading toward the woods at the opposite end of the parking lot. "And they're off!" she shouted over her shoulder. "Old Schneider's first out of the gate and holds the lead. Milton Black moves up on the outside. Leulah Maloney is coming up from fifth place. On the final turn it will be Jade and Blue battling it to the finish line." She laughed.

"What's she talking about?" asked Nigel staring after her.

"Who the hell knows," said Jade.

"Get going, thoroughbreds! We have to get there in the next four hours, otherwise we'll be hiking in the dark!"

"Great," said Jade, rolling her eyes. "She's finally lost it. And she couldn't lose it when we were buoyed by civilization. No, she had to lose it now, when we're in the middle of nowhere, when it's all snakes and trees and no one to come to our rescue but a fleet of friggin' rabbits."

Nigel and I looked at each other. He shrugged.

"What the hell?" he said. Flashing his tiny smile, a pocket mirror catching light, he started after her.

I held back, watching the others. For some reason, I didn't want to go. I felt, not dread or apprehension, only an awareness that something grueling was looming in front of me, something so vast I couldn't see all of it, and I didn't know if I had the strength to take it on (see *Nothing but a Compass and an Electrometer: The Story of Captain Scott and the Great Race to Claim Antarctica*, Walsh, 1972).

Tightening the straps of my backpack, I headed after them.

A few yards in front of me, at the opening of the trail, Jade tripped on a root. "Oh, stunning. Simply stunning," she said.

The northwest passage of Bald Creek Trail (a dotted black line on Hannah's map) started out amiably enough, broad-shouldered as Mrs. Rowley, my second-grade teacher at Wadsworth Elementary, puffy with mulch and late afternoon sunshine, and fine, wispy, flyaway pines like the hair loosened from her ponytail at the end of the day. (Mrs. Rowley possessed the enviable knack for turning all "frowns upside down," and all "snuffles into smiles.")

"Maybe this isn't so bad," said Jade, turning around and grinning as she trudged along in front of me. "I mean it *is* kind of fun."

An hour later, however, after Hannah's yell for us to "keep right at the fork," the road revealed its true character; it resembled not Mrs. Rowley, but the prickly Ms. Dewelhearst of Howard Country Day who dressed in dirt browns, with a posture taking cues from an umbrella handle and a face so withered she looked more walnut than human. The trail shriveled, forcing us to proceed single file and in relative silence as we skirted past painful brambles and weeds. ("Not a twitter during the examination or I'll hold you back a grade and your life will be in ruins forevermore," said Ms. Dewelhearst.)

"This freaking *hurts*," said Jade. "I need a local anesthetic for my legs."

"Stop complaining," said Charles.

"How's everyone doing?" shouted Hannah at the front, walking backward up the hill.

"Marvelous, marvelous. This is fucking Candy Land."

"Only a half hour to the first lookout point!"

"I'm going to throw myself off," said Jade.

We trudged on. In the woods, with its endless procession of malnourished pines and lop-eared rhododendrons and wan gray rocks, time seemed to speed up and slow down without provocation. I fell into a strange lull as I lumbered along in the very back, staring for minutes at a time at Jade's red kneesocks (hiked up over her jeans; some precaution against rattlesnakes), the thick brown roots caterpillaring through the trail, the splotches of fading gold light staining the ground. The seven of us seemed to be the only things alive for miles (apart from a few invisible birds and a gray squirrel skittering up a tree's torso) and one couldn't help but wonder if Hannah was right, if this experience she'd forced us into was, in fact, a gateway to something else, some brave new understanding of the world. Pines frothed, imitating the ocean. A bird fluttered up, up, swiftly, like an air bubble, to the sky.

Oddly enough, the only person who appeared not to have fallen under this plodding spell was Hannah. Whenever the path stiffened into a straight line, I could see she'd hung back to walk with Leulah and talked animatedly—a little *too* animatedly—nodding and looking over at Lu's face as if to memorize her expressions. And every now and then, she laughed, an abrupt and harsh sound, puncturing the bland peace of everything.

"Wonder what they're gossiping about," said Jade.

I shrugged.

*　　*　　*

We reached the first vista, Abram's Peak, around 6:15 P.M. It was a large rock promontory off to the right of the trail that opened up, like a stage, to reveal a grand expanse of mountains.

"That's Tennessee," Hannah said, shading her eyes.

We stood next to her in a line, staring at Tennessee. The only immediate sound was Nigel unwrapping the blueberry Pop-Tart he'd removed from his backpack. (As fish are impervious to drowning, Nigel was impervious to all Quietly Profound Moments.) The cold air tightened my throat, my lungs. The mountains hugged each other sternly, similar to the way men hugged other men, not letting their chests touch. Thin clouds hung around their necks, and the mountains farthest away, the ones passed out against the horizon, were so pale, you couldn't see where their backs ended and the sky began.

The view made me sad, but I suppose everyone, when happening upon a sprawling expanse of earth, all light and mist, all breathlessness and infinity, felt sad—"the enduring gloom of man," Dad called it. You couldn't help but think, not only about shortages of food, safe water, shockingly low averages of adult literacy and life expectancy in various developing nations, but also that shopworn thought about how many people were, at this precise moment, being born, and how many were dying, and that you, like some 6.2 billion others, were simply between these two ho-hum milestones, milestones that felt earth shattering while they were happening, but in the context of Hichraker's 2003 edition of the *World Geographical Factbook*, or M. C. Howard's *Finding the Cosmos in a Grain of Sand: The Nativity of the Universe* (2004) they were ordinary, run-of-the-mill. It made one feel as if one's life was no more imperative than a pine needle.

"*Fuck you!*" Hannah screamed.

The sound didn't echo, as it would in a Looney Tune, but was swallowed immediately, like a thimble hurled at the sea. Charles turned and stared at her. The look on his face clearly indicated he thought she was crazy. The rest of us shifted like nervous cattle in a boxcar.

"*F–Fuck you!*" she shouted again, her voice hoarse.

She turned to us. "You should all say something." She took another deep breath, tipped her head back and closed her eyes in the manner of someone preparing to sunbathe on a deck chair. Her eyelids trembled, her lips too.

"*Let me not to the marriage of true minds admit impediments!*" she screamed.

"You okay?" Milton asked her, laughing.

"There's nothing funny about this," Hannah said with a serious face. "Put some muscle into it. Pretend you're a bassoon. And then say something. Something that comes from your soul." She took a deep breath. "*Henry David Thoreau!*"

"*Don't be afraid to be afraid!*" Leulah gasped rather abruptly, sticking out her chin like a child in a spitting contest.

"Nice," said Hannah.

Jade huffed. "Oh, God. I guess we're going to be born again from this ex-perience?"

"I can't hear you," Hannah said.

"This is fucking *ridiculous!*" Jade shouted.

"Better."

"Dang," said Milton.

"Wimpy."

"*Dang!*"

"Jenna Jameson?" shouted Charles.

"Is it a question or an answer?" said Hannah.

"*Janet Jacme!*"

"*Get me the fuck out of here!*" screamed Jade.

"*Set limits and goals with equal precision!*"

"*I want to fucking go home!*"

"*Say hello to my leetle friend!*" yelled Nigel, his face red.

"*Sir William Shakespeare!*" shouted Milton.

"He wasn't a sir," said Charles.

"Yes, he was."

"He wasn't knighted."

"Let it go," said Hannah.

"*Jenna Jameson!*"

"Blue?" Hannah asked.

I didn't know why I hadn't shouted anything. I felt like a person who couldn't unstick their stutter. I believe I was trying to think of someone with a decent last name, someone who deserved this privilege of being sent into the wind. Chekhov, I'd been about to say him, but he seemed too stilted, even if I added the first name. Dostoevsky was too long. Plato seemed irritating, as if I were trying to one-up everyone by choosing the Very Root of Western Civi-lization and Thought. Nabokov, Dad would have approved, but no one, Dad included, seemed certain of the pronunciation. ("NA-bo-kov" was incorrect, the pronunciation of amateurs who bought *Lolita* under the impression it was a bodice ripper; yet "Na-BO-kov" fired like a defunct pistol.) It was even worse with Goethe. Molière was an interesting choice (no one had yet men-tioned a Frenchman) but there was a problem shouting the guttural *R*. Racine was too obscure, Hemingway too macho, Fitzgerald fine, but in the end it was unforgivable what he did to Zelda. Homer was a good choice, though Dad said *The Simpsons* had bastardized his reputation.

"*Be—be true to yourself!*" shouted Leulah.

"*Scorsese!*"

"*Behave yourself!*" said Milton.

"That's not a good one," said Hannah. "Never behave yourself."

"*Never behave yourself!*"

"*Just do it!*"

"*Be all that you can be!*"

"Don't rely on the sound-bites of American advertising to tell you how you feel," said Hannah. "Use your own words. What you have to say, what's in your heart, is always powerful."

"*Full-sleeved tattoos!*" shouted Jade. Jade's face was now screwed up with emotion like a ringing out washcloth.

"Blue, you're thinking too much," said Hannah, turning to me.

"I—uh—" I said.

"*The Canterbury Tales!*"

"*Mrs. Eugenia Sturds! May she live happily ever after with Mr. Mark Butters but may they not procreate and terrorize the world with their offspring!*"

"Say the first thing that comes into your head—"

"*Blue van Meer!*" I blurted.

It slipped out like a big catfish. I froze. I prayed no one had heard me, that it'd swum into the air, far ahead of everyone's ears.

"*Hannah Schneider!*" shouted Hannah.

"*Nigel Creech!*"

"*Jade Churchill Whitestone!*"

"*Milton Black!*"

"*Leulah Jane Maloney!*"

"*Doris Richards my fifth-grade teacher with the incredible tits!*"

"*Hell yeah!*"

"You don't have to be lewd to be passionate. Dare to be real. To be serious."

"*Never listen to the awful things people say about you because they're jealous!*" Leulah pushed her hair out of her tiny, demure face. She had tears in her eyes. "*One—one must persevere despite great adversity! One can never give up!*"

"Don't just be that way here," Hannah said to us. She pointed at the mountains. "Be that way down there."

* * *

The remaining hike to Sugartop Summit (now a disturbing dotted line on our keyless map) took another two hours and Hannah told us we needed to pick up the pace if we wanted to get there before dark.

As we walked, the light weakening, bony pines crowding closer and closer around us, Hannah again became engrossed in a private conversation, this time with Milton. She walked very close to him (*so* close that, at certain moments, she with her great blue backpack and he with his red one, collided at the shoulders like bumper cars). He nodded at something she said, his large frame hunched down on the side where she walked, as if she was causing him to erode.

I knew how complimentary it could feel when Hannah talked to you, when she singled you out—opened your meek cover, boldly creased the spine, stared inside at your pages, searching for the point at which she'd stopped reading, anxious to find out what happens next. (She always read with great concentration, so you thought you were her favorite paperback until she abruptly put you down and started to read another with the same intensity.)

Twenty minutes later, Hannah was talking to Charles. They broke into screechy seagull laughter; she touched his shoulder, pulling him to her, their arms and hands for a moment entwined.

"Aren't *they* the happy couple," said Jade.

Not fifteen minutes later, Hannah was walking next to Nigel (I could tell from his lowered head and sideways glances, he was listening to her a little uneasily), and soon, she was in front of me talking to Jade.

Naturally, I assumed she'd eventually move back to talk to *me*, that this was a Hannah–Student Conference, and I, bringing up the rear, was the last on the list. But when they finished their conversation—Hannah was encouraging Jade to apply for a summer internship at *The Washington Post* ("Remember to be kind to yourself," I also heard her say)—she whispered something more, gave her a quick kiss on the cheek, and then hurried to the front of our procession without so much as a glance in my direction.

"Okay! Don't worry, guys!" she shouted. "We're almost there!"

I was a mixture of indignation and melancholy by the time we reached Sugartop Summit. One tries not to pay attention to blatant favoritism ("Not everyone can be a member of the Van Meer Fan Club," noted Dad), but when it is so unashamedly flung in one's face, one can't help but feel hurt, as if everyone else gets to be pine needles, but one is forced to be sap. Mercifully, the others didn't realize she hadn't talked to me, and so when Jade threw her backpack to the ground, stretched her arms over her head, a big smile sunseting her face and said, "She really knows what to say, you know what I mean? *Amazing,*" I admit I lied; I nodded in emphatic agreement and said, "She does."

"Let's try to get the tents up first," Hannah said. "I'll help with the first one. But go take a look at that view! You'll be speechless!"

Despite Hannah's patent enthusiasm, this campground I found dreary and anticlimactic, especially after the sprawling majesty of Abram's Peak. Sugartop Summit comprised a circular dirt clearing flanked by mangy pines, and a blackened campfire where a few logs had recently burned, soft and gray around their edges like the muzzles of old dogs. Off to the right, beyond a cluster of boulders, was a bald rock ledge, narrow as a nearly closed door, where one could sit and spy on a naked, purplish mountain range sleeping under a shabby bedspread of fog. By now, the sun had drained away. Runny oranges and yellows clogged the horizon.

"Someone was here five minutes ago," said Leulah.

I turned from the lookout point. She was standing in the middle of the clearing, pointing at the ground.

"What?" asked Jade next to her.

I walked over to them.

"Look."

In front of the toe of her boot was a cigarette butt.

"It was burning three seconds ago."

Crouching down, Jade picked it up as one picks up a dead goldfish. Carefully, she sniffed it.

"You're right," she said, throwing it on the ground. "I can smell it. *Great.* All we need. Some mountain scab waiting for nightfall to come fuck us all in the ass."

"*Hannah!*" shouted Lu. "We have to get out of here!"

"What's wrong?" asked Hannah.

Jade pointed at the cigarette butt.

"This is a very popular place to camp," Hannah said.

"But it was burning," Leulah said, her eyes saucered. "That's how I saw it. It was orange. Someone's here. Watching us."

"Don't be ridiculous."

"But none of us were smoking," said Jade.

"It's *fine*. It was probably a hiker stopping for a rest on his way up the trail. Don't worry about it." Hannah strolled back over to Milton, Charles and Nigel, who were trying to set up the tents.

"It's all such a joke to her," said Jade.

"We have to leave," said Leulah.

"That's what I've been saying from the beginning," said Jade, walking away. "Would anyone listen to me? *No*. I was the killjoy. The wet blanket."

"Hey," I said to Leulah, smiling. "I'm sure it's okay."

"Really?"

Despite having no evidence to back up my claim, I nodded.

※　※　※

Half an hour later, Hannah was starting a campfire. The rest of us were sitting on the bald rock eating rigatoni with Newman's Own Fra Diavolo tomato sauce, heated up on the ministove, and French bread hard as igneous rock. We faced the view, even though there was nothing to see but a cauldron of darkness, a dark blue sky. The sky was a little nostalgic; it didn't want to let go of the last frayed streak of light.

"What would happen if you fell off this rock thing?" asked Charles.

"You'd die," said Jade through pasta.

"There's no sign or anything. No 'Please Remain Alert.' No 'Bad Place to Get Wasted.' It's just there. You fall? Too damn bad."

"Is there any more parmesan cheese?"

"Wonder why it's called Sugartop Summit," said Milton.

"Yeah, who cooks up the lame names?" asked Jade, chewing.

"Rural folk," said Charles.

"The best part is the quiet," said Nigel. "You never notice how loud everything is until you're up here."

"I feel sorry for the Native Americans," said Milton.

"Read Redfoot's *Dispossessed*," I said.

"I'm still hungry," said Jade.

"How're you still hungry?" asked Charles. "You ate more than everyone. You commandeered the hot pot."

"I didn't commandeer anything."

"Thank God I didn't go in for seconds. You probably would've bitten my hand off."

"If you don't eat enough, your body goes into starvation mode and then when you eat a slice of angel food cake your body treats it like it's penne à la vodka. You balloon within twenty-four hours."

"I don't like the fact that someone was here," Leulah said suddenly.

Everyone looked at her, startled by her voice.

"That cigarette butt," she whispered.

"Don't worry about it," Milton said. "Hannah's not worried. And she goes camping all the time."

"Anyway, we couldn't leave now if we wanted to," said Charles. "It's the middle of the night. We'd get lost. Probably *would* stumble into whatever it is that wanders around—"

"Convicts," said Jade, nodding.

"And that guy who bombed abortion clinics."

"They found him," I said.

"But you didn't see Hannah's face," said Leulah.

"What was wrong with her face?" asked Nigel.

Lu looked forlorn in her blue windbreaker, her arms hugging her knees, that Rapunzeled cord of hair roping her left shoulder, touching the ground.

"You could tell she was as scared as I was. But she didn't want to say so because she thought she had to be an adult, responsible and everything."

"Anyone pack a firearm?" asked Charles.

"Oh, I should have brought Jefferson's," Jade said. "It's *this big*. Adorable. She keeps it in her underwear drawer."

"We don't need guns," said Milton, lying back, staring at the sky. "If I had to go—I mean if it was *really* my fuckin' time—I wouldn't mind doing it here. Under these stars."

"Well, you're one of those contented morbid people," said Jade. "I for one will do anything I can to make sure my number doesn't come up for at least seventy-five years. If that means shooting someone in the head or biting off some parkie's chu-chu, so be it." She looked in the direction of the tents. "Where is she anyway? Hannah. I don't see her."

We carried the plates and pots back to the clearing and found Hannah eating a granola bar in front of the fire. She'd changed her clothes. She was wearing a green-and-black checkered button-down shirt. She asked us if we were still hungry and when Jade responded in the affirmative, suggested we make S'mores.

As we roasted marshmallows and Charles told his ghost story (cab driver, ghoulish fare), I became aware that Hannah, sitting on the opposite side of the fire, was staring at me. The campfire jack-o-lanterned everyone, made them orange, carved certain parts of their faces away, and the sockets around her dark eyes, blazing with light, appeared unusually hollow, as if they'd been further dug out with a spoon. I smiled as fiddle-dee-deeishly as I could, then pretended to be entranced with the Art of Roasting a Marshmallow. Yet, when I glanced at her not a minute later, her gaze hadn't budged. She held on to my eyes, then, almost imperceptibly, pointed to her left, toward the woods. She touched her wristwatch. Her right hand motioned *Five*.

"And then the cab driver turned around," Charles was saying. "The woman was gone. All that was left on the seat? *A white chiffon scarf.*"

"That's *it?*"

"Yeah," said Charles, smiling.

"Suckiest ghost story I ever heard."

"Sucked *balls—*"

"If I had a tomato I'd be throwing it at your head."

"Who knows that one about the dog with no tail?" asked Nigel. "He goes around looking for it. Terrorizing people."

"You're thinking of 'The Monkey's Paw,' " said Jade, "that awful short story you read in fourth grade but will remember for the rest of your life for unknown reasons. That and 'The Most Dangerous Game.' Right, Retch?"

I nodded.

"There *is* one about a dog, but I can't remember it."

"Hannah knows a good one," said Charles.

"I don't," said Hannah.

"Come *on.*"

"No. I'm an awful storyteller. Always have been." She yawned. "What time is it?"

Milton checked his watch. "A little after ten."

"We really shouldn't stay up too late tonight," she said. "We need to be rested. We're starting early tomorrow."

"Great."

Needless to say, Fear and Anxiety typhooned through me. None of the others appeared to have noticed Hannah's signal, not even Leulah, who'd forgotten all about the ominous cigarette butt. Now, rather blissfully, she ate her S'more (lint of melted marshmallow on her lip), smiling at whatever Milton was going on about, those tiny dimples splintering her chin. I sat on my knees and stared at the fire. I considered ignoring her (*"When in doubt, feign oblivion"*), but after five minutes, I noticed with horror Hannah was staring at me again, this time expectantly, as if I was playing Ophelia and had gotten so deep into character, into the throes of mental illness, I was missing all my cues, forcing Laertes and Gertrude to ad-lib. From the sheer force of her gaze, I found myself standing up, dusting myself off.

"I'll–I'll be right back," I said.

"Where're you going?" asked Nigel.

Everyone stared at me.

"To the bathroom," I said.

Jade giggled. "I'm *dreading* that."

"If the Native Americans could do it," said Charles, "so can you."

"Native Americans also scalped people."

"Might I suggest dry leaves? A bit of moss?" said Nigel smirking.

"We have toilet paper," Hannah said. "It's in my tent."

"Thanks," I said.

"In my bag," she said.

"Is there any more chocolate?" Jade asked.

I walked to the other side of the tents where it was dark and sandpapery and waited for my eyes to adjust. When I was certain no one had followed me, when I could hear their voices crackling with the fire, I stepped into the woods. Branches rubber-banded against my legs. I turned around and saw with surprise that the pines had fallen into place behind me, like those hippie beads decorating a doorway. Slowly, I moved along the arc of the clearing, back in the trees, so no one would see me, and stopped somewhere near the far left side, where I thought Hannah had pointed.

The campfire was close, some ten yards in front of me, and I could see Hannah still sitting with the others, resting her head in her hand. Her face looked so sleepy and satisfied, for a second I wondered if I'd been hallucinating. I told myself that if she didn't appear in three minutes, I'd go back and never speak to that crazy woman again—rather, *two* minutes, for two minutes was all it took for almost half of the nuclei in a lump of aluminum-28 to decay, for one to die from VX exposure (pronounced "VEEKS"), for 150 Sioux men, women and children to be shot at the Battle of Wounded Knee in 1890, for a Norwegian woman in 1866 by the name of Gudrid Vaaler to give birth to a son, Johan Vaaler, future inventor of the paper clip.

Two minutes was enough time for Hannah.

Heart of Darkness

I watched her stand up and say something to them. I heard my name, so I guessed she said she wanted to check on me. She walked toward the tents and out of sight.

I waited another minute, watching the others—Jade was doing her exaggerated impression of Ms. Sturds during Morning Announcements, feet wide apart, that bizarre rocking movement as if she were a ferry crossing a choppy English Channel ("This is a very scary time for our country!" Jade cried, clapping her hands together, eyes bulging)—and then I heard spine cracks of branches and leaves, and saw Hannah coming toward me, her face smudged by the dark. When she saw me, she smiled and pressed a finger to her lips, motioning for me to follow her.

Obviously, this surprised me. I didn't have my flashlight and the wind was picking up; I was wearing nothing more substantial than jeans, a T-shirt, the sweatshirt Dad had given me from the University of Colorado at Picayune and a windbreaker. But she was already moving swiftly away, weaving in and out of the trees, and so, with a quick glance back at the others—they were laughing, their voices tightly woven together—I headed after her.

Out of earshot from the campground, I was going to ask what we were doing, but when I looked at her, I saw the focused, intense look on her face, and it silenced me. She removed a flashlight—she was wearing one of those fanny packs in black or dark blue, which I hadn't noticed before—but that meek circle of white light could barely shove back the dark, illuminating nothing but a handful of skinny tree-shins.

We followed no path. At first I tried keeping a mental Hansel and Gretel trail of crumbs, noticing the irregularities—discoloration of bark, okay, giant toadlike rock next to that dead tree, skeleton branches stretched out in an upside-down crucifixion, that's promising—but such distinctions were rare and ultimately pointless, and after five minutes, I stopped and walked blindly next to her, like a man no longer dog-paddling, allowing himself to drown.

"They'll be fine for a little while," she said. "But we don't have much time."

I don't know how long we walked. (In what turned out to be an unbearable oversight, I was not wearing a watch.) After ten minutes or so, she stopped suddenly, and, unzipping the pouch around her waist, removed a map—different from the one she'd given us, colored, much more detailed—as well as a tiny compass. She studied them.

"A little farther," she said.

We walked on.

It was odd, the blind way I followed, and even now, I can't quite explain why I went, without protest or questions or even fear. During those episodes in one's life in which one *assumes* one will be paralyzed with dread, one isn't. I floated, as if I was doing nothing more than riding the mechanical brown canoe on the Enchanting Amazon River Ride at Walter's Wonderworld in Alpaca, Maryland. I noticed peculiar details: Hannah chewing the inside of her lip (the way Dad did when grading a unexpectedly apt paper), the toe of my leather boot kicking the flashlight beam, the pine trees' restless shifts and heaves, as if they were all unable to sleep, the way she placed her right hand, every minute or two, on that satchel clipped around her waist, like a pregnant women touching her stomach.

She stopped walking and checked her watch.

"This is good," she said, turning off the flashlight.

Slowly my eyes calibrated to the darkness. We appeared to be standing in a spot we'd walked through five minutes before. I could make out the fine corduroy of all those trees enveloping us, and Hannah's rapt face, shiny, a sort of bluish mother-of-pearl.

"I'm going to tell you something," she said, staring at me. She took a deep breath, exhaled, but said nothing. She was nervous, worried even. She swallowed, took another beleaguered breath, pressed her hand to her collarbone and left it there, a white, wilting hand-corsage. "I'm terrible at this. I'm good at other things. At math. Languages. Orders. Making people comfortable. I'm horrible at this."

"At what?" I asked.

"Truth." She laughed, a weird choking sound. She hunched up her shoulders and looked up at the sky. I looked too, because looking up at the sky was contagious, like yawns. There it was: hoisted into the air by the trees, a heavy black patch, the stars, little rhinestones like the ones in June Bug Rachel Groom's cowboy boots.

"I can't blame anyone, you know," Hannah said. "Just myself. Everyone makes choices. God, I need a cigarette."

"Are you okay?" I asked.

"No. *Yes.*" She looked at me. "I'm sorry."

"Maybe we should head back."

"No, I–I understand if you think I'm nuts."

"I don't think you're nuts," I said, though as soon as I said it, of course, I began to wonder if she was.

"It's not bad, what I have to tell you. More for *me.* Awful for me. Don't think I don't know *how* awful. How sick. Living like this—oh, you're afraid. I'm sorry. I didn't mean for it to be like this, deep in the enchanted forest, I know, it's a little medieval. But it'd be impossible to talk without one of them coming up, Hannah this, Hannah that. Oh, *God.* It's impossible."

"What's impossible?" I asked, though she didn't seem to hear me. She appeared to be saying these things to herself.

"When I thought about how I was going to say it—God, I'm a coward. Deluded. Sick. Sick." She shook her head, touched her hands to her eyes. "See, there are people. Fragile people, that you love and you hurt them, and I–I'm pathetic, aren't I? Sick. I hate myself, I really do. I . . ."

In many ways, there is nothing more disturbing than an adult who reveals herself not to be an Adult and all that word is supposed to imply—not solid, but leaking, not fixed, but seriously unglued. It was like being in first grade again, watching some adorable hand puppet rising up, revealing the monstrous human attached. Her chin crinkled with strange unknown emotions. She wasn't crying, but her dark mouth curled down at the edges.

"You'll listen to what I say?" Her voice was low, quivery like a grandmother's, but needy like a child's. She stepped forward, a little too close to me, her black eyes swerving over my face.

"Hannah—?"

"Promise me."

I stared at her. "Okay."

This seemed to calm her slightly.

"Thank you."

Again, she took a deep breath—but didn't speak.

"Is this about my father?" I asked.

I wasn't sure why, without thinking about it, that particular question flew out of my mouth. Maybe I hadn't quite gotten over the revelation of Kitty: if Dad had lied so smoothly about *her*, it was entirely possible he'd lied about other clammy trysts with St. Gallway staff. Or perhaps it was a reflex; throughout my life, without explanation, teachers had pulled me aside in hallways and lunchrooms, by cubbyholes and jungle gyms, and as I hyper-ventilated, waited to hear I'd been bad, would be harshly punished, that I'd botched a Unit Test and would be held back a year, they always surprised me by leaning in with their grayed eyes and coffee breaths and asking me inane questions about Dad (Did he smoke? Was he single? / When's a good time to call and mingle?). Frankly, if I was to form a hypothesis for such cases of being bizarrely singled out, it'd be: It All Comes Down to Dad. (Even he up-held this premise; if a supermarket check-out person was sullen, Dad con-cluded it was because of the condescending way Dad had accidentally looked at him while piling our groceries on the conveyor belt.)

I couldn't gauge Hannah's reaction, however. She stared at the ground, her mouth open a little, as if in shock, or perhaps she hadn't heard me and was trying to think of something to say. And as we stood in that endless car-bonated fizz of trees and I waited for her to respond with "Yes," or "No," or "Don't be crazy"—a few yards behind us, there was a small but distinct *shift* of something.

My heart lurched. Instantly, Hannah switched on the flashlight, pointing it in the direction of the noise and to my horror, the light actually *snagged* something—a reflection of some kind, a pair of glasses—and then it began crashing away from us, barging through the branches and bushes and pine needles and leaves on what was, indisputably, two feet. I was too horrified to move or scream, but Hannah clamped a hand over my mouth and held it there until we couldn't hear it anymore, until there was only the stark night and the sound of the wind shivering in the trees.

She turned off the flashlight. She pressed it into my hand.

"Don't turn it on unless you have to."

I could barely hear her, she spoke so quietly.

"Take this, too." She handed me a thick piece of paper, the map. "A pre-caution. Don't lose it. I have the other one, but I'll need this when I come back. Stay here. Don't say a word."

It happened so quickly. She squeezed my arm, let it go, began to move away in the direction of that *thing*, which I wanted to believe was a bear or wild boar—the most widely distributed land animal, known for running over 40 mph and ripping meat off a man's bones faster than a truck driver could eat a buffalo wing—but I knew in my heart, it wasn't. No reference book could second-guess the truth: it had been a human being close to us, what zoologist Bart Stuart calls in *Beasts* (1998), "the most vicious animal of all."

"Wait." My heart felt as if it was being toothpaste-squeezed into my neck. I started to follow her. "Where are you going?"

"I said stay here."

It was a harsh voice and it stopped me cold.

"I bet that was Charles," she added gently. "You know him—so jealous. Don't be afraid." Her face was large, serious, and even though she smiled, that small smile floating there like a Fall Webworm Moth in the dark, I knew she didn't actually believe what she said.

She leaned forward, kissed me on the cheek. "Give me five minutes."

Words tangled in my mouth, in my head. But in the end, I just stood there. I let her go.

"Hannah?"

I began to snivel her name after a minute or two, when I could still hear her footsteps and the realization I was standing alone in this wild jungle hit me, when the woods' indifference seemed to imply I'd probably die here, shivering, alone, lost, a statistic to be tacked to a police station's bulletin board, my stiff-smiling class picture (I hoped they didn't use the one from Lamego High) stuck to the front of a local newspaper, some article about me hashed, rehashed, then recycled into toilet paper or used for house training a pet.

I called her name at least three or four times, but she didn't answer and soon, soon I couldn't hear her anymore.

*　*　*

I don't know how long I waited.

It felt like hours, but the night whirred on, without interruption, so maybe it was fifteen minutes. It was the one thing, oddly enough, I found utterly unbearable: not knowing the time. I understood in full why convicted murderer Sharp Zulett had written in his surprisingly glib autobiography *Living in the Pit* (1980) (a book I wrongly once thought exceedingly hyper and melodramatic), that "in the fleapit"—the "fleapit" was the pitch-black four-by-nine-foot cell at Lumgate, the maximum-security federal prison outside of Hartford—"you have to make yourself let go of the rope of Time, let yourself float there in the dark, live in it. Otherwise you'll go mad. You'll start to see devils. One guy came out of the fleapit after only two days, and he'd pulled out his own eye" (p. 131).

I did my best to live in it. Aloneness settled over me, heavy, like that thing they put over you during X-rays. I sat down on the prickly pine-needled ground, and soon found myself unable to move. Sometimes I thought I heard her coming back, that sweet munch of footsteps, but it was nothing but the trees crashing their arms together as if pretending, in the escalating wind, to play the cymbals.

Whenever I heard an awful noise, one I couldn't identify, I told myself it was nothing but Chaos Theory, the Doppler Effect or the Heisenberg Uncertainty Principle applied to lost people in the dark. I think I repeated the Heisenberg Uncertainty Principle in my head at least one thousand times: the mathematical product of the combined uncertainties of concurrent measurements of position and momentum in a specified direction could never be less than Planck's constant, h, divided by 4π. This meant, rather encouragingly, that my uncertain position and zero momentum and the Beast Responsible for the Sound's uncertain position and uncertain momentum had to sort of null each other out, leaving me with what is commonly known in the scientific world as "wide-ranging perplexity."

When a person is unaided and terrified for over an hour (again, an approximation), the fear becomes part of the person, another arm. You stop noticing it. You wonder what other people—people who never let others "see them sweat" to use a familiar phrase—would do in your shoes. You try to let that guide you.

Dad said at the end of his Musical Chair Survival: The Quintessence of Predicaments seminar at the University of Oklahoma at Flitch, that one or two individuals in times of crisis turn into Heroes, a handful into Villains, the rest into Fools. "Try not to be a simpering idiot, the Fool category, where one descends into simian simpering, paralyzed by the desire to just die, quickly, painlessly. They want to roll over like possums. Well, *decide*. Are you a man or are you a nocturnal animal? Do you have courage? Can you comprehend the meaning of 'do not go gentle into that good night'? If you're a worthwhile human being, if you're not just filler, Styrofoam, stuffing for a Thanksgiving

turkey, garden mulch—you must fight. *Fight.* Fight for what you believe in."
(When Dad said the second-to-last "fight," he slammed his fist onto the
podium.)

I stood up, my knees stiff. I turned on the flashlight. I hated the seedy
light the flashlight made. I felt as if I was shining it into an orgy of trees,
gaunt, naked bodies crowding together to hide themselves. Little by little, I
began to proceed in what I guessed was the direction Hannah had gone. I followed the flashlight, playing a little game with myself by pretending I wasn't
directing it, but God was (with the help of a few bored angels), not because
He favored me over everyone else on earth in a quandary, but because it was
a slow night, and He had very little on his radar in terms of Widespread Panic
or Genocide.

At certain times, I stopped, listened, tiptoed around grimy thoughts of
being followed, raped and killed by an enraged parkie with pointy teeth and
a chest like a sandbag, my life ending up nothing more than an agonizing ?
in the vein of Violet Martinez. I concentrated instead on the laminated map
Hannah had given me, labeled at the top, "The Great Smoky Mountain National Park" (underneath this headline, rather meekly: "Courtesy of Friends
of the Smokies") with its helpful labels and blobs of mountains, color corresponding to elevation—"Cedar Gorge," I read, "Gatlinburg Welcome Center," "Hatcher Mountain," "Pretty Hollow Gap," "6,592 ft. above sea level."
Having no inkling where I was, I'd have been just as well off with a page from
Where's Waldo? (Handford, 1987). Still, I took great care to shine the flashlight onto it, study all those squiggly lines and the pleasant Times New Roman font, that prim Key, little pledges, little pats on the back, assuring me
that in this dark there was an Order, a Grand Scheme of Things, that the
armless, headless tree standing in front of me, was somewhere, a speck, on
the map *here,* and all I needed to do was find the thing that would link the
two elements and suddenly (with a little poof of light) the night would flatten
and divide into asparagus green squares I could follow home, A3ing, B12ing,
D2ing back to Dad.

I also couldn't stop thinking about the blueprint of a story Hannah had
mentioned back in the fall (no details, only bare bones dimensions of what
happened)—the occasion in the Adirondacks when she'd saved the life of a
man who injured his hip. She'd said she "ran and ran," eventually finding
campers with radios and I thus started mentally cheerleading: perhaps I, too,
would come across Campers with Radios, perhaps Campers with Radios were
simply around the bend. But the longer I walked and the trees swarmed like

prisoners wanting to be fed, the more it occurred to me I was as likely to find Campers with Radios as I was to find a brand-new Jeep Wrangler parked in a clearing with keys in the ignition and a full tank of gas. There was nothing here, nothing but me, the branches, the quicksand darkness. I couldn't help but wonder what screwy environmentalists were always complaining about, the "diminishing environment" and such, because there was a surplus, an overkill of Environment; it was time to come in here and start clear-cutting, put up Dunkin' Donuts and a parking lot as far as the eye could see, big, square and exposed, lit up at midnight like an August afternoon. In such a wonderful place, one's shadows were not mangled but drifting behind you in long neat lines. You could take a protractor to them and effortlessly determine the exact angle to your feet: thirty degrees.

I'd been walking for a while, maybe an hour or so, forcing my head to float on these rickety rafts of thought to avoid sinking—when I first heard the noise.

It was so acute, so rhythmic and confident, the entire night-tarred world seemed to quiet itself like sinners at church. It sounded—I stood very still, tried to reign in my breathing—like a child swinging. ("A child swinging" sounds très horrorfilmesque, but I found nothing immediately frightening about the sound.) And though it appeared to fly in the face of reason and common sense, without thinking very much, I began to follow it.

It ceased every now and then. I wondered if I was hearing things. Then it resumed, shyly. I walked on, the flashlight thrusting all those pines back, trying to think, trying to figure out what it could be, trying not to be afraid, but pragmatic and strong like Dad, trying to follow his Determination Theory. I found myself channeling Ms. Gershon of AP Physics, because whenever there was a question in class, she never answered it outright, but turned to the dry-erase board and without a word, dully wrote out five to seven bullet points explaining the answer. She always stood at a forty-five-degree angle to the dry-erase board because she was shy about her back. And yet Ms. Pamela "PMS" Gershon's back told stories; there was a spot of thinning hair on the back of her head, her pants in tan and taupe clung to her like baggy second skins, her bottom was squashed like a sat-upon Sunday hat. Ms. Gershon, if she were here, would attempt to illuminate all there was to illuminate about this sound, this child on a swing, writing at the top of the dry-erase board (she stood on tiptoe, her right arm high above her head as if she were rock climbing): "Phenomenon of a Child on a Swing in a Heavily Wooded Region: The Seven-Point Spectrum of Conceptual Physics." Her first bullet point would read: "*As Atoms:* Both Child on a Swing and Swing are composed of small moving particles," and her last bullet point would read, "*As Einstein's Special Theory of Relativity*: if a Child on a Swing had a Twin who boarded a space-ship and traveled close to the speed of light, the Twin would return to Earth younger than the Child on the Swing."

Another step forward, the sound was louder now. I found myself in a small open space paved with pine needles, fragile, trembling bushes at my feet. I turned, my yellow light shuffling, tripping like a roulette ball across the tree trunks, and then it stopped.

She was astoundingly close, hanging by her neck by an orange rope three feet above the ground. Her tongue bulged from her mouth. My flashlight electrified her giant eyes and the green squares on her checkered shirt. And her inflated face, her expression—it was so inhuman, so sickening, I still don't know how I knew, in that instant, it was she. Because it *wasn't* Hannah, it was unreal and monstrous, something no textbook or encyclopedia could ever prepare you for.

And yet, it was.

*   *   *

The aftermath of seeing her has been locked away into an unassailable prison cell of Memory. ("Witness traumatization," Sergeant Detective Fayo-nette Harper later explained.) Despite nights lying awake, trying all sorts of probing keys, I cannot recall my screams, or falling down, or running so fast that I sideswiped something and cut open my left knee, which would need three stitches, or even letting go of the map she'd asked me to hold on to in that dry whisper like a piece of paper touching your cheek.

I was found the next morning, at approximately 6:45 A.M. by one John Richards, age 41, on a trout fly-fishing excursion with his son, Ritchie, 16. My voice had ripped to nothing. My face and hands were so covered in needle-like scratches and mud, a little bit of my own blood, too, they told Dad when they first saw me—(close to Forkridge Trail, nine miles from Sugartop Sum-mit) sitting against a tree, a dead-eyed look on my face, still gripping a dying flashlight—they thought I was the boogeyman.

One Flew Over
the Cuckoo's Nest

I opened my eyes and found myself on a bed in a curtained cubicle. I attempted to speak, but my voice was a scrape. A white flannel blanket covered me from chin to woolly green ankle sock. I seemed to be wearing a light-blue cotton hospital gown patterned with faded sailboats, an Ace bandage on my left knee. Jabbering incessantly, everywhere, was hospital Morse Code: beeps, toots, rings, clicks, a page for Dr. Bullard to pick up Line 2. Someone was talking about a recent trip to Florida with the wife. A square piece of gauze and a small hypodermic needle were stuck into my left hand (mosquito), which was linked by a thin tube to a bag of clear liquid hanging over me (mistletoe). My head, rather my whole body, felt helium-ballooned. I stared at the folds of the spearmint curtain on my left.

It swooshed. A nurse came in. She swooshed it closed behind her. She glided over to me as if she wasn't on feet but casters with wheel locks.

"You're awake," she announced. "How do you feel? Are you hungry? Don't try to talk. Sit tight and let me change this bag and then I'll get the doctor."

She replaced the IV-bag and wheeled herself away.

I smelled latex and rubbing alcohol. I stared at the ceiling, at the white rectangles mottled with brown specks like vanilla ice cream. Someone was asking where Johnson's crutches were. "They were labeled when he came in." A woman was laughing. "Married for five years. The key is to act like it's your first date every day." "Got kids?" "We're trying."

Another swoosh and a small tan doctor appeared, girlishly boned with crow-black hair. Around his neck he wore a plastic Backstage Pass that featured, beneath a pixilated picture of himself with the skin tone of a jalapeño, a barcode, as well as his name: THOMAS C. SMART, SENIOR ER RESIDENT. As he walked over to me, his considerable white lab coat whimsically floated out behind him.

"How're we doing?" he asked. I tried to speak—my *okay* came out like a knife spreading jelly on burnt toast—and he nodded understandingly, as if he spoke the language. He jotted something down on his clipboard, and then asked me to sit up and take slow, deep breaths as he pressed the icy stethoscope into my back in different places.

"Looking good," he said with a tired fake smile.

In a gust of white, a swoosh—he disappeared. Once again, I stared at the glum spearmint curtain. It trembled whenever someone rushed past it on the opposite side, as if it were afraid. A phone rang, was hastily answered. A stretcher rolled down the hall: chick peeps of wobbly wheels.

"I understand, sir. Fatigue, exposure, no hypothermia, but dehydration, the cut to her knee, other minor cuts and scrapes. Evident shock too. I'd like to keep her here a few more hours, have her eat something. Then we'll see. We'll give her a prescription for the knee pain. A mild sedative too. The stitches will come out in a week."

"You're not following me. I'm not talking about stitches. I want to know what she's been through."

"We don't know. We notified the park. There are rescue personnel—"

"I don't give a flying *fuck* about rescue personnel—"

"Sir, I—"

"Do not *sir* me. I want to see my daughter. I want you to get her something to eat. I want you to find her a decent nurse, not one of these guinea pigs who'd unwittingly kill any kid with an ear infection. She needs to go home and *rest*, not relive whatever *ordeal* she's been through with some bozo, some *clown* who couldn't even graduate from high school, who wouldn't know a motive if it bit him on the *ass*, all because some chicken-'n-biscuits police force doesn't have the proficiency to figure it out themselves."

"It's standard, sir, with these sorts of mishaps—"

"*Mishaps?*"

"I mean—"

"A mishap is spilling Kool-Aid on a white carpet. *A mishap is losing a fucking earring.*"

"She–she'll only speak to him if she's up to it. You have my word."

"You're going to have to do a lot better than your word, Doctor what does that thing say, Dr. Thomas, Tom *Smarts?*"

"Actually, it's without the *s.*"

"What is that, your *stage* name?"

I rolled off the bed and, making sure my arm and the other plastic cords to which my chest was attached did not fully tear out of whatever machine I was rigged to, I walked the few feet to the curtain, the bed reluctantly trolley-ing after me. I peered out.

Standing next to the large white administrative hexagon in the middle of the Emergency Room was Dad, in corduroy. His gray-blond hair flopped across his forehead—something that happened during lectures—his face was red. In front of him stood White Lab Coat, clasping his hands and nodding. To his left, behind the counter, sat Fuzzy Hair and, faithfully at her side, Mars Orange Lipstick, both of them gazing at Dad, one pressing a phone re-ceiver to her pink neck, the other pretending to scrutinize a clipboard but eavesdropping.

"Dad," I scraped.

He heard me immediately. His eyes widened.

"Jesus Christ," he said.

* * *

As it turned out, although I had no recollection of it whatsoever, I'd ap-parently been quite the Talk Show Host with John Richards and his son, when they carried me, their limp bride, half a mile to their pickup truck. (White Lab Coat was very informative when he explained, where memory was concerned, I could "expect anything and everything"—as if I'd only bumped my head, as if I'd merely had a head-on collision.)

With what I imagine to be the energized yet charred voice of someone recently struck by lightning (over 100 million volts of direct current) with di-lated pupils and splinter sentences I told them my name, address, telephone number, that I'd been on a camping trip in the Great Smoky Mountains, that something *bad* had happened. (I actually used the word *bad.*) I didn't re-spond to their direct questions—I was unable to tell them specifically what I'd seen—but apparently I repeated the words "She's departed" throughout the forty-five minute ride to Sluder County Hospital.

This detail was particularly unsettling. "She's Departed" was a grim nurs-ery song Dad and I used to sing on the highways when I was five, learned in

Ms. Jetty's kindergarten in Oxford, Mississippi. It followed the generic melody of "Oh, My Darlin' Clementine": *"She's departed, she's a nowhere, she's my girl and she's a-gone / She went drownin' in the river, washed up somewhere in Babylon."*

(Dad learned most of this after bonding with my two knights in shining armor in the Emergency waiting room, and though they left well before I was awake, Dad and I later sent them a thank-you note and three hundred dollars' worth of new fly-fishing equipment blindly purchased from Bull's-eye Bait and Tackle.)

Due to my bizarre lucidity, Sluder County Hospital had been able to contact Dad immediately, also alert the Park Ranger on duty, a man by the name of Roy Withers, who began a search of the area. It was also why the Burns County Police dispatched an officer from their Patrol Unit, Officer Gerard Coxley, to the hospital, so he could talk to me.

"I've already made arrangements," Dad said. "You're not talking to anyone."

Once again I was behind the spearmint curtain in the spongy bed, mummified by heated flannel blankets, trying to eat with one pipe cleaner arm the turkey sandwich and chocolate chip cookie Mars Orange Lipstick had brought me from the cafeteria. My head felt like that colorful balloon they used in the classic film *Around the World in 80 Days*. I seemed to be able only to stare at the curtain, chew and swallow, and sip the coffee Fuzzy Hair had brought according to Dad's specific instructions ("Blue likes her coffee with skim milk, no sugar. I like mine black."): stare, chew, swallow, stare, chew, swallow. Dad was on the left side of the bed.

"You're going to be fine," he said. "My girl's a champion. Not afraid of anything. We'll get you home in an hour. You'll rest. Soon be right as rain."

I was aware Dad, all Trumanish voice and Kennedyesque grin, was repeating these cheerleader phrases to inspire team spirit in himself, not me. I didn't mind. I'd been given some sedative via the IV and hence felt too balmy to grasp the full extent of his anxiety. To explain: I'd never actually *told* Dad about the camping trip. I'd told him I'd be spending the weekend at Jade's. I didn't *mean* to be deceitful, especially in lieu of his newfound McDonald's-styled approach to parenting (Always Open and Ready to Serve), but Dad despised outdoor activities such as camping, skiing, mountain biking, parasailing, base jumping and, even more, the "dimwitted dulls" who did them. Dad had not even the remotest desire to take on the Forest, the Ocean, the Mountain or the Thin Air, as he detailed extensively in "Man's Hubris and the National World," published in 1982 in the now-obsolete *Sound Opinions Press*.

I present Paragraph 14, the section entitled "Zeus Complex": "The ego-centric Man seeks to taste immortality by engaging in demanding physical challenges, wholeheartedly bringing himself to the brink of death in order to taste an egotistical sense of *accomplishment*, of *victory*. Such a feeling is false and short-lived, for Nature's power over Man is absolute. Man's honest place is not in extreme conditions, where, let's face it, he's frail as a flea, but in *work*. It is in building things and governing, the creation of rules and ordinances. It is in work Man will find life's meaning, not in the selfish, heroin-styled rush of hiking Everest without oxygen and nearly killing himself and the poor Sherpa carrying him."

Due to Paragraph 14, I didn't tell Dad. He'd never have let me go, and though I hadn't especially wanted to go myself, I also didn't want the others to go and have a mind-blowing experience without me. (I had no idea how mind-blowing it would actually be.)

"I'm proud of you," Dad said.

"Dad," was all I could scuff. I did manage to touch his hand and it responded like one of those mimosa plants, but in the opposite way, opening.

"You will be fine, little cloud. Fine. Fine as a fiddle."

"Fit," I scratched.

"Fit as a fiddle."

"Promise?"

"Of course I promise."

＊　　＊　　＊

An hour later, my voice had begun to tiptoe back. A new nurse, Stern Brow (illicitly kidnapped by White Lab Coat from another floor of the hospital, in order to placate Dad) took my blood pressure and pulse ("Doin' fine," she said before humphing off).

Although I felt bug-snug under the sunshine lights, the hospital beeps, clicks and toots soothing as fish noises one hears in the ocean while snorkeling, gradually, I noticed my memory of the night before had begun to show signs of life. As I sipped my coffee listening to the aggravated mutters of a croaky gentleman recovering from an asthma attack on the other side of the curtain ("Reely now. Got to get home and feed my dog." "Just another half hour Mr. Elphinstone."), suddenly I was aware Hannah had snuck into my head: not as I'd seen her—*God no*—but sitting at her dining room table listening to one of us, her head tilted, smoking a cigarette, then ruthlessly stabbing it out on her bread plate. She did that on two occasions. I also thought about the heels of her feet, a tiny detail not many others noticed: sometimes they were black and so dry, they resembled pavement.

"Sweet? What's the matter?"

I told Dad I wanted to see the policeman. Reluctantly, he agreed and twenty minutes later I was telling Officer Coxley everything I could remember.

According to Dad, Officer Gerard Coxley had been waiting patiently in the Emergency waiting room for over three hours, shooting the shit with the attendant nurse and other Low Priority patients, drinking Pepsi and "reading *Cruising Rider* with such an immersed expression I could tell it's his secret instruction manual," Dad reported with distaste. Yet Still Life patience appeared to be one of Gerard Coxley's predominating characteristics (see *False Fruits, Drupes and Dry Fruits*, Swollum, 1982).

He sat with his long skinny legs crossed like a lady's on the low blue plastic chair Stern Brow had carried in for the occasion. He balanced a withered green notepad on his left thigh and wrote on it, left-handedly, in ALL CAPS, with the speed of an apple seed burgeoning into a ten-foot tree.

Midforties, with messy auburn hair melting over his head and the drowsy squint of a late-August lifeguard, Officer Coxley was also a man of reductions, of distillations, of one-liners. I was propped up with pillows (Dad shadowing Coxley at the foot of the bed), trying my hardest to tell him *everything*, but when I completed a sentence—a complex sentence, full of invaluable details painstakingly mined from all that darkness, because confusingly, none of it seemed real anymore; every recollection now seemed Mr. DeMille-lighted in my head, all klieg lights and special effects and lurid stage makeup, pyrotechnics, atmospherics—after all of this, Officer Coxley would write down only one, *maybe* two words.

ST. GALLWAY 6 KIDS HANA SCHEDER TEACHER DEAD? SUGARTOP VIOLET MARTINEZ.

He could shrink any plot of Dickens into haiku.

"Only a few more questions," he said, squinting at his e.e. cummings poem.

"And when she came and found me in the woods," I said, "she was wearing a large satchel, which she hadn't had on before. Did you get that?"

"Sure I got it." SATCHEL

"And that person who followed us, I want to say it was a man, but I don't know. He was wearing large glasses. Nigel, one of the kids with us, he wears glasses, but it wasn't him. He's very slight and he wears tiny spectacles. This person was large and the glasses were large. Like Coke bottles."

"Sure." BOTTLES

"To reiterate," I said, "Hannah wanted to tell me something."

Coxley nodded.

"That was the reason she took me away from the campsite. But she never got to tell me what it was. That was when we heard this person near us and she went after him."

By now my voice was nothing more than wind, at its most emphatic, a jet stream, but I wheezed on and on, in spite of Dad's concerned frown.

"Okay, okay. I got it." CAMPSITE Officer Coxley looked at me, raising rambutan-eyebrows and smiling as if he'd never had an Eyewitness quite like me before. In all probability, he hadn't. I had a disturbing feeling Officer Coxley's experience with Eyewitnesses was geared not toward murder or even burglary, but motor vehicle accidents. The fifth of his series of questions (posed in such a bland voice, one could almost see the paper labeled EYE-WITNESS QUESTIONNAIRE thumbtacked to the station bulletin board next to a sign-up sheet for the 52nd Annual Auto Theft Weekend Roundtable and the Police Intra-Personals Corner, where department singles posted their Seek-ings in twenty-eight words or less) had been the supremely disheartening: "Did you notice any problems at the scene of the mishap?" I think he was hoping I'd say, "Out-of-order traffic signal," or "Heavy foliage obscuring a stop sign."

"Have any of them been found yet?" I asked.

"We're working on it," said Coxley.

"What about Hannah?"

"Like I said. Everyone's doing their job." He ran a thick podlike finger down the green notepad. "Now can you tell me more about your relationship to—?"

"She was a teacher at our school," I said. "St. Gallway. But she was more than that. She was a friend." I took a deep breath.

"You're talking about—"

"Hannah Schneider. And there's an 'i' in her last name."

"Oh, right." I

"Just to be clear, she's the person I think I saw . . ."

"Okay," he said, nodding as he wrote. FRIEND

At this point, Dad must have decided I'd had enough, because he stared at Coxley very intensely for a moment and then, as if deciding something, stood up from the end of the bed (see "Picasso enjoying high times at Le Lapin Agile, Paris," *Respecting the Devil*, Hearst, 1984, p. 148).

"I think you must have everything then, Poirot," Dad said. "Very methodical. I'm impressed."

"What's that?" asked Officer Coxley, frowning.

"You've given me a new respect for law enforcement. How many years on the job now, Holmes? Ten, twelve?"

"Oh. Uh, going on eighteen now."

Dad nodded, smiling. "Impressive. I've always loved the lingo—DOA, DT, OC, white shirts, skels—isn't that right? You'll have to forgive me. I've watched more than my share of *Columbo*. I can't help but regret never going into the profession. May I ask how you got into it?"

"My father."

"How wonderful."

"His father too. Go back generations."

"If you ask me, there aren't nearly enough young people going into the force. Bright kids all go for the high-flying jobs and does it make them happy? I doubt it. We need sound people, *smart* people. People who know their head from their elbows."

"I say the same thing."

"Really?"

"Good friend of mine's son went to Bryson City. Worked as a banker. Hated it. Came back here, I hired him. Said he'd never been happier. But it takes a special kind of man. Not everyone—"

"Certainly *not*," said Dad, shaking his head.

"Cousin of mine. Couldn't do it. Didn't have the nerves."

"I can imagine."

"I can tell straight off if they're going to make it."

"No kidding."

"*Sure*. Hired one guy from Sluder County. Whole department thought he was great. But me. I could tell from the look in his eyes. It wasn't there. Two months later he ran off with the wife of a fine man in our Detective Division."

"You never know," said Dad, sighing as he glanced at his watch. "As much as I'd love to keep talking—"

"Oh—"

"The doc out here, I think he's pretty good, he suggested Blue get home to rest and get her voice back. I guess we'll wait to hear about the others." Dad extended his hand. "I know we're in good hands."

"Thank you," said Coxley, rising to his feet, shaking Dad's hand.

"Thank *you*. I trust you'll contact us at home in the event of additional questions? You have our telephone number?"

"Uh, yes, I do."

"Terrific," said Dad. "Let us know any way we can be of service."

"Sure. And best of luck to you."

"Same to you, Marlowe."

And then, before Officer Coxley knew quite what had happened to him, before *I* knew what had happened to him, Officer Coxley was gone.

One Hundred Years
of Solitude

In severe circumstances, when you inadvertently witness a person dead, something inside of you gets permanently misplaced. Somewhere (within the brain and nervous system, I'd imagine) there's a snag, a delay, a stumbling block, a slight technical problem.

For those who've never had such bad luck, picture the world's fastest bird, the Peregrine Falcon, *Falco peregrinus*, splendidly diving toward its quarry (unwitting dove) at over 250 mph, when abruptly, seconds before its talons are to strike a lethal blow, it feels light-headed, loses its focus, goes into a tailspin, *two bogies, three o'clock high, break, break, Zorro got your wingman*, barely managing to pull up, up, righting itself and floating, quite shaken, to the nearest tree on which it could once again get its bearings. The bird is fine—and yet, afterward, really for the rest of its life span of twelve to fifteen years, it is never able to nosedive with quite the same speed or intensity of any of the other falcons. It is always a little off-center somehow, always a little *wrong*.

Biologically speaking, this irreparable change, however minute, has no right to occur. Consider the Carpenter Ant, who allows a fellow ant recently found dead on the job to remain where he is a total of fifteen to thirty seconds before his lifeless body is picked up, hauled out of the nest, and tossed into a pile of debris composed of bits of sand and dust (see *All My Children: Fervent Confessions of an Ant Queen*, Strong, 1989, p. 21). Mammals, too, take an equally humdrum view of both death and bereavement. A lone tigress will defend her cubs against a roving male, but after they are slaughtered she will "roll over and mate with him without hesitation" (see *Pride*, Stevens-Hart, 1992, p. 112). Primates do mourn—"there is no form of grief as profound as a chimpanzee's," declares Jim Harry in *The Tool-Makers* (1980) — but their anguish tends to be reserved only for immediate family members. Male chimpanzees are known to execute not only competitors but also the young and disabled both inside and outside their clan, occasionally even eating them, for no apparent reason (p. 108).

Try as I might, I could summon none of the *c'est la vie* sangfroid of the Animal Kingdom. I began to experience, over the course of the next three months, full-blown insomnia. I'm not talking about the romantic kind, not the sweet sleeplessness one has when one is in love, anxiously awaiting the morn so one can rendezvous with a lover in an illicit gazebo. No, this was the torturous, clammy kind, when one's pillow slowly takes on the properties of a block of wood and one's sheets, the air of the Everglades.

My first night home from the hospital, none of them, not Hannah, Jade or the others, had been found. With the rain blathering endlessly against the windows, I stared at my bedroom ceiling and was aware of a new sensation in my chest, the feeling that it was caving in like an old piece of sidewalk. My head was seized by dead-end thoughts, the most rampant of which was the Moving Picture Producer's Yen: the tremendous and supremely unproductive desire to scrap the last forty-eight hours of Life, rid myself of the original director (who obviously didn't know what He was doing) and reshoot the entire affair, including substantial script rewrites and recasting the leads. I sort of couldn't *stand* myself, how safe and snug I was in my wool socks and navy flannel pajamas purchased from the Adolescent Department at Stickley's. I even resented the mug of Orange Blossom tea Dad had placed on the southwest corner of my bedside table. (It read, "A Stitch in Time Saves Nine" and sat there like an unpopped blister.) I felt as if my fortunate rescue by the Richardses was akin to a first cousin with no teeth and a tendency of spitting when he talked — downright embarrassing. I had no desire to be the Otto Frank, the Anastasia, the Curly, the Trevor Rees-Jones. I wanted to be with the rest of them, suffering what they were suffering.

Given my state of turmoil, it will come as no surprise that in the ten days following the camping trip, St. Gallway's Spring Break, I found myself embarking on a sour, irksome and altogether unsatisfying love affair.

She was an insipid, fickle mistress, that two-headed she-male, otherwise known as the local news, WQOX News 13. I started seeing her three times a day (*First News at 5, News 13 at 5:30, Late Night News at 11:00*), but within twenty-four hours, with her straight talk, shoulder pads, ad-libs and commercial breaks (not to mention that backdrop of faux sun permanently setting behind her) she managed to strong-arm her way into my unhinged head. I couldn't eat, couldn't *try* to sleep without supplementing my day with her half-hour programming at 6:30 A.M., 9:00 A.M., noon and 12:30 P.M.

Like all romances, ours began with great expectation.

"We have your local news next," said Cherry Jeffries. She was dressed in Pepto-dismal pink, had hazel eyes, a tight smile reminiscent of a tiny rubber band stretched across her face. Thick, chin-length blond hair capped her, as if she were a ballpoint pen. "It's called the Sunrise Nursery School, but the D.S.S. wants the sun to go down on the center after multiple allegations of abuse."

"Restaurant owners protest a new tax increase by city hall," chirped Norvel Owen. Norvel's sole distinguishing characteristic was his male pattern baldness, which mimicked the stitching of a baseball. Also of note was his necktie, which appeared to be patterned with mussels, clams and other invertebrates. "We'll talk about what it means for you and your Saturday night on the town. These stories coming up."

A green square popped up and hovered at Cherry's shoulder like a good idea: SEARCH.

"But first, our top story," said Cherry. "Tonight an intensive search continues for five local high school students and their teacher reported missing in the Smoky Mountain National Park. Park authorities were alerted early this morning after a Yancey County resident found a sixth student near Route 441. The student was admitted to a local hospital for exposure and was released in stable condition earlier this evening. The Sluder County Sheriff says the group entered the park Friday afternoon, expecting to camp for the weekend, but later became lost. Rain, wind and heavy cloud cover have decreased visibility for the rescue squads. But with temperatures staying well above freezing, Park rangers and Sluder County Police stay optimistic the others will be rescued without injury. Our hearts go out to all the families and everyone involved in the search."

Cherry glanced down at the blank piece of paper on the plastic blue desk. She looked up again.

"People are horsing around at the Western North Carolina Farm Center with the arrival of a brand new pony."

"But this is no ordinary horse, of course, of course," piped Norvel. "Mackenzie is a Falabella Miniature Horse standing a little over two feet tall. Curators say the pony originates from Argentina and is one of the rarest breeds in the world. You can go see Little Mac for yourself at the petting corral."

"It happens every year," said Cherry, "and its success depends on *you*."

"Later," said Norvel, "details on Operation Blood Drive."

By the following morning, Sunday, my fly-by-night infatuation had congealed into obsession. And it wasn't just the news I was anticipating, yet still had not heard—that rescue teams had at last found them, that Hannah was alive and safe, that Fear (renowned for its hallucinogenic qualities) had conjured everything I'd heard and seen. There was something undeniably gripping about Cherry and Norvel (Chernobyl, I called them) a quality that forced me to withstand six hours of talk shows (one theme of significance, "From Frog to Prince: Extreme Male Makeovers") and cleaning commercials featuring housewives with too many stains, kids and not enough time, to catch their second segment together, *Your Stockton Power Lunch* at 12:30. A wide and triumphant smile elbowed through Cherry's face when she announced *she* was the sole anchor this afternoon.

"We're power lunching today with breaking news," she said, frowning as she arranged the blank papers in front of her, though visibly thrilled to preside over the *entire* blue desk, rather than merely the right-hand side. The white piping of her navy suit, edging around her shoulders, patch pockets and cuffs, delineated her petite frame like white lines marking sudden swerves of an unlit road. She blinked at the screen and looked grave. "A Carlton County woman was found *dead* this afternoon by rescue workers searching the Smoky Mountain National Park. This is the latest development in the search for five local high school students and a teacher that began yesterday. News 13's Stan Stitwell is live at the rescue center. Stan, what are the police saying?"

Stan Stitwell appeared, standing in a parking lot, an ambulance parked behind him. If Stan Stitwell had been wine, he wouldn't be robust or full bodied. Stan would be fruity, acidic, with a hint of cherry. Limp brown hair hung into his forehead like wet shoelaces.

"Cherry, Sluder County Police have not yet made a statement, but we hear they've positively identified the body to be that of Hannah Louise Schneider, a forty-four-year-old teacher at the St. Gallway School, the well-known private school in West Stockton. Park personnel had been searching for her and the five other students for over twenty-four hours now. Authorities haven't yet told us what condition the body was in, but minutes ago, detectives arrived on the scene to determine if there was foul play."

"And the five students, Stan. What's the latest on them?"

"Well, despite the bad conditions out here, rain, wind, heavy fog, the search continues. An hour ago rescue teams managed to get a National Guard helicopter into the air, but they had to bring it back due to bad visibility. But, still, in the past two hours or so, at least twenty-five more civilians have joined the volunteer search effort. And as you can see here behind me, the Red Cross and a medical team from the University of Tennessee have set up operations for food and aiding injuries. Everyone's doing what they can to make sure the kids get home safe."

"Thank you, Stan," said Cherry. "And News 13 will continue to keep you updated as the story unfolds."

She glanced down at a blank piece of paper on her desk. She looked up again.

"Up next, it's the little things in life you take for granted. Today, as part of our 'Wellness' series, we'll show you a lot of time and money goes into designing that little thing your dentist wants you to use twice a day. News 13's Mary Grubb has the story of the toothbrush."

I watched the rest of the news, but there was no further mention of the camping trip. I found myself noticing all the Little Things about Cherry: her eyes scurrying across the teleprompter, the way her facial expressions morphed between the Look of Restrained Dismay (salon heist), the Look of Deep-seated Sorrow (infant dead in apartment fire), the Look of Quiet Community Consciousness (battle revs up between motocross riders and trailer-owners in Marengo) with the ease of trying on slips in a dressing room. (Staring at the blank papers in front of her seemed to be the switch that prompted this mechanical expression-wipe, similar to shaking an Etch A Sketch.)

And the next morning, Monday, when I dragged myself out of bed at 6:30 to catch "Waking You Up in the Morning!" I observed the maniacal way Cherry unilaterally leeched all attention from Norvel, rendering him an appendix, a hubcap, an extra packet of salt one misses at the bottom of a bag of fast food. Norvel, if one visualized him with a full head of sandy hair, had probably once been competent, perhaps even *commanding* in his news delivery, but like a Dresden church with Byzantine architecture on the eve of February 13, 1945, he'd been in the wrong place at the wrong time. Paired with Cherry, prey to her Ways to Upstage by Way of Large Plastic Earrings, her Modes of Stealing Thunder Via the Application of More Eye Makeup than a Drag Queen, not to mention the Art of the Indirect Castration (i.e., "Speaking of toddlers, Norvel has the story of a new Montessori day care center opening up in Yancey County.")—it had left him in ruins. He spoke his allotted portion of the broadcast (forgettable stories about mayoral appearances and farm animals) in the uncertain, rickety voice of a woman on a diet of pineapples and cottage cheese, her spine emerging from her back like a banister when she bent over.

I knew she was bad news, that it wasn't the most wholesome of affairs.

I just couldn't help myself.

✺   ✺   ✺

"Five local high school students were found *alive* this morning by rescue personnel in the Great Smoky Mountains following an intensive two-day search," said Cherry. "This is the latest development in the story after the body of their teacher, Hannah Louise Schneider, was recovered yesterday. We're live outside the Sluder County Hospital with News 13's Stan Stitwell. Stan, what can you tell us?"

"Cherry, there were cheers and tears here as Park rescue squads brought to safety the five high school seniors missing since Saturday. The heavy fog and showers tapered off early this morning and K-9 rescue dogs were able to track the students from a popular Park campsite known as Sugartop Summit to another section more than twelve miles away. Police say the kids had become separated from Hannah Schneider and the sixth student found on Saturday. They tried to locate a path out of the park but became lost. One of the male students is allegedly suffering from a broken leg. Otherwise, they're all confirmed in stable condition. A half hour ago they were admitted to the Emergency Room, which you can see just behind me. They're being treated for cuts and scrapes and other minor injuries."

"That's great news, Stan. Any word from the police about the teacher's cause of death?"

"Cherry, Sluder County Police have issued no statements about the body of the woman found, except to say that for the progress of the investigation, all evidence will be held at this time. We'll have to wait for the Sluder County coroner's ruling, which is expected next week. For now, everyone's relieved the kids are safe. They're expected to be released from the hospital later today."

"Great, Stan. And News 13 will keep you tuned as news breaks in this camping tragedy."

Cherry looked down at the piece of paper and looked up again.

"It's small. It's black. It's something you shouldn't leave home without."

"Find out what it is," said Norvel, blinking at the camera, "in our 'Get Technical' series. Coming up next."

I watched the program until the very end, when Cherry smiled and twittered, "Have a great morning!" and the camera zoomed away from her and Norvel like a fly zipping around the studio. From her triumphant grin, it appeared she was hoping the camping tragedy would be her claim to fame, her Fifteen Minutes (That Could Potentially Lead to a Full Half Hour), her First-Class Ticket to Somewhere (with Fully Reclining Seats and Champagne before Takeoff). Cherry seemed to see it all twisting into the distance like a four-lane highway: "The Cherry Jeffries Talk Show: Spill Your Heart Out," CHAY-JEY, a conservative clothing line for the serious blond working woman ("No longer an oxymoron"), "Cherry Bird," the Cherry Jeffries Fragrance for Women in Motion, the newspaper article in USA Today, "Move over Oprah, Here Comes Cherry." A car commercial roared onto the screen. I noticed Dad standing behind me. His tattered leather bag, stuffed with legal pads and periodicals, hung heavily around his shoulder. He was on his way to the university. His first seminar, Conflict Resolution in the Third World, started at 9:00 A.M.

"Perhaps it's not a wise idea to watch anymore," he said.

"And do what instead," I asked blandly.

"Rest. Read. I have a new annotated copy of De Profundis—"

"I don't want to read De Profundis."

"Fair enough." He was silent for a moment. Then: "You know, I could phone Dean Randall. We could go somewhere for the day. Drive to a—"

"Where?"

"Perhaps we could take a picnic to one of those lakes people are always praising to the high heavens. One of these local lakes with ducks."

"Ducks."

"You know. Paddleboats. And geese."

Dad walked around to the front of the couch, ostensibly so I'd peel my eyes off the TV and look at him.

"To get on the highway," he said. "It might remind us that no matter the tragedy, there's always a world beyond it. 'Whither goest thou, America, in thy shiny car in the night?' "

I continued to stare at the TV, my eyes sore, my thin bathrobe, the color of tongues, limp around my legs.

"Did you have an affair with Hannah Schneider?" I asked.

Dad was so shocked he didn't immediately speak. "I—*what?*"

I repeated the question.

"How can you ask such a thing?"

"You had an affair with Eva Brewster, so maybe you also had an affair with Hannah Schneider. Maybe you had an affair with the entire *school* and kept me in the dark—"

"Of course not," Dad said irritably, then he took a deep breath and added very quietly, "I did *not* have an affair with Hannah Schneider. Sweet, you should stop this . . . *brooding*—it isn't good. What can I do? Tell me. We can move somewhere. California. You always wanted to go to California, didn't you? Any state you like . . ."

Dad was grabbing at words the way drowning people grab at floating bits of plywood. I didn't say anything.

"Well," he said, after a minute. "You have my office number. I'll be home around two to check on you."

"*Don't* check on me."

"Sweet."

"What?"

"There's that macaroni—"

"In the fridge, which I can reheat for lunch—yes, I *know*."

He sighed and covertly I glanced over at him. He looked as if I'd punched him in the face, as if I'd spray-painted PIG on his forehead, as if I'd told him I wished he was dead.

"You'll call if you need anything?" he asked.

I nodded.

"If you'd like, on my way home I can pick up a few videos from—what is that—?"

"Videomecca."

"Right. Any requests?"

"*Gone with the Fucking Wind*," I said.

Dad kissed me on the cheek and walked through the hall to the front door. It was one of those instances one feels as if one's skin has abruptly become thin as one layer of phyllo dough on a triangle of baklava, when one *desperately* doesn't want the other person to go, but one doesn't say anything in order to feel isolation in its purest form, as a periodic table of element, one of the noble gases, Iso[1].

The front door closed, locked. To the far-off tune of the blue Volvo driving away, it slipped over me, sadness, deadness, like a sheet over summer furniture.

*   *   *

I guess it was shock, the body's spin on distress, what Jemma Sloane drearily refers to on p. 95 of her book on "confrontational children," *Raising Goliath* (1999): "child coping mechanisms." Whatever the psychological grounds, for the next four days following their rescue (as my beloved Chernobyl reported during *First News at Five*, returned to their homes like damaged parcels) I adopted the character and deportment of a nasty ninety-year-old widow.

Dad had to work, so I spent the rest of Spring Break alone. I said little. What I did say tended to be to myself or to my colored companion, the TV (Chernobyl proved more enjoyable than any show-offy grandchild). Dad was the grossly underpaid yet loyal caretaker who showed up at regular intervals to make sure I hadn't burned down the house, that I ate my prepared meals and didn't fall asleep in strange positions that could lead to injury or death. He was the nurse who held his tongue when I was irritable, in the off chance I keeled over.

When I felt up to it, I ventured outside. The rueful weekend of rain had given way to conceited sunshine. It was too much—the glare, the grass like straw. The sun harassed the yard with a shamelessness I'd never noticed before, inundating the leaves, scalding the pavement. Also offensive were the earthworms, those vagrants, visibly hungover from the downpour, so wasted they were unable to mobilize and fried themselves into orange french fries all over the driveway.

I scowled, kept my bedroom shades pulled, hated everyone, felt grouchy. As soon as Dad drove away in the morning, I rummaged through the kitchen trash to retrieve the latest *Stockton Observer*, which he'd thrown out early in the morning, so I wouldn't see the headlines and fester over what had happened. (He didn't know my well-being was a lost cause; I had little appetite and sleep remained likely as phoenix eggs.)

Around five o'clock, before he came home, I returned the newspaper to the trash can, carefully repositioning it below last night's rigatoni with tomato sauce (the UNCS Political Science Department assistant, Barbara, had given Dad a few "comfort food" recipes; supposedly they'd been the rock that helped some wayward stepson, Mitch, through rehab). It was a stealthy exercise, much like hiding one's medication in the elastic of a fitted sheet, crushing it up with a soupspoon, using it to fertilize geraniums.

"Teacher Death Shocks School," "Dead Woman Beloved Teacher, Community Activist," "Investigators Hold Details of Local Death"—these were the keyed-up articles about it, us, *her*. They rehashed the specifics of the rescue, the Stockton community's "shock," "disbelief" and "sense of loss." Jade, Charles, Milton, Nigel and Lu all got their names and grinning yearbook pictures in the paper. (I did not—another blow for being the first found.) They quoted Eva Brewster: "We can't believe it." They also quoted Alice Kline, who'd worked with Hannah at the Burns County Animal Shelter: "It's so sad. She was the happiest, kindest person in the world. All the dogs and cats are waiting for her to come back." (When someone died prematurely they routinely become the Happiest, Kindest Person.)

Apart from "Investigation Continues into Park Death," which explained that her body had been discovered two miles from Sugartop Summit, that she had been hanging by an electrical cord, none of the other articles said anything new. After a while, I found it all stomach-turning, especially the editorial, "WNC Murder, Evidence of Voodoo," by R. Levenstein, some "local critic, conservationist and Web blogger" speculating that her death was occult related. "The police's continuing reluctance to disclose the details of Hannah Schneider's death steers the astute observer to a conclusion local authorities have been trying to cover up for years: *there is a growing populace of witches in Sluder and Burns Counties.*"

No, it wasn't like it was in the Olden Days.

Due to my new fondness for trawling through the trash, I was able to locate something else of note Dad had discarded for the sake of my mental health, The St. Gallway Bereavement Pack. Judging from the date on the large manila envelope in which it'd come, apparently The Pack had been launched with the velocity of a Tomahawk cruise missile as soon as news of the catastrophic event hit school radars.

The Pack included a letter from Headmaster Havermeyer ("Dear Parents: We are saddened this week by the death of one of our dearest teachers, Hannah Schneider . . ."), an overexcited article from a 1991 issue of *Parenting* magazine, "How Children Grieve," a schedule of counseling times and room numbers, Crisis Team constituents, a pair of 24-hour 800-numbers to call for psychological assistance (1-800-FEEL-SAD, and another I find difficult to remember, 1-800-U-BEWAIL, I believe) and a tepid postscript about a funeral ("A date for Ms. Schneider's memorial service has yet to be arranged.").

One can imagine how strange it was for me to read these carefully prepared materials, to realize they were talking about Hannah, *our* Hannah, the Ava Gardnered person across from whom I'd once eaten pork chops—how scary and sudden the shift from Living to Dead. Chiefly unsettling was the fact that The Pack mentioned nothing of how she'd died. True, The Pack had been prepared and mailed well before the Sluder County Coroner's Office would release its autopsy report. Yet the omission was bizarre, as if she hadn't been murdered (a sensational word; if I had my way there'd be something a little more serious at the intersection of Death, Murder and Slaughter— Mauleth, perhaps). Instead, according to The Pack, Hannah had simply "passed"; she'd been playing poker and decided not to take another card. Or, reading Havermeyer's spongy wording, one had the sense she'd been seized ("taken from us"), King-Kong-style ("without warning") by the gigantic, smooth hand of God ("she's in good hands"), and though such an event was gruesome ("one of life's toughest lessons") everyone should nail a grin to their face and continue robotically with daily life ("we must continue on, loving each day, as Hannah would've wanted").

*   *   *

St. Gallway's Grief Management began, but certainly did not end, with The Bereavement Pack. The day after I found the thing, Saturday the 2, Dad received a phone call from Mark Butters, Head of the Crisis Team.

I eavesdropped on the conversation from my bedroom phone with Dad's silent complicity. Prior to Butters' appointment to the Crisis Team, he'd never been a confident man. He had the complexion of baba ghanoush and his flabby body, even on bright, sunny days, reminded one of nothing more robust than a much-used carry-on suitcase. His most obvious personality trait was his suspicious nature, the unflagging conviction that he, Mr. Mark Butters, was the secret subject of all student jokes, quips, puns and personal asides. Over his table at lunch, his eyes searched student faces like drug dogs in an airport for the chalky residue of ridicule. But, as evidenced by his sonorous, newly confident voice, Mr. Butters had simply been a person of untapped potential, a man who needed only a Tiny Calamity in order to shine. He'd given up Hesitation and Doubt with the surprising ease of anonymously returning erotica in the middle of the night to the RETURNS slot at the video store, had effortlessly replaced them with Authority and Daring.

"Your schedule permitting," said Mr. Butters, "we'd like to arrange a half-hour session with both you and Blue in order to discuss what's happened.

You'll be sitting down with myself and Havermeyer, as well as one of our child counselors."

"One of your *what*?"

(Dad, I should mention, did not believe in anyone's counsel except his own. He thought psychotherapy promulgated nothing more than a great deal of handholding and shoulder massaging. He despised Freud, Jung, Frasier and any person who thought it fascinating to instigate a lengthy discussion of his/her own dreams.)

"A counselor. To share your concerns, your daughter's concerns. We have on hand a very competent, full-time child psychologist, Deb Cromwell. She's come to us from The Derds School in Raleigh."

"I see. Well, I have only one concern."

"Oh?"

"Yes."

"Great. Hit me with it."

"*You.*"

Butters was silent. Then: "I see."

"My concern is that for the entire week your school has remained mute—out of terror, I suppose—and now, at long last, one of you has mustered the courage to come forward, at, what time is it, *three-forty-five* on a Saturday afternoon. And all you have to say is that you'd like us to schedule a time to come in and be psychoanalyzed. Is that correct?"

"This is a just a preliminary question-and-answer session. Bob and Deb would like to sit down with you, have a one-on-one—"

"The true intention of this phone call is to intuit whether or not I plan to sue both the school and the Board of Education for negligence. Am I right?"

"Mr. Van Meer, I'm not going to try to argue with—"

"Don't."

"What I *will* say is that we wish—"

"I wouldn't say or wish anything if I were you. Your reckless—let me rephrase that—your *deranged* staff member took *my* child, a *minor,* on a weekend field trip *without* securing parental permission—"

"We're well aware of the situa—"

"Endangered her life, the lives of five other minors *and,* let me remind you, managed to get herself killed in what is looking like a highly disgraceful fashion. I am *this* close to calling a lawyer and making it my life's ambition to ensure that you, that headmaster of yours, Oscar Meyers, and *every* person associated with your third-rate institution ends up wearing stripes and leg irons for the next forty years. Furthermore, in the off chance my daughter *does* wish to share her concerns, the last person with whom she'd choose to do so would be a private-school counselor named *Deb*. If I were you, I wouldn't call here again unless you wish to beg for clemency."

Dad hung up.

And though I wasn't in the kitchen with him, I knew he didn't slam down the phone, but gently returned it to the wall, much in the manner of putting a maraschino cherry atop a sundae.

Well, I *did* have concerns. And Dad was right; I had no intention of sharing them with Deb. I had to share them with Jade, Charles, Milton, Nigel and Lu. The need to explain to each of them what had happened from the moment I left the campground to those seconds I saw her dead was so overpowering, I couldn't think about it, couldn't *attempt* to outline or ABC it on note cards or legal pads without feeling dizzy and dumb, as if I were trying to contemplate quarks, quasars and quantum mechanics, all at the same time (see Chapters 13, 35, 46, *Incongruities*, V. Close, 1998).

Later that day, when Dad left to go buy groceries, I finally called Jade. I estimated I'd given her enough time to recover from the initial shock (perhaps she'd even continued on, loving each day, as Hannah would've wanted).

"Who's calling please?"

It was Jefferson.

"This is Blue."

"Sorry, honey. She's not taking calls."

She hung up before I could say anything. I called Nigel.

"Creech Pottery and Carpentry."

"Uh, hello. Is Nigel there? This is Blue."

"*Hey* there, Blue!"

It was Diana Creech, his mother—or rather, adopted mother. I'd never met her, but had talked to her countless times on the phone. Due to her loud, jocular voice, which snowplowed everything and anything you said, whether it be a lone word or the Declaration of Independence, I envisioned her as a large, cheery woman who wore men's overalls covered with clay smears from her own gigantic fingers, fingers that in all probability were wide as naked rolls of toilet paper. When she talked, she took big bites out of certain words, as if they were bright green, solid Granny Smiths.

"Let me go see if he's awake. Last time I looked in on him he was sleeping like a baby. That's all he's been doing for the past two days. How are *you*?"

"I'm okay. Nigel's all right?"

"*Sure.* I mean, we're still in *shock.* Everyone is! 'Specially the school. Have they called? You can tell they're nervous about a lawsuit. *Obviously* we're waiting to hear what the police say. I told Ed they should have made an arrest by now or come forward and *said* something. Silence is inexcusable. Ed says no one has a *clue* what happened to her and that's why they're holding out. What I *will* say is that if somebody *did* do it—'cuz I don't want to think about the *other* possibility, not yet—you can be sure he's on his way to Timbuktu with a fake passport in a first-class seat." (The few times I'd spoken to her on the phone, I noticed Diana Creech always managed to stick the word *Timbuktu* into the conversation as many youths stuck in *like* or *whatever.*) "They're dragging their *feet.*" She sighed. "I'm sad about what's happened, but I'm thankful you guys are safe. But you turned up Saturday, didn't you? Nigel said you weren't with them. Oh, *here* he comes. Hold on, sugar."

She put the receiver down and walked away, the sound of a Clydesdale trotting down on a cobblestone street. (She wore clogs.) I heard voices and then the hooves again.

"Mind if he calls you back? He wants to eat something."

"Sure," I said.

"You take care now."

No one answered when I called Charles.

At Milton's, the answering machine picked up, a whine of violin accompanied with a woman's fanciful voice, "You've reached Joanna, John and Milton. We're not home . . ."

I dialed Leulah. I sensed she'd be the most unglued out of all of us, so I hesitated calling her, but I had to talk to someone. She answered on the first ring.

"Hey, Jade," she said. "Sorry about that."

"Oh, it's Blue actually." I was so relieved, I oil-spilled. "I'm glad you picked up. How are you? I–I've been going crazy. I can't sleep. How are you?"

"Oh," said Leulah. "This isn't Leulah."

"What?"

"Leulah's asleep," she said in a strange voice. I could hear, on her end, a television. It was thrilled about house paint, only a single coat necessary for total coverage, Herman's Paints are guaranteed to last five years regardless of exposure to rainfall and wind.

"Can I take a message?" she asked.

"What's wrong?"

She hung up.

I sat down on the edge of my bed. The bedroom windows were crammed with late-day light, soft, yellow, the color of pears. The paintings on the wall, oil landscapes of pastures and cornfields, looked so shiny they might have still been wet. I might have run my thumb through them and made a finger painting. I began to cry, dumb, lethargic tears, as if I'd cut into a scarred old gum tree and the sap could barely leak out.

This, I remember distinctly, was the worst moment—not the insomnia, not my wasted courtship of the TV, not the endless chanting in my head of a certain hysterical phrase that became less alive the more I said it—*someone killed Hannah, someone killed Hannah*—but this awful desolate feeling, desert-island aloneness. Worst of all, I knew it was the beginning of it, not the middle or the end.

Bleak House

In 44 B.C., ten days after he stabbed Caesar in the back, Brutus probably felt the same way I did when the student body returned to St. Gallway for the commencement of Spring Term. Brutus, strolling down the dusty roads of the Forum, doubtless came face-to-face with the harsh realities of "Corridor and Country Road Ostracism," with its principal tenets, "Keep a wide girth," and "As you come closer, fasten your eyes to a point immediately north of the leper's head so for a second he/she thinks you're acknowledging his/her pitiable existence." Brutus most likely became well versed in "Modes of Seeing Through," the most startling of which were the "Pretend Brutus Is a Diaphanous Scarf" and "Pretend Brutus Is a Courtyard-Facing Window." Though he once drank watered-down wine with the perpetrators of this unspoken cruelty, once sat next to them at Circus Maximus and rejoiced in the overturning of a chariot, once bathed with them, naked, in both the hot *and* the cold pools of the public baths, these things meant nothing now. Because of what he'd done, he was and always would be their object of disgrace.

At least Brutus had done something productive, albeit controversial, carrying out a meticulously laid plan to seize power for what he believed to be the continued well-being of the Roman Empire.

I, of course, had done nothing at all.

"See, if you remember, everyone *thought* she was amazing, but I always thought there was something hair-raising about her," said Lucille Hunter in my AP English class. "Ever watch when she's taking notes?"

"Huh-uh."

"Barely looks up from the page. And when she's taking an essay test she mouths what she's writing the whole time. My grandmother in Florida, who my mom says is *totally* going senile, does the same thing while watching *Wheel of Fortune* or writing checks."

"*Well*," said Donnamara Chase, leaning forward in her seat, "Cindy Willard told me this morning that Leulah Maloney announced to her *entire* Spanish class that . . ."

For some reason, it perpetually slipped both Lucille and Donnamara's meager minds that my assigned seat in Ms. Simpson's AP English class was, and always had been, immediately behind Donnamara's. The girl handed me *The Brothers Karamazov* handouts still warm from the Faculty Lounge copier and seeing me, nervously bared her long and pointy teeth (see "Venus Flytrap," *North American Flora*, Starnes, 1989).

"Wonder if she'll leave school," mused Angel Ospfrey, four seats away.

"Absolutely," whispered Beth Price. "Expect some announcement in the next few weeks that her dad, Account Executive for Whatever Corp, was recently promoted to Regional Manager of the Charlotte branch."

"Wonder what her last words were," said Angel. "Hannah's, I mean."

"From what I hear Blue doesn't have too long to say hers," said Macon Campins. "Milton *detests* her. He said, and I quote, that if he ever meets her in a dark alley, he'll 'Jack-the-Ripper her ass.' "

"Ever heard that old wives' tale," asked Krista Jibsen in AP Physics, "that it's okay never to be wealthy or famous or whatever because if you never had it, you won't miss it? Well—and I bet this is how Blue feels—if you've tasted fame, then lost it, that's like, extreme torture. You end up with a cocaine addiction. You have to spend time in rehab. And when you come out you make vampire movies that go straight to video."

"You got that off the Corey Feldman *True Hollywood Story*," said Luke "Trucker" Bass.

"Well, I heard Radley's mom is over the moon," said Peter "Nostradamus" Clark. "She's throwing a Return-to-Power party for Radley because after undergoing such an ordeal, the girl won't be able to hold onto Valedictorian."

"I heard from a very reliable source—wait. No. I feel bad spreading it around."

"What?"

"She's a *full-scale* lesbian," sang Lonny Felix that Wednesday during Physics Lab 23, "Symmetry in Physical Laws: Is Your Right Hand Really Your Right Hand?" "The *Ellen* kind, by the way. Not the Anne Heche kind, when you can go either way." Lonny pony-tossed her hair (long, blond, the texture of Wheaties) and glanced toward the front of the room where I was standing with my lab partner, Laura Elms. She hunched closer to Sandy Quince-Wood. "Guess Schneider was one, too. That's why they went off together in the middle of the night. How two women get it on is beyond my comprehension but what I *do* know is that something went fatally wrong during the sex act. That's what the police are trying to figure out. That's why it's taking so long for them to have a verdict."

"That same thing was on *CSI: Miami* last night," said Sandy distractedly as she wrote in her lab manual.

"Little did we know what's going on on *CSI: Miami* is happening right here in our physics class."

"For gosh sakes," said Zach Soderberg, turning around to look at them. "Would you guys keep it down? Some of us are trying to figure out these laws of reflection symmetry."

"Sorry, Romeo," said Lonny with a smirk.

"Yes, let's try to keep things quiet, shall we?" said our substitute teacher, a bald man named Mr. Pine. Pine smiled, yawned and stretched his arms high over his head revealing sweat stains the size of pancakes. He resumed his scrutiny of a magazine, *Country Life Wall & Windows*.

"Jade's trying to get the Blue girl kicked out of school," whispered Dee during second period Study Hall.

Dum scowled. "For what?"

"Not murder, but like, coercion or brute force or something. I heard her pleading her case in Spanish. I guess Hannah was all *bueno*. Then she goes off with this Blue person and five minutes later ends up *muerto*. It's all *not* going to hold up in court. They're going to declare a mistrial. And no one can use a race card to get her off."

"Stop acting like you're all Greta van Susteren with an eyelift because here's a breaking headline for you. You're *not*. Neither are you Wolf Blitzer."

"What's *that* supposed to mean?"

Dum shrugged, tossing her crumpled copy of *Startainment* on the library table. "It's like so, obvious. Schneider pulled a Sylvia Plath."

Dee nodded. "Not a terrible assumption actually. Think about my last Intro to Film class."

"What about it?"

"I *told* you. The woman was supposed to give us an essay test on the Italians, *Divorce Italiano Style*, *L'Avventura*, *Eight and a* Friggin' *Half*—"

"Oh, yeah—"

"But when we showed up, all prepared and everything, yet again she was all flailin' and flappin'. It'd *totally* slipped her mind. She played it off, said not having the test was our surprise, but everyone was creeped out— it was *ob*vious she was blowin' those excuses out the wazoo. She plain old-fashioned for*got*. So she hastily puts in *Reds*, which isn't even *Italian*, right? *Plus* we'd already seen it nine times because three days in a row she forgot to bring in *La Dolce* Friggin' *Vita*. The woman had no teach cred, was hope-lessly ding-headed, suffered epizootics of the blowhole and was full of booty-cheddar. But what kind of teacher forgets their own *essay* test?"

"A bugged-out teacher," whispered Dum. "One who's mentally unstable."

"Damn straight."

Unfortunately, my instinctive response to overhearing campus-wide chitchat of the aforementioned kind was not The Pacino (godfather-styled vengeance), The Pesci (urges to stick a ballpoint pen in someone's throat), The Costner (flat, frontierlike amusement), The Spacey (scathing verbal re-taliation accompanied by a blank facial expression) nor The Penn (blue-collared bellows and moans).

I can only compare how I felt to being inside an austere clothing store when one of the workers silently follows you around to make sure you don't steal anything. Though you have no *intention* of stealing anything, though you've never come close to stealing anything in your life, knowing they see you as a potential shoplifter unexpectedly turns you into a potential shoplifter. You try not to peer suspiciously over your shoulder. You peer suspi-ciously over your shoulder. You try not to look at people sideways or sigh arti-ficially or whistle or shoot people nervous smiles. You look sideways, sigh, whistle, shoot nervous smiles and put your extremely sweaty hands in and then out of your pockets over and over again.

*   *   *

Not to complain *all* of St. Gallway was hashing me over like this, and certainly not to whimper about such abysmal treatment or feel sorry for my-self. There were some extraordinary kindnesses, those first few days back at school, such as the moment my old lab partner, Laura Elms, who at four-feet-nine and approximately ninety to ninety-five pounds typically exuded the personality of rice (white, easy on the stomach, went well with every kid), suddenly snatched my left hand as it was copying down $F = qv \times B$ from the dry-erase board: "I totally know what you're going through. One of my best friends found her father dead last year. He was outside on their driveway washing their Lexus when he just collapsed. She ran outside and she totally didn't recognize him. He was this really weird blueberry color. She went crazy for a while. All I'm saying is if you ever want to talk I'm here for you." (Laura, I never took you up on your offer, but please accept my thanks. I apologize for the rice comment.)

And there was Zach. If velocity affected the mass of all objects, it wouldn't affect Zach Soderberg. Zach would be the Amendment, the Correction, the Tweak. He was a lesson in durable materials, a success story of sustainable good moods. He was c, the constant.

On Thursday, in AP Physics, I returned from the bathroom to find a mysterious folded piece of notebook paper sitting on my chair. I didn't open it until class was over. I stood very still, right in the middle of the hallway with all those kids gushing past me with backpacks, sagging hair and lumpy jackets, staring at the words, at his schoolgirl's handwriting. I was refuse in a river.

IIOW ARE YOU
I'M AROUND
IF YOU WANT TO TALK

ZACH

I kept the note folded in my backpack for the rest of the day and surprised myself by deciding I *did* want to chat with him. (Dad said it never hurt to glean as many perspectives and opinions as possible, even those one suspects will be unsophisticated and Calibanesque.) Throughout AP World History, I found myself fantasizing about going home not with Dad, but with Patsy and Roge, having a supper not of spaghetti, lecture notes, a one-sided debate of J. Hutchinson's *The Aesthetic Emancipation of the Human Race* (1924), but roasted chicken, mashed potatoes, a discussion of Bethany Louise's softball tryouts or Zach's recent paper on The American Dream (the most ho-hum of paper topics). And Patsy would smile and squeeze my hand while Roge embarked on an impromptu sermon—if I was lucky, "The Fourteen Hopes."

As soon as the bell rang, I hurried out of Hanover along the sidewalk to Barrow, up the stairs to the second floor where I'd heard Zach had his locker. I stood just inside the doorway and watched him in khaki pants and a blue-and-white striped shirt talking to that Rebecca girl, the one with prehistoric carnivore eyeteeth. She was tall, propping a stack of spiral notebooks against her jutted-out hip, her other bony arm hooked on the top of the lockers so she resembled an angular Egyptian character scrawled on papyrus. And something about the way Zach gave her his full attention (aware of no one else in the hall), the way he smiled and ran that giant hand through his hair made me realize he was in love with her, that they were doubtlessly both Kinko's employees always shoulder-to-shoulder and engaged in tons of color-copying, and now I'd stand there trying to talk to him about Death with that Hieroglyph breathing down my neck, her eyes sticking to my face like smashed figs, bushy black hair flooding her shoulders like the River Nile—I couldn't do it. I spun around, darted back into the stairwell, shoved open the door and raced outside.

∗   ∗   ∗

I also can't overlook the Good Samaritan Kindness of another occasion, that Friday in Beginning Drawing, when I, exhausted from the sleepless nights, dozed off in the middle of class, forgetting about my Line Drawing of Tim "Raging" Waters, who'd been chosen to sit at the center of this week's Life Drawing Circle.

"What on earth is wrong with Miss Van Meer?" roared Mr. Moats, glaring down at me. "She's green as El Greco's ghost! Tell us what you ate for breakfast and we'll make a point of avoiding it."

Mr. Victor Moats was, for the most part, a gentle man, but at times, for no rhyme or reason (perhaps it was moon phases) he relished degrading a student in front of the class. He snatched my Strathmore drawing pad from the easel and held it high over his seal-slick head. Immediately, I saw the tiny disaster: there was nothing, nothing at all in the Pacific Ocean of the white page, except way down in the lower right-hand corner, I'd drawn Raging the size of Guam. I'd also drawn his leg over his muddled face, which would have been fine if Mr. Moats hadn't spent ten minutes at the beginning of class detailing the essentials of life drawing and proportion.

"She is not concentrating! She must be dreaming about Will Smith or Brad Pitt or any number of brawny heartthrobs, when what she should be doing is—*what? Can someone please inform us what Miss Van Meer should be doing instead of wasting our time?"*

I gazed up at Mr. Moats. If it'd been any Friday *before* Hannah's death, I'd have turned red and apologized, perhaps even sprinted to the bathroom, locked myself in the handicapped stall and wept over the toilet seat, but now, I didn't feel anything. I was impassive as a blank sheet of Strathmore drawing paper. I stared up at him, as if he wasn't talking about me but about some other wayward kid named Blue. I felt all the embarrassment of a desert cactus.

I *did* notice, however, that the entire class was nervously glancing around at each other, carrying out some impressive routine of alarm like tree-dwelling Guenon monkeys alerting each other to the presence of a Crowned Eagle. Fran "Juicy" Smithson widened her eyes at Henderson Shoal and Henderson Shoal, in response, widened his eyes in the direction of Howard "Beirut" Stevens. Amy Hempshaw bit her lip and removed her caramel hair from behind her ears and lowered her head so it swiftly covered half of her face like a trap door.

What they were signaling to each other, of course, was that Mr. Moats, notorious for preferring the works of Velázquez, Ribera, El Greco and Herrera the Elder to the company of his clam-faced Gallway coworkers (who neither dreamt about, nor were overly eager to wax poetic on, the genius of the Spanish Masters) had also apparently thrown out, unopened, all recent interoffice mail delivered daily to his Mailbox in the Faculty Lounge.

Hence he had not familiarized himself with Havermeyer's "Emergency Memorandum," nor the article written by the National Teaching League, "Preparing a Student Body for Grief" or, most critically, that confidential list prepared by Butters entitled, "Ones to Watch," which included my name, as well as the Bluebloods': *"These students in particular will be affected by the recent loss. Pay close attention to their behavior and academic performance and alert myself or our newly appointed counselor, Deb Cromwell, of any abnormalities. This is a very delicate situation."* (These confidential faculty documents had been stolen, Xeroxed and illicitly trafficked among the student body. By whom, no one knew. Some said it was Maxwell Stuart, others said Dee and Dum.)

"Actually," said Jessica Rothstein across the room, crossing her arms, "I think it's okay to excuse Blue today." Her kinky brown curls, which at distances greater than fifteen feet resembled one thousand wet wine corks, trembled in perfect unison.

"Is that so?" Mr. Moats spun around to face her. *"And why is that?"*

"She's been through an *ordeal*," said Jessica loudly, displaying the thrilling conviction of a young person who knows she's Right, the old guy in front of her (who should, in theory, have Maturity and Experience working for him) Flat-Out Wrong.

"An ordeal," repeated Moats.

"Yes. An ordeal."

"What sort of ordeal are we talking about? I'm intrigued."

Jessica made a face of exasperation. "She's had a *rough week*." She was desperately glancing around the room now wishing someone else would take over. Jessica preferred to be Captain of this rescue, making the phone call, giving the order. Jessica had no desire to be the Private who flew the HH-43F helicopter from Bin Ty Ho Airbase, emergency-landed in enemy territory, crawled through rice paddies, waterholes, elephant grass and landmines with over seventy pounds of ammo and C-rations tied to her, carrying the wounded solider seven miles and spending the night on the mosquitoed bank of the Cay Ni River before boarding a rescue bird coming at 0500 hours.

"Miss Rothstein enjoys beating around the bush," said Moats.

"I'm just saying she's had a hard time, okay? That's all."

"*Well, life isn't a cakewalk, is it?!*" asked Moats. "Eighty-nine percent of the world's most valuable art was created by men living in rat-infested flats. You think Velázquez wore Adidas? *You think he enjoyed the luxuries of central heating and twenty-four-hour pizza delivery?!*"

"No one's talking about Velázquez," said Tim "Raging" Waters, slumped on the stool at the center of the Life Drawing Circle. "We're talking about Hannah Schneider and how Blue was with her when she *died*."

Usually no one, including myself, paid any attention to Raging, so typical his sullen voice and the bumper stickers all over the trunk of his car, I LOVE PAIN, BLOOD TASTES GOOD and the words scrawled in black permanent marker all over his backpack, RAGE, ANARCHY, GO F*CK YOURSELF. Whiffs of cigarette smoke followed in his wake like a Just-Married convertible trailing cans. But he said her name, and it floated out into the center of the room like an empty rowboat and—I don't know why—in that moment, I think I would've run away with that pale angry kid if he'd asked me to. I loved him desperately, an agonizing, overwhelming love, for three, maybe four seconds. (That was how things were after Hannah died. You didn't notice someone and when you did you *adored* him/her, wanted to have his/her offspring, until the moment passed as abruptly as it had come.)

Mr. Moats didn't move. He raised a hand to his green plaid vest and kept it pressed there, as if he was going to be sick, or else he was trying to remember words to a song he once knew.

"I see," he said. Gently, he returned my sad Strathmore pad to my easel. "Resume your drawings!"

He stood next to me. When I started drawing again, beginning with Raging's leather shoe in the middle of the page (a brown shoe, on the side of which a word was scrawled, *Mayhem*), Mr. Moats, oddly enough, bent down next to me so his head was inches from the white paper. I sort of glanced over at him, reluctantly, because like the sun, it was never a good idea to stare directly into a teacher's face. Inevitably, you noticed things you wished you hadn't—sleep, moles, hairs, wrinkles, some calloused or discolored patch of skin. You were aware there was a sour, vinegary truth to these physical details, but you didn't want to know what it was, not yet, because it'd directly affect one's ability to pay attention in class, to take notes on the many stages of club mosses reproduction, or the exact year and month of the Battle of Gettysburg (July 1863).

Moats didn't say anything. His eyes traveled all over my blank paper stopping on Raging down in the corner with his leg over his face, and I watched him, spellbound by his craggy profile, a profile that bore a striking resemblance to the southeastern coast of England. And then he closed his eyes, and I could see how upset he was, and I started to wonder if perhaps he'd loved Hannah. I was aware too how strange adults were, how their lives were vaster than they wanted anyone to realize, that they actually stretched on and on like deserts, dry and desolate, with an unpredictable, shifting sea of dunes.

"Maybe I should start over on another piece of paper," I said. I wanted him to say something. If he said something, it meant he might bear extreme heat, freezing temperatures at night, the odd sandstorm, but otherwise be all right.

He nodded and stood up again. "Continue."

*　　*　　*

That day after school, I went to Hannah's classroom. I'd hoped nobody would be there, but when I walked into Loomis, I saw two freshman girls taping things—it looked like Get Well Soon cards—to Hannah's door. On the floor to their right was a giant picture of Hannah, as well as a pile of flowers—carnations for the most part, in pinks, whites and reds. Perón had mentioned them on the intercom during Afternoon Announcements: "The outpouring of flowers and cards shows us that, despite our different backgrounds we can band together and support each other, not as students, parents, teachers and administrators, but as human beings. Hannah would be overwhelmed with joy." Immediately, I wanted to leave, but the girls had seen me so I had no choice but to continue down the hall.

"Wish we could light the candles."

"Let *me* do it. You're going to ruin the whole design, Kara—"

"Maybe we should light them anyway. For *her* sake, you know?"

"We *can't*. Didn't you listen to Ms. Brewster? It's a fire hazard."

The taller, pale girl was taping a large card to the door, which sported a giant gold sun and read, "A star has dimmed . . ." The other girl, bowlegged, with black hair, was holding an even larger card, this one handmade with crude orange lettering: TREASURED MEMORIES. There were at least fifty more cards propped up on the floor around the flowers. I bent down so I could read a few.

"Rest in peace. Love, the Friggs," wrote the Friggs. "C U N HEV N," wrote Anonymous. "In this world of bitter religious hatred and unmitigated violence against our fellow man, you were a shining star," wrote Rachid Fox-glove. "We'll miss you," wrote Amy Hempshaw and Bill Chews. "I hope you're reincarnated as a mammal and our paths cross again, sooner rather than later because when I go to med school I doubt I'll have a life," wrote Lin Xe-Pen. Some cards were introspective ("Why did it happen?") or harmlessly irreverent ("It'd be cool if you could send me a sign that indicates there's a discernible afterlife, that it's not just eternity in a box because if that's what it is, I'd rather not go through with it."). Others were filled with remarks suitable for Post-its, for shouts out of unrolled windows of cars driving away ("You were an awesome teacher!!!").

"Would you be interested in signing the Condolence Card?" the black-haired girl asked me.

"Sure," I said.

The inside of the Condolence Card was graffitied with student signatures and read: "We find peace and comfort knowing you are now in a Perfect Place." I hesitated signing, but the girl was watching me so I squeezed my name between Charlie Lin and Millicent Newman.

"Thank you very much," said the girl, as if I'd just given her enough change to buy a soft drink. She taped the card to the door.

I walked outside again and stood in the shade of a pine tree in front of the building until I saw them leave, and then returned inside. Someone (the black-haired girl, self-appointed Executor of the H. Schneider Memorial) had placed a plastic green tarp beneath the flowers (all stems pointing in the same direction), as well as a clipboard next to the door that read, "Sign here and pledge a special amount to raise money for the Hannah Schneider Hummingbird Garden. (Minimum donation $5.)"

To be honest, I wasn't especially thrilled with all the grief. It felt artificial, as if they'd taken her away somehow, stolen her, replaced her with this frightening smiling stranger whose giant color faculty photo was laminated and propped up on the floor by a squat unlit candle. It didn't look like her; school photographers, armed with watery lighting and smeary neutral backgrounds, cheerfully leveled everyone's uniqueness, made them look the same. No, the real Hannah, the cinematic one who sometimes got a little too drunk with her bra straps showing, she was being held against her will by all these limp carnations, wobbly signatures, humid sentiments of "Missing U."

I heard a door slam, the stark punctuation of a woman's shoes. Someone pulled open the door at the end of the hall, letting it slam. For one mad moment, I thought it was Hannah; the slim person walking toward me was wearing all black—a black skirt and short-sleeved shirt, black heels—exactly what she wore the first time I saw her, all those months ago in Fat Kat Foods.

But it was Jade.

She looked pale, gutter-thin, her blond hair slicked back in a ponytail. As she passed under the fluorescent lights the top of her head flashed a whitish green. Shadows swam through her face as she walked, staring at the floor. When she finally noticed me, I knew she wanted to turn back, but didn't let herself. Jade hated all retreats, U-turns, backpedaling, and second thoughts.

"I don't have to see you if I don't want to," she said as she stopped in front of the flowers and cards. She leaned down and inspected them, a pleasant, relaxed smile on her face as if she were peering in at cases of expensive watches. After a minute, she turned around and stared at me.

"You planning to stand there all day like a moron?"

"Well, I—" I began.

"Because I'm not going to sit here and lug it out of you." She put a hand on her hip. "I assumed because you've called me like some lunatic stalker for the past week you had something decent to say."

"I do."

"What?"

"I don't understand why everyone's angry at me. I didn't do anything."

Her eyes widened in shock. "How can you not understand what you *did?*"

"What did I do?"

She crossed her arms. "If you don't know, Retch, I'm not going to tell you." She turned and leaned down to inspect the cards again. A minute later, she said: "I mean, you disappeared on *pur*pose and made her go look for you.

Like some weird game or something. No, don't even *try* to say you went to the bathroom because we found that roll of toilet paper still in Hannah's backpack, okay? And then you—well, we don't know what you did. But Hannah went from laughing with us without a care in the world to hanging from a tree. Dead. You did something."

"She signaled for me to get up and disappear into the woods. It was her idea."

Jade made a face. "When was this?"

"Around the campfire."

"Not true. I was there. I don't remember her—"

"No one saw her but me."

"*That's* convenient."

"I left. She came and found me. We walked into the woods for ten minutes, then she stopped and said she had to tell me something. A secret."

"Ooo, what was the *secret*? That she sees dead people?"

"She never told me."

"Oh, *God*."

"Someone followed us. I didn't see him clearly but I think he was wearing glasses, and then—this is the part I can't figure out—she went after him. She told me to stay where I was. And that's the last time I saw her." (It was a white lie, of course, but I'd decided to remove the fact I'd seen Hannah dead from my history. It was an appendix, a functionless organ that could become infected and thus it could be surgically removed without upsetting any other part of the past.)

Jade stared at me, skeptical. "I don't believe you."

"It's the truth. Remember the cigarette butt Lu found? Someone had been there."

She looked at me, eyes wide, and then shook her head. "I think you have a serious problem." She allowed her bag to fall to the floor, on its side. It belched up two books, *The Norton Anthology of Poetry* (Ferguson, Salter, Stallworthy, 1996 ed.) and *How to Write a Poem* (Fifer, 2001). "You're desperate. And completely sad and embarrassing. Whatever your lame excuses are, no one gives a shit. It's over."

She was waiting for me to protest, fall to my knees, moan, but I couldn't. I sensed the impossibility of it. I remembered what Dad said once, that some people have all of life's answers worked out the day they're born and there's no use trying to teach them anything new. "They're closed for business even though, somewhat confusingly, their doors open at eleven, Monday through

Friday," Dad said. And the trying to change what they think, the attempt to explain, the hope they'll come to see your side of things, it was exhausting, because it never made a dent and afterward you only ached unbearably. It was like being a Prisoner in a Maximum-Security Prison, wanting to know what a Visitor's hand felt like (see *Living in Darkness*, Cowell, 1967). No matter how desperately you wanted to know, pressing your dumb palm against the glass right where the visitor's hand was pressed on the opposite side, you never would know that feeling, not until they set you free.

"We don't think you're like, psychotic, or a Menendez brother," Jade said. "You probably didn't do it on purpose. But *still*. We talked it over and decided if we're honest with ourselves we can't forgive you. I mean, she's gone. Maybe that doesn't mean anything to you, but it means the world to us. Milton, Charles *loved* her. Leulah and I adored her. She was our *sister—*"

"That's breaking news," I interrupted. (I couldn't help myself; I was Dad's daughter and thus prone to blowing the whistle on Hypocrisy and Double-Talk.) "Last I heard, you thought she was responsible for estranging you from mint chocolate chip ice cream. You were also worried she was a member of the Manson Family."

Jade looked so enraged, I wondered if she was going to fling me to the linoleum and rip out my eyes. Instead, her lips shrunk and she turned the color of gazpacho. She spoke in pointy little words: "If you're so dumb that you can't understand why we're upset beyond all possible *belief*, I'm not having this conversation. You don't even know what we went through. Charles went out of his mind and fell off a *cliff*. Lu and Nigel were hysterical. Even Milton broke down. *I* was the one who hauled everyone to safety, but I'm still traumatized by the experience. We thought we were going to die, like those people in the movie when they're stuck in the Alps and forced to eat each other."

"*Alive*. Before it was a movie, it was a book."

Her eyes widened. "You think this is a joke? Don't you *get* it?"

She waited, but I *didn't* get it—I really didn't.

"Whatever," she said. "Stop calling my house. It's annoying for my mother to have to talk to you and give you excuses."

She leaned down and picked up her bag, heaving it up onto her shoulder. Primly she smoothed back her hair, displaying the self-consciousness of the Ones Making an Exit; she was well aware that a great deal of Exiting had been done before her, for millions of years and millions of different reasons, and now it was her turn and she wanted to do a decent job. With a prim smile on her face, she picked up *The Norton Anthology of Poetry* and *How to Write a Poem*, took great pains to tuck them neatly into her bag. She sniffed, pressed her black sweater over her waist (as if she'd just completed a first round of interviews at Whatever Corp.) and began to make her way down the hall. As she walked away, I could tell she was considering joining the elite subgroup within the Ones Making an Exit, a sect reserved for the wholly unsentimental and the completely hard-boiled: The Ones Who Never Looked Back. She decided against it, however.

"You know," she said smoothly, turning to look at me. "None of us could figure it out."

I stared back, unaccountably afraid.

"Why *you?* Why Hannah wanted to bring you into our little group. I'm not trying to be rude, but from the beginning none of us could *stand* you. We called you 'pigeon.' Because that's how you acted. This grimy pigeon clucking around everyone's feet desperate for crumbs. But she *loved* you. 'Blue's great. You have to give her a chance. She's had a tough life.' Yeah, *right.* It didn't make sense. No, you have some weirdly dreamy home life with your virtuoso dad you blather on about like he's the fucking second coming. But no. Everyone said I was mean and judgmental. Well, now it's too late and she's dead."

She saw the look on my face and did a *Ha.* The Ones Making an Exit had to have a *Ha*, a truncated laugh that brought to mind videogame Game Overs and typewriter dings.

"Guess that's life's little joke," she said.

At the end of the hall, she pushed open the door and was illuminated for a second by a puddle of yellow light, and her shadow was tossed, elongated and thin, in my direction like piece of towrope, but then she stepped nimbly through the doorway, and the door slammed and I was left with the carnations. ("The only flower that, when given to someone, is only marginally superior to giving dead ones," Dad said.)

The Big Sleep

The next day, Saturday, April 10, The Stockton Observer finally published a terse article on the coroner's findings.

LOCAL WOMAN'S HANGING
DEATH RULED SUICIDE

The death of Burns County woman, Hannah Louise Schneider, 44, was ruled a suicide by Sluder County Coroner's Bureau yesterday afternoon. Cause of death was determined to be "asphyxiation due to hanging."

"There was no evidence whatsoever of foul play," said Sluder County Coroner Joe Villaverde yesterday.

Villaverde said there was also no evidence of drugs, alcohol or other toxins in Schneider's body and the manner of death was consistent with suicide.

"I'm basing my ruling on the autopsy report as well as the evidence found by the sheriff's department and state legislators," Villaverde said.

Schneider's body was found March 28 hanging from a tree by an electrical cord in the Schull's Cove area of the Great Smoky Mountains National Park. She had accompanied six local high school students on a camping trip. The six students were recovered without injury.

"This can't have happened," I said.

Dad looked at me, concerned. "My dear—"

"I'm going to be sick. I can't take this anymore."

"They just might be right. One never knows with—"

"They're not right!" I screamed.

*   *   *

Dad agreed to take me to the Sluder County Sheriff's Department. It was astonishing he actually consented to my outlandish, fitfully proposed demand. I assumed he felt sorry for me, noticed how pale I looked of late, how I could barely eat, didn't sleep, how I sprinted downstairs like a Beat junkie looking for a fix to catch *First News at Five*, how I reacted to all questions, both ordinary and existential, with a five-second transatlantic delay. He was also familiar with the quotation, "When your child is seized by an idea with the zeal of a fundamentalist Bible salesman from Indiana, stand in his or her way at your own risk" (see *Rearing the Gifted Child*, Pennebaker, 1998, p. 232).

We found the address on the Internet, climbed into the Volvo and drove for forty-five minutes to the station, located west of Stockton in the tiny mountain town of Bicksville. It was a bright, chipper day, and the flat, sagging police building sat like an exhausted hitchhiker on the side of the road.

"Do you want to wait in the car?" I asked Dad.

"No, no, I'll come in." He held up D. F. Young's *Narcissism and Culture Jamming the U.S.A.* (1986). "I've brought some light reading."

"Dad?"

"Yes, sweet."

"Let me do the talking."

"Oh. By all means."

The Sluder County Sheriff's Department was a single ransacked room that resembled the Primates section of any midlevel zoo. All efforts, within budget, had been made to lead the ten or twelve captive policemen to believe they were in their natural environment (bleating phones, cinder-block walls painted taupe, dead plants with leaves like tendriled bows on birthday presents, chunky filing cabinets lined up in the back like football players, Department star patches barnacling their clay brown shirts). They were given a restricted diet (coffee, donuts) and plenty of toys to play with (swivel chairs, radio consoles, guns, a ceiling-suspended TV hiccupping the Weather Channel). And yet there remained the unmistakable whiff of artificiality to this habitat, of apathy, of everyone simply going through the motions of being a law enforcer, as struggling for survival was no longer an immediate concern. "Hey, Bill!" shouted one of the men pacing in the very back by the water cooler. He held up a magazine. "Check out the new Dakota." "Already did," said Bill, coma-staring at his blue computer screen.

Dad, with a look of unmitigated distaste, sat down in the only seat available in the front, next to a fat and faded girl wearing a tinseled halter top, no shoes, her hair so coarsely bleached it resembled Cheetos. I made my way to the man behind the front desk flipping through a magazine and chewing a red coffee stirrer.

"I'd like to speak to your chief investigator, if he or she is available," I said.

"Huh?"

He had a flat red face, which, discounting his yellowed toothbrush mustache, recalled the bottom of a large foot. He was bald. The topmost part of his head was grease-spattered with fat freckles. The name tag under his police badge read A. BOONE.

"The person who investigated the death of Hannah Schneider," I said. "The St. Gallway teacher."

A. Boone continued to chew the coffee stirrer and stared at me. He was what Dad commonly called a "power distender," a person who seized the moment in which he/she possessed a marginal amount of power and brutally rationed it so it lasted an unreasonable amount of time.

"What's your business with Sergeant Harper?"

"There's been a grave error in judgment regarding the case," I said with authority. It was essentially the same thing Chief Inspector Ranulph Curry announced at the beginning of Chapter 79 in *The Way of the Moth* (Lavelle, 1911).

A. Boone took my name and told me to have a seat. I sat down in Dad's chair and Dad stood next to a dying plant. With a look of faux-interest and admiration (raised eyebrow, mouth turned down) he handed me a copy of *The Sheriff's Starr Bulletin*, Winter, Vol. 2, Issue 1, which he detached from the bulletin board behind him, along with a small sticker of an American Eagle crying an iridescent tear (America, United We Stand). In the section of the newsletter on p. 2, "Activity Report" (between Famous/Infamous and Bet You Didn't Know . . .) I read that Sergeant Detective Fayonette Harper, for the last five months, had made the greatest number of Fall Arrests in the entire department. Detective Harper's Fall Captures included Rodolpho Debruhl,

WANTED for murder; Lamont Grimsell, WANTED for robbery; Kanita Kay Davis, WANTED for welfare fraud, theft and receiving stolen property; and Miguel Rumolo Cruz, WANTED for rape and criminal deviant conduct. (In contrast, Officer Gerard Coxley had the lowest number of Fall Arrests: only Jeremiah Golden, WANTED for unauthorized use of a motor vehicle.)

Additionally, Sergeant Harper was featured in the black-and-white team photo of the Sluder County Sheriff's Dept. Baseball League on p. 4. She was standing on the right, at the very end, a woman with a sizable crooked nose, and all other features crowded around it as if trying to keep warm on her arctic white face.

Twenty-five, maybe thirty minutes later, I was sitting next to her.

*   *   *

"There's a mistake with the coroner's report," I announced with great conviction, clearing my throat. "The suicide ruling is wrong. You see, I was the person with Hannah Schneider before she walked into the woods. I know she wasn't going to go kill herself. She told me she was coming back. And she wasn't lying."

Sergeant Detective Fayonette Harper narrowed her eyes. With her salt-white skin and bristly lava hair, she was a harsh person to take in at close range; it was a swipe, whack, a kick in the teeth no matter how many times you looked at her. She had broad, doorknobbish shoulders and a way of always moving her torso at the same time as her head, as if she had a stiff neck.

If the Sluder County Sheriff's Department was the Primates section of any midlevel zoo, Sergeant Harper was obviously the lone monkey who chose to suspend disbelief and work as if her life depended on it. I'd already noticed she narrowed her eyes at everyone and everything, not only at me and A. Boone when he escorted me over to her desk at the back of the room ("All right," she said with no smile as I sat down, her version of "Hello!"), but she also narrowed her eyes at her TO BE FILED paper tray, the exhausted rubber-and-metal Hand Stress Reliever next to her keyboard, the sign taped above her computer monitor that read, "If you can see, look, and if you can look, observe," even at the two framed photographs on her desk, one of an elderly woman with cotton-hair and an eyepatch, the other of herself and what I assumed was her husband and daughter; in the photo they bookended her with identical long faces, chestnut hair and obedient teeth.

"And why do you say that," Sergeant Harper asked. Her voice was dull and low, a combination of rocks and oboe. (And that was how she asked questions, not bothering to hoist up her voice on the end.)

I repeated, for the most part, all that I'd told Officer Coxley in the Sluder County Hospital Emergency Room.

"I don't mean to be rude," I said, "or disrespectful to your–your systematized process of upholding the law, which you've been doing for years, probably quite effectively, but I don't think Officer Coxley wrote down the specifics of what I told him. And I'm a very pragmatic person. If I *thought* there was even the slightest chance of the suicide ruling being true, I'd accept it. But it's not feasible. First, as I said earlier, someone followed us from the camping ground. I don't know who it was, but I heard him. We both did. And second, Hannah wasn't in that kind of *mood.* She wasn't depressed—at least, not at *that* moment. I'll admit she had her moments of being down. But we all do. And when she left me, she was acting very sane."

Sergeant Harper hadn't moved a muscle. I became acutely aware (particularly from the way her eyes gradually drifted away from me before being jerked, by a certain emphatic word of mine, back to my face) she'd seen my type before. Housewives, pharmacists, dental hygienists, banking clerks, undoubtedly they'd all come to plead their cases, too, with their hands clenched, their perfumes rancid, their eyeliner skid-marking their eyes. They sat on the edge of the same uncomfortable red chair I was sitting on (which made woolly nonfigurative prints on the back of one's bare legs) and they wept, swore on a range of Bibles (Today's English, King James, Illuminated Family Edition) and graves (Grandma's, Pa-paw's, Archie who died young) that, whatever the charges against dear Rodolpho, Lamont, Kanita Kay and Miguel, it was lies, all lies.

"Obviously, I know how I sound," I tried, attempting to iron the twinges of desperation out of my voice. (I was slowly gathering Sergeant Harper didn't do twinges of desperation, nor did she do pangs of longing, worries to distraction or hearts broken beyond all possible repair.) "But I'm *positive* someone killed her. I know it. And I think she deserves for us to find out what really happened."

Harper thoughtfully scratched the back of her neck (as people do when they vehemently disagree with you), leaned to the left of her desk, pulled open a file cabinet and, narrowing her eyes, removed a green folder an inch thick. The labeled tab, I noted, read #5509–SCHN.

"Well," she said with a sigh, slapping the file on her lap. "We *did* account for the person you think you heard." She flipped through the papers—photocopied, typewritten forms, too small a font for me to make out—until she stopped on one, glancing through it. "Matthew and Mazula Church," she read slowly, frowning, "George and Julia Varghese, two Yancey County couples, were camping in the area at the same time as you and your peers. They stopped at Sugartop Summit around six, rested for an hour, decided to continue on to Beaver Creek two and a half miles away, arriving around eight-thirty. Matthew Church confirmed he was wandering the area looking for firewood when his flashlight went dead. He managed to make his way back to the site around eleven and they all went to bed." She looked at me. "Beaver Creek is less than a quarter of a mile from where we found her body."

"He said he saw Hannah and me?"

She shook her head. "Not exactly. He said he heard deer. But he'd had three beers and I'm not sure he knows what he saw or heard. It's a wonder he didn't find himself lost, too. But you probably heard him wandering around, crashing through the brush."

"Does he wear glasses?"

She thought about this for a moment. "I think he does." She frowned, scanning the paper. "Yes, here it is. Gold frames. He's nearsighted."

Something about the way she'd said that particular detail, *nearsighted*, made me think she was lying, but when I sat up imperceptibly and tried to glimpse where she was reading, she closed the file quickly and smiled, her thin, chapped lips pulling away from her teeth like tinfoil off a chocolate bar.

"I've been camping," she said. "And the truth is, when you're up there, you don't know *what* you're seeing. You came across her hanging there, am I right?"

I nodded.

"The brain dreams up things to protect itself. Four out of every five witnesses are completely unreliable. They forget things. Or later on, they think they saw things that weren't there. It's witness traumatization. Sure, I'll consider witness testimony, but in the end I can only consider what I can see in front of me. The facts."

I didn't hate her for not believing me. I understood. Because of all the Rodolphos, Lamonts, Kanita Kays and Miguels and other delinquents she caught red-handed wearing dirty underwear, watching cartoons, eating Cocoa Puffs, she assumed she knew everything there was to know about The

World. She had seen the bowels, the guts, the innards of Sluder County and thus no one could tell her anything she didn't already know. I imagined her husband and daughter found this frustrating, but they probably tolerated her, listened to her over a dinner of sliced ham and peas, all silent nods and supportive smiles. She looked at them and loved them, but noticed a chasm between them, too. They lived in Dream Worlds, worlds of homework, appropriate office conduct, unspoiled milk mustaches, but she, Fayonette Harper, lived in Reality. She knew the ins and outs, the tops and bottoms, the darkest, most mildewed corners.

I didn't know what else to say, how to convince her. I thought about standing up, knocking over the red chair and shouting, "This is a veritable outrage!" as Dad did when he was at a bank filling out a deposit slip and none of the ten pens at the Personal Banking Counter had ink. A middle-aged man always arrived out of the blue, zipping, buttoning, tucking in shirttails, palming wisps of antenna-hair off his forehead.

Sensing my frustration, Detective Harper reached out, touched the top of my hand, then abruptly sat back again. It was a gesture intended to be comforting but one that came off like putting a nickel in a casino slot machine. You could tell Sergeant Harper didn't know what to do with Tenderness or Femininity. She treated them like frilly sweaters someone had given her for a birthday that she didn't want to wear, yet couldn't throw away.

"I appreciate your efforts," she said, her whiskey-colored eyes seeing, looking, observing my face. "You know. Coming out here. Trying to talk to me. That's why I decided to see you. I didn't *have* to see you. The case is closed. I'm not authorized to discuss it with anyone but immediate family. But you came here out of worry, which was nice. The world *needs* nice. But I'll be straight with you. We have no doubts about what happened to your friend, Hannah Schneider. The sooner you accept it, the better."

Without saying anything more, she leaned across her desk, picked up a blank sheet of white paper and a ballpoint pen. In five minutes, she drew four tiny detailed drawings.

(I've often thought back to this moment, perpetually awed by the simple brilliance of Sergeant Harper. If only everyone, to prove a point, didn't resort to pushy words or aggressive action, but quietly took out a pen, blank paper and *drew* their reasons. It was shockingly persuasive. Unfortunately, I didn't notice this treasure for what it was, and didn't think to take her drawing with me when I left the station. Hence, I've had to draw my own approximations of what she sketched, so meticulously that, intentionally or not, what she'd drawn actually looked a little like Hannah [Visual Aid 26.0].)

"These here are the kinds of marks left on a body when you got a murder," Sergeant Harper said, pointing to the two sketches on the right side of the paper and glancing at me. "And you can't fake it. Say you decide to strangle someone. You'll leave a mark on the neck that's straight across like this one here. Think of it. The hands. Or say you use a rope to kill 'em. Same thing. Most of the time, it comes with bruising too, or fractured cartilage 'cause the perp'll use more force than necessary due to adrenalin."

She pointed to the other two drawings on the left.

"And this over here is how it looks when someone does it suicide. See? Rope's an upside-down V from the hanging position, the rope being pulled up. Usually there's no evidence of a struggle on the hands, fingernails or neck unless he had second thoughts. Sometimes they try to get out of it because it hurts so bad. See, most people don't do it right. Real hangings, like in the old days, you had to fall straight down, six to ten feet, and you cut straight through the spinal cord. But your average suicide, he'll do it off a chair with the rope tied to a ceiling beam or a hook, and he'll only fall two or three feet. It's not enough to sever the spine so he chokes to death. Takes a couple minutes. And that's how your friend Hannah did it."

"Is it possible to murder someone and have an upside-down V?"

Detective Harper leaned back in her chair. "It's possible. But unlikely. You'd have to have the person unconscious maybe. String them up that way.

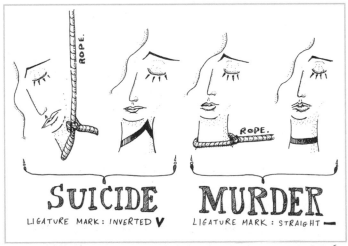

SUICIDE   MURDER
LIGATURE MARK: INVERTED V   LIGATURE MARK: STRAIGHT ▬

VISUAL AID 26.0

Else take them by surprise. Be a trained assassin like in the movies." She chuckled, then shot me a suspicious look. "That *didn't* happen."

I nodded. "She used an electrical cord?"

"It's fairly common."

"But she didn't have an electrical cord when I was with her."

"She probably had it in the pouch around her waist. There was nothing in it but a compass."

"What about a suicide note?"

"Didn't leave one. Not everyone does. People with no family usually don't. She was an orphan, after all. Grew up at the Horizon House, a group home for orphans in New Jersey. She had no one. Never did."

I was so surprised I couldn't immediately speak. Like an unexpected result in a Physics lab, this ruthlessly canceled out all I'd believed about Hannah. Of course, she'd had never told us anything about her past (apart from a few anecdotes, dangled like sausages in front of hungry dogs before snatching them away), and yet I'd assumed her childhood had been teeming with sailboats, lake houses and horses, a father with a pocket watch, a mother with bony hands who never left the house without her Face (a childhood that, funnily enough, overlapped my own mother's in my head).

I hadn't pulled such a past out of thin air—had I? No, the way Hannah lit cigarettes, put her profile on display like an expensive *vahze*, chaise-longued over everything, the way she idly picked out words for sentences as if choosing shoes—these details hinted, however loosely, she'd come from a privileged background. There was, too, all that rhetoric she'd droned on about at Hyacinth Terrace—"*It takes years to overturn this conditioning. I tried my whole life.*"—words symptomatic of "Waiting Room Righteousness," but also another one of Dad's phrases, "Bloated Plutocrat Guilt," perpetually "slipshod and short-lived." And even in Cottonwood, when Hannah had slipped into the Country Styles Motel, Room 22, after Doc, one could just have easily assumed she was entering a La Scala opera box for Mozart's *Così Fan Tutte* (1790), so straight her spine, so heiressesque the angle of her chin.

Sergeant Harper took my silence for grudging acknowledgment. "She tried it once before, too," she went on. "The exact same way. Electrical extension cord. Right in the woods."

I stared at her. "*When?*"

"Just before she left the home. When she was eighteen. Almost died."

Harper leaned forward so her big face hovered six inches from mine.

"*Now*"—she leaned in another inch, her voice raspy—"I've told you more than enough. And you got to listen. Time and again, I've seen innocent people get ruined by these things. And it's no good. Because it's not them that did it. It's between that person and God. So you got to go home, get on with life, not think about it. She was your friend and you want to help her. But I'll tell you, plain as day, she planned it all along. And she wanted the six of you there for it. You understand me?"

"Yes."

"Someone who would do that to innocent children isn't worth getting worked up over, understand?"

I nodded.

"Good." She cleared her throat, picked up Hannah's file and slid it into the filing cabinet.

*   *   *

A minute later, Dad and I were walking to the car. Heavy sun drooped over Main Street, made it a compost heap of mushy shadows falling off the hot cars hunched along the curb, and the spindly parking signs, and the bicycle dead on its side, chained to a bench.

"Everything's fine now, I trust?" he asked merrily. "Case closed?"

"I don't know."

"How did Big Red treat you?"

"She was nice."

"You two seemed to have a rather tantalizing conversation."

I shrugged.

"You know, I don't think I've ever seen a woman so obscenely orange in all my life. You suppose her hair naturally sprouts from her head that precise shade of carrots, or do you think it's a special kind of peroxide rinse one buys in the hope that it will temporarily blind people? A deliberate police weapon for her to use against the dissolute and depraved."

He was trying to make me laugh, but I only shaded my eyes and waited for him to unlock the car.

Justine

Hannah's Memorial Service, held the following Friday, April 16, was a sham. It was a Gallwanian ceremony, so naturally there was no coffin. On Tuesday, when Havermeyer announced the date of the service (also that we were free from class afterward, a Hannah Holiday) he further clarified in a voice with the unmistakable tone of an Epilogue or Afterword, that Hannah had been buried in New Jersey. (It was a dismal prospect. I'd never even heard Hannah say *New Jersey*.)

And so it was only us that day, the students, the faculty dressed in earth tones, the St. Gallway Choral Society (seventeen humdrum kids who'd recently tacked the word *Society* onto the end of their name in order to taste exclusivity) and St. Gallway's part-time chaplain, who wasn't Reverend Alfred Johnson, Preacher Johnson or Evangelist Johnson, but the spayed and sanitized *Mr.* Johnson. Supposedly he'd gone to divinity school, but "as what" nobody knew. He was a minister of indeterminate denomination, a truth Headmaster Havermeyer forbade him to disclose or even indirectly allude to during his Friday morning service, in order to avoid offending the one kid whose parents were Latter-Day Saints (Cadence Bosco). In the St. Gallway Admissions Catalogue, *Higher Learning, Higher Grounds*, the two-story stone chapel was described as a "sanctuary," technically unaffiliated with a particular religion (though during the holiday season, there were "secular tidings"). It was simply a "house of faith." Exactly which faith was anybody's guess. I doubt even *Mr.* Johnson knew. Mr. Johnson didn't wear a vicar's collar but khakis and short-sleeve polo shirts in forest green and royal blue, giving him the air of a golf caddy. And when he talked about a Higher Power, he used words like *gratifying*, *restorative* and *life-changing*. It was something that "got you through the tough times," which "any young person could manage with a little hard work, trust and tenacity." God was a trip to Cancun.

I sat with the seniors, second pew from the front, staring down at the play I'd brought with me, *A Moon for the Misbegotten* (O'Neill, 1943) in order to avoid any eye contact with the Bluebloods. Apart from Jade and Nigel (whose mother had dropped him off one morning directly in front of the Volvo—which I stalled leaving by unzipping and zipping my backpack until he disappeared inside Hanover), I hadn't seen the others a single time.

I'd heard tidbits of rumor: "I can't remember what I ever saw in Milton," said Macon Campins in AP English. "I was next to him in Biology and he totally doesn't look hot anymore." "Joalie broke up with him for that very reason," said Engella Grand. During Morning Announcements and lunch (occasions when I hoped to sneak a speedy look at one of them the way Dad and I had peeked inside the trailer of the world's smallest she-male at the Screamfest Fantasy Circus) they were nowhere to be found. I could only assume their parents had made some sort of arrangement with Mr. Butters and all five of them were attending rigorous morning and afternoon counseling sessions with Deb Cromwell. Deb, a short, yellow-complexioned woman, slow in movement and fatty in word (a walking wedge of Camembert) had made herself right at home in Hanover Room 109, erecting a variety of posters and cardboard displays. On my way to AP Calculus, as I darted past her room, I noticed, unless Mirtha Grazeley had wandered in (probably by accident, they said she often confused other rooms in Hanover with her office, including the Men's Room), Deb was always sitting in there alone, keeping herself occupied by paging through her own Depression pamphlets.

Now, behind us on the balcony, the Choral Society started to sing, "All Glory, laud, and honor," and the Bluebloods were still missing. I was just starting to presume, yet again, they were marooned in Deb Cromwell's office, Deb turning them on to the pleasures of Self-Acceptance and Letting Go, when Deb herself, a smile gooped onto her face, hastened into the chapel with Ms. Jarvis, the school nurse, lumping herself onto the end of a pew where Havermeyer was sitting with his wife, Gloria, so massively pregnant she looked like she'd been pinned to the ground by a boulder.

Then, I heard someone gasp—it was Donnamara Chase sitting behind me; she needed smelling salts—and most of the school, including a few teachers, swiveled around to watch the five of them saunter in, single file and self-loving (see *Abbey Road*, The Beatles, 1969). They were head to toe in black. Milton and Nigel looked like ninjas (one XS, the other XL), Leulah, in a long-skirted, high-necked chiffon number, looked vaguely vampiric. Jade was blatantly ripping off Jackie at Arlington (saucer-sized sunglasses on her head and a vintage black alligator handbag were stand-ins for the veil and John-John). Charles was the charred elephant bringing up the rear. He was in black, too, but the giant plaster cast on his left leg (ankle to upper thigh) jutted out like a giant ivory tusk. As he limped along with his crutches, glowering at the floor, disturbingly pasty and thin, his face wet with sweat (gold hair stuck in Os along his forehead like soggy Cheerios in a bowl) I felt sick—not because I wasn't with them or dressed in black (I hadn't thought about my outfit; I'd put on a stupid short floral thing), but because he looked so unlike that first time I'd seen him, when he tapped my shoulder during Morning Announcements back in the fall. He was a different person. If once he'd been a *Goodnight Moon* (Brown, 1947), now he was a *Where the Wild Things Are* (Sendak, 1963).

The Bluebloods wedged themselves into the row in front of me.

"We gather here today in this sacred haven both to grieve and to give thanks," began Mr. Johnson in the pulpit. He licked his lips as he paused to glance down at his papers. (He was always licking his lips; they were like potato chips, salty and addictive.) "Since our beloved Hannah Schneider left us over three weeks ago, throughout our community there have been resounding accolades, words of warmth and kindness, stories of how she affected our lives in ways both great and small. Today, we join together to give thankfulness for being blessed with such an extraordinary teacher and friend. We give thanks for her kindness, her humanity and caring, her courage in adversity and the overwhelming joy she brought to so many. Life is eternal and love is everlasting and death is nothing but a horizon and a horizon is nothing but the boundary of our sight."

Johnson went on and on, giving an equal amount of eye contact to every third of the congregation with the mechanized surety of a sprinkler system, most likely having learned this from a course, How to Give a Mesmerizing Sermon, with its concepts of Bringing Everyone In and Evoking a Feeling of Togetherness and Universal Humanity. The speech wasn't terrible, but it wasn't at all specific to Hannah. It was teeming with She Was a Lights and She Would Have Wanteds, mentioning nothing of her *real* life, a life, which Havermayer and the rest of the administration were now all deeply afraid of, as if they'd secretly discovered asbestos in Elton House or found out Christian Gordon, St. Gallway's Head Chef, had Hepatitis A. I could almost see the paper on the podium filled with (*Insert Deceased's Name Here*) (see www.123eulogy.com, #8).

When it was over, the Choral Society erupted, marginally off-key, into "Come Down O Love, Divine," and students began to spill out of the pews, smiling, laughing, loosening their ties, tightening their ponytails. I took my last contraband look at the Bluebloods, shocked at how still they sat, how stony their faces. They hadn't whispered or grimaced a single time during Johnson's speech, although Leulah, as if feeling my eyes on her, had abruptly turned her doilied face in my direction during Eva Brewster's Psalms Reading and, teeth clenched so her cheek dented, looked *straight* at me. (But then, almost immediately, she'd turned into one of those Highway Window Gazers; Dad and I would speed past them in the Volvo all the time, and they always stared past us, at something infinitely more interesting than our faces: the grass, the billboards, the sky.)

As Havermeyer made his way down the aisle, smiling a lead pipe smile with no joy behind it, rolling Gloria along next to him, and Mr. Johnson after her, jolly as Fred Astaire fox-trotting with one helluva girl ("Have a great day everybody!" he sang), without a word to anyone, chins held at the exact angle Hannah held hers while salsaing with her wineglass to Peggy Lee's "Fever" (or at dinner, pretending to be interested in one of their meandering stories), one by one, the Bluebloods rose and paraded down the aisle, disappearing into the bright bland day waiting for them.

*   *   *

I'd forgotten to tell Dad it was a half day, so I hurried down the deserted first floor of Hanover to use the pay phone.

"Olives," I heard someone shout behind me. "Wait up."

It was Milton. I wasn't exactly overjoyed at the prospect of chatting with him—who knew what sort of abuse I'd have to endure, unleashed by that tepid memorial service—but I forced myself to stand ground. "Never retreat unless death is certain," wrote Nobunaga Kobayashi in *How to Be a Shogun Assassin* (1989).

"Hey," he said with one of his sloth smiles.

I only nodded.

"How ya doin'?"

"Great."

He raised his eyebrows at this and shoved his big hands into his pockets.

Yet again, he took his Grand Ole Time with conversation. One Ming Dynasty rose and fell between the end of one sentence and the beginning of the next.

"I wanted to talk to you," he said.

I didn't say a *word*. Let the big ninja do the talking. Let *him* scrounge around for a few sentences.

"Well." He sighed. "I don't see how she coulda killed herself."

"Not bad, Quiet Man. Now why don't you tie that notion into a noose and see if it's strong enough to hang yourself?"

He looked stunned, maybe even flabbergasted. Dad said it was nearly impossible to flabbergast a person in this tawdry day and age, when "kinky sex was mundane," "a flasher in a trench coat in a public park, routine as cornfields in Kansas," but I think I'd done it to this kid—I really did. Obviously, he wasn't used to my tough ranchero tone of voice. Obviously, he wasn't used to the *new* Blue, Blue the Conqueror, the Hondo, King of the Pecos, Blue Steel, the feral Born to the West Blue, that Lucky Texan, that Lady from Louisiana, who shot from the hip, sat tall in the saddle and rode the lonely trail. (Obviously, he'd never read *Grit* [Reynolds, 1974]. It was what Buckeye Birdie said to Shortcut Smith.)

"Want to get the hell out of here?" Milton asked.

I nodded.

※   ※   ※

I suppose everyone has his/her Open Sesame, his/her Abracadabra or Presto Chango, the arbitrary word, event or unforeseen signal that knocks a person down, causes him/her to behave, either permanently or for the short term, out of the blue, contrary to expectation, from nowhere. A shade is pulled, a door creaks open, some kid goes from Geek to Glamour Boy. And Milton's Hocus-Pocus, his Master Key, happened to be a flowy sentence in Mr. Johnson's generic speech, a speech Dad would call "stirring as a wall of cinder blocks," indicative of the "Hallmark fever infecting our politicians and official spokesmen of late. When they speak, actual words don't emerge, but summer afternoons of draining sun and tepid breeze and chirping Tufted Titmice one would feel gleeful shooting with a handgun."

"When he said that thing about Hannah bein' like a flower," Milton said, "like a rose and all, I felt kinda moved." His big right arm lumber-rolled on top of the steering wheel as he edged the Nissan between the cars and out of the Student Parking Lot. "I couldn't stay angry 'bout what happened, 'specially not at my girl, Olives. I tried telling Jade and Charles it wasn't your fault, but they're not seein' straight."

He smiled. It was like one of those Viking ships in amusement parks, swerving up onto his face, dangling there for a few seconds nearly vertical to the ground, before swinging off again. Love, or more accurately, *infatuation* ("Take as much care with words expressing your sentiments as you will crafting your doctoral dissertation," Dad said.) was one of those no-good drifter emotions. After everything that happened, I didn't think I felt a *thing* for Milton, not anymore; I assumed my feelings had skipped town. But now he smiled, and there they were, those old sweaty sentiments slinking down the road again, waiting for me to acknowledge them by the bus station in a greasy wife-beater, cowboy hat, muscles frighteningly potholed and slick.

"Hannah told me I had to take you to her house when we got back from the camping trip. I figured we'd head over there, if you can handle it."

I glanced over at him, confused. "What?"

He let my words sit on the dock of the bay for at least thirty seconds before answering.

"Remember Hannah had those private conversations with each us hikin' up the mountain?"

I nodded.

"That's when she said it. I forgot about it 'til a couple of days ago. And now—"

"What did she say?"

" 'Take Blue to my house when you get back. Just the two of you.' She repeated it three times. Remember how crazy she was that day? Orderin' everyone around, screamin' off mountaintops? And when she said it, I didn't even recognize her. She was *mean*. Still, I laughed it off and said, 'I don't get it. You can have Blue over anytime.' Instead of answering directly, she only repeated the sentence. 'Take Blue to my house when you get back. You'll understand.' She made me swear I'd do it and that I wouldn't say anything to the others."

He switched on the radio. His shirtsleeves were rolled up to his elbows, so when he shifted gears, the cute burnt toes of the tattoo angel became visible like the edge of a seashell peeking out of sand.

"What was strange," he continued in his buffalo voice, "was that she said *you*. 'When *you* get back.' Not when *we* get back. Well, I've been thinking about the *you*. It can only mean one thing. She never planned to return with us."

"I thought you didn't think she committed suicide."

He seemed to tobacco-chew this for a minute, squinting in the sun, shoving down the sun visor. We were speeding along the highway now, barreling through the thickened sunshine and the limp-rag shadows of the trees standing stiffly on the shoulder of the road. They held their branches high in the air—as if they knew the answer to an important question, as if they hoped to be called on. The Nissan was old and as Milton shifted the gears it rattled like one of those famished motel beds one feeds quarters to, a bed I'd never seen firsthand, though Dad claimed he'd counted seven within a one-mile radius in Northern Chad. ("They don't have running water or bathrooms, but never fear, they have beds that buzz.")

"She was sayin' good-bye to us during those talks," he said, clearing his throat. "She told Leulah, 'Never be scared to cut your hair.' And Jade. She said, 'A lady should be a lady even when she removes her little black dress'— whatever the hell *that* means. She told Nigel to be himself, then somethin' about wallpaper. 'Change the wallpaper as much as you like and screw how much it costs. You're the one who has to live there.' And she said to me, before the thing about you, she said, 'You just might be an astronaut. You just might walk on the moon.' And Charles—no one knows what she said to him. He refuses to say. But Jade thinks she confessed she loved him. What'd she say to you?"

I didn't answer, because obviously Hannah hadn't said anything to me, not a single sentence of encouragement, however inscrutable and bizarre it sounded (no offense to Milton, but frankly, he didn't strike me as the astronaut type; it was dangerous for a kid that size to float through the shuttle at zero gravity).

"See, I don't want to believe suicide," he went on thoughtfully, "because it makes me feel stupid. In hindsight, though, it adds up. She was always alone. That *hair*cut. Then, there's what happened to the Smoke guy. And her thing for truckers who eat at Stuckey's. Shit. It was all just sittin' there. Obvious. And we didn't see it. How's it possible?"

He looked to me for help, but obviously I didn't have a decent answer. I watched his eyes ski down the front of my dress, stopping somewhere around my bare knees.

"Any idea why she'd want me to take you to her house? *Alone?*"

I shrugged, but the way he asked made me wonder if Hannah, after my flat-falling attempt to fix her up with Dad (mind you, that'd been B.C., or, before I knew about Cottonwood; A.C., or after Cottonwood, I'd sort of decided, for health reasons, she really wasn't Dad's dish), wanted to return the favor and had decided to tuck this sexy question mark of a sentence into Milton's breast pocket, thereby ensuring at some point, in the Big-Bang aftermath of the camping trip (it was a simple scientific principle: after explosions, new beginnings) we'd conveniently find ourselves together, alone, in her empty house. Maybe she'd caught wind of my fixation from Jade or Lu or had figured it out on her own, given my graceless behavior at dinner. (I wouldn't be surprised if all Fall and Winter Semester I'd had bird-nervous eyes: at Milton's slightest movement, instantly airborne.)

"Hopefully, she left you a suitcase full of cash," Milton said, smiling lazily. "And maybe if I'm nice, you'll split it with me."

*   *   *

As we approached Hannah's house, slipping past the pastures, the quiet barns, the horses waiting like men in bus stations (the sun had cemented their hooves to the grass), the corkscrew tree, that little patch of hill where Jade always floored the Mercedes so the car flew over the top and our stomachs flipped like pancakes, I told Milton my account of what happened on the mountain. (As with Jade, I omitted the section where I found Hannah dead.)

When he asked me what I thought Hannah was going to tell me, why she'd led me away from the campground, I lied and said I didn't have a clue.

Well, it wasn't exactly a lie. I *didn't* know. But it wasn't as if I hadn't outlined, in the middle of the night, in meticulous detail, in the library silence of my room, on my Citizen-Kane desk (switching out my light if I heard Dad skulking around the stairs to make sure I was asleep), the Infinite Possibilities.

After laying some groundwork, I'd concluded there were two generalized schools of thought arising from this mystery. (This wasn't including the possibility Milton had just disclosed, that Hannah might have wanted to hand me a few lukewarm good-byes—that one day I'd be strolling Mars, or that I shouldn't hesitate to repaint my house in a flamboyant color since I was the one who lived there—stale, crumbly, oyster-cracker phrases she could have easily said to me as we hiked the trail. No, I'd have to assume what Hannah wanted to tell me was entirely different, more vital than anything she'd whispered to the Bluebloods.)

The first school of thought then, was that Hannah wished to confess something to me. It was an attractive idea, considering her hoarse voice, moth-moving eyes, the fitful starts and stops of her sentences as if she were operated by sporadic electricity. And *what* she wanted to confess could be any number of things, ranging from the crass to the crazy—her Cottonwood habit, for example, or an accidental affair with Charles, or that somehow she'd managed to kill Smoke Harvey; or perhaps she'd cultivated (another one of Jade's shot put accusations, flung out with all her might, then forgotten as she strolled back to the locker room for stretches) a secret association with the Manson Family. (Incidentally, I still had Hannah's copy of *Blackbird Singing in the Dead of Night* stored in a bottom desk drawer. My heart had stopped when I'd overheard Dee mention in second period Study Hall that Hannah had asked her Intro to Film class if anyone had removed a book from her desk. "Some bird book," Dee said with a shrug.)

If *this* thesis was true—that Hannah had hoped to disclose a secret—I could only surmise she chose me to confess to, over say, Jade or Leulah, because I looked unthreatening. Maybe she sensed, too, I'd read all of Scobel Bedlows Jr., his essays on judgments; basically, you weren't allowed to have any so long as "devastation was directed inwards, at yourself, never other people or animals" (see *When to Stone*, Bedlows, 1968). Hannah also seemed to have had an innate understanding of Dad and perhaps she figured I was already a highly forgiving person, that I did my best to treat shortcomings like hobos I'd found dozing on my porch: take them in and maybe they'll work for you.

The second school of thought, and obviously the more disturbing one, was that Hannah wanted to disclose a secret All About Me.

I was the only one, out of all of them, who hadn't washed ashore and been collected by Hannah after some tempest of a home life. I'd never run off with an old Turk, tried to throw my arms around the torso of a trucker (and strained to touch my hands together on the other side), suffered a street-life blackout, had a parent who was a junkie or in maximum-security prison. I wondered if Hannah knew a secret that revealed me to be like them.

What If Dad really wasn't my dad, for example? What If he'd found me like some penny on a public promenade? What If Hannah was my real mother who'd given me up for adoption because no one wanted to get married in the late eighties; everyone wanted to go roller-skating and wear shoulder pads? Or What If I had a fraternal twin named Sapphire who was everything I wasn't—gorgeous, athletic, funny and tan with a carefree laugh, blessed not with an Osmium Dad (the heaviest metal known to man) but a

Lithium Mom (the lightest) who slaved not as a vagabond professor and essayist, but was simply a waitress in Reno?

Such paranoid What Ifs caused me, on more than a few occasions, to run downstairs into Dad's study and quietly rummage through his legal pads, his unfinished essays and faded notes for *The Iron Grip*, to stare at the photographs: the picture of Natasha at the piano, and the one of her and Dad, standing outside on a lawn in front of a badminton net, holding racquets, arms pretzeled, wearing antique outfits and expressions that made them look as if it was 1946 and they'd survived a World War, rather than the year it *really* was, 1986, and they were surviving the Brat Pack and Weird Al.

These frail photographs cordoned off my past again, made it staunch and impermeable. I did, however, venture asking Dad a few off-hand yet probing questions, and Dad responded with a laugh.

Dad, on Secret Bastard Siblings: "Don't tell me you've been reading *Jude the Obscure*."

Milton had no further light to shed on this conundrum—why Hannah had singled me out, why I wasn't with them when Charles, trying to ascend a jutting rock promontory in order to get a sense of direction, perhaps spot an electrical tower or a skyscraper sign for a Motel 6, "fell down this Grand Canyon sorta thing and started to yell so loud we thought he was bein' stabbed." After I finished telling Milton the remainder of my story, which had drooled a little into my confrontation with Jade in Loomis, he only shook his head in bewilderment and said nothing.

By then we were inching down Hannah's deserted drive.

*   *   *

For lack of a better plan—embarrassingly inspired by Jazlyn Bonnoco's *Fleet Book Evidence* (1989)—I suggested to Milton, maybe Hannah wanted us to find a clue in her house, a treasure map or old letters of blackmail and fraud—"something to tell us about the camping trip or her death," I explained—we decided to peruse her possessions as discreetly as we could. And Milton read my mind: "Let's start with the garage, huh?" (I suspected we were both afraid to enter the actual house, for fear we'd find some specter version of her.) The wooden one-car garage, standing a decent distance from the house with a flabby roof, crusty windows, looked like a giant matchbox that'd been in someone's pocket too long.

I'd been worried about what had happened to the animals, but Milton said Jade and Lu, who'd hoped to adopt them, found out they'd gone to live with Richard, one of Hannah's coworkers from the animal shelter. He lived on a llama farm in Berdin Lake, north of Stockton.

"It's fuckin' sad," Milton said, pushing open the side door to the garage. "Because now they're gonna be like that dog."

"What dog?" I asked, glancing at Hannah's front porch as I followed him inside. There was no POLICE LINE DO NOT CROSS tape on the door, no immediate sign anyone had been there. "Old Yeller?"

He shook his head and switched on the light. Neon light spilled through the hot, rectangular room. There wasn't space for two tires, much less an entire *car*, which explained why Hannah always parked the Subaru in front of the house. Heaps of furniture—blistered lamps, injured armchairs, carpets, chairs—not to mention a few cardboard boxes and random camping gear—had been brutally tossed on top of each other like bodies in an open grave.

"*You* know," Milton said, stepping around one of the boxes. "In *The Odyssey*. The one always waitin' for his master."

"Argos?"

"Yeah. Poor old Argos. He dies, doesn't he?"

"You want to stop please? You're making me . . ."

"What?"

"Depressed."

He shrugged. "Hey, don't mind me."

* * *

We dug.

And the longer we dug, through backpacks, boxes, armoires and armchairs (Milton was still fixated on his suitcase-full-of-cash idea, though now he figured Hannah could have stuffed the unmarked bills into seat cushions and goose-down pillows), the more the experience of digging (Milton and I, cast as unlikely Leading Man and Woman) became sort of electrifying.

Scrutinizing those chairs and lamp shades, something began to happen: I started to imagine myself a woman named Slim, Irene or Betty, a dame who wore penciled skirts, a cone bra, had zigzag hair over an eye. Milton was the disillusioned tough-guy with a fedora, bloody knuckles and a temper.

"*Yep*, just makin' sure the old girl didn't leave us somethin'," Milton sang cheerfully as he gutted an orange couch cushion with the Swiss Army knife he'd found an hour ago. "No stone unturned. Because I'd hate her to be an Oliver Stone movie."

I nodded, opening an old cardboard box. "If you end up a well-publicized mystery," I said, "you no longer belong to yourself. Everyone steals you and turns you into anything they want. You become their cause."

"Uh huh." Thoughtfully, he stared down at the cottage-cheesed foam. "I hate open-ended stuff. Like Marilyn Monroe. What the hell *happened?* Was she gettin' too close to somethin' and the president had to shut her up? That seems *crazy*. That people can just take a life, like it's—"

"Free fruit."

He smiled. "*Yeah*. But then maybe it *was* an accident. Stars align a crazy way. Death happens. Could just as well've been the lottery or a broken leg. Or maybe she had a thought that she couldn't go on. We all have thoughts like that, only she decided to act on hers. She forces herself to. Because she thinks that's what she deserves. And maybe seconds later she knows she was wrong. Tries to save herself. But it's too late."

I stared at him, unsure if he was talking about Marilyn or Hannah.

"S'how it always is." He was setting aside the seat cushion, picking up an ashtray and turning it over, staring at the bottom of it. "You never know if there's a conspiracy or it's just how things unravel, the—I don't know, one of . . ."

"Life's hairball pincurves."

His mouth was open, but he didn't go on, apparently floored by a Dadism I'd always thought kind of irritating (it was a sentence you could find in his *Iron Grip* notes if you were patient enough to sit through his handwriting). He pointed at me.

"That's good, Olives. *Very* good."

I criss-crossed, detoured, fell out of the past.

After two hours of searching, although we'd found no *direct* clue, Milton and I had managed to dig up all kinds of different Hannahs—sisters, cousins, fraternal twins, stepchildren to the one we'd known. There was Haight-Asbury Hannah (old records of Carole King, Bob Dylan, a bong, tai chi books, a faded ticket to some peace rally at Golden Gate Park on June 3, 1980), Stripper Hannah (I didn't feel comfortable going through *that* box, but Milton exhumed bras, bikinis, a zebra-striped slip, a few more complicated items requiring directions for assembly), also Hand Grenade Hannah (combat boots, more knives), also Hannah, Missing Person Possessed (the same folder full of Xeroxed newspaper articles Nigel had found, though he'd lied about there being "fifty pages at *least*"; there were only nine). My favorite, however, was Madonna Hannah who material-girled out of a sagging cardboard box.

Beneath a raisined basketball, among nail polish, dead spiders and other junk, I found a faded photograph of Hannah with cropped, spiky red hair and brilliant purple eye shadow painted all the way to her eyebrows. She was singing onstage, a microphone in hand, wearing a yellow plastic miniskirt, beetle-green-and-white striped tights and a black corset made from either garbage bags or used tires. She was midnote, so her mouth was *wide* open — you could possibly pop a chicken egg in there and it'd disappear.

"Holy fuck," Milton said, staring down at the photograph.

I turned it over, but there was nothing written on it, no date.

"It's her isn't it?" I asked.

"Hell yeah, it's her. Shit."

"How old do you think she is?"

"Eighteen? Twenty?"

Even with boy-short red hair, clown-like makeup, eyes wincing due to the angry look crashing through her face, she was still gorgeous. (Guess that's absolute beauty for you: like Teflon, impossible to deface.)

*   *   *

After I found the photograph and looked through the last cardboard box, Milton said it was time for the house.

"Feelin' good, Olives? On your game?"

He knew about an extra set of keys under the geranium pot on the porch, and jamming the key into the dead bolt, suddenly his left hand reached back and found my wrist, squeezing it, letting go (a bland gesture one did with a stress ball; still, my heart leapt, did an agitated "Ahh," then fainted).

We crept inside.

Surprisingly, it wasn't frightening — not in the least. In fact, in Hannah's absence, the house had taken on the solemn properties of a lost civilization. It was Machu Picchu, a piece of ancient Parthian Empire. As Sir Blake Simbel writes in *Beneath the Blue* (1989), his memoir detailing the *Mary Rose* excavation, lost civilizations were never frightening, but fascinating, "reserved and riddle-filled, a gentle testament to the endurance of earth and objects over human life" (p. 92).

After I left a message for Dad telling him I had a ride home, we excavated the living room. In some ways, it was like seeing it for the first time, because without the distractions of Nina Simone or Mel Tormé, without Hannah herself gliding around in her worn-out clothing, I was able to really see things: in the kitchen, the blank notepad and ballpoint pen (BOCA RATON it read in fading gold) positioned under the 1960s phone (the same spot and type of notepad on which Hannah supposedly had scrawled *Valerio*, though there were no exciting indentations on the page I could shade over with light pencil—as TV detectives do so effectively). In the dining room, the room where we'd eaten a hundred times, there were actually objects Milton and I had never seen before: in the big wooden and glass display case behind Nigel and Jade's chairs, two hideous porcelain mermaids and a Hellenistic Terracotta female figure, approximately six inches tall. I wondered if Hannah had just received them as gifts a few days prior to the camping trip, but judging by the thick dust, they'd been there for months.

And then, from the VCR in the living room, I ejected a movie, *L'Avventura*. It was fully rewound.

"What's that?" Milton asked.

"An Italian movie," I said. "Hannah was teaching it in her film class." I handed it to him and picked up the video box, alone on the coffee table. I scanned the back.

"Laventure?" Milton asked uncertainly, staring down at the tape with his mouth pushed to the side. "What's it about?"

"A woman who goes missing," I said. My words made me shiver a little.

Milton nodded and then, with a frustrated sigh, tossed the videotape onto the couch.

We combed the remaining rooms downstairs, but found no revolutionary relics—no drawings of bison, aurochs or stags from flint, wood or bone, no carving of Buddha, no crystal reliquary or steatite casket from the Mauryan Empire. Milton suggested Hannah might have kept a diary, so we made our way upstairs.

Her bedroom was unchanged from the last time I'd seen it. Milton checked her bedside and vanity table (he found my copy of *Love in the Time of Cholera*, which Hannah had borrowed and never returned) and I did a quick tour of the bathroom and closet, finding those things Nigel and I had exhumed: the nineteen bottles of pills, the framed childhood photos, even the knife collection. The only thing I *didn't* find was that other schoolgirl picture, the one of Hannah with the other girl in uniforms. It wasn't where I thought Nigel had put it—in the Evan Picone shoe box. I looked for it in some of the other boxes along the shelf, but after the fifth one, I gave up. Either Nigel had put it back somewhere else, or Hannah had moved it.

"I've lost steam," Milton said, leaning against the part of Hannah's bed where I was sitting. He tilted his head back so it was less than an inch from my bare knee. A strand of his black hair actually slipped off his sticky forehead and *touched* my bare knee. "I can smell her. That perfume she wore."

I looked down at him. He looked like Hamlet. And I'm not talking about the Hamlets enamored with the language, the ones always thinking ahead to the upcoming sword fight or where to stress the line (Get *thee* to a nunnery, Get thee to a *nunn*ery), not the Hamlet worried about how well his tunic fits or whether he can be heard in the back. I'm talking about the Hamlets who actually start to wonder if they should be, or *not* be, the ones who are bruised by Life's Elbows, Kidney Punches, Head Butts and Bites on the Ear, the ones who, after the final curtain, can barely speak, eat or take off their stage makeup with cold cream and cotton balls. They go home and do a lot of staring at walls.

"Goddamn miserable," he said almost inaudibly to the overhead light. "Guess we should go home. Forget this stuff. Call it a day."

I let my left hand fall off my bare knee so it touched the side of his face. It had a dampness to it, a humidity of basements. Immediately, his eyes slipped onto me and I must have had an Open Sesame look on my face because he grabbed me and pulled me down onto his lap. His big sticky hands covered both sides of my head like earphones. He kissed me as if biting into fruit. I kissed him back, pretending to bite into peaches and plums—nectarines, I didn't know. I think I also made funny noises (egret, loon). He gripped my shoulders, as if I was the sides of a carnival ride and he didn't want to fall out.

I'd imagine it occurred a great deal during excavations.

Yes, I'd wager quite a bit of money that more than a few hips, knees, feet, and bottoms have rubbed up against royal sepulchres in the Valley of the Kings, hearth remains in the Nile Valley, Aztec portrait beakers on an island in Lake Texcoco, that a lot of fast, rabbity sex transpires on Babylonian-dig cigarette breaks and Bog Mummy examination tables.

Because, after a strenuous dig with your trowel, your pickax, you've seen that sweaty compatriot of yours from every critical angle (90, 60, 30, 1), also in a variety of lights (flashlight, sun, moon, halogen, firefly) and all of a sudden you're overwhelmed with the feeling that you under*stand* the person, the way you understand stumbling upon the lower jaw and all the teeth of *Proconsul Africanus* meant not only that the History of Human Evolution would be transformed, forever afterward mapped with a little more detail, but also that your name would be up there with Mary Leakey's. You, too, would be world renowned. You, too, would be entreated to write lengthy articles in *Archaeological Britain*. You feel as if this person next to you was a glove you'd managed to turn inside out, and you could see all the little strings and the torn lining, the hole in the thumb.

Not that we did It, mind you, not that we had blank-faced handshake sex rampant among America's twitchy youths (see "Is Your Twelve-Year-Old a Sex Fiend?", *Newsweek*, August 14, 2000). We did take off our clothes, however, and roll around like logs. His angel tattoo said hello to more than a few freckles on my arm and back and side. We scratched each other accidentally, our bodies blunt and mismatched. (No one tells you about the frank lighting or lack of mood music.) When he was on top of me, he looked calm and inquisitive, as if he were lying at the edge of a swimming pool, staring at something shiny at the bottom, contemplating diving in.

I will thus confess a stupid truth regarding this encounter. For a minute afterward, lying on Hannah's bed with him, my head on his shoulder, my skinny white arm garlanding his neck, when he said, wiping his drenched forehead, "Is it fuckin' hot in here or is it me?" and I said without thinking, "It's me," I sort of felt—well, fan*tastic*. I felt as if he was my American in Paris, my Brigadoon. ("Young love come like roseth petals," writes Georgie Lawrence in his last collection, *So Poemesque* [1962], "and like lightning boltheth flees.")

"Tell me about the streets," I said softly, staring at Hannah's ceiling, square and white. Then I was horrified: without thought, the sentence had drifted out of my mouth like a boat Victorian people float around on with parasols, and he hadn't immediately answered so obviously I'd blown things. That was the problem with the Van Meers; they always wanted more, had to dig deeper, get dirtier, doggedly cast their fishing line in the river over and over again, even if they only caught dead fish.

But then he answered, yawning: "Streets?"

He didn't continue, so I swallowed, my heart on the edge of its seat.

"I just meant . . . when you were involved with your . . . *gang*—you don't have to talk about it if you don't want to."

"I'll talk about anythin' with you," he said.

"Oh. Well . . . you ran away from home?"

"No. You?"

"No."

"*Wanted* to on plenty of occasions, but I never did."

I was confused. I'd been expecting shifty eyes, words jamming in his throat like coins in a faulty pay phone.

"But then how did you get your tattoo?" I asked.

He turned his right shoulder around and stared at it, the corners of his mouth plunging down. "My older bro, fuckin' John. His eighteenth birthday. He and his friends took me to a tattoo parlor. Total shithole. We both got tattoos, only he royally fucked me, because *his*, freakin' salamander, is *this big*"—he displayed the width of a blueberry in his fingers—"an' he talked me into getting *this monster* motherfuckin' can of worms. You shoulda seen my mom's face." He chuckled, remembering. "Never seen her so pissed. It was *classic*."

"But how old are you?"

"Seventeen."

"Not twenty-one?"

"Uh, not unless I fell into a coma."

"You never lived on the streets?"

"What?" He scrunched up his face like he had sun in his eyes. "I can't even sleep on those fuckin' couches at Jade's. I like my own bed, Sealy Posturepedic or whatever—hey, what's with the questions?"

"But Leulah," I persisted, my voice crashing out of my mouth now, determined to hit something. "When she was thirteen she ran away with a–a Turkish math teacher and he was arrested in Florida and he went to jail."

"*What?*"

"And Nigel's parents are in prison. That's why he has a preoccupation with suspense novels and is vaguely pathological—he doesn't feel guilt and Charles was adopted—"

"You can't be serious." He sat up, looking down at me like I was *loco*. "Nigel feels stuff. He still feels bad for ditchin' that kid last year, what's his name, sits next to you in Mornin' Announcements and second of all, Charles is *not* adopted."

I frowned, feeling that vague sense of irritation when tabloid stories turned out not to be true. "How do you know? Maybe he just never said anything."

"Ever met his mom?"

I shook my head.

"They could be brother and sister. And Nigel's parents aren't in *prison*. Jesus. Who told you that?"

"But what about his *real* parents?"

"His *real* parents own that pottery place—Diana and Ed—"

"They didn't serve time for shooting a police officer?"

That particular claim made Milton guffaw (I'd never heard a real guffaw, but what he did was definitely one) and then, seeing I was serious and more than a little worked up—blood was rushing into my cheeks; I'm sure I was red as a carnation—he lay back and rolled toward me so the bed went *ugh*, and his puffy lips and eyebrows and the tip of his nose (on which stood, rather heroically, a freckle) were inches from my own.

"Who told you this stuff?"

When I didn't answer, he whistled.

"Whoever he is, he's a nut case."

Quer pasticciaccio brutto de via Merulana

"I do not believe in madness," Lord Brummel notes dryly at the end of Act IV in Wilden Benedict's charming play about the sexual depravity of the British upper class, A Bev'y of Ladies (1898). "It's too uncouth."

I agreed.

I believed in the madness of destitution, drug-induced madness, also Dictator Dementia and Wartime Whacked (with its tragic subsets, Frontline Fever, Napalm Non Compos Mentis). I could even confirm the existence of Checkout-Aisle Crackers, which abruptly afflicts an ordinary, unassuming person standing behind a man with seventy-five exotic grocery items, none of which sport price tags, but I did *not* buy Hannah's madness, even though she had the hair for it, had killed or hadn't killed herself, had slept or hadn't slept with Charles, had picked up strange men and shamelessly fashioned lavish lies out of the plain cotton histories of the Bluebloods.

Thinking about it, I felt dizzy, because it'd been such a classy con; she'd been Yellow-Kid Nickel, the most acclaimed confidence man in history, and I'd been the easy mark, the fall guy, the unwitting casino.

"If Jade rode a *mile* in some cruddy eighteen-wheeler then I'm Elvis reincarnated," Milton said as he drove me home.

Naturally, I now felt dim for believing her. It was true. Jade wouldn't go fifty feet unless there was fur, silk or fine Italian leather involved. Sure, the girl disappeared into handicapped stalls with men who had faces like busted-up Buicks, but that was simply her brand of thrill, her bump of cocaine at fifteen minutes a pop. She wouldn't ride out of the parking lot with one of them, much less into a sunset. I'd also completely overlooked how much the girl shirked responsibility. She had trouble dropping a History class. "Can't deal with the paperwork," she said, the paperwork being a slip of paper requiring three lines to be filled out.

When I admitted to Milton Hannah had told me these stories, he declared her certifiable.

"In your defense, I see how you'd believe her," he said, stopping the Nissan by my front door. "If she told me that story about myself, that I'd joined a gang—hell, that my parents were aliens—I'd probably believe it. She made everythin' real." He hooked his fingers on the steering wheel. "So that's it, I guess. Hannah was bojangled. Never woulda guessed it. I mean, why go through the trouble to invent that shit?"

"I don't know," I said grimly as I climbed from the car.

He blew me a kiss. "See you Monday? You. Me. A movie."

I nodded and smiled. He drove away.

And yet, as I made my way upstairs to my room, I realized that in my life, if I'd known someone certifiable, it wouldn't be Hannah Schneider. No, it'd be June Bug Kelsea Stevens whom I caught in Dad's bathroom having a conversation with herself in the mirror ("You look *mar*velous. No, *you* look marvelous. No, *you* loo—how long have you been standing there?") or even June Bug Phyllis Mixer who treated her skittish Standard Poodle like a ninety-year-old grandmother ("Up-see-daisies. Good girl. That too much sun for you? No? What would you like for lunch, honey? Oh, you want my sandwich."). And poor June Bug Vera Strauss, whom Dad and I found out later had been manic for years—looking back, she'd had actual signs of lunacy: her eyes were severely depressed (literally, into her face) and when she talked to you, there was something scary about it, as if she were actually addressing a ghost or some sort of poltergeist hovering just behind your left shoulder.

No, in spite of mounting evidence to the contrary, I didn't believe that was the trapdoor out of the maze—that Hannah Schneider was simply nutty as a fruitcake. Any professor worth his salt would throw out that sort of essay, if some kid dared to turn in such an ill-considered, hackneyed Thesis. No, I'd read *The Return of the Witness* (Hastings, 1974) *and* its sequel and I'd *watched* Hannah; I'd seen how she'd marched so assuredly up that trail (there'd been a discernible jaunt in her step) and she'd shouted off that mountaintop with conviction, *not* despair (there were vast differences in a voice's timbre between those emotions).

There had to be another reason.

In my room, I threw down my backpack and removed the materials I'd filched from Hannah's house from the front of my dress and my shoe. I hadn't wanted Milton to know I was swiping things. I'd started to feel more than a little embarrassed by the way my mind was working. He'd said, "Look who's sleuthin'," "Olives' got her sleuth on," "That's so *sleuthy*, baby," six times and it'd sounded less and less cute the more he said it, and so, when we climbed into his Nissan I'd said I'd left my birthstone necklace on the bureau in Hannah's garage (I didn't have, nor had I ever had, a birthstone necklace) and while he waited, I ran inside and grabbed those materials I'd already set aside in the cardboard box in the back corner. I shoved the thin folder of Missing Person articles down my dress so it was pressed around my waist, put the photograph of Hannah with the spiky rockstar hair into my shoe, and when I climbed back into the car and he said, "Got it?" I grinned, pretending to zip it into the front pocket of my backpack. (He wasn't the most perceptive person; I sat stiffly the entire ride home as if perched on pinecones and he didn't bat an eye.)

Now, I switched on the bedside lamp and opened the manila folder.

The shock with which the revelation came to me wasn't because the idea was particularly intricate or inspired, but because it was so excitingly *obvious*, I hated myself for not considering it sooner. I read the newspaper articles first (Hannah appeared to have gone to a library and photocopied them from grainy microfiche): two from *The Stockton Observer* dated September 19, 1990, and June 2, 1979, "Search for Missing Backpacker Underway," "Roseville Girl, 11, Found Unhurt," respectively; another from *The Knoxville Press*, "Missing Girl Reunited with Father, Mother Charged"; one from Tennessee's *Pineville Herald-Times*, "Missing Boy Prostituted," and finally "Missing Woman Found in VT, Using Alias," from *The Huntley Sentinel*.

I then read the last page, the book excerpt, which concluded the story of Violet May Martinez, the day she disappeared from the Great Smoky Mountains on August 29, 1985.

97.

the group was one person short. Violet was nowhere to be found.

Mike Higgis searched the parking lot and questioned strangers who'd parked there, but no one had seen her. After an hour, he contacted the National Park Service. The Park immediately launched a search, closing the area from Blindmans Bald to Burnt Creek. Violet's father and sister were notified and they brought Violet's clothes so the search dogs could identify her smell.

Three German Shepherds tracked Violet to a single spot by

a paved road, 1.25 miles from the last place Violet was seen. The road led to U.S. 441 leading out of the Park.

Ranger Bruel told Violet's father, Roy Jr., that could mean Violet made her way there and was picked up by someone in a vehicle. She also could have been abducted against her will.

Roy Jr. rejected the idea Violet had planned her disappearance. She did not have a credit card or identification with her. She had taken no money from her checking or savings accounts prior to the trip. She was also looking forward to her 16th birthday the following week at Roller-Skate America.

Roy Jr. tipped the police off to a potential suspect. Kenny Franks, 24, released January 1985 from a correctional institution for violence and theft, had seen Violet at the mall and become infatuated. He'd been spotted at Besters High and harassed Violet with phone calls. Roy Jr. contacted the police and Kenny left her alone, though his friends reported he still was obsessed with her.

"Violet said she hated him, but she still wore the necklace he gave her," said her best friend Polly Elms.

Police investigated the possibility of Kenny Franks having a hand in her disappearance, but sources testified on Aug. 25 he'd been working all day as a busboy at Stagg Mill Bar & Grill and was cleared of suspicion. Three weeks later he moved to Myrtle Beach, S.C. Police investigated if he was in contact with Violet, but no evidence to support this claim ever emerged.

A Final Enigma

The search for Violet ended September 14, 1985. With 812 searchers, including Park Personnel, Rangers, the National Guard and FBI, no further leads in her disappearance came to light.

On October 21, 1985, at Jonesville Nations Bank in Jonesville, Florida, a black-haired woman tried to cash a check from Violet's checking account, made payable to "Trixie Peanuts." When the teller informed the woman she'd have to deposit the check and wait for it to clear, the woman left with it and never returned. The bank teller, when presented with a picture of Violet, was unable to confirm it was she. The woman was never seen in Jonesville again.

Roy Jr. swore his daughter would never have cause to disappear from her life. Her friend Polly thought otherwise.

"She was always talking about how much she hated Besters and hated being a Baptist. She got good grades so I think she could plan it so people thought she was dead. That way they'd stop looking for her and she'd never have to come back."

Seven years later, Roy Jr. still thinks of Violet every day.

"I put it with God now. 'Trust in the Lord with all your heart,' " he quotes from Proverbs 3:5, 6, " 'and lean not on your own understanding.' "

All of the articles in the folder were not merely concerning Missing Persons, but disappearances that had appeared to have been staged—definitively, in the case of the *Huntley Sentinel* article, which detailed the vanishing of a fifty-two-year-old woman, Ester Sweeney of Huntley, New Mexico, married to her third husband, Milo, and owing over $800,000 in back taxes and credit card bills. Police ultimately concluded she'd ransacked her home, slashed her kitchen screen and her own right arm (her blood was found in the foyer) in order to make it look like a violent break-in. She was found three years later in Winooski, Vermont, living under an assumed name and married to her fourth husband.

The other articles were more informative, detailing police procedures, a National Park abduction, search methods. The Missing Backpacker article specified the ways the National Guard conducted a search of Yosemite: "Rangers, after screening search-and-rescue volunteers for physical fitness, employed a grid system, assigning each group sequential areas of the Glacier Point area to sweep."

I couldn't *believe* it. And yet it wasn't unheard of; according to the *Almanac of American Strange Habits, Tics and Behaviors* (1994 ed.) one in every 4,932 United States citizens planned their own kidnapping or death.

Hannah Schneider had not meant to die, but to disappear.

Somewhat sloppily (and it wasn't exactly meticulous work; if she'd been a Doctoral Candidate her advisor would've reprimanded her for lethargy), Hannah had compiled these articles as exploratory research before she made a break for it, took it on the lam, copped a sneak, polished off her former life like a button-man did a squealer.

Anjelica Soledad de Crespo, a pseudonym for the drug-trafficking heroine of Jorge Torres's stirring nonfiction portrait of the Pan-American narcotics cartel, *For the Love of Corinthian Leather* (2003), fed up with *la vida de las drogas*, had designed a similar death for herself, though she'd ventured to La Gran Sabana in Venezuela and appeared to tumble over a thousand-foot falls. Nine months prior to the supposed accident, a boat of nineteen Polish tourists had gone over in the same fashion—three of the corpses were never recovered due to the powerful undercurrents at the waterfall's base, which held the bodies under in a vicious spin cycle until they were ripped to shreds, then devoured by crocodiles. Anjelica was declared dead within forty-eight hours. The truth was, she'd slipped out of her rowboat, making her way to the scuba gear planted for her on a convenient rock formation, which she'd donned and, fully submerged, swam the four miles to a location upriver where her handsome lover, Carlos, originally from El Silencio in Caracas, awaited her in a tricked-out silver Hummer. They hightailed it to an uninhabited section of the Amazon, somewhere in Guyana, where they still live.

I stared at the ceiling, racking my brain to recover every detail from that night. Hannah had changed into heavier clothes while we were eating dinner. When she came to find me in the woods, she wore a satchel around her waist. As she led me away, she'd known exactly where she was going because she'd walked resolutely, checking the map and compass. She'd intended to tell me something, a confession of some kind, then abandon me. Using the compass, she'd intersect with a predetermined trail, which would lead to one of the minor Park roads, then to U.S. 441 and a campground where a car awaited her (perhaps it was Carlos in a silver Hummer). By the time we were rescued and she was declared missing—a lag time of at least twenty-four hours, most likely longer, given the weather conditions—she'd be states away, maybe even Mexico.

And maybe the stranger who'd come upon us had not been so strange. Maybe *he* was Hannah's Carlos (her *Valerio*) and the ambush, the "Give me five minutes," the "I said stay here," had been a hoax; maybe she'd *intended* to go after him all along, and together they'd make their way to the trail, the road, car, Mexico, margaritas, fajitas. In this case, when I was found, I'd report to authorities someone had come upon us, and when no sign of Hannah turned up, when German Shepherds tracked her to a spot on a nearby road, the police would suspect Kidnapping or other Foul Play, or, that she'd *planned* to vanish, in which case, unless she was WANTED for something, they'd do little. (Detective Harper had not hinted at Hannah having a criminal record. And I could only assume she wasn't related to the Bonanno, Gambino, Genovese, Lucchese or Colombo crime families.)

Sure, it was a brutal thing she'd done, to purposefully abandon me in the dark, but when people were desperate they did, with little conscience, all kinds of brutal things (see *How to Survive "The Farm," Louisiana State Prison at Angola*, Glibb, 1979). Yet, she hadn't been totally without concern; before she left me, she'd given me the flashlight, the map, told me not to be afraid. And during the afternoon hike up Bald Creek Trail, on four or five occasions, she'd pointed out on our maps, not only our location, but the fact that Sugartop Summit was only four miles away from the Park's main road, U.S. 441.

If I could determine the reason Hannah had wished to flee her life, I could determine who'd killed her. Because it'd been a first-rate rub out, a button man well acquainted with autopsies, because he'd understood the consequence of the ligature marks, how to make them look like suicide. He'd planned in advance the ideal spot for the lynching, that small, round clearing, and thus he'd known she was running away and what trail she was taking to reach the road. Maybe he'd been wearing night-vision goggles, or hunter's camouflage—like the disturbing kind I'd seen in Andreo Verduga's Wal-Mart shopping cart in Nestles, Missouri, ShifTbush™ Invisible Gear, Fall Mix, "the accomplished hunter's dream"—and, "instantly invisible in his woodland surroundings," he'd stepped onto a tree stump or some other sturdy, elevated position, silently waiting for her, poised with the electrical cord in a noose, which was in turn rigged to the tree. As she stumbled past, trying to find her way, trying to find *him*—because she'd known who he was—he looped it over her head, wrenching his end of the rope hard so she rose into the air. She didn't have time to react, to kick or scream, to organize the last thoughts of her life. ("Even the devil deserves last thoughts," wrote William Stonely in *Ash Complexions* [1932].)

As I reenacted this scene in my head, my heart began to thud. Sickening chills began to inchworm down my arms and legs, and then, rather abruptly, one more detail fell motionless at my feet like a lead-poisoned canary, like a pugface nose-toasted by a mean right to his chin.

Hannah had instructed Milton to take me to her house, *not* to play matchmaker (though perhaps that played a part; I couldn't discount the movie posters in her classroom), but so I, a thought-ridden and inquisitive person, would engage in a little gumshoe: *"You're such a perceptive person; you don't miss anything,"* she'd told me that night at her house. She had not foreseen her death, and thus presumed, after she'd disappeared, when the search party turned up no trace of her, the Bluebloods and I would be left with the maddening question of what had happened, the kind of question that could *kill* a person, turn a person into a Bible-spewer, a rocking-horsed corn-shucking mountie with no teeth. And thus I, along with Milton, had been meant to discover, sitting entirely alone on that strangely immaculate coffee table (ordinarily littered with ashtrays and matchbooks, *National Geographics* and junk mail) an item that would be our reassurance, the end to her story: a film, *L'Avventura*.

I felt faint. Because it was chic, oh, yes, it was *brilliant*, très Schneideresque: neatly precise yet sweetly hush-hush. (It was an act of personal punctuation even Dad would've considered nimble.) It was thrilling because it illustrated a premeditation, a craftiness of action and mind of which I hadn't thought Hannah capable. She was hurtfully beautiful; sure, she could listen to you, and rumba remarkably well with a wineglass; she could also pick up men like they were socks cluttering the floor, but for a person to orchestrate, however gently, such a subtle end to her life—at least, her life as everyone at St. Gallway knew it—that was something else, something dramatic, yet sad, because this murmur of an ending, this classy question mark, had not happened.

I tried to calm myself. ("Emotion, especially excitement, is the enemy of dick work," said Detective Lieutenant Peterson in *Wooden Kimono* [Lazim, 1980].)

L'Avventura, Michelangelo Antonioni's lyrical black-and-white masterpiece of 1960 happened to be one of Dad's favorite films and thus, over the years, I'd seen it no less than twelve times. (Dad had a soft spot for all things Italian, including curvy women with poofy hair and Marcello Mastroianni's squints, shrugs, winks and smiles, which he tossed like overripe cherry tomatoes at women strolling Via Veneto. When Dad fell into a Mediterraneo Bourbon Mood, he'd even do bits of *La Dolce Vita* with pitch-perfect, seedy Italian flair: *"Tu sei la prima donna del primo giorno della creazione, sei la madre, la sorella, l'amante, l'amica, l'angelo, il diavolo, la terra, la casa . . ."*)

The film's simple plot unraveled as follows:

A wealthy socialite, Anna, goes on a yachting trip with her friends off the coast of Sicily. They go ashore to sunbathe on a deserted island. Anna wanders away and never returns. Anna's fiancé, Sandro, and her best friend, Claudia, search the island, and subsequently, all of Italy, pursuing a variety of dead-end clues and embarking on a love affair of their own. At the film's end, Anna's disappearance remains as mysterious as the day she disappeared. Life continues—in this case, one of hollow desire and material excess—and Anna is all but forgotten.

Hannah had hoped I'd find this film. She hoped—no, she *knew*—I'd perceive the similarities between Anna's unexplained tale and her own. (Even their names were virtually identical.) And she was confident I'd explain it to the others, not only that she'd planned this departure but that she wanted us to move on with our lives, with dancing barefoot with a wineglass, with shouting off of mountaintops ("Living Italian-Style," as Dad was fond of saying, though being Swiss-born it was violently against nature for him to follow his own advice).

"*L'Avventura*," Dad said, "has the sort of ellipsis ending most American audiences would rather undergo a root canal than be left with, not only because they loathe anything left to the imagination—we're talking about a country that invented spandex—but also because they are a confident, self-assured nation. They *know* Family. They *know* Right from Wrong. They know God—many of them attest to daily chats with the man. And the idea that none of us can truly know anything at all—not the lives of our friends or family, not even ourselves—is a thought they'd rather be shot in the arm with their own semi-automatic rifle than face head on. Personally, I think there's something terrific about not knowing, relinquishing man's feeble attempt to control. When you throw up your hands, say, 'Who knows?' you can get on with the sheer gift of being alive, rather like the *paparazzi*, the *puttane*, the *cognoscenti*, the *tappisti* . . ." (Around here, I always tuned Dad out, because when he went on in Italian he was like a Hell's Angel on a Harley; he loved to go fast and loud and for everyone to stop in the streets and stare at him.)

By now, it was after 6:00 P.M. The sun was loosening its grip on the lawn and frilly black shadows had collapsed all over my bedroom floor like skinny widows killed with arsenic. I rolled off the bed, putting the folder and photo of punk-rocked Hannah in the top left desk drawer (where I also kept her Charles Manson paperback). I considered calling Milton, telling him everything, but then I heard the Volvo swerving down the driveway. Moments later, Dad was in the hall.

I found him by the front door, which he hadn't closed because he was reading the front page of South Africa's *Cape Daily Press*.

"You've got to be kidding me," he muttered disgustedly, "poor disorganized fools—when will the madness—no, it *won't* end, not until they educate—but it's possible, crazier things have happened . . ." He glanced at me, a dour expression on his face, before returning to the article. "They're slaughtering more rebels in the D.R.C., sweet, some five hundred—"

He looked at me again, startled. "What's the matter? You look exhausted."

He frowned. "Are you still not sleeping? I went through quite a nasty period of insomnia myself, Harvard '74—"

"I'm fine."

He studied me, about to argue, then decided against it. "Well, never fear!" With a smile, he folded the newspaper. "Remember what we're doing tomorrow or have you forgotten our bid for a day of repose? The great Lake Pennebaker!"

I *had* forgotten; Dad had been planning the day trip with all the excitement of Britain's Captain Scott planning the world's first expedition to the South Pole, hoping to beat Norway's Captain Amundsen in the process. (In Dad's case, he hoped to beat the retirees so he'd be first in line for a paddle-boat and a picnic table in the shade.)

"A lake excursion," he went on, kissing me on the cheek before picking up his briefcase and moving down the hall. "I must say I'm stirred by the idea, especially since we'll be catching the tail end of the Pioneer Crafts Fair. I think you and I both require an afternoon in the sun, to take our minds off the flabby state of the world—though something tells me when I see the onslaught of RVs I'll realize I'm not in Switzerland anymore."

Things Fall Apart

By Monday morning, I hadn't slept a wink, having spent Saturday night and most of Sunday reading all 782 pages of *The Evaporatists* (Buddel, 1980), a biography about Boris and Bernice Pochechnik, husband-and-wife Hungarian grifters who, some thirty-nine times, staged their deaths and rebirths under aliases with the meticulous choreography and grace of the Bolshoi Ballet doing *Swan Lake*. I'd also reexamined disappearance statistics in the *Almanac of American Strange Habits, Tics and Behaviors* (1994 ed.), learning that while two out of every thirty-nine adults who absconded from their lives did so out of "sheer boredom" (99.2 percent of these were married, the ennui a result of a "lackluster spouse"), twenty-one out of the thirty-nine did so because of heat, the "iron-cleated sole of the law descending quickly upon them"; they were criminals—petty crooks, con artists, embezzlers and felons. (Eleven out of thirty-nine did so due to drug addiction, three out of thirty-nine because they were "made" and fleeing the Italian or Russian mobs and two for unknown reasons.)

I'd also finished *The History of Lynching in the American South* (Kittson, 1966), and it was in that book I'd made my most exciting discovery: popular among Georgia slave owners and later reemerging during the second founding of the Ku Klux Klan in 1915, there was an effective hanging technique supposedly invented by Judge Charles Lynch himself, nicknamed "The Flying Demoiselle" due to the "quick soaring motion of the body as it is yanked into the air" (p. 213). "This method stayed popular due to its convenience," the author Ed Kittson writes on p. 214. "A man with sufficient musculature could hang someone single-handedly, without the assistance of a mob. The noose and pulley is detailed but easy to learn with practice: a type of running bowline, tightening under strain, usually a Honda Knot, coupled with a Logger's Hitch, around a strong tree limb. Once the victim is pulled three to six feet into the air depending on the slack, the Logger's Hitch tightens and holds like a constrictor knot. Some thirty-nine lynchings transpired in this manner in 1919 alone." The accompanying Visual Aid featured a lynching postcard— "common souvenirs in the Old South"—and written along the edge, was "1917, Melville, Mississippi: 'Our Flying Demoiselle / his body soars, his soul goes to hell' " (p. 215).

Enthused by this illuminating development, during second period Study Hall I opted to blow off Operation Barbarossa in my AP World History textbook, *Our Life, Our Times* (Clanton, 2001 ed.) opting instead to tackle *Death Codes* (Lee, 1987), a gory little paperback I'd brought from Dad's library penned by Franklin C. Lee, one of L.A.'s greatest private snoopers, which I'd started reading during first period. ("Blue! Why are you sitting in the back?" Ms. Simpson had demanded in AP English, visibly aghast; "Because I'm solving a *homicide*, Ms. Simpson, because no one else will get off their ass and do it for me," I'd wanted to shout—but didn't, of course; I said there was a glare on the dry-erase board and I couldn't see from my usual seat.) Dee and Dum, by the Hambone Bestseller Wish List, had just started their daily round of gossip, egged on by their accomplice, Little Nose Hemmings—Mr. Fletcher with *The Ultimate Crossword Omnibus* (Johnson ed., 2000) once again turning a blind eye—and I was just about to stalk over and tell them to shut their mugs (it was incredible, the resolve crime-solving gave a person) when I began to eavesdrop on their conversation.

"I heard Evita Perón telling Martine Filobeque in the Teacher's Lounge she thinks the Hannah Schneider suicide verdict's a load of dung," reported Little Nose. "She said she knew for a *fact* Hannah didn't commit suicide."

"What else?" said Dee, narrowing her eyes suspiciously.

"Nothing—they noticed me standing by the photocopier and that was the end of their conversation."

Dee shrugged, looked uninterested and calmly studied her cuticles.

"I'm all sick of talking about Hannah Schneider," she said. "Total media overexposure."

"She's out like carbs," explained Dum with a nod.

"Besides, when I told my mom some of the films we'd been watching in her class, movies that were totally black marketed to us, *never* on the syllabus, Mom wigged. She said it was obvious the woman was captain of team nutjob, *totally* schizophrenical—"

"Mixed up," translated Dum, "all jumbled inside—"

"Natch, mom wanted to launch a complaint with Havermeyer, but then she figured the school's been through enough. Admissions applications are in a downward spiral."

Little Nose wrinkled her nose. "But don't you wanna know what Eva Brewster was talking about? She must know a secret."

Dee sighed. "I'm sure it's something along the lines of Schneider pregnant with Mr. Fletcher's child." She raised her head, throwing a grenade-gaze at the poor, unwitting bald man across the room. "It was going to be a carnie." She giggled. "The world's first living crossword omnibus."

"They were going to name it *Sunday Times* if it was a boy," said Dum.

The twins erupted into squealish laughter and slapped each other five.

*   *   *

After school, standing outside of Elton, I watched Perón making her way to the Faculty Parking Lot (see "Leaving Madrid, June 15, 1947," *Eva Duarte Perón*, East, 1963, p. 334). She wore a short, dark purple dress with matching pumps, thick white tights and carried an enormous stack of manila folders. A lifeless beige sweater was knotted around her waist, about to fall off, one of the arms dragging on the ground like a hostage being hauled away.

I was a little afraid, but I made myself go after her. (" 'Keep tightening the screws on those chippies,' " entreated Private Peeper Rush McFadds to his partner in *Chicago Overcoat* [Bulke, 1948].)

"Ms. Brewster."

She was the kind of woman who, when hearing someone shout her name, didn't turn around but continued to charge forward as if riding a moving platform on an airport concourse.

"Ms. Brewster!" I caught up to her at her car, a white Honda Civic. "I was wondering if we could talk."

She slammed the door to the backseat where she'd placed the folders and opened the driver's seat door, brushing her mango-colored hair off her face.

"I'm late for a spin class," she said.

"It won't take long. I—I'd like to make amends."

Her blue eyes pounced on me. (It was probably the same daunting stare she gave Colonel Juan, when he, along with the other flabby Argentine bureaucrats, voiced a lack of enthusiasm for her latest great idea, the joint Perón-Perón ballot for the 1951 election.)

"Shouldn't it be the other way around?" she asked.

"I don't care. I wanted you to help me with something."

She checked her watch. "I can't right now. I'm due at Fitness Exchange—"

"It doesn't have anything to do with my Dad, if that's what you're worried about."

"What's it have to do with?"

"Hannah Schneider."

She widened her eyes—evidently that topic was even less favorable than Dad—and she pushed the car door wider so it hit my arm.

"You shouldn't be worrying about that stuff," she said. Struggling against the purple dress, which had the effect on her legs of a narrowed napkin ring, she heaved herself into the driver's seat. She jingled her car keys (on the key-chain, a bright pink rabbit's foot), jamming one in the ignition quickly, like she was knifing someone. "You want to talk to me tomorrow I'll be here. Come to the office in the morning, but right now I do have to go. I'm late." She leaned forward, grabbing the handle to slam the door, but I didn't move an inch. The door hit my knees.

"Hey," she said.

I stood my ground. (" 'I don't care if they're giving birth, don't let a witness fly the coop,' " ordered Miami Police Detective Frank Waters to his immature partner, Melvin, in *The Trouble with Twists* [Brown, 1968]. " 'No brush offs. No rain checks. You don't want them to reflect. Surprise a witness and he'll inadvertently send his mother to the slammer.' ")

"For God's sake, what's the matter with you?" Evita asked with irritation, letting go of the handle. "What's *that* look—listen, someone dying isn't the end of the world. You're sixteen for Pete's sake. Your spouse left you, you got three kids, mortgages, diabetes—*then* we'll talk. Concentrate on seeing the forest through the trees. If you want, like I said, we can talk tomorrow."

She was turning on the charm now: smiling up at me, making sure her voice curled sweetly on the ends like gift-wrap ribbons.

"You destroyed the only thing I have left of my mother in the world," I said. "I think you can spare five minutes of your time." I stared down at my shoes and did my best to look miserable and *melanchólica*. Evita responded only to the *descamisados*, the shirtless ones. Everyone else was a complicit member of the oligarchy and hence, worthy of imprisonment, blacklisting, torture.

She didn't immediately respond. She shifted, the vinyl seat moaning beneath her. She pressed the hem of her purple dress over her knees.

"You know, I was out with the girls," she said in a quiet voice. "I had a few kamikazes at El Rio and I got thinking about your father. I didn't mean—"

"I understand. Now what do you know about Hannah Schneider?"

She made a face. "Nothing."

"But you don't think she committed suicide."

"I never said that. I don't have a clue what happened." She looked up at me. "You're a strange girl, you know that? Does *pa* know you're running around, intimidating people? Asking questions?"

When I didn't respond, she checked her watch again, muttered something about spinning (something told me there was no spin class, no Fitness Exchange, but I had bigger fish to fry), then yanked open the glove compartment, removing a packet of Nicorette gum. She shoved two pieces in her mouth, swung her left then her right leg out of the car, crossing them and making a big to-do about it, like she'd just sat down at the bar at El Rio. Her legs were like giant thick candy canes minus the red stripe.

"I know what you do. Next to nothing," she said simply. "My only concern was that it didn't seem like her. Suicide, especially hanging yourself—I guess, I could understand pills, *maybe*—but not hanging."

She fell silent for a minute, chewing thoughtfully, staring out across the parking lot at the other hot cars.

"There was a kid couple years back," she said slowly, glancing at me. "Howie Gibson IV. Dressed like a prime minister. Couldn't help it, I guess. He was a fourth and everyone knows sequels don't do well at the box office. Two months into Fall Term his mother found him hanging from a hook he'd put up in his bedroom ceiling. When I found out"—she swallowed, crossed and recrossed her legs—"I was sad. But I also wasn't surprised. His dad, a third, obviously no blockbuster himself, he was always here to pick him up in the afternoon in a big black car and when the boy got in, he sat in the back, like his dad was the chauffeur. Neither of them ever talked. And they drove away like that." She sniffed. "After it happened we opened up his locker and there was all kinds of stuff taped to the door, drawings of devils and upside-down crosses. Actually, he was a pretty talented artist, but let's just say in terms of subject matter, he wasn't going to be designing any Hallmark cards. The point is—you saw signs. I'm not an expert, but I don't think suicide happens out of nowhere."

She fell silent again, examining the ground, her purple pumps.

"I'm not saying Hannah didn't have her share of problems. Sometimes she'd stay late and there was no reason for her to—*film* class, what do you do, you pop in the DVD. I got the feeling she hung around because she needed someone to talk to. And sure, she had a lot of lint in her head. At the beginning of every school year, it was always her last. 'Then I'm getting out, Eva. I'm going to Greece.' 'What're ya gonna do in Greece?' I'd ask. 'Love myself,' she'd say. Oh, *boy*. Usually I have zero tolerance for that kind of self-help crap. I've never been the type to buy improvement books. You're over forty and you *still* haven't won friends or influenced people? You're still the poor dad, not the *rich* dad? Well, I hate to break it to you, but it ain't gonna happen."

Eva was laughing about this to herself but then, suddenly, the laugh fluttered awkwardly in her mouth and flew away, and she sniffed, staring after it maybe, at the sky and the sun tucked into the trees with a few wispy clouds.

"There were other things, too," she went on, chewing the Nicorette with her mouth open. "Something awful happened in her twenties, a man was involved, her friend—she didn't go into details, but said not a day went by when she didn't feel guilt over what she'd done—whatever it was. So sure, she was sad, insecure, but vain too. And vain people don't hang themselves. They complain, they whine, make a lot of noise, but they don't string themselves up. It'd ruin their looks."

She laughed again, this time a pushy laugh, one she probably used on the radio soap opera *Oro Blanco*, a laugh to intimidate bacon-fingered Radiolandia writers, beef-backed generals, yoke-cheeked compadres. She blew a small bubble and popped it in her teeth, a smacking sound.

"What do *I* know? What does anyone know about what goes on in someone's head? In early December she asked to take a week off so she could go to West Virginia, to see the family of that man who drowned at her house."

"Smoke Harvey?"

"Was that his name?"

I nodded and then remembered something. "She invited you to that party, didn't she?"

"What party?"

"The one taking place when he died."

She shook her head, puzzled. "No, I only heard about it afterward. She was pretty upset. Told me she wasn't sleeping at night due to the situation. Anyway, she ended up not taking the vacation. Said she felt too guilty to face the family, so maybe I didn't know the extent of her guilt. I tried telling her you have to forgive yourself. I mean, one time I was asked to watch a neighbor's cat when they went to Hawaii—one of those long-haired jobs straight off a Fancy Feast commercial. Thing *hated* me. Every time I went into the garage to feed it, it jumped onto the screen door and hung there by its claws like Velcro. One day, by accident, I pressed the button to the garage door. It hadn't gone up three inches before the thing motored out of there. Left track marks. I went outside, searched for hours, couldn't find it. A couple days later, the neighbors came back from Maui and found it flattened on the road, right smack in front of their house. Sure, it was my fault. I paid for the thing. And I felt terrible about it for a while. Had nightmares where the thing was coming after me with rabies—red eyes, claws, the whole shebang. But you have to move on, you know. You have to find your peace."

Maybe it had to do with her bastardized birth and impoverished Los Toldos upbringing, the trauma of seeing Augustin Magaldi naked at fifteen, shoving to great political heights the wide load of Colonel Juan, the twenty-four-hour workdays at the *Secretaria de Trabajo* and the *Partido Peronista Feminino*, looting the National Treasury, stockpiling her closet with Dior— but she had, at some point over the years, become uninterrupted asphalt. Somewhere, of course, there had to be a crack in her where a tiny seed of apple, pear or fig might fall and flourish, yet it was impossible to locate these minuscule fractures. They were constantly being sought and filled.

"You have to lighten up, kiddo. Don't take it so hard. Adults are complicated. I'm the first to admit—we're sloppy. But it doesn't have anything to do with you. You're young. Enjoy it while it lasts. Because later, that's when things get really tough. The best thing to do is keep laughing."

One of my pet peeves was when an adult imagined they had to encapsulate Life for you, hand you Life in a jar, in an eyedropper, in a penguin paperweight full of snow—A Collector's Dream. Obviously Dad had his theories, but he always expounded on them with the silent footnote that they weren't answers, per se, but loosely applied *suggestions*. Any one of Dad's hypotheses, as he well knew, applied solely to a smidgin of Life rather than the entire thing, and *thinly* applied at that.

Eva checked her watch again. "Now I'm sorry, but I do want to make it to my spin class." I nodded and moved out of the way so she could close the door. She started the engine, smiling at me like I was a tollbooth collector and she wanted me to lift the barrier so she could drive on. She didn't immediately reverse out of her parking space, however. She turned on the radio, some jittery pop tune, and after a second or two of digging through her purse, unrolled the window again.

"How is he, by the way?"

"Who?" I asked, even though I knew.

"Your *pa*."

"He's great."

"Really?" She nodded, tried to look casual and disinterested. Then her eyes inched back over to me. "You know, I'm sorry about that stuff I said about him. It wasn't true."

"It's okay."

"No, it isn't. No kid should hear those things. I'm sorry about it." She was giving me the once over, her eyes climbing my face as if it was a jungle gym. "He loves you. A lot. I don't know if he shows it, but he does. More than anything, more than—I don't even know what to call it—his political hooey. We were at dinner once and we weren't even talking about you and he said you were the best thing that ever happened to him." She smiled. "And he meant it."

I nodded and pretended to be entranced by her left front tire. For some reason, I didn't love discussing Dad with random people who had nectarine hair and careened between insults, compliments, terseness and compassion like a driver three sheets to the wind. Talking about Dad with these kinds of people was like talking about stomachs in the Victorian Age: inappropriate, gauche, a perfectly sound reason to look through them at future assemblies and balls.

She sighed resignedly when I didn't say anything, one of those adult throw-in-the-hand-towel sighs that indicated they didn't understand teenagers and were delighted those days were far behind them. "Well, take care of yourself, kiddo." She was rolling up the window, but stopped again. "And try to eat something once and a while—you're about to disappear. Have some pizza. And stop worrying about Hannah Schneider," she added. "I don't know what happened to her, but I do know she'd want you to be happy, all right?"

I smiled stiffly as she waved at me, reversed (her brakes sounded as if they were being tortured), then barreled out of the Faculty Parking Lot, her white Honda the limousine to carry her through the poorest pig-pungent *barrios* where she'd wave from an unrolled window to the hungry, enchanted people in the streets.

＊　＊　＊

I'd told Dad he didn't need to pick me up. When Milton drove me home on Friday, we'd arranged to meet at his locker after school and I was now a half hour late. I hurried up the stairs to the third floor of Elton, but the hall was empty apart from Dinky and Mr. Ed "Favio" Camonetti standing in the doorway of his Honors English classroom. (As many people enjoy hearing details of the hot and heavy, I shall quickly mention: Favio was Gallway's hottest male instructor. He had a bronzed, Rock-Hudsony face, was married to a plump nondescript woman who wore pinafores and appeared to think he was just as sexy as everyone else did, though personally, I thought his body resembled an inflated raft suffering from a clandestine pinprick.) They stopped talking as I walked past.

I walked up to Zorba (where Amy Hempshaw and Bill Chews were vined together in an embrace) and then the Student Parking Lot. Milton's Nissan was still parked in his assigned space, so I decided to check the cafeteria, and when I found no one, Hypocrite's Alley in the basement of Love, the center of St. Gallway's black market, where Milton and Charles sometimes rubbed noses with other frantic students trafficking illegal Unit Tests, Final Exams, Straight-A Student Notes and Research Papers, trading sexual favors for a night with the latest copy of *The Trickster's Bible*, a 543-page ghostwritten manual on how to swindle one's way through St. Gallway, categorized by teacher and text, method and means. (A few titles: "A Room of One's Own: Taking the Makeup Test," "Toy Story: The Beauty of the TI-82 and the Timex Data Link Watch," "Tiny, Handwritten Diamonds on the Soles of Your Shoes.") As I made my way along the dark corridor, however, peering in the small rectangular windows of the seven musical practice rooms, I saw shady figures huddled in the corners, on piano benches, behind the music stands (no one practicing any musical instruments, unless one counts body parts). Not one was Milton.

I decided to try the clearing behind Love Auditorium; Milton sometimes went there to smoke a joint between classes. I hurried back up the stairs, through the Donna Faye Johnson Art Gallery (modern artist and Gallway alumnus Peter Rocke '87 was deep in his Mud Period and showing no signs of surfacing), out the backdoor with the EXIT sign, across the parking lot with the scabbed Pontiac parked by the garbage dump (they said it was the jam jar of a long-lost teacher found guilty of seducing a student) quickly making my way through the trees.

I saw him almost immediately. He was wearing a navy blazer and leaning against a tree.

"Hi!" I shouted.

He was smiling, and yet as I neared, I realized he wasn't smiling because he saw me, but at something in the conversation because the others were there too: Jade sitting on a thick fallen branch, Leulah on a rock (holding onto her braided hair as if it were a ripcord), Nigel next to her and Charles on the ground, his giant white cast jutting out of him like a peninsula.

They saw me. Milton's smile curled off his face like unsticky tape. And I knew immediately, I was a boy band, a boondoggle, born fool. He was going to pull a Danny Zuko in *Grease* when Sandy says hello to him in front of the T-Birds, a Mrs. Robinson when she tells Elaine she didn't seduce Benjamin, a Daisy when she chooses Tom with the disposition of sour kiwi over Gatsby, a self-made man, a man engorged with dreams, who didn't mind throwing a pile of shirts around a room if he wanted to.

My heart landslided. My legs earthquaked.

"Look what the cat dragged in," said Jade.

"Hi, Retch," Milton said. "How are you today?"

"What the fuck's *she* doing here?" asked Charles. I turned to look at him and saw, with surprise, that simply due to my close proximity his face had turned the angry shade of Red Imported Fire Ants (see *Insecta*, Powell, 1992, p. 91).

"Hello," I said. "Well, I guess I'll see you late—"

"Hold on a minute." Charles had stood up on his good leg and begun to hobble toward me, awkwardly, because Leulah was holding one of his crutches. She held it out to him, but he didn't take it. He chose to hobble, as veterans sometimes do, as if there is greater glory in the hobble, the shamble, the limp.

"I want to have a little *talk*," he said.

"Not worth it," said Jade inhaling her cigarette.

"No, it is. It *is* worth it."

"Charles," warned Milton.

"You're a fucking piece of shit, you know that?"

"Jesus," Nigel said, grinning. "Take it easy."

"No, I'm *not* going to take it easy. I–I'm going to kill her."

Although his face was red and his eyes bulged from his face in the manner of a Golden Mantella, he was on a single leg, and thus as he leered at me, I wasn't afraid. I knew very well if it came down to it I could push him over with very little force and spirit away before any of them could catch me. At the same time, it was highly unsettling to think I was the reason his features contorted into the wrenched expression of an infant in a delivery room; why his eyes were so narrowed they looked like cardboard slits you stick pennies or dimes into, thereby donating to Kids with Cerebral Palsy, *so* unsettling that the thought actually crossed my mind maybe I *did* kill Hannah, maybe I suffered from schizophrenia and had been under the influence of the malevolent Blue, the Blue who took no prisoners, the Blue who ripped people's hearts out and ate them for breakfast (see *The Three Faces of Eve*). It could be the only reason why he hated me so, why his face was so wounded, scrunched up and bumpy like tire treads.

"You want to kill her and end up in juvie hall for the rest of your life?" asked Jade.

"Bad plan," said Nigel.

"You'd be better off hiring a bounty hunter."

"I'll do it," said Leulah, raising her hand.

Jade stubbed out her cigarette on the bottom of her shoe. "Or we could stone her like they do in that short story. When all the townspeople descend and she starts to scream."

" 'The Lottery,' " I said, because I couldn't help myself (Jackson, 1948). I shouldn't have said it though, because it made Charles gnash his teeth and jut out his face out even more, so I could see the minute spaces between his bottom teeth, a little white picket fence. I felt his broiler-hot breath on my forehead.

"You want to know what you did to me?" His hands trembled, and on the word *did* some of his spit jumped ship, landing somewhere on the ground between us. "You *destroyed* me—"

"Charles," said Nigel warily, walking up behind him.

"Stop acting like a madman," Jade said. "If you do something to her she'll get you kicked out. Her superhero dad will make sure of it—"

"You broke my fucking leg in three places," Charles said. "You broke my heart—"

"*Charles*—"

"And you should know, I think about killing you. I think about stringing you up by your ungrateful little neck, and—and leaving you for dead." He swallowed loudly. It sounded like a rock dropped in a pond. Tears stormed his red eyes. One actually threw itself over the wall, sliding down his face. "Like you did to her."

"*Fuck*, Charles—"

"Stop."

"She's not worth it."

"Yeah, man. She's a terrible kisser."

There was a silence, and then Jade sizzled with laugher.

"She is?" Charles instantly stopped crying. He sniffed and wiped his eyes with the back of his hand.

"The worst. She's like kissin' tuna."

"*Tuna?*"

"Maybe it was sardines. Shrimp. I don't remember. I tried to block it from my mind."

I couldn't breathe. Blood was flooding into my face, as if he hadn't spoken, but kicked me in the face. And I knew it was one of those devastating moments in Life when one had to address one's congress, pull The Jimmy Stuart. I had to show them they were not dealing with a wounded, fearful nation, but an awakened giant. Yet I couldn't retaliate with any old cruise missile. It would have to be a Little Boy, a Fat Man, a gigantic head of cauliflower (bystanders would later claim they saw a second sun) with scorched bodies, the chalky taste of atomic fission in the pilots' mouths. Afterward I might feel regret, probably think the inevitable, "My God, what have I done?" but that never stopped anyone.

Dad had a small black book he kept on his bedside table, *Words of a Glowworm* (Punch, 1978), which he turned to at night, when he was tired and craved something sweet the way some women craved dark chocolate. It was a book of the most powerful quotations in the world. I knew most of them. "History is a set of lies generally agreed upon," Napoleon said. "Lead me, follow me, or get out of my way," said General George Patton. "On stage I make love to twenty-five thousand people and then I go home alone," moaned Janis Joplin, bleary of eye and disheveled of hair. "Go to Heaven for the climate, Hell for the company," said Mark Twain.

I stared at Milton. He couldn't look at me, but pressed against the trunk of that tree, as if he wished it would eat him.

" 'We are all worms,' " I said carefully, " 'but I do believe I am a glowworm.' "

"What?" asked Jade.

I turned and began to walk away.

"What was *that?*"

"That's what you call *taking a moment.*"

"Did you see her? She's totally possessed."

"Find an exorcist!" Charles shouted, and laughed, a sound like poured gold coins, and the trees bore the sound up with their perfect acoustics and made it float in the air.

When I reached the parking lot, I encountered Mr. Moats walking to his car with textbooks under his arm. He looked startled when he saw me coming out of the trees, as if he thought I was the ghost of El Greco.

"Blue van Meer?" he called out uncertainly, but I didn't smile or speak to him.

I'd already started to run.

The Nocturnal Conspiracy

It was one of the biggest scandals of Life, to learn the cruelest thing someone could say to you was that you were a terrible kisser.

One would think it'd be worse to be a Traitor, Hypocrite, Bitch,
Whore or any other foul person, worse even to be a Way-out-there, a Welcome
Mat, a Was-Girl, a Weasel. I suspect one would even fare better with "bad in
bed," because everyone has an off day, a day when his/her mind hitchhikes
on each and every thought that cruises by, and even champion racehorses
such as Couldn't Be Happier, who won both the Derby and the Preakness in
1971, could suddenly come in dead last, as he did at the Belmont Stakes. But
to be a terrible kisser—to be *tuna*—was the worst of all, because it meant you
were without passion, and to be without passion, well, you might as well be
dead.

I walked home (4.1 miles), replaying that humiliating remark again and
again in my head (in slo-mo, so I could mentally draw agonizing little circles
around my every instance of fumbling, holding, intentional grounding and
personal foul). In my room, I broke down into one of those headachy weeps
one would *think* would be reserved for the death of a family member, for terminal illness, the end of the world. I cried into my clammy pillowcase for
over an hour, the darkness swelling in the room, the night slinking up
and crouching in the windows. Our house, the elaborate, empty 24 Armor
Street, seemed to wait for me, wait like bats for darkness, an orchestra for a
conductor, waiting for me to calm myself, to proceed.

Stuffy of head and crimson of eye, I rolled off my bed, wandered downstairs, played the message from Dad about dinner with Arnie Sanderson, re-

moved from the fridge the Stonerose Bakery chocolate cake Dad had brought home the other day (part of the Van Meer Brighten Up Blue Initiative) and grabbing a fork, carried it up to my room.

"We're tucking you in tonight with breaking news," sang the imaginary Cherry Jeffries of my head. "It took not the police force, not the National Guard, Park Rangers, K-9, the FBI, CIA, Pentagon, not preachers, clairvoyants, palm readers, dream catchers, superheroes, Martians, not even a trip to Lourdes, but simply a brave, local area teen to solve the murder of Hannah Louise Schneider, age forty-four, whose death had been erroneously declared a suicide by the Sluder County Sheriff's Department just last week. A gifted senior at the St. Gallway School in Stockton, Miss Blue van Meer, who happens to have an I.Q. that will knock your pants off, 175, flew in the face of adversity from teachers, students, and fathers alike when she deciphered a range of nearly imperceptible clues leading her to the woman's killer, now in police custody and awaiting trial. Dubbed the Schoolgirl Sam Spade, Miss Van Meer has not only been a regular on the talk-show circuit, from *Oprah* and Leno to the *Today* show and *The View*, also gracing the cover of this month's *Rolling Stone*, but she's also been invited to the White House to dine with the President who, despite her tender age of sixteen, asked her to serve as a U.S. Ambassador on a thirty-two-country Goodwill Tour promoting peace and world freedom. All of this prior to her matriculation at Harvard this fall. Christ. Isn't that something else, Norvel? Norvel?"

"Oh. Uh, yes."

"It just goes to show you that this world isn't falling apart too bad. Because there are real heroes out there and dreams really do come true."

I had no choice but to do what Chief Inspector Curry did when facing a dead end in one of his investigations, as he did on p. 512 of *Conceit of a Unicorn* (Lavelle, 1901), when "every door remains bolted and every casement firmly latched, concealing the wickedness at which we, my esteemed Horace, may only fitfully turn our discouraged minds to, much as the lean mongrel wandering our city of slate and stone, poking through rubbish, fraught for a careless scrap of mutton dropped by an unwary merchant or solicitor on his journey home. Yet, there is hope! For remember, my dear lad, the starving dog misses naught! When in doubt, *return to the victim*! He will light your way."

I pulled out a neon pink five-by-seven note card and wrote out a list of Hannah's friends, the few names I knew. There was the late Smoke Harvey and his family who lived in Findley, West Virginia, and the man from the animal shelter, Richard Something, who lived on the llama farm, and Eva Brewster, Doc, the other men from Cottonwood (though I wasn't sure one could classify them as friends, more acquaintances).

All things considered, it was a paltry list.

Nevertheless, I decided to begin, somewhat confidently, with the top, a member of the Harvey family. I hurried down to Dad's study, switching on his laptop and typing Smoke's name into the People Search on Worldquest.

There was no record of him. There were, however, fifty-nine other Harveys, also a record of one Ada Harvey in Findley registered on one of the advertising links, www.noneofyourbusiness.com. Ada, I remembered, was one of Smoke's daughters; Hannah had mentioned her during the dinner at Hyacinth Terrace. (I remembered, because her name was one of Dad's most beloved books, Nabokov's *Ada or Ardor* [1969].) If I paid just $89.99 to the Web site, I could not only obtain Ada's home telephone number, but her address, birthday, background check, public record report, National Criminal Record Search, as well as a satellite photo. I ran upstairs into Dad's bedroom and took one of his extra MasterCards out of his bedside table drawer. I decided to pay the $8.00 for her phone number.

I returned to my room. I wrote out a list of detailed questions on three other five-by-seven note cards, each neatly labeled at the top, CASE NOTES. After I'd reviewed the questions three, maybe four times, I slipped downstairs to the library, uncapped Dad's fifteen-year-old George T. Stagg bourbon, took a swig straight from the bottle (I wasn't yet completely at ease with shamus work, not yet, and what detective didn't dip the bill?) and returned to my room, taking a few moments to collect myself. " 'Youse got to picture the steel bed the stiff is on an' make that your manner, broads,' " Sergeant Detective Buddy Mills demanded of his relatively bashful all-male police force in *The Last Hatchet Job* (Nubbs, 1958).

I dialed the number. A woman answered on the third ring.

"Hello?"

"May I please speak to Ada Harvey?"

"This is she. Who's callin' please?"

It was one of those scary, antebellum, I-do-declare Southern voices, purdy, feisty and preternaturally elderly (all wrinkle and quiver no matter the age of the person).

"Um, hello, my name is Blue van Meer and I—"

"Thank you very much, but I'm not interested—"

"I'm not a telemarketer—"

"No, *thank* you, much obliged—"

"I'm a friend of Hannah Schneider's."

There was a sharp gasp, as if I'd stuck her in the arm with a hypodermic needle. She was silent. Then she hung up.

Puzzled, I pressed Redial. She picked up instantly—I could hear a television, a soap opera repeat, a woman, "Blaine," then, "How *could* you?"—and Ada Harvey slammed down the receiver, hard, without a word. On my fourth attempt, it rang fifteen times before the operator recording came on informing me my party was unavailable. I waited ten minutes, ate a few bites of chocolate cake and tried a fifth time. She answered on the first ring.

"The *nerve*—you don't stop I'm goin' to call the authorities—"

"I'm not a friend of Hannah Schneider's."

"No? Well, who the heck are you then?"

"I'm a stude—I'm an investigator," I amended hastily. "I'm a private investigator employed"—my eyes veered onto my bookshelf, landing between *The Anonymous* (Felm, 2001) and *Party of the Third Degree* (Grono, 1995)—"by an anonymous third-degree party. I was hoping you could help me by answering a few questions. It should only take five minutes."

"You're a private investigator?" she repeated.

"Yes."

"Then the Lord wears pantaloons and saddle shoes—how old are you? You sound no bigger than a minute."

Dad said one could dig up a great deal about a person from his/her phone voice and from the sound of hers, she was in her early forties and wore brown leather flats with tiny tassels on them, tassels like miniature brooms sweeping the tops of her feet.

"I'm sixteen," I admitted.

"And you said you work for *who?*"

It wasn't a good idea to keep lying; as Dad said: "Sweet, your every thought walks through your voice holding a giant billboard advertisement."

"Myself. I'm a student at St. Gallway, where Hannah taught. I–I'm sorry I lied before but I was afraid you'd hang up again and I"—frantically, I stared down at my CASE NOTES—"you're my only lead. I happened to meet your father, the night he died. He seemed to be a fascinating person. I'm sorry about what happened."

It was a detestable thing to do, to drag people's deceased family members into it, in order to get what one wants—any mention of Dad dead, I'd doubtlessly sing like a magpie—but it was my only hope; it was obvious Ada was on the fence between hearing me out and hanging up and leaving the phone off the hook.

"Because," I went on shakily, "your father and the rest of your family were, at one time, friends with Hannah, I was hoping—"

"*Friends?*" She spit out the word like it was rancid avocado. "We were not *friends* with that woman."

"Oh, I'm sorry. I thought—"

"You thought *wrong.*"

If before her voice had been miniatured and poodled, now it was rott-weilered. She didn't go on. She was what was commonly called in the gumshoe world, "one helluva cemented dame."

I swallowed. "So, then, uh, Ms. Harvey—"

"My name is Ada Rose Harvey Lowell."

"Ms. *Lowell.* You weren't acquainted with Hannah Schneider at all?"

Again, she didn't say anything. A car commercial was assaulting her liv-ing room. Hurriedly, I scribbled "None?" in my CASE NOTES under question #4, "What is the nature of your relationship with Hannah Schneider?" I was just about to move on to #5, "Were you aware of her scheduled camping trip?" when she sighed and spoke, her voice stark.

"You don't know what she was," Ada said.

Now it was my turn to stay silent, because it was one of those dramatic comments that come up halfway into a sci-fi action movie, when one charac-ter is about to inform the other character what they're dealing with is not "of this earth." Still, my heart began to clang in my chest like a voodoo funeral march in N'awlins.

"What *do* you know?" she asked with a note of impatience. "*Anything?*"

"I know she was a teacher," I tried quietly.

This elicited an acerbic, "Heh."

"I know your father, Smoke, was a retired financier and—"

"My father was an in*ves*tigative *jour*nalist," she corrected (see "Southern Pride," *Moon Pies and Tarnation,* Wyatt, 2001). "He was a banker for thirty-eight years before he was able to retire and pursue his first loves. Writin'. And true crime."

"He wrote a book, didn't he? A–a mystery?"

"*The Doloroso Treason* was *not* a mystery. It was 'bout the illegal aliens and the Texas border and the corruption and drug smugglin' that goes on."

(She callously squashed the word *aliens*; it became *Aileens*.) "It was a huge success. They gave him a key to the city." She sniffed. "What else?"

"I–I know your father drowned at Hannah's house."

She gasped again; this time it sounded like I'd slapped her across the face in front of a hundred guests at a toffee pull. "My father did *not*"—her voice was trembly and shrill, the scrape of Lee Press-On Nails down pantyhose—"*I*— *Do you have any idea who my father was?*"

"I'm sorry, I didn't mean to—"

"He was hit by a tractor-trailer when he was *four* riding his tricycle. Broke his back serving in Korea. Got trapped in a car that went over Feather Bridge and *then* went out the window like they do in the movies. He'd been bit *twice*—once by a Doberman, another time a Tennessee rattler, and almost had a shark attack off the coast of Way Paw We, Indonesia, only he'd watched a special on the Nature Channel and remembered to punch it straight in the nose, which is what they tell you to do when one's comin' at you only most people don't have the guts to do it. Smoke *did*. And now you're tryin' to tell *me* his medication mixed with a little Jack was going to finish him off? Makes me sick. He'd been takin' it for six months and it had no effect, *period*. That man could be shot in the head six times and he'd go right on—you mark my words."

To my horror, her voice tore a hole on "words"—a sizable hole by the sound of things. I wasn't positive, but I think she was crying too, an awful held-back hiccuping sound that faded into the mumbles and elevator music of the soap opera, so you couldn't tell the difference between her drama and the one on television. It was very possible she'd just said, "Travis, I'm not gonna lie and say I don't have feelings for you"—not the woman on the TV, and it was also possible the woman on the TV, not Ada, was crying over her dead father.

"I'm sorry," I said. "I'm just kind of, confused—"

"I didn't put it all together 'til later," she sniffled.

I waited—enough time for her to stitch together, however crudely, the hole in her voice.

"You didn't put what . . . together?"

She cleared her throat.

"Do you know who The Nightwatchmen are?" she asked. " 'Course you don't . . . don't even know your own name, probably—"

"I do, actually. My father's a political science professor."

She was surprised—or maybe relieved. "Oh?"

"They were radicals," I said. "But apart from an incident or two in the early seventies, no one's sure if they actually existed. They're more a–a beautiful idea, fighting against greed—than something real." I was paraphrasing bits of "A Quick History of the American Revolutionary" (see Van Meer, *Federal Forum*, Vol. 23, Issue 9, 1990).

"An incident or two," Ada repeated. "Exactly. So then you know about Gracey."

"He was the founder. But he's dead, isn't he?"

"Other than one other person," Ada said slowly, "George Gracey is the only known member. And he's still wanted by the FBI. In '70 . . . no, '71, he killed a West Virginia Senator, put a pipe bomb in his car. A year later, he blew up a building in Texas. Four people died. He was caught on tape so they made a sketch of him, but then he dropped off the face of the earth. In the eighties there was an explosion in a townhouse in England. Homemade bombs. People had heard he was livin' there, so they assumed he was dead. There was too much damage to recover the teeth on the bodies found. That's how they identify, you know. Teeth records."

She paused, swallowing.

"The Senator killed was Senator Michael McCullough, Dubs's uncle on his mother's side, my great uncle. And it happened over in Meade, twenty minutes from Findley. Dubs said it all the time when we were growin' up: 'I'll fly to the ends of the earth to bring that sonuvabitch to trial.' When Dubs drowned, everyone believed the police. They said he'd had too much to drink and it was an accident. *I* refused to believe it. I stayed up all night goin' through his notes even though Archie cussed me out, said I was crazy. But then I saw how it all went together. I showed Archie and Cal too. And *she* knew of course. She knew we were on to her. We'd called the FBI. That's why she hanged herself. It was death or prison."

I was bewildered. "I don't understand—"

"*The Nocturnal Conspiracy*," Ada said softly.

Trying to follow this woman's logic was like trying to watch an electron orbit a nucleus with the naked eye.

"What's *The Nocturnal Conspiracy*?"

"His next *book*. The one he was writing on George Gracey. That's what he was going to call it and it was going to be a bestseller. Smoke tracked him down, see. Last May. He found him on a fantasy island called Paxos, livin' high off the hog."

She drew a shaky breath. "You don't know what it felt like, when the police called and told us our father, the one we'd just seen two days before at Chrysanthemum's baptism, was gone. Snatched from us. We hadn't heard the name *Hannah Schneider* in all our lives. At first, we thought she was the loud divorcée the Rider's Club had trouble nominatin' for treasurer, but that was Hannah *Smithers*. Then we think, maybe she was Gretchen Peterson's cousin who Dubs took to the Marquis Polo Fundraiser, but that's Lizzie Sheldon. So"—by this point, Ada had ripped out most of her punctuation, some of her pauses, too; her words stampeded into the receiver—"after *two* days of this, Cal takes a look at the picture I asked the police to get for us and what do you know? He says he remembers her talkin' to Dubs at the Handy Pantry way back in June, when they were coming back from Auto Show 4000—this is a *month* after Dubs got back from Paxos. So Cal says, yeah, Dubs went inside the Handy Pantry to get gum and this same woman shimmied up to him. Cal has a photographic memory. 'It was her,' he said. Tall. Dark hair. A face shaped like one of those Valentine chocolate boxes and Valentine's was Dubs' favorite holiday. She asked for directions to Charleston and I guess they stayed talkin' for so long, Cal had to get out of the car to go get him. And that was *it*. When we went through Dubs' things, we found her number in his address book. Phone records showed he called her at least once or twice a week. She knew how to play it, see. After my mother, there's never been anyone special—I–I still talk about him in the present. Archie says I have to stop that."

She paused, took another labored breath, started to speak again. And as she talked, I was struck by the image of one of those itsy-bitsy garden spiders that decide to make their web not in some sensible corner, but in a gigantic space, a space so huge and far-fetched, in it one could fit two African Elephants end to end. Dad and I watched such a determined spider on our porch in Howard, Louisiana, and no matter how many times the wind unrigged the mooring, how many times the web buckled and sagged, unable to hold itself up between the fake columns, the spider went on with its work, climbing to the top, free-falling, silk thread trembling behind it, dental floss in the wind. "She's making sense of the world," Dad said. "She's sewing it together as best she can."

"We *still* don't know how she managed it," Ada went on. "My father was two hundred and forty pounds. It *had* to be poison. She injected him with something, between his toes . . . cyanide maybe. 'Course the police swore they checked all that and there was no sign. I just don't see how it was possible. He liked his whiskey . . . won't lie about that. And there was his medication—"

"What kind of medication was it?" I asked.

"Minipress. For blood pressure. Dr. Nixley told him you're not supposed to drink with it but he had before and it never messed with him. He drove home all by himself from the King of Hearts Fundraiser right when he first went on it and I was there when he got home. He was *fine*. Believe me, if I thought he *wasn't* fine I'd have caused a stink. Not that he would've listened."

"But Ada"—I kept my voice subdued, as if we were in a library—"I really don't think Hannah could've possibly—"

"Gracey was in contact with her. He told her to kill Smoke. Like she'd done with all the others. She was the temptation, see."

"But—"

"She's the *other one*," she interrupted flatly. " 'Other than *one* other person.' The other member—weren't you listening?"

"But I *know* she's not a criminal. I talked to a detective here—"

"Hannah Schneider's not her real name. She ripped it off a poor missing woman who grew up in an orphanage in New Jersey. She's been livin' as that girl for years. Her real name's Catherine Baker and she's wanted by the FBI for shootin' a police officer right between the eyes. Twice. Somewhere in Texas." She cleared her throat. "Smoke didn't recognize her because no one's sure what Baker actually looks like. 'Specially *now*. They have old testimony, a composite that's twenty years old—in the eighties everyone had weird hair, freaky looks—*you* know those awful leftover hippies. And she's blond in the sketch. Says she has blue eyes. Smoke *had* the picture, along with the stuff on George Gracey. But it's one of those things—it could be a drawin' of *me*, you know. Could be a drawin' of anyone."

"Could you send me copies of his notes? For research purposes?"

Ada sniffed and though she didn't exactly agree to send them I gave her my mailing address. Neither of us spoke for a minute or two. I could hear the end credits of the soap opera, the outburst of another commercial.

"I just wish I'd been there," she said faintly. "I have a sixth sense, see. If I'd gone to the Auto Show, I could've gone in with him when he went to get the gum. I would've seen what she was doin'—prancin' by in tight jeans, sunglasses, pretendin' it was a coincidence. Cal swore he saw her a couple days before, too, when he and Smoke were in Winn-Dixie pickin' up ribs. He said she walked right by with her empty shoppin' cart, all gussied up like she was goin' somewhere, and she looked straight at Cal, grinned like the Devil himself. 'Course, there's no way of knowin' for sure. It gets busy on Sundays—"

"What did you say?" I asked quietly.

She stopped talking. The abrupt change in my tone of voice must have startled her.

"I said there's no way of knowin'," she said apprehensively.

Without thinking, I hung up the phone.

Che Guevara Talks to Young People

The Nightwatchmen have always gone by a variety of names—
Nächtlich, or "Nocturnal," in German, also *Nie Schlafend*, or
"Never Sleeping." In French, they are *Les Veilleurs de Nuit*. Membership, in its supposed heyday, 1971 to 1980, is wholly unknown;
some say it was twenty-five men and women across America; others
claim over a thousand around the globe. Whatever the truth—and,
alas, we may never know it—the movement is whispered about with
greater enthusiasm today than at its zenith (an Internet search yields
over 100,000 pages). Its present-day popularity as part history lesson,
part fairy tale, is a testament to The Freedom Ideal, a dream to liber-
ate all people, regardless of their race or creed, a dream that, no matter how fractured and cynical modern society becomes, will not die.

Van Meer,
"*Nächtlich*: Popular Myths of Freedom Fighting,"
Federal Forum, Vol. 10, Issue 5, 1998

Dad had raised me to be a skeptical person, a person unconvinced until
"the facts line up like chorus girls," and so I had not believed Ada Harvey—
not until she'd described the Winn-Dixie incident (or perhaps a little before,
with "tight jeans" and "sunglasses"); then, it'd sounded as if she were describing not Smoke and Cal in Winn-Dixie, but Dad and me at Fat Kat in September, when I'd first seen Hannah in Frozen Foods.

If that weren't enough to knock the wind out of me, she had to go
entirely Southern Gothic, dragging the Devil and his grin into it, and when-

ever someone with a fudgethical Southern accent said *devil*, one inevitably felt they knew something one didn't—as Yam Chestley wrote in *Dixiecrats* (1979), "The South knows two things through and through: cornbread and Satan" (p. 166). After I hung up, my bedroom stalagmited with shadows, I stared at my CASE NOTES on which I'd written in famished handwriting Officer Coxley–style haiku (NIGHTWATCHMEN CATHERINE BAKER GRACEY).

My first thought was that Dad was dead.

He, too, had been Catherine Baker's target, because he, too, had been working on a book about Gracey (it was the logical explanation for Hannah stalking us the same way she'd stalked Smoke Harvey), or, if he wasn't at work on a book ("I'm not certain I have the stamina for another book," Dad admitted in a Bourbon Mood, a sad acknowledgment he never made in daylight), then an article, essay or lecture of some kind, his own *Nocturnal Conspiracy*.

Of course—I ran across the room to switch on the overhead light and thankfully, the shadows were instantly whisked away like out-of-fashion black dresses in a department store—I reminded myself, Hannah Schneider was dead (the petit four of truth I knew for certain) and Dad was safe with Professor Arnie Sanderson at Piazza Pitti, an Italian restaurant in downtown Stockton. Still, I felt the need to hear his sandpaper voice, his "Sweet, don't be preposterous." I ran downstairs, tore through the Yellow Pages and dialed the restaurant. (Dad didn't have a cell phone; "So I may be available to others twenty-four hours, seven days a week like some minimum-waged dunderhead working in Customer Service? Much obliged, but no thank you.") It took only a minute for the hostess to identify him; few sported Irish tweed in spring.

"Sweet?" He was alarmed. "What's happened?"

"Nothing—well, *every*thing. Are you okay?"

"What—of course. What's the matter?"

"Nothing." A paranoid thought occurred to me. "Do you trust Arnie Sanderson? Maybe you shouldn't leave your food unattended. Don't get up to go to the bathroom—"

"*What?*"

"I've discovered the truth about Hannah Schneider. I know why someone killed her, or–or she killed herself—I haven't quite figured that part out yet, but I know *why*."

Dad was silent, obviously not only weary of the name, but thoroughly unconvinced. Not that I *blamed* him; my breathing was a madwoman's, my heart was teetering like a wino in a jail cell—altogether an unconvincing figure of truth and forethought.

"Sweet," he said gently, "you know, I dropped off *Gone with the Wind* earlier this afternoon. Perhaps you should watch it. Have a piece of that chocolate cake. I should be no more than an hour." He began to say something more, something that started with, "Hannah," but that word yoga-twisted in his mouth so it came out "hands"; he seemed afraid to say her name, in case it encouraged me. "You sure you're all right? I can leave *now*."

"No, I'm fine," I said quickly. "We'll talk when you get home."

I hung up (infinitely reassured; Dad's voice was a pack of ice on a sprain). I collected my CASE NOTES and raced downstairs to the kitchen to brew some coffee. ("Experience, intellectual prowess, forensics, fingerprints, footprints—sure, they're important," wrote Officer Christina Vericault on p. 4 of *The Last Uniform* [1982]. "But the essential element of crime solving is a fine French Roast or Colombian blend. No murder will be solved without it.") After jotting down a few additional details from the Ada Harvey conversation, I hurried downstairs to Dad's study, switching on the lights.

Dad had only written one relatively short piece about The Nightwatchmen, published in 1998, "*Nächtlich*: Popular Myths of Freedom Fighting." Every now and then, too, for his Civil War seminars, he included on reading lists a more extensive commentary about their methodologies, an essay out of Herbert Littleton's *Anatomy of Materialism* (1990), "The Nightwatchmen and Mythical Principles of Practical Change." With little trouble, I located both on the bookshelf (Dad always purchased five copies of any *Federal Forum* issue in which he was featured, not unlike a paparazzi-hungry starlet when her picture graces "Around Town" in *Celebrastory Weekly*).

I returned to Dad's desk with the two publications. To the left of his laptop sat a hefty stack of legal pads and various folded foreign newspapers. Curious, I paged through them, my eyes having to adjust to decode his barbed-wire handwriting. Unfortunately, their subject matter had nothing to do with The Nightwatchmen or the whereabouts of George Gracey (thus paralleling Smoke's story like a dream). Instead, they featured Dad's obvious cause célèbre, civil upheaval in the Democratic Republic of the Congo and other nations of Central Africa. "When Will Killing Stop?" demanded the awkwardly translated editorials in *Afrikaan News*, the small Cape Town political newspaper. "Where Is Champion for Freedom?"

I put those papers aside (returning them to their original order; Dad knew snooping the way dogs smell fear) and began my orderly investigation into The Nightwatchmen (or *"Mai addormentato,"* as they were called in Italian and apparently 決して眠った in Japanese). First, I read Dad's *Federal Forum* article. Second, I browsed the long-winded Chapter 19 in the Littleton book. Lastly, I turned on Dad's laptop and searched for the group on the Internet.

In the years since 1998, the number of pages referencing the radicals had mushroomed; the 100,000 had become 500,000. I scanned as much as I could, no resource excluded for bias, romanticism or even conjecture ("Within prejudice grows all kinds of remarkable truths," Dad said): encyclopedias, history texts, political Web sites, Leftist blogs, Communist and Neo-Marxist sites (a favorite, www.thehairyman.com—alluding to Karl Marx's lionlike appearance), conspiracy and anarchist Web sites, sites about cartels, cults, hero worship, urban legends, organized crime, Orwell, Malcolm X, Erin Brockovich and something out of Nicaragua called Champions of Che. It seemed the group was like Greta Garbo when she first went into retirement: mysterious, impossible to pin down and everyone wanted a piece of her.

It took me a little over an hour to look through everything.

When I finished, my eyes were red, my throat dry. I felt drained and yet—scandalously alive (pronounced "a-LIVE"), giddy as the bright green Darning Needle Dragonfly that careened into Dad's hair at Lake Pennebaker, making him dance like a marionette, go "Ahhhhh!" and barge through a crowd of geriatrics wearing yellow visors identical to the yellow halo Christ sports in old frescoes.

My heart-thumping excitement was not simply because I knew so much about The Nightwatchmen I felt oddly confident I could deliver a Dadified lecture on them, my voice a tidal wave, rising up, up over the shabbily combed heads of his students, and not because, rather incredibly, Ada Harvey's information had held up heroically upon further examination like the British blockade against the Germans in the First Battle of the Atlantic during World War I. My exhilaration wasn't even because Hannah Schneider—all that she'd done, her strange behaviors, her lies—had suddenly come crashing open at my feet like the outer stone sarcophagus of Pharaoh Heteraah-mes when Carlson Quay Meade, in 1927, fumbled his way through a murky mummy cache high up in the cliffs of the Valley of the Kings. (For the first time, I could crouch down, take my oil lantern directly to Hannah's bone-smooth face, see, in startling detail, its every angle and plane.)

It was something else, too, something Dad once said after recounting those final hours in the life of Che Guevara. "There is something intoxicating about the dream of liberty and those who risked their lives for it—particularly in this whiny day and age, when people can barely manage to roll off their Barcalounger to answer a doorbell for a pizza delivery, much less a cry for freedom."

I'd *solved* it.

I couldn't believe it. I'd recovered the values of both *x* and *y* (with the vital assistance of Ada Harvey; I wasn't vain like many applied mathematicians, desperate to appear unaccompanied in the Annals of History). And I felt both terror and awe—what Einstein experienced in the middle of the night in 1905 in Bern, Switzerland, after waking from a nightmare in which he'd witnessed two pulsing stars crashing together creating strange waves in space—a vision that would inspire his General Theory of Relativity.

"It vas ze sceriest end most beautiful sing I haf ever seen," he said.

I hurried over to Dad's bookshelf again, this time pulling Colonel Helig's treatise on murder from the shelf, *Machinations Idyllic and Unseen* (1889). I paged through it (so old, pages 1–22 dandruffed out of the spine), searching for the passages that would cast the last puddles of light on this sprawling truth I'd uncovered, this surprising—and obviously, treacherous—New World.

*   *   *

The oddest insight into the workings of The Nightwatchmen (an incident Dad would deem evidence of "a legend's potential to be worn like a trench coat, used for good, warding off the rain, and evil, streaking through a park, frightening children") was an episode detailed on www.goodrebels .net/nw, in which two eighth graders from an affluent Houston suburb committed suicide together on January 14, 1995. One of them, a thirteen-year-old girl, had written a suicide note—posted on the Web site—and in stark handwriting, on frighteningly sweet stationery (pink, rainbows) she'd written: "We hereby eliminate our selfs in the name of The Nightwatch Men and to show our parents their money is dirty. Death to all oil pigs."

The creator of the site (when you clicked on "About Randy" he revealed himself to be an emaciated woolly-mammoth type with a serious red mouth zipped tightly into his face, of indeterminate age) complained about this, the "heritage" of The Nightwatchmen being abused in such a fashion, because "nowhere in their manifestos do they say kill yourself because you're rich. They're champions against capitalist abuses, not wacko members of the

Manson Family." "Death to all pigs," of course, was written in blood on the front door of Cielo Drive (see *Blackbird Singing in the Dead of Night: The Life of Charles Milles Manson,* Ivys, 1985, p. 226).

According to most sources, Randy was correct; nowhere in the manifestos of *Nächtlich* did they urge suicide under any circumstance. In fact, there were no manifestos at *all* penned by the group, no pamphlets, brochures, outlines, recorded sound-bites or fervently worded essays detailing their intentions. (It was a choice Dad would deem remarkably astute: "If rebels never broadcast who they are, their enemies will never be sure of what they're fighting.") The only paper evidencing the group's existence was a single notebook page attributed to George Gracey, dated July 9, 1971, marking the birth of The Nightwatchmen—at least, as the nation, the police and the FBI knew it. (It wasn't a welcomed nativity; The Establishment already had their hands full with the Weather Underground, Black Panthers and Students for a Democratic Society, among a handful of other "hallucinating hippie quacks," as Dad called them.)

On that day in 1971, a Meade, West Virginia, policeman discovered this notebook page Scotch-taped to a telephone pole ten feet from where Senator Michael McCullough's white Cadillac Fleetwood Seventy-five had exploded in a wealthy residential community known as Marlowe Gardens. (Senator Michael McCullough climbed inside and was killed instantly in the blast.)

The Nightwatchmen's sole manifesto could be read on www.mindfucks .net/gg (and Gracey was no Spelling Bee Winner): "Today dies a crooked and gluttonus man"—it was true, at least literally; McCullough allegedly weighed three hundred pounds and suffered from scoliosis—"a man who gets rich by the suffering of women and children, a greedy man. And so I, and the many with me, will be The Nightwatchmen, helping to divest this nation and the world of the capitalistic greed contemptuous of human life, undermining democrisy, blindfolding its people, forcing them to live in the dark."

Dad and Herbert Littleton supplied insight into the objectives of The Nightwatchmen, inferred from the 1971 assassination, as well as Gracey's subsequent explosion of an office building in downtown Houston on October 29, 1973. Littleton reasoned Senator McCullough had become the group's first known assassination due to his involvement in a 1966 toxic waste scandal. Over seventy tons of toxic waste had been dumped illegally into the West Virginia Pooley River by Shohawk Industries, a textiles manufacturing plant, and by 1965, the tiny, impoverished coal mining towns of Beudde and Morrisville had suffered an increase in cancer among its low-income population. When the scandal broke, McCullough, then the governor, voiced his outrage and grief and his highly publicized, heroic mandate to clean up the river, never mind the price tag (what it cost taxpayers), had won him a seat in the senate the following election year (see "Governor McCullough Visits Five-year-old Boy with Leukemia," *Anatomy*, Littleton, p. 193).

In truth, however, in 1989, Littleton exposed McCullough had not only known about the dumping, and the toll it would take on the communities downstream, but he'd actually been well compensated for keeping mum, an amount estimated between $500,000 and $750,000.

The Houston bombing of 1973 illustrated, according to Dad, The Nightwatchmen's resolve to wage war against "capitalistic greed and exploitation on a global scale." The target was no longer a single man but the corporate headquarters of Oxico Oil & Gas (OOG). An AN/FO-based (Ammonium Nitrate/Fuel Oil) explosive was planted on the executive floor by George Gracey masquerading as a maintenance man; a security camera taped him hobbling out of the building early that morning, as well as two other figures wearing ski masks beneath janitor caps—one purportedly a woman. The blast killed three high-ranking executives, including the company's long-time President and CEO, Carlton Ward.

Littleton contended the assault was provoked by Ward's approval, in 1971, of a secret cost-saving initiative for Oxico's South American oil refining interests. The proposal outlined that Oxico should stop lining their crude oil waste pits throughout refinery fields in Ecuador, allowing seepage and severe environmental contamination, yet saving $3 per barrel—an action "illustrative of the flagrant disregard for lost human life in favor of amiable profit margins." By 1972, toxic drilling waters were actively contaminating the freshwater supply of more than thirty thousand men, women and children; and by 1989, five different indigenous cultures faced not only escalating cancer rates and severe birth defects but also total extinction (see "Girl Without Legs," *Anatomy*, Littleton, p. 211).

The Houston bombing marked a sea change in tactics for The Nightwatchmen. It was then, according to Dad, that "the reality of whiny radicals ended and the legend began." The Oxico executive assassinations disheartened (others said "defeated") the sect; it did nothing to modify South American refinery policies—it only strengthened building security, forced the maintenance crews to suffer increasingly vigorous background checks, many losing their jobs; and an innocent secretary, a mother of four, had been killed in the explosion. Gracey was forced to go underground. The second to last confirmed sighting of him was in November 1973, a month after the Houston bombing; he was spotted in Berkeley, California, eating at a diner close to the university with an "unidentified dark-haired child, a girl between thirteen and fourteen years of age."

If The Nightwatchmen had once been highly visible—if solely through their use of explosives—in January 1974, Gracey and the twenty to twenty-five other members resolved to carry out their goals wholly unseen, according to Dad, "without pomp and circumstance." While most revolutionaries (even Che himself) might consider such a move unwise and self-defeating—"What is civil war if it isn't fought in the open, deafeningly, colorfully, so the masses are encouraged to take up arms," contends Lou Swann, Dad's artless Harvard peer who'd penned the well-received *Iron Hands* (1999); "He purloined my title," Dad noted sourly—it was actually a strategic shift Dad would deem both clever and highly sophisticated. In his various essays on insurrection, Dad maintained: "If fighters for liberty are forced to use violence, they must do it silently to be effective in the long term" (see "Cape Town Fear," Van Meer, *Federal Forum*, Vol. 19, Issue 13). (This actually wasn't Dad's idea; he'd plagiarized it from *La Grimace* [Anonyme, 1824].)

For the next three or four years, The Nightwatchmen did just that; silently, they restructured, educated and recruited. "Membership tripled not only in America, but internationally," reported a Dutch theorist who ran a Web site called "De Echte Waarheid," "The Real Truth." They supposedly formed a tangled web, a mysterious network with Gracey poised at the center surrounded by other "thinkers," as they were called, and spangling the outside of this maze, countless ancillary members—the majority never meeting Gracey or even each other.

"No one knows what most members were up to," wrote Randy on www.goodrebels.net.

I had an inkling. Charlie Quick in *Prisoners of War: Why Democracy Won't Stick in South America* (1971) (a regular on Dad's syllabus), wrote of a necessary period of "gestation," when it was beneficial for a potential freedom fighter to do nothing but "learn everything about his enemy—including what he has for breakfast, his brand of aftershave, the number of hairs on his left big toe." Perhaps that's what each member had been assigned to do, collect (with the precision and patience of collecting butterfly specimens, even the rare, shy species) personal information on the men Gracey deemed their targets. Hannah had shown this level of detail when discussing the Harvey family at Hyacinth Terrace; she'd known the Civil War story about his house, Moorgate, and intimate particulars about people she'd never met, probably never even *seen*. Maybe Gracey was like Gordon Gekko ("You stop sending me information and you start getting me some.") and each of the ancillary members were Bud Foxes ("He had lunch at La Cirque with a group of well-dressed heavyset bean counters.").

(After scribbling these speculations in my CASE NOTES, I read on.)

During this particular period, the group also abandoned the too-obvious, too-unproductive Group Meeting—in March 1974, police had come close to raiding one of their gatherings in an abandoned Braintree, Massachusetts, warehouse—in favor of more covert, well-disguised meetings, private "one on ones." According to www.livingoffthegrid.net/gracey, these encounters typically began "at a roadside diner, truck stop or local dive bar and continued in a Holiday Inn or some other cheap motel—the intention being that the meeting would look to observers like a random pick-up, a one-night-stand," and hence, "totally unremarkable." (Obviously, I wanted to jump for joy when I read this, but I made myself stay focused, reading on.)

According to www.historytheydonttellyou.net/nachtlich, in early 1978, whispers of a renewed, silent presence of The Nightwatchmen began to surface again, when MFG Holdings CEO Peter Fitzwilliam died in an electrical fire at his fifty-acre Connecticut estate. Fitzwilliam had been in clandestine merger talks with Sav-Mart, the discount retailer. In the aftermath of his death, the negotiations fell apart and by October 1980, MFG (whose manufacturing sweatshops in Indonesia were deemed by Global Humanitarian Watch "some of the most atrocious in the world") had filed for bankruptcy. Their stock had gone to zero.

In 1982, Gracey's radicals—now purportedly going by the name *Nie Schlafend* (also проснитесь в ноче according to www.mayhem.ru, Russian for "awake in the night")—were again discussed throughout countless left-wing and Conspiracy Theory journals (*Liberal Man*, and something called *Mind Control Quarterly*) when the four Senior Managers, directly responsible for the design and distribution of the Ford Pinto, ended up dead within a three-month period. Two died from sudden cardiac arrest (one, Howie McFarlin, was a health nut and exercise freak), another from a self-inflicted gunshot wound to the head and the last, Mitchell Cantino, drowned in his own swimming pool. Cantino's autopsy revealed his blood-alcohol level to be

.25 and a large dose of a Methaqualone was found in his system, a sedative prescribed by his doctor for sleeplessness and anxiety. He'd been in the process of divorcing his wife of twenty-two years, and she told police he'd confessed he'd been dating another woman for six months.

"Said her name was Catherine and that he was madly in love. I never saw her but I know she was a blonde. When I went to the house to pick up some of my clothes, I found blond hair in my comb," Cantino's ex-wife informed police (see www.angelfire.com/save-ferris80s/pinto).

Police ruled the drowning an accident. There was no evidence "Catherine," or any other person, had been present at Cantino's house on the night of his death.

It was during this period, 1983–1987, that Catherine Baker—or at the very least, her myth—began to materialize. She was referred to on countless Web sites as the Death's Head Hawkmoth, or *Die Motte*, as she was called on an anarchist site out of Hamburg (see www.anarchieeine.de). (Apparently everyone in the group had a nickname. Gracey was Nero. Others [none of them ever identified with an actual person and widely disputed] were Bull's-Eye, Mohave, Socrates and Franklin.) Dad and Littleton barely mentioned The Moth in their essays; she appeared as a postscript in Littleton's piece and Dad only mentioned her toward the end, when discussing the "power of the freedom fairy tale, when men and women fighting injustice are assigned attributes of movie stars and comic book heroes." I could only assume this slight was because while Gracey's identity was real, both documented and validated—he was Turkish in origin, had undergone hip surgery following an unknown accident, leaving his right leg a half-inch shorter than his left— Catherine Baker's life was cast with more hairpin curves, loopholes, murk and Muddy Footprints Leading Nowhere than the plot of a film noir.

Some claimed (www.geocities.com/revolooshonlaydees) she'd never *technically* been linked to The Nightwatchmen, and the fact that the town of the last confirmed George Gracey sighting and the location of her own brutal crime happened within two hours (and twenty-three miles) of each other, was simply a coincidence and, subsequently, an overeager conclusion of "extremist ties" by the FBI.

There was no way of knowing for certain if, on September 19, 1987, the blonde spotted with Gracey in a Lord's Drugstore parking lot in Ariel, Texas, was the *same* blonde pulled over by a State Trooper on a deserted road off Highway 18 outside Vallarmo. Fifty-four-year-old Trooper Baldwin Sullins, following the 1968 blue Mercury Cougar onto the shoulder of the road, radioed headquarters to say he was on a routine stop for an extinguished taillight. And yet, something unusual about the woman must have made him ask her to step out of the vehicle (according to www.copkillers.com/cbaker87, he'd asked to see the inside of her trunk, where Gracey was hiding), and as she climbed from the driver's seat wearing blue jeans and a black T-shirt, she pulled out an RG .22 handgun, commonly called a Saturday Night Special or Junk Gun, and shot him twice in the face.

(I'd hoped Ada Harvey had been embellishing that particular detail; I'd wanted the Unintentional Tugged Trigger, the Slipped My Mind Safety Off, but sadly, it seemed Ada was not prone to ornamentation.)

Trooper Sullins had called in the Mercury Cougar's license plate tags before he'd left his police car, and the car was registered to one Mr. Owen Tackle of Los Ebanos, Texas. It soon came to light Tackle had put the car up for sale at Reece's Cars-for-Less in Ariel three months prior, and a tall blonde, who gave her name as Catherine Baker, had purchased the car the day before, paying in cash. Seconds before the shooting, a Lincoln Continental happened to drive by, and it was that driver's testimony—Shirley Lavina, age 53—that led to the police sketch of Catherine Baker, the only certified portrait of her in existence.

(A grainy posting of the composite is featured on www.american outlaws.net/deathmoth and Ada Harvey was right; it looked nothing like Hannah Schneider. In fact, it could very well have been a rendering of June Bug Phyllis Mixer's Standard Poodle.)

There were hundreds of other details to read about *Die Motte* (according to www.members.aol/smokefilledrooms/moth, she looked like Betty Page, while www.ironcurtain.net claimed people mistook her for Kim Basinger) and it was these details—not to mention the startling reappearance of "Lord's Drugstore" (where Hannah had said *Jade* had been stopped by police at the end of her phony road trip)—that made me wonder if I might faint from sheer incredulity. But I forced myself to press on with an unyielding countenance and bearing, much like old British pinch-faced spinster, Mary Kingsley (1862–1900), the first female explorer, who without batting an eyelash traveled up the crocodile-ridden Ogooué River in Gabon to study cannibalism and polygamy.

While some sources contended Catherine Baker was British and French in origin (even Ecuadorian; according to www.amigosdaliberdade.br her twin had died from stomach cancer due to the Oxico-contaminated water, prompting her to join the group), the resounding, and least refuted idea, was that she was the same thirteen-year-old Catherine Baker who'd been reported missing by her parents in New York City the summer of 1973. She was also "almost certainly" the "unidentified dark-haired child, a girl between thirteen and fourteen years of age" who'd been spotted with Gracey in Berkeley, November of that same year, a month after the Houston bombing.

According to www.wherearetheynow.com/felns/cb3, the parents of the mislaid Catherine Baker had been stratospherically wealthy. Her father was a Lariott, a descendant of Edwards P. Lariott, the American capitalist and oil tycoon, once the second richest man in the United States (and archenemy of John D. Rockefeller) and it was her rebellious spirit, a disenchantment with her home life and a childish infatuation with Gracey (who some estimated she'd met in New York, early in 1973) that had motivated her to escape her life of "capitalist privilege and excess," never to return to it again.

Naturally, to me, this rarefied upbringing looked infinitely more at home around the bare and bony shoulders of Hannah Schneider than Sergeant Detective Harper's contention that she'd been an orphan, raised at the Horizon House in New Jersey—a difference between a mink stole and a Member's Only. If Ada Harvey was to be believed (and thus far, there was no reason not to), Fayonette Harper's mistake was that she'd investigated the life of Hannah Schneider the Missing Person, the orphan whose identity Catherine Baker had apparently absconded with (the overcoat she'd donned and blithely strolled out of the store with, without paying). And yet, frustratingly, I couldn't confirm Ada's conjecture as fact or fiction; searching for "Hannah Schneider" and "Missing Person" yielded not a single result, which I initially found strange until I remembered what Hannah herself had said that night at her house: *"Runaways, orphans, they're kidnapped, killed—whatever the reason, they vanish from public record. They leave behind nothing but a name, and even that's forgotten in the end."*

It had happened to the person whose name she'd taken.

As I read the first startling details about Catherine Baker's life (www .greatcommierevolt.net/women/baker was particularly well researched, replete with bibliography and links to Additional Reading), I started sprinting like an Errand Boy all the way back to that conversation with her, when I was alone at her house, retrieving her every word, expression and gesture, and when I dumped that splintered cargo at my feet (something "night," police officer, The Gone), I turned around and sprinted back for more.

Hannah had claimed it was the truth about the Bluebloods, when in fact, it was her own past she'd narrated between all those cigarettes and sighs. She'd assigned each of them a portion of her own history, neatly sewing it into them using an invisible appliqué stitch, garnishing it with a few erroneous, baroque details ("prostitute, junkie," "blackouts") in order to floor me, make it look so astonishing, it had to be real.

It'd been *her* father, not Jade's, *"from oil money, so he had the blood and suffering of thousands on his hands."* And it had been *she* who'd run away from home, from New York to San Francisco, and those six days of travel had "changed the course of her life." When she was thirteen, she, not Leulah, had absconded with a Turkish man ("handsome and passionate," she'd called him) and she, not Milton, had wanted something to believe in, something to keep her afloat. She joined, not a "street gang," but "something *night*"—The Nightwatchmen.

She'd cut out the police officer killing from her own past and tacked it onto Nigel's parents as if dressing paper dolls.

"Life hinges on a couple of seconds you never see coming," she'd said broodingly (*so* broodingly, I should have known she could only be talking about herself, a tenet of Dad's Life Story principle: "People will always reserve The Brood, The Glower and The Heathcliff-Styled Mope, for their *own* Story, never someone else's—call it the narcissism that leaks out of Western culture like oil from an Edsel.").

"Some people pull the trigger," Hannah had said (a palpable glower on her face), *"and it all explodes in front of you. Other people run away."*

Leading criminologist Matthew Namode wrote in *Chokes Alone* (1999) that individuals who suffer a serious trauma—a child who'd lost a parent, a man who'd committed a single brutal crime—"may often, subconsciously or no, obsess over a lone word or image that may be directly traced back to the incident" (p. 249). "They repeat it when they're nervous, or idly doodle it in the margins of a piece of paper, write it on a windowsill or in the dust along a shelf, often a word so obscure it may be impossible for outsiders to discover the shattering ordeal at its root" (p. 250). In Hannah's case, it *wasn't* obscure: Leulah saw the word Hannah had unknowingly scribbled all over the notepad by the telephone, but in Hannah's haste to hide the paper from her, Leulah had misread it. Perhaps it had not said, "Valerio," but "*Vallarmo*," the Texan town where Hannah had killed a man.

And then—at this point I had Box Office Mojo; if they'd stuck me on a track I would've broken some hurtling records; in front of the high jump, I'd have soared *so* high, spectators would swear I had wings—I realized the truth behind the camping story Hannah had told us.

Hip injury, hip surgery, one leg shorter than the other: the man whose life she'd saved on the camping trip, the man who'd injured his hip, was George Gracey. He'd been living in the Adirondacks. Or perhaps she'd invented that detail; maybe he'd been hiding along the Appalachian Trail or in the Great Smokies like the Vicious Three detailed in *Escaped* (Pillars, 2004). Perhaps this was why Hannah had become a seasoned mountaineer; it'd been her responsibility to bring him food and supplies, keep him alive. And presently, he was living in Paxos, an island off the western coast of Greece, and Greece was where Hannah had told Eva Brewster she longed to go at the beginning of every St. Gallway school year, so she could "love herself."

But then—why had she decided to tell me her Life Story in such a roundabout way? Why had she been living in Stockton, not with Gracey in Greece? And what were the present movements of *Nächtlich*—if any at all? (Solving crime-related questions was like trying to rid one's house of rodents; you kill one, blink, six more dart across the floor.)

Perhaps Hannah had decided to tell me because she sensed I, out of all the Bluebloods, had the wits to solve the riddle of her life (Jade and the others weren't methodical enough; Milton, for one, had the mind—and body, for that matter—of a Jersey Cow). *"Ten years from now—that's when you decide,"* Hannah had said. Obviously, she'd wanted *some*one to know the truth, and not now—later, after she'd staged her disappearance. The night I'd shown up on her doorstep, she'd undoubtedly known all about Ada Harvey, and had been uneasy about what that dogged and determined Southern Belle (desperate to avenge the death of Big Daddy) might uncover and reveal to the FBI: Hannah's true identity and crime.

She and Gracey *couldn't* be together for security's sake; they were still wanted by the Feds and thus it was crucial to cut off all contact, reside on opposite sides of the globe. Or else, their romance had gone flat as uncapped Pellegrino; "The shelf life of any great love is fifteen years," wrote Wendy Aldridge, Ph.D., in *The Truth About Ever After* (1999). "After that you need a serious preservative, which can seriously harm your health."

The resounding belief was that, even today, *Nächtlich* was alive and well. (Littleton supported this claim though he had no evidence. Dad was more skeptical.) "Thanks to inspirational recruitment," wrote Guillaume on www.hautain.fr, "they have more members than ever. But you can't go and join. That's how they remain unseen. They choose *you*. *They* decide if you're suitable." In November 2000, an executive at the center of an accounting fraud, Mark Lecinque, had unexpectedly hanged himself at his family home twenty minutes north of Baton Rouge, a pistol—fully loaded, apart for a single bullet—was found on the floor next to him. His apparent suicide was a shock, because Lecinque and his lawyers had acted smug and haughty when interviewed on network television. It was thus whispered his death had been the vigilante work of *Les Veilleurs de Nuit*.

Other countries, too, claimed similar silent assassinations of bigwigs, magnates, industrialists and corrupt officials. The anonymous editor-in-chief of www.newworldkuomintang.org wrote that between 1980 and the present, more than 330 moguls in thirty-nine countries, including Saudi Arabia (men with a combined net worth of $400 billion) had been "quietly, efficiently disposed of" thanks to The Nightwatchmen, and though it was unclear if such sudden deaths actually benefited the downtrodden and oppressed, at the very least, it sent corporations into a temporary state of upheaval, forcing them to focus immediate attentions on resolving internal leadership problems, rather than looking outward to the land and people they might sacrifice to turn a profit. Countless employees also started to complain of a steep decline in productivity in the years following the death of the CEO or various trustees—what some referred to as a "never-ending bureaucratic nightmare." It was nearly impossible to get any work done or for anyone to make a final decision, because so many managers from different departments were required to sign off on the tiniest of ideas. Some Web sites, particularly those out of Germany, suggested members of *Nächtlich* were employed as supervisors at these behemoth conglomerates, their aim being to fan the flames of inertia by means of endless mandatory paperwork, circuitous checks and balances and labyrinthine red tape. Thus, the corporation, day after day, burning millions in what was becoming an endless waiting game, would "slowly eat itself from the inside out" (see www.verschworung.de/firmaalptraume).

I liked to believe *Nächtlich* was still active, because it meant Hannah, during her monthly trip to Cottonwood, had not been collecting men like they were tin cans she'd hoped to recycle as we'd all believed. No, she'd been engaged in prearranged encounters, "private one-on-ones" intended to *appear* like seedy one-night stands, while in fact, they were a platonic exchange of vital information. And perhaps it'd been Doc, sweet Doc with his relief-

map face and retractable trellis legs who'd informed Hannah about the recent movements and probing inquiries of Smoke Harvey and following *that*
rendezvous—the first week of November—Hannah decided she had to kill
him. She had no choice, if she wished to preserve her former lover's hiding
place in Paxos, his sanctum sanctorum.

But how had she done it?

It was the question that stumped Ada Harvey, but after reading about the
other *Nächtlich* assassinations, I could now answer it with my eyes closed
(also with a little help from Connault Helig's *Machinations Idyllic and Unseen*).

If rumor could be believed, The Nightwatchmen, following their post–
January 1974 creed of invisibility, employed correspondingly traceless murder
techniques. Their repertoire had to include something akin to "The Flying
Demoiselle," described in *The History of Lynching in the American South*
(Kittson, 1966). (In my opinion, Mark Lecinque of Baton Rouge had been
killed this way, as his death was ruled a straightforward suicide.) They also
must use another, more impermeable method, a procedure first documented
by Connault Helig, the London surgeon summoned by a bamboozled police
force to examine the body of Mary Kelly, the fifth and final victim of Leather
Apron, commonly known as Jack the Ripper. A venerated, if furtive man
of medicine and science, in Chapter 3, Helig details at length what he con-
siders to be "the only flawless stealthy execution that exists in all the world"
(p. 18).

It was flawless because technically it wasn't murder, but a calculated
setup of fatal circumstances. The plan was executed not by one person, but
by a "consortium between five and thirteen like-minded gentlemen," who
each, on the chosen day, independently committed an act assigned by the
central planner, "the engineer" (p. 21). Viewed individually, these acts were
lawful, even ordinary, and yet in a concentrated period of time, they combined to elicit a "perfectly lethal state of affairs, in which the intended victim
has no choice but to die" (p. 22). "Each man acts alone," he writes on p. 21.
"He does not know the faces, actions or even the final aim of those with
whom he operates. Such ignorance is imperative, for his lack of knowledge
maintains his virtue. Only the engineer will know the design from inception
to end."

Detailed knowledge of the victim's personal and professional life was
mandatory, in order to effectively isolate the "ideal poison" to facilitate the

"slaying" (pp. 23–25). It could be any possession, weakness, physical handicap or idiosyncrasy of the doomed individual—a cherished gun collection, perhaps, the steep flight of stairs outside Belgravia townhouse (which became "startlingly slippery in the wee hours of a brisk February morning"), a secret affinity for opium, foxhunting upon skittish stallions, hobnobbing under rickety bridges with disease-ridden streetwalkers or most conveniently of all, a daily dose of medication prescribed by the family physician—the concept being that all weapons utilized against the prey were his/her own, and thus the death would appear accidental to even the "craftiest and most inventive of investigators" (p. 26).

This was how Hannah had done it—rather, how *they'd* done it, because I doubted she'd acted alone at the costume party, but had a number of ghouls to assist her, most of them conveniently wearing masks—*Elvis: Aloha from Hawaii*, maybe; *he'd* looked squinty eyed and suspicious, or the astronaut Nigel and I had overheard speaking Greek to the Chinese woman in the gorilla suit. ("Membership expanded not only in America but internationally," reported Jacobus on www.deechtewaarheid.nl.)

"The primary gentleman, whom we shall hereafter refer to as One, will prepare the poisons prior to the day in question," Helig writes on p. 31.

Hannah had been One. She'd ingratiated herself with Smoke, pinpointed his poisons: his blood-pressure medication, Minipress, and his favorite booze, Jameson, Bushmills, maybe Tullamore Dew ("*He liked his whiskey . . . I won't lie about that*," Ada had said). According to www.drug data.com the medicine was "incompatible with alcoholic beverages," and when combined, the individual may suffer the effects of "syncope," dizziness, disorientation, even a loss of consciousness. Hannah herself had acquired the drug—or perhaps she'd had it already; perhaps that nineteen-bottle stash of prescription pills in her bedroom cabinet was never for herself, but for her hit jobs. She pulverized a predetermined quantity (the exact amount of the daily dosage, so the elevated levels of the drug discovered in the autopsy could be easily explained in the absence of other signs of foul play; the coroner would assume the victim accidentally took his dosage twice on the day in question). She dissolved the powdered drug into the alcohol and served it to him when he arrived at the party.

"One," writes Helig on p. 42, "is accountable for relaxing the victim, ensuring his defenses are down. It may serve the group well if One is a person of great physical beauty and charm."

They passed Nigel and me on the stairs, went to her bedroom, talked, and shortly thereafter, Hannah excused herself, maybe under the guise of getting them another drink, taking both glasses with her, heading downstairs to the kitchen, rinsing them out in the sink, destroying the only piece of incriminating evidence in the entire plot—and so concluding what Helig designated the initial setup, "The First Act." She never returned to him for the rest of the night.

The Second Act comprised the seemingly random relay race that "gently guides the man toward his own conclusion" (p. 51). Hannah must have known Smoke would wear the olive-green Red Army uniform, and thus the assigned individuals knew not only his physical description but also what costume to watch for. Two, Three, Four, Five (and I wasn't certain how many there were)—they appeared at prearranged locations, approaching him, introducing themselves, handing him another drink, chatting breathlessly as they escorted him from the bedroom, down the stairs, outside onto the patio, each of them bold, engaging, ostensibly drunk. Perhaps one or two of them were men, but the majority were women. (Ernest Hemingway, who wasn't keen on the fair sex, wrote, "a young dame with pretty eyes and a smile can make an old man do just about anything" [p. 278, *Journals*, Hemingway, 1947].)

This carefully choreographed relay continued for an hour or two until Smoke was positioned by the edge of the pool, his face swollen and red, his eyes unable to pick themselves up off the scales and angel wings and dorsal fins to see where he was standing. His head was a bag of feed for chickens. That was the moment Six, standing in a group, bumped into him, making him lose his balance, fall, and Seven—Seven must have been one of the rats playing Marco Polo—made certain he was helpless, if not holding his head under water, then simply ensuring he splashed, drifted to the opposite end of the pool, the deep end, and was left alone.

And so the victim dies, completing the Second Act, "the most noteworthy Act of our little tragedy" (p. 68). The Third Act begins the moment the body is found, ending with each implicated person "dispersing into the world like the withered petals off a dead flower, never to come together again" (p. 98).

*   *   *

I rubbed my eyes after scribbling this last bit into my CASE NOTES (now occupying twelve pages of a college-ruled legal pad), threw down my pen and pressed my head into the back of Dad's office chair. The house was quiet. In the lone window by the ceiling, darkness clung like a flimsy night-gown. The wood-paneled wall, where my mother's six cases of butterflies and moths had once hung, stared back at me, expressionless.

Remembering old Smoke Harvey, shadowing him through the costume party, his Long Night's Journey into Death—it rained all over the parade of secret revolution against corporate greed.

That was the problem with causes, the cheap toy within their Happy Meal; inevitably, there came a point when they looked exactly like their enemy, when they became what they fought so hard against. Freedom, Democracy—the big breathy words people shouted with their fists in the air (or else whispered, wimpy looks in their eyes)—they were beautiful mail-order brides from far-flung countries, and no matter how long you insisted they stick around, when you actually took a good look at them (when you stopped feeling woozy in their presence), you noticed they never *actually* fit in; they barely learned the customs or language. Their transplant from a text-book into the real world was slipshod, rickety at best.

"Just as no imposing character in a book may be cleverer than its minus-cule author," Dad remarked in his lecture "Landlocked Switzerland: They're Nice and Neutral Only Because They're Tiny," "no government can be greater than its governors. And provided we're not invaded by Little Green Men any time soon—reading a week's worth of *The New York Times*, I'm not so sure that'd be a bad thing—these governors will always be mere humans, men and women, cute little paradoxes, forever capable of astound-ing compassion, forever capable of astounding cruelty. You'd be surprised—Communism, Capitalism, Socialism, Totalitarianism—whatever *ism* it happens to be doesn't matter all that much; there will always be the tricky balance be-tween the human extremes. And so we live our lives, make informed choices about what we believe in, stand by them. That's all."

It was 9:12 P.M. and Dad still wasn't home.

I turned off his computer, returned the copy of *Federal Forum* and the other books to the bookshelf. Gathering together my notes, I switched off the study lights and hurried upstairs to my room. I threw the papers on my desk, took a black sweater out of my closet and pulled it over my head.

I was going back to Hannah's. And I had to go, not tomorrow, not in the bleaching daylight that killed everything, made it laughable, but *now*, while the truth was still squirming. I wasn't finished. I couldn't tell anyone about my theory now. No, I needed something else, physical evidence, facts, papers—Minipress in one of those nineteen prescription bottles, a photograph of Hannah and George Gracey hand in hand or an article from *The Vallarmo Daily*, "Policeman Shot, Woman Escapes," dated September 20, 1987—something, *any*thing that would handcuff Hannah Schneider to Catherine Baker to Smoke Harvey to The Nightwatchmen. *I* believed it, of course. I *knew* Hannah Schneider was Catherine as surely as I knew a turtle could weigh a thousand pounds (see "Leatherback Turtle," *Encyclopedia of Living Things*, 4th ed.). I'd been with her in her living room and on the mountaintop, painstakingly collected those splinters of her Life Story she'd scattered on the ground. I'd always suspected something beautiful and grotesque lived in her shadows, and now, finally, here it was, shyly inching out of the gloom.

But who'd believe me? Lately, my average of persuading others of my beliefs was around zero for eight. (I'd make an appalling missionary.) The Bluebloods thought I'd killed Hannah, Detective Harper thought I had Witness Traumatization and Dad seemed to be deathly afraid I was soft-shoeing into madness. No, the rest of the world, including Dad, needed proof to believe in something (it was a crisis the Catholic Church faced with its rapidly diminishing numbers) and *not* the kind of proof that was a faint shadow darting through a doorway, a hiccup on the stairs, but proof like a stout Russian schoolmarm standing directly under a floodlight (and unwilling to budge): three chins, frantic gray hair (barely pacified by bobby pins), a big orange skirt (under which an adult orangutan could hide fully undetected) and a pince-nez.

I'd find this proof if it killed me.

As soon as I finished tying my shoes, however, I heard the Volvo cruising into the driveway—a snag in my plan. Dad would never let me go to Hannah's *now*, and by the time I'd explained everything, fielded every one of his tenacious, sticky questions (trying to convince Dad of something new, one had to be outfitted like God in Genesis), the sun would be rising and I'd feel as if I'd just fought off a Giant Squid. (I'll admit, too, even though *I* felt I'd proved it satisfactorily, I was nevertheless afraid that, unlike the Boltzmann Constant, Avogadro's Number, Quantum Field Theory, Cosmic Inflation, my feeble premise could very well collapse within twenty-four hours. I had to get moving.)

I heard Dad enter the front door, chuck his keys onto the table. He was humming "I Got Rhythm."

"Sweet?"

Wildly, my eyes veered around the room. I ran to a window, unlatched it, heaved the thing up with all my might (it hadn't been opened since the

Carter Administration), then the rusty screen. I stuck my head out, looked down. Unlike a clammy family drama on network television, there was no mighty oak with ladderlike branches, no lattice, rose-garden grill or well-situated fencing—only a three-story drop, a sloping ledge above the bay window in the dining room and a few feeble strands of ivy clinging like hair to a sweater.

Dad was playing messages on the answering machine, his own, about dinner with Arnie Sanderson, then Arnold Schmidt of *The New Seattle Journal for Foreign Policy* who spoke with a lisp and slurred the last four digits of his phone number.

"Sweet, you upstairs? I brought home some food from the restaurant."

Hastily, I slipped on my backpack, swung one leg out the window, then the other, awkwardly sliding onto my elbows. I dangled there for a minute, staring down at the shrubs far under my feet, noting I could very well die, at the very least, break both arms and legs, maybe even my back, end up a paraplegic—*then* what sort of crimes would I be able to solve, which of Life's Great Questions would I ever answer? It was a moment I was supposed to wonder if It Was Worth It, and so I did: I wondered about Hannah and Catherine Baker and George Gracey. I pictured Gracey in Paxos, tan as rawhide holding a margarita by an infinity pool, the ocean jaded in the distance, skinny girls fanning out on either side of him like celery sticks on a dip tray. How faraway Jade and Milton had become, and St. Gallway, even Hannah—her face was already receding like a set of history dates I'd crammed into my head for a Unit Test. How lonely and absurd one felt dangling out a window. I took a giant breath, opened my eyes—I wasn't the sort of drip who *closed* her eyes, not anymore; if this was my last moment before total paralysis, before it all went haywire, I wanted to go down seeing it: the huge night, the grass shivering, the headlights of a passing car scissoring through the trees.

I let go.

"Good Country People"

The bit of roofing jutting out like stiffened, hair-sprayed bangs over the dining room's bay window braced my plummet to the earth, and though my entire left side was scratched by the side of the house and the rhododendrons in which I landed, I stood up, brushed myself off, remarkably unscathed. Obviously, I now needed a car (if I risked creeping through the front door for the Volvo keys, I risked encountering Dad) and the only decent place that came to mind, the only person who might help was Larson at the BP gas station.

Twenty-five minutes later, I was dinging into the Food Mart.

"Look who's come back from the dead," announced the intercom. "Beginnin' to think ya bought a car. Beginnin' to think you didn't like me."

Behind the bulletproof glass, he crossed his arms and winked at me. He wore a black T-shirt with the sleeves cut off that read, CAT! CAT! Next to the batteries stood his latest girlfriend, a string-bean blonde in a short red dress eating potato chips.

"*Senorita*," he said. "I missed ya."

"Hi," I said, hurrying to the window.

"What's goin' *on*? How come ya haven't come seen me? Ya been breakin' my *corazón*."

String Bean surveyed me skeptically, licking salt off her fingers.

"How's high school?" he asked.

"All right," I said.

He nodded and held up an open book, *Learning the Spanish Language* (Berlitz, 2000). "Been doin' some studyin' myself. Came up with a plan to break into the film industry. You stay here, you gotta do it from the ground up, too many people. Go to a foreign country? You can be a big fish in a little pond. I decided on Spain. I hear they need actors—"

"I need your help," I blurted. "I–I was wondering if I could borrow your truck again. I promise to have it back in three or four hours. It's an emergency and—"

"Typical *chica*. Only comes to see ya when she wants somethin'. Can't ask yer pops cuz things are rough with him—you don't have to tell me. I pick up on the *símbolos*. The *signs*."

"It's not about my father. It's something that happened at school. Did you hear about the teacher who died? Hannah Schneider?"

"Killed herself," said String Bean through shards of potato chips.

"Sure," said Larson, nodding. "Been thinkin' 'bout that. I was wonderin' how yer pops was. The male species mourns different from women. Before he left, my pops was datin' Tina who worked at Hair Fantasy, took her out only a week after my stepma died of brain cancer. I had a fit. But he sat me down, told me people show their loss different, is all. Got to respect the mournin' process. So if yer pops starts datin' again, can't hold it against him. I'm sure he's upset. A lot of people come through here, all different kinds, an' I can spot real love like I kin spot an actor who's not in the moment, just readin' lines—"

"Who are you talking about?"

He smiled. "Yer pops."

"My pops."

"Figure he's pretty broken up."

I stared at him. "Why?"

"Well, yer girl ups and dies on ya—"

"His *girl?*"

"Sure."

"Hannah Schneider?"

He stared at me.

"But they barely knew each other." As soon as I said it, the sentence sounded absurdly frail. It curled, began to fall apart like an empty straw wrapper when a drop of water falls on it.

Larson didn't continue. He looked uncertain; sensing he'd stumbled into the wrong stairwell, he couldn't decide if he should keep going down or back the way he came.

"What made you think they were a couple?" I asked.

"Way they looked at each other," he said after a moment, leaning forward so his freckled forehead was an inch from the glass. "She came in here while he waited in the car once. Smiled at me. Bought Tums. The other time they paid for gas with a credit card. Didn't get out of the car. But I saw her. Next thing I know her picture's in the paper. Her face was so pretty, it gets etched in yer mind."

"Are you positive? It wasn't a–a woman with yellow-orange hair?"

"Oh, yeah, I saw *her*. Crazy blue eyes. No. This one was the one in the newspaper. Dark hair. Looked like she wasn't from around here."

"How many times did you see them?"

"Two. Maybe three."

"I can't—I have to"—my voice was scary, coming out in clumps—"Excuse me," I managed to say. And then, all at once, the convenience store became highly inconvenient. I whirled around, because I couldn't look at Larson's face anymore, and the whole place looked smeared, out of focus (or else all gravitational fields had gone limp). As I turned, my left arm smacked the display of greeting cards, and then I crashed into String Bean who'd left her position by the batteries to go get a cup of scalding coffee the size of a small child. It erupted all over us (String Bean screaming, wailing about her burnt legs), but I didn't stop or apologize; I lurched forward, my foot hit the rack of beaded eyeglass chains and angel air fresheners, the door dinged and finally, the night jammed into my face. I think Larson might have shouted something, "Make sure yer ready fer the truth," in his chainsaw accent—but maybe it was the screeches of the cars as they honked to avoid hitting me, or my own words as they skidded through my head.

The Trial

I found Dad in the library.

He wasn't surprised to see me—but then, I can't remember a time when Dad was ever surprised, except when he leaned down to pet June Bug Phyllis Mixer's chocolate Standard Poodle and the thing leaped into the air in an attempt to bite his face, missing it by half an inch.

I stood in the doorway for a minute, staring at him, unable to speak. He put his reading glasses in their case with the air of a woman handling pearls.

"I gather you didn't watch *Gone with the Wind*," he said.

"How long did you date Hannah Schneider?" I asked.

"Date?" He frowned.

"Don't lie. People saw you with her." I opened my mouth to say more, but couldn't.

"Sweet?" He leaned forward slightly in his reading chair, as if to better observe me, as if I was an interesting principle of Conflict Resolution scrawled across a blackboard.

"I hate you," I said in a quivering voice.

"Excuse me?"

"*I hate you!*"

"My God," he said with a smile. "I—this is an interesting turn of events. Rather ridiculous."

"*I'm not ridiculous! You're ridiculous!*" I lurched around, yanked a random book from the bookshelf behind me and hurled it at him, hard. He deflected it with his arm. It was *Portrait of the Artist as a Young Man* (Joyce, 1916) and it fell open at his feet. Instantly, I grabbed another, *Inaugural Addresses of the Presidents of the United States* (Bicentennial ed. 1989).

Dad stared at me. "For God's sake, get a hold of yourself."

"You're a liar! You're an ape!" I screamed, throwing it at him. *"I hate you!"*

He deflected that one too. "The use of the phrase, *I hate you*," he said calmly, "is not only untrue, it's—"

I threw *A Tale of Two Cities* (Dickens, 1859) at his head. He deflected it, so I grabbed more, as many as I could hold in my arms like some mad, starving woman ordered to grab as much food as she could from a cafeteria buffet. There was *The Strenuous Life* (Roosevelt, 1900), *Leaves of Grass* (Whitman, 1891), *This Side of Paradise* (Fitzgerald, 1920), a very heavy, green hardback— *A Description of Elizabethan England* (Harrison, 1577), I believe. I launched all of them at him, rapid fire. He repelled most, though *Elizabethan England* hit him on the right knee.

"You're a sick, sick liar! You're evil!"

I threw *Lolita* (Nabokov, 1955).

"I hope you die a slow death riddled with unbearable pain!"

Although deflecting the books with his arms, and sometimes legs, Dad didn't stand up or try to restrain me in any way. He remained in his reading chair.

"Get a hold of yourself," he said. "Stop being so melodramatic. This isn't a miniseries on AB—"

I hurled *The Heart of the Matter* (Greene, 1948) at his stomach, *Common Sense* (Paine, 1776) at his face.

"Is this necessary?"

I threw *Four Texts on Socrates* (West, 1998). I picked up *Paradise Lost* (Milton, 1667).

"That's a rare edition," Dad said.

"Let it be the blow to kill you then!"

Dad sighed and shielded his face. He caught the book in his hands and closed it, placing it neatly on the side table. Immediately, I hurled *Rip Van Winkle & the Legend of Sleepy Hollow* (Irving, 1819), hitting him in the side.

"If you would collect yourself and behave as a rational person, I might be inclined to tell you how I came to know the supremely unhinged Miss Schneider."

Discourse on Inequality (Rousseau, 1754) struck his left shoulder.

"Blue, *really*. If you would simply calm down. You're inflicting more harm on yourself than me. *Look* at yourself—"

A large-fonted *Ulysses* (Joyce, 1922), thrown over my head backhandedly after tossing The King James Bible as a decoy, managed to avert his dodge, knocking him on the side of his face, close to his left eye. He touched where the spine of the book hit him and looked at his hand.

"Are you finished bombarding your father with the Western canon?"

"Why did you lie?" My voice was hoarse. "Why do I always find out you lie to me?"

"Sit *down.*" He moved toward me but I aimed a battered edition of *How the Other Half Lives* (Riis, 1890) at his head. "If you could calm down, you might spare yourself the stress of getting so hysterical." He took the book from me. That soft part just under a person's eye—I don't know what it's called—it was bleeding. A beadlike drop of blood glistened there. "Now calm down—"

"Don't change the subject," I said.

He returned to his chair.

"Are you going to be reasonable?"

"*You should be reasonable,*" I said loudly, though not as loud as before because my throat hurt.

"I understand what you must think right now—"

"Every time I go somewhere I find out something from other people. Things you didn't tell me."

Dad nodded. "I understand completely. Who were you with tonight?"

"I don't reveal my sources."

He sighed and put his hands in perfect This-is-the-church-this-is-the-steeple architecture. "It's really quite simple. You introduced us again on the occasion she drove you home. Sometime in October, wasn't it? You remember?"

I nodded.

"Well, the woman called me shortly thereafter. Said she was worried about you. You and I weren't on the best of terms, if you recall, so naturally, I was concerned and accepted her invitation to meet for dinner. She chose a rather inappropriately ornate restaurant, Hyacinth something, and over the course of the seven-course meal proceeded to inform me it was a *swell* idea for you to start seeing a child psychiatrist to work out some issues you had with your deceased mother. Naturally, I was livid. The sheer *gall* of the woman! But then, when I came home, *saw* you—saw your hair, the natural color of feldspar—I began to worry if perhaps she was right. Yes, it was an idiotic, *insulting* assumption on my part, but all the same, I've always been nervous, raising you without your mother. You could say it's been my Achilles' heel. And so I had dinner with her two more times, in order to discuss the possibility of your *seeing* someone, at the end of which I realized, not only did you *not* need help, *she* needed help. And rather urgently." Dad sighed. "I know you liked her, but she was not the most stable of people. She called my office a few times after that. I told her you and I had managed to work things out, that we were *fine*. And she accepted it. Shortly thereafter, we flew to Paris. I hadn't talked to or heard anything about her since. Until she committed suicide. Tragic, certainly, but I can't say I was surprised."

"When did you send her the barbaresco orientals?"

"I—the *what?*"

"*Obviously* you didn't buy them for Janet Finnsbroke who dates back to the Paleozoic Period. You bought them for Hannah Schneider."

He stared at me. "Yes. I—well, I didn't want you to—"

"Then you were madly in love with her," I interrupted. "Don't lie. *Say* it—"

Dad laughed. "Hardly."

"No one buys barbaresco orientals for someone they're not in love with."

"Then call Guinness. I am the first, my dear." He shook his head. "I *told* you. I thought she was rather sad. I sent her flowers after one of our dinners, after I told her, rather harshly, what I thought of her—that she was one of those despairing people who concoct madcap theories about others—and doubtlessly for herself—purely for entertainment as their own lives are so dull. Such people wish to be bigger than they actually are. And naturally, when one speaks one's mind—tells someone the truth, or one's personal version of it—it never goes over well. Someone always ends up crying. Remember what I've always said about truth, standing in a long black dress in the corner, feet together, head down?"

"She's the loneliest girl in the room."

"Precisely. Contrary to popular belief, no one wants anything to do with her. She's too depressing to be around. Trust me, everyone prefers to dance with something a little sexier, a little more comforting. And so I sent flowers. I didn't know what kind they were. I asked the florist to pick something—"

"They were barbaresco oriental lilies."

Dad smiled. "Well, now I know."

I didn't say anything. The position at which Dad was sitting, turned away from the lamplight, made his face old. The wrinkles on his face textured him. Lines cut toward his eyes and along his face, in his hands, tiny tears all over him.

"So it was you calling that night," I said.

He looked at me. "What?"

"The night I ran away to her house. You called her."

"Who?"

"Hannah Schneider. I was there when the phone rang. She said it was Jade, but it wasn't Jade. It was you."

"Yes," he said softly, nodding. "Maybe that's right. I did call her."

"See? You—you have an entire *relationship* with her and you—"

"*Why do you think I called her?*" Dad shouted. "That nut job was my only lead! I didn't know the names or telephone numbers of any of those other pieces of fuzz you'd befriended. And when she told me you'd just material-ized on her doorstep, immediately I wanted to come get you, but again, she proposed one of her squishy psychoanalytic ideas and I, being something of a fool when it comes to my daughter as we've *well* established this evening, I went along with it. 'Leave her alone. We need to talk. Just us girls.' Dear *God*. If there's one supremely puffed-up concept in all of Western Culture, it's the *talk*. Doesn't anyone remember that cute little phrase, which I happen to find rather illuminating? Talk is cheap?"

"Why didn't you say something?"

"I suppose I was embarrassed." Dad gazed at the floor, the landfill of books. "After all, you were completing your application to Harvard. I didn't wish to upset you."

"Maybe I wouldn't have been upset. Maybe I'm more upset *now*."

"Granted, it wasn't the wisest decision, but it was a decision I thought best at the time. Anyway, this business with Hannah Schneider is finished. May she rest in peace. The school year's nearly over." Dad sighed. "It's one for the books, is it not? I think Stockton is certainly the most theatrical town in which we've lived. It has all the elements of a good piece of fiction. More passion than Peyton Place, more frustration than Yoknapatawpha County. And it's certainly up there with Macondo in terms of sheer elements of the bizarre. It has sex, sin and that most painful quality of all, youthful disillu-sionment. You're ready, sweet. You no longer need your old pa."

My hands were cold. I walked over to the yellow couch in front of the windows and sat down.

"It's not all finished with Hannah Schneider," I said. "You have blood here." I showed him.

"You got me, huh," he said sheepishly, touching his face. "Was it the Bible or *An American Tragedy*? I'd like to know for symbolic purposes."

"There's more about Hannah Schneider."

"I might need stitches."

"Her real name was Catherine Baker. She was an old member of The Nightwatchmen. She murdered a policeman."

My words were like a ghost passing through Dad; not that I'd ever seen a ghost passing through a person, but his face drained of color—fell out of him like water poured from a bucket. He stared at me, expressionless.

"I'm not kidding," I said. "And if you want to confess something about your own involvement, recruiting or–or murder or blowing up one of your capitalist Harvard colleagues, you'd better do it right now, because I'm going to know everything. I won't stop." The resolve in my voice surprised Dad, but especially me; it was as if my voice was stronger than I was. It threw itself onto the ground, leading the way like slabs of stone.

Dad was squinting. He looked as if, suddenly, he had no idea who I was. "But they never existed," he said slowly. "Not for thirty years. They're a fairy tale."

"Not necessarily. It's all over the Internet that—"

"Oh, the *In*ternet," Dad interrupted. "As powerful a source as they come. If we open that gate, we must also usher in Elvis, still alive and kicking, pop-up ads—I don't understand why you're bringing up The Nightwatchmen. You've been reading my old lectures, *Federal Forum*—?"

"The founder, George Gracey, is still alive. He lives in Paxos. A man named Smoke Harvey drowned in Hannah's swimming pool last fall and he'd tracked him down and—"

"Of course," Dad nodded, "I remember her whining about it—obviously yet another reason why she went bananas."

"No," I said. "She *killed* him. Because he was researching a book about Gracey. He was going to expose him. All of them. The entire organization."

Dad raised his eyebrows. "Well, you've obviously done quite a bit of work figuring this out. Go on."

I hesitated; Burt Towelson wrote in *Guerrilla Girls* (1986) to preserve the purity of any investigation one had to be vigilant about whom one spoke to concerning the scary truths that had emerged; but then, if I couldn't trust Dad, I couldn't trust anyone. He was staring at me as he'd stared at me a thousand times before, whenever we moseyed through my thesis for an upcoming research paper (his expression interested but doubtful he'd be wowed) and so it seemed an inevitable thing to walk him through my theory, My Grand Scheme of Things. I began with Hannah plotting her own exit because of what Ada Harvey knew, how she left me *L'Avventura*, "The Flying Demoiselle," the costume party, a version of Connault Helig's elimination technique employed to murder Smoke, Hannah's history of the Bluebloods paralleling Catherine Baker's history, her preoccupation with Missing Persons and, finally, my telephone conversation with Ada Harvey. In the beginning, Dad stared at me as if I was a lunatic, but as I went on, he began to hang on my every word. In fact, I hadn't seen Dad this engrossed since he obtained a newsstand copy of the June 1999 issue of *The New Republic*, in which his lengthy satiric response to an article entitled, "Little Shop of Horrors: A History of Afghanistan," had been printed in the Letters section.

When I finished, I expected him to hurl questions at me, but he remained thoughtfully silent for a minute, maybe two.

He frowned. "So who killed poor Miss Schneider?"

Naturally, Dad would have to ask the *one* question I had only a rickety-bridge answer to. Ada Harvey had said she thought Hannah had committed suicide, but since *I'd* heard that stranger bounding through the trees, I tended to think someone in *Nächtlich* had done it; Hannah had been a liability when she'd killed the State Trooper, and with Ada telephoning the FBI and the possibility of her capture, Gracey, the entire group's clandestine existence was at risk. But I didn't know any of this for certain, and as Dad said, one should never "dribble speculation like a leaky garbage bag."

"Well, I'm not sure, exactly," I said.

He nodded and said nothing more.

"Have you written about *Nächtlich* recently?" I asked.

He shook his head. "No. Why?"

"Remember the way we met Hannah Schneider—she was in Fat Kat Foods and then she reappeared at the shoe store?"

"Yes," he said, after a moment.

"Ada Harvey described the same thing when she told me how Hannah met her father. She'd planned the whole encounter. So I was worried maybe you were her next victim, because you were writing something—"

"Sweet," Dad interjected, "as flattered as I'd be for Miss Baker to choose me as her target—never been anyone's target before—there *is* no Nightwatchmen, not any longer. They're considered by even the most laid-back of political theorists to be a mere fantasy. And what are fantasies? What we use to pillow ourselves against the world. Our world, it's a cruel parquet—*murder* to sleep on. Besides, this isn't the age of revolutionaries, but an age of isolationaries. Man's proclivity today is not to unite, but to cut himself off from others, step on them, grab as much *dough* as he can. As you know too, history is cyclical and we're not due for another uprising—even a silent one—for another two hundred years. More to the point, I remember reading an in-depth piece about Catherine Baker being a Parisian gypsy in origin, so however thrilling it may sound, it's still rather tenuous to assert Schneider and Baker were the same woman. Given the odd way she told all of this to you, how do you know she didn't simply read a book, a real *page-turner* about the mysterious Catherine Baker, then let her imagination run wild? Maybe she wanted you to believe, for *every*one to believe before she killed herself, that *that* had been her life, a life of upheaval and causes—she, Bonnie, some other dope, Clyde. That way she might live forever, *n'est-ce pas?* She'd leave behind a thrilling Life Story, not the dreary editorial that was her truth. Such are the lies people tell. And they're a dime a dozen."

"But what about the way she met Smoke—?"

"All we know for certain is that she liked to pick up men in *food settings*," Dad said with authority. "She was looking for love amidst frozen peas."

I stared at him. He *did* have a few infinitesimal points. On www.iron butterfly.net the author claimed Catherine Baker had been a French gypsy. And given the heaving-bodice posters in Hannah's classroom, I could conceive how it was *some*what plausible she might devise a more exciting life for herself. Just like that, Dad could poke serious holes in my rowboat theory, make it look embarrassingly overdesigned and ill considered (see "De Lorean DMC-12," *Capitalist Blunders*, Glover, 1988).

"So I'm nuts," I said.

"I didn't say that," he said sharply. "Certainly, your little theory is elaborate. Far-fetched? Absolutely. But it is, in a word, remarkable. And rather exciting. Nothing like news of silent revolutionaries to get the blood rushing into one's head—"

"You believe me?"

He paused and turned his face up to the ceiling to consider this, as only Dad could consider things.

"Yes," he said simply. "I do."

"*Really?*"

"Of course. You know I've a soft spot for the far-fetched and fantastical. The wholly ludicrous. I suppose there are a few details to further shape—"

"I'm not crazy."

He smiled. "To the ordinary, untrained ear you might sound slightly un-hinged. But to a Van *Meer*? You sound rather ho-hum."

I leapt from the couch and hugged him.

"*Now* you wish to hug me? So I take it you've forgiven me for not telling you about my imprudent encounters with that strange and wayward woman, whom we shall now call, given her subversive connections, Blackbeard?"

I nodded.

"Thank God," he said. "I don't think I could have survived another blitzkrieg of books. Especially with that twenty-pound edition of *The World's Famous Orations* still on the shelf. Do you feel like eating something?" He brushed hair off my forehead. "You've grown too thin."

"All of this must have been what Hannah wanted to tell me on the mountain. Remember?"

"Yes—but how are you planning to dispense your findings? Will we coauthor a book, entitled, say, *Mixed Nuts: Conspiracies and Anti-American Dissidents in Our Midst* or *Special Topics in Calamity Physics*, something with a bit of rumba to it. Or will you write a bestseller with all the names changed, the proverbial, 'Based on a true story,' written on the first page to sell more copies? You'll have the entire country terrified that unhinged ac-tivists are working as teachers in their schools, poisoning the minds of their dear dullard children."

"I don't know."

"Now *here's* an idea—you'll simply jot it down in your diary, an anecdote for your grandchildren to read upon your death when they go through your belongings neatly arranged in an antique steamer trunk. They'll sit around the dinner table, murmuring in incredulous voices, 'I can't believe Grandma did that, all at the tender age of sixteen.' And via this diary, which will be auc-tioned at Christie's for nothing less than $500,000, a story of small town terror will float away by word of mouth into one of magical realism. Blue van Meer will be said to have been born with a pig's tail, the troubled Miss Schneider driven to fanaticism due to a love that went unrequited for centuries, a *Love in the Time of Cholera*, and your friends, the Miltons and the Greens, they will be the revolutionaries staging thirty-two armed uprisings and losing every one. And we can't forget your dad. Wise and withered in the background, the *General in His Labyrinth* on his seven-month river voyage from Bogotá to the sea."

"I think we'll go to the police," I said.

He chuckled. "You're pulling my leg."

"No. We *have* to go to the police. Immediately."

"Why?"

"We just have to."

"You're not being realistic."

"Yes, I am."

He shook his head. "You're not thinking. Let's say there's truth to it. You'll need evidence. Testimonials of former group members, manifestos, recruitment processes—which will all be rather difficult to find, won't they, if your suspicions about undetectable murder tactics are correct. More important, there's an inherent risk when someone comes forward, pointing a finger. Have you thought about *that*? Coming up with a theory is all very thrilling, but if there's truth to it, it's no longer a round of *Wheel of Fortune*. I won't allow you to draw attention to yourself, assuming, of course, any of this is true, which we will probably never know with any certainty. Going to the police is gallant for simpletons, for nitwits—but what purpose would it serve? So the sheriff can have a story for his donut break?"

"No," I said. "So lives can be saved."

"How touching. Just whose life are you saving?"

"You can't just go kill people because you don't like what they're doing. That makes us animals. Even—even if we can never find it we still have to try for . . ." I trailed off into silence, because I wasn't exactly sure what we had to try for. "Justice," I said weakly.

Dad only laughed. " 'Justice is a whore who won't let herself be stiffed and collects the wages of shame even from the poor.' Karl Kraus. Austrian essayist."

" 'All good things may be expressed in a single word,' " I said. " 'Freedom, justice, honor, duty, mercy. And hope.' Churchill."

" 'As thou urgest justice, be assured / Thou shalt have justice more than thou desirest.' *Merchant of Venice*."

" 'Justice wields an erratic sword / grants mercy to fortunate few / Yet if man doesn't fight for her / 'Tis chaos he's left to.' "

Dad opened his mouth to speak, but stopped, frowning. "Mackay?"

"Gareth van Meer. 'The Revolution Betrayed.' *Civic Journal of Foreign Affairs*. Volume six, issue nineteen."

Dad smiled, tilted his head back and gave a very loud "*Ha!*"

I'd forgotten about his "*Ha!*" Usually he reserved it for faculty meetings with a Dean, when a fellow colleague said something humorous or stirring and Dad was slightly perturbed *he* hadn't thought to say it, so he said a very loud *Ha!*, partly an expression of annoyance and partly to suck the room's attention back to him. Now, however, when he looked at me, unlike those faculty meetings with a Dean (Dad allowed me to sit in the corner whenever I was out sick with a mild head cold and, without stirring, swallowing all potential sneezes, I listened to the assembled Ph.D.s with chalky complexions and thinning hair, speaking in weighty voices of Knights at the Round Table) Dad had big, bare tears shivering there, ones that threatened to slide shyly from his eyes like modest girls in bathing suits removing their towels, making a slow, embarrassed move toward the pool.

He stood, put a hand on my shoulder and moved past me to the door.

"So be it, my Justice-seeker."

I sat in front of the empty chair for another moment or two, surrounded by the books. They all had a silent, haughty perseverance about them. They weren't going to be destroyed by any launch at a human, oh no. With the exception of *The Heart of the Matter*, which had belched up a clump of pages, the others were intact, gleefully open and showing off their pages. Their tiny black words of wisdom remained in perfect order, sitting in pristine rows, unmoving, attentive like schoolchildren impervious to the influence of a naughty child. *Common Sense* was open next to me, peacocking its pages.

"Stop moping and get in here," called Dad from the kitchen. "You must eat something if you're going to wage war on flabby-armed, potbellied radicals. I don't think they age all that well, so you'll probably be able to outrun them."

Paradise Lost

For the first time since Hannah died, I slept through the night. Dad called such sleeps "The Sleep of Trees," which was not to be confused with "The Sleep of Hibernation" or "The Sleep of Dead-Tired Dogs." The Sleep of Trees was the most absolute and rejuvenating of sleeps. It was only darkness, no dreams, a leap forward in time.

I didn't stir when the alarm went off, nor did I wake up to hear Dad shouting from downstairs the Van Meer Vocabulary Wake-up Call.

"Wake up, sweet! Your word of the day is *pneumococcus!*"

I opened my eyes. The phone was ringing. The clock by my bed read 10:36 A.M. The answering machine clicked on downstairs.

"Mr. Van Meer, I wanted to notify you that Blue is not in school today. Please call us and give a reason for her absence." Eva Brewster curtly recited the number to the main office and hung up. I waited for Dad's footsteps to come through the hall to find out who'd called, but I heard nothing but the clinking of silverware in the kitchen.

I climbed out of bed, stumbled into the bathroom, splashed water on my face. In the mirror, my eyes looked unusually large, my face thin. I was cold, so I pulled the comforter off my bed, wrapped it around me and walked with it down the stairs.

"Dad! Did you call the school?"

I entered the kitchen. It was empty. The clinking I'd heard was the breeze through the open window hitting the silverware wind chime over the sink. I switched on the downstairs light and called into the stairwell.

"Dad!"

I used to dread a house without Dad in it. It could feel empty as a can, a shell, a blind desert skull of a Georgia O'Keefe painting. Growing up, I had a variety of techniques to avoid the truth of the house without Dad. There was "The Watch *General Hospital* with Very Loud Volume" (surprisingly comforting, more than one would imagine) and the Put On *It Happened One Night* (Clark Gable without an undershirt could distract anyone).

Late morning light poured through the windows, bright and vicious. I opened the refrigerator and saw with some surprise, he'd made a fruit salad. I reached in, picked out a grape, ate it. Also in the refrigerator was lasagna, which he'd attempted to cover with too small a piece of tinfoil; it left two corners and a side exposed like a winter coat leaving entire shins bare, half the person's arms and neck. (Dad was always unable to correctly eyeball the required length for tinfoil.) I ate another grape and called his office.

The Political Science Department assistant answered the phone.

"Hey, is my dad there? It's Blue."

"Hmm?"

I glanced at the clock. He didn't have a class until 11:30 A.M. "My dad. Dr. Van Meer. Can I talk to him please? It's an emergency."

"He's not coming in today," she said. "There's that conference in Atlanta, right?"

"Excuse me?"

"I thought he went to Atlanta, replacing the man who was in the car accident—?"

"*What?*"

"He requested permission for a substitute this morning. He won't be in for the—"

I hung up.

"Dad!"

I left the comforter in the kitchen, raced down the stairs to his study, switching on the overhead light. I stood in front of his desk, staring at it.

It was bare.

I yanked open a drawer. It was empty. I yanked open another. It was empty. There was no laptop, no legal pads, no desk calendar. The ceramic mug was empty too, where he usually kept his five blue ink pens and five black ink pens next to the green desk lamp from the agreeable Dean at the University of Arkansas at Wilsonville, which also was gone. The tiny bookshelf next to the desk was completely empty too, apart from five copies of Marx's *Das Kapital* (1867).

I sprinted up the stairs, through the kitchen, down the hall, yanking open the front door. The blue Volvo station wagon was parked where it always was, in front of the garage door. I stared at it, at the egg-blue surface, the rust around the wheels.

I turned back inside and ran to his bedroom. The curtains were open. The bed was made. Yet his old sheepskin loafers purchased at Bet-R-Shoes in Enola, New Hampshire, were not capsized beneath the television, nor were they beneath the upholstered chair in the corner. I moved toward the closet and slid open the door.

There were no clothes.

There was nothing—nothing but hangers jittering along the pole like birds, frightened when people stepped too close to the bars to stare at them.

I ran into his bathroom, swung open the medicine cabinet. It was bare. So was the shower. I touched the side of the tub, feeling its stickiness, the few remaining drops of water. I looked at the sink, a trace of Colgate toothpaste, a tiny drop of shaving cream dried on the mirror.

He must have decided we're moving again, I told myself. *He went to fill out a Change-of-Address card at the Post Office. He went to the supermarket for moving boxes. But the station wagon wouldn't start, so he called a taxi.*

I went into the kitchen and played the answering machine, but there was only the message from Eva Brewster. I looked on the counter for a note, but there wasn't one. Again, I called the Political Science Department assistant, Barbara, pretending I knew all about the conference in Atlanta; Dad said there was "a motor-mouth on Barbara, coupled with the foul stench of the ridiculous." (He cheerfully referred to her as "the Haze woman.") I called the conference by a specific name, quickly decided beforehand. I think I called it SPOUFAR, "Safe Political Organization for the Upholding of First Amendment Rights," or something to that effect.

I asked her if Dad had left a number where she could contact him.

"No," she said.

"When did he notify you?"

"Left a message at six this morning. But, wait, why don't you—?"

I hung up.

I wrapped the comforter around me, turned on the television, watched Cherry Jeffries in a yellow suit the color of a road sign with shoulder pads so sharp they could cut down trees. I checked the clock in the kitchen, the clock in my bedroom. I walked outside and stared at the blue station wagon. I sat in the driver's seat and turned the key in the ignition. It started. I ran my hands along the steering wheel, over the dashboard, stared at the backseat, as if there might be a clue somewhere, a revolver, candlestick, rope or wrench carelessly left behind by Mrs. Peacock, Colonel Mustard or Professor Plum after killing Dad in the library, conservatory or billiard room. I examined the Persian carpets in the hall, searching for singular imprints of shoes. I checked the sink, the dishwasher, but every spoon, fork and knife had been put away.

They'd come for him.

Members of *Nächtlich* had come for him in the night, placed a linen handkerchief (embroidered with a red N in the corner) dabbed with a bit of sleeping potion over his unsuspecting snoring mouth. He hadn't been able to struggle because Dad, although tall and hardly skinny, wasn't a fighter. Dad preferred intellectual debate to physical assault, eschewed contact sports, considered wrestling and boxing "faintly preposterous." And although Dad respected the art of karate, judo, tae kwan do, he himself had never learned a single move.

They'd meant to take me, of course, but Dad had refused. *"No! Take me instead! Take me!"* And so the Nasty One—there was always a Nasty One, the one who had scant regard for human life and bullied the others—pressed a gun to his temple and ordered him to call the university. "And you'd better sound normal or I'll blow your daughter's brains out while you watch."

And then they made Dad pack his own bags in the two large Louis Vuitton duffle bags June Bug Eleanor Miles, age 38, had given to Dad so he'd remember her (and her spiky teeth) every time he packed his bags. Because even though, sure, they were "revolutionaries" in the classical sense of the word, they were not barbarians, not South American guerrillas or Muslim extremists who relished the odd beheading every now and then. No, they held fast to the belief that all human beings, even those held against their will, waiting for certain political demands to be met, required his/her personal belongings, including corduroy pants, tweed jackets, wool sweaters, Oxford shirts, shaving kits, toothbrushes, razors, soaps, dental floss, peppermint exfoliating foot scrubs, Timex watches, GUM cufflinks, credit cards, lecture notes and old syllabi, notes for *The Iron Grip*.

"We want you to be comfortable," said the Nasty One.

*   *   *

That night, he still hadn't called.

No one had, with the exception of Arnold Lowe Schmidt of *The New Seattle Journal of Foreign Policy*, telling the machine how thawry he was that Dad had declined hith invitathon of writhing a cover pieth on Cuba, but to pleath keep the periodical in mind if he wanthed "a preeminent repothitory for the publicathon of hith ideath."

Outside, I walked around the house some twenty times in the dark. I stared into the fishpond, devoid of fish. I returned inside, sat on the couch watching Cherry Jeffries, picking at the half-eaten bowl of fruit, which the radicals had allowed Dad to prepare before they carried him away.

"*My daughter has to eat!*" Dad commanded.

"Fine," said the Nasty One. "But be quick about it."

"Would you like some help cutting the cantaloupe?" asked another.

I couldn't stop picking up the phone, staring at the receiver, asking, "Should I report him missing to the police?" I waited for it to tell me, "Yes, Definitely," "My Reply Is No" or "Concentrate and Ask Again." I could call the Sluder County Sheriff's Department, tell A. Boone I had to speak to Detective Harper. "Remember me? The one who talked to you about Hannah Schneider? Well, now my father's missing. Yes. I keep losing people." Within an hour, she'd be at the door with her pumpkin hair and complexion of refined sugar, narrowing her eyes at Dad's vacant reading chair. "Tell me the last thing he said. Does your family have a history of mental illness? Do you have anyone? An uncle? A grandmother?" Within four hours, I'd have my own green folder in the filing cabinet next to her desk, #5510-VANM. An article would appear in *The Stockton Observer*, "Local Student Angel of Death, Witness to Teacher's Demise, Now Missing Father." I hung up the phone.

I searched the house again, this time not allowing myself to whimper, not allowing myself to miss a thing, not the shower curtain, or the cabinet under the bathroom sink full of Q-tips and cotton balls, or even the roll of toilet paper inside of which he might have taken a moment to scrawl, *They've taken me do not worry* with a toothpick. I examined every book we'd returned to the shelves the night before in the library, for he might have swiftly slipped a page of legal paper into its pages on which he'd written, *I'll get out of this I swear.* I turned over every one, shook them, but found nothing at all, apart from *The Heart of the Matter* losing another clump of pages. This searching continued until Dad's bedside clock read that it was after 2:00 A.M.

Denial is like Versailles; it isn't the easiest thing to maintain. To do so took an astounding amount of resolve, oomph, chutzpah, none of which I had, starfished as I was across the black-and-white tiles of Dad's bathroom floor.

Clearly, I had to accept the notion of Dad's kidnapping being up there

with the Tooth Fairy, the Holy Grail or any other dream concocted by people
bored to tears with reality, wanting to believe in something bigger than themselves. No matter how charitable these radicals were, they wouldn't have permitted Dad to pack each and *every one* of his personal items, including
checkbooks, credit cards and statements, even his favorite needlepoint by
June Bug Dorthea Driser, the tiny, framed "To Thine Own Self Be True,"
which had been hanging to the right of the kitchen telephone, now gone.
They also would have put their foot down when Dad took a half hour
to cherry-pick the selection of texts he wished to take with him, Maurice
Girodias' Olympia Press 1955 two-volume edition of *Lolita*, *Ada or Ardor*, the
Paradise Lost he hadn't wanted me to throw, the hulking *Delovian: A Retro-
spective* (Finn, 1998), which featured Dad's favorite work, the appropriately ti-
tled *Secret* (see p. 391, #61, 1992, Oil on linen). Also missing was *La Grimace*,
Napoleon's Progress, *Beyond Good and Evil* and a photocopy of "In the Penal
Colony" (Kafka, 1919).

My head throbbed. My face felt tight and hot. I pulled myself out of the
bathroom into the middle of Dad's spongy bedroom carpet, the one thing he
loathed about the house—"one feels as if one is walking on marshmallows"—
and began to cry, but after a while, my tears, either bored or frustrated, sort of
quit, threw in the towel, stormed off the set.

I didn't do anything but stare at the bedroom ceiling, so pale and quiet,
dutifully holding His tongue. Somehow, out of pure exhaustion, I fell asleep.

* * *

For the next three days—frittered away on the couch in front of Cherry
Jeffries—I found myself imagining Dad's final moments in our house, our
beloved 24 Armor Street, setting of our last year, our last chapter, before I
"conquered the world."

He was all plan and calculation, all bird-quick glances to his wristwatch,
five minutes fast, silent steps through our dim-drenched rooms. There was
nervousness too, a nervousness only *I'd* be able to detect; I'd seen him before
a new university, giving a new lecture (the barely discernible trembling of index fingers and thumbs).

The change in his pocket rattled like his withered soul as he moved
through the kitchen, downstairs to his study. He turned on only a few lamps,
his desk lamp and the red one on his bedroom nightstand that drowned the
room in the jelly-red of stomachs and hearts. He spent a great deal of time or-

ganizing his things. The Oxford shirts on the bed, red on top, followed by blue, blue patterned, blue-and-white stripe, white, each folded like sleeping birds with wings tucked under them, and the six sets of cufflinks in silver and gold (including, of course, his favorite, those 24-karat ones engraved with GUM, given to Dad for his forty-seventh birthday by Bitsy Plaster, age 42, a misprint by the jeweler due to Bitsy's bubbly handwriting) all tucked into the Tiffany felt pocket like a bag of prized seeds. And then there were his socks herded together, black, white, long, short, cotton, wool. He wore his brown loafers (he could walk fast in them), the gold and brown tweed (faithfully hanging around him like an old dog) and the old khaki slacks so comfortable he claimed "they made the most unbearable tasks bearable." (He wore them trudging through the "squishy Thesis Statements, fetid quagmires of Supporting Evidence" inevitably found within student research papers. They even allowed him to feel no guilt as he wrote C- next to the kid's name before continuing on, relentlessly.)

When he was ready to load the boxes and duffle bags into the car—I didn't know what waited for him; I imagined a simple yellow cab driven by some sea urchin driver with goose-bumped hands, tapping the steering wheel to Public Radio's *Early Bluegrass Hour*, waiting for John Ray Jr., Ph.D., to emerge from the house, thinking about the woman he left at home, Alva or Dottie, warm as a dinner roll.

When Dad knew he'd forgotten nothing, when it was all gone, he walked back inside and up to my room. He didn't turn on a light, or even look at me as he unbuckled my backpack and perused the legal pad on which I'd scrawled my research and theory. After he reviewed what I'd written, he returned it to the bag and hung it on the back of my desk chair.

He was incorrect putting it there. That wasn't where I'd put it; I'd placed it where I always did, at the end of my bed on the floor. Yet, he was pressed for time and no longer needed to worry about such details. Such details mattered very little now. He probably laughed at the Irony. At the most unlikely of moments, Dad took time to laugh about the Irony; or, perhaps it was one instance he didn't have time to, because if he moved toward Laughter, he might have to continue down that shoulderless, exitless road of Feeling, which could lead one, rather swiftly, into Whimpering, Full-on Howling and he didn't have time for that kind of detour. He had to get out of the house.

He looked at me as I slept, memorizing my face as if it was a passage of an extraordinary book he'd come across, the crux of which he wished to commit to memory in the off chance he found use for it during an exchange with a Dean.

Or else, staring at me—and I like to think this was the case—Dad came undone. No book tells one how to look at one's child one is leaving forever and will never see again (unless it's clandestinely, after thirty-five, forty years, and only then from a great distance, through binoculars, a telephoto lens or an $89.99 satellite photo). One probably gets close and tries to determine the exact degree of the nose from the face. One counts freckles, the ones never noticed before. And one also counts the faint creases in the eyelids, in the forehead, too. One watches the breathing, the peaceful smile—or, in the absence of such a smile, one willfully ignores the gaping, wheezing mouth, in order to make the memory polite. One probably gets a little carried away, too, introducing a little moonlight to silver the face, covering up those dark circles under the eyes, sound-looping adorable insects—better still, a gorgeous night bird—to lessen the cold, cell silence of the room.

Dad closed his eyes to make sure he knew it by heart (forty-degrees, sixteen, three, one, a sea way of breathing, peaceful smile, silvery eyes, enthusiastic nightingale). He pushed the comforter close to my check, kissed me on the forehead.

"You'll be fine, sweet. You really will."

He slipped from my room, downstairs, and outside to the taxi.

"Mr. Ray?" asked the driver.

"*Dr.* Ray," Dad said.

And just like that—he was gone.

The Secret Garden

The days shuffled by like bland schoolgirls. I didn't notice their individual faces, only their basic uniform: day and night, day and night.

I had no patience for showers or balanced meals. I did a lot of lying on floors—childish certainly, but when one can lie on floors without anyone seeing one, trust me, one will lie on a floor. I discovered, too, the fleeting yet discernable joy of biting into a Whitman's chocolate and throwing the remaining half behind the sofa in the library. I could read, read, read until my eyes burned and the words floated like noodles in soup.

I ditched school like a boy with rusty breath and glue-stick palms. Instead, I took up with *Don Quixote* (Cervantes, 1605)—one would think I'd have driven to Videomecca and rented porn, at the very least *Wild Orchid* with Mickey Rourke, but alas, no—then some steamy paperback I'd kept hidden from Dad for years called *Speak Not, My Love* (Esther, 1992).

I thought about Death—not suicide, nothing that histrionic—more a begrudged acknowledgment, as if I'd snubbed Death for years, and now, having no one else, I had no choice but to exchange pleasantries with him. I thought about Evita, Havermeyer, Moats, Dee and Dum forming a nighttime Search Party, wielding torches, lanterns, pitchforks, clubs (as bigoted townspeople did when hunting a monster), discovering my wasted body slung over the kitchen table, arms limp at my sides, my head facedown in the crotch of Chekhov's *The Cherry Orchard* (1903).

Even when I tried to collect myself, pull myself together as Molly Brown had done in that *Titanic* lifeboat, or even find a productive hobby like the Birdman of Alcatraz, I failed. I thought *Future*. I saw *Black Hole*. I was spaghettified. I didn't have a friend, driver's license or survival instinct to my name. I didn't even have one of those Savings Accounts set up by a conscientious parent so their kid could learn Money. I was a minor, too, would remain so for another year. (My birthday was June 18.) I had no desire to end up in a Foster Home, the Castle in the Sky of which was to be supervised by a pair of retirees named Bill and Bertha, who wielded their Bibles like handguns, asked me call them "Mamaw" and "Papaw," and got tickled pink every time they stuffed me, their brand new turkey, with all the fixins (biscuits, poke salad and possum pie).

Seven days after Dad left, the phone began to ring.

I didn't answer it, though I remained poised by the answering machine, my heart banging in my chest, in case it was he.

"Gareth, you're causing quite a stir around here," said Professor Mike Devlin. "I'm wondering where you are."

"What on earth have you *done* with yourself? Now they say you're not coming back," said Dr. Elijah Masters, Chairman of the English Department and Harvard Alumni Interviewer. "I'll be sorely disappointed if that is the case. As you know, we have an unfinished chess game and I'm beating you to a pulp. I'd hate to think you've disappeared simply so I have to forgo the pleasure of telling you, 'Checkmate.'"

"Dr. Van Meer, you must call the office as soon as possible. Again, your daughter Blue has not appeared in class all week now. I hope you're aware that if she does not begin to make up some of the work, the idea of her graduating on time will be more and more—"

"Dr. Van Meer, this is Jenny Murdoch who sits on the front row of your Patterns of Democracy and Social Structure seminar? I was wondering if Solomon is now going to be in charge of our research papers, because he's like, *totally* giving us new parameters. He says it only has to be seven to ten pages. But *you* wrote on the syllabus twenty to twenty-five, so everyone's totally baffled. Some clarification would be much appreciated. I also wrote you an e-mail."

"Please call me as soon as possible at my home or office, Gareth," said Dean Kushner.

I'd told Dad's assistant, Barbara, that I'd written down the incorrect contact number for Dad at the conference and asked her to let me know as soon as she heard from him. She hadn't called however, so I called her.

"We still haven't heard," she said. "Dean Kushner's having a heart attack. Solomon Freeman is going to have to take over his classes for finals. Where *is* he?"

"He had to go to Europe," I said. "His mother had a heart attack."

"Ohhh," said Barbara. "I'm sorry. Is she going to be all right?"

"No."

"Gosh. That's so sad. But then why hasn't he—?"

I hung up.

I wondered if my steady stupor, my inertia, marked the onset of madness. Only a week ago I'd believed madness to be a far-fetched idea, but now I recalled a handful of occasions when Dad and I encountered a woman muttering expletives as if she was sneezing. I wondered how she'd become that way, if it was a debutante's dreamy descent down a grand flight of stairs or else a sudden misfire in the brain, its effects immediate, like a snakebite. Her complexion was red like raw dishwasher hands and the soles of her feet were black, as if she'd meticulously dipped them in tar. As Dad and I passed her, I held my breath, squeezed his hand. He'd squeeze back—our tacit agreement he'd *never* allow me to wander the streets with my hair like a bird's nest, my overalls marred with urine and dirt.

Now I could, with no trouble at all, wander the streets with hair like a bird's nest in overalls of urine and dirt. The That's-Ridiculous, the Don't-Be-Absurd had happened. I'd be selling my body for a frozen Lender's bagel. Obviously, I'd been wrong all along about madness. It could happen to anyone.

*   *   *

For those who are *Marat/Sade* aficionados, I must deliver bad news. The shelf life of a depressed torpor for any otherwise healthy individual is ten, eleven, at the most, twelve days. After that, the mind can't help but notice such a disposition is as much use as a one-legged man in an arse-kicking contest, and that, if one didn't stop bouncing around like a big girl's blouse, Pimms and strawberries, Bob's your uncle and God save the bloody Queen, one just might not make it (see *Go See a Man About a Dog: Beloved Englishisms*, Lewis, 2001).

I didn't go mad. I got mad (see "Peter Finch," *Network*). Rage, not Abe Lincoln, is the Great Emancipator. It wasn't long before I was tearing through 24 Armor Street, not limp and lost, but throwing shirts and June Bug needlepoints and library books and cardboard moving boxes marked THIS END UP like Jay Gatsby on a rampage, searching for something—even if it was something minor—to give me proof of where he'd gone and why. Not that I let myself hope I'd discover a Rosetta Stone, a twenty-page confession thoughtfully tucked into my pillowcase, between mattresses, in the icebox:

"Sweet. So now you know. I am sorry, my little cloud. But allow me to explain. Why don't we start with Mississippi . . ." It wasn't likely. As Mrs. McGillicrest, that penguin-bodied shrew from Alexandria Day informed our class, so triumphantly: "A deus ex machina will never appear in real life so you best make other arrangements."

The shock of Dad gone (*shock* didn't do it justice; it was astonishment, stunned, a bombshell—astunshelled), the fact he had blithely hoodwinked, bamboozled, conned (again, too tepid for my purposes—hoodzonked) me, me, *me*, his daughter, a person who, to quote Dr. Luke Ordinote, had "startling power and acumen," an individual who, to quote Hannah Schneider, did not "miss a thing," was so improbable, painful, impossible (impainible), I understood now Dad was nothing short of a madman, a genius and imposter, a cheat, a smoothie, the Most Sophisticated Sweet Talker Who Ever Lived.

Dad must be to secrets as Beethoven is to symphonies, I chanted to myself. (It was the first of a series of stark statements I'd concoct in the ensuing week. When one has been hoodzonked, one's mind crashes, and when rebooted, reverts to unexpected, rudimentary formats, one of which was reminiscent of the mind-bending "Author Analogies" Dad devised as we toured the country.)

But Dad wasn't Beethoven. He wasn't even Brahms.

And Dad not being an unsurpassed maestro of mystery was regrettable, because infinitely more harrowing than being left with a series of obscure, incomprehensible Questions—which one can fill in at one's whim without fear of being graded—was having a few disquieting Answers.

My rampage through the house uncovered no evidence of note, only articles about civil unrest in West Africa and Peter Cower's *Inside Angola* (1980), which had fallen in the crevice between Dad's bed and bedside table (as nutritionless pieces of evidence as they come) and $3,000 in cash, crisply rolled up inside June Bug Penelope Slate's SPECIAL THOUGHTS ceramic mug kept on top of the refrigerator (Dad had purposefully left it for me, as the mug was usually reserved for loose change). Eleven days after he left, I wandered down to the road to collect the day's mail: a book of coupons, two clothing catalogues, a credit card application for Mr. Meery von Gare with 0% APR financing and a thick manila envelope addressed to Miss Blue van Meer, scrawled in majestic handwriting, the handwriting equivalent of trumpets and a stagecoach pulled by noble steeds.

Immediately, I ripped it open, pulling out the inch-thick stack of papers. Instead of a map of the South American White Slavery network with rescue instructions, or Dad's unilateral Declaration of Independence ("When in the Course of human events, it becomes necessary for a father to dissolve the paternal bands which have connected him to his daughter . . ."), I found a brief note on monogrammed stationery paper clipped to the front.

"You asked for these. I hope they help you," Ada Harvey had written, then scrawled her loopy name beneath the knot of her initials.

Even though I'd hung up on her, hacked off her voice without a word of apology like a sushi chef chopping off eel heads, exactly as I'd asked, she'd sent me her father's research. As I raced back up the driveway and into the house with the papers, I found myself crying, weird condensation tears that spontaneously appeared on my face. I sat down at the kitchen table and carefully began to page through the stack.

Smoke Harvey had handwriting that was a distant cousin of Dad's, minuscule script blustered by a cruel northeasterly. THE NOCTURNAL CONSPIRACY, the man had written in caps in the top right corner of every page. The first few papers detailed the history The Nightwatchmen, the many names and apparent methodology (I wondered where he'd gotten his information, because he referenced neither Dad's article nor the Littleton book), followed by thirty pages or so on Gracey, most of it barely readable (Ada had used a photocopier that printed tire treads across the page): "Greek in origin, *not* Turkish," "Born February 12, 1944, in Athens, mother Greek, father American," "Reasons for radicalism unknown." I continued on. There were photocopies of old West Virginia and Texas newspaper articles detailing the two known bombings, "Senator Killed, Peace Freaks Suspected," "Oxico Bombing, 4 Killed, Nightwatchmen Sought," an article from *Life* magazine dated December 1978, "The End of Activism," about the dissolution of the Weather Underground, Students for a Democratic Society and other dissident political organizations, a few papers about COINTELPRO and other FBI maneuverings, a tiny California article, "Radical Sighted at Drugstore," and then, a newsletter. It was dated November 15, 1987, *Daily Bulletin*, Houston Police Department, Confidential, For Police Use Only, WANTED BY LOCAL AND FEDERAL AUTHORITIES, Warrants on file at Harris County Sheriff Warrant Section, Bell 432-6329—

My heart stopped.

Staring back at me, above "Gracey, George. I.R. 329573. Male, White,

VISUAL AID 35.0

43, 220, Heavy build. Fed. Warrant #78-3298. Tattoos on right chest. Walks with limp. Subjects should be considered armed and dangerous"—was Baba au Rhum (Visual Aid 35.0).

Granted, in the police photo, Servo sported a dense steel-wool beard and mustache, both doing their best to scrub out his oval face, and the photograph (a still taken from a security camera) was in sloppy black and white. Yet Servo's burning eyes, his lipless mouth reminiscent of the plastic gap in a

Kleenex box with no Kleenex, the way his small head stood up against his bullying shoulders—it was unmistakable.

"He always hobbled," Dad had said to me in Paris. "Even when we were at Harvard."

I grabbed the paper, which also featured the sketch of Catherine Baker, the one I'd seen on the Internet. ("Federal Authorities and the Harris County Sheriff's Department are asking for public assistance in obtaining information leading to the Grand Jury indictment of these persons . . ." it read on the second page.) I ran upstairs to my room, yanked open my desk drawers, and dug through my old homework papers and notebooks and Unit Tests, until I found the Air France boarding passes, some Ritz stationery, and then, the small piece of graph paper on which Dad had scribbled Servo's home and mobile telephone numbers the day they'd left me and gone to La Sorbonne.

After some confusion—country codes, reversing ones and zeros—I managed to correctly dial the mobile number. Instantly, I was met with the hisses and heckling of a number no longer in service. When I called the home number, after a great deal of "*Como?*" and "*Qué?*" a patient Spanish woman informed me that the apartment wasn't a private residence, *no*, it was available for weeklong lettings via Go Chateaux, Inc. She pointed me toward the vacation Web site and an 800-number (see "ILE-297," www.gochateaux.com). I called the Reservations line and was curtly told by a man that the apartment hadn't been a private residence since the company's inception in 1981. I then tried to wrench free whatever info he had on the individual who'd leased the unit the week of December 26, but was informed Go Chateaux wasn't authorized to disclose their client's personal records.

"Have I done what I could to assist you on this call?"

"This is a matter of life and death. People are being *killed*."

"Have I satisfied all of your questions?"

"No."

"Thank you for calling Go Chateaux."

I hung up and did nothing but sit on the edge of my bed, stunned by the blasé response of the afternoon. Surely, the sky should have split open like plumber's pants; at the very least, smoke should be unraveling from the trees, their topmost branches singed—but no, the afternoon was a dead-eyed teenager, a weathered broad hanging around a dive bar, old tinsel. My revelation was *my* problem; it had nothing whatsoever to do with the bedroom, with the light like drunk wallflowers in shapeless gold dresses slouching

along the radiator and bookshelf, the windowpane shadows like idiot sun-
bathers sprawled all over the floor. I remembered picking up Servo's cane after it had toppled off the edge of a *boulangerie* counter, rapping a woman
standing behind him directly on her black shoe making her gasp and light up
red like she was a twenty-five-cent theme park game of sledgehammer and
bell, and the top of the walking stick, a bald eagle head, had been hot and
sticky from Servo's steak-fat palm. As I returned the cane to the spot by his elbow, he'd tossed words over his left shoulder, hastily, like he'd spilled salt:
"Mmmm, merci beaucoup. Need a leash for that thing, don't I?" I supposed
it was no use berating myself for not quilting together, in a more timely
fashion, these obviously well-matched scraps of life (How many men had I
ever known with hip trouble? *None but Servo* was the pitiful answer) and
naturally (though I resisted) I thought of something Dad had said: "A surprise
is rarely a stranger, but a faceless patient who's been reading across from you
in the waiting room the entire time, his head hidden by a magazine but his
orange socks in plain view, as well as his gold pocket watch and frayed
trousers."

But if Servo was George Gracey, what did that make Dad?

Servo is to Gracey as Dad is to—suddenly, the answer came lurching out
of hiding, hands up, throwing itself to the ground, begging for forgiveness,
praying I wouldn't flay it alive.

I raced to my desk, seized my CASE NOTES, scoured the pages for those
odd little nicknames I'd taken such haphazard note of, eventually finding
them cowering at the bottom of Page 4: Nero, Bull's-Eye, Mohave, Socrates
and Franklin. It was farcically obvious now. Dad was Socrates, otherwise
known as The Thinker according to www.looseyourrevolutioncherry.net—of
course, he'd be Socrates—who else would Dad be? Marx, Hume, Descartes,
Sartre, none of those nicknames were good enough for Dad ("out-of-date,
blubbering scribblers"), and he wouldn't be caught dead going by Plato
("hugely overhyped as a logician"). I wondered if one of The Nightwatchmen had dreamt up the nickname; no, it was more likely Dad himself had
casually suggested it in private to Servo before a meeting. Dad didn't do well
with subtlety, with off the cuff; when it came to All Things Gareth, Dad wore
indifference like a socialite thin as a cheese cracker forced to lunch in a football jersey. My eyes were staggering down the page now, through my own
neatly written words: "January 1974 marked a change in tactics for the group
from evident to invisible." In January 1974, Dad had been enrolled in Harvard's Kennedy School of Government; in March 1974, "police had come

close to raiding one of The Nightwatchmen's gatherings in an abandoned Braintree, Massachusetts, warehouse"; Braintree was less than thirty minutes from Cambridge, and thus The Nightwatchmen had been less than thirty minutes from Dad—a highly likely intersection of two moving bodies across Space and Time.

It must have been Dad's admittance into The Nightwatchmen that led to their shift in strategy. "Blind Dates: Advantages of a Silent Civil War" and "Rebellion in the Information Age" were two of Dad's most popular *Federal Forum* essays (every now and then he still received fan mail), and it was a Primary Theme that had served as the basis for his highly regarded Harvard dissertation of 1978, "The Curse of the Freedom Fighter: The Fallacies of Guerrilla Warfare and Third-World Revolution." (It was also the reason he called Lou Swann a "hack.") And then there was Dad's palpable Moment of Turning, a moment he spoke lovingly about in a Bourbon Mood (as if it were a woman he'd seen in a train station, a woman with silky hair who tilted her head close to the glass so Dad saw a cloud where her mouth should be), when he stood on Benno Ohncsorg's stiff shoelace at a Berlin protest rally and the innocent student was shot dead by police. This was when he realized that "the man who stands up and protests, the lone man who says *no*—he will be crucified."

"And that was my Bolshevik moment, so to speak," Dad said. "When I decided to storm the Winter Palace."

When charting what I knew to be my life, somehow I'd managed to omit an entire continent (see *Antarctica: The Coldest Place on Earth*, Turg, 1987). *"Always content, aren't you, to hide behind the lecture podium?"* I'd overheard Servo shouting at Dad. Servo was the "hormonal teenager," Dad, the theorist. (Frankly, Servo had hit the nail on the head; Dad didn't like dishwasher soap on his hands, much less the blood of men.) And Servo doubtlessly paid Dad well for his theorizing. Though Dad, over the years, had always pleaded poverty, when it came down to it, he could still live it up like Kubla Kahn, renting an ornate house like 24 Armor Street, staying at the Ritz, shipping a 200-pound, $17,000 antique desk across the country and lying about it. Even Dad's choice of bourbon, George T. Stagg, was considered by *Stuart Mill's Booze Bible* (2003 ed.) "the Bentley of all bourbons."

In Paris, had I come upon them arguing about Hannah Schneider, or the encroaching problem of Ada Harvey? *Highly hysterical, problem, Simone de Beauvoir*—the overheard conversation was a mule; it wouldn't come back willingly. I had to coax and cajole it, tug it back into my head, so by the time

I lined up the shards of conversation for inspection, I was just as confused as when I began. My head felt hollowed out with a spoon.

*　　*　　*

After the initial sting, my life—jam packed with highways, Sonnet-a-thons, Bourbon Moods, notable quotations by people who were dead—it peeled away with remarkable ease.

Frankly, I was astonished how unfazed I felt, how unflappable. After all, if Vivien Leigh suffered from hallucinations and hysteria, requiring shock treatment, ice packing and a diet of raw eggs simply by working on the set of *Elephant Walk* (a film no one had ever heard of except descendants of Peter Finch), surely it'd be conceivable, maybe even mandatory for me to develop *some* form of dementia over the fact my life had been a Trompe l'Oeil, Gonzo Journalism, *The $64,000 Question*, the Feejee Mermaid, a Hitler Diary, Milli Vanilli (see Chapter 3, "Miss O'Hara," *Birds of Torment: Luscious Ladies of the Screen and Their Living Demons*, Lee, 1973).

After my Socratic revelation, however, the subsequent truths I unearthed weren't nearly so jaw dropping. (One can only be so hoodzonked before one's hoodzonk maxes out like a credit card.)

In the ten years we'd traveled the country, Dad appeared to have been concerned, not so much with my education, but with a rigorous Nightwatch-men staffing exercise. Dad had been their powerful Head of HR, his voice intoxicating as the Sirens, most likely directly responsible for that "inspirational recruitment," detailed by Guillaume on www.hautain.fr. It was the only logical explanation: every professor who'd come to dinner over the years, the quiet young men who listened with such intensity while Dad delivered his Sermon on the Mount, his story of Tobias Jones the Damned, his Determination Theory—"*There are wolves and there are brine shrimp*," he'd said, going for the Hard Sell—not only were they *not* professors, they didn't exist.

There was no hearing-impaired Dr. Luke Ordinote spearheading the History Department at the University of Missouri at Archer. There was no fig-eyed Professor of Linguistics Mark Hill. There *was* a Professor of Zoology Mark Hubbard but I couldn't speak to him because he'd been on sabbatical in Israel for the last twelve years studying the endangered Little Bustard, *Tetrax tetrax*. Most chillingly, there was no Professor Arnie Sanderson who taught Intro to Drama and History of the World Theater, with whom Dad had had a riotous dinner the night Eva Brewster destroyed my mother's butterflies, also at Piazza Pitti the night he'd disappeared.

"Hello?"

"Hello. I was trying to get in touch with an Associate Professor who taught in your English Department in the fall of 2001. His name is Lee Sanjay Song."

"What's the name?"

"*Song.*"

There was a brief pause.

"No one by that name here."

"I'm not sure if he was full- or part-time."

"I understand, but no one by that—"

"Perhaps he's left? Moved to Calcutta? Timbuktu? Maybe he was flattened by a bus."

"Ex*cuse* me?"

"I'm sorry. It's just—if anyone knows *any*thing, if there's someone else I could talk to I'd be grateful—"

"*I* have supervised this English Department for twenty-nine *years* and I assure you, *no* one with the last name of Song has ever taught here. I'm sorry I can't be of better assistance, miss—"

Naturally, I wondered if Dad too had been an imposter professor. I'd witnessed him speaking in lecture halls on a handful of occasions, but there were more than a few colleges I *hadn't* visited. And if I hadn't seen with my own eyes the closet-office Dad referred to as his "cage," his "crypt," his "and they think I can sit in this catacomb and come up with novel ideas to inspire the featureless youths of this country"—perhaps it was similar to that tree falling in a forest. It never happened.

I was entirely off the mark on this front. Everyone and their grandmother had heard of Dad, including a few departmental secretaries who'd just been hired. It seemed, wherever Dad went, he'd left a blinding Yellow Brick Road of adulation in his wake.

"How *is* the old boy?" inquired Dean Richardson of University of Arkansas at Wilsonville.

"He's fantastic."

"I've often wondered what happened to him. Thought of him the other day when I came across a Virginia Summa article saluting Mideast policies in *Proposals*. I could just hear Garry howling with laughter. Come to think of it, I haven't seen an essay of his in a while. Well, I suppose it's tight these days. Mavericks, nonconformists, those who march to the beat of their own drum, speak up, they're not finding the same forums they used to."

"He's managing."

Obviously, if a corner of one's life ended up covertly cultivating a shocking amount of slime mold, one must switch on unflattering fluorescent lights (the cruel kind of chicken coops), get down on one's hands and knees and scrub *every* corner. I thus found it necessary to investigate another thrilling possibility: What If June Bugs were not June Bugs, but Spanish Moon Moths (*Graellsia isabellae*), the most captivating and well bred of all the European moths? What If they, too, like the bogus professors, were gifted individuals Dad had meticulously handpicked for The Nightwatchmen? What If they only *pretended* to bond vigorously to Dad as lithium does to fluorine (see *The Strange Attractions of Opposite Ions*, Booley, 1975)? I wanted it to be true; I wanted to pull my boat up next to theirs, rescue them from their wasted African violets and quivery-voiced phone calls, from their tepid waters with nothing flourishing in them, no reefs, parrot or angelfish (and certainly no sea turtles). Dad had left them stranded on that boat, but I'd set them free, send them away on a powerful Trade Wind. They'd disappear to Casablanca, to Bombay, to Rio (everyone wanted to disappear to Rio)—never heard of, never *seen* again, as poetic a fate as any they could hope for.

I began my investigation by calling Information and obtaining the telephone number of June Bug Jessie Rose Rubiman, *still* living in Newton, Texas, and *still* heiress to the Rubiman Carpeting franchise: "Mention his name *one* more time—know what? I'm still considering finding out where he lives, coming into his bedroom while he sleeps and chopping off his doohickey. That's what that son-of-a-bitch's got coming to him."

I ended my investigation by calling Information and obtaining the telephone number of June Bug Shelby Hollow: "Night watch? Wait—I won a free Indiglo Timex?"

Unless June Bugs were skilled actresses in the tradition of Davis and Dietrich (suitable for the A movies, not the B or C movies), it seemed evident that the only moth flying through this sticky night, doggedly figure-eighting (like a confused kamikaze pilot) around every porch light and lamppost, refusing to be deterred even if I switched out the lights and ignored her, was Hannah Schneider.

That was the startling thing about this business of abandonment, of finding oneself so without conversation, one's thoughts had the entire world to themselves; they could drift for days without bumping into anyone. I could swallow Dad calling himself Socrates. I could swallow The Nightwatchmen too, hunt down every whisper of their workings like a private detective desperate to find The Missing Dame. I could even swallow Servo and Hannah as lovers (see "African Egg-Eating Snake," *Encyclopedia of Living Things*, 4th ed.). I could assume Baba au Rhum hadn't always rattled and Mmmmed; back in the stringy-haired summer of 1973, no doubt he'd cut an arresting rebel figure (or resembled Poe just enough that thirteen-year-old Catherine decided to be his Virginia forevermore).

What I *couldn't* swallow, couldn't stare at with the naked eye, was *Dad* and Hannah. I noticed, as the days drifted past, I kept tucking that thought away, saving it like a grandmother for a Special Occasion that would never come. I attempted and sometimes succeeded diverting my mind (*not* with a book or play and, yes, reciting Keats was an idiotic idea, boarding a row-boat for refuge in an earthquake) but with TV, shaving and Gap commercials, prime-time melodramas with tan people named Brett declaring, "It's payback time."

They were gone. They were giant specimens splayed in glass cases in dim, deserted rooms. I could stare down at them, ridicule my stupidity for never noticing their blatant similarities: their awe-inspiring size (personas larger than life), brightly-colored hind wings (conspicuous in any room), their spined caterpillar beginnings (orphan, poor little rich girl, respectively), taking flight solely at night (their endings swathed in mystery), boundaries of their distribution unknown.

If a man bemoaned a woman as noisily as Dad ("commonplace," "strange and wayward," a "sob story," he'd called her), behind Curtain #1 of such severe dislike there was almost always a brand new Sedona Beige Love parked there, big, bright and impractical (destined to break down within the year). It was the oldest trick in the book, one I never should have fallen for, having read all of Shakespeare, including the late romances, and the definitive biography of Cary Grant, *The Reluctant Lover* (Murdy, 1999).

BUTTERFLIES FRAGILE. Why, when I forced myself to consider Dad and Hannah, did that old moving box crash into my head? They were the words Dad almost always used to describe my mother. After the fuss of *battement frappés* and *demi-pliés*, the Technicolor Dream dress, those words often showed up like unwanted, impoverished guests at a splendid party, embarrassing and sad, as if Dad was talking about her glass eye or absence of an arm. At Hyacinth Terrace, her black eyes like clogged drains, her mouth stained plum, Hannah Schneider had said the same frilly words, spoken not to the others but to me. With a stare pressing down on me, she'd said: "*Some people are fragile, as—as butterflies.*"

They'd used the same delicate words to describe the same delicate person.

Time and again, Dad handpicked a cute slogan for a person and rudely bumper-stuck it to them for all ensuing conversations (Dean Roy at the University of Arkansas at Wilsonville had been the uninspired "sweet as candy"). Hannah must have heard him say it once when describing my mother. And just as she'd blatantly recited Dad's favorite quotation to me at the dinner table (happiness, dog, sun) and planted Dad's favorite foreign film in her VCR (*L'Avventura*) (Hannah was now dusted, cast in ultraviolet light; I could see Dad's fingerprints all over her), she had tantalizingly tossed me that phrase, thereby letting bits of her dark secret, the hot one she'd clutched tightly in her hands, fall through her fingers, so that I might see it, follow it like the barest trail of sand. Not even when I was alone with her in the woods did she have the guts (*Mut*, in German) to let go of it, throw it all into the air so it showered over our heads, got caught in our hair and mouths.

The truth they'd hidden (Dad with Fifth Symphony ferocity, Hannah messily) that they'd known each other (since 1992, I calculated) in the movie-poster sense of the word (and I'd never know if they were *Il Caso Thomas Crown* or *Colazione da Tiffany* or if they'd flossed their teeth next to each other three hundred times), it didn't garner a gasp from me—not a whimper or wheeze.

I only went back to the moving box and sat on my knees, running my fingers through the velvet splinters, the antennae and forewings and the thoraxes and torn mounting papers and pins, hoping Natasha had left me a code, a suicide letter identifying her traitorous husband just as she'd identified the part of the Red-based Jezebel that indicated it was repugnant to birds—an explanation, a puzzle to pore over, a whisper from the dead, a Visual Aid. (There was nothing.)

By then, my CASE NOTES filled an entire legal pad, some fifty pages, and I'd remembered the photograph Nigel had shown me in Hannah's bedroom (which she must have destroyed before the camping trip since I'd been unable to find it in the Evan Picone shoe box), the one of Hannah as a girl with the blonde floating away from the camera lens and on the back, written in blue pen, 1973. And I'd driven the Volvo to the Internet café on Orlando, Cyberroast, and matched the gold-lion insignia, which I recalled from the pocket of Hannah's school uniform blazer, to the crest of a private school on East 81st Street, the one Natasha had attended in 1973 after her parents made her quit the Larson Ballet Conservatory (see www.theivyschool.edu). (*Salva veritate* was their irksome motto.) And after staring for hours at that other photo of Hannah, the one I'd stolen from her garage, Rockstar Hannah of the Rooster-Red Hair, I'd realized why, back in January, when I'd seen her with the madwoman haircut, I'd felt that persistent itch of déjà vu.

The woman who'd driven me home from kindergarten after my mother died, the pretty one in jeans with short red porcupine hair, the one Dad had told me was our next-door neighbor — it had been Hannah.

I cut out pieces of evidence from every other conversation I could remember, gluing them together, awed, but also sickened by the resulting graphic collage (see "Splayed Nude Patchwork XI," *The Unauthorized Biography of Indonesia Sotto*, Greyden, 1989, p. 211). "*She had a best friend growing up*," Hannah had said to me, cigarette smoke pirouetteing off her fingers, "a beautiful girl, fragile; they were like sisters. She could confide in her, tell her everything under the sun — for the life of me, I can't remember her name." "There are people. Fragile people, that you love and you hurt them, and I—I'm pathetic, aren't I?" she'd said to me in the woods. "Something awful happened in her twenties, a man was involved," Eva Brewster had said, "her friend — she didn't go into details, but not a day went by when she didn't feel guilt over what she'd done — whatever it was."

Was Hannah the reason Servo and Dad (in spite of their dynamic working relationship) warred with each other — they'd loved (or perhaps it was never anything so grand, simply a case of poorly wired electricity) the same woman? Was Hannah why we moved to Stockton, remorse over her dead best friend who committed suicide from a broken heart, the reason she'd showered me with breathy compliments and squeezed me against her bony shoulder? How was it possible scientists were able to locate the edge of the observable universe, the Cosmic Light Horizon ("Our universe is 13.7 billion light years long," wrote Harry Mills Cornblow, Ph.D., with astounding confidence in *The ABCs of the Cosmos* [2003]) and yet, mere human beings stayed so fuzzy, beyond all calculation?

Yes, Not Sure, Probably, and Who the Hell Knew were my answers.

Fourteen days after Dad was gone (two days after I received the cordial greeting from Mr. William Baumgartner of the Bank of New York notifying me of my account numbers; in 1993, the year we left Mississippi, it seemed Dad had set up a trust fund in my name) I was downstairs in the storage room off of Dad's former study, weeding through the shelves piled with damaged *stuff*, most of it belonging to the owner of 24 Armor Street, though some of it was junk Dad and I had accumulated over the years: matching lamps in mint green, a marble obelisk paperweight (a gift from one of Dad's worshipful students), a few faded picture books of little consequence (*A Travel Guide to South Africa* [1968] by J. C. Bulrich). I happened to push aside a small flat cardboard box Dad had marked SILVERWARE and saw, next to it, wedged in the corner behind a crinkled, jaundiced newspaper (the grimly titled, *Rwandan Standard-Times*), Dad's Brighella costume, the black cloak in a ball, the bronze mask with its peeling paint and fishhook nose sneering at the shelves.

Without thinking, I picked up the cloak, shook it loose and pressed my face into it, a sort of embarrassing, lost thing to do, and immediately, I noticed a distantly familiar smell, a smell of Howard and Wal-Mart, Hannah's bedroom—that old Tahitian acidic sap, the kind of cologne that barged into a room and held it up for hours.

But then—it was a face in a crowd. You noticed a jaw, eyes or one of those fascinating chins that looked like a needle and knotted thread had been stuck and pulled tightly through the center and you wanted, sometimes were desperate, to glimpse it one last time, but you couldn't, no matter how hard you fought through the elbows, the handbags, the high-heeled shoes. As soon as I recognized the cologne and the name panthered through my head, it slipped out of sight, drowned somewhere, was gone.

Metamorphoses

I knew something screwballed and romantic would happen on Graduation Day, because the morning sky wouldn't stop blushing over the house and when I opened my bedroom window, the air felt faint. Even the girlish pines, crowded in their tight cliques around the yard, shivered in anticipation; and then I sat down at the kitchen table with Dad's *Wall Street Journal* (it still turned up for him in the wee hours of the morning like a john returning to a street corner where his favorite hooker had once strutted her stuff), switched on WQOX News 13 at 6:30 A.M., *The Good Morning Show with Cherry*, and Cherry Jeffries was missing.

In her place sat Norvel Owen wearing a tight sports jacket the blue of Neptune. He wove his chubby fingers together, and with his face glowing, blinking as if someone was shining a flashlight in his eyes, he began to read the news without a single comment, plea, passing remark, or personal aside about the reason for Cherry Jeffries' absence. He didn't even throw out a bland and unconvincing, "Wishing Cherry the best of luck," or "Wishing Cherry a speedy recovery." Even more astonishing was the show's new title, which I noticed when the program cut to commercial: *The Good Morning Show with Norvel*. The Executive Producers at WQOX News 13 had erased the very *being* of Cherry with the same ease of deleting an eyewitness' "uhs," "ers," and "see heres" out of a top news story in the Editing Room.

With his half-a-slice-of-pineapple grin, Norvel turned the floor over to Ashleigh Goldwell who did Weather. She announced Stockton could expect "high humidity with an eighty percent chance of rain."

Despite this dismal forecast, as soon as I arrived at St. Gallway (after running my last few errands, Sherwig Realty, the Salvation Army), Eva Brewster made the announcement over the intercom that proud parents would *still* be ushered to their designated metal folding chairs on the field in front of the Bartleby Sports Center *precisely* at the stroke of 11:00 A.M. (Five chairs maximum were allotted per student. Any relative spillover would be relegated to the bleachers.) The ceremony would *still* begin at 11:30. Contrary to the circulating rumors, all events and speakers would proceed as scheduled, including the post-ceremony Garden Hour of Hors d'oeuvres (music and entertainment provided by the Jelly Roll Jazz Band and those St. Gallway Fosse Dancers who were not graduating) where parents, faculty and students alike could circle like Pallid Monkey Moths among the whisperings of Who Got in Where and the sparkling cider and the calla lilies.

"I've telephoned a few radio stations and the rain isn't forecast until later this afternoon," Eva Brewster said. "As long as all seniors line up on time we should be fine. Good luck and congratulations."

I was late leaving Ms. Simpson's classroom in Hanover (Soggy Ms. Simpson: "Can I just say, your presence in this classroom has been an honor. When I find a student who demonstrates such a deep understanding of the material . . .") and Mr. Moats also wished to detain me when I turned in my Final Drawing Portfolio. Even though I'd been meticulous in making sure I looked and behaved exactly as I had before my abrupt hiatus from school, a total of sixteen days—dressing the same, walking the same, having the same hair (these were the clues people bloodhounded when trying to chase down Domestic Apocalypse or a Deteriorating Psyche), it still seemed Dad's desertion had altered me in some way. It had revised me, but only very slightly—a word here, a bit of clarification there. I also felt people's eyes on me all the time, though not in the same envious way as in my Blueblood Heyday. No, it was the adults who noticed me now, always with a brief yet baffled stare, as if they now noticed something old within me, as if they recognized themselves.

"Glad to know things are back on track," Mr. Moats said.

"Thank you," I said.

"We were worried. We didn't know what had happened to you."

"I know. Things became hectic."

"When you finally let Eva know what'd happened, we were relieved. You must be going through a lot. How's your father doing by the way?"

"The prognosis isn't good," I said. It was the scripted sentence I'd sort of relished saying to Ms. Thermopolis (who responded by reminding me they can do wonders "fixing" cancer as if it was just a bad haircut) and Ms. Gershon (who speedily changed the subject back to my Final Essay on String

Theory), even Mr. Archer (who stared at the Titian poster on the wall, rendered speechless by the ruffles in the girl's dress), but now I felt bad when it rendered Moats visibly sad and mute. He nodded at the floor. "My father died of throat cancer too," he said softly. "It can be grueling. The loss of the voice, a failure to communicate—not easy for any man. I can't imagine how tough it'd be for a professor. Modigliani was plagued with illness, you know. Degas. Toulouse too. Many of the greatest men and women in history." Moats sighed. "And next year you're at Harvard?"

I nodded.

"It'll be hard, but you must concentrate on your studies. Your father will want it that way. And keep drawing, Blue," he added, a statement that seemed to comfort him more than me. He sighed and touched the collar of his textured magenta shirt. "And I don't say that to just anyone, you know. Many people should stay far, far away from the blank page. But *you*—you see, the drawing, the carefully considered sketch of a human being, animal, an inanimate object, is not simply a picture but a blueprint of a soul. Photography? A lazy man's art. Drawing? The thinker, the *dreamer*'s medium."

"Thank you," I said.

A few minutes later, I was hurrying across the Commons in my long white dress and flat white shoes. The sky had darkened to the color of bullets and parents in pastels drifted toward Bartleby field, some of them laughing, clutching their handbags or the hand of a small child, some of them fluffing their hair as if it was goose-feather pillows.

Ms. Eugenia Sturds had mandated that we "load" (we were bulls to be unleashed in a ring) in the Nathan Bly '68 Trophy Room no later than 10:45 A.M., and when I pushed open the door and made my way into the crowded room, it seemed I was the last senior to arrive.

"No disturbances during the ceremony," Mr. Butters was saying. "No laughter. No fidgeting—"

"No clapping until all names are called—" chimed Ms. Sturds.

"No getting up and going to the *bath*room—"

"Girls, if you have to pee, go now."

Immediately, I spotted Jade and the others in the corner. Jade, wearing a suit in marshmallow white, hair slicked into a *mais oui* twist, reviewed her reflection in a pocket mirror, rubbing lipstick off her teeth and smacking her lips together. Lu was standing quietly with her hands together, looking down, pitching forward and backward on her heels. Charles, Milton and Nigel were discussing beer. "Budweiser tastes like fuckin' rabbit piss," I heard Milton remark loudly, as I skirted to the other side of the room. (I'd often wondered what they talked about now that Hannah was gone and I was sort of relieved to know it was hackneyed and had nothing to do with The Eternal Why; I wasn't missing much.) I pushed past Point Richardson, Donnamara Chase sniffing in distress as she dabbed a wet napkin along a blue pen streak across the front of her blouse, Trucker wearing a green tie with tiny horse heads floating in it and Dee safety-pinning Dum's crimson bra straps to her dress straps so they didn't show.

"I all can't fathom why you told mom eleven forty-five," Dee said heatedly.

"What's the big deal?"

"The procession's the big deal."

"Why?"

"Mom's all not going to be able to take pictures. Because of your *mal á la tête* mom's all missing our last day of childhood like a crosstown bus."

"She said she was going to be *early—*"

"Well, I didn't see her and she's wearing that highly visible purple outfit she wears to *every*thing—"

"I thought you forbade her to wear the highly visible—"

"It's starting!" squawked Little Nose, perched on the radiator at the window. "We have to go! *Now!*"

"Grab the diploma with the right, shake with the left, or shake with the left, grab with the right?" asked Raging Waters.

"Zach, did you see our parents?" asked Lonny Felix.

"I gotta pee," said Krista Jibsen.

"So this is it," Sal Mineo said solemnly behind me. "This is the end."

Even though the Jelly Roll Jazz Band had broken into "Pomp and Circumstance," Ms. Sturds callously informed us No One Was Graduating Anywhere until everyone calmed down and formed the alphabetized line. We tapewormed, exactly as we'd practiced all week. Mr. Butters gave the signal, opened the door with *American Bandstand* flourish and Ms. Sturds, as if unveiling a solid new line of mules, arms raised, her floral skirt jitterbugging around her ankles, stepped out onto the lawn in front of us.

The sky was a massive bruise; someone had punched it in the kisser. There was an uncouth wind, too. It wouldn't stop teasing the long blue St. Gallway banners hanging on either side of the Commencement Stage, and then, growing bored, turned its attention to the music. In spite of Mr. Johnson's cries for the Jelly Roll Jazz Band to play louder (for a second I thought he was shouting, "Sing out, Louise!" but I was wrong), the wind intercepted the notes, sprinting away with them across the field and punted them through the goal posts, so all that was audible was a few shabby clangs and honks.

We filed down the aisle. Parents frothed excitedly around us, clapping and grinning, and slow-motion grandmothers tried to take *foe-toes* with cameras they handled like jewelry. A wiry lizard-photographer from Ellis Hills, trying to blend in, scurried ahead of our line, crouching, squinting as he peered through his camera. He stuck out his tongue before snapping a few quick pictures and scuttling away.

The rest of the class made their way into the metal folding chairs in the front and Radley Clifton and I continued up the five steps to the commencement stage. We sat down in the chairs to the right of Havermeyer and Havermeyer's wife, Gloria (finally relieved of the boulder she'd been carrying, though now she had an equally disturbing pale, rigid, Plexiglas appearance). Eva Brewster was next to her and she tossed me a comforting smile but then almost immediately took it away, like lending me her handkerchief but not wanting it to get dirty.

Havermeyer sauntered toward the microphone and talked at length about our unparalleled achievements, our great gifts and glowing futures, and then Radley Clifton gave his Salutatorian Speech. He'd just begun to philosophize—"An army marches on its stomach," he said—when the wind, obviously contemptuous of all scholars, truth-seekers, logicians (anyone who tried to address The Eternal Why) I-Spied-With-My-Little-Eye Radley, joking with his red tie, mocking his hair (neatly combed, the color of cardboard), and just when one thought the mischief would subside, it started to rag on the neat white pages of his speech, forcing him to lose his place, repeat himself, stutter and pause so Radley Clifton's Graduation Credo came out jarring, conflicted, confused—a surprisingly resonant life philosophy.

Havermeyer returned to the podium. Strands of sandy hair daddylonglegged across his forehead. "I now introduce to you our class Valedictorian, a highly gifted young woman, originally from Ohio, who we were honored to have at St. Gallway this year. Miss Blue van Meer."

He pronounced Meer *mare*, but I tried not to think about it as I stood up, smoothed down the front of my dress and, in the moderate but perfectly respectable burst of applause, made my way across the rubberized stage (supposedly there'd been a bad wipeout a few years prior: Martine Filobeque, cunning pinecone, girdle). I was grateful for the applause, grateful people were generous enough to clap for a kid who wasn't theirs, a kid who, at least academically, had outtangoed their own kid (as decent a reason as any Dad would find to crack "so *this* what they call 'outstanding.' "). I set the papers on the podium, pulled down the microphone and made the mistake of glancing up at the two hundred heads facing me blankly like an expansive field of mature white cabbage. My heart was trying out new moves (The Robot, something called The Lightning Bolt) and for a harrowing second I wasn't sure I'd have the courage to speak. Somewhere in the crowd Jade was smoothing her gold hair back, sighing, "Oh, *God*, not the pigeon again," and Milton was thinking, tuna tataki, salade niçoise—but I quarantined these thoughts as best I could. The edges of the pages seemed to panic too, trembling in the wind.

"In one of the first well-known Valedictorian Speeches," I began; somewhat disconcertingly my voice boomeranged over everyone's coiffed head, presumably reaching the tall man in the blue suit in the very back, a man I'd *thought*, for a split second, was Dad (it wasn't, unless like a plant without light, Dad without me had withered, lost serious amounts of hair), "transcribed in 1801 at Doverfield Academy in Massachusetts, seventeen-year-old Michael Finpost announced to his peers, 'We will look back on these golden days and remember them as the best years of our lives.' Well, for each of you sitting before me, I really hope that's not the case."

A blonde in the front row of the Parents Section wearing a short skirt crossed, uncrossed her legs and did a restless swinging gesture with them, a stretch of some kind, also a movement used at airports to direct planes.

"And I–I'm not going to stand here and tell you, 'To Thine Own Self Be True.' Because the majority of you won't. According to the Crime Census Bureau America is experiencing a marked increase in grand larceny and fraud, not only in cities but rural vicinities as well. For that matter, too, I doubt any of us in four years of high school have managed to locate our self in order to be true to it. Maybe we've found what hemisphere it's in, maybe the ocean—but not the exact coordinates. I'm also"—for a terrifying second my hobo concentration fell off the train, the moment started to speed by, but then to my relief it managed to shake itself off, sprint, hurtle on board again—"I'm also not going to tell you to wear sunscreen. Most of you won't. *The New England Journal of Medicine* reported in June 2002 skin cancer in the under-thirty demographic is on the rise and in the Western World, forty-three out of every fifty people consider even plain-looking people twenty times more attractive when they're tan." I paused. I couldn't believe it; I said *tan* and a little seismic laughter quaked through the crowd. "No. I'm going to try to assist you with something else. Something practical. Something that might help you when something happens in your life and you're worried you might never recover. When you've been knocked down."

I noticed Dee and Dum, front row, fourth from the left. They stared up at me with evenly weirded-out faces, half-smiles caught up in their teeth like skirt hems caught in pantyhose.

"I'm going to ask that you seriously consider modeling your life," I said, "not in the manner of the Dalai Lama or Jesus—though I'm sure they're helpful—but something a bit more hands-on, *Carassius auratus auratus*, commonly known as the domestic goldfish."

There was party favor laughter, little bits of it strewn here and there for fun, but I pressed on.

"People make fun of the goldfish. People don't think twice about swallowing it. Jonas Ornata III, Princeton class of '42, appears in *The Guinness Book of World Records* for swallowing the greatest number of goldfish in a fifteen minute interval, a cruel total of thirty-nine. In his defense though, I don't think Jonas understood the glory of the goldfish, that they have magnificent lessons to teach us."

I glanced up and my gaze smacked right into Milton, first row, fourth from the left. He had tilted his chair back and was talking to someone behind him, Jade.

"If you live like a goldfish," I continued, "you can survive the harshest, most thwarting of circumstances. You can live through hardships that make your cohorts—the guppy, the neon tetra—go belly up at the first sign of trouble. There was an infamous incident described in a journal published by the Goldfish Society of America—a sadistic five-year-old girl threw hers to the carpet, stepped on it, not once but twice—luckily she'd done it on a shag carpet and thus her heel didn't *quite* come down fully on the fish. After thirty harrowing seconds she tossed it back into its tank. It went on to live another forty-seven years." I cleared my throat. "They can live in ice-covered ponds in the dead of winter. Bowls that haven't seen soap in a year. And they don't die from neglect, not immediately. They hold on for three, sometimes four months if they're abandoned."

One or two restless people were dribbling into the aisles, hoping to escape my notice, a silver-haired man needing to stretch his legs, a woman bouncing a toddler, whispering secrets into its hair.

"If you live like a goldfish, you adapt, not across hundreds of thousands of years like most species, having to go through the red tape of natural selection, but within mere months, weeks even. You give them a little tank? They give you a little body. Big tank? Big body. Indoor. Outdoor. Fish tanks, bowls. Cloudy water, clear water. Social or alone."

The wind taunted the edges of my papers.

"The most incredible thing about goldfish, however, is their memory. Everyone pities them for only remembering their last three seconds, but in fact, to be so forcibly tied to the present—it's a gift. They are free. No moping over missteps, slip-ups, faux pas or disturbing childhoods. No inner demons. Their closets are light filled and skeleton free. And what could be more exhilarating than seeing the world for the very first time, in all of its beauty, almost thirty thousand times a day? How glorious to know that your Golden Age wasn't forty years ago when you still had all your hair, but only *three seconds* ago, and thus, very possibly it's *still* going on, this very moment." I counted three Mississippis in my head, though I might have rushed it, being nervous. "And this moment, too." Another three seconds. "And this moment, too." Another. "And this moment, too."

Dad never talked about not moving people during a lecture. He never talked about the funny human need to impart something, *any*thing, to someone, build a tiny bridge to them and help them across, or what to do when the crowd twitched ceaselessly like a horse's back. The endless sniffing, the clearing of throats, fathers' eyes that skate boarded one side of a row to the other side of a row, doing a 180-ollie around the hot mom, sixth from the right—he never said a *word*. Standing around the rim of the football field the hemlocks stood tall, watching protectively. The wind tugged the sleeves of a hundred blouses. I wondered if that kid, far end, third row, red shirt (oddly gnawing his fist and frowning at me with James-Deanian intensity) if *he* knew I was an imposter, that I'd secretly cut out only the beautiful part of the truth and discarded the rest. Because, in reality, goldfish were having as rough a time with life as the rest of us; they expired all the time from the shock of new temperatures and the faintest shadow of a heron prompted them to hide under rocks. And yet, maybe it didn't matter so much what I said or didn't say, what I kissed on the cheek or what I gave the cold shoulder. (My god, Red Shirt, hands clamped over his mouth, biting his fingernails, he was now sitting *so* far forward, his head was nearly a flowerpot on the sill of Sal Mineo's shoulder. I didn't know who he was. I'd never seen him before.) Lectures and Theories, all Tomes of Nonfiction, maybe they deserved the same gentle treatment as works of art; maybe they were human creations trying to shoulder a few terrors and joys of the world, composed at a certain place, at a certain time, to be pondered, frowned at, liked, loathed and then one went to the gift shop and bought the postcard, put it in a shoe box high on a shelf.

The end of my speech was a disaster, the disaster being that nothing happened. Obviously, I'd hoped—as all people do when they stand before an audience, show a bit of leg—for culmination, illumination, a flake of sky to loosen, crash down on everyone's stiff hair like the big chip of plaster on which Michelangelo in the Sistine Chapel had taken a stab at God's index finger, when, in 1789 it unexpectedly freed itself from the ceiling, hitting Father Cantinolli on the head and sending a bevy of visiting nuns into eye-rolling seizures; when they came to, their prevailing line of defense for all actions, from the sacred to the seedy, was "because God told me to" (see *Lo Spoke Del Dio Di Giorno*, Funachese, 1983).

But if God existed, today, like most days, He chose to remain mum. There was only wind and faces, yawning sky. To applause that might as well have been laughter on a late, late show (it had the same sense of obligation), I returned to my chair. Havermeyer began to read the list of graduating names, and I didn't pay much attention, until he came to the Bluebloods. I saw their Life Stories flash before my eyes.

"Milton Black."

Milton lumbered up the stairs, his chin held at that deceitfully sweet angle, around 75 degrees. (He was a lethargic coming-of-age novel.)

"Nigel Creech."

He smiled—that wristwatch catching light. (He was an unsentimental comedy in Five Acts, sequined with wit, lust and pain. The last scene tended to end on a sour note, but the playwright refused to revise.)

"Charles Loren."

Charles hobbled up the stairs with his crutches. (He was a romance.)

"Congratulations, son."

The sky had yellowed, performing one of its best magic tricks, overcast yet making people squint.

"Leulah Maloney."

She skipped up the stairs. She'd cut off her hair, not as harshly as Hannah, but the result was just as unhappy; the blunt pieces banged against her jaw. (She was a twelve-line poem of repetition and rhyme.)

Raindrops the size and texture of wasps started to zing off the shoulder pads of Havermeyer's navy blazer, also off some mother wearing a pink sun

hat that sun-rose high over her head. Instantly, umbrellas blossomed—a garden of black, red, yellow, a few striped—and the Jelly Roll Jazz Band began
to pack up their instruments, evacuating to the gym.

"Things aren't looking good, are they?" Havermeyer noted with a sigh.
"Better hurry things along." He smiled. "Graduating in the rain. For those of
you who think this is a bad omen, we do have some spots available in next
year's senior class, if you'd like to wait for an exit that looks a little more
promising." No one laughed and Havermeyer started to read the names
quickly, jerking his head up and down: microphone, name, microphone;
God was fast-forwarding him. It was difficult to hear what name he was on because the wind had found the microphone and sent ghostly, theme park,
"Woooooooos" out across the crowd. Havermeyer's wife, Gloria, stepped up
onto the stage and held an umbrella over his head.

"Jade Churchill Whitestone."

She stood up, carrying her orange umbrella Statue-of-Liberty-style, and
grabbed her diploma from Havermeyer as if doing him a favor, as if he was
handing her his résumé. She stalked back to her seat. (She was a breathtaking book written in a bleak style. She often didn't bother with "he said" or
"she said"; the reader could figure it out. And now and then a sentence made
you gasp it was so beautiful.)

Soon it was Radley's turn to go, and then my own. I'd forgotten my umbrella in Mr. Moats' classroom and Radley was holding his over himself and a
strip of rubberized commencement stage on his other side, so I was getting
drenched. The rain was an oddly soothing temperature, just right, Goldi-
locks' porridge. I stood up and Eva Brewster with her small pink cat umbrella, muttered "Christ," and shoved hers into my hands. I took it, but felt
bad because the rain started to stick to her hair and bang against her forehead. I quickly shook Havermeyer's cold pruned hand and returned to my
seat, handing the umbrella back to her.

Havermeyer rushed his closing—something about luck—the crowd ap-
plauded and began to disband. There were the wet picnic mechanics of moving inside—do we have everything, where'd Kimmie go, what's my hair
doing, it's seaweed, *hell*. Dads with pained faces wrenched toddlers out of
chairs. Mothers in soggy white linen were unaware they admitted to the
world their underwear.

I waited another minute, doing my About-To act. One doesn't look suspiciously alone, without blood relation, if one appears industriously About To

do something, and so I stood up, made a big deal of removing the mythical rock from my shoe and scratching the fictitious itch on my hand, another one on the back of my neck (they were like fleas), pretending I'd lost something somewhere—granted, for that I didn't have to pretend. Soon I was alone with the chairs and the stage. I slipped down the stairs and began to make my way across the field.

In the past few weeks, when I'd imagined this day, I'd pictured, at this precise moment, Dad, making a Grand Final Appearance (for One Night Only). Just as I figured all along—there he'd be, far in front of me, a black figure on an empty hill. Or else he'd have climbed up into the topmost branches of one of those hulking oaks, decked in Tiger Striped camouflage in order to spy, unobserved, on my graduation proceedings. Or else he'd be sealed inside a limousine, which, just as I realized it was he, came swooping down Horatio Way, almost knocking me over, cruelly reflecting me back to me before roaring around the curve, past the stone chapel and the wooden Welcome to The St. Gallway School sign, disappearing like a whale in a sound.

But I saw no swarthy black figure, no limousine and not a single lunatic in a tree. In front of me, Hanover Hall, Elton and Barrow lounged like dogs so old they wouldn't raise their heads if you threw a tennis ball at them.

"Blue," someone shouted behind me.

I ignored the voice, continuing up the hill, but he called out again, closer this time, so I stopped and turned. Red Shirt was walking quickly toward me. Instantly, I recognized him—well, let me revise that. Instantly, I was aware I'd inadvertently done the highly improbable thing of following my own advice—all that goldfish business—because it was Zach Soderberg, sure, yet I'd never seen him before in my life. He looked radically different, because sometime between our last AP Physics class and graduation, he'd decided to shave his entire head. And it wasn't one of those heads plagued with disturbing potholes and dents (as if tipping people off to the fact the brain inside it was a bit squishy), but a pleasantly strong head. His ears, too, were nothing to be ashamed of. He looked brand new, a newness that hurt the eyes and was unsettling, which was why I didn't say, "Sayonara, kid," and break into a sprint, because the Volvo was packed, waiting for me in the Student Parking Lot. I'd said so long to 24 Armor, tallyho to the Citizen Kane desk, returned the three sets of house keys to Sherwig Realty in a sealed manila envelope, including a handwritten Thank-You note to Miss Dianne Seasons, throwing in a few !!! for good measure. I had organized road maps in the glove compartment. I had neatly divided the states between North Carolina and New York (like they were equitable pieces of birthday cake) into audio-tapes from the Bookworm Library on Elm (most of them pulpy thrillers Dad would loathe). I had a license with an unfortunate picture and I planned to drive in every sense of the word.

Zach noticed my surprise at his new haircut and ran a hand over the top of his head. It probably felt like velveteen on a threadbare fainting couch. "Yeah," he said sheepishly. "Last night I decided to turn over a new leaf." He frowned. "So where are you going?" He was standing close to me, holding the black umbrella over my head so his arm was stiff as a drying rail on which one could hang wet towels.

"Home," I said.

This surprised him. "But it's just getting good. Havermeyer's dancing with Sturds. There's mini quiche." His bright red shirt was doing that butter-cup experiment to his chin—you held it there and if it glowed the person liked butter. I wondered what it meant when red glowed there.

"I can't," I said, hating how stiff it sounded. If he'd been police and I'd been guilty, he would have known, immediately.

He studied me and then shook his head, as if across my face someone had written an incomprehensible equation. "Gosh, you know, I liked your speech . . . I mean . . . *man.*"

Something about the way he said that made me feel the urge to laugh—only the urge, though; it lost steam somewhere around my collarbone.

"Thanks," I said.

"The part about the—what was it . . . when you talked about art . . . and who you are as a person . . . and *art* . . . that was so amazing."

I had no idea what he was talking about. Nowhere in my speech had art or who I was as a person been mentioned. They weren't secondary or even tertiary themes. But then, as I stared up at him, so tall—strange, I'd never no-ticed the minute creases at edges of his eyes; his face was cheating, throwing out hints of the man he'd become—I noticed perhaps that was the point; if we wanted to listen to someone, we heard what we needed to in order to inch closer. And there was nothing wrong with hearing art, or who they were as a person, or goldfish; each of us could choose whatever materials we liked for our rickety boat. There'd been something, too, in his leaning *so* far forward, so awkwardly trying to get to me (giving goosenecked lamps a run for their money), wanting to catch every word I threw into the air, not wanting to let one hit the ground. I liked this little bit of truth, tried to think it twice, three times, so I wouldn't forget it, so I could think about it on the highway, the best place to think about things.

Zach cleared his throat. He'd turned to squint at something, at Horatio Way, the part where it squeezed past the daffodils and the birdbath, or maybe higher up, the roof of Elton where the weathervane pointed at something off-screen.

"So I take it if I invited you and your dad to join us tonight at the club for the roast beef buffet, you'd say no." He looked back at me, his eyes touching my face the sad way people look out, put their hands on windowpanes. And I remembered, in the click-stutter of Mr. Archer's slide projector, that tiny painting trapped in his house. I wondered if it was still there, hanging bravely at the end of the hallway. He'd said I was like that painting, that unmanned boat.

He arched an eyebrow, another tiny talent I'd never noticed. "Can't tempt you? They have great cheesecake."

"I actually have to get going," I said.

He accepted this with a nod. "So I take it if I asked if I could . . . see a little of you over the summer—and it doesn't have to be the *whole* you, by the way. We could decide on . . . a *toe*. You'd say it's impossible. You have plans 'til you're seventy-five. You have grass stuck to your shoes, by the way."

Startled, I leaned down and wiped the grass caked to my sandals, which hours ago had been white but now were blotchy and purpled like old ladies' hands.

"I'm not going to be here this summer," I said.

"Where're you going?"

"To visit my grandparents. Maybe somewhere else." ("Chippawaa, New Mexico, Land of Enchantment, Homeland of the Roadrunner, Blue Gamma Mosquito Grass, the Cutthroat Trout, Industries, mining, silver, *pot*ash . . .")

"You and your dad, or just you?" he asked.

The kid had an uncanny ability to nail every question, again and again. Dad was the first to debunk the No Wrong Questions policy thrown out to make dimwits feel better about themselves; *yes*, whether one wanted to accept it or not, there were a handful of right questions and billions of wrong ones and out of these, out of *all* of these, Zach had selected the one that made me feel like I'd sprung a leak in my throat, the one that made me afraid

I'd cry or fall over, also causing an outbreak of those pretend itches on my arm and neck. Dad probably would have liked him—that was the funny thing. This one, this bull's-eye, would have impressed Dad.

"Just me," I said.

And then I walked away—without really realizing it. I headed up the wet hill, across the road. Not upset or crying or anything like that—no, I was remarkably fine. Well, not *fine* ("Fine is for dulls and slows.") but something else—something I actually didn't have a word for. I felt a shock from the blankness of the pale gray sky on which it was possible to draw anything, art or goldfish, as tiny or as huge as I wanted.

I continued up the sidewalk, past Hanover and the lawn in front of the cafeteria littered with branches, and the Scratch, the rain turning it all to soup. And Zach, without "Wait," or "Where are you—?" he stayed *right* there, right by my right shoulder without needing to chat about it. We walked without formula, hypothesis or detailed conclusion. His shoes moved cleanly through the rain, fishtail splashes in a pond, the fishes themselves mysteries— mine too. He held the umbrella a precise distance over my head. And I tested it—because Van Meers always had to test things—inching a little outside the shelter of it, imperceptibly to the right; I accelerated, slowed, paused to wipe more grass off my shoes, curious if I could get a small percentage of my knee or elbow, *some* part wet, but he held it over my head with remarkable consistency. By the time we reached the top of the stairs and the Volvo, and the trees crowding the road danced, but only very slightly—they were extras after all, not wanting to distract from the leads—not a new drop of rain had touched me.

Final Exam

Directions. This all-inclusive final examination will test your deepest understanding of giant concepts. It consists of three sections to be completed to the best of your ability (percentage of Final Grade specified in parentheses): 14 True or False Questions (30%), 7 Multiple Choice Questions (20%) and 1 Essay (50%).[1] You may have a clipboard to write upon, but no supplemental textbooks, encyclopedias, legal pads or extraneous papers. If you are not presently sitting with one seat between you and anyone else, please arrange for this now.

Thank you and good luck.

Section I: True/False?

1. Blue van Meer has read too many books. T/F?
2. Gareth van Meer was a handsome, charismatic man of big (and often long-winded) ideas, ideas that just might, when vigorously applied to reality, have unpleasant consequences. T/F?
3. Blue van Meer was blind, and yet one can't hold it against her, because one is almost always blind when it comes to considering oneself and one's immediate family members; one might as well be staring with naked eyes at the sun, trying to see in that blinding ball sunspots, solar flares and prominences. T/F?
4. June Bugs are incurable romantics, known to turn up at even the most

---

1. I suggest using a No. 2 pencil on the off chance you make a mistake in your initial perceptions and, provided you have a little bit of time left, wish to change your answer.

formal gatherings with lipstick on their teeth and hair as frazzled as any businessman stuck in rush hour traffic. T/F?

5. Andreo Verduga was a gardener who wore heavy cologne, no more, no less. T/F?

6. Smoke Harvey clubbed seals. T/F?

7. The fact that Gareth van Meer and Hannah Schneider have the same sentence underlined—"When Manson listened to you it was like he was drinking up your face," on p. 481 of their respective copies of *Blackbird Singing in the Dead of Night: The Life of Charles Milles Manson*—probably doesn't mean as much as Blue would like to think. The most she should take from this tidbit is that they both found the behaviors of lunatics fascinating. T/F?

8. The Nightwatchmen still exist, at the very least, in the minds of conspiracy theorists, neo-Marxists, bloodshot-eyed bloggers and champions of Che, also individuals of all races and creeds who take pleasure in the thought that there may be teaspoons of, if not *justice*, per se (justice tends to hold up in the hands of men the way Chabazite does in HCl—disintegrating slowly, often leaving slimy residue) then a simple leveling of a tiny section of the world's playing field (currently without referee). T/F?

9. The Houston police photograph of George Gracey is *unquestionably* Baba au Rhum; Blue can conclude this simply from the man's unmistakable eyes, which are like two black olives pushed deep into a plate of hummus—no matter if the rest of the head, in the grainy picture, is obscured with facial hair denser than the neutron (10^{18} kg/m^3). T/F?

10. Each of the impromptu films Hannah played for her Intro to Film class, movies that—as Dee revealed to her sister, Dum—*never* appeared on the actual syllabus, had subversive themes, evidence of her freaky flower chile politics. T/F?

11. Hannah Schneider, with the help of other Nightwatchmen (rather sloppily) killed a man, to the infinite exasperation of Gareth van Meer; while he took pleasure in his role as Socrates (the job fit him like a bespoke suit from Saville Row)—touring the country, lecturing new recruits about Determination and other compelling ideas detailed in countless *Federal Forum* essays, including "Viva Las Violence: Transgressions of the Elvis Empire"—Gareth *still* preferred to be a man of theory, not violence, the Trotsky, rather than the Stalin; you may recall, the man eschewed all contact sports. T/F?

12. In all probability (though admittedly, this is the conjecture of someone with little more than a remembered photograph to go on), Natasha van Meer killed herself upon learning that her best friend, with whom she attended the Ivy School, had been having a hot-breathy affair with her husband, a man who adored the sound of his own voice. T/F?

13. One can't really believe it, but Life is, rather confusingly, both sad and funny at the same time. T/F?

14. Reading an obscene number of reference books is greatly advantageous to one's mental health. T/F?

Section II: Multiple Choice

1. Hannah Schneider was:

   A. An orphan who grew up at the Horizon House in New Jersey (which required its children to wear uniforms; the house seal, a gold pegasus that could also pass for a lion if one squinted, was stitched into the jacket on the breast pocket). She wasn't the most attractive of children. After reading *The Liberation's Woman* (1962) by Arielle Soiffe, which featured an extensive chapter on Catherine Baker, she found herself wishing *she'd* done something that bold with her life, and in a moment of gloomy restlessness found herself hinting to Blue that she was, in fact, that fearless revolutionary, that "hand-grenade of a woman" (p. 313). In spite of these efforts to align her life with something a bit more majestic, she was nevertheless in jeopardy of turning into her worst fear, one of The Gone, if it weren't for Blue writing about her. Her house is currently #22 on Sherwig Realty's "Hot List."

   B. Catherine Baker, equal parts runaway, criminal, myth, moth.

   C. One of those lost civilization women, poorly lit but with astonishing architecture; many rooms, including an entire banquet hall, will never be found.

   D. Flotsam and jetsam of all the above.

2. Miss Schneider's passing was really:

   A. A suicide; in a sloppy moment (and she'd had many), when she'd danced too long with her wineglass, she'd slept with Charles, an error in judgment that began to corrode her from the inside out, prompting her to spin fantastical stories, hack off her hair, end her life.

B. Murder by a member of The Nightwatchmen (*Nunca Dormindo* in Portuguese); as Gareth "Socrates" and Servo "Nero" Gracey hashed over during their emergency powwow in Paris, Hannah was now a liability. Ada Harvey was digging too deep, was weeks away from contacting the FBI, and thus Gracey's freedom, their entire antigreedian movement, was at risk; she had to be eliminated—a difficult call ultimately made by Gracey. The man in the woods, the person Blue is positive she heard as surely as she knows the Bumblebee Bat is the smallest mammal on earth (1.3 in.), was their most sophisticated button man, Andreo Verduga, decked in ShifTbush™ Invisible Gear, Fall Mix, the accomplished hunter's dream.

C. Murder by "Sloppy Ed," the member of the Vicious Three still at large.

D. One of those muddy events in life, which one will never know with certainty (see Chapter 2, "The Black Dahlia," *Slain*, Winn, 1988).

3. Jade Churchill Whitestone is:

A. A phony.

B. Beguiling.

C. Irksome as a stubbed toe.

D. An ordinary teenager who couldn't see the sky through the air.

4. Making out with Milton Black was like:

A. Kissing squid.

B. Being sat upon by an *Octopus vulgaris*.

C. Doing a jackknife into Jell-O.

D. Floating on a bed of frontal lobes.

5. Zach Soderberg is:

A. A peanut butter sandwich with the crusts cut off.

B. Guilty of lion sex performed in Room 222 at The Dynasty Motel.

C. *Still*, after a myriad of explanations and Visual Aids presented to him by Blue van Meer as they toured the country for a summer in a blue Volvo station wagon, somewhat disturbingly unable to grasp even the most rudimentary concepts behind Einstein's General Theory of Relativity. He is currently learning to recite pi out to sixty-five decimal places.

D. An Oracle of Delphi.

6. Gareth van Meer abandoned his daughter because:

   A. He had had enough of Blue's paranoia and hysterics.

   B. He was, to quote Jessie Rose Rubiman, "a pig."

   C. He finally had the guts to take a stab at immortality, follow his life-long dream to go play Che in the Democratic Republic of the Congo; this was what he and his sham professors across the country had been organizing in secret; this was also why countless African newspapers were found strewn around the house in the immediate aftermath of his departure, including *Inside Angola*.

   D. He couldn't bear to lose face with his daughter, Blue, Blue who always thought The World of him, Blue who, even after learning he was an intellectual outmoded as the Great October Soviet Socialist Revolution of 1917, a disaster-prone dreamer, a showboat theorist (and only a very minor one), a philanderer whose illicit affairs caused the suicide of her mother, a man who doubtless *will* end up like Trotsky if he isn't careful (ice pick, head), *still* can't help but think The World of him, Blue who whenever she is running late to her lecture, "American Government: A New Perspective," or passing by a park with trees that whisper overhead as if they wish to let slip a secret, can't help but wish to find him sitting on a wooden bench, in tweed, waiting for her.

7. Blue's detailed theory of love, sex, guilt and murder scrawled across fifty pages of a legal pad is:

   A. 100% Truth, as things are 100% Cotton.

   B. Preposterous and delusional.

   C. A frail web spun by a garden spider, not in some sensible porch corner, but in a massive space, a space so huge and far-fetched one could easily fit two Cadillac DeVille Stretch Limos in it, end to end.

   D. The materials Blue used for her boat, in order to pass without serious injury through a harrowing patch of sea (see Chapter 9, "Scylla and Charybdis," *The Odyssey*, Homer, Hellenistic Period).

Section III: Essay Question

Many classic films and published academic works do their best to shine tiny lights on the state of American culture, the surreptitious sorrow of all people, the struggle for selfhood, the generalized bewilderment of living. Nimbly utilizing specific examples from such texts, structure a sweeping argument around the premise that, while such works are enlightening, amusing, comforting, too—particularly when one is in a new situation and one needs to divert the mind—they can be no substitution for experience. For, to quote Danny Yeargood's exceptionally brutal memoir of 1977, *The Edgycation of Eyetalians*, life is "one blow after another and even when you're on the ground, you can't see nothin' 'cause they hit you on the part of the head where sight comes from, and you can't breathe 'cause they kicked you in the stomach where breathin' comes from, and your nose's all blood 'cause they held you down and punched you in the face, you crawl to your feet and feel fine. Beautiful even. Because you're alive."

Take all the time you need.

Acknowledgments

I am deeply indebted to Susan Golomb and Carole DeSanti for their tireless enthusiasm, criticism and sound advice. Many thanks to Kate Barker, and also to Jon Mozes for his feedback on those early drafts (making the imperative suggestion that I replace *high heels* with *stilettos*). Thank you to Carolyn Horst for meticulously dotting the i's and crossing the t's. Thank you to Adam Weber for being the most big-hearted friend on earth. Thank you to my family, Elke, Vov and Toni and my amazing husband, Nic, my Clyde, who graciously watches his wife disappear daily into a dark room with her computer for ten to twelve hours at a time and asks no questions. Most of all, I thank my mother, Anne. Without her inspiration and extraordinary generosity, this book would not be possible.